WHITE HAVEN HUNTERS

BOOK ONE - THREE

TJ GREEN

White Haven Hunters Books 1-3

Mountolive Publishing

©2022 TJ Green

All rights reserved

eBook ISBN 978-1-99-004741-1

Paperback ISBN: 978-1-99-004742-8

Cover Design by Fiona Jayde Media

Editing by Missed Period Editing

Contents

One   3

Two   9

Three   16

Four   24

Five   30

Six   34

Seven   42

Eight   48

Nine   53

Ten   58

Eleven   63

Twelve   70

Thirteen   76

Fourteen   81

Fifteen   87

Sixteen   93

Seventeen   99

Eighteen   109

Nineteen   115

Twenty   121

Twenty-One   126

Twenty-Two   131

Twenty-Three   136

Twenty-Four   142

One   153

Two   157

Three   165

Four   170

Five   175

Six   181

Seven   187

Eight   193

Nine   199

Ten   204

Eleven   209

Twelve   214

Thirteen   220

Fourteen   226

Fifteen   231

Sixteen   241

Seventeen   249

Eighteen   254

Nineteen   258

Twenty   263

Twenty-One   269

Twenty-Two   275

Twenty-Three   280

Twenty-Four   287

Twenty-Five   292

Twenty-Six   297

Twenty-Seven   302

Twenty-Eight   307

Twenty-Nine   312

Thirty   319

One   327

Two   332

Three   337

Four   345

Five   352

Six   356

Seven   363

Eight   371

Nine   378

Ten   384

Eleven   391

Twelve   398

Thirteen   407

Fourteen   414

Fifteen   420

Sixteen   426

Seventeen   434

Eighteen   443

Nineteen   451

Twenty   457

Twenty-One   463

Twenty-Two   471

Twenty-Three   479

Twenty-Four   487

Twenty-Five   494

Twenty-Six   500

Twenty-Seven   505

Twenty-Eight   513

Author's Notes   520

About Author   522

Also By   524

                                                                529

                                                                531

SPIRIT OF THE FALLEN

WHITE HAVEN HUNTERS BOOK ONE

TJ GREEN

One

Shadow watched Gabe roll his shoulders and square up, ready to attack again. He held the sword easily, like it weighed nothing, and she assessed his stance, deciding how he would strike this time.

If she was honest, it didn't really matter; she was pretty confident she'd best him, despite his strength. She had agility on her side. She raised an eyebrow at him, and the corner of her mouth turned up as he narrowed his eyes at her.

"Feeling pleased with yourself, aren't you?"

She shrugged. "Why wouldn't I? I've beaten you twice this morning."

"Just to remind you, I haven't fought with a sword for a long time."

"Well then, this is the perfect way for you to learn!"

He prowled around the perimeter of the barn where they had set up their practice area, and she mirrored his actions. The barn was rustic and basic, but it was solid, giving them adequate protection from the rain and the winds that blew in across the moor above White Haven. The ground was made of beaten earth and it was covered in sawdust and straw, providing a reasonably soft landing when they tumbled and rolled.

Gabe struck quickly, covering the space between them in a split-second, and she parried, reminding herself that his lightning-quick reflexes were similar to her own.

"You know, I'm still recovering from my encounter with the Empusa," she reminded him as she retaliated.

He continued to attack, and responded in between swings of his sword. "Well, if you involve yourself with the affairs of the White Haven witches, what do you expect?"

"They needed my help!"

He laughed. "And you saw a way to help yourself!"

"That is not true!" She glared at him, furious, and rolled under his legs, swinging aggressively at his calf, and he dived over her, on the attack immediately.

She regained her footing and circled him again. The Nephilim's size still impressed her. He was a good deal taller than she was, and muscular. Over the last couple of months since she had first met him, his dark brown, almost black hair had grown a few inches, and he wore it swept back, showing his hard-edged jaw. He smirked at her. He'd caught her off balance and they both knew it.

"I hit a nerve," he told her. "It distracted you."

"I like the witches. You make me sound like a mercenary."

"I thought that's exactly what you are."

"Sometimes I've had to be, but not always by choice."

She struck at him, whirling across the room like a dervish, and they traded blow for blow, up close and personal. She tried to press her advantage, pinning him against the wall in a dusty corner of the barn. He let her draw closer, watching her with a gleam in his eye.

"And now?" he asked.

"Now I need to make a life. I'm about to earn a lot of money."

"You think. If Beckett doesn't short-change you." He was referring to Harlan Beckett, the American man who worked for the Orphic Guild, the mysterious organisation that obtained occult and arcane objects for private buyers.

"If he does, I won't sell!"

They were inches apart, her sword under his chin, the cold blade against his neck.

"You're good, Shadow, but you need to be careful. Your overconfidence may cost you one day."

She smirked and dropped her weapon, backing away from him. "It hasn't yet."

"Hasn't it? You're stuck here, aren't you? If you hadn't forced your way past the coven's perimeter circle on Samhain, you'd be back in the Otherworld by now." He held his sword loosely, stepping close to her again, his dark eyes holding her gaze. "I'm serious. You should be more careful."

Shadow fell silent for a moment, knowing he was right. She had been reckless that night. The energy of the Wild Hunt had heated her blood and made her act rashly, but in her defence, she really hadn't thought anyone would stop Herne. The Cornwall Coven witches may not have fey magic, but their magic was strong, and they commanded it well. She refused to let Gabe intimidate her. "I'm fey. I'm faster than any human. And you."

He grinned. "You might be faster, but you're not stronger, and one day I'll beat you at sword fighting, too." He headed to the hook on the wall and pulled a towel free, wiping the sweat from his face. It may have been cold out, but they had both become hot while they fought. "Have you heard from Beckett?"

He always called Harlan by his surname, and Shadow detected a brooding resentment behind his words. "I'm expecting his call any minute. The last time I spoke to him, he said he'd found a buyer and was negotiating a price." She grabbed her own towel, putting her sword in her scabbard while she dried off.

"Where have you put the Empusa's sword?"

"Somewhere safe, don't you worry."

"I'm not about to steal it! Are you sure you wouldn't be better off keeping it?"

She shook her head. "I've examined it carefully, on my own and with El, and we can't find any special qualities or hidden powers, other than its age and skilled forging and design. It's unique, and the pair of them together would sell for a small fortune, but El is refusing to sell hers." She was referring to Elspeth, one of the White Haven witches who owned The Silver Bough jewellery shop, and who was particularly adept with metalwork.

She continued, "We've even tested them together, and still can't detect anything unusually magical—you know, enhanced abilities when used at the same time."

It had been over two weeks since Shadow and the White Haven witches had fought and defeated Caitlin, and retrieved The Callanish Ring. Caitlin had turned into the Empusa in the campgrounds of the Crossroads Circus, and fortunately they had been helped by the Raven King and the Green Man. Shadow was sure they wouldn't have defeated her without them. The Raven King had taken her and her relatives to the Underworld to face justice. The Empusa had carried two swords that had made the fight particularly difficult, and Shadow had to reluctantly admit that she had met her match.

That night, when she had escorted Harlan away from the wild forest that had sprung up under the command of the Green Man, they had talked for quite a while about how they could help each other. He had promised to discuss their meeting with the director of the London branch, and said he knew of several potential customers for the sword.

Gabe flung his towel on a long bench that ran across one side of the barn and pulled on a sweatshirt. "I can't believe El won't sell it."

"She loves weaponry, and besides, I think she's still testing hers." Shadow was pulling on her jacket when the phone in her pocket rang, and she answered it, aware that Gabe was watching her. "Harlan, we were just discussing you."

His voice was low. "Only good things, I hope! You'll be pleased to know that one of my clients wishes to make you an offer." He named an impressive sum. "Obviously we'll be taking a commission, but be assured this is the best possible price—for both of us." He paused, and then added, as if he sensed some reluctance from her, "I haggled hard, and I'm excellent at it."

Shadow grinned. She and Gabe had discussed how much to accept, and although they had never negotiated arcane objects before in this world, Shadow had done it plenty of times in the Otherworld. She'd learnt to quadruple any price offered, and knew collectors would pay. But, if Harlan was taking a commission, it was in his best interest to get the highest price, too.

"You know what, Harlan, I bet I could make it go higher, but as this is the start of our beautiful friendship, I'll accept that. Just tell him that I won't be so generous next time. And that's in both our interests."

Harlan's tone hardened. "You know that he'll pay much more for the pair."

"But the other is not for sale, so let it drop," she said sharply. Of all the witches, El was her favourite. She called her 'sister' for a reason. She was similar in height to her, and her love of gems, weapons, metalwork, and forging made her interests comparable to her own. In a world where she was finding her feet, her friendship with El had been unexpected. There was an edge to her that she liked, and Shadow was not about to betray her.

He sighed. "Fine. I have your account, so I'll organise the deposit straight away, but I need to get the sword before we complete the transaction. How do you fancy a trip to our headquarters?"

"In London?" Shadow asked, staring wide-eyed at Gabe.

"Yes. I'll introduce you to the director, too. You've intrigued him."

"Hold on." Shadow thought quickly. She was sure she could handle this on her own, but she'd like backup, just in case. She'd be on their ground, not hers, and that would put her at a disadvantage with an organisation she knew nothing about. She covered the phone and said to Gabe, "I need to take the sword to London. Will you come?"

He nodded straight away. "Sure, I'll get Nahum to take over at Caspian's warehouse."

Harlan hadn't met Gabe, and Shadow wasn't sure if this would be an issue, but she pressed the phone back to her ear. "No problem, but I'm bringing Gabe. He's my partner, after all."

There was a slight pause before he answered. "Okay, I'm confident I can make the director agree."

A wave of suspicion washed over her. "Why wouldn't he?"

"He's just wary about people he doesn't know coming into our branch," Harlan said smoothly. "We tend to restrict visitors, and he knows about you, but not Gabe."

"Tell him we work together, and if you want the sword, he'd better say yes."

"He will. Shall we say Friday at one? That should give you time to get here."

"Sure, send me your address."

"I'll text it. See you soon," he said, and rang off.

Shadow realised she'd been holding herself tensely, and she took a deep breath of relief. She raised an eyebrow at Gabe, who was still leaning against the wall, watching her. "We're on."

He nodded. "Good. We'll take the train in—it will be easier than driving."

Shadow had never travelled by train before, and had only just got used to cars and bikes. There was nothing like them in the Otherworld, but they made getting around much simpler. She couldn't decide whether that was a good thing or not. "London is big. Do you know where we're going?"

"No, but that's what maps and taxis are for. We'll be fine." He pushed away from the wall and headed to the door. "I'll go and speak to Nahum, and then I'm heading to the shower. What are you up to?"

Shadow still had a lot of nervous energy, especially after the phone call, and she needed peace and quiet. "I need to ride. I think I'll head to Ravens' Wood." The ancient forest that had grown in a matter of moments was the place she felt most at home now, and she spent long periods of time there.

Gabe held the barn door open for her and then headed to the house, calling over his shoulder, "Sure, I'll see you later."

Within ten minutes, Shadow had saddled her horse, Kailen, and was riding across the moors towards the wood that bordered White Haven Castle. It was early March, and spring flowers were starting to appear. Hedgerows were buzzing with life, and the birds were busy making nests and preparing for their small broods. She paused on a rise along the downs and inhaled deeply, smiling at the scent. She could feel new life all around her and it settled in her blood, making her even more restless. At the foot of the hills she could see White Haven nestling in the folds of the valley, the jumble of buildings heading down to the harbour. She couldn't see it all from here, but her mind filled in what was obstructed, and she thought of her friends in their shops and businesses. It was mid-afternoon, and the sea was a brittle blue, the waves choppy with the brisk wind that cut through her jacket.

This was home now, and she considered herself lucky. Despite her less than auspicious arrival, she had been welcomed, albeit cautiously, and she had to admit that she liked it here. White Haven's charm was infectious, more so if you embraced magic. The land rustled with it, especially since Imbolc and the appearance of the Green Man. It made her feel closer to the Otherworld, the place she'd most likely never see again. And she could see beings here that she knew no one else could.

She was distracted by one of them now, a small, wizened figure that popped up out of nowhere. It was a tiny pixie with brown and green skin, skinny limbs, and an angular face. Her heart swelled, and she laughed and waved, but it didn't reciprocate. They were grumpy creatures, and it scowled at her and then disappeared with a *pop*. She had been surprised when she had first seen them; she hadn't thought that any creature from the Otherworld would be here, and they gave her hope that she'd find others. Admittedly, they weren't like the pixies in the Otherworld, which were taller, brawnier, and vicious fighters. These were their smaller cousins, and their size helped them remain unseen. And they were also stuck here, like she was.

Kailen stamped his feet, eager to be off, and she turned him towards Ravens' Wood and let him race, crouching low against him. It was exhilarating, and it was with reluctance that she slowed down to cross the lane and enter the leafy shadows of the old forest.

Silence fell like a cloak, and she slipped from Kailen's back, leading him along the ancient paths. It felt warmer in here, and bright green leaves were already unfurling around her. She meandered for a while before she spotted a familiar figure kneeling in the undergrowth. It was Briar, the earth witch, and she must have heard her, because she looked up and smiled.

"Shadow! I was just thinking about you. How are you?"

"I'm well, thank you. You look full of spring." It was an odd thing to say, but it was true. Briar's eyes gleamed with old magic, and her dark hair fell thick and wild down her back. She was wearing a heavy jumper and one of her long skirts, and she'd taken her boots off, so her bare feet could wriggle into the earth.

Briar stood up, brushing grass off her clothing. She'd been gathering roots and herbs, and an overflowing basket sat to the side. "This spring I feel more acutely than any other. My blood sings with it! And look at my hair!" She dragged her fingers through it. "It resists all attempts to comb it. It's nuts."

"That's the Green Man for you. He's wild, and he's a part of you now." Shadow frowned. "I must have lost my touch. Normally, no one can hear me coming, but you did."

"The earth told me." She gestured around her. "This place feels you, you must know that. It feels me, too. I can't work out whether I feel wilder here, or more at peace. It's so weird. Hunter likes it, too."

"Your wolf-shifter? That doesn't surprise me. I told you he had a sort of fey blood."

For once, Briar didn't deny their relationship, and she laughed. "I told him that, and I think he quite liked it. And what about you? Did you hear from Harlan?"

Shadow nodded as she stroked Kailen's side. "Yes, he's found a buyer for the sword and offered me a lot of money. We're going to London on Friday to complete the deal."

"That's great," Briar said, nodding. "It will help you establish yourself here." A note of caution entered her voice. "But don't go alone. London is big and confusing, and I know you're not stupid, but it's very different from here."

"I'm going with Gabe. I thought it was important to have support." She hesitated as she recalled their earlier conversation, and she wondered what Briar would think. "He tells me I'm too headstrong."

Briar frowned. "You are, but you know that. And I know you've told Harlan that you're fey, but you really shouldn't tell anyone else. You need to be careful about who you trust with that knowledge. Gabe doesn't tell anybody about what he is, and we don't reveal that we're witches, other than to our close friends."

Shadow felt a ripple of unease pass through her, but she shrugged it off. "I'm fey. Anyone with any sense should take that as a warning not to mess with me."

"And it also makes you a target. Some people are devious. You must have fey like that in your world."

"Of course we do. I'm not a child. I'm years older than any of you, and have been in some interesting situations in my lifetime, and dealt with fey who are considerably more dangerous than most humans."

Briar just regarded her quietly, her dark eyes solemn. "I know, but you're new to our world, and it's important that you understand its dangers. Many people hate things that are different. It scares them—or makes them greedy. Be careful."

Shadow's annoyance increased, but as she felt Briar's magic roll off her, she sensed the wisdom in her words, which was strange from someone so young. In her race's years, Briar was like a new-born, but she was uncanny. She drew her strength from the earth, and that in itself imparted wisdom beyond normal years. And besides, she meant well.

Shadow softened her stance and smiled. "Thanks, I'll try. Anyway, you're busy, so I'll leave you to it." She turned, ready to head deeper into the forest. "Say hi to the others."

Briar nodded. "I will."

But as Shadow walked away, she felt Briar's calm regard like a weight between her shoulder blades, and she shrugged, eager to dismiss her concerns.

Friday would be fine, and it would open her up a whole new world.

Two

The headquarters of the Orphic Guild was located in an impressive building made of pale grey stone in a very exclusive area of London.

Gabe watched it from across the street, Shadow next to him. They had arrived slightly early in order to stake it out, but so far no one had gone in or out. His eyes roved over the exterior, noting the discrete cameras and alarm system, the brass plaque that announced its name, the shiny black front door, and its general air of smart respectability that made it seem impressively expensive. He hated places like this. They made his skin crawl. It reminded him of all the rich people he'd ever dealt with, and most of them were completely selfish and egocentric. No matter that it was over 2,000 years later than his previous life, the entitlement of the affluent never changed.

Shadow stirred. "We're not going to see anything from here today."

He kept his eyes on the building, but said, "You're probably right. I'm sure it will have a back entrance anyway for anyone who needs discretion."

"Don't we?" she asked.

He turned to her, needing to look down to meet her stare. "No. We're not the rich buyers who want to keep their anonymity. We're the workforce, never forget that. You can be damn sure they won't."

"You know they might have spotted us?"

"Probably, but we're not hiding. Are you ready?"

Shadow firmly gripped the sturdy black case that contained the Empusa's sword, and fire lurked behind her eyes. "In a minute," she said, distracted by the busy street, and she frowned as she studied the comings and goings. Her stance looked easy, but it wasn't, and Gabe knew she'd leap into action if something untoward happened.

Gabe admired her attitude. She had been completely separated from her kind, but that hadn't slowed her down. If anything, it had spurred her on to make a life for herself in this strange world that was full of technology, so different from her own. He knew he'd made the right decision all those weeks ago when he offered her a place to stay. He'd watched her pacing in the iron cage and recognised her fire as being similar to his own. He respected that. And he'd wanted to keep an eye on her. She was like a firecracker that was liable to go off at any point, and he didn't want her bringing disaster to their doors.

Besides, he and Shadow had lots in common. Awakening in this world had been hard for the Nephilim too, he reflected, but like Shadow they knew they were stuck here and were determined to make it work on their terms as much as possible. That meant acclimatising to modern culture. They'd arrived naked, and with no money, and had stolen clothes and cash, bought fake identification, and rented the old farmhouse that was well out of the way from anyone else.

Gabe was a warrior, and had also been an occasional mercenary with flexible morals. He and his kind had been revered and feared equally, and most of the time he had displayed his huge wings as a symbol of his difference and power. Here it was impossible, and he kept them hidden. While Shadow had revealed who she was to some people, Gabe hadn't. The witches and Newton were the only ones who knew what they were, and he aimed to keep it that way. He'd told Shadow not to divulge what they were to Harlan, and he hoped she'd honour that.

Shadow looked up at him, her violet eyes bright with the anticipated meeting. "Okay, I'm ready." She crossed the street, and Gabe's gaze lingered on her shapely figure, before quickly focusing on the job at hand. There were added benefits to her living with them, too.

Shadow rang the doorbell, and they heard a corresponding chime from deep within the building. In a few moments, the door was opened by a man in his thirties wearing a sharp dark grey suit, and a suspicious frown. He looked them up and down imperiously. "You must be Shadow." He stared at Gabe, and he had to look up to meet his eyes. "Were we expecting *you*?"

Gabe smiled coolly. "Yes, you were. Gabe Malouf." He held out his hand and gripped the other man's in his own tightly before releasing it.

"Ah yes, I do remember your name being mentioned."

He didn't introduce himself, but instead led the way into the large reception hall, which had an elaborately tiled floor, a sweeping stairway, and doors on either side, and then turned into the room on the right, which was decorated with expensive furnishings, many antique. "Take a seat, and I will let Mr Becket know you're here."

He left them alone, and Gabe grinned. "He's an ass."

"I think you intimidated him."

"I think he was trying to intimidate me. He failed." Gabe paced around, a wry smile on his face. "I think this room is meant to intimidate, too. Is it working?"

Shadow shook her head, amusement in her eyes. "No. I'm intrigued as to how much money this place makes. I may not know much about this world, but expensive stuff is the same everywhere." She frowned. "There's nothing here that looks remotely occult, though."

Gabe heard footsteps, and a voice interrupted them. "No, you won't find anything like that in this part of the building."

A tall man was in the doorway. His dark grey hair was swept back from his face, and he had a trace of stubble across a square jaw. He was dressed informally in jeans and t-shirt, and his blue eyes focussed on Shadow first as he stepped forward to shake her hand. "Hey Shadow, welcome to the Orphic Guild. I'm glad you could make it."

"Harlan. Good to see you, too. This is Gabe," she said, introducing him.

Both men eyed each other suspiciously, and Gabe was acutely aware that he was being assessed as to how much of a threat he was. That was okay. He was used to it. Again he was given a cool but firm handshake. "Hi, sorry we didn't meet last time."

Gabe smiled. "Me, too. This is quite some place!"

Harlan looked pleased. "It is, isn't it? The owner has very defined tastes, and is responsible for how it looks, even though he's not here that often. Our director, Mason Jacobs, oversees the branch, and ensures everything remains pristine." He nodded at the case in Shadow's hand. "Is that the sword?"

"It is. Want to see it again?"

"Not here. I'll take you to Mason's office, upstairs." As he led them out of the room and up the grand, sweeping staircase, he said, "The ground floor rooms are for administrative staff. The next floor is where the offices for the collectors and the director are."

Gabe's gaze travelled over the expensive artwork and antique furniture, which was mixed with modern, sleek design elements. He didn't know much about modern design, but he was certainly beginning to know what it looked like. He'd done his homework before coming here, and he also knew that Eaton Place was one of the most exclusive addresses in London. He idly wondered who the director was, and was about to ask more about him when Harlan stopped in front of a polished wooden door.

Harlan knocked as he told them, "This is Mason's office."

A voice called, "Come in."

Harlan opened the door and ushered them through.

This room was as impressive as the rest of the building, but the colours were muted and the furnishings modern, except for the huge antique desk and Persian rug on the floor. A man who Gabe estimated to be in his fifties rose from his seat behind the desk and walked around it to greet them. He had a short beard, grey hair, and a slim build. His suit was immaculate and clearly tailored, and Gabe realised that, like everything in this place, it was designed to impress. And there was something about him that Gabe didn't like.

Harlan made the introductions, and Mason offered them seats in the tan leather chairs that clustered around a table. "Please sit, the coffee will be here shortly. You do drink coffee, I hope?" His voice was clipped and assured, without any discernible accent, other than English.

"Of course," Shadow said, sitting nonchalantly and placing the case on the floor. "As long as it's good."

Mason looked slightly affronted. "I can assure you, it's excellent."

Gabe took his seat and noticed Harlan suppressing a smile. That was good. He liked Shadow, he could tell, but he was pretty sure Mason saw them as merely commodities.

Mason continued in his smooth voice, "I'm glad to finally meet you. Harlan has kept me apprised of the negotiations. You came by the sword in a very unusual way."

"You managed to get the Ring of Callanish in a very unusual way, too," she countered, amused. "Are all of your acquisitions obtained in such a manner?"

Mason looked slightly put out to be answered with a question. "We deal with arcane and occult objects, and as such they often come from unusual and sometimes dangerous places. Our collectors consequently have special skills," he nodded towards Harlan, "and we use contractors, too. That's what I would like to discuss with you today, once I have seen the sword."

He held her gaze in his own steely one, and Gabe realised he hadn't looked at him once since their first greeting. Amusing. Maybe he thought he was more bodyguard than partner.

A knock at the door broke their conversation, and the man who had let them in to the building entered with a tray containing an antique coffee pot, cups, and a platter of tiny cakes and pastries. He wordlessly put the tray on the table and left.

"Excellent, thank you, Robert," Mason murmured. "Harlan, would you be so kind?"

Harlan was already rising to pour coffee and offer the refreshments, and Gabe realised this was a longstanding ritual. He took a cup from Harlan and sipped his coffee, recognising an Arabic brew. Mason was right. It was excellent.

Shadow asked, "Would you like to see the sword now?"

"Yes, please," Mason said, sipping his coffee.

Shadow unpacked it from the case and placed it on the table, and Mason's eyes fired with excitement. He placed his cup down, pulled a pair of glasses from his pocket, and lifted the curved blade.

"Magnificent." He examined it carefully, almost reverentially, and then looked up at Shadow. "It has some slight marks, and what looks like a nick along the edge, so it's not pristine."

Shadow raised an eyebrow. "It's an ancient weapon that belonged to Hecate's servant. I think you'll find she used it often. And of course, we had quite a heated battle. My own sword is made from one of the strongest metals ever forged. The clash of our blades rang across the forest that night." She was using her fey glamour, Gabe could tell. There was a swell of power around her that was subtle, but to his eye it was unmistakable. He was pretty sure, however, that Mason wouldn't know that. He'd just feel overwhelmed. Shadow continued, a trifle smugly, "You should thank me. I've added to its provenance."

Mason's carefully manufactured expression glazed as he placed the sword back on the table. "Ah yes, I heard you defeated a mysterious creature to get it."

She nodded. "With help. The Empusa had arrived straight from the Underworld, so it was a tricky fight."

"I've certainly heard of her," he confessed. A gleam entered his eyes. "You couldn't capture her?"

"That would be like trying to catch the wind," Shadow said sharply.

Gabe stared at Mason and spoke for the first time, a dangerous edge to his voice. "Why would you want to capture the Empusa?"

Mason looked at him properly, his eyes narrowing, and for a second didn't answer, his discomfort apparent. "I just thought it would be interesting to see such a creature up close, that's all." He sipped his coffee casually, trying to make it look as if his comment was nothing.

Shadow lowered her voice. "I saw it 'up close.' It would have killed you in a second." Her gaze ran over him dismissively. "You're too soft, too weak. She would have broken you like a doll."

Gabe winced inwardly. Ouch.

Mason didn't respond, instead turning back to Gabe. "Sorry, I didn't catch your name earlier. Are you a friend of Shadow's?"

"I'm her business partner."

"Oh! Yes, of course, Harlan told me." Mason glanced between the two of them, no doubt weighing their relationship up. "You didn't mention that though, Shadow."

She shrugged and smiled. "It doesn't matter to you, does it? Now, are you happy with the sword? I would like to finalise our deal. I have other things to do today."

They didn't really, other than a celebratory pub lunch. Both Gabe and Shadow had embraced the English pub culture.

Mason nodded, still trying to control the conversation. "Of course. The client who is buying this will be very happy with it. As you say, it has provenance, particularly its unexpected arrival in this world." He looked slightly awkward as he asked, "What about its sister sword?"

"It's not for sale, and never will be," Shadow told him.

"Just checking," he replied. "Harlan tells me you might be interested in more work in the future?"

"Yes, both of us are, actually, as long as we can fit it into our schedule."

"Of course." He rose to his feet as he brought the meeting to a close. "Excellent. We look forward to working with you again." Mason nodded at Harlan. "Please transfer the money."

There was a flurry of handshakes before they exited the room. Gabe was the last one out and he turned, catching Mason staring at him with a frown. Gabe smiled and closed the door.

———◆◇◆———

As soon as Harlan had dealt with Shadow and Gabe, he returned to Mason's office, knocking softly before he entered.

Mason was standing with his back to the room, looking out of the window onto Eaton Place below, and he turned, a cut glass crystal tumbler in his hand with a healthy measure of amber liquid. Whiskey, no doubt. It was his favourite drink.

"Is she what you expected?" Harlan asked as he joined him.

"No, not at all." Mason headed to the cabinet where he kept a small bar. "Whiskey? I think you should join my celebration."

Harlan knew better than to refuse. His charming boss was also ruthless, and these celebratory drinks didn't happen often, so that meant he must be impressed by Shadow.

"Of course, thank you."

Harlan waited patiently while Mason poured a couple of fingers of whiskey and passed him the glass, raising his own in salute. "Well done. She was a good find."

"She was, but I have no idea of what to really make of her, or her partner."

Mason returned to the window, watching the pedestrians and the cars coming and going on the street below.

"I saw them walk towards the Palace," Mason noted. He meant Buckingham Palace, which was a short stroll away. "I wonder how they met. I especially wonder about her.

Did you say she's fey? She doesn't seem any different." He levelled a narrow, accusatory glare at Harlan.

"She may not, but I can assure you she is. She uses glamour to disguise herself. But I detected her energy—well, her magic really, while I was investigating in White Haven. There's a lot of magic in that town, but hers feels unique. It's why you employ me." Harlan had been doing his job for a long time, and he'd honed his skills in the paranormal world, often at great risk to his life.

"How did you say you found her?"

"I followed her when she left Happenstance Books, Avery Hamilton's book store. She knew I was behind her and confronted me, so over a drink in the closest pub, I explained what I wanted. It was clear from the start that we had mutual interests."

"And she took you to the castle?"

"Yes, when it was obvious that Avery wouldn't help, Shadow was my next option." Harlan sipped his whiskey, recalling the night the ancient forest grew in White Haven. He'd dreamt about it time and time again, until the event itself seemed like a dream. "I met her at an agreed rendezvous along the lane, and she took me to the edge of the field and left me with her horse, another Otherworldly animal. I saw it all happen—it was extraordinary. The rush of magic and power was unlike anything I've experienced before, and as you know, I've seen my fair share." He'd been gazing into his drink, but he looked at Mason now, and was taken aback by the fervent gleam in his eyes, but Harlan hid his surprise well. "When she came for me, with the witch called Reuben, her magic was obvious, and I could see the fey in her. She'd unleashed it for a while, and her Otherness glowed within her."

"You admire her," Mason said, watching him carefully.

"Yes. She's very honest—well, with the witches and me at least. She was stranded here after the witches defeated the Wild Hunt on Samhain."

Mason's hand tightened on his glass for a brief second, his face becoming taut. "You didn't tell me that."

"Sorry, didn't I? I guess we've been too busy finding the right buyer and arranging the sale. It's earned us a good commission."

"And her partner, he's not fey?"

Harlan shook his head. "No." He didn't like to admit that he knew nothing about Gabe. He was very reserved. All he knew was that he ran a security firm that employed a handful of men, and Shadow lived with them.

Mason fell silent, looking out of the window again, but his gaze was distant. Harlan had to remind himself that no matter how useful Mason's contacts were, and no matter how efficiently he ran the London office, he wasn't as good at detecting magic and the Otherworldly like Harlan and the other collectors. It's why Mason had moved from being a collector to becoming the director at such a young age. That put Harlan at a distinct advantage, not that he ever showed that.

Mason finally looked at him. "I can't think of a job we need her for at the moment. Can you?"

Harlan ran through their current workload. They had a number of regular clients, and they also had some who approached them for single commissions. The Guild's role was to source suitable objects by keeping an eye on auction houses, both legitimate and those of a more private nature, and advising them accordingly. Or it could be that the client would identify an object and employ them to get it. As an organisation, they were flexible. Whatever the client wanted they would find, within reason. At present they were working a few contracts, but nothing they couldn't handle. But Mason would know that more than anyone. He had oversight of everything.

"No. She has a select set of skills. I suggest we use her carefully."

Mason gave one of his most calculating smiles. "I agree. In the meantime, try and find out a little more about Mr Malouf. We employed a fey once before, but it was long before my role here. He was tricky, I know that much. Did you see her fight the Empusa?"

"No, I was too busy watching the meteoric rise of the ancient forest, and hoping I wasn't about to end up dead."

"Shame. I'd like to know how good she is." Mason returned to his desk, and pulled his phone towards him, a distinctly calculating look on his face. He had a mobile phone, but Mason was old-fashioned and hardly ever used it. "Thanks, Harlan. If you have no other business, take the rest of the afternoon off. You've earned it."

Harlan drained his glass and headed for the door. It was Friday, and he had plans for the weekend, so he wasn't about to hang around. "Thanks. You too."

As he exited the room, he wondered just who Mason might be calling, but if he had any thought of eavesdropping, it was quickly dispelled when he saw Robert coming towards him, treading as softly as a cat. He was Mason's private secretary, and as slippery as a mongoose.

"Business concluded?" Robert asked sharply.

"Like clockwork," Harlan answered, refusing to bite back. He grinned broadly. "Have a nice weekend." He added asshole silently to himself, and as he headed to the stairs, shrugged off the trickle of concern Mason's fervid gleam had given him.

Three

G abe joined Shadow at the table and placed her beer in front of her.
   They sat in the corner of a busy pub, both with their backs to the wall so they could watch the patrons' activities. Shadow was still full of nervous energy, and she picked up her pint and took a long drink. When she finally put it down, she sighed. "That's better."

"The meeting went well. Pleased?"

"Very. I'm not sure if I like Mason, though. Something about him made me uncomfortable."

"Me too," he agreed, nodding thoughtfully. "But we don't know him. He could treat everyone like that. At least he looked at you most of the time. He ignored me completely."

"That's because I'm prettier."

"Pretty annoying," he shot back.

"Pretty useful, actually. Have you seen our account?" She pulled her phone out of her pocket, brought up the app for their bank, and then passed it to him.

Gabe grinned, animating his normally serious face. He had a good sense of humour, but didn't often show it. "That's a solid start," he said, settling himself against the back of his seat.

"Do you think you'll eventually stop the security work?"

"Maybe. But for now we're contracted to Caspian, and I'll honour that. Besides, the discipline of daily work is good." He referred to Caspian Faversham, who was the director of Kernow Industries, and was a powerful witch from an old magical family. Gabe had secured a contract to provide security at Caspian's main warehouse in Harecombe, the town next to White Haven.

Shadow watched him over the rim of her glass. He was cagey about his history, but his physique and bearing betrayed his warrior past, and dictated his future, to an extent. All the Nephilim were close, despite the fact that they weren't all from the same region—they'd told her that much. Other than Gabe and Nahum, who had the same Angel father, the others had different fathers, and that might mean some of their powers differed too; but again, that was pure speculation on her part.

"You seem to know what your life will be here."

Gabe laughed. "Do I? What makes you say that?"

"You seem confident, not worried about change or this strange world we live in."

"Change is inevitable—it's how we deal with it that's important. And this world is no different to how it was in my time, not really. There's just more technology."

She wasn't sure what her future would be, and she mused aloud, "At least I'll have the money to pursue trying to find my way back home."

He frowned. "You should listen to the witches. They're right. You're stuck here. Isn't that what the Raven King said, too?"

"I refuse to accept that. There are portals between this world and ours, but they're well hidden. However, I'm creative and good at finding things."

"So, now what?"

"Now I make a list of the most probable places and start there. Dan has already helped me with this."

"Dan from Avery's shop? You're nuts. That could take forever."

"I've got a long time." As she said it, she felt a weight settle within her. She did have a long time, and the prospect of endlessly trying to get home and trailing around a whole list of mystical places suddenly didn't seem that exciting. What was she thinking? She pushed her doubts aside. She had to try.

As if he'd read her mind, Gabe said softly, "We are as long-lived as you, probably. We need to think smartly about what we do with our lives. No social media, no showy lifestyles. We need to blend in, like the witches. And we'll have to move at some point, pretend to die, and reinvent ourselves."

"But I like White Haven, and I like Ravens' Wood."

"I don't mean now, but we will in the future."

Shadow had a vision of her life as a fugitive, and she wasn't sure if that excited her or depressed her, but Gabe had said 'we.' She liked that. It made her feel less lonely. She finished her pint. "Have we got time for another?"

"I think so. Your round," he said, pushing his glass towards her.

When they arrived back at the farmhouse that night, it was late. Three of the Nephilim were at home, all playing on one of the games consoles in their large living room at the side of the house, overlooking the moors.

When they first moved in, the place was bare, and Gabe hadn't wanted to spend their earnings on luxuries, but as they'd made more money and secured better jobs, they pooled their cash and bought more goods. Most of the Nephilim were from the ancient Middle East and the Mediterranean, except for Barak, who was from Ethiopia. Their decorations reflected those styles. Various tables were dotted around, and lamps lit dim corners. As well as a couple of long low sofas, there were also huge cushions and thick rugs spread across the wooden floor. Nahum still liked to smoke a hookah, and one stood to the side of the fireplace. That was the other thing they all agreed on—a fire that blazed pretty much all day if they were in. They all liked the warmth, and even though they could tolerate the cold easily, they didn't like to.

Tonight, the only light came from the fire and the large TV mounted on the wall, and Nahum, Ash, and Zee lounged in front of it, yelling at each other, surrounded by half-full bowls of crisps and discarded beer bottles.

The Nephilim loved war and action games, and competed furiously. They thrived on physical combat, and consequently picked up the occasional injury. That was okay; they healed fast, a gift from their fathers. However, new technology meant they had found other ways to fight, and this was safer. Gabe watched the screen, still amazed at the quality of the picture. He would never have imagined that this would be the future of mankind, and he couldn't decide if it was good or bad. At least these games were better than actual war, and they'd all had their far share of that.

Shadow was as competitive as any of them, and she hustled Zee along on the couch, grabbing a controller. "I want in!"

"Too late," Ash told her, distracted. "I'm about to kick Nahum's butt."

"No way!" Nahum objected. His fingers punched the controller aggressively before groaning loudly as his character experienced a grisly death.

Ash grinned. "Told you!"

"You must have cheated."

"Yeah, right," Ash said, standing and stretching. Ash, short for Asher, hadn't cut his hair like some of the other Nephilim, and it fell below his shoulders. He wore a short beard under intense hazel eyes. "It must be time for another beer."

Zee was already setting up the next game, but shouted, "For me, too!" Zee had a new scar on his cheek from his encounter with the Wild Hunt. He looked around at Gabe. "How did business go?"

"Successfully. We closed our first deal! I like Harlan, but not Mason Jacobs," he told them as he thought back over their meeting. "There's something slippery about him, but there is also potential for future work."

"There's still more going on in that place than we know, though," Shadow said. Her violet eyes shone with fey light. She eased her glamour when she was around them, and her Otherness was more obvious.

"Of course there is," Gabe admitted. "We'll probably never know half of it."

Zee frowned. "That doesn't matter though, does it, as long as they pay us?"

"True, and we were paid well today," Gabe said. "But I like to have the full picture. I'm a strategist." He sat on the end of the sofa and reached absently for some crisps, pondering the best way to find out more about the Orphic Guild. He could ask Newton, the DI and head of paranormal investigations for the Cornwall and Devon police, but he was wary of involving him in their business. However, they had skills, too.

He looked at Nahum, who looked back at him warily. He was physically similar to Gabe, but while Gabe had brown eyes, Nahum's were blue. Otherwise, they both had thick dark hair, and were square-jawed and olive-skinned. Back in their old life, they had worked together all the time; Nahum was his right-hand man, and all the others knew it.

Nahum put the game controller down. "Why do I get the impression you have a job for me?"

"Beckett and Jacobs know me, but they have no idea about the rest of us. How would you like to hang around in London for a while and check out their place?"

Nahum's eyes gleamed with intrigue. "Sounds good. What exactly am I looking for?"

"Visitors, unusual behaviour..." Gabe shrugged. "I don't know exactly, but I just want to find out more about them. They have lots of money, and I want to know how legitimate it is."

Shadow sat cross-legged, watching him. "You think they're lying?"

"I don't know, but that's the trouble. You might find nothing significant, Nahum, and that's okay. Just hang around and watch. We've got enough cash to put you up in a decent hotel."

"When do you want me to go?"

"In a couple of days, maybe even tomorrow if we can get a room booked quickly. Is there much happening at the warehouse?"

Nahum spent most of his time there, splitting his shifts mainly with Othniel and Barak, but the other Nephilim took their turns, too. Caspian had originally planned to fire his regular security team, but in the end on Gabe's advice had kept them on, and the Nephilim were in charge of them, allowing them time to pursue other avenues of business.

Nahum shrugged. "No. Everything is going smoothly, although Caspian is away at the moment, and I'm dealing with Estelle on everyday matters. There's a big shipment expected in tonight, though, so that's why Barak and Niel are there. She insisted on needing two of us." Estelle was Caspian's sister, and she was as mean as a snake.

Gabe groaned. "She makes life so awkward."

"I like her," Nahum said, a wicked grin on his face. "Awkward is fun."

"You're so weird," Shadow told him.

Nahum just laughed as Ash came back into the room with a handful of bottled beers, and handed them out. "Nahum has always had a thing for feisty females."

Feisty was one word for her, but Gabe had better ones. "It's unlike Caspian to be away for so long."

"Just business, I guess," Nahum speculated.

Shadow laughed. "You men know nothing. Avery has broken his heart, and he headed off to clear his head."

Gabe grunted in surprise. "Caspian likes Avery? I thought he hated the White Haven witches."

Shadow looked at him in disbelief. "You're such an idiot sometimes. Don't you notice anything? That last business with the Empusa had him and Alex almost at each other's throats over her. It's only the fact that Alex is Mr Cool that he didn't punch him."

"Interesting," Gabe said thoughtfully. "Avery is a little too quiet for my liking. I don't get it."

Zee just grinned. "You're as bad as Nahum. You like women with a temper." He slid his gaze toward Shadow, who was too busy setting the game up to notice.

Gabe did not dignify his dig with a response. "I presume Eli is out tonight with another woman?" Eli was proving popular with the ladies in White Haven, and working at Briar's Charming Balms Apothecary meant he met lots of them.

Ash reached for a controller as he answered. "You presume correctly. He must be exhausted."

"The best kind of exhaustion, right?" Nahum said, smirking.

Gabe rolled his eyes. "Let's hope he doesn't catch something."

"That's the beauty of being us though, isn't it?" Nahum replied. "We don't get diseases! Anyway, Gabe, what's my plan?"

"I'll sort the hotel out tomorrow, and get you a train ticket. The Orphic Guild is in an exclusive part of London, so I'll book you a room as close as we can afford. If you find out anything and think you need help, we'll send backup."

"No, don't bother with a train," Nahum said with a grimace. "I hate public transport. I'll drive. Find me a hotel with parking."

"Fair enough. But call me every day with updates."

"And now can we stop talking business?" Shadow asked. "I want to fight one of you, and I'm going to win."

"Game on," Zee said, picking up the spare controller and settling himself in front of the TV.

Gabe popped the cap off his bottle, leaned back in his seat, and settled in to watch the fun.

The next morning, Shadow had a last-minute panic attack after selling the Empusa's sword, despite the fact that they'd tested it extensively, and she phoned El to arrange to meet her for another check on the remaining weapon. El had suggested that they meet at the smithy that she used to make her bigger pieces of metalwork, such as her daggers and swords.

The blacksmith was situated just out of town, in a hamlet called Polkirt. Shadow had never been there before, and she was looking forward to going. Because it was located in such a small place, it was easy to ride to, and she raced across the fields on Kailen. There was a cool wind blowing, and by the time she arrived at the forge, her cheeks were flushed from the journey.

She dismounted, tying Kailen to a fence surrounding the courtyard. El's Land Rover was already there, next to a black van, and on the building was a sign that read, Dante's Forge. She headed to the open door of the old stone building, and as soon as she stepped inside, the heat of the furnace hit her, as did the resounding clang of metal on metal. She squinted to see into the dark interior. The windows were small and grubby with long-accumulated dirt, and mostly blocked with shelving and a random assortment of objects that were stacked on the counter that ran along walls. A fire dominated one end of the room, and a well-built man was hammering out a long piece of hot metal on the anvil. At his side, watching him closely, was El.

As usual, El was an arresting sight. Her long, white-blonde hair was cascading down her back, and she wore black jeans tucked into leather biker boots, and a blood red leather jacket that matched her scarlet lipstick. Her rings, necklaces, and piercings glinted in the low light. The man next to her had dreadlocks pulled back from his face with a bandana, and sweat beaded his brow. As Shadow approached, El turned and saw her, and headed to her side, hugging her tightly.

"Shadow! Good to see you, I'm so glad you could meet me here. It's my second favourite place on Earth!"

The noise stopped as the man halted his work and looked around. He laughed. "Is it?"

"You know it is!" She threw her arms wide. "All this stuff! I love it. And of course, you're here too, I guess that helps."

"Oh, thanks," he said dryly, but he was obviously joking, and it was clear they had a good friendship. He dunked the long piece of metal into a water butt, where it hissed and steamed, and then slipped his thick leather gloves off and shook Shadow's hand with a strong grip. "I'm Dante. Welcome to my smithy." He wore a grubby t-shirt, jeans, and work boots, with a heavy apron protecting his chest, and when he smiled, he revealed white, even teeth that looked even whiter against his black skin. But it was his eyes that were so arresting; they were a pale sea green, lively with intelligence, and there was something about him that radiated trust.

"Thanks. This is a very interesting place. And it's hot!"

He laughed. "My family is from Jamaica; we're used to the heat. That's partly why I opened this place, so I don't freeze to death in English winters."

Shadow frowned, trying to place where Jamaica was. She'd been studying maps and reading all sorts of books as she tried to figure out how this world worked. She was familiar with England and Europe, and Gabe and the other Nephilim had taught her about the Middle East and the Mediterranean, but Jamaica? And then it struck her. It was a Caribbean Island and the birthplace of reggae. Zee had made her listen to Bob Marley, and she loved it.

"I love Bob Marley," she told him. "I should visit there one day."

"Everyone loves Bob Marley," he said, winking. "If they don't, there's something wrong with them."

"Too right," El agreed. She pulled the Empusa's curved bronze sword out of her bag and placed it on a wooden table laden with objects. "So why are you worried about the swords, Shadow? We've tested them to death!"

She shrugged. "I wouldn't say worried, but I sold mine yesterday, and then had a last-minute fear that we missed something." She was cautious about what she said, as she wasn't sure how much Dante knew about El and the events a few weeks ago with the Empusa.

El's eyes widened. "You've sold it already? Wow. Who to?"

"There were a few interested parties, from what I could gather. Harlan wasn't exactly forthcoming on the details."

"Neither of those things surprises me." She looked at Dante. "This bronze sword has a twin."

He folded his arms across his chest. "You were holding out on me! I thought that thing was unique!"

"It is, well, they are. They came from the same place."

"Say no more. The less I know, the better."

An impish grin appeared on El's face. "Trust me. There's nothing dodgy about how we got them, it's just unusual."

"I'm used to your unusual, remember?"

"This was more unusual than most." El turned to Shadow. "He may look rough and ready, but his skills go far beyond smithy work. He knows metal and weapons manufacturing and their history really well. Dante was the one who told me about the sword's worth."

He frowned at her, but he was teasing. "What do you mean by rough and ready?"

"You know exactly what I mean. He has a degree in art history," El said, "so he's very good at dating things."

"Some things," Dante explained. "I worked in a museum a long time ago, and I specialised in weapons and war, but working in a museum bored the crap out of me, so now I work for myself. But," he tapped his head, "it's still up here, and I still keep myself up to date with research and auction prices." He picked up the blade, examining it. "This is called a Sickle Sword, and they are commonly associated with power. It was believed they were the swords that Gods carried."

The myths were right. It was surprising how much of the truth trickled through time. Shadow nodded. "A Sickle Sword? Yes, that makes sense, but we have a different name for them—the Crescent Moon Sword."

Dante frowned. "I've never heard of that before. Where are you from?"

El interrupted, "A long way from here. How old is it?"

Dante was still frowning at Shadow, but he said, "Typically 2500 BCE onwards. Often they're badly damaged, so won't fetch a huge amount, a few thousand at the most, but this one is incredibly well-preserved, with a high level of detail. Depending on the provenance, that would affect the price."

Shadow thought about the money currently sitting in their account. "I sold mine for more than a few thousand, so obviously the provenance mattered to them."

El smiled. "Excellent. I keep this on my wall at home. It looks amazing. And I'm still not selling."

"Fair enough, but we needed the money, and it starts off our relationship with the Guild." Shadow eyed the sword speculatively. "So, other than its unusual background, there's definitely nothing to worry about otherwise?"

"No," El reassured her. "We've examined it here extensively, and Dante didn't notice anything particularly worrying."

Dante nodded in agreement as he leant back against a heavy wooden table scarred by years of work, still holding the sword. He ran his hand across the surface admiringly. "It's skilfully made, and as I said, well-preserved, but I couldn't see anything different about its manufacture."

"Did you work in London?" Shadow asked.

"Sure, twenty or so years ago. It's where the best museums are, and the only place to find the big auction houses."

"Have you ever heard of a place called the Orphic Guild? It's not an auction house, as such..."

He narrowed his eyes as he thought for a moment, and then shook his head. "I don't think so. Where is it based?"

"Eaton Place."

Dante whistled. "Wow. That's an expensive address. They must do well. Who runs it?"

"Mason Jacobs. He's an older man, grey hair, smart suit, very slick. But he doesn't own it. Someone else does, but I don't know his name."

"It still doesn't ring any bells, sorry."

Shadow smiled. "It's fine. I'm just curious about them."

Dante shrugged. "If they got you over a few thousand for the sword, then they clearly know what they're doing."

Shadow looked at the objects stacked around the room. "What do you make?"

"Garden stuff, mainly. I work with wrought iron. I make fencing and hanging baskets, but also gates, decorative things, and swords and daggers on occasion—like today."

Shadow shivered at the mention of iron, but Dante didn't notice, as he'd already given the sword back to El and was heading to the fire. He poked it, and the flames roared back to life. "Now, I need to get on with it. You're welcome to stay and watch. I'm showing El some tips and tricks."

El nudged her. "Come on. You'll enjoy it. He's the best. I'll take you for a pub lunch later. I'm meeting Reuben—you can tell us about your deal."

Reuben, El's partner, was a keen surfer and water witch with a dry sense of humour she wasn't always sure how to take, but he was fun to be around. "All right. You're on," she said as she followed El to Dante's side.

Four

Harlan was at lunch with William Chadwick, one of his most demanding clients, and more than most people, had the ability to annoy the crap out of him. He tried not to show it.

It was Monday, and his weekend had been busy. He'd gone out for dinner with a very attractive American woman who worked at one of the smaller auction houses, and they exchanged news over items that would benefit them both. Occasionally, these meetings became something more than business, but not this weekend. He'd headed home slightly drunk on expensive wine, and slept late on Sunday. To clear his head, he'd gone out on his Moto Guzzi motorbike, enjoying its speed and power, and then he spent the rest of the day relaxing.

Chadwick frowned. "What do you mean you can't find it?"

"Just what I said. All trace of it has disappeared."

"But it's an ancient document rumoured to have been written in the fifteenth century and stored for years in the library of Thomas Norton. There was a lot of buzz around it! It can't just have disappeared."

Harlan took a deep breath and counted to ten. Well, tried to. He made it to five when Chadwick said, "Harlan! Are you deaf?"

Do not punch him, you'll be fired. "No. I know exactly what it was rumoured to be, and believe me, I've been following those rumours for weeks, but now the chatter has stopped. It's gone!" He stared at his client to reinforce his words. Chadwick was an ugly man with pockmarked, sallow skin and beady eyes that even his silk shirt and Italian suit couldn't improve. "I can only presume that someone has already bought it."

"I want to put in a better offer."

"And if I ever find out who bought it, I'll make sure to make that offer, but for now, I don't even know who to approach."

Chadwick's eyes blazed and he snorted like a pig. "I bet it's Cavendish."

"Perhaps. I can contact him if you wish, but as you know, I can't guarantee anything. Or it may have been stolen, although potentially that would make waves."

Chadwick leaned back in his seat and fell silent, and Harlan could practically see his brain cells whizzing around as he thought through his options. Harlan also leaned back and sipped his wine, hoping to ease the tension. Chadwick was an old and valued client, part of a group of very rich and obsessive collectors of alchemical documents. However, he was not a member of the Order of the Midnight Sun, and consequently loathed them. Cavendish was a member of the Order, hence the accusation. And Chadwick could well be right. Competition for such manuscripts was intense. Especially between practising magicians, which they all were. Even those who belonged to the Order were competitive with each other, but others who were not members actively sought to deprive them of any opportunity to obtain ancient texts.

This business was cutthroat. Many of them may have had worldly aspirations, but it didn't stop them from being mean. The thing was, the Orphic Guild also did work for the Order; they worked for anyone who hired them, but as far as Harlan knew, they had not had anything to do with this particular document.

Chadwick stirred out of his long, thoughtful silence. "No, leave it for now. Rumours may resurface. They sometimes do if you wait long enough."

Harlan nodded, relieved. "Of course, but I will continue to listen for any news, as always."

"Good. Let's move on to my other issue." He shuffled forward and lowered his voice, pushing his empty plate out of the way as he did so. "I have found the ancient tomb of a man I have been researching my whole life! I need to get in there for the grave goods, but I can only get so far. I want help."

Harlan had leant forward as well to better hear him, and for a moment thought he'd misheard. "You mean you've already broken into it?"

"Yes! But I believe I've only reached a false outer tomb. The real one is there, but hidden by a veil of magic." He widened his eyes as he said the final word, uttering it almost as a whisper. "I need you to help me get in."

"Forgive me for seeming dense, but you are a magician and alchemist. You deal with the magical all the time. Why can't you handle this?"

Chadwick narrowed his eyes in annoyance. "Because my magic is bound with ritual and research. This is beyond my ken. It's wilder—different."

Interesting. Chadwick had pretty much admitted where his magic ended. "You think it's mystical in nature?"

"Isn't that what I said?"

"I need more details. What is it, and where is it?"

"You can help then? Because I've never asked for this type of assistance before."

Harlan eased back, eager to be further than inches away from this annoying little man. "We have many contacts in the occult and arcane community, as you well know. I am sure that once I have the full details, I can find someone to help you."

"I trust the information will be kept a secret? To the best of my knowledge, I am the only one who knows about this."

"Have I ever been less than discrete?" A note of annoyance crept into Harlan's voice; he simply couldn't help it. "I recently successfully negotiated the Empusa's sword for you, and ensured that you won the bid!"

"I just had to be certain. The sword is magnificent, by the way." A feral glint entered Chadwick's eyes.

"I hope you appreciate how hard that was to come by," Harlan told him. "The Empusa met an unpleasant end, and not by my hand. Now, give me some more details!"

Chadwick flinched and smiled tightly. "Fair enough. As I said, I have been investigating an ancient shaman and Druid for many years. He was reputed to have strange powers. I recently found his burial site. It's close to Belas Knap."

"Sorry, I'm not sure I know what that is."

"Belas Knap is a chambered long barrow, from the Neolithic times. It's in Gloucestershire, and particularly well-preserved."

Harlan had already pulled out his phone, and he typed the name in, waiting impatiently for the information to load while Chadwick talked.

"I found a reference to his tomb in an obscure text, and initially thought it was referring to the existing barrows, as there are a few in that area. But then I realised it was another one, as yet unfound."

Harlan looked at his screen and then at Chadwick with disbelief. "Are you nuts? Belas Knap is well known and heavily researched, and is owned by English Heritage. The surrounding area has been farmed for years. There can't possibly be anything close by."

"Wrong. Belas Knap is set in the corner of a field on a rise, only accessible by a public footpath called the Cotswold Way, and yes, part of the surroundings are farmlands, but it is also next to a small wood that has been undisturbed for ages. That's where I found the tomb."

Harlan folded his arms and stared at Chadwick. "You're proposing an archaeological dig?"

"No! Aren't you listening? I have been in it already! I dug out the entrance myself, and once inside, the place is accessible, but..." He paused as he tried to articulate his experience and then repeated his earlier assumption. "There's something there that stops me from progressing further, and I think it's magic."

Harlan reassessed Chadwick in the light of this news. He hadn't thought he had it in him to do grubby field research, which meant that whatever he hoped was there, must be worth it. "I take it you have disguised the entrance again?"

"Of course, but I have the GPS coordinates, and am prepared to give them to you, if you have someone who can break through the magic at the site."

"I have a very good idea who we could use, but I would have to check first."

Chadwick smiled. "Excellent. If your contact agrees, we will organise the contract. I would like to act as soon as possible."

"What are you prepared to pay?"

"The usual hourly rate, all expenses, plus your cut. And I want to be there, too."

Harlan winced. He was going to ask Shadow, obviously, but he wasn't sure she'd agree to a witness. "I'll see what I can do."

Gabe leaned against the corner of Caspian's warehouse, situated on the outskirts of Harecombe, watching the unloading of the containers that had been delivered from the quay. There were half a dozen men milling around, and despite his relaxed demeanour, Gabe watched them like a hawk.

This shipment had been delayed for a variety of reasons, and Estelle was anxious. She emerged from the inner office, striding purposefully to his side with a scowl on her face. Her long, dark hair was swept up into a chic chignon, and she wore an expensive outfit. Unfortunately, the hard hat and fluorescent jacket she also wore covered them both up, but Gabe knew Estelle well enough now to know her vanity was more bound up with her magic than her appearance, although she always looked immaculate.

Watching the unloading, she asked, "Any issues?"

"None. The manifest matches up so far. We should be finished in a few minutes." He checked his watch. It was nearly three in the afternoon, and he was finishing soon. Barak was due to arrive to cover the evening shift, and Gabe was looking forward to contacting Nahum and hearing his update on the Orphic Guild.

Estelle's expression relaxed. "Good. Our buyers are getting impatient. I see you've brought Shadow today?"

She nodded to where Shadow stood talking to the driver. She was an arresting sight in her black fatigues, even with the fluorescent jacket and obligatory hard hat. She'd complained bitterly about wearing them, but in the end hadn't had a choice.

He nodded. "She has some free time right now, so she's doing some shifts this week. Barak and Niel need a break. I must admit I didn't think she'd agree, but she's easily bored, and curious."

Estelle raised an eyebrow. "A dangerous combination."

"And then some."

Estelle watched her for a while, and then said, "Caspian likes her, actually, and he's hard to please. Although if I'm honest, I think his judgement is waning at the moment."

Gabe twitched his lips with amusement. She could only be referring to the fact that he now liked and worked with the White Haven witches. "Oh, I don't know. He employed me." He winked at Estelle, and she looked at him coolly, but he heard her heart rate rise and her pupils dilated slightly. Okay, that was interesting. Does Estelle like him?

However, before she could speak, Shadow joined them.

"There are some strange items in that delivery," she noted. "Bound for a private address in London."

Estelle's tone was sharp. "It is not your job to pry about the inventory. You just make sure it matches."

Shadow stared at Estelle, who stared back. "I am merely commenting. You can't check something off without reading it."

Gabe saw Shadow's hand move to the small knife she kept strapped to her thigh, hidden by glamour to most people. He intervened swiftly. "Of course not, Shadow, but best to keep such information to yourself. We have to pretend we haven't read it, if you know what I mean."

Her violet eyes turned to him now. "I'm not about to blab it at the pub."

"I know. If I didn't trust you, you wouldn't be here," he said softly.

"Lucky me."

"Lucky both of you," Estelle said. "I'm the one who's paying you."

"I think you mean Caspian is," Shadow shot back.

Estelle's hand balled at her side, and Gabe felt a faint spark of magic before she clearly thought better of it. She glared at Gabe instead. "Keep her on a leash, or I won't let her back in." She turned her back on them and headed to the office. In seconds, the door slammed behind her.

Gabe looked at Shadow with impatience. "Could you stop being a smart mouth just once?"

"She's the smart mouth, not me," she said, bristling. "Anyway, you like my smart mouth."

"I like it sometimes, but Estelle doesn't, and that's who is important right now. I'm trying to cultivate a relationship with her."

"Really? I think you'll find she's incapable. She certainly hates women. And she has what is commonly called a Resting Bitch Face."

Shadow looked very pleased with herself, and Gabe couldn't help laughing.

"Where on Earth did you hear that? Oh wait, El?"

She grinned. "Of course. All the witches hate her."

"Well, you need to get over it. Today, she's your boss." He looked away as the last of the shipment was wheeled into the warehouse behind them. "Anyway, we're done here for now. Barak will be here soon." He steered her up the stairs towards the mezzanine floor and the office they used next to the manager's room. It was small, containing a couple of chairs, a desk and computer. Half a dozen additional monitors displayed what was filmed in various places around the grounds, and a window looked out on the warehouse floor. He headed to the corner and turned the kettle on to boil, getting mugs ready at the same time.

Shadow leaned against the wall, and said, "I heard from Harlan earlier. He's offered me another job."

"Us, I think you mean!"

She wrinkled her nose. "Yes, us. It sounds intriguing. We have to go to a place called Gloucestershire and find a Druid burial site."

"That is intriguing. Who for?" he asked, turning around to face her.

"He didn't say. I said I'd discuss it with you first, once he emailed me some more details."

Gabe almost dropped the cup he was holding. "You actually said you'd consult me?"

Shadow looked offended. "Yes! We are partners!"

"Have you had a recent head injury?"

"No! Was that wrong?"

There was hope for her, yet. "No, it was very right. Well done!"

"Thank you, Mr Patronising. Shall I show you the job?"

"Please do!"

She pulled her phone from her pocket and started scrolling, just as Barak walked in. He nodded as he entered. "Coffee for me too, Gabe."

Barak was as big and muscular as the rest of them, but where some of the Nephilim were lean with muscle, Barak was heavier set, with huge biceps and thighs. He was from Africa originally, and his skin was a deep mahogany colour. He kept his hair clipped short and he was clean-shaven, showing off his strong jaw and generous mouth, but his eyes were gentle and humorous, and of all of them, he was the joker.

He grinned at Shadow. "Finally getting some work out of you, then?"

"Your cheek will get you nowhere! I have a new job, thank you!"

"We do!" he said, reiterating Gabe's early comment. "Do you need my help?"

"No, thank you," she answered primly. And then she frowned. "I don't think so, anyway. Here, you can both look at what Harlan has sent through."

Gabe took the phone from her, and scrolled through the short message and the images of Belas Knap and the woods. "Sounds straightforward, but what do you think?" He passed the phone to Barak for his opinion.

Barak scanned the message and shrugged. "Agreed. It's hidden, and easy to do at night with little local risks. But I'd take a couple of us to keep watch." He looked at Shadow. "It all comes down to the magic that's there, though. Can you handle it?"

"It really depends on what's going on. I should be able to see through a glamour, but it's hard to say until I'm there."

That was enough for Gabe. He was anxious to get more work utilising their unique talents. Security was fine, but they could do more, and he didn't want the team getting restless and doing anything rash. "Sounds good. Tell Harlan that you accept the job. We'll plan for the middle of the week."

"There's one more thing," Shadow said hesitantly. "The man who's hiring us wants to be there, too."

"Why?"

"I guess he wants to ensure we don't mess up or steal whatever it is we find."

That would undoubtedly make life harder. If they needed to use their special abilities, he didn't want outsiders to see. He frowned. "Can you say no?"

"I don't think so."

"Bollocks. We'll just have to put up with him, then."

Five

G abe drove his SUV onto the small car park at the base of the walk to Belas Knap, and looked at Shadow and Niel. "Ready?"

"Always," Niel said, already halfway out of the passenger door. "I need to stretch."

It had taken them almost four hours to get to the site, and it was now early afternoon. The skies were grey and Gabe felt a chill wind slice through him. He headed to the boot and pulled out his thick coat, and next to him, Shadow grabbed hers.

"Just one other car," she noted, looking around the lot.

"Good, let's hope it's quiet at the site, too," Gabe said. It was a fifteen-minute walk from the car park to the site, but it was part of a long, popular walking track called the Cotswolds Way. With luck, the weather would keep people away.

Niel pulled his jacket on and looked up at the sky. "I think it might rain. That will make it very unpleasant tonight."

"We can't help that," Gabe told him. He shut the boot and locked up, asking Shadow, "Did you tell Beckett we're arriving early?"

She shook her head, a mischievous glint in her eye. "No, I just said we would meet him later."

"Good. I don't like people hanging over my shoulder when I investigate."

Gabe headed to the sign that said, *Belas Knap Long Barrow, Ancient Monument*, and set a good pace up the path. The walk featured a mixture of fields and woodland, but rather than try to find the GPS coordinates he had been given to the hidden tomb, he headed straight for the burial site.

It was a steep climb in some places, but the view at the top was spectacular, and Gabe looked around appreciatively. "What a place to be buried!" They were surrounded by fields, and the land fell away below them, brooding under a cloudy sky. A small wood was next to the chamber, but Gabe could see other wooded areas not too far away.

"It's so quiet," Shadow observed. "I like it."

Gabe knew what she meant. The isolated location, devoid of modern buildings and technology meant the land spoke to them, and he knew Shadow felt that more than he did. Niel was already exploring the site, heading past the false entrance, and they followed him as he ducked into one of the stone chambers. Gabe had to bend almost double to get in, but as soon as he entered the tiny space he heard muted voices, as if someone was whispering in his ear.

"Niel, do you hear that?"

Niel nodded, his eyes wide. "The voices of the dead. They're restless."

"The dead?" Shadow said, her voice rising. "You hear the dead?"

"Not all of the time," Gabe confessed, "but in certain places, yes. It's a sign of a place's power."

"Can you tell what they're saying?" she asked.

Gabe paused, listening intently, the hairs on his arms lifting as the voices swirled around him. "Snatches of words, pleas to the Gods, but they're too quiet."

Niel shuffled past him, heading back outside, and they followed, Gabe straightening with relief.

Niel laughed dryly. "This place is almost as old as we are. I like it. In fact, I like this land. It has layers of civilisations here." Niel was a big blond man, who looked as if he'd been hewn from rock. A beard and sideburns adorned his face, and his hair was swept back from his head into a small ponytail.

Shadows hands were on her hips and she stared at both of them. "Can you all hear the dead?"

"To a degree," Gabe told her. "A gift from our fathers, along with other things."

"Can you ever understand them?"

"Sometimes, depending on what they need to tell us, or how agitated they were at death." He shrugged, wondering how to explain what was to him something he had experienced all his life.

"Can you hear them in White Haven, too?"

"No. The place is too busy."

"I did once," Niel said, "up at Old Haven Church when the witch was doing blood magic. The dead didn't like it."

Gabe hadn't known that and he looked at Niel, surprised. "You never said."

"I presumed you'd heard them, too. But I was patrolling the wood all the time, at the boundary of the cemetery. Maybe that's why."

"Can you speak to them?" Shadow asked.

Gabe shook his head. "They are echoes really, not sentient. They're trapped in repeated cycles. But we can't see them," he added, suspecting he knew what Shadow would ask next.

Shadow shuddered. "I'm glad I just hear the earth. I certainly don't want to listen to what's buried beneath it." She looked around, her eyes bright with curiosity. "I've been reading about this place. It's aligned north to south, which is unusual, apparently. Many think the design of the tomb echoes the shape of a woman kneeling down."

"Do you?"

She narrowed her eyes as she stepped back and looked at the tomb. "Perhaps."

"A celebration of a Goddess, then?" Gabe asked. "Mother Earth, possibly. We had such beliefs."

"I thought your God was the only God?" Shadow said scathingly, as she walked up the turfed sides of the tomb to stand on the top.

He walked next to her, trying to keep the disdain from his voice. "So my father would have me believe, but it's not true. There are too many Gods to count, and they all covet worship."

She paused on the rise and looked at the lay of the land, but her eyes were concentrating on something else. "Your angel father?"

He tried not to sound impatient. "Yes, that one. And no, he's not a sylph."

She ignored his jibe. "Is he still alive? If you're superhuman, it would suggest he had immortality."

Gabe found it a strangely painful subject, but he answered her honestly. "He was alive, not that I saw him often, and then the flood came, a punishment to me and my kind for our perceived heresies, and I have no idea what happened to him, because I don't feel him now."

"What about when you were in the Underworld with the other spirits? Did you not hear whispers about them?"

"No. That place was crowded and tormented, and we were there for millennia. I look back to my time before the flood as if it was a dream. A sometimes bloody, battle-filled dream, but a dream nonetheless." Gabe wasn't quite sure why he was having this conversation now, on an ancient burial chamber, with the dead whispering beneath his feet, but maybe just being here was the reason. He had talked to the other Nephilim about it on occasion, but he sensed that it was a topic they would rather bury, along with their past. The betrayal of their fathers burned deep.

She looked at him, her violet eyes bright with intelligence. "You're part of myth and legend. Giants, according to some stories. I've read about you."

He smiled. "I know. I see all of your books lying around."

"Don't you want to read them?"

"Someday. The other guys have looked at them, and have told me enough. There are truths in there, but plenty of lies, too. Of more interest to me is what happened after the flood."

"Why?"

Gabe shrugged. "Unfinished business, I suppose."

"You should tell me what you were really like all those years ago. I could correct the stories," she teased.

"Some things should live beneath veils of illusion," Gabe said, "the better to protect us now. It's a strange world we walk in, and not all dangers are as obvious as we expect."

His voice was soft, and standing so close to Shadow he saw her vulnerability up close, something she normally hid so well. But he was starting to see the real Shadow now, and he liked it, more than he cared to admit.

She stared at him for a moment more, and in the silence he heard the soft thumping of her heart as they were both caught in stillness. And then she looked away, down the bank towards the dry stone wall and the wood beyond.

"Let's head into the wood and find the hidden burial site so we can go and eat. I'm starving." With that declaration she walked away, and after a moment's pause to look around once more, he followed.

It was gloomy beneath the trees, and Shadow led the way, following the directions programmed into her phone. The signal was spotty up here, but she forged ahead into the undergrowth, virtually disappearing at times. Gabe blinked as if to clear his vision, and there she was again, a perfect blend of light and shadow. He laughed to himself. She was certainly well named.

Gabe and Niel were right beyond her, and despite their bulk, they moved quietly. Unfortunately, they weren't alone. There were paths through the woodland, and every now and again, they heard the distant bark of a dog and a raised voice, and Niel muttered, "Bloody dogs."

Shadow stepped unerringly forward, pushing through a thick stand of trees and bushes, slipping through their tangled branches with ease as if they parted for her. As he followed, Gabe noted a few broken branches and some disturbed ground in places, and realised it was probably where their mysterious employer had come through, because Shadow didn't disturb a thing. They followed her up a steep rise and into a small space surrounded by dense bushes on all sides, which protected them from casual onlookers. There was still a heavy canopy of branches overhead, just starting to bud with leaves. Shadow pointed to the mound of rocks against the bank that was smothered in torn ivy and other ground-covering plants. "It's under there."

Niel looked at it sceptically. "Really? Because it looks like a pile of crap to me!"

"Can't you feel it?" Her eyes gleamed. "There's something on the other side."

"Good or bad?" Gabe asked.

"I'm not sure yet."

"That's what worries me," Gabe said.

Niel grunted. "Too late to be having second thoughts now."

"No, it's not. We can pull out anytime we want—not that I'm suggesting we do," Gabe said reassuringly. "I just like to know the odds." He looked at Shadow. "Is it fey magic?"

"I can't tell. Shall we look?"

He shook his head. "We'll wait for tonight; best not to upset the client. Let's just check the area before we go, and then we'll pick the keys up for the cottage and find a pub for lunch. What time are we meeting Harlan later?"

"About seven," Shadow told him.

"Excellent," Niel said, pushing his way back through the bushes. "There's nothing like a pint before a night of grave robbing."

Six

Harlan met Chadwick in the bar of the hotel they had both booked into for their arranged meeting. He hadn't really wanted to be at the same place as his client, but it was the easiest thing to do, and besides, Mason had sort of insisted on it.

Chadwick was as well groomed as always, and he had a glass of white wine in front of him, which for some inexplicable reason annoyed Harlan. *Why couldn't he just order a pint?* Harlan almost defiantly ordered the local beer and sat opposite him.

"Are you looking forward to tonight?"

"I am! I've been searching for this burial site for a long time."

"Perhaps you'd like to share exactly why that is? You've been very coy." *And perhaps that was the reason for his nervousness*, Harlan reflected. He was usually well prepared for these events, but Chadwick had refused to reveal any details. "You should know by now that you can trust us."

"I do trust you," Chadwick said smoothly, "but I'm also suspicious. I wouldn't like to think that someone else would beat me to it when I'm so close." He leaned forward, his eyes filled with a maniacal gleam. "That's why I have to be there."

"Why?"

"Why don't I wait and tell you all together? What time are we meeting your hunters?"

"They'll be here at any moment. In fact," he looked around, hearing the door swing open and voices behind him, "I think they're here."

Shadow was standing next to Gabe and another man that Harlan hadn't met before who looked like a marauding Viking, and they stood to meet them. Shadow smiled, and her eyes darted to Chadwick, before resting on Harlan. "Harlan, fancy meeting you so soon!"

"Aren't I lucky?" he said, amused. "This is William Chadwick, our client. Chadwick, this is Shadow, Gabe, and—"

"Niel," the large blond man supplied, shaking his hand and then Chadwick's.

"Three of you?" Chadwick said, sitting again after greeting them. "I'm not sure you'll all be needed."

"Oh, trust me, we will," Gabe replied, smiling charmingly while flashing his perfect teeth. "Seeing as we've been told very little, I like to be prepared."

Harlan looked at him, impressed. "Me, too. Chadwick has been worried about security, but is obviously ready to tell us now."

Chadwick glanced down at his glass as they settled themselves at the table. "I believe I have found the burial place of a Druid and bard called Kian. He should have his ritual objects buried with him, and I want them."

"Have they any particular significance?" Harlan asked.

"Not really, but the fact that they have been masked with some sort of magic may suggest otherwise."

Harlan started to get an uneasy feeling. "Is it something that could cause danger?"

"I thought you liked danger, Harlan?"

"I don't mind it, but I'd rather know what we're facing."

"And seeing as I'm the one who'll be breaking through the magic, I'd really like to know more," Shadow said, a dangerous edge to her voice.

Chadwick sipped his drink, unperturbed. "Well, as I said, he's a Druid, and therefore whatever went with him to his grave would have been his personal objects. A window into his world."

"Surely most things would have rotted away?" Niel asked, sipping the pint he'd brought with him to the table.

"Perhaps, but I have to see anyway."

Gabe leaned forward, his curiosity piqued. "There must be something of value?"

Chadwick just looked at him. "It is *all* of value. A powerful Druid who wielded magic and served the old Gods. That must be what protects his grave, even now."

Harlan hated it when his clients became fervid about the old Gods. It almost always caused trouble. Like the Callanish Ring did. *Which reminded him...* "Shadow, Chadwick is the man who brought the Empusa's sword."

Shadow turned to him, frowning. "Oh! And what are you doing with it?"

"Nothing. It is displayed on my wall. Harlan hasn't exactly said how you came to own it, but I'm very grateful you did. "

"I had help," Shadow said, cagily. "Let's hope tonight is not so tricky."

Niel nudged her. "It's just some grave robbing, Shadow."

"And what skills do you two bring tonight?" Chadwick asked, looking at Gabe and Niel.

"Just security," Gabe said nonchalantly. "Hanging about in woods at night could have consequences. What else can you tell us about this Druid?"

Chadwick spread his hands wide. "Nothing. He was the Druid for a powerful tribe, and travelled between here and Breton, and well, did what Druids do! Protected his people and pacified the Gods. But they were revered for their knowledge. Surely you know that?"

"But why him?" Gabe insisted.

"Not many names make it through history. Most are lost in time. His name is found in documents written much later, and his deeds were impressive. But he was overshadowed by one of his contemporaries—or near contemporaries, at least—Merlin."

"Merlin!" Harlan exclaimed.

"But no one's heard of Kian, which is good for me," Chadwick said brightly.

Gabe pushed his chair back. "Fine. In that case, we'll meet you there at midnight, at Belas Knap. I trust you'll be wearing something more suitable?"

"Of course." Chadwick looked slightly affronted.

"Good. Wouldn't want you to damage your nice suit," Gabe told him, and he nodded at Harlan as he left the table.

"Until tonight then," Shadow said, all smiles as she and Niel followed Gabe out of the room.

Harlan watched them leave and then looked back at Chadwick. "Well, that was short and sweet."

If Chadwick was perturbed, he didn't show it. "Excellent. To tonight." And he raised his glass, downed his drink, and ordered another.

Shadow stood on top of Belas Knap again and gazed across the dark fields, enjoying the cool night air on her skin. There was a pale crescent moon rising, and it gave off a faint light that silvered the fields.

She could see well in the dark—better than most humans, she'd realised—but maybe not as well as Gabe and Niel, who seemed as comfortable at night as in the day. Gabe stood silently next to her, but Niel stood below them, by the path, while they waited for Harlan to arrive.

They'd come back early, and once again had walked around the ancient site and along the edge of the woods, making sure no one was there.

"This place has more power at night," Gabe observed, stirring out of his silence.

She nodded. "I know. I feel the weight of its years. Can you hear the dead?"

"Faintly. Remember to keep your powers as secret as possible, Shadow. Be careful tonight. I'm not sure I trust Chadwick."

"I'm not sure I do either, but it's unlikely he'll put us in danger. He wants his Druid objects very badly."

Earlier that evening, when they had returned to the cottage they'd rented for the night, they had tried to find out more about the Druid Kian, but had failed miserably. They would need to do proper research to discover anything significant, and even then Shadow suspected they would require more unusual resources than they had access to at the moment.

Gabe pointed to the path where dark shapes were coming into view. "They're here. Good. I want to get this done."

Harlan was in his sturdy leather boots, jeans, and a jacket, but Chadwick was in hiking clothes and he didn't waste time on pleasantries. He nodded at them and simply said, "I'll lead."

He brought them over the break in the dry stone wall and into the foliage, leading them confidently to the burial site. It was dark under the trees, and Chadwick's torch flashed along the ground. Shadow was behind him, and the rest followed closely, Gabe at the rear. When they reached the covered cairn of stones against the slope, Gabe stepped into the enclosed area with them, but said to Niel, "Just patrol around the edges."

Niel gave a short jerk of his head, and then disappeared silently into the trees.

"How do you want to play this?" Harlan asked Chadwick, who was already pulling on sturdy leather gloves.

"Help me clear the entrance," Chadwick grunted as he started work. "And someone keep the torch on it."

Gabe pulled gloves out of his pocket and started to move the rocks, while Shadow stood next to Harlan, who kept his torch trained on the spot, and watched. Within a few minutes they had cleared the ivy and pulled the stones away, revealing a small hole in the side of the bank. Chadwick stopped and took out his own torch out, shining it inside.

Shadow shuddered, feeling a strange, unrecognisable power drift out of the opening and swirl around them. Interesting. This was a type of fey magic, but it felt darker somehow. Only Gabe caught her movement, as Chadwick was too busy peering into the tomb.

Concerned, he asked, "Are you okay?"

"It feels odd. Do you sense it?"

"I'm afraid not."

Harlan looked between them, worried. "What is it?"

"I'm doing what you hired me to do," Shadow told him. "I sense a strange sort of power, stronger now that the tomb is open."

Chadwick grinned, a gleam of excitement in his eyes. "You feel it? Good. Beyond this entrance is a short passageway, but you'll have to crouch. At the end is a square, stone-walled tomb, but I feel I'm not seeing everything properly."

They seemed to be making a lot of noise, but around them was silence, and Shadow was glad that Niel was out there, somewhere. Chadwick continued to clear the stones, and with Gabe's help they moved quickly until the entire entrance was revealed.

Chadwick stepped back, inviting her forward, and Shadow stared down the passage. Chadwick's torchlight showed nothing but an earth floor and rock walls that were crumbling in places. Tree roots had thrust through the walls, and debris and stones were scattered across the ground. She glanced up at Gabe's worried face, and placed her hand on the knives sheathed against her thigh.

Chadwick cleared his throat behind her. "I'll go first."

"No, you won't," she said, turning quickly and throwing a hand out to stop him. "It's too small, and you'll get in my way."

"No, I have to see," he said, his voice rising with annoyance.

"And you will, when I've finished."

Gabe put in, "It's going to be a tight squeeze if I come, too."

"No one is coming, including you," Shadow said to Harlan as he looked as if he might protest. If she had to do anything odd, she certainly didn't want Harlan or Chadwick seeing it. She turned back to Gabe. "If there's room further down I'll call for you, but only you!" She shot a warning glance at Chadwick to emphasise her point.

Shadow pulled her knife out and edged down the low passageway, ducking her head and stooping. In her left hand she held her torch, knowing it would look too odd to Chadwick not to use it. The passageway led downwards and then turned left, and she picked her way slowly, careful not to trip and twist her ankle. It was musty, the strong earthy smell of decay almost overpowering. Dust rose around her, and she lifted her jacket across her mouth. She felt as if the roof might collapse at any moment, and it was with relief when the passage opened into a small square room as Chadwick had said.

A low rock shelf had pottery objects on it, and a stone coffin lay on the left. The top had been pushed open and bones were inside it. Shadow wondered why Chadwick would think there was more to this tomb, but she turned her torch off and let her eyes adjust to the dark. The prickle of power was stronger here, and it seemed to be coming from the back wall. Chadwick was a ritual magician, which was probably why he could feel it, too.

Gabe called from behind, his voice low. "Shadow, are you okay?"

"I'm fine. Come on through." There was enough room for both of them, just about. *Damn tombs.* They were damp and cold, and she remembered why she'd stopped doing this kind of thing in the Otherworld.

She heard a short, sharp whistle, and then within seconds Gabe was next to her, his shoulders covered in dust, still ducking due to the low ceiling. "Sorry, I called Niel to guard the entrance. I didn't entirely trust Chadwick not to follow us. What have you found?"

"This wall at the back is either enhanced or constructed with fey magic." She placed her hand on the cold stone, pushing her energy out of her fingers and into the rock. "It's odd. The power that's protecting whatever's beyond here is strong. But who did this?"

Gabe stood next to her and felt the wall, too. "Maybe it's like you said before. Years ago, the boundaries between worlds were weaker. Perhaps your magic was shared."

She handed her blade to Gabe. "Let me try something." She placed her hands on the wall again, closed her eyes, and concentrated on the feeling beneath her fingers. It felt as if her palms were sinking into the rock, and she pushed harder.

"It's working!" Gabe cried. "It's shimmering!"

Shadow hadn't had the occasion to use her power like this before, and she started to feel drained. Within seconds, the wall snapped back into place, solid and unyielding. She sighed and stepped away. "I'm going to try something else."

She pulled her sword out of its scabbard, and directed her fey energy down through the dragonium blade, forged from some of the most powerful creatures to exist in her world—dragons. When the blade was humming with magic, she pushed it into a seam in the rock, satisfied when cracks started spreading across the surface. She focused even harder, aware of Gabe watching intently. "Nearly there," she said, now certain it was an illusion.

Within a few minutes, the wall vanished with a *crack*, revealing another passageway behind it.

"Yes!" she exclaimed.

Gabe grinned. "It's heading towards Belas Knap."

"Is it?"

"Yes. Can't you tell? Maybe his tomb is beneath the others. Come on."

This passage was bigger than the first. Again, the floor was of beaten earth, but the walls were made of layered stonework, and although some of the stones had dislodged, it was generally in a good state, allowing Gabe to set a quick pace. The path ran undisturbed in almost one straight line, deviating only slightly in a few places. Along the wall were recessed shelves where objects were placed: animal bones, bird skulls, unusually shaped crystals, and other decayed items. Finally, they paused on the threshold of the hidden tomb.

"As I thought," he said softly. "I think we're pretty much dead centre of Belas Knap. This place must have had great significance at one point."

The vault was circular in design, again made of layers of thick rock, rising to a shallow domed roof. In the middle of the space was a long, rectangular stone, like an altar, and on it was a human skeleton, grave goods arranged around it.

"Are you okay in there?" Harlan called, his voice faint.

"Yes, give us a few more moments," Shadow shouted back, and then said to Gabe, "Let's see what's so precious about this place first."

The roof was higher than that of the passage, allowing them to stand upright. Various objects were also on shelves in here, such as goblets, plates, dried things that may have been food, animal skins, and a carved walking stick that was almost as tall as Shadow. What looked like a leather bag lay upon the coffin itself.

"It all looks harmless enough, although this—" she said, pointing to the wooden staff, "has a hum of power about it." She examined it closely, seeing carvings along its length.

"A walking stick?" Gabe said, confused.

"It reminds me of staffs the shamans in our world carry."

"What about the jewellery? Any magic there?" He pointed to the rings and thick bracelets on another shelf.

"Faint only." She peered into the gloom. "I can't see anything suspicious, can you?"

Gabe shook his head. "No, nothing. I'll call Chadwick."

He headed to the end of the passage, leaving Shadow standing alone, and she flashed her torch around the tomb again. She noticed a small, polished flat stone sitting within the jawbone of the skull, and she picked it up, observing strange markings on it. Why was a stone placed in the jaw? But before she could consider it further, she saw a black shape manifest out of the bones, and she blinked, thinking her eyes were playing tricks.

Shadow backed away and kept her torch trained onto the area, holding the stone awkwardly. She held her sword in her other hand, ready to defend herself, although she wondered how a blade would help fight a ghost, or whatever that was. A wave of power rolled around her, and she stepped back again.

For endless seconds nothing seemed to happen, and she realised she was holding her breath. And then Gabe was next to her, Harlan and Chadwick behind him.

"What's up, Shadow?" Gabe asked, looking concerned at her raised sword. "Have you seen something?"

As soon as he spoke, the black shape manifested again and smacked Shadow in the chest, throwing her against the wall behind her. The torch and stone clattered to the floor. In seconds she was on her feet and she slashed forward, missing Gabe by inches as the mysterious entity retreated.

Harlan and Chadwick were still in the entrance, their torches flashing, and Harlan yelled, "What the hell is happening?"

Then it launched again at Shadow and Gabe, who was still standing next to her. This time, the two of them collided with each other against a far wall, and another wave of power rolled across the tomb.

"Is that a ghost?" Chadwick shouted, sounding both alarmed and excited. "It must be Kian! The Druid!"

"Why in Herne's balls is it attacking us?" Shadow said, outraged.

"I think it has a lot of pent-up energy," Gabe suggested, pacing the perimeter as he watched the black shape in the middle of the room.

"Yeah, well, so do I," Shadow replied. Determined not be defeated by a dead Druid, she pulled her fey magic towards her, and then sent it out like a punch, straight at the bulk of Kian's shade.

Within seconds the spirit disappeared, leaving all four of them looking around wildly. Harlan and Chadwick wouldn't have seen her magic, but they might have felt it. Hopefully, in the semidarkness they wouldn't notice.

"Where did it go?" Harlan asked, spinning around.

Chadwick trained his torch down the passage behind them. "Maybe it fled for the entrance?"

"In that case," Gabe said, "it's gone, and there's not much we can do about it."

"What about Niel?" Harlan asked. "For a ghost, it sure contained a lot of energy."

"Niel will be fine," Gabe reasoned, but even so, he looked worried. "Maybe you should do what you need to, Chadwick, so we can get out of here."

Harlan agreed. "Yeah. I'd rather be outside if he comes back."

Chadwick, however, didn't look so sure. In fact, he was grinning like a madman. "To have found his tomb is one thing, but his ghost! This is too good!" He looked at Shadow. "I'm impressed! You did it."

"That's what you pay me for."

Chadwick was already prowling around, flashing his torch everywhere and taking photos as he examined every inch of it.

Harlan frowned at her sword that she still held, just in case. "Where were you concealing that?"

"Nowhere special," she said, raising an eyebrow. "But it came in handy for breaking the illusion. It's not really that useful for ghosts."

"No, I guess not."

Harlan still looked uneasy, and he shone his torch around the stonework. "This is an impressive place. He must have been revered to have merited such a special burial."

"Yeah, but why hide the entrance?" Gabe asked uneasily.

"Because he was like royalty," Harlan suggested. "They didn't want anyone stealing his valuables and ruining his afterlife."

Chadwick was already gathering up all the grave goods and packing them in his bags. He grinned at them. "You did well. Harlan was right to choose you two."

"We'll finish the payment as soon as we leave the tomb, then," Harlan told him.

"Of course." Chadwick was barely listening, and when he came to the long wooden staff, he stroked it almost reverently.

Gabe pulled Shadow to the entrance and whispered, "Entities don't just disappear. I don't like this."

"We broke the seal. It has no need to stay here now."

Gabe looked doubtful. "Things that carry that much power don't disappear so easily."

"Maybe it's scared of my magic," she suggested, her voice low and her back to the others.

"Really? Or is he in one of those objects?" He nodded to where Chadwick was closing up his bags, laden with the stolen items.

"Then it will be his problem," Shadow told him. "Ready, Chadwick?"

He nodded, a satisfied smirk on his face, and Shadow led them out into the cool night air.

Niel sighed with relief when he saw them emerge. "I was just starting to get worried. Success?"

"Of course," Shadow said confidently. "You really shouldn't doubt me."

Niel gave her a withering look. "Silly me."

"I don't suppose an overly energetic ghost headed this way?" Gabe asked hopefully.

"Ghost? No." Niel looked confused. "What the hell did you do back there?"

"Kian didn't like his grave being disturbed," Harlan told him, still looking spooked.

Shadow started piling up the stone and debris against the hole in the bank again, and Niel helped her. "I think we should keep this sealed, but I have a feeling someone will spot it sooner rather than later."

Gabe turned to Chadwick, who was busy securing his bags. He'd given Harlan the staff to hold. "Chadwick, the Druid's ghost was in there, and it didn't seem to like being disturbed. You have his grave goods now, so be careful."

Chadwick straightened up. "I'm not scared of a restless spirit."

"Maybe you should be. It manifested enough energy to throw me into a wall." He rolled his shoulders. "That doesn't happen to me very often!"

Chadwick eyes travelled across Gabe muscular physique. "I guess not. But it didn't attack all of us!"

"True, but I'm just not convinced it's gone for good."

Chadwick was already turning away, dismissing his opinion. "Thank you, but I've been doing this for a while." He hoisted the bags on to his shoulders and set off through the trees, the staff once again in his hands.

Harlan watched his retreating back. "I'm sure he'll be fine. He really has been doing this for years. He's one of our oldest clients. I better go. We're in the same car. Thanks, guys! You'll get your payment later."

Harlan left, and Gabe helped Shadow and Niel close the tomb, muttering under his breath. "Well, don't say I didn't warn him."

Seven

When Harlan arrived in London the following day, he headed straight to the office, knowing that Mason would call him in at some point for an update.

He considered the previous night a resounding success. Chadwick was overjoyed at finally breaking into the tomb, and had babbled about it all the way back to the hotel. Harlan shuddered just at the thought of it, even as he looked around at his richly appointed office, which was soothing in its normality. He hadn't seen Chadwick at breakfast as he'd checked out early, returning to his Gothic pile in Highgate.

There were many things Harlan enjoyed about his job, and the money was especially good, but he hated ghosts. When he'd first entered this line of work, it was because he had a deep interest in mythology and mythical magic objects. Not only did he study them extensively, amassing his own impressive private library, but he'd also obtained a few of those objects for himself. Small goods much like they had found last night, but without the ghost that lurked in the tomb.

It was during the course of his grave investigations—he hated to use the term tomb raiding, he wasn't Lara Croft or Indiana Jones—that he'd come across the Orphic Guild. He'd never even thought this type of work existed until he'd been approached by a much younger Mason Jacobs, who had already given up fieldwork. He winced at how long ago that was. Olivia James, another collector, was his first contact, and they had met during the pursuit of a very interesting Incan statue with reputed strange powers. He had, by the skin of his teeth, beaten her to it. But she was the one with the better buyer and the higher profit margin. They had made a deal, and the rest was history.

Olivia was English, but based in San Francisco at the time, before she had been called back to the London branch. Within a few years, he had followed. The Orphic Guild was bigger than most people realised—by design. In addition to the London office, there was the U.S. branch in San Francisco, a branch in Rome, and one in Paris.

Harlan was still wearing his jeans, boots, and leather jacket, and he flung his backpack into the corner, threw his jacket over the closest chair, and then headed up to the Guild's library on the second floor. He wanted to research Kian, the Druid. He hated being a step behind, and last night he'd felt he was just that. Chadwick was infuriating, and he'd allowed his money and influence to stop him pressing for details long before he should have. He vowed he wouldn't allow that to happen again. That everything went well was more of a testament to Shadow and Gabe than his own efforts. The trouble was, he had to be careful with Chadwick, because he was a very old client and personal friend of Mason's. Damn politics.

He pushed through the double doors into the library, relieved to see that it was empty. The smell of old pages, musk, and vanilla filled his senses and he inhaled deeply, before heading directly to the section he thought would be of most use. With luck he'd get a few hours of peace before he needed to speak to Mason. He searched quickly, pulling book after book off the shelf, rummaging through them. He found half a dozen that should help, and then turned to some of the older texts and papers that he couldn't take home. Finding a comfortable chair, he settled down to read.

When his phone rang, shadows were stretching across the floor, and Harlan's shoulders ached. He answered quickly, the noise jolting him out of his studies. As predicted, it was Mason calling him to his office for an update. He confirmed he'd be with him in fifteen minutes, and then frowned at the papers in front of him. He had found virtually nothing on the Druid, other than passing references, and nothing that suggested his burial site. Maybe he should speak to Aidan Deveraux. He was another collector who specialised in that period. Not for the first time did he wish that Mason would employ a full-time librarian. It would make all their lives so much easier.

Aiden answered within seconds. "Harlan. It's been a while. How's London?"

"The usual. How's Scotland?"

"Freezing! The snow is virtually impassable in places, but I'm holed up at the castle, and fed and watered, so that's okay."

Harlan laughed. No one had wanted to be in the far north of Scotland at this time of year, but as Aiden was already there investigating the origins of the Crossroads Circus and trying to find the actual crossroads, it made sense he should stay and taken on the new case. "I trust there are roaring fires and whiskey?"

"Those are about the only plus points. The family is arguing non-stop. But that's tedious, and I doubt it's what you've phoned about."

Harlan told him about the tomb beneath Belas Knap, and how he wanted to find out more about the Druid, Kian.

"Belas Knap has a burial beneath it?" Aiden asked, shocked. "There have long been rumours of one! In fact, excavations years ago found the ruins of a small stone circle in the centre, but that was all."

"The entrance was well over a hundred metres away, and the tomb itself was very deep. Look, I know you're lacking in specific resources, but will you see what you can find out?"

"Sure. But why do you care? It's over now, isn't it? Chadwick has his treasures, and you've confirmed the usefulness of another hunter."

"You're probably right," Harlan admitted, "but I can't shake this feeling I have. Maybe I need a good night's sleep."

"All right, I'll see what I can find and I'll be in touch."

Mason had just ended his own call when Harlan walked into his office, and he was beaming. "Great job last night. Chadwick is very happy." He gestured for Harlan to sit. "Do you know how long he's been looking for that tomb?"

"No."

"Almost twenty years, but it's been his obsession for far longer, ever since he found some archaic old documents."

Harlan eased back in his chair, feeling the previous 24 hours catching up with him. "What's so special about Kian?"

"He's one of the great Druids of the dark ages. Rumoured to have been around slightly earlier than Merlin, although Merlin got all the fame."

"You believe Merlin existed?"

Mason laughed. "Of course, but probably not quite as the stories suggest."

"Why aren't there stories about Kian? I must admit, I've been trying to find some information myself."

"Chadwick hasn't told me much. It's part of his life's great work, but you know these alchemists...they have many, varied interests. He's planning to write about it, so he's understandably cagey. He doesn't want anyone stealing his thunder."

Harlan laughed. "Does anyone care, apart from him?"

"Maybe not," Mason said, shaking his head. "But, he thinks his own great obsessions are everyone's. Anyway, he wants to invite Shadow to dinner to thank her."

Harlan shifted uneasily in his chair. "Really? He doesn't normally do things like that!"

"Like I said, it's been a long time, and this is the end of his search. He knows it took a special kind of person to break the magic that sealed the tomb. He's planning to go back to the site at some point, to investigate it more fully—in private, you understand."

"Of course. But he should go soon. It's very obvious that the bank has been disturbed now, and quite frankly it's a death trap. The passageways are partially collapsed in some places."

Mason nodded. "I'll call Shadow and extend the invite, but I just wanted to say well done. I presume you have other jobs to keep you busy now?"

"Sure," Harlan said, rising to leave. "There are a few occult objects coming up for auction this week that I need to contact some clients about, and one of our long standing searches might have thrown up a few clues to an alchemical document."

"Excellent. I'll leave you to it."

As Harlan shut the door, he reflected on how little Mason seemed to know about Kian too, but he didn't seem to care. Maybe Harlan was reading too much into it. Their clients looked for all sorts of strange things; the Callanish Ring was only one of them. All had the power to wreak destruction, but they trusted their clients to do the right thing.

He headed to his office, shaking his head. He needed a hot meal, whiskey, and bed.

----◆----

It was a slow drive back to White Haven for Gabe and the others, and Gabe fumed at the tail of traffic in front of him. He wanted to speak to Nahum, anxious to see if he'd found out anything interesting, but he knew ringing at lunch time was the best time to call.

When he pulled into the farmhouse courtyard, all of the cars and bikes were gone, except for Barak's, and Gabe realised he was probably sleeping after his night shift.

"What are you up to now, Shadow?" he asked, as all three headed to the kitchen.

"I need to ride Kailen. I hate being cooped up in that car. Then I'm meeting Dan."

"Dan from the bookshop?" Niel asked, opening the fridge and pulling out half a dozen eggs.

"Yes, we're going to Tintagel this afternoon."

Niel frowned. "I think I've heard of that. Has it got a castle?"

She nodded and leaned against the counter, watching him prepare a second breakfast. "Yes. It's very famous."

Gabe had settled at the table, and felt his stomach grumble. They'd all eaten earlier, but he was already hungry again. "Breakfast for me too, please, Niel. Is that the King Arthur castle?" he asked Shadow.

She nodded, starting to prepare cups for the coffee that was percolating on the bench. "And food for me!"

Niel groaned. "I'm not the bloody cook!"

"But your breakfasts are amazing, you know they are," she said cheekily, and dodged out of the way as he flicked a tea towel at her. "I'll make you dinner later. I'll bring back rabbits again, and start a stew before I go out with Dan," she added brightly. "And yes, it's the King Arthur castle, at least according to all those myths these people love so much."

By these people, Gabe knew she meant humans. Their layers of history were muddied and confused, a mixture of the real and imagined. It was a way of grounding themselves in the world, figuring out what was important, and a rare chance to keep some magic in their common lives. It was the same as when he was first alive, just the stories were different.

"Why are you going there?" he asked.

"Dan suggested it would be a good place to start with my investigation of places where boundaries could break. Although, he also said it was one of the most popular tourist attractions in Cornwall, and there were probably better spots to look for boundary magic." She slid a cup of coffee onto the bench next to Niel, and one in front of Gabe, and then sat opposite him, while Niel continued to cook. "But I thought I'd start there—even though it might not really be his castle."

The smell of bacon began filling the room as Niel started cracking eggs. "Who's this King Arthur dude?"

"He's a famous king who saved Britain from attack and united the people. He's in the Otherworld now, so I know that he's not made up. Which means," she said, her eyes wide, "if *he's* real, what else is?"

Niel looked at her, surprised. "He's in the Otherworld? How did that happen?"

She sipped her drink thoughtfully. "I'm not entirely sure. Something to do with a spell in exchange for his sword, Excalibur. It was created by the Forger of Light—he's very famous where I'm from. Or should I say infamous? Anyway, the Lady of the Lake wanted it to happen, so Merlin agreed, and they made a long-winded spell."

Gabe smiled. He doubted it was a long-winded spell at all, but Shadow loved to either play things down or exaggerate; there was no middle ground with her.

Niel nodded. "Interesting. So why do you think Tintagel Castle might not be his?"

Shadow snorted. "Because so many places here are associated with him! They can't all be true. But, Dan is happy to show me around, so why not?"

Niel finished plating up their bacon, eggs, and toast, placed a plate in front of them all, and joined them at the table. "Of course he is. He fancies you."

"Just a sign of his good taste, then," she said, as she tucked into her food.

Niel shot a look at Gabe and he laughed. It was a relief that they all got on so well. When he had asked Shadow to stay with them, he'd done so in a fit of guilt. He thought he had killed her, but instead she'd feigned death and escaped after the witches defeated the Wild Hunt, forcing it to return to the Otherworld. When he went back to move her body, and that of a male fey who had also been killed, she had vanished, and he had spent weeks tracking her down before finally capturing her in Old Haven Wood. A pure-blood fey was adept at hiding in woodlands.

He'd felt slightly guilty about keeping her in an iron cage in the basement for so long, but he'd had no idea what to do with her. It was Zee who finally made him free her, and much pressure from Alex and Avery, two of the witches. If he had just let her leave, where the hell else would she have gone? He'd rather she stayed here where he could keep an eye on her. And yes, she was nice to look at. But she also had a good sense of humour, was a great fighter, and wasn't intimidated by the overly-testosteroned Nephilim. She was a great fit.

"What are you doing today?" she asked Niel.

"Going back to bed before I head to the warehouse this evening. I need all my strength if I'm to put up with Estelle."

"That bitch," Shadow grumbled under her breath, but before Gabe could say anything to defend Estelle, his phone rang, and he left the other two sitting at the table in order to answer it. He leaned on the counter and looked over the fields outside, rubbing the stubble on his chin as he absently thought he must shave. "Morning, Nahum."

"Hey, Gabe."

"You sound tired."

"I had a late night watching Eaton Place. You don't sound so sharp yourself."

"I was tomb hunting, and we found a restless spirit."

"That's more interesting than my job." He sounded bored.

"No intriguing revelations about the Orphic Guild, then?"

"None. I watched it for almost 24 hours, just in case, and all I've seen are regular staff coming and going like clockwork. Mason Jacobs puts in the longest hours. He's there sometimes until nine at night."

Gabe was disappointed. "I guess I should be relieved that there's nothing out of the ordinary happening. Well, within reason."

Nahum laughed. "Yeah, running an organisation that hunts for the occult is anything but normal, but I know what you mean. I've noticed they have a rear entrance, accessed by another road, very discrete, but I guess that's only to be expected. I've only seen a couple of people go in that way, though."

"How did you manage that?"

"I flew up on the roof at night and found myself a nice spot to watch from all day."

"Very creative!"

"Do you want me to stay here?"

Gabe sighed as he thought about it. "Just for a few more days. I doubt you'll discover anything, but it will make me happy."

"Sure. I'll head there again shortly."

He rang off and Gabe turned around to see Niel and Shadow staring at him expectantly. "He's found nothing," he told them. "Which is a good thing, right?"

"Yes," Niel answered. "Your arrangement with them is already proving lucrative, so don't mess it up." He directed this at Shadow, and she rose to her feet disdainfully.

"How dare you. I'm going to shoot rabbits, so you better not get in my way, or you'll find an arrow in your back."

She turned and stalked out of the room and Niel grinned at Gabe. "I really enjoy winding her up. She bites so easily."

"You won't be saying that when she actually takes a chunk out of you."

Niel rose to his feet and dumped the dirty plates in the sink. "That's going to give me some very sweet dreams. Later, brother." And with that parting shot, he headed to bed.

Eight

Shadow stood on the cliff top overlooking the ruins of Tintagel Castle and gasped. "That is quite impressive."

Dan grinned at her. "I knew you'd love it! Who doesn't, though? It's magnificent."

Shadow narrowed her eyes and tried to imagine how it would look completely intact. "It's in such a commanding place. No wonder history says King Arthur was born here."

It was a beautiful day on which to see Tintagel, too. It was early afternoon, and the spring sunshine was warm, the sky a pale blue, and clouds like feathers scudded across it. Shadow felt as if she were on top of the world. She turned to look along the cliffs that ran on either side, and then down to the waves crashing below.

"Come on," Dan said, eager to show her more. "Wait until you're inside it. We can go over the bridge. It's fairly new."

Shadow saw the steps below, winding up the face of the cliff. "But we have to walk the steps later."

"Of course. Merlin's cave is down there, too. The tide is out so we'll be able to get in."

She followed Dan, enjoying his infectious excitement. As he walked, he told her some of the tales, and she explored the ruined rooms, stroking the stonework. They eventually ended up on the beach, the cliffs towering over them, and she looked into the gloom of the cave, trying to find a quiet moment—which was difficult with half a dozen tourists around them.

"I don't think he really lived in this!" she said, turning her nose up.

Dan laughed. "Me neither. He'd surely drown at high tide. I doubt even his magic would keep him dry. But it's romantic, as so many of the King Arthur tales are."

He led the way inside, the damp sand squelching beneath their feet, and remembering their encounter in the tomb, she asked, "Have you ever heard of a Druid called Kian?"

"Kian? No, I don't think so. Should I have?"

"Not really, but I raided his tomb last night."

Dan spun around, his mouth falling open. "What on Earth were you doing that for?"

"Another assignment. We met his ghost, and he wasn't happy."

"I wouldn't be happy if you raided my tomb, either," Dan said. He looked at the other people close by, and pulled her out and up the stairs. "Let's find a nice patch of sun and an ice cream and you can tell me all about it."

By the time they were once again on the cliff top, Shadow was hot and breathless, and accepted an ice cream cone gratefully. The grass was warm beneath her and she gazed across the sea, feeling as if she could release her own wildness here, and blend in effortlessly.

"Go on," Dan prompted, sitting next to her, cross-legged.

In between bites, she told him what had happened the night before, and about Chadwick.

Dan frowned at her. "I can't say I approve of stealing from tombs. Those things are our cultural heritage! Everything we find tells us more about our past!"

She poked her tongue out at him. "Spoilsport!"

"Thief!" he shot back.

"If it wasn't for Chadwick's investigation, no one would have found it, anyway!"

Dan shrugged. "I suppose, but I still don't approve. But, if I'm honest, I had a feeling the Orphic Guild would do this sort of thing. Did you say Chadwick is an alchemist?"

"Among other things."

"Wow, Old School. I don't think there are many around anymore!"

Shadow felt she should confess her ignorance. "I must admit, I'm not really sure what one is."

"They were the forerunners of modern scientists, studying a strange mix of philosophy, magic, astrology and other esoteric things. They were chiefly known for searching for immortality and trying to turn lead into gold." He laughed at her puzzled face. "I have no idea if they still do that, or whether it's all just research-based now. If I remember correctly, they did have a resurgence in the early twentieth century, I think. That's about a hundred years ago for you!"

"We have fey who do such things, although it's less about the search for immortality. We already have long lives. It's more about the search for potent objects. Of course magic is normal in our world, although some of us possess more of it than others."

Dan looked surprised. "Don't you all have the same amount?"

"No. I can't do what the witches do here. My magic is attuned to the earth. I can't cast spells. But other fey who come from the powerful old families have special magic, enhanced by jewels or objects. But again, they don't really use spells. Of course we have a few witches and magicians too, and bards who weave magic with their words, and other types of fey who look quite different to me."

Dan's face took on a dreamy quality. "I wish I could go there. To think it even exists is amazing."

As he spoke, Shadow saw a pixie pop up in the distance, scowling at the humans, and she turned away, trying not to laugh. She wasn't sure whether to tell Dan or not, but decided against it. Maybe one day.

"There's still a lot of magic in this world, Dan. It's just hidden, smothered in technology. But you know that, you work with a witch! If you ever feel that it's missing in your life, just visit Ravens' Wood." She shivered, as a cool wind picked up and silvered the grass along the cliff top.

"True," Dan said, standing and pulling her to her feet. "Come on, let's go to the gift shop, and then I'll take you home. Over the next few days I'll read up on alchemists. You've piqued my curiosity now."

As they walked towards the shop, Shadow's phone rang, and she frowned at the unknown number. "Hello? Shadow speaking."

"Excellent, this is Mason Jacobs, my dear. Remember me?"

"Of course."

"I have spoken to Mr Chadwick today, who is so pleased with your help last night that he has invited you and Gabe to dinner, to show his thanks."

"Really? He's paying us!" Shadow said, not sure if she wanted to go to dinner with such an annoying man. "That's enough."

"No, no," Mason persisted. "He's really keen. This is something he's been looking for, for nearly half of his life. It could mean more lucrative work for you, too."

He left that comment hanging for a moment, and Shadow felt that to refuse would be rude, more than anything. They did not want to annoy Chadwick or Mason.

"Fine, that's very generous of him. I can speak to Gabe about it. When was he thinking?"

"Saturday night? He lives in London. You could book a hotel, make a weekend of it. There are many amazing sights to see around here."

She nodded, pausing outside the shop, and Dan waited with her, trying not to appear as if he was eavesdropping. "Okay. I'll call you to confirm."

She could practically hear Mason preening on the other end of the phone. "Excellent! I look forward to hearing from you."

She groaned as he hung up. Thank the Gods Harlan wasn't as formal.

"What's up?" Dan asked.

"I've been invited to dinner with the alchemist, Chadwick!"

"Great," Dan said, looking mischievous. "You can report back. Now come on in and I'll buy you a King Arthur key ring!"

It was seven in the evening before Shadow saw Gabe again.

As soon as she arrived home, she started cooking her rabbit stew, and the rich smells drifted around the house. She knew it amused the Nephilim that she liked to cook, because she was anything but domestic; in fact, Eli had called her feral one night after she'd thrown her dagger at him and it had lodged in the wall mere inches from his head. But there was something soothing about the chopping, preparing, and balancing of flavours that quieted her overactive mind.

She could hear the shouts of Barak, Ash, and Eli from the living room where they were again fighting on the games console, the air ripe with insults that should have made her blush if she wasn't storing them for use later. Niel had already left for the warehouse, and Zee was at The Wayward Son, working the evening shift.

Gabe entered the kitchen, his hair still damp from the shower. He had jeans on and nothing else, and her eyes ran across his broad, sculpted chest before eventually resting on his amused face.

"Looked enough?" he asked.

"Well, if you insist on walking around displaying yourself like a prized cock, what do you expect?"

"I'm hoping you mean cockerel?" he asked, holding her gaze challengingly.

"What else would I mean?" She turned back to the pot and stirred it slowly, her tongue in her cheek as she tried to suppress a smirk.

"And for the record, I am not a cockerel, either. I'm looking for a clean t-shirt."

"I am not your laundry woman, so how would I know where it is?"

"If you remember anything at all, the laundry room is the other side of this one. I'm simply passing through."

He strode past her and she turned to watch his retreating back, admiring the sculpted muscles there too, and wondering where he put those huge wings. Herne's horns! These Nephilim stirred her blood like no other. Not that anything would ever happen between them, especially Gabe. They were housemates, with a business to run. But there was no harm in looking.

When he returned, he'd pulled on a clean white t-shirt, and if she was honest, that looked almost as good as his bare chest. She distracted herself from her thoughts by grabbing a loaf of crusty bread and started to slice it. "I heard from Mason today. We've been invited to dinner with Chadwick, on Saturday night."

Gabe groaned, as she knew he would. "You're kidding, I hope. That sounds like the most boring evening ever." He reached into the fridge and pulled out two bottles of beer, automatically popping them both and handing her one. "Why?"

"He's very grateful for our help."

"He paid us."

"I know, that's what I said. But Mason insisted, and it felt rude to say no. Especially if we want more business!"

Gabe grimaced. "Did you say this Saturday?"

"Yep."

"I can't go. I need to be at the docks, the one in Falmouth. There's another big shipment due, and Estelle wants me there."

"Does she, now?" she asked, wondering what else Estelle might want to do with Gabe. He frowned at her insinuation, and she moved on. "Great, I'll cancel."

"No. You should go. You're right. It's very important to keep our clients happy." He smiled smugly.

She threw her head back and groaned. "How very convenient! I don't want to go on my own! It could be awkward." She brightened then. "Nahum could come. He's already in London."

"No. I want to keep him an unknown entity. Perhaps Harlan could join?"

"That could work. I like Harlan."

Gabe clinked her beer with his own. "There you go, then. I'm sure Chadwick won't mind. Although, Harlan might."

"I'm so charming that I'm certain he'd love to accompany me."

Gabe's smile was tight. "You so are. Now, is that ready to eat, or am I going to die of starvation?"

Nine

S hadow negotiated the train and tube easily, checking into her hotel in London by mid-afternoon on Saturday.

She was staying at the same place as Nahum, and as agreed, at five on the dot, there was a knock at her door. She opened it to find him leaning against the opposite wall, and he gave her a lazy smile.

"You made it."

"Of course I made it, I'm not an idiot." She turned and headed inside as he followed.

"Always so touchy!"

"Only when people insinuate things."

He sighed. "I wasn't insinuating anything. It was just a greeting." He shook his head. "You are such hard work sometimes."

"Am not!" She headed to the mini bar and pulled out a beer. "May I offer you a drink in an effort to soothe your delicate sensibilities?"

"My delicate sensibilities! Yes, you can." He took the bottle from her, popped the cap, and sipped while he paced around the room. "Are you all set for tonight?"

She gestured to a black, slim-fitting dress hanging against the door, and strappy heels waiting on the floor. "Of course. I'm making an effort."

Nahum almost choked. "I never thought I'd see the day!" His eyes flitted from the dress to her and back again. "And heels? Can you even walk in them?"

Shadow glared at him over her bottle. "Of course I can." She winced. "Admittedly, I practised. El helped."

Nahum laughed. "Go El! Did she give you the outfit, too?"

"You don't think I'd buy one?" she asked, mildly affronted.

"No. You don't seem the shopping type."

"I am if it's for weapons! You should see the market in Dragon's Hollow. Weapons to die for!"

"Isn't that an oxymoron?" He smirked at her, and sat down in a chair next to a small table.

She grinned at him. "You know exactly what I mean." Nahum was very charming, just like the other Nephilim, despite the smirk on his face.

"So you're hoping to make an impression tonight?"

"I've already made an impression," she replied smugly. "But business is business. And besides, I could still kick your ass in a dress."

"Never suggested you couldn't. Although, I do wonder where you'll put your knife," he said, raising an eyebrow.

"Let me worry about that!"

"Is Harlan picking you up?"

She nodded, and sat on the bed. "At six-thirty. Apparently, Chadwick lives in a Victorian Gothic house on the edge of some park. I'm intrigued! I've never been invited to dinner before. Well, not here anyway. I just eat with you lot, or at the pub with the witches!" She reflected for a moment. "I think I'm quite excited. It will be interesting to see where he lives, what he cooks..."

Nahum smiled. "It's strange, isn't it, this new life?"

"Do you think so, too?"

"Of course! We all do. We're living outside of our time, and although I'm growing used to all of this," he gestured around expansively, "I still find myself needing to stop and orient myself sometimes."

Shadow regarded him silently for a moment, and then voiced something she had been thinking for some time. "I'm lucky to be living with all of you. You, more than anyone, understand how weird this life is."

"Well, at least we're in the world we were born in, unlike you," he said softly. "But it's virtually unrecognisable."

She frowned. "I actually don't know what I'd have done if Gabe hadn't asked me to stay! I thought I'd live in the wood, but that's ridiculous, really."

"You would have managed. You are fey, after all," he said, a hint of sarcasm to his tone.

Now she knew he was teasing her. "And you're cheeky."

He laughed and stood. "I better go. I just wanted to make sure you were okay. I'll be watching the Guild again later. Phone if you need me."

"Is it really worth watching it?" she asked, following him to the door.

"I don't think so, but it keeps Gabe happy. He's thorough, and he's always done the right thing, for as long as I've known him."

"He's a decent half-brother, then?"

"The best. But, we're all like brothers, regardless. We're unique. And we were all betrayed by those who supposedly loved us." His eyes darkened for a moment, and he opened the door before he could say anything else, as if he felt he'd shared too much. "Just be careful tonight. And yes—" he held a hand up, palm outwards. "I know you can look after yourself! More importantly, have fun!"

He winked and left the room, and Shadow watched him go, wondering exactly what he meant by *betrayed*.

◆◯◆

Harlan pulled his car onto the gravelled drive in front of Chadwick's Gothic home, all turrets and arched windows and chimneys, and Shadow studied it for a moment.

"This is a cool place. It's a bit like a small castle!"

Harlan laughed. "It's not as old as it looks. In the nineteenth century, a lot of these were built by the Victorians after there was a resurgence of interest in all things Gothic."

"Have you been here before?"

"Once, years ago." He raised an eyebrow. "I feel very privileged to be asked again!"

"Thank the Gods I put a dress on then," Shadow said, amused. She pointed to the old Jaguar in the driveway. "Is that Chadwick's?"

"No, that's Mason's. It's his pride and joy."

They exited the car and headed to the front door that was positioned beneath a huge stone archway and rang the bell, hearing it tone deep within the house. In seconds, Chadwick was ushering them in. "Excellent, welcome!" His eyes swept across them both approvingly. "My dear, you look just fabulous in that dress!"

Shadow smiled, self-consciously smoothing it over her slender hips. "Thank you. I felt the occasion warranted it."

Harlan tried not to laugh. It might have fit like a glove but he could tell she was entirely uncomfortable wearing it. To be fair, he wasn't all that comfortable in his suit. Give him his jeans and bike leathers any day.

However, all thought of discomfort left him when he looked around. He'd forgotten how overpowering this place was. The house was decorated dramatically, with dark paper and gilt patterns. Side lights were dim, and the flooring was a mixture of tiles and thick rugs.

Shadow was equally impressed. "Wow. I even feel like I'm in a castle."

Chadwick looked smug. "I like to think I'm the King of the Castle when I'm home." He led them along the hallway and into a large drawing room, also dimly lit, and with a roaring fire in a stone fireplace that was easily half as tall as the room. Mason was standing in front of it, holding a glass of wine.

"Our guests of honour! Good drive over?"

"As good as can be expected on a Saturday night," Harlan said dryly. "At least it's not raining, but I don't think it will last. There are a lot of clouds out there."

"Forget the weather!" Chadwick said, pouring them white wine. "You're here now, and I have a selection of food you won't believe. Although," he looked sheepish, which was very unlike Chadwick, "I confess that I didn't cook. My chef came in earlier and prepared everything, assisted by my housekeeper!"

Shadow was pacing around the room, glass in hand, studying it with narrowed eyes. "You have a lot of things!" she observed.

The whole house was an exhibit, Harlan thought. Paintings and prints jostled for space upon the walls. Vases, figurines, and other objects, were crowded on occasional tables and shelves.

"I do love art and beautiful pieces," Chadwick admitted. "When I buy something, I have to display it to perfection!"

"There are so many different styles here," Harlan observed. "I had no idea you were such a magpie!"

"That's because he only uses us for certain items," Mason said. "Where do you keep your more unusual collections?"

"My arcane treasures? In other rooms, slightly less public than this one. I'll show you later." He looked at them knowingly, fellow conspirators in the occult business. "But first, *hors d'oeuvres!*"

For the next half an hour or so they all chatted politely, and Harlan had to admit Chadwick was the perfect host. He lead them to the dining room, also decorated dramatically, and they sat at a table covered with white linen and dressed with glassware and silver, while Chadwick carried in the dishes himself. That seemed odd, and gave Harlan the faintest prickling of unease. He knew that Chadwick's housekeeper lived at the house and helped him with everything. He was a rich bachelor, and not used to looking after himself.

They had eaten the starters and the main course, when Harlan asked, "Where's your housekeeper, Chadwick?"

He answered quickly. "She has the night off! Heading to the cinema, I believe. I've had to manage."

"And doing so beautifully," Mason said smoothly, shooting Harlan a look of annoyance.

Chadwick pressed on. "Anyway, my dear, tell me a little about you." He fixed Shadow with an intent stare and she shuffled uncomfortably.

"There's nothing interesting about me. I was brought up a long way from here, but have recently settled in Cornwall. A place called White Haven."

"And what do you do, other than help find treasures?"

"Not a lot. I work with Gabe in his security business."

"The man you were with the other night."

"Yes, that's right, and Niel, who was also there." She was answering politely enough, but Harlan could tell she was wary about saying too much. He hoped Mason hadn't said anything about where she was really from, either.

"They are uncommonly large men," he said sharply.

"They are distantly related. Sort of cousins. They're all big."

"But you said Gabe couldn't be here tonight?"

"Unfortunately not. Gabe sends his apologies. He's tied up with his other business. Thanks for letting me come with Harlan instead."

"And how did you meet them?"

"We met on Halloween last year, at a party!" She shrugged, a hint of amusement in her eyes. "We hit it off! I live with them now."

"Just the two of them?"

"Yes." Shadow sipped her wine, and Harlan exchanged a nervous glance with Mason. "And what about you? Have you lived here long?"

He brushed it off. "It seems like forever." He pushed away from the table. "I'll bring dessert."

"Do you need help?" Harlan asked, moving his chair as if to rise. He felt guilty watching him trip back and forth to the adjoining kitchen on his own.

"No!" Chadwick smiled as if he realised he'd answered too abruptly. "I'm fine."

In the brief moments they had before he returned, Harlan said to Shadow, "Sorry. I wasn't expecting him to quiz you."

Shadow shrugged. "That's okay, it's just conversation. No harm done."

Mason spoke quietly. "I must admit, he doesn't seem quite right tonight. He normally loves to talk about himself."

Before anyone could answer, Chadwick returned with a tray of chocolate desserts in glass goblets. "I hope you all like chocolate. They're divine."

They all murmured their assent, and Harlan started to eat, the rich flavour filling his mouth. He barely noticed Shadow's frown as she looked across at Chadwick and placed her spoon down. And then he felt very dizzy, the room began to spin, and everything went black.

Ten

S hadow was on her feet in seconds, and she pulled her dagger out of the sheath strapped to her inner thigh.

Mason and Harlan were facedown on the table, unconscious, while Chadwick looked at her with cold, calculating eyes.

"You know, it's generally not polite to poison someone at dinner!" she said, half-inclined to slit his throat right now.

"I've never been one to follow convention. More importantly," Chadwick asked, "why aren't you affected?"

"I could taste the drug in my food." She could taste it still, a bitter residue disguised by the bitter chocolate. It had given her a faint buzz, but nothing more, and she shook her head, clearing the last of it away.

A slow, evil smile crept across Chadwick's face. "I knew it. You're fey."

"You're ridiculous. Have you gone insane?"

"Who else could have penetrated the magic that sealed my tomb?"

All evening she'd been looking at him, feeling something was amiss, and clearly so had Harlan and Mason. Suddenly, it hit her.

Chadwick wasn't Chadwick anymore.

"Kian, I presume?" She stood, frozen, her knife poised, deciding not to comment on his accusation.

He leaned back in his chair, watching her. "At your pleasure."

"I really don't think it is. What do you want?"

"My freedom!"

"You seem to have it. Why did you invite us here?"

"Because I wanted to speak to you!"

She shot a glance at Mason and Harlan, relieved to see they were still breathing. "You're not planning on killing them, then?"

"No. The poison was just to shut them up. You're the one I want."

"Why?"

He didn't answer. Instead, he studied her, and she wondered what he was waiting for. And then she wondered what *she* was waiting for. She should act now. Bury her knife in his chest and watch him die. That would be the end of it. Except that would also be the end of Chadwick, an innocent man, and potentially Kian's spirit would find another body to inhabit.

Shadow repeated her question, her irritation rising. "Why do you want me?"

"I needed to know what you are. And now I do. But your friends aren't fey."

"And neither am I."

"Liar." With a swift movement, he pulled an unusual-looking gun from under the table, took aim, and shot at her chest.

With lightning reflexes, she dived for cover behind a large stuffed sofa, and peeking around it, released the knife without hesitation. It flew at Chadwick, but he ducked and rolled out of the way surprisingly quickly, and her dagger missed him and landed in the wall.

Shadow could smell iron in the air. It must be the bullets. She didn't know much about guns, but she was pretty sure he didn't need an iron bullet to kill her. Any would do. He didn't seem to want to take a chance. Kian rose to his feet, raised the gun, and marched across the room, ready to fire again.

Shadow cursed the fact that she hadn't brought her sword, or another knife, and realised even with her speed she couldn't get to the one embedded in the wall that quickly. She picked up the nearest object to hand, which was a solid wooden-carved head on a small table, and threw it at Chadwick.

It hit his left arm, spinning him around, and he yelled in pain. The gun fired, shooting wildly up at the ceiling, and a shower of plaster rained down. He ran from the room and she raced after him, kicking her heels off, and retrieving her dagger as she went.

He dashed through the kitchen and out the other side, into a hallway. A couple of doors stood open, all with light coming from them, but Kian was nowhere in sight.

Shadow paused, catching her breath and listening for sounds of movement. A *thump* came from one of the rooms ahead, and she ran, only slowing as she reached the threshold. She edged forward until she could see the whole space.

It was full of Chadwick's collections. Plinths and tables had been placed with care, and objects were lit with soft spotlights. A collection of antique swords was on the wall, the familiar shape of the Empusa's blade in the centre. But there was no Kian.

Double doors leading to a connected room were on the left, and after satisfying herself that it was safe, she crossed to them, deciding to get another weapon on the way. She picked the Empusa's, wishing it was her own sword instead, but it would be better than nothing. She chided herself for not suspecting something sooner. Even Harlan had said that Chadwick was being surprisingly generous with his thanks. She remembered Gabe telling her he didn't think the spirit had gone, and she'd dismissed him, like an idiot.

The room beyond was in darkness, and she turned the lights off in the one she was in before she advanced, trusting that her eyesight was better than his. She dropped to the floor, waiting for her vision to adjust, and within seconds saw movement ahead.

She crept forward, wondering what to do with him. Her best options were to capture him or knock him unconscious, while they figured out a way to expel Kian from Chadwick. Alex, the witch, would know how.

She could see Kian clearly now, crouching as he tried to hide behind a piece of large, bulky furniture. She could just make out his leg, and crossing the threshold, she continued to ease towards him, only stopping when she heard a whirring noise and a clang overhead. She looked up in time to see a cage dropping on her.

Thank the Gods for high ceilings. She dived to the side and the cage crashed down, missing her by inches. Kian stood and shot at her, and she threw her knife at him simultaneously. It landed in the centre of his chest and he jerked back, hitting the wall before sliding to the floor, and she felt a searing pain as the bullet hit her left thigh. And then the most peculiar thing happened.

She watched Kian's shade leave Chadwick's inert form, its boundaries surprisingly clear. She could see his features, and a red gleam behind his eyes, before the spirit disappeared through the wall.

Damn it.

Despite the pain, she stood up, limped to the door, and entered the hall beyond. Kian was swifter than her now, already close to the kitchen.

Herne's hairy balls. He must be heading for Harlan and Mason.

Her wounded thigh burned, and blood dripped down her leg as she hobbled after him.

She'd just reached the dining room when she saw Kian's ghost grin at her from where he stood between Harlan and Mason. He was shockingly solid, and she briefly wondered why he needed to inhabit another body. He was of average height, with a dark shock of hair, thick eyebrows, and an intense stare. She could even make out his clothes—a loose shirt and trousers, covered by a long robe with a cowl hood. Mason was already rousing, his head lifting from the table, but Harlan was still inert. He was also closest to her, and she grabbed him, hauling him off the chair and onto the floor with her all strength. But she couldn't protect both of them. Not that she had any idea of how to protect a body from possession.

Kian sank into Mason, and with a jerky movement, he stood on shaking legs. He paused for moment, grinning maliciously at Shadow. "Until next time!"

He ran out the door, and within seconds she heard a car engine roar to life, the spatter of gravel, and then silence fell.

Bollocks!

She sat besides Harlan, feeling for his pulse. The beat was strong and regular, and with an inward sigh of relief, she called Nahum, relieved when he picked up quickly.

"Hey, Shadow. Isn't it a little rude to be ringing someone else at a dinner party?"

"Not when your host is dead."

His lazy, teasing tone disappeared immediately. "What? Are you okay?"

"I've been shot with an iron bullet and I'm bleeding all over the floor. Harlan's unconscious, and Mason has been possessed."

"Give me your address. I'm coming right now."

"No! I need you to wait and see if Mason turns up at the Guild. If he does, follow him. Besides, I have no idea where I am."

"You really don't do things by halves."

"No shit. I'll find the address and text it to you, but until then, watch for Mason."

She rang off, and slapped Harlan's face. "Harlan, wake up!"

He groaned and then went limp again.

Deciding to give him a few more moments of blissful unconsciousness, she examined her leg. The bullet had taken a chunk from her outer thigh, about two thirds of the way up, and it was still bleeding profusely. She grabbed a napkin from the table and pressed it to the wound, wincing from the pain, and then decided to call Gabe.

He answered quickly. "I've just heard from Nahum. You should have called me first."

Shadow's temper started to rise. "Well, excuse me! And yes, I'm all right, thanks, other than missing a large portion of my blood!"

He hesitated, and then said, "Sorry, worry makes me cross. Besides, you do sound fine!"

"Asking wouldn't go amiss, just so you know!"

There was a longer pause, and Shadow could almost see him trying to control his temper. "Nahum will bring you home."

"I think he should stay here, actually. To try to find Kian."

"Fill me in, on everything," he ordered.

Shadow took her time, describing the evening as best she could. "I'm going to wake Harlan now, I hope, and then... I don't know," she sighed, suddenly weary, "We need to decide what to do next."

"You shouldn't get involved with the police."

"I don't think I have much choice." Part of her wanted to run, but as the witches kept reminding her, that wasn't the way this world worked.

"No, probably not." His voice was serious, and Shadow knew he'd be weighing up the implications of this for all of them. "Ask Harlan for Mason's address, and tell Nahum. It might be worth him checking there, too."

"That's true. Harlan is still unconscious, but as soon as I have it, I'll send it. I'll call you later."

Shadow hung up and turned to Harlan again.

"Harlan! Wake up!"

She shook his shoulders, relieved to see his eyes finally flicker open. "Shadow? What's going on?" He lifted his head, confused. "Why am I on the floor?"

"You were drugged."

His eyes focussed and he sat up. "What? Ow! My head hurts, and I feel sick." He lifted his hand to his head. "I was eating. Did you say drugged?"

Shadow filled him in on what happened, and as she talked, Harlan started to look less pasty and more worried.

"Chadwick is dead?"

She nodded. "Sorry. It was him or me. As it was, he took a chunk out of me." She gestured to her leg.

Harlan leaned over. "Show me."

She lifted the napkin, showing him her wound, and fresh blood started to well again. "It stings, which I suppose is to be expected. I'm not sure if the iron bullet is making it worse."

He examined it and then said, "Did you say Mason is possessed?"

She nodded. "Again, it was either you or him, and I could protect you because you were closer." She paused, frowning. "Protect might not be the right word. How do you stop a ghost? Anyway, he was next to Mason, so... Not the most logical choice for him. You're younger, fitter—but there you go."

Harlan smiled briefly. "Thank you. I appreciate not being possessed, but," he glanced at her wound again, "we need to clean that."

Shadow pressed the napkin back into place. "Later. For now, can you find something to strap it up?"

Harlan nodded, and rising on still shaky feet, headed to the kitchen, returning with a fresh towel, which he proceeded to wrap tightly around the wound.

"That's the best I can do. We need to get you to a hospital."

"No way. I'd rather see Eli or Briar, the earth witch. She's the best healer I know. They'll ask uncomfortable questions in a hospital. What are we going to do about Chadwick?"

Harlan stood and extended a hand to her, pulling her to her feet. "Can you walk?"

"Just about."

"Lean on me." He proffered her his right arm, and they made their way slowly through the kitchen and down the rear corridor to the room where Chadwick's body lay. It was pretty obvious that he was dead, but leaving Shadow leaning on a chair, Harlan bent down and felt Chadwick's pulse. "He's definitely dead. Damn it."

A million things raced through Shadow's mind. "What now? Do we call the police?"

Harlan rubbed his face wearily. "There's a detective we use for cases like this. She's used to the paranormal."

"Someone like Newton, you mean?"

"Yeah." He turned to her, his eyes full of sadness. "I liked Chadwick, most of the time. He was annoying and impatient, but he didn't deserve this."

"I take it he doesn't live with anyone else?"

"No. He hadn't had time for relationships. He's a confirmed bachelor. His close friends were other eccentrics... And us." He looked around at the ornate furnishings and rich fabrics. "Ironic, isn't it? The very thing he's been looking for years to discover has killed him." He frowned as he focussed on a corner of the room. "Is that Kian's staff?" It was propped against shelving, as if it had been put there and then forgotten, and he collected it and handed it to Shadow. "I can still feel power in this, can you?"

She held it carefully, and nodded. "I can." She felt a faint hope stir. "You know, I think he forgot this in the rush to escape."

"Good. We can use it to bargain with." He pulled his phone out. "I'd better call Maggie."

"Is that the detective?"

He grinned for the first time since he'd regained consciousness. "Oh, yes. You're gonna love her!"

Eleven

G abe sat on the sofa in the living room of the farmhouse, and gazed vacantly at the TV. The sound was muted and he wasn't even focussing on the picture. He was deciding what do with the situation in London.

"Trouble?" Niel asked, handing him a beer and sitting in the chair opposite him. It was past midnight, but they all kept late hours, and he had just returned home from the warehouse.

"Yeah." He looked at Niel bleakly. "Shadow was attacked earlier this evening by the ghost of Kian—the spirit from the Druid tomb. Chadwick is dead."

Niel's jaw dropped. "How?"

Gabe ran through the details. "Nahum is trying to track Mason, aka Kian, without success, and I'm waiting to hear back from Shadow. She's being interviewed by the police. A woman called Maggie."

"This is really bad."

"I know. But Shadow says this detective knows the paranormal world, and hopefully she won't be arrested and thrown in jail."

Niel snorted. "Like that would hold her!"

"But it would make life tricky."

"What can we do?"

"Absolutely sod all for now. We need to figure out what Kian wants with Shadow. But she needs to heal first."

Niel frowned. "Isn't she like us? Can't she heal quicker than humans?"

"Not like we can. And she was shot with an iron bullet, which doesn't help."

His voice rose with surprise. "He knew what she was?"

"Apparently, yes."

"This keeps getting worse." Niel stood and paced to the fire.

Gabe thought through his conversation with Shadow again, feeling despondent. "She thinks Kian wants his own body, but we have no idea how he'll recover that. And in the meantime, we have to try to get him out of Mason's body without killing him."

"Why didn't he kill Harlan and Mason?"

"Good question. According to what he said to Shadow, he just wanted them out of the way so he could get her alone." He scratched his chin, perplexed. "He was either trying to kill her, or wound her badly enough to kidnap her."

Niel's back was to the fire, his voice grim. "We regained our bodies through blood. Is that what he'll do?"

Niel had voiced the very thing that Gabe was thinking. "We have to consider that it's a possibility. I'm pretty pissed that our first job has already caused bloodshed."

"You didn't do it on purpose."

"I promised Alex. I take my promises seriously."

"You couldn't have foreseen this," Niel said, trying to reassure him. "We'll honour our promises by stopping Kian. But, we need to know why he wants Shadow, and what he'll do next!"

Gabe nodded. "It must mean something that her magic opened his tomb."

"That's what worries me. He was sealed in for a reason. Why? What was so bad about Kian that his burial place was hidden with fey magic? Why would the fey even become involved in sealing a Druid's tomb?"

Silence fell as Gabe tried to make sense of Kian's actions. "Maybe fey blood is what he really needs, not human. That's why he made a cage for her. He must have acted quickly in the last few days since we released him. Make the cage, invite her to dinner, drug the others..."

"And now he's hiding, biding his time until he can trap her."

"We need to get her back here," Gabe said decisively. "She'll be better protected with all of us around."

Niel barked out a laugh. "Ha! I don't think she'll see it like that."

"She's not stupid. She'll know she's a target, and for all her skills, she'll still need help. I'll get Nahum to bring her home."

"Shadow might be right. He may be of more use staying in London, looking for Mason."

"No. Harlan can do that. He knows the city better, and has connections there. I'll call Nahum now."

<hr />

Harlan watched Maggie, officially known as Detective Inspector Milne, walk around the room where Chadwick's body lay.

She was what he called a 'ball buster,' in American slang. And he didn't mean that affectionately. She was of average height and size, with light brown hair and blue eyes, and at first glance, you'd almost dismiss her as insignificant. But those were the only average things about her. Once you got to know her, she was unforgettable. Maggie was intelligent, short-tempered, had a great sense of humour, and swore like a trooper. She was currently in full flow.

"Christ almighty, Harlan! You really are an A-1 shit! Look at this place!" She flung her arms wide. "It's the mother lode of all occult shit put together! And a cage? A fucking cage? Is this the fucking Wicker Man?"

Harlan had been trying to calm her down, unsuccessfully, for the last half an hour. "I know how it looks, but we'll find him. The whole thing has been unexpected!"

"Un-fucking expected? You really are taking the piss! And you!" She rounded on Shadow, who sat in a chair in the corner, looking far more amused that she should. "Your knife is in that man's chest!"

Shadow smiled smugly. "I know that. I put it there. It was an excellent shot, if I may say so. I was on the floor, bent and twisted, and had just escaped that landing on me." She pointed at the cage, which lay inside the entrance of the room, next to the connecting door. "I impressed myself."

Maggie stood in front of her, hands on her hips. "Well, lucky you! I now have all this shit to report on! And did you say a resurrected Druid?" She'd turned back to Harlan at this point, and glared at him.

Harlan, for all his bravado, wilted under her gaze. "Yes, we think so. The only person who knew much about him is dead."

"Fucking unbelievable!"

Harlan could feel his balls shrinking already. "I know, sorry." He sounded lame, even to his own ears. "But I have someone who's trying to track him down, and I can call Olivia to help. She's in town at the moment."

Maggie scowled. "That's all I need, more bloody Orphic meddling!"

"It's called help, Maggie. We like to clean up our own shit."

"No, no, no." She pointed at him. "You don't get away with this that easily. This will eat into my time. I'm already dealing with enough paranormal crap in this seething hotbed of weirdness that's called London, and you've just added to it!"

"What are you going to do about Shadow?" Harlan asked, trying to bring her back to his current concern.

Maggie addressed him with a narrowed eyed glare. "I'll need a statement, obviously. But because it's very clear that this was an attempted kidnapping and imprisonment," she swivelled to Shadow, "and that you were shot, I won't hold you or charge you. It's pretty obvious you were defending yourself."

Harlan sighed with relief. It was what he was hoping for, but he hadn't wanted to presume. "Thank you. We both appreciate that, don't we, Shadow?" He looked at her expectantly.

"Yes, thank you. I really had no choice." To her credit, she looked genuinely contrite. "I liked Chadwick, too."

"Can we give our statements here?" Harlan asked, eager to avoid going to the station.

Maggie nodded and yelled, "Walker! Get your arse in here and take their statements!"

A tall, skinny man with blond hair and a short beard appeared in the doorway, a look of weary resignation on his face. Detective Sergeant Ted Walker had worked with Maggie for a couple of years, and seemed to cope well with her regular verbal abuse. "I'm not deaf, Maggie." He looked at Harlan. "Who wants to go first?"

Harlan jumped in, "Do Shadow first, then she can get going and have her leg looked at. I'd like to stay and go through some of Chadwick's papers once my statement is done."

Walker glanced at Maggie, who nodded and said, "But keep out of the dining room for now, and this room, until we've gathered evidence." She pointed at the gun on the floor next to Chadwick's body. "Is that a Flintlock?"

Harlan nodded, thinking it was the perfect choice for using an old iron bullet—not that he'd tell Maggie that. She didn't need to know the significance of an iron bullet to Shadow. "Weapons were another of Chadwick's interests. Fortunately, their aim is usually off."

"Tell my leg that," Shadow said snarkily. She looked pale now, and tired, and Harlan guessed that even fey had their physical limits.

Walker must have thought so too, as he headed to her side, and sat in the next chair. "Let's get started. Name?"

"Shadow Walker of the Dark Ways, Star of the Evening, Hunter of Secrets. But you can shorten it to Shadow Walker, and then we'll have matching names." Shadow looked at him, amused.

Harlan saw Walker look at her with wide-eyed amazement, as if he was going to ask more, but then he just shrugged. "Yes ma'am."

Harlan suppressed a grin, and Maggie shot him a look. "Don't think I'm not going to investigate her."

He echoed Walker. "Yes ma'am." And then he sat down and waited his turn.

When Shadow emerged from Chadwick's home later that evening, she passed through the police cordon and official vehicles, limping on her now increasingly sore leg, and found Nahum a short distance down the road, as they'd arranged on the phone.

He exited the car and opened the passenger door. "I was getting worried." He frowned at the staff that she was using to lean on. "What's that?"

"It's from Kian's tomb. I thought I should bring it with me."

He jerked his head toward the house and the police cars. "Doesn't that count as evidence?"

She grinned. "Yes, but I disguised it with enough glamour to get it past them. It's too important to leave there." She eased into the car, and after Nahum put the staff on the back seat, he drove away before anyone could stop them.

The car was warm, and Shadow relaxed for the first time in hours. "That was an ordeal. Remind me never to be interviewed by the police again."

He shot her a swift look. "Try not to stab anyone again."

"It was kill or be killed! I'll miss that dagger…" Now that they were safely away from the house, she pulled the Empusa's sword from her jacket, where she'd hidden it with her magic. "I got this, too."

Nahum was concentrating on driving, but he looked at it with surprise. "You've stolen it?"

"Well, he doesn't need it anymore. And besides, I think it has more useful qualities than we initially realised." She leaned against the seat, the warmth of the heater making her sleepy. The evening seemed like a dream now, and she thought back to when she'd picked the sword up and saw Kian's shade fleeing Chadwick's dead body. "I think it makes you see spirits more clearly. That's what it appeared like, anyway. The whole thing happened so quickly."

"Really? That's intriguing. Have you spoken to Gabe?"

"Only briefly, just after I phoned you. I haven't had time since."

"Okay. Tell me what happened, as much as you can remember, and then you can sleep on the drive home."

"Wait," she sat up, confused. "Aren't we going to the hotel? My bag's there."

"I've packed everything, and checked you out already. Is that okay?" He looked suspicious. "You haven't hidden anything in the hotel room, have you?"

"No." She leaned back again, relieved not to have to do anything else, and kicked her heels off. "Why do women wear these things?"

"Because you look hot as hell in them. Did you chase him in those?"

She laughed. "No! I took them off. Did you search for him? Mason, I mean?"

"Of course. I staked out the Guild for another hour or so, and then went to Mason's address. But he didn't show at either place, and there's nothing else I can do at the moment. Gabe wants us both home. Now stop getting distracted and tell me what happened, before you forget the details."

They arrived home at four in the morning. A few lights were on in the farmhouse, the usual selection of cars and bikes on the driveway, and there was also a car Shadow didn't recognise.

As soon as Nahum pulled into the courtyard, Gabe opened the front door and ran over, closely followed by Niel. Gabe helped Shadow get out of the car, while Nahum headed to the boot for the bags.

"I'm fine, honestly," Shadow said, reassuring Gabe, but wincing. She felt horribly stiff and slow.

He ignored her. "Liar. Briar's already here." He glanced at Nahum. "Any updates?"

"No, nothing new. The drive was uneventful." He turned to Niel. "The staff and the Empusa's sword are on the back seat. Can you get them?"

"Sure," Niel said, already opening the rear doors. "That's all we need, Kian's magic stick."

"It's important!" Shadow said, frowning.

"Yeah, yeah," he muttered.

"Send Briar and Eli over," Gabe said to him, and then led Shadow to her own room in the outbuilding she had made her home. It was warm and the lighting was low, and he escorted her to her bed.

"Wait," she said. "I can't sleep in this dress. I'll ruin it. It's probably already ruined, actually—there's blood all over it. Can you grab me a t-shirt? Top drawer."

She struggled with the zip, and when Gabe returned, he placed her clothing on the bed and turned her around. "Allow me."

Shadow was suddenly self-conscious—which was ridiculous. She felt a tingle run through her as air rushed across her skin when Gabe unzipped her dress down to the small of her back.

"Can you manage?" he asked, a rough edge to his voice.

She looked over her shoulder to find his dark eyes fixed firmly on her face. "Yes, thanks." She wriggled out of it and it fell to the floor, and Gabe quickly turned his back. She smiled to herself at his unexpected gentlemanly behaviour, and then chided herself. Why was she surprised? Gabe was always a gentleman. She swiftly pulled the t-shirt over her head and slid into bed, stacking pillows behind her. "All done."

Gabe picked the dress up off the floor, and placed it on the back of a chair. "Do you need anything? A drink, some food?"

She smiled at him gratefully as she considered her options. Whiskey was tempting, but instead she said, "Hot chocolate, really hot and sweet please."

"Sure thing." He paused for a moment, his gaze serious. "I was very worried. I'm glad you're okay."

"Thanks. I'm sorry to be a pain. I've caused us all a lot of trouble, haven't I?"

"No. You were defending yourself."

"But the police—"

He cut her off. "Stop. We'll talk about it tomorrow."

Nahum interrupted them as he brought in her bag and dumped it on the floor. "You'd be better off staying in the house, where we're closer."

"I'm going to sleep in here, too," Gabe told him.

Shadow protested. "Why? I'll be fine!"

"If by some weird chance Kian's found where you live, I don't want you to be attacked in the middle of the night."

"But—"

"No! I've made my mind up. Nahum, get the guys together. I'll be over in a moment."

Nahum nodded and left them to it, and Shadow noticed a pile of blankets and pillows stacked on the sofa next to wood burner on the far side of her cabin. A few weeks before, Gabe had insisted she have the wood burner installed, rather than deplete her magic to keep the smokeless fire going in the middle of the room.

She looked at Gabe. "Seriously, you do not need to do this."

"You're weak. You couldn't possibly defend yourself if something attacked. I've got this."

Shadow's natural instinct to argue reasserted itself. "I don't need protecting! I could still fight!"

"We don't even know what we're fighting. I don't know if I could fight it. It's some weird ghost with a powerful energy." He ran his hands through his hair, frustrated, and turned as there was a soft knock at the door.

Briar peered inside. "It's only me and Eli." She entered, Eli on her heels, and headed to Shadow's side.

Eli had been an apothecary, amongst other things in the past, and that's why he liked to work with Briar. He was one of the calmest Nephilim, quiet and considered, and an undeniable ladies man. His soft brown eyes were made for seduction. He wore his hair tousled, but was clean-shaven usually. Not tonight, however. Stubble grazed his cheeks.

"Hey, you two," Shadow said, trying to sound brighter than she was feeling. "You could have seen me in the morning, you know."

"No, we couldn't," Briar replied, as she pulled a table close to the bed, set her bag on it, and opened it up. "We need to act now. You look a peculiar colour."

"I do?" Shadow's hands flew to her face.

Eli laughed. "You're very pale, and I think there's a tinge of green there, too."

Gabe was already heading to the door. "I'll leave you to it." He looked at Shadow. "I'll be back with your drink."

Before he'd even left, Briar was easing the blankets back, revealing her injured leg, and she started to unwrap the towel. Eli, in the meantime, was filling a bowl with hot water from the sink in the corner, and he brought it to the table. He threw a handful of herbs in, and added some clean cloths. A rich smell filled the air, something honeyed and sweet.

Briar frowned. "You bled a lot. This towel is stiff with it."

Shadow winced as Briar pulled it off her wound, taking scabs and clots with it. "I didn't think it was that deep."

Blood immediately started to well again, and Briar tutted. "Liar. It's going to leave a nice scar."

"That's okay. I have a few. Sword fights will do that to you."

Briar looked up at Eli. "Can you prepare the poultice? I'll clean the wound."

He nodded. "Sure."

Eli worked silently, but Briar whispered under her breath as she cleaned the dried blood away. Shadow felt Briar's magic swell, and a lightness came over her as the throbbing in her leg began to ease. "That's better already."

Briar smiled. "Good."

Gabe returned before they'd finished, and handed Shadow her drink. He looked at the wound and frowned, shaking his head as he left again. Sleep started to steal over Shadow, and she sipped, savouring the rich hot chocolate. It was delicious. Gabe didn't mess about. It was actual melted chocolate and cream, with a dash of cinnamon, exactly as she liked it.

She watched Briar put the poultice on her leg, and felt warmth spread up and across her body, meeting the hot balm of the chocolate in her stomach. By the time she'd drained the cup, she couldn't keep her eyes open, and easily fell into a dreamless sleep.

Twelve

Maggie glared at Harlan as he signed his official statement. "We've checked the rest of the premises, and there are no more bodies anywhere, thank Christ, or the lurking shades of the fucking undead. Just watch what you're doing!"

"Scout's honour," he said, saluting.

She shot him a filthy look and marched back to the kitchen, and after a quick search on the ground floor, trying to find Chadwick's study, Harlan headed upstairs.

Other than the living room, drawing room, dining room, and the two rooms with the connecting door, there was only the kitchen and utility room downstairs. By the time he'd finished his statement, the coroner had arrived with SOCO, and Harlan was keen to keep out of the way.

The stairs were in the middle of the unusual house, and they swept up into darkness. Harlan paused as he reached the landing, listening carefully, but other than the muffled voices coming from below, he could hear nothing. From first impressions, the overpowering decorating didn't stop on the ground floor. Richly patterned wallpaper, ornate woodwork, and oriental furniture was clearly going to be a feature everywhere.

Harlan moved methodically, opening one door after another, finding Chadwick's bedroom at the rear of the house overlooking the garden. He also found a spare bedroom, followed by another room that housed more of Chadwick's collected artefacts. Finally, he found the study, lined with books and prints.

Harlan sighed with relief, slipped inside, and shut the door firmly behind him. Chadwick had obviously been in there earlier that day. A fire was smouldering in the fireplace, and lamps were lit. And, it was a mess. Books and papers were strewn everywhere, and Harlan wasn't sure if this was Chadwick's normal way of working, or if Kian, in Chadwick's body, had been looking for something specific. Harlan hoped for the former.

Logic dictated that as Chadwick's latest discovery, the details of Kian's burial must be accessible on his desk somewhere, although as he started searching, Harlan became more and more convinced there was little order applied to the mess. Chadwick was a magpie.

There were old books, new books, first editions, illustrated manuals, and arcane papers that should really have been in a museum. The source for the burial and any information about Kian must be old, surely. Harlan abandoned the desk after a fruitless search, and headed instead to a large table in the centre of the room. Under the chaotic paperwork, he saw what looked like the edge of a map, spread across the surface. What he had assumed to be objects on display were actually holding down the corners, to stop it rolling up again. He quickly pushed the papers aside and frowned. It was a map of Belas Knap and the surrounding area, and there were marks all over it.

It looked as if Chadwick had narrowed his search down to the Neolithic burial site a while ago, and had been testing theories ever since. Harlan rummaged around some more, finding book after book on Neolithic burials, and then books on Druid religions. He was getting closer. And then a thought struck him. Where were the other grave objects? Shadow had taken the staff, but what about the old leather bag, the pottery and the jewellery?

Harlan sighed. He could be here for hours.

A headache was beginning its slow, insidious advance when Maggie found him in Chadwick's bedroom. He'd figured that this was the next best place to look when the study refused to reveal any secrets.

"I wondered where you'd snuck off to." She looked around. "Christ. How did he sleep in here? It's as creepy as hell."

Harlan straightened from his examination of the chest of drawers, amused. "I don't know... It has a certain charm, if you like Hammer House of Horror films."

"I don't. I have enough of this crap in my day-to-day life. I feel like Peter bloody Cushing is about to leap out on me."

"I wish he would. I could use some help right now."

Maggie walked around the room, her sharp eyes everywhere. "What are you looking for?"

"Grave goods, taken from the tomb of our ghost. They could be important."

"You're sure he didn't take them?"

"No, he ran out of here too quickly, in Mason's body. They have to be here somewhere. And so does information on who Kian was and why he was sealed in his tomb, despite the fact that he was dead."

Maggie shook her head. "You probably should have asked that before you opened it!"

"You know how it works, Maggie! We're hired to help find these objects, and we trust our clients have done their homework."

"And you don't double check?" She snorted. "That's a big fat fucking recipe for disaster, isn't it?"

Harlan took a deep breath, and repeated what he'd said to others before. "We check up on as much as we can. But we've worked with some of our clients for years! Chadwick is not a demon-raiser! He loves the occult, the old, and the arcane, like we all do. He wants to—" Harlan corrected himself, "He wanted to unlock life's secrets. It's what many of them want. All of the members of the Order of the Midnight Sun are the same, too."

"That bunch of new age alchemists. Of course they are." She was dismissive of the group.

"They are actually intelligent people, who follow the old teachings, and their predecessors were the forerunners of scientists!"

"Yeah, yeah. Well, now Chadwick's dead, and we have a rogue ghost on the loose." She frowned. "Where did you find Shadow?"

"Ah!" He'd been expecting this question, and had decided to keep it simple. "In White Haven. She helped me on another job. She's very resourceful."

Maggie crossed her arms in front of her and tapped her foot. "That Cornish village?"

"It's a town."

"I've been hearing things about that place. They had a vampire issue just before Christmas."

"Really? I had no idea. I was there because of the Crossroads Circus."

She raised her eyebrows as understanding dawned. "Oh! You dealt with whoever had caused the deaths that had been trailing after that show?"

He winced. "Not exactly, but I helped, in my small way. That's how I met Shadow."

"She doesn't live in London?"

"No. White Haven."

"Good. She's trouble, I can tell." She changed the subject abruptly. "Have you looked under the bed?"

"Isn't that a bit obvious?"

"I suggested it for a reason!"

Harlan frowned at her, and feeling foolish, dropped to the floor, lifted the valance, and squinted into the darkness. He groaned. The bed was old-fashioned with a high base, and underneath it were shabby boxes. He pulled them out and laid them on the richly coloured eiderdown.

Maggie grinned. "Told you."

"They could be old clothes!" Harlan protested, but he opened one that was the least covered in dust. A worn leather bag and the other grave goods were inside. "Bingo! But this doesn't make sense. Why would he hide them in his own house? Chadwick would be examining these like a kid at Christmas!"

"Perhaps Kian hid them?" Maggie shrugged. "Whatever—you owe me." She leaned closer. "I'm amazed they aren't more decayed!"

"Me too," Harlan murmured, lifting them gently. "They're dirty, and although the leather bag is rotting, it's in far better shape than I'd have thought. Maybe it was the magic protecting the tomb?"

Maggie pointed at the rings, torques, and a large, ornate cloak clasp. The metal was dull, but their engravings were intriguing. "He had influence, and money. What's in the pouch?"

Harlan opened it gently, dislodging a flurry of dust. Inside were old bones—a bird skull, a skull of some type of small mammal, claws, feathers, and beads.

"Looks more like a shaman's bag to me," Maggie suggested, "but what do I know?" She walked towards the door. "You've got fifteen more minutes, and then we lock up and you have to go. I've put an alert out for Mason's car, but haven't heard anything yet. I'll tell you if I do."

"Sure." Harlan nodded. "I'll hurry. And thanks, Maggie. I appreciate this."

"Just try not to leave a trail of death in your wake!"

Gabe and the other Nephilim were beyond tired, and their tempers were short.

They were in the living room, and music played softly in the background while they argued about the meaning of the symbols drawn on the staff and the translations of the words they had deciphered. Being a Nephilim meant they understood all languages, modern and ancient, and that applied to written languages, too.

Nahum frowned. "'Those who choose the dark path will reap its rewards.' Well, that's suitably cryptic and ominous. Sounds like mumbo jumbo to me."

"But do you feel its power?" Gabe asked.

"Sure. But I don't know where its power is coming from." Nahum held the staff under the light. It was the height of an average man, and made of what looked to be oak. The symbols were carved down the entire length. Some were delicate, others made with thicker stokes.

Ash took it from him. "None of these symbols look particularly magical to me. Some are just images—these are of the moon," he pointed to them. "And these are rudimentary animals —this one's a deer, and these are the carvings of stag horns."

Zee was sprawled on the sofa. "Was it used in rituals? I mean, I presume it's more than a walking stick with some dire warning on it!"

"Possibly," Ash said, nodding. He placed it against the wall, next to the fire, where they all could see it, and sat down again.

"Perhaps we're focusing on the wrong thing," Niel suggested. "It may have power, and we know what's written on it, but there might be other important things we're missing."

"Yeah, like why he wanted to get Shadow," Ash pointed out. "And why didn't he kill Harlan and Mason while he had the chance."

"Let's not forget that he shot her," Gabe said.

Nahum shrugged. "Sounds like he was only intending to wound her—it would have been easier to catch her if she was injured. The gun was insurance, and sensible self-defence."

"He knew she was fey, though! How?" Zee asked.

"Because she broke the seal on his tomb," Niel reminded them. "There were other objects, too. We should find them. It would help to know more about who he was."

"Let's hope Harlan is on to that. In the meantime, what else can we do?" Nahum asked.

Gabe stood and stretched, touching the ceiling with his outstretched fingers. "I think we need to go back to the tomb. See if there's something we've missed. We can go tonight." He checked his watch. "Briar and Eli should be finishing up soon. I'll sleep over there, and see you all in a few hours. Who's up for later?"

There was a show of hands, and Gabe grinned. "Road trip, then!"

Gabe had only been asleep for a short while when he heard movement in the room and he sat up quickly, blinking in the gloom.

But it was only Shadow, stirring from her bed. She sat on the edge of it, reaching for water, and nodded at Gabe. "Morning. I can't believe you slept on that sofa—it's barely big enough! So we weren't attacked, then?"

He groaned as he stretched. "I'm not sure I'd call it sleep. And no, we weren't. How's your leg?"

She stood, testing her weight. "It feels so much better. The pain is dull rather than sharp. That has to be good, right?"

"I'd say so." Gabe tried not to stare. Her t-shirt was long, but he could still see a lot of thigh. A bandage was wrapped around the wound. "Briar will be back to check that later today. I don't think she completely trusted Eli."

Shadow laughed. "Poor Eli. Although to be fair, he doesn't have Briar's magic."

Gabe checked his watch and found it was almost ten in the morning. Five hours of sleep would have to do; he managed on far less in the old days, when they waged war. He was growing soft with age, he reflected, as he stood up and gathered his blankets, rolling them neatly and putting them in the corner. He hesitated to tell Shadow the plans the group had discussed, but he couldn't really keep them a secret. "We're going back to the tomb tonight. I'd like to suggest you stay here—"

She didn't let him finish his sentence. "No way! I'm coming, too."

"You're injured!"

"Don't nanny me!"

"Shadow, will you please see sense? First, there's that hike up the hill from the car park. Your wound could start bleeding again!"

She grinned at him. "Or, you could fly me up there! If you're strong enough."

She was baiting him, and he knew it. "Of course I'm strong enough."

"It will be night, and no one will see us. That place is deserted! And surely you want to stretch your wings?"

Damn it. He hated it when she was right, but he wasn't about to concede that now. "I'll think about it."

"Sure you will. Are you going to cook me breakfast, too?"

"Don't push your luck. I'll meet you in the kitchen. Do you need help getting dressed?" She just stared at him. "No."

"Fine!" He didn't know whether he was relieved or disappointed. He chided himself on the way out of the door. You're relieved, you idiot!

Niel was already cooking, and the smell of bacon filled the room. He looked up when Gabe entered. "She okay?"

"Fine. As annoying as usual. She wants to come tonight."

Niel laughed, his white teeth flashing. "Did you really expect anything else?"

"No." Gabe headed to the coffee machine and made a drink, strong enough to stand the spoon in it. He inhaled deeply, and took a sip; it was so hot it almost scalded his tongue. "Are you making some for us?" He nodded to the breakfast supplies.

"Of course. The others are getting up, too. Only Barak is out."

Gabe was about to say more when his phone rang. He glanced at the screen. "It's Beckett." He answered quickly. "Morning, any news?"

"Only bad, I'm afraid. The police haven't found Mason's car yet, so we have no idea where he is."

"Shit." Gabe moved to the window and looked out across the fields. It was raining, and the moors disappeared into a hazy mist. "He could be heading to us, but we have no way of knowing."

"Presume the worst, but hope for the best." Beckett sighed, and Gabe could hear the worry in his voice. "Mason knows where you live. I have no idea how this possession business works, but he must have access to whatever is in Mason's head—if his possession of Chadwick's body is any indication. How's Shadow?"

"She's fine." Gabe paused. "Thanks for getting her out of there with no charges."

"We have Maggie to thank for that. Listen, I managed to find those grave goods last night, but I still haven't found anything that could tell us who Kian is. I'm going to keep looking. They've sealed the house, but I'll try and sneak back in anyway."

Gabe was unsure of how much to share with Beckett, but he seemed to be fairly upfront with him. "We're going back to the tomb tonight. I want to give it a thorough check."

"Is that wise?" Beckett asked.

"Maybe not, but like you, I want to cover all of our bases."

"All right. I'll let you know if I find anything else. I may even drive to White Haven."

"Fair enough. You be careful, too, Beckett. He might come looking for those grave goods."

Gabe rang off, and turned to find Shadow already sitting at the table. She was fully dressed, and the Empusa's sword was next to her. She was sipping her coffee and watching him with a speculative look on her face, while Niel continued to cook. Gabe heard movement on the floor above, and the sound of feet on the stairs.

"What's happened? Is Harlan okay?" she asked.

"He's fine. Let's hang on for the others, and I'll update you all at once."

"I have news for you, too," she said enigmatically.

"Great," Niel groaned. "Sounds like life is about to get more complicated."

Thirteen

Shadow finished listening to Gabe's updates, and studied the other Nephilim. They had all just eaten, and their plates were pushed into the middle of the table. Their appetites were huge. Shadow couldn't fathom why they weren't obese. Must be their sylph ancestry. It was rare to see a fat fey. Their genetic makeup didn't work that way. And yes, she was still sure their fathers were sylphs. She sensed a kind of magic in them, and was convinced it was fey blood. But the language thing was weird. As far as she knew, speaking multiple languages was not something sylphs could do—unless they were some sort of super-sylph.

Gabe interrupted her thoughts. "What's your news, then?"

Shadow lifted the Empusa's sword from where it rested next to her chair, and placed it on the table. "I had a strange experience with this last night, when I was chasing Kian's ghost. I pulled it off the wall, because I only had my dagger and wanted to have another weapon." She paused, remembering the moment when Kian's spirit left Chadwick's dead body. "It was really odd. I killed Chadwick, and Kian's ghost left it, but the weird thing was that it wasn't a shadowy shape like it had been before. It was almost solid—like an actual body. I could see that he had dark hair, a thin face, and a wiry build. By the time I'd scrambled to the door, he was at the far end of the corridor, but I could still see him clearly." She looked at the Empusa's sword. "I think it's because of that."

Nahum was sitting next to her, and he picked it up. "I thought you and El had examined it and decided there was nothing special about it?"

"We did! I even went to her friend Dante's forge the other day to double check. He agreed that it wasn't unusual in any way. Dante said it was virtually impossible to say where it had been forged or how, though."

"But I guess there wasn't a ghost in the room, was there?" Nahum asked.

Zee leaned on the table, his chin on his hands. "You're saying that sword allows you to see the dead?"

"It seems to." She shrugged. "Well, that's my impression. I obviously haven't had a chance to test that theory again. But once I got to the kitchen, I saw him, just as clearly as I do you, before he sank into Mason's body."

"I think it's great news," Gabe said. "I wonder if it would injure a spirit, too."

"A sword that fights ghosts!" Eli laughed. "Wow! *That* would increase its value."

"I'm not selling it again!" Shadow exclaimed. "That's mine now. It's not like Chadwick will miss it. I'll see if I can borrow El's too, just for the next few days."

Nahum passed the sword around the table for the rest of the Nephilim to examine it. As Niel held it, he said, "You know, that does make a lot of sense. The Empusa was Hecate's servant, is that right?"

"Yes, straight from the Underworld," Shadow told him.

Niel nodded. "It makes sense she would carry weapons that would allow her to see the dead and fight them."

"But she was from there," Eli said. "Surely she wouldn't need that kind of help?"

Gabe shrugged. "Maybe she was like some kind of Underworld enforcer."

"Whatever the reason," Zee said, "it puts us at a distinct advantage to have them." He turned to Shadow. "Did Kian know you could see him properly?"

"Hard to say. I don't think so. I didn't do anything that gave it away...well, other than talking to him. But," she said, taking a deep breath, "that brings me to the next thing I noticed. Kian was fey."

"What?" they exclaimed, pretty much as one.

Shadow continued. "I could tell from his ears, and the way his face was shaped. He had a long, narrow chin like some fey do."

"Well shit, that puts a new perspective on things," Gabe said. "Are you sure?"

"Very sure. I've been thinking on it all night. Well, before I fell asleep," she conceded. "I've been trying to decide if I was imagining it. But it also makes sense for other reasons. Did you know that Avery's ancestor, Helena's ghost, is in her flat?"

Eli nodded. "I did. Briar has mentioned it. Sounds freaky to me." He shuddered, as most people did at the mention of ghosts.

"I asked why she allowed her to stay, because you know—creepy, and apparently Helena possessed her once. I wondered why Avery wasn't worried that she'd try to possess her again, but Briar told me that you have to invite a ghost in. That they just can't slide in whenever they want. Alex prepared a potion for Avery, and then she said an invocation that allowed it to happen." The Nephilim were silently watching her, a couple starting to nod with understanding. "It's been playing on my mind. I couldn't work out how Chadwick had been possessed. He wouldn't have invited Kian in—I doubt it, anyway. He was a collector!"

"Of course," Zee said thoughtfully. "But a fey spirit might not need to be invited in."

"Exactly!"

"That's just brilliant," Ash said, not sounding like it was at all. "Does that mean it could possess any of us?"

Shadow winced. "In theory. But who knows how weird you are? You might be immune to possession. Or it could be he triples his powers if he possesses one of you!"

"Please stop talking," Zee said, rising to his feet and gathering the plates up. "This keeps getting worse."

"Better we know what we're up against!" she shot back.

Eli stood, too. "I'm heading to the barn to work out. Anyone want to join me?"

Shadow knew what that meant. It was sparring time.

"Sure," Niel said, "give me five."

Zee shook his head. "Not me, I need to go to the pub. I'm covering the lunch shift. I don't think there's anything else I can do here—Gabe?"

Gabe nodded. "No, go ahead. I'll have to decide what we do next. I'll ring Barak and update him, too."

Shadow stood as well, trying to hide the grimace when she felt the injury to her leg tighten. "Can you take me to White Haven with you? It will save Briar coming here to check my wound. And then I can see El."

Zee nodded. "Sure. Ten minutes?"

"Great."

She headed to the door, but Gabe called her back. "Are you going to get the second sword?"

"Yes. Why?"

"Be careful. Kian could be here, and he could be anyone!"

———————◆○◆———————

Harlan looked at Olivia's worried face, and wondered what, if anything, he could say to reassure her.

"He needs him. He won't kill him."

"But Mason might be killed accidently, just like Chadwick! Poor Mason!" Olivia rose from the leather chair where she'd been sitting, and started to walk around his office, picking things up and putting them down randomly. "We have to tell the staff."

"Do we?" Harlan asked, watching her. "Or will we scare them unnecessarily? Most people who work here just have admin duties, filing, bills, or look for acquisitions. Most of them have no idea of some of the things we really deal with! Half the staff would probably resign! And," he raised his hand as Olivia rounded on him, "I know that's their prerogative to leave, but they won't be at risk. They know nothing, and can't achieve anything for Kian."

Olivia paused, her face pinched, and her lips pressed together tightly. "No, you're right. Although, I wish you'd told me sooner."

"Yes, sorry. That was an oversight. I should have spoken to you before I called Maggie." As he said it, Harlan half-wondered if Olivia could be Kian right now. And then he shook his head. No. Chadwick was different last night. There were subtle clues that he wasn't behaving normally, but he would never have presumed possession. Now, of course, it all made sense. But Olivia was her usual self. "We need to work out how to save Mason and catch Kian without further bloodshed."

Olivia nodded. "Where are the grave goods?"

"In my safe." He headed across the room and pulled aside some books from the shelves, exposing the safe behind. He punched in his code and drew out the box he'd put everything in, and then placed it on the round table he used for meetings.

Olivia started rifling through the objects. "Just the usual grave goods, really. Nothing that rings any alarm bells."

"There was also a staff that was marked with strange symbols, but Shadow has that. She claimed it had power."

Olivia looked startled. "That sounds more interesting!"

"Bollocks!" Harlan said, exasperated. "Why the hell didn't I ask Chadwick more about this tomb?"

"Because you trusted him. I take it you aren't any wiser as to who Kian is?"

"Other than some Druid who clearly pissed a lot of people off? No. I need to get back into Chadwick's house."

"Breaking a police cordon?" Olivia raised an eyebrow, a smirk on her face. "What would Maggie say to that?"

"What Maggie doesn't know won't hurt her." Even as he said it, Harlan wondered how he was going to manage it. In theory, by tonight, no police would be there, but Chadwick had an alarm system...

"I know his security code."

"You read my mind! For the alarm? How?"

"He's good friends with Mason. Best buds. He sent me round there once to get something when Chadwick was away on one of his trips."

Harlan looked at her sceptically. "And you remember it?"

She rolled her eyes. "I wrote it down! I'm not stupid. These things come in handy—like for now!"

Harlan winked at her. "Oh, Olivia. How are you still single?"

She grinned. "Like you, I take my job far too seriously, and get my pleasure along the way." She ran her finger across his chin. "Would you like some company tonight?"

He blinked and stuttered as several images flooded his mind from one night years ago in a hotel room, during a snow storm. His one and only night spent with Olivia, and it had been memorable for so many reasons. She'd worn her very sexy Louboutin shoes, and not much else.

"Naughty." She wagged a finger. "Breaking into Chadwick's house, I mean."

"Oh, that. I suppose so. I preferred the other option."

"It was not an option. That was your mind teasing you." She stepped away, amused. "Give me all the details. I can tell I need to get your thoughts out of the gutter."

———◆○◆———

Briar looked at Shadow's wound. "Excellent. This looks so much better. Far more so than I expected, actually."

"I'm fey," Shadow said nonchalantly, already feeling stronger. "I've always healed quickly, and beside, you are a very good healer."

Briar's eyes were wide, and she looked as if she were trying to suppress a smile. "Thank you. I wish I could say you were a better patient. You shouldn't be walking on it so often."

"There's too much to do!"

They were in the sunroom at the back of Briar's house, and Shadow was lying on the low couch pushed into the corner. While Briar worked Shadow looked around at the herbs growing on the sills, and the eclectic mix of decor. It was very Briar. Outside the window, in her tiny courtyard, a tangle of vines and climbing plants were already sending up bright green growth.

Briar said, "I'm going to put another poultice on it and strap it up, and then I want to see you tomorrow." Her small hands were deft and sure, and as she dressed the wound, she uttered a spell. Once again, Shadow felt warmth creeping up her leg and across her body.

"Your magic is strong. I feel the Green Man's spirit in you."

Briar looked up. "He's never far away anymore."

There was a ring of bright green around Briar's dark eyes that Shadow didn't remember seeing before. "Your eyes have changed."

"I know." She dropped her gaze, concentrating on finishing the dressing. "He's getting stronger with the arrival of spring."

"Not like possession?" Shadow asked, suddenly anxious.

Briar laughed. "No, not at all. He's just—around. It's like his sap runs through my blood."

Shadow smiled. "That's an interesting way of putting it."

"It's the only way I can describe it. I've always felt an affinity for spring—most gardeners and earth witches do. It's just enhanced now." She finished the dressing and straightened up. "I have to remember to rein him in. Anyway, you're done," she said, changing the subject.

Shadow stood, pulling her combats trousers on. It was difficult to wear her tight jeans at the moment because of the bandage. "Which one of you witches is the best at dealing with spirits? Is it Alex?"

Briar nodded. "You thinking about your wayward spirit?"

"Yes."

"Definitely Alex." Briar checked her watch. "He'll be in the pub now. You could get lunch in there. And any of us will help if you need it."

"Thanks, but we're trying to clean up our own mess."

"Sometimes things just happen, despite our best intentions. It has to us. I mean it. We're happy to help." She paused, frowning. "How are you getting to the pub if Zee dropped you here?"

"I was going to walk."

Briar tutted. "No! It's too far."

"It takes ten minutes!"

Briar lived on one of the charming, winding lanes around White Haven, and it was a short stroll to the town centre.

"You'll aggravate your wound. I tell you what—I'll take you. Any excuse for a lunchtime tipple!"

Shadow smiled. "I could meet El there, too! I love pubs! We have them in the Otherworld too, you know."

Briar laughed. "Well, you're hanging out with the right people, then! I'll grab my keys."

Fourteen

S hadow sat at the bar on their usual stools at The Wayward Son, and scanned the room.

It was Sunday lunchtime, and very busy. The smell of roast meat scented the air, and the pub was loud with chatter. The English loved their Sunday lunches. It was something she'd learnt very early on, and she had to admit it was a tradition she liked. Not right now, though. Niel's breakfast had filled her up.

Zee headed over to take their order. "I should have known you'd come here. Pint of Skullduggery Ale, I presume." He smiled at Briar. "And white wine?"

Briar laughed. "You know me so well."

"How's your patient?" he asked, filling her glass.

Briar wrinkled her nose. "Not being nearly as compliant as she should be."

"Nothing new there, then."

Shadow shot him a filthy look. "I'm right here!"

"I know. And here I was hoping for some peace and quiet." He placed her pint in front of her. "Did you get in touch with El?"

Shadow bit back a rude response. She was trying to be less argumentative, and it didn't sit easily with her. "She's on her way. Is Alex here?"

"In the kitchen." He leaned forward. "If you're going to talk business, head to the rear lounge. There's a table free. I'll send El and Alex through."

"Good suggestion," Briar said, and grabbing her drink she led the way to the room Alex had spelled to keep quiet for the locals.

Within minutes El arrived, looking very glam for a Sunday, and Alex was right behind her. He slid into his seat staring at all three of them, intrigued. "You all look like you're up to something!"

"Me?" Shadow said, wide -eyed. "I'm never up to anything!"

"Oh, please. Pull the other one!" Alex had shoulder-length dark hair and stubble always grazed his chin. He favoured old jeans and older t-shirts, and despite the wet, miserable day, he wasn't wearing long sleeves, revealing his tattoos, although he had nowhere near as many as some of the Nephilim. "Zee has told me about your wayward ghost."

"Ghost?" El said, suddenly paying attention.

"Should I wait for Avery or Reuben?" Shadow asked. Alex lived with Avery now, and El and Reuben were a couple. Together with Briar, they made up the White Haven Coven.

"No, Avery is seeing her grandmother, and Reuben is surfing," Alex said, sipping his pint. "I'll tell Avery later."

El nodded. "I can fill Reuben in. Now, tell all! What's happened?"

Shadow relayed how they'd found the tomb and released the spell on it, and then the attack by Kian's ghost the night before. "Now we have to find Kian, and get him out of Mason's body without hurting him. If he's even still possessing him. We have no idea where he may be, but suspect he'll probably come here, after me."

"Wow." El leaned back in her chair. "And you think this ghost is fey?"

"Yes. I can tell—just like you can tell that I'm not human without my glamour. There are subtle differences."

"Not so subtle if you ask me," Alex said. "It's a bit worrying to know a fey spirit can invade your body without your permission."

"Are there any circumstances where that could be true for any ghost?" Briar asked.

Alex looked out of the window, deep in thought. "I couldn't say categorically no, but it would be unusual. Possession is usually demonic. I have spells that can help with exorcism, but I'm not sure how effective they'd be in this circumstance. I'm sure I could adapt one. Of course," he said, brightening, "there is another, simpler option."

"Yes?" Shadow watched him, hoping it was something they could do without needing the witches.

"You could drug Mason, then Kian couldn't use his body."

Briar frowned. "I thought you said that he possessed Mason when he was drugged, and he woke up when Kian was inside him?"

"He was already rousing," Shadow reminded her. "They only had a light sedative. He wanted to get me on my own. Maybe a stronger one would work. But it would have to be safe, too. I have no problem killing anyone, but Mason is an innocent man. I could do without a second death on my hands. The whole police thing really complicates matters, too." She said police distastefully, as if the word was bitter on her tongue.

"I could make a potion that would work," Briar said. "You could slip it in a drink, or food. But, it would be hard to get close enough to do that without him knowing."

"I could poison an arrow tip!" Shadow suggested, becoming excited. "I could craft a fine one, like a dart. That would be easier. Could you make something powerful enough to work in a tiny quantity? Or even something that could go on the end of my knife? One small cut would be sufficient to administer the drug."

"Wow. You do like your hands-on weaponry, don't you," Alex said, amused.

"It's what I do best. I've always been told to work with my strengths!"

"Sage advice," El agreed.

"Yes, I could do that," Briar said, thoughtfully. "I could reduce it to absolute potency and put it in a cream or gel. When do you need it?"

"As soon as possible. Kian seems to want me, and we think that's to resurrect his own body using some unknown ritual."

"But what happens when he's in spirit form?" Alex asked, dropping his voice. "How do you stop him then? I could at that point banish it, probably. I've done it before with human spirits."

Shadow grinned. "Oh, that's where the Empusa's sword comes in. I've found out what it does!"

El looked at her, shocked. "It does something? But we tested it!"

"There's no way we could have known this until we tested it with a ghost. When I held it last night, I saw him clearly. I think I could injure the spirit, too. Or else, what's the point of it?"

"Chadwick, the man you killed, he was your buyer?"

"Yes. I've stolen it back. And I'm wondering if I could borrow yours? It may be that its effects are enhanced when used together."

"Consider it done!" El said, suitably intrigued. "But you should set some kind of trap. You want to fight him on your terms, not his."

"That's a great idea," Briar agreed. "Either by the farm, or Ravens' Wood. You draw strength from there."

Shadow nodded, as she thought it through. If she could lure him to her preferred place that would be better. "I like the idea of using the wood. But he's fey, too. It could work to his advantage."

Alex looked confused. "How the hell did a fey end up beneath Belas Knap? And did you say it was fey magic that had sealed the tomb?"

"Yes, part of it. It is odd. We have no idea who he is, or why he's there. Harlan has found the grave goods, but he's still trying to find Chadwick's research. That should tell us something about him."

"Do you like Harlan?" El asked.

Shadow nodded. "Yes, he's seems honest enough. He helped me out last night. Gabe likes him too, and that doesn't happen often. He's usually very suspicious!" She checked her watch. "I'd better not be too late. We're travelling to Belas Knap again tonight."

"All right," El said. "Let's drink up, and we'll go get the sword."

Harlan pulled up halfway down the street from Chadwick's house, deciding to advance on foot. It was just past ten at night, and very dark. It had been raining for most of the day, and thick clouds still covered the sky.

He glanced at Olivia. "Are you ready?"

"I was born ready," she said, already exiting the car. "It's a good thing this place is so green. At least we'll have some cover."

Harlan locked up and nodded, falling into step next to her as they strolled down the road. The houses all had drives, and plenty of shrubs to offer privacy.

Olivia tucked her arm into Harlan's, in an effort to look like they were a couple out for an evening walk, and when they reached Chadwick's drive, they ducked under the police tape, and kept to the shadows along the edge. The drive ended in a small turning circle, and a side gate led to the rear of the house. As soon as they got closer, a sensor triggered the security light, and they hurried to the front door.

"Bloody hell!" Olivia said, annoyed. "This place is lit up like a sodding Christmas tree!"

"Very sensible, really," Harlan said. "He has a lot to steal!"

Harlan had managed to swipe the spare keys before he'd left the previous night. He'd spotted them on a hook in the kitchen, and he used them now. The alarm started to beep, and Olivia quickly entered the code, both sighing with relief when it worked.

"Thank God he hadn't changed it," Olivia said. She paused in the darkness, and Harlan could barely see her.

The house felt eerie, its silence thick and heavy around them, the smell of the food they'd eaten the night before still lingering. "Shit. I feel terrible doing this."

"It's the right thing to do. We're avenging Chadwick's death, and let's face it, only he knows anything about Kian."

"We think," Harlan reminded her.

"Oh, come on," Olivia said in hushed tones. "We know these guys. They don't share anything if they think they're on to something big, and this was his life's passion. Where to?"

"The study again. There were papers everywhere. I didn't have long enough to get a proper look."

"Okay," she said, pulling a torch out of her bag. "Why don't you head up, I'll check the rooms down here, and then join you."

Harlan nodded, and taking out his own flashlight out, headed up the stairs and down the hall. When he reached the study door, he pushed it open, keeping his light pointed down. The windows were screened with heavy velvet curtains, and when he'd made sure they were drawn tightly, he flicked the lamps on.

The table was still covered with papers and books, slightly obscuring the map. He was relieved to see the police hadn't taken everything. But why would they? It was well away from the crime scene and probably seemed unconnected. He looked at the documents despondently. He must have missed something last night; he just needed to be more organised. He quickly started making orderly piles of related work, but most of the books were obscure texts on the end of the Roman Empire in Britain. That was interesting. Chadwick had suggested that Kian was from a similar time to that of Merlin, and of all the research that had been done, the most likely time frame for that was around 500 AD—if you believed King Arthur was a real figure. The myths were boundless.

Harlan looked at the map again. Kian was buried long after the original building of Belas Knap, but research of the site suggested that it had been used for centuries afterwards. *Why was Kian buried beneath it? Was he greatly respected, or more likely, feared?*

Harlan stepped back from the table, frustrated. Chadwick must have had handwritten notes somewhere. He slowly turned, scanning the room. There must be a safe, or a secure hiding place. He was halfway through pulling out books and lifting pictures off the wall when he heard a shout from downstairs.

Olivia.

He raced on to the landing and peered over the bannister, down into the darkened hall. There was another shout and loud thumps. Someone was attacking Olivia, and with luck they may not know he was here, too. *One good thing*, he assured himself as he sprinted down the stairs, *was that Olivia was very capable of looking after herself.*

He headed in the general direction of the noise and Olivia yelled out, "I know it's you, Kian! Don't think I'm fooled by your new skin suit!"

There was another *thump*, and Harlan ran, finally pausing outside an open doorway. A fallen torch illuminated two figures wrestling on the ground. He raced in, threw his arm around the neck of the man straddling Olivia, and hauled him off her.

They stumbled and fell, and the man rolled onto Harlan, trapping him. He repeatedly jabbed his elbow into Harlan's gut, forcing him to let go, before jumping to his feet to grab a bag that was lying to the side. But Olivia was now standing and she tackled him unexpectedly, and they crashed into a bookcase. The man threw Olivia off, pushing her with such force that she fell onto a table and landed on the floor, winded. Before Harlan could get close, the man rushed out and down the passageway.

"Grab him!" Olivia yelled.

But Harlan was already in pursuit, and in the seconds it took him to reach the kitchen, their attacker had escaped through the back door and was sprinting across the garden.

Harlan watched him go. It was pointless to follow him. He risked being possessed himself, or injuring the man who was now possessed. And besides, he knew his identity. It was Kent Marlowe, a member of the Order of the Midnight Sun.

Olivia joined him, wincing as she put a hand to her lower back. "Bollocks! That hurt. Why aren't you chasing him?"

"Because that's Kent Marlowe. Don't you recognise him?"

Olivia groaned. "Shit. I do now. I haven't seen him for ages. What the hell is Kian doing in Kent's body?"

Harlan locked the door. "And importantly, where is Mason?"

"Oh crap! He better not have hurt him!" She fumbled in her pocket. "Bollocks. I've lost my phone." She headed down the hall to the room where they'd been fighting, and Harlan followed, thinking furiously.

"Why Kent Marlowe? He's a research guy, not an action hero."

"Oh, really," Olivia grumbled. "He seemed pretty action-heroey to me. I think I've broke a rib." She retrieved her torch and flashed it around the room, eventually getting onto her hands and knees to look under tables. "Got it!" she said triumphantly as she picked it up.

But Harlan was distracted by the upended bag that Kian had abandoned, and a sprawl of papers on the floor. He shone his own torch down, feeling a flutter of excitement as he knelt and searched through them. "Hey, Livy. I think we've found Chadwick's research. He must have come back for it."

Before she could reply, her phone rang, and he paid scant attention while she answered, until he heard her exclaim, "Mason! Are you okay?" Harlan looked up at her anxious face, relieved when she said, "Thank God. Where are you?" There was a pause before she nodded. "Yes, of course. We'll call Maggie and we'll be there soon!"

She ended the call, and Harlan asked, "Is he really all right?"

"I think so. He sounded shocked and confused. He's just woken up in a dark house, and he had to go the street to work out where he was."

"Which is, of course, Kent Marlowe's house?"

"Bingo." Olivia was already heading to the door. "Come on, we have to go. Bring the notes."

"Give me a minute," he told her. "Help me search. We don't want to miss anything, and I am not coming back here again!"

Olivia shot him a long look. "One minute, and then we leave. And you need to call Maggie to get her to meet us there."

Fifteen

G abe exited his SUV at the base of the Cotswold Way, the path leading to Belas Knap, and stretched as Shadow, Niel, Ash, and Barak exited, too. It was close to midnight, and after their almost four-hour drive, he felt cramped.

There was a light breeze, and clouds were heavy overhead, the air carrying the promise of rain; he inhaled deeply, savouring the night scents.

"I'm looking forward to seeing this place," Barak said. "It sounds suitably ghostly."

Gabe grunted. "And small! I had to crouch to get in."

Shadow nodded in agreement. "But only the Gods know why someone would make the tomb so inaccessible."

"So it's hard to raid and steal grave goods, obviously," Ash told them. "Although, it clearly didn't work."

"It did for a long time!" Niel argued, walking to the path.

Gabe was about to follow, but then noticed Shadow's hand touch her leg wound, and he remembered her earlier suggestion. "Why don't we fly, boys?"

"Is that wise?" Barak asked. He turned, scanning the car park and the sky above them. "There are no other cars here," he pointed out.

"But there's a path from the other direction," Niel reminded him.

Gabe grinned, sick of following rules and playing human all the time. "I don't care. Let's live a little." He pulled his jacket and t-shirt off, throwing them in the SUV. "I'll take Shadow for a ride." He looked at her, eyebrow cocked. "Ready?"

Her gaze drifted down his chest and back to his eyes, amused. With one quick flex of his shoulders he unfurled his enormous wings, and enjoyed seeing Shadow gasp as they spread out, twice his height on either side of him, and thick with tawny feathers that swept to his feet.

Gabe groaned with pleasure as he lifted them up and down, feeling the wind already ruffling them. "That feels good!"

Barak whooped, and throwing his t-shirt off, did the same, unfurling wings that were as black as the night sky. "Brother, that's the best suggestion you've made all day!"

Without waiting, Barak lifted into the air with ease, manoeuvring himself with dexterity and grace. Ash and Niel quickly followed suit, until Gabe was the only one still standing. He held his hand out to Shadow. "Want a lift?"

"I think I should walk." Her eyes did not echo her words. She watched the others circling the car park, envy in her gaze, and glanced back at Gabe. "You make it look so easy."

"It is, to us. It's like walking is for you. Or sword fighting. It's instinctive." They flew often at the farmhouse. It was secure there, private and protected from prying eyes. It was one of the reasons he'd chosen it. But although they lived with Shadow, they didn't usually fly in front of her. It wasn't for any other reason than the freedom of being with his brothers.

She studied his wings, taking in their span, and then circled behind him. He smiled, enjoying her admiration. "How do you hide them?" she asked. "They're huge!"

"Magic," he said, winking. When she stood before him again, he held his arms out. "Come on. I promise I won't drop you."

She gave him a long look, her violet eyes almost hooded, and then stepped close, her back to his chest. Gripping her tightly, he rose into the air, laughing at her sharp intake of breath.

"Herne's horns!" she exclaimed. He felt her stiffen and tense, her arms wrapped around his strong ones that were circling her waist. Her fingers dug into his skin and liked it more than he should. She was breathless when she whispered, "This is so freaky."

"Relax," he murmured in her ear. "I've got you."

"Easier said than done!"

He smiled. She was light and easy to carry, and he lifted them higher. In seconds they were above the tree line, and the road, car park, and fields were laid out around them. The rise of Belas Knap was ahead, black against the night sky.

"Looks good to me," Niel said, flying closer. His wings were a pale grey on top and darker underneath, which made it harder to detect him from below. "Let's go."

Gabe followed the others, but rather than land straight away, Gabe circled above, his keen eyes taking in the landscape and design of the burial site. "I can see why humans think it looks like a kneeling woman."

Shadow huffed. "People love to see the female form in everything! I find it demeaning."

"You should find it flattering. And besides, she's called Mother Earth for a reason. She was even called that, or a version of it, when I was first alive. She gives life to all. Perhaps the shape of Belas Knap is about returning the dead to the womb of the Earth."

Shadow didn't answer, and he flew over the fields and then the woods that lay alongside them, which were larger than he first realised. The roads beyond were quiet, and he saw only occasional headlights winking through the lanes as they dipped behind hedges. Niel had already landed and was checking the small tombs, but Ash and Barak were still circling over the area. The night air caressed his skin, and the feel of it through his feathers was almost as pleasurable as a woman's touch. *God knows it had been a long time since he'd experienced that.* He'd been like a monk since they'd arrived back from the spirit lands. Most of them had, except for Eli.

Pushing those thoughts behind him, he asked Shadow, "What do you think of flying?"

"I like it, although I'd much rather be doing it myself. It's scary putting my life in someone else's hands." She shivered slightly, and he gripped her tighter.

"Just like it?" He sounded annoyed, but he wasn't really. He was teasing her. He had decided long ago that teasing Shadow was one of his life's greatest pleasures. "I am flying, woman!"

"All right. It's amazing! I love it. I'm jealous." She twisted her head to look at him. "Bastard."

He laughed, pleased to have provoked her, and then a piercing whistle from Niel gave them the all-clear. They swooped down to join him, landing on top of Belas Knap, and Gabe released Shadow, a beat slower than he should have.

"No one's here," Niel told them. "I've read that sometimes people spend the night in one of the tombs, but not tonight. The wood should be deserted, too."

"Let's go, then," Gabe said, reluctantly hiding his wings. He led them down the bank and onto the narrow path through the trees, but Shadow slipped ahead of him, and once again, she disappeared, despite his good eyesight. Her capacity to just vanish was unnerving. She might have been jealous of his ability to fly, but he was jealous of her vanishing tricks.

He continued regardless, remembering the way easily, and within ten minutes they were back at the blocked entrance to the tomb. They quickly dismantled the stones, revealing the passage beyond.

"You weren't kidding about the size," Barak said. His hand was on the bank as he bent down to peer inside.

"Just be careful with those ridiculously oversized shoulders of yours," Shadow said. "You might get stuck! I'll go first."

As she entered, Gabe said, "One of us should wait here, anyway. I don't want to be sealed in there, and it *is* a tight space."

"I'm happy to wait," Barak said, already pacing around.

"And me," Niel agreed.

"Good, I need to see this," Ash said, and he followed Shadow, leaving Gabe to enter last.

Once inside, Gabe was quickly reminded of how dirty and ruined the initial passage was. As they crouched, walking awkwardly, trickles of earth slid down, and Ash broke away roots that had breached the walls, something they hadn't bothered doing before, trying to make their progress easier. They reached the false tomb with relief.

"What exactly are we searching for?" Ash asked, looking around.

"Anything!" Gabe said. "Marks on the stonework or floor, or something unusual about the objects, although I don't think there'll be much of significance here. These items were designed to fool anyone who found it into thinking this was the tomb proper."

Ash nodded. "While we're here, though, we may as well check."

They spent a short while examining the small alcoves, finding cups, bowls, and small animal bones, before Shadow sighed, frustrated. "There's nothing useful here. Let's carry on." She hadn't bothered using her torch up to this point, but now she pulled it out, and flashed it down the passageway, explaining, "I don't want to miss anything."

Every now and again they stopped, noting symbols etched onto the stones, swirls and shapes that made no sense. Gabe rested his hands on them. "These feel like they were carved only recently. They're pristine."

"That's because no one's ever seen them before," Ash pointed out. "We had many such tombs where I came from, but they were ornate, and lots were lined with gold. That's Kings for you. " He pulled his phone from his pocket. "I'm going to take some photos. I'd like to see if we can find anything out later."

Gabe nodded. "I'll follow Shadow, she's disappeared. Again. "

"It can't be easy knowing that a fey ghost wants to capture you. I'd be pretty pissed if a ghost Nephilim was trying to catch me for some dodgy reason." He gave Gabe a knowing grin. "She certainly makes life interesting."

He grunted. "That's one way of putting it." He left Ash laughing and headed to the main tomb, where he could see torchlight flashing around. When he reached Shadow's side, her expression was bleak. "Are you okay?"

"Not really. I still feel his energy in here. It's dark, twisted. I should have paid more attention to it before." She looked at him, meeting his eyes. "You were right, and I should have listened. Restless ghosts don't just disappear."

He placed a hand on her shoulder and squeezed. "But what would that have changed? Nothing. Chadwick would still have taken the grave goods, and we can't perform exorcisms. If that would even work." He recalled what Shadow had told him about her chat with the witches.

She nodded, turning her attention back to the room, and sweeping the torch up to the roof. "Did you notice the flat stone in the dome centre? It's different to the rest."

Gabe squinted upwards. The roof was high at the point, well beyond even his reach, and it was impossible to fly to. His wings were too big for the tight space. "It has spirals marked on it, too. Get on my shoulder—see if you can touch it."

He crouched down and once she was in place, he gripped her legs and lifted her slowly. "You okay?"

"Fine, I can reach it."

Ash joined them again. "What are you doing?"

"Checking the roof, dummy, what does it look like?" she called down.

"I can see that!" he said, impatiently. "Why?"

"That is not what you asked first," she retorted. "It has marks on it. Do you think it opens?"

Gabe couldn't look up, it was too hard with Shadow on his shoulders, but he frowned at Ash. "Isn't that likely to bring the roof down on our heads?"

"Yes! Hey Shadow, don't do anything rash!"

"But it's in a sort of frame. I can see it. I'm going to try." She thrust the torch at Ash and he took it, aiming the beam of light where she worked.

Before they could object, Shadow was already pushing at the central stone, and Gabe could feel her wriggling above him. "Seriously? Shadow, what the hell are you doing?" Gabe yelled, debating whether to lower her to the floor, although part of him was intrigued. Was there something above them? A trickle of earth and tiny stones showered down. "Shadow!"

Ash's eyes narrowed with worry. "She's going to kill us all!"

"Will you please trust me?" she said, annoyed, and then grunted. "Damn it. Nothing's happening!"

"Good," Gabe said, and squatted before she could cause any damage.

Shadow huffed as she slid from his shoulders. "There must be something else here, apart from his bones!"

"It's a bloody tomb. What else do you expect?" Ash asked.

Her eyes widened. "Oh, no! I just remembered what happened right before Kian's spirit rose out of those bones." She started to examine the floor methodically, sifting through the debris of earth and small stones.

Gabe willed himself to be patient, trying to ignore Ash's obvious amusement. "Shadow, can you explain what you're looking for?"

"In all the excitement of being attacked by a murderous spirit, I'd forgotten that I found a stone in Kian's jaw. It was polished and flat, with strange symbols on it."

Gabe groaned. "You took it out, didn't you?"

"Of course! I wanted to see it. But then the spirit rose up and assaulted me, and I dropped it."

"For fuck's sake! That's what probably triggered its escape, you bloody Muppet! Why didn't you say so before?"

She stood up and poked him in the chest. "I am not a Muppet! I just forgot! I was attacked, remember." And then she scowled. "What is a Muppet, anyway? It sounds derogatory."

"It's meant to be. They're stupid, brainless puppets."

"Calm down children," Ash said, stepping between them, his lips twitching. "Why don't we all look for it now, and we can debate Muppets and their merits later." He turned to Shadow. "Where were you?"

She pointed to the wall on their right. "Over there, but it could have gone anywhere."

"Let's take a section each then, and get this done," Ash said, immediately heading to the far corner.

Shadow gave Gabe one final scowl before turning her back on him, and he took a deep breath and counted to ten, before starting his own search.

It wasn't long before he heard a shout from Ash. "Is this it?" He pointed his torch at the stone in his hand.

Shadow sighed with relief. "Yes. Can you interpret those symbols?"

Ash nodded, looking grim. "It's a rune sigil for silence—a sort of binding of the tongue and body."

"And you took it out of his mouth!" Gabe said, shaking his head.

"Well, I didn't know that at the time, did I?" Shadow said, annoyed.

Ash pocketed the stone. "At least we know what triggered Kian's escape, but it won't help us find him." He examined the doorway. "The swirling signs that are all along the passageway are inscribed here, too. I think this is purely decoration to honour the dead, before they sealed him in, but there's nothing here to indicate why he needed to be locked away for eternity."

"I think we should take his bones," Shadow said, dusting her trousers off.

"Why?" Gabe asked.

"I just think we should. His spirit is separate from his body now, but maybe we can use his bones to control him or banish him. And if I'm honest, I don't really want to come here again, so we should take everything."

Gabe felt increasingly uncomfortable about the tomb. Kian's dark energy still seeped from the stones. Tombs often were elaborate and detailed, celebrating the dead within them, but this was different. "Maybe Kian had some power over death. Maybe that's why they had to treat his body so carefully. Maybe death wasn't merely death for him? We've already messed so much up, is taking the bones really a good idea? And just to remind you, he's hunting you for some reason. This could make him even more annoyed."

"It's the only thing left to take. The significant grave goods have gone, including the staff." Shadow paused thoughtfully. "I just think we should."

Ash shrugged. "I'm not convinced. I'm with Gabe—this feels wrong!"

Shadow ignored their protestations and started to collect the bones anyway, placing them in the bag she had brought with her, before flashing them her most dangerous smile. "Trust me! I'm fey!"

"Yeah, and look what happened..." Gabe muttered to her retreating back. He stared at Ash. "The next time I suggest going into business with a fey, remind me of this moment."

Sixteen

Mason looked grey, and far older than his years.

He was slumped in a chair in Kent's living room, staring vacantly at the wall. Olivia sat next to him, holding his hand. "Can you remember anything?"

Mason shook his head. "Not really. I felt as if I was buried alive. I had flashes of awareness. Of being in my car, and then I was gone again. Until about an hour ago, when I woke up on the floor." He swallowed and took a few deep breaths. "I feel sick."

They had arrived ten minutes ago, to find Kent's door wide open and Mason sitting in the hall, shivering. As yet, Maggie hadn't turned up, and while Olivia had settled Mason in the lounge, Harlan prowled around the house, looking for anything that might help them. However, he'd found nothing of note, except for a half-consumed meal that must have been interrupted.

Kent Marlowe was well respected in the Order of the Midnight Sun. He was a similar age to Harlan, he would guess, and was known for his love of the occult, particularly magical rituals. All of the Order had eclectic interests, some more than others. Kent was an academic though, not a practising magician, and his home reflected that. It was far more ordinary than Chadwick's house.

Mason started to shiver, and Olivia looked at Harlan anxiously. "He's in shock. We need to get him seen by a doctor." She picked up a woollen blanket that was placed across the back of the sofa, threw it around Mason's shoulders, and then stood decisively. "I'll make some tea."

Harlan rolled his eyes. "Sure. Tea solves everything!"

"He needs something hot and sweet! It always works."

"Maybe throw a shot of brandy in it," Harlan called after her.

While Olivia headed to the kitchen, Harlan paced off his nervous energy, trying to work out where Kian would go next, but it was impossible to know at this stage. "Mason, can you remember what Kian was thinking, or doing?"

Mason blinked once and shook his head. "I don't think so. I felt he was sifting through my brain for things."

"That's because he was. He was looking for someone to help him, and Kent Marlowe is it." He rubbed his face wearily. "He headed back to Chadwick's, too. Fortunately, we interrupted him."

The screeching of brakes called him to the window, and he saw Maggie's car in the drive. Harlan took a deep breath, steeling himself for what was to come. "She's here," he shouted to the kitchen, not needing to explain what he meant to Olivia.

He headed to the door to let Maggie in, but she was already hammering on it when he got there. "All right, all right. I'm here."

Maggie barrelled into the hall, shaking the water off her jacket as she went. It had started raining since they'd arrived. "Bloody hell," she said, not wasting time. "Another kidnapping! For fuck's sake. You and your sodding Orphic Guild!"

"Can I remind you that I am not responsible for this? This was Chadwick's doing. I did what I always do, enable an acquisition!"

"Without any thought of the consequences!"

"And I help, too!" he yelled back, now very grumpy. "We keep objects of power away from the general population. Objects that could do immense harm in the wrong hands. You're happy for us to do our job then, aren't you?"

Maggie paused and took a deep breath. "Sorry. I'm tired. I had just got into bed when you called."

Harlan calmed down, slightly mollified. "I'm tired, too. And I'm worried. I have no idea where Kent Marlow has gone, but he will be in his own car. That's something."

"Okay. At this stage if we find him, I don't think we'll stop him, just monitor him," she said thoughtfully. She glanced down the hall. "What state is Mason in?"

"Not a good one. We might have to take him to the hospital." He led the way to the elegant sitting room and found Olivia pressing a cup of tea into Mason's hands.

Olivia nodded. "Hey, Maggie. Life is getting weird."

"Not for me, it's not. It's always this bloody weird. Christ!" She looked at Mason, focussing on him fully as she took in his appearance. "He looks like shit."

Mason stared into the mug, mute.

"Maybe you should get him checked out," Maggie said. "Although, he might be better after getting a good night's sleep in a warm bed. And food. Has he eaten in the last twenty-four hours?"

"Hard to know," Harlan told her. He leaned against the wall, his arms folded across his chest, exhausted. If he sat down now, he might never get up again. "He can't remember anything."

Maggie sighed. "Okay, let me get my head around this. You manage to wake a spirit from his tomb, who has become actively aggressive. He inhabits Chadwick, who tries to catch Shadow. She kills him and he hops into Mason, and now body-hops again, into Kent. What is he trying to achieve? And why does he want Shadow?"

Harlan exchanged a worried glance with Olivia. "I don't know why he wants Kent, but I presume it's because he studies ritual magic. He's an expert on it. Maybe his knowledge compliments Kian's. We believe Kian was a Druid who would have protected his tribe and his King." He'd already decided he wouldn't tell Maggie about their encounter with him at Chadwick's house. Not yet, anyway.

"So he would have practiced magic, of a sort," Maggie said thoughtfully. She narrowed her eyes at Harlan. "What aren't you telling me about Shadow?"

"Nothing. She's new to the Guild, but she has useful skills and will, hopefully, continue to help us in the future."

Maggie tapped her toe. "You're a shit liar. I checked her out. There's nothing about her anywhere until a few months ago. And nothing much about this Gabreel, who she lives with, either. He didn't exist on paper until September of last year! The same story for the other six guys registered at that address."

That gave Harlan a momentary shock, and his eyes must have betrayed it. He hadn't checked on Gabe, particularly. It didn't seem necessary. The Guild wasn't the police. They didn't run background checks on their contractors. They couldn't.

Maggie laughed. "So, you didn't know! You're slipping, Harlan. You get your contractors to do all sorts of things. Surely you should investigate them!"

"I had first-hand experience of working with Shadow. I trust her, and I trust Gabe."

"But you know nothing about him, or the other six men. That's eight of them living in a farmhouse, with no background at all! But they all have IDs and they all pay taxes!"

"Well, there you go then," Harlan said, relieved ever so slightly.

"Just because they pay their taxes doesn't make them good guys! It makes them smart! Do you even know who they work for?"

"Gabe? No idea." He shot a look at discomfort at Olivia, but she was mute, listening with interest.

"Kernow Industries. He and his crew do surveillance for them at their main warehouse in Harecombe."

"Great! I'm sure they must have done security checks on them. They have to be legit."

She was silent for a moment, considering him. "I have a contact down in White Haven. DI Newton. I haven't met him personally, but I hear good things about him. He's heading up their recently formed paranormal division. I bet he knows something."

"I met him after the Crossroads Circus problem ended. He seems decent." Harlan cast his mind back to the night of the fight with the Empusa, when Ravens' Wood had sprung up in a matter of hours. "He's good friends with the witches down there."

"Well, in that case, I must ring him." She gave Mason another long, speculative look. "We have to presume that having failed to catch Shadow once, he'll try again. That's good. She's bait."

"Maggie!" Harlan protested. "That's not cool."

"It is if it means catching some bastard rogue ghost. We need to exorcise it!"

"We are working on it. Trust me. Shadow will have a plan! She has no wish to get captured."

"I guess not," she agreed, begrudgingly. "Well, it's clear I'm getting nothing out of him now. Where's he going tonight?"

"He can come to my place," Olivia said. "I have a spare bed, and I'm happy to look after him."

Harlan nodded gratefully. "Thanks. I'll help you get him settled in."

Maggie headed for the door. "I'll have a quick look around and then lock up. I'll call you in the morning, Livy. Now, you three get out of here, and if I hear anything about Kent's car, I'll let you know."

———◦◦◦———

Shadow finished her conversation with Harlan, put her phone in her pocket, and stared at Kian's bones, which she had laid out in a corner of their barn.

She hadn't bothered to place them in order, but had instead piled them on each other, his skull on the top. The sockets looked back at her balefully, and she glared at them. "What are you up to, you devious old fey?"

"I don't think he's going to tell you," Gabe said from behind her, and she spun around.

"How did you sneak up on me so quietly?"

He smirked as he stood next to her, his arms folded across his chest. "I'm Nephilim, remember?"

"And huge! You're rarely quiet."

"Just goes to prove I can be when I want to be! Why are you talking to the bones?"

"Obviously I'm not expecting them to answer me. I'm musing out aloud."

"Good. Just checking that the iron in your blood hadn't addled your brain."

She decided to ignore his sarcasm. "I'm trying to recall what I know about certain rites that allow the spirit to transcend death in fey. It would involve dark magic, but I guess it could be done." She studied the hard planes of Gabe's face, and the stubble that grazed it. He looked tired, but she guessed she did, too. It was lunchtime on Monday, and those who had gone to Belas Knap had grabbed a few hours' sleep like her, and woke late. "You transcended death. How?"

Gabe met her eyes briefly and then looked at Kian's skeleton. "We didn't really. We died in the Great Flood that swept the Earth. It was sent as a punishment by God to kill us and the rest of the population who were deemed unworthy." Gabe had a good sense of humour, but it was often buried beneath what seemed an unequal burden of grief, and it showed now. His eyes were haunted.

"And what did you do that deserved that?"

"Rebel against our destiny."

"Wow." For a second, words failed Shadow, but if she didn't ask now, she may never get another opportunity. It was rare for Gabe to open up. "And what was your destiny?"

"We are half-angels, a bridge between the divine and the human. We could walk the Earth, unlike our angel fathers. We were bred for fighting, and to do our fathers' bidding."

He fell silent, and Shadow had to prompt him again. "Which was?"

"Controlling people, making war, herding the innocent to follow God's will. Our size and skills gave us a superior advantage. For a while, it made me arrogant. All of us, in fact." He was still staring at the bones, but it was clear he was seeing something entirely different. "I didn't like it, in the end. It felt wrong. I don't like to use my strength against others who are weaker and don't deserve it. We stopped following our fathers' orders and were punished for it, and those we then tried to protect were punished for our rebellion."

"I've read about the flood in history books. How big was it?"

"It pretty much killed everyone in the Mediterranean and the Middle East, except a chosen few. I don't believe that it really was worldwide—I think that's myth. But, what do I know? What I do know is that our fathers let us drown." Shadow felt the enormity of the event roll through her, and she was speechless. He finally turned to look at her. "Harsh, wasn't it?"

"That's one word for it."

"I drowned, as did all of my brothers, and our spirits ended up in the spirit world. An eternity of nothingness, in a dark place. And then we saw our chance, a glimpse of life and light again."

Shadow nodded, recalling a conversation she'd had with the witches. Curiously, they had been cagey about it, too. "Alex's spell that opened a portal."

"Yes. But only seven of us escaped."

"There were more of you?"

"My brothers were many. They are there still."

Shadow leaned against the barn wall, thinking that Gabe's history was far more complex than she could have imagined. She would probably only ever know a fraction of it; the histories she had read revealed only fragments. "I'm sorry they were left behind. But how did you regain your bodies? I don't understand how that's even possible."

"I had to kill someone and take his blood. It gave me enough strength to finally transform my spirit form into my physical body. We killed cattle, when we could."

"Oh. So that's why Newton doesn't like you. How many people did you kill?"

"Enough. We broke our centuries-old pact when we took innocent mortal lives to regain our bodies."

"Is your father alive?"

"He was immortal, so he should be. But I have not heard from him, and I'm glad of it. And neither have the others."

"I still think they are some kind of fey, a sylph."

"I no longer care what you think. I know what I know."

Shadow felt guilty. "I don't mean to demean your parentage. You may be right. Maybe this God of yours did have winged servants who bred with humans, but I really do sense some kind of fey blood. Fey bred with them, all the time at one point, when the veil between worlds was thin." She nodded at Kian's bones. "Look at them. Look at me. Look at you! We are like humans in many ways."

"We used human blood to regain our bodies. I fear he will do the same. With yours. Fey blood for a fey body."

"I have no intention of letting him do that. Briar is making me something to drug him. I aim to kill his spirit when he emerges from whoever he's possessing."

"Sounds easier said than done."

"I know." It was a half-formed plan, at best. "Harlan has phoned me. Kian moved bodies again, into a man called Kent Marlow who is an expert on ritual magic. He must need to use his knowledge. The good news is that Harlan has found Chadwick's notes—or some of them, at least. He hasn't read them yet, not properly anyway."

"Good, that's something. Kian has stayed in London then?"

"I suspect he will be here soon enough."

Gabe nodded. "Let's hope that he won't try to jump into our bodies."

"But what does he want?"

"Ultimately? To live like anyone else, surely? We'll keep a watch now and every night until this is over."

Shadow looked at Kian's remains. *Did he need these? Should she destroy them?* Gabe was spirit-only and he had regained his fully physical form without them, but he was Nephilim. *What was a Druid capable of? Whatever it was, she would stop him.*

"I need to get out," she said. "I'm going for a ride. I'll be safe enough on horseback."

He considered her for a moment. "I suppose you will. But don't stay out long, and take your bronze swords."

She nodded, heading to the stables. However, before she saddled Kailen, she spent some time with the horse of the fallen fey warrior. Shadow didn't know either of their names, but she had decided to call the beast Stormfall, after the night of their arrival. She stroked his soft nose and looked into his eyes. "I'm sorry your master is dead," she whispered. He was a fine animal, as tall as her own and as swift, like all horses from the Otherworld. Fortunately, the Nephilim were good riders, and many of them took him out for exercise, particularly Ash.

She didn't know his rider, so it would be wrong to say she'd grieved for his death, but she had grieved for the loss of one of her kind. Like her, he had been recruited for the Hunt at Herne's request. He'd been tall, fair-skinned, with fire in his eyes. He'd been the one to break the circle, and she followed, foolishly, as had one other. But he had died, killed by the Nephilim. She suspected it was Niel, but they hadn't said, and she didn't ask. The other fey had managed to get back to Herne and to the Otherworld when the witches forced them out through the doorway between worlds.

What if Kian did regain his body? What then? Would she forever fear him, or would he become an ally? She sighed, resting her head against Stormfall's neck. Just because he was fey didn't make him trustworthy, or a friend. He had been enough of a threat to others for him to be sealed in with fey magic. Perhaps he had crossed to this world because other fey had been hunting him. *Had he died naturally, or had someone killed him?*

Shadow thought again of Kian's remains. She had given them a cursory examination, but there were no obvious signs of trauma. No smashed bones or tell-tale cracks across the skull. He could still have died a violent death, though. A knife between the ribs, along the throat, or into the stomach would leave no marks on bone.

She took a deep breath and turned away. She didn't need to know who he was or what he'd done to kill him. She saddled up Kailen and headed out into the fresh air, leaving her speculation for another time.

Seventeen

When Harlan arrived in White Haven, the shops were just closing. He headed for the one place he knew he'd find a familiar face and some food before he visited Shadow—The Wayward Son, Alex's pub.

Harlan hadn't left London until the early afternoon, having been late to bed after helping Olivia with Mason the previous night. Olivia had already phoned to say that Mason was much better today, but he hadn't heard from Maggie yet. He'd decided to travel to White Haven anyway, and rather than examine Chadwick's notes at home, planned to do it once he arrived. They were in the trunk, with his overnight bag. Tucked inside the latter were his shotgun and a pack of salt-filled shells. It was the best protection he had against a rogue ghost.

He managed to find a park along the quayside, and when he stepped outside, he inhaled the fresh sea air. This place was a balm for the senses after London. He wasn't sure if it was his imagination, but he thought he could feel magic. When he'd come here a few weeks ago chasing the Crossroads Circus, he'd been suspicious of the town after everything he'd heard, but not anymore. Even the presence of powerful witches didn't put him off. Was that a mark of how he lived far more in the magical world than he did the normal? Maybe. White Haven felt remarkably safe, despite the magic, and that was a credit to the witches.

He pushed through the door of Alex's pub, relieved to see that it wasn't too busy. There was a table by the fire that would do nicely for his purposes. He headed to the bar to place his order, immediately seeing Alex serving another customer, and he waited patiently for his turn, scanning the menu to pass the time. But it wasn't Alex who served him; it was a tall man with broad shoulders, a scar down his cheek, and brooding eyes.

He nodded at Harlan in greeting. "What would you like?"

"The steak, medium rare, and a pint of Skullduggery Ale, please." The beer seemed fitting, considering his situation.

"Sure," he said, starting to ring up his order. "You're American."

"I am."

"You wouldn't happen to be Harlan Beckett, would you?"

Harlan looked at him, shocked. "What if I am?"

The man laughed and he instantly looked far less formidable. "Don't worry, you're not in trouble. I live with Shadow—as a housemate only, you understand!" He looked as if the alternative was horrific.

"I get it." Harlan laughed as he relaxed. "How do you know who I am?"

"We don't get many Americans this time of year. And Gabe said you'd be coming." He placed his pint in front of him. "I'm Zee."

Harlan shook his hand, remembering his conversation with Maggie. This man was as tall and broad-chested as Gabe and Niel, which was unusual. He couldn't help wondering about the rest of them. "I understand there are a few of you in that farmhouse."

Zee nodded and cocked an eyebrow. "Yeah, eight of us. Fun times."

"Never a dull moment, eh?"

"That's one way of putting it. Where are you staying?"

"I haven't decided. There are a couple of hotels I thought I'd try, but I needed food first."

Zee leaned on the bar and lowered his voice. "Have you come to help us find our rogue ghost?"

"Sort of. I've found Chadwick's papers, but I haven't had a chance to read them properly yet. I'm hoping they will tell us something useful." He broke off as Alex approached, a wary look in his eye. Harlan reached over and shook his hand, keen to establish good relations. "Hey, Alex. Great to meet you again."

"You too, I think. You're not chasing anything else, are you?"

Harlan laughed. "Just the ghost. I was telling Zee that I found Chadwick's papers. I need to study them, but I'd like to see Gabe and Shadow later."

"We keep late nights," Zee told him. "Give him a call after you've eaten. He won't mind."

"You still driving that Mercedes?" Alex asked.

Harlan had a jolt of surprise as he wondered how Alex knew what car he drove, and then realised they'd probably researched him, too. "It's outside now."

"Well, if you value your suspension, I suggest you take it slow. Did I hear you say you need a place to stay?"

"Yeah. I'd hoped I'd get a room easily at this time of year."

Alex looked uncertain. "You might, but my flat, upstairs, is empty at the moment. It's furnished, and it will take only a few minutes to make up the bed if you want to stay there. No charge, either. As long as you don't raid the alcohol stores tonight."

That sounded perfect. "You don't mind? It's not like you know me that well."

"I know you well enough. And besides, I think you know better than to cross a witch." He said the word witch quietly, an amused look on his face.

"I sure do. Thanks, Alex. And you can trust me with your whiskey."

When Harlan pulled into the farmhouse's courtyard a few hours later, he found a large man blocking his way and he halted, uncertain, as the man strode around to his window.

He was well built and again very tall, and very similar in appearance to Gabe—olive-skinned and dark-haired. Were all these men related?

Harlan introduced himself. "I'm expected, I hope."

"You sure are," he answered. "Park over here and head to the front door."

Harlan felt like saluting, but he resisted the urge, and instead did as he was told. He hoped he was guarding the gate just because of their unusual situation; otherwise, things were really odd here. When he exited the car, the man had already disappeared, and he crossed the yard feeling invisible eyes on his back.

Shadow answered his knock within seconds and led him inside. "Hey, Harlan. You want a drink?"

He looked around with curiosity as she brought him down the hall, which was bare, except for a couple of prints on the wall. "You got any beer?"

She laughed. "Of course we have. I'll grab a few before I introduce you to everyone." He followed her into the kitchen, which was far cleaner than he expected for a house full of men. He must have looked surprised, because she said, "Gabe keeps these guys on their toes. Although, to be honest, they're all house-trained. More than I am, anyway."

She flashed him a cheeky grin, her beauty catching him off guard. She had relaxed her glamour, or whatever it was she used to mask her Otherness, and he felt lost suddenly in her violet eyes. Her Otherness was uncanny, though he knew it was stupid to say that. Of course she was uncanny, she was fey, but her glamour was so effective it was easy to forget who she really was. He took a deep breath to ground himself, and when she passed him his beer, he clutched it like a man clinging to a life raft, and swiftly took a gulp.

"You look like you've seen a ghost." She grinned again. "Sorry. Poor choice of words."

Harlan decided honesty was the best policy. "It's easy to forget you're fey when you cover it up, and tonight you haven't. It's unnerving. Sorry if that's uncool to say."

"It's fine. I'm home now, so I don't need to bother."

"And the guard in the courtyard. Is that normal?"

"No. That's Nahum, and it's just what we're doing while Kian is on the loose. No one wants any nasty surprises at night."

He leaned against the counter, glad to have the chance to speak to her on her own. "Gabe and the others know you're fey, then."

Shadow watched him steadily, gauging his reaction. "Of course. They're fine with it."

"And you're okay with them knowing?"

"I had no choice when we first met," she said enigmatically, "but yes, I am. I'm okay with you knowing too, and the witches, but it was Avery and Alex who told me to use glamour. Of course they're right. I'd never fit in, otherwise. Gabe agrees. He says I'm too rash. So, from now on, I'm very choosy as to who knows about me!" She shrugged. "This place is not like home. I'd be a freak if everyone knew."

"Well, I feel very privileged, then," he said, raising his bottle in salute. "But there are a few of us who straddle two worlds, you know, and you happen to have stumbled upon some of them—me and the Orphic Guild, included."

"So I gather. I'm lucky to be in White Haven, and have Ravens' Wood to visit." She frowned. "I'm surprised more people here don't see the magic that still exists, despite mankind's attempt to bury it."

"People like to rationalise everything away. If science can't explain it, then it must be your imagination."

"How very sad and dreary they are."

He laughed. "They are indeed. Tell me, these men you live with. Are they paranormal in any way? The ones I've met so far are big guys."

"They're all big. Come and meet the rest," she said, and she led the way back down the hall, ignoring his question, Harlan noticed.

He heard them before he saw them. Loud shouts and swearing filtered down the hall, and when Shadow opened the door to a large living room on the side of the house, he paused for a moment, taking stock of the space.

There were four men sitting either on the sofa or floor cushions, cursing each other as they played a game screened on the TV dominating the wall. The lighting was low, a fire burned in the fireplace, and he noted the room had an oriental feel to it. There were two huge maps of the world on the rear wall, one modern, and the other old. A few pins were on it and he wondered what they were for. Gabe was on the sofa next to Niel, and two men he hadn't met before were on the floor. Both looked to be from the Mediterranean from what he could discern, Greek maybe. One had long hair, and the other's was shorter. And yes, they were also big, broad-shouldered, and clearly very competitive.

"Oi!" Shadow shouted to be heard over the noise, and she headed to the sofa and gestured Harlan toward the armchair. "Harlan has arrived."

Gabe barely glanced at him. "Hey Beckett, be with you in a minute!" The others grunted their greetings as a volley of gunfire filled the room.

They were all playing together, some combat game he didn't recognise.

Shadow rolled her eyes. "They're obsessed. Don't worry, they're generally civil when they're not trying to kill everything in sight. Do you play?"

"Not for years. Do you?"

"Yeah, I like to remind them who's the better fighter every so often."

The man on the floor in front of her laughed dryly. "Sure you do. I am fey!" he mimicked.

Shadow smacked a cushion off his head. "Sod off, Eli," she said. "Why aren't you out seducing unsuspecting women tonight?"

"So I can annoy you, Shadow, why else?" he retorted, without taking his eyes off the screen.

Harlan stared at him for a few moments. "I know you. You work with Briar!"

"Sure do," he said, shooting him a grin.

Shadow pointed to the other man on the floor. "That's Ash. He works with Reuben, and sometimes at Caspian's. And you saw Nahum outside. There are only another two who you haven't met. Barak is at the warehouse right now, and Zee's at the pub."

"I met Zee, actually. I'm staying at Alex's old flat tonight."

Shadow gave him a wry smile. "So you've seen most of our happy household, then."

Harlan tried to relax, but it wasn't easy with so much testosterone in the room. "It's an interesting setup you have here."

There was a final flurry of gunfire and a lot of cheering as they completed the end of the scene, and then the screen suddenly froze as someone paused the game. There was a general shuffling as they all grabbed beers and swivelled to look at him, and Harlan tried not to show his discomfort at the intensity of their stares. There was something about these men, something strange he couldn't place.

"Sorry," Gabe said again. "That level's been killing us. We had to get through it."

"I know the feeling, although I haven't played for a while," he answered. "Sorry to have disturbed your evening."

"It's fine," Niel answered, looking at him curiously. "Have you found our missing ghost?"

"I'm afraid not, but he's in another body now. A man named Kent Marlowe."

Gabe nodded. "Shadow told us, thanks for phoning. Who is he?"

Harlan paused, wondering how accepting of unusual news these men were. They lived with a fey and knew about an escaped ghost, so they must be broad-minded. "Kent is a ritual magician, although less of a practicing one than someone who researches the knowledge. He's a member of the Order of the Midnight Sun. It's an organisation that devotes its time to esoteric learning."

Gabe glanced at the others. "What kind of esoteric learning?"

"Alchemy, astronomy, divination, communing with angels and demons, unlocking the secrets of eternal life, ritual magic...and more, no doubt."

Eli raised an eyebrow. "That's quite a list."

"They're an interesting bunch," Harlan acknowledged. "But generally harmless. Well, they have been so far."

"You think Kian has stolen Kent's body because of his knowledge?" Gabe asked.

"It's the only reason I can think of. Kian is a Druid, and I imagine would be an expert in magical rites, but what the hell do I know? Maybe he needs a refresher? Maybe he just needs someone to understand what he wants to do? I mean, what can a ghost see or do in someone's body?"

Ash spoke for the first time, a trace of an accent in his voice. "He's got a plan though, that's for sure. He's setting things up carefully."

Harlan nodded reluctantly. "Yes, you're right. He was very determined last night, too. We ran into him when me and Olivia went back to Chadwick's house to find his notes. He attacked us both."

"Who's Olivia?" Niel asked.

"My colleague. She's a collector, like me. She's good, and can take care of herself—which is lucky, because he assaulted her while she was on her own. Fortunately, we got what he found, and he escaped empty-handed." He pointed to the bag at his feet. "Chadwick's notes on Kian."

"Why would he have wanted those?" Eli asked, puzzled.

"I can only assume to stop us from seeing them—to keep us in the dark."

"Have you read them yet?" Gabe asked.

"Just started, but if I'm honest, I can't find anything that will benefit us. They're just notes about his life, the approximate time of his existence, the king he was linked to—a local king you understand, the head of a tribe in the dark ages. It looks like they're assembled from hundreds of different sources, some the barest of references. It will be my bedtime reading later." He shrugged. "I know I'm staying in a spell-protected pub, but I didn't want to leave them there."

"Sensible," Niel acknowledged. "With luck, if Kian is being methodical about his plans, he won't attack tonight."

"Unless he prepares very quickly," Shadow said. She'd curled up in the corner of the sofa, listening to the exchange. "I'll be carrying the Empusa's swords everywhere with me now."

"Maybe you should leave one in here, for us," Eli suggested. "Just in case."

"Nahum's got one at the moment, and the other one is there." She pointed to where it sat on the side table, its curved blade wickedly sharp.

Harlan held his hand up, confused. "What's the relevance of the Empusa's swords?"

Shadow looked at him, wide-eyed. "Shit! Haven't I told you? I found out what they can do. The bearer can see spirits —and hopefully, banish them. When I accidentally killed Chadwick, I saw Kian's ghost! So clearly that I could tell that he's fey."

Harlan thought he was imagining things. "Fey?"

"Sorry. I'd forgotten I hadn't told you."

"That's pretty important, Shadow!" he said, annoyed.

At least she had the grace to look embarrassed, and she repeated, "Really sorry! That's why we think he wants me, in particular."

"But what if we're wrong?" Ash said to Shadow. "He might not be coming for your blood. He might want something else. Or someone else."

Harlan tried to bury his annoyance, feeling like he was playing catch-up with this evolving situation. "I've brought the grave goods with me, if anyone wants to see them. I'm not sure how they'll help."

"No harm in looking," Ash said, and pointed to the long, low coffee table in front of the fire. "Put them here." He started to clear cups, bowls of crisps, and empty beer bottles from the surface, and Eli quickly helped him as Harlan unpacked.

He placed the old leather bag out first. "It's rotted quite a lot, but not as much as I expected."

The others crowded around, picking up the items as Harlan unloaded them.

"Rings and torcs," Niel noted. "The torcs look like silver. He was wealthy."

"Or had a wealthy benefactor," Ash said. He had spread out the contents of the bag. "These look like herbs, and these are runes." The *click-clack* of wood on the table drew Harlan's attention. "For divination."

"If he was considered dangerous, and his tomb sealed, why bury his personal items with him?" Gabe asked. "Wouldn't you destroy them?"

Shadow stood to get the staff, which was still propped in the corner of the room, and she laid it next to the other objects. "Why insult the dead more than you need to?"

"Exactly," Ash said. "You still honour the dead, for fear of retribution. We did."

Harlan looked at him, wondering what the hell he meant, then decided now was not the time to press for information. "Did you decipher anything on the staff?"

"We did," Gabe nodded. "'Those who choose the dark path will reap its rewards.'"

"Great. Suitably ominous, then," he said, feeling more unsettled.

"I see nothing in here of particular concern," Eli said, still sifting through the items. "It just confirms he's a Druid, or a shaman."

"A fey shaman," Shadow reminded them. "I'm more interested in knowing why he was here." She turned to Harlan. "We found something else in the tomb—something I'd forgotten about when we were attacked." She fished in her pocket and then handed him a small, flat stone. "I took this out of Kian's jawbone. A few seconds after that, his ghost attacked us." She leaned back, frowning. "I should have known better."

Harlan looked with curiosity at the seemingly innocuous object, examining the marks etched into its surface. "What do the symbols mean?"

Ash answered. "It's a sigil that binds the tongue and the body. We think removing it broke a spell on Kian's spirit."

"Wow. They really didn't like him, did they?"

"Apparently not," Gabe said, shooting an impatient look at Shadow. "And now he's out, thanks to us!"

"To be honest," Harlan said, "there was nothing in the fake tomb to suggest of what was beyond it. Nothing. How were we supposed to know what the magic was hiding? It could have just been a very wealthy burial! And who would think a stone would have bound him after death? It's very easy in hindsight to criticise our behaviour. I've been annoyed with myself ever since, but the reality is, we couldn't have known unless they had slapped a big warning on it."

"Which would have told everyone that something was there, anyway," Niel said, nodding.

"And," Harlan continued, "if you hadn't been here, Shadow, we couldn't have gotten through the fey magic."

"It's fate," Shadow said, her eyes widening.

"More like an unfortunate confluence of actions," Eli said.

Harlan addressed Ash, confused. "How do you know what the marks on the stone mean?"

Ash shot an amused glance at Gabe before answering. "It's a skill."

"To read old markings that haven't been read for hundreds of years?"

Ash shrugged. "Yes."

Harlan studied them all again, one by one; their height, build, and the intensity that lurked behind their eyes. Now that he was with a few of them, he sensed a latent power. Something different. He couldn't help himself. "Who are you?"

"We're nothing and no one," Gabe answered flatly.

"We're working together. Honesty would be nice," Harlan pointed out.

"Honesty has a time and a place," Gabe said. "We're cautious, that's all." He moved on swiftly, instead asking his own questions. "How is Mason now? Does he remember anything of what Kian wanted?"

Harlan paused, unwilling to change the subject, but faced with their blank but pleasant expressions, he realised he didn't have a choice. "I wish," he said, regretfully. "He feels like he's been hit with a sledge hammer. He doesn't remember much at all, unfortunately."

"Damn it," Gabe said, sighing. "Tell us more about the Midnight Sun."

"They've been around for a very long time, hundreds of years. The Order was formed in the sixteenth century, and then became very popular in the 1800s. They were all alchemists originally, searching for the meaning of life, but they also studied metaphysics, astrology, divination, and astral travel." Harlan shrugged. "I think that's still the focus for quite a few of them, but other members are interested in other occult things."

Gabe sipped his beer. "How many are in the Order?"

Harlan laughed. "That's difficult to say for sure. They're very secretive. I know a few of them, but most I have no idea about. And I believe there are various initiation levels, too."

"There have always been such organisations," Eli said, "for as long as man has existed. They may call themselves different things, but their intent is the same."

Ash agreed. "To unlock the secrets of the world. And some secrets are dangerous."

There was something about the way they looked at each other that unsettled Harlan, as if they knew facts he didn't. "I think the danger is part of the appeal. They may look like regular men and women, but those appearances are deceptive. However," he shrugged again, "that's what the Orphic Guild does, too. We search for the lost items of the world, to buy them for others."

"The secrets just below the surface of everyday life," Niel said, wryly. "Be careful what you wish for, isn't that the saying?"

Harlan tried to shrug off his unease. "It's certainly led me to a few interesting experiences, and the situation with Kian is one of them. And of course I'm sitting here with a fey," he said, looking at Shadow. "I wasn't expecting that."

"An unexpected pleasure, though," she said, a challenge in her voice. "You're very privileged."

Eli groaned. "Will you shut up? Privileged? You're a pain in the ass. We have a watch on the house because a fey ghost wants your blood. If you ask me, he's welcome to it."

In seconds, Shadow's dagger appeared in her hands as if from nowhere, and she whipped it to Eli's neck, but equally quickly, in a blur of movement Harlan barely saw, he grabbed her wrist in his hand, staring her down.

"You do that again, and I'll break your arm, Shadow."

"Trust me, if I wanted you dead, you would be. That's a warning."

"You could try," he said softly.

At this moment, Harlan wasn't sure who he would put his money on to come out on top; he was just glad they hadn't turned on him.

"Shadow, put your damn blade away," Gabe said, glaring at her. "You really need to learn to take a joke."

"He wasn't joking," Shadow retorted.

Eli looked amused. "No, I wasn't."

"Shadow is one of us now," Gabe said staring at Eli, and then at the other two. "You know that, and if you've forgotten, get used to it."

Shadow smirked at Eli, and her dagger disappeared again. "We're in business together, remember?"

"How could I forget?"

Gabe ignored both of them and addressed Harlan. "Have you any idea what to do with Kian? Our plan is vague, at best. Stop him from kidnapping Shadow whilst trying to kill his ghost without harming the host."

"I haven't got much else to offer, unfortunately, other than to try to find out more about him."

"Briar's making me a potion to drug him," Shadow said. "Well, a paste I hope, something to put on my knife, or a dart. I'm picking it up tomorrow. If I can drug the host, Kian will have to leave the body, and I can slay him using the Empusa's sword."

"You trust the fact that he'll arrive here at some point, then?"

"If he wants me, he'll have to."

Harlan nodded, thinking of what Maggie had said. "So you're the bait."

"I guess I am."

"You look way more comfortable with that idea than I would be."

"Without wishing to annoy my colleagues," she shot a vitriolic look at Eli, "I have faith in my abilities."

"Even with your injured leg?"

"I've had worse, and it's healing well. Thanks to Briar."

"And me!" Eli said, refusing to let her get away with anything.

Harlan tried not to laugh. "Maggie is keeping an eye out for Kent's stolen car, so if she finds it, I can warn you. But her resources are small when it comes to surveillance cameras and such. I should caution you about her, though."

"Why?" Shadow asked warily.

Harlan paused, debating just how much to say, but had to admit he wondered how they'd react, especially considering their response to his earlier question. "She's very interested in all of you, particularly because she believes that none of you existed six months ago."

"She can be as interested as she wants," Gabe said evenly. "We work, pay our taxes, and don't cause trouble."

"Who's Maggie?" Ash asked.

"The detective who leads the paranormal team in London," Harlan told him. "She's well versed in the occult world, and likes to know everything. She's going to speak to Newton about you."

"So be it," Gabe said, looking more at ease with the news than Harlan expected. "Our arrival caused some initial concerns, but since then we have only helped the witches here."

Harlan noted that he didn't say where he'd arrived from or why they'd raised concerns, but he wasn't going to ask anymore. *Not yet.* He finished his beer, and placed the empty bottle on the table, along with the stone. "Well, it's good to have met you all. I wanted to let you know that I'm here, and happy to help. I'm as responsible for this mess as anyone, and I'm not going until it's over. Shall I leave the grave goods with you?"

Ash answered, "Yes, please." He was still examining the items.

"You have his bones too, is that right?" Harlan asked.

Shadow nodded. "I decided that we needed them, I'm not sure why."

"Maybe you should try putting the stone back in the jaw," he suggested.

"Maybe we should," she said thoughtfully.

Harlan stood to leave, and realised he was exhausted. He wanted nothing more than bed, but that would still be a few hours away. He had more reading to do first. "I'll keep you updated with what I find out."

The other men stood as well, all reaching to shake his hand, and Gabe said, "Thanks, Harlan, we appreciate it. If we ever form a more concrete plan, we'll tell you."

Shadow escorted him to the door, and after he'd said goodbye, he headed swiftly to the car, aware that Nahum was out there, somewhere, still watching. If anything, the meeting with Gabe and the others had raised more questions than provided answers, but he was glad for one thing. At least they were on his side, because he definitely didn't want to be their enemy.

Eighteen

G abe joined Nahum outside once Harlan had left. He was sitting on the roof of one of the outbuildings, leaning against the chimney, his wings wrapped around him for warmth.

"Anything out there?"

Nahum shook his head. "Nothing but the wind and a few cars heading into White Haven."

"Good." Gabe shuffled himself into a more comfortable position. "I wonder if Kian knows where we live? It's hard to know how much he extracted from Mason."

"Unless Mason has a phenomenal memory, it's unlikely. But maybe he went by the office in the middle of the night. It's possible, I guess. He could have looked at the files."

"If he doesn't know, he'll have to ask around. That will slow him down."

"What did Harlan have to say?"

"He's found Chadwick's papers, and will tell us if he discovers anything useful. He also told us the detective, Maggie, is interested in who we are."

Nahum gave him a crooked smile. "We knew it would happen eventually. She'll talk to Newton, I suppose."

"Yes. That's okay. She knows more about the paranormal world than he does, by the sound of it. She's worked in it longer. We'll just be one more non-human group to know about."

"But Nephilim? Do you really think she's come across us before?"

"It would be something if she had, brother," Gabe said softly. "But I doubt it. No one had escaped before us."

"You've read our vague history. It sounds like some of us didn't die in the flood."

Gabe looked to the horizon, a distant black line barely discernible from the dark, cloudy sky. He could see the sea from here, but not White Haven; it was tucked in the folds of the valley. The farmhouse was high on the hill, and it caught the wind, but it afforded them views across the moors, as well as the sea. It was open, and Gabe liked that. You couldn't be trapped up here. It was the perfect spot.

He thought on what Nahum had said. "It's speculation, nothing more. The flood took everything."

"But there are written records, and we're in the Bible!"

"Stories to promote a God, that's all. The tales about us are wrong and vague at best," Gabe insisted.

"But there were hundreds of us, spread across the east, Canaan, and the Mediterranean. We didn't know all the Nephilim. Some might have survived if they reached the mountains in time. Or our fathers could have found more willing females and created more of us."

Gabe looked at Nahum, his expression barely discernible in the dark. "Say some of them did. They would be long dead by now. Our lifespans are great, but we are not immortal. You are talking about thousands of years. The land doesn't even look the same. It's impossible to know where we were with any accuracy." He was frustrated, and he knew he sounded it. For months they had been trying to work out where their old home was in the modern world, but everything had changed. "I don't even see any place names that are familiar."

"We'll find out one day," Nahum said, reassuringly. "We're collecting books and old maps that will help. But if I'm honest, I don't know why it worries you so much. We're here now, and in a good situation. That's all that matters."

Gabe nodded, knowing Nahum was right, but he couldn't help it. He had a need to establish himself in the modern world. "I think it's because we were ripped from our existence so quickly. I feel I have unfinished business."

"With what? Who? We were fighting battles that didn't mean anything to us, other than the money. Except for Eli, who was smart enough to stay out of it. At least we're not doing that anymore."

"You know who I have unfinished business with."

"With our father? Forget him. He's not worth our time. We were tools for him, nothing else. And he was fallen, damned."

"He let us die."

"He let lots of people die. They all did." He snorted. "They were never Angels of Mercy. The flood was probably sent to kill them, as well as us. They had angered their God and created us out of spite. A merciful God, my ass. You've heard the witches talk, and Shadow. Gods have their own agendas, and ours was no different. Let it go, Gabe."

"I can't. Since we've been here, our time before the flood seems like a dream. I can't help but think that we must have been created for more than to be our fathers' weapons on Earth."

"You're looking for meaning where there is none. Our destiny was to bring death and destruction, and at one point we did it well—too well. And then we sought independence." Nahum smiled. "We were kings and princes, once."

"We'll never be that again."

"And I wouldn't want to be." Nahum's eyes gleamed. "We have more freedom now than we ever had. No responsibilities, no one to dictate what we do. Our plan with Shadow is a good one."

"It is. I've been thinking about this Guild. It has resources, arcane knowledge."

"You want to use it for your own research."

"Our research, our history."

"We know it, we were there!"

Gabe fell silent. He wasn't the only one to think this way. The more he thought back on their old life, the more he realised there were secrets they weren't privy to. Some of the others thought so, too. If they had resources, they should use them. But he would let it drop, for now.

He surveyed the hushed landscape, and knew he wouldn't sleep for hours. "I don't think Kian will come tonight, but I'll take your place. Head inside and rest."

"Thanks," Nahum said, and passed him the curved bronze sword. "You'll need this, just in case. But Gabe, don't get caught up in our past. It's behind us now."

Gabe watched him jump from the roof and land as lightly as a cat, and wished he could feel the same way.

Shadow looked at the thick paste in the pot. "How much do I need?"

"A smear, only. It's concentrated, but even if you use more than you need to, it won't kill anyone. It's a heavy sedative, but it shouldn't interfere with breathing," Briar told her. "And of course, there's magic in there, too. It's very effective."

"Thanks," she answered, slipping it into her pocket. "With the sword and the paste, I feel like we have a chance of success."

Shadow and Briar were talking in Briar's herb room in her shop. It was early and Shadow had arrived with Eli, riding on the back of his bike. Despite yesterday's argument, she liked Eli. They may spat occasionally, but he was generally even-tempered and a good healer, just not quite as good as Briar. She knew he wasn't particularly excited by their deal with Harlan, but he went along with it anyway, and she sensed he blamed her for the arrangement. He was right about that. She was responsible, but Gabe had agreed quickly enough. Eli was in the shop now, opening up.

"Just be careful with it," Briar warned her. "If you get some in a scratch, you'll end up putting yourself to sleep. Right, let me see your leg."

Shadow slipped her trousers off and sat on the small sofa in the corner of the room, watching Briar deftly pull the bandage off. "It feels much better already," she told her.

Briar looked pleased as she examined the wound. "It looks good. I'll put the salve on it and another light dressing. You should be able to do it yourself from now on. Or ask Eli." She grinned. "Just don't mix the pots up."

Shadow laughed. "I won't."

"What are you doing now?"

"Heading to Avery's shop to see Dan. I want to ask him about tombs and bones."

"I hear he took you to Tintagel the other day."

"It's a beautiful spot," Shadow admitted. "I can see why people love it. But no portals to the Otherworld there."

Briar tightened the dressing and stood up, giving her space to dress. "Did you think there would be?"

"No, not really. I guess I'm getting used to this place, anyway." Shadow headed to the door. "I'd better let you get to work, and I need to go, too. Gabe is picking me up soon, and we're going to the warehouse."

"I hear Caspian is back. Say hi to him for me, and tell Avery I'll see her later."

When they re-entered the main shop, a couple of people were already browsing the shelves despite the early hour, and one young woman was leaning on the counter, looking doe-eyed at Eli. He chatted to her easily, and Shadow could tell he had another admirer.

"Does this happen often?" she asked Briar, nodding at them talking.

She rolled her eyes. "All the time, but it's good for business, and he treats them well. I guess it's a win for everyone."

Shadow laughed, waved goodbye, and stepped outside. It was another brisk spring morning, and she strolled up the winding lanes to Happenstance Books. But she hadn't gone far when she saw Harlan sheltering in the doorway to a gift shop, staring down the street, and she hurried to his side. "Can you see Kian?"

He barely glanced at her. "I thought I had, but now I'm not so sure." He rubbed his face with his hand. "I think I'm overtired."

His chin was covered in day-old stubble, and there were dark rings beneath his eyes. "Did you sleep at all?" she asked.

"For a few hours. I was reading until late. I want to see Dan, and Avery too, I guess, so I'm heading there now. I'm starving as well, which doesn't help matters. I should have eaten first."

"I'll treat you. I'm going your way, and I'm buying cakes for bribery purposes."

Harlan walked up the street with her. "You want to see Dan, too?"

"He said he'd do some research for me, so I just want to learn what he's found." She spotted the shop she wanted, and stopped. "Wait here, I won't be a minute."

She ducked inside and chose half a dozen pastries, feeling her stomach rumbling already, and then bought a coffee for her and Harlan. By the time she got outside again, he was sheltering within the deep porch, and gestured to her to get behind him.

"He's here."

She tried to peer over his shoulder. "Where?"

"Walking up the street, just dawdling, really."

"He hasn't seen you, then?"

"Not yet, and I'd like to keep it that way."

Shadow chaffed at not being able to see. "Should we try and follow him?"

"It's tempting, but the street's not busy enough. If we step out now, he's likely to spot us. At least we know he's here, in White Haven."

"I feel we should do something!"

"Like what? We can't challenge him. Oh, hold on."

"What?"

"He's going into a shop, now's our chance." In a split-second, Harlan grabbed her arm and pulled her up the road at a fast trot. "At least Avery's shop is along the next street."

"Shouldn't we be going the other way?" she protested. "We can spy on him!"

"No. We're not ready."

"I'm not saying we engage in battle right now!"

"If he spots us and feels cornered, who knows what might happen? We must wait."

Harlan's hand was under her elbow, almost propelling her around the next corner, and then he pushed her behind him in a way that Shadow had to admit made her feel both resentful and protected. He looked back down the street, ignoring the strange glances they were getting.

After a few moments he was satisfied, and he sighed. "Good. We dodged him for now."

He tried to walk on, but Shadow stopped him, feeling increasingly annoyed. "Harlan, I need to see him. I have no idea what he looks like, and meeting him in the open is actually the safest thing to do! He's not stupid. I'm going to find him."

She turned and marched back down the road, Harlan hot on her heels.

"Shadow, this is dumb!"

"No, it's not! Which shop was he in?"

"I'm not telling you," he said petulantly.

She stopped in the middle of the pavement, glaring at him. "Don't be ridiculous!"

"You're the one being ridiculous. How can you protect yourself carrying pastries and coffee?"

Shadow itched to drop the goods, grab him, and throw him against the wall, but decided to soften her approach. "If I don't know what he looks like, how will I defend myself?"

Harlan sighed heavily. "Damn it. He was in the little occult shop that sells crystals, incense, and things."

"There are a million of those in White Haven!" She thrust his coffee at him, freeing up one hand. "Take that and show me!"

He walked around her, leading the way. "He went into Spells and Shells."

The shops were in old buildings with doors set back from the road, and they were close to Spells and Shells when Harlan paused, hand on her arm. "That's him!"

A man with fine, sandy blond hair emerged from the entrance, a package in his hands. He looked up, saw them, and froze, and then glancing around at the other shoppers, stood his ground, a grim smile on his face.

Shadow didn't hesitate, and trying to ignore the twinge in her leg, marched to his side. "Kian, how nice to see you again."

"And you Shadow, Harlan."

"Whatever you're planning, I'll stop you," she told him coolly.

"But that's the problem, isn't it?" he said softly. "You have no idea what I'm planning."

Shadow glanced at the package, wondering what was in it. "I presume it involves me."

"Maybe, maybe not. I may not need you."

"Then why are you here?"

"That's my business. But I will thank you for my freedom. I wasn't sure I would ever get it again."

"My mistake," Shadow admitted. "Which is why I'll make sure I put you back where you belong."

Kian looked infuriatingly smug. "You'll try, of course. I'm going to walk away now. Please don't follow me, if you value Kent's life."

Harlan leaned into him. "You'd better not hurt him, Kian."

"Or what?" he sneered, oblivious to the curious onlookers. "You have no way to stop me, and the more you annoy me, the more likely Kent will get hurt, understood?

Although, I'm not the one who killed Chadwick." He shot Shadow a vicious smile, which sent her hand reaching for her knife, and then walked away, leaving Shadow and Harlan staring after him.

"Bollocks," Shadow said, using her favourite English curse. "I really wanted to sink my knife into his gut."

"I'm very grateful you didn't," Harlan said with a tight smile. "And at least you know what he looks like now. Let me see if I can find out what he bought."

He left Shadow watching Kian until he was out of sight, and when he returned, he said, "He bought some herbs—wormwood and valerian."

"What will they do?"

Harlan directed her back up the hill. "We'd better ask a witch!"

By the time they got to Happenstance Books, they were both stewing on their encounter, and they pushed through the door with relief.

Avery, the redheaded witch who owned the shop, was already heading towards them, a worried look on her face. "What's happened?"

"Kian is in town," Harlan told her. "We've just had an unpleasant chat outside of Spells and Shells. I assume Alex has told you what's going on?"

Avery ushered them into the recesses of the shop. "He did. Anything I can do?"

"Not at the moment, other than offering some shelter in case he decides to follow us. He suggested he didn't need Shadow, but I'm not convinced." He looked at the section of books surrounding them. "The Gothic and Horror section. How apt!"

Avery laughed, but Shadow protested loudly. "I don't need sheltering, thanks! I'm not a child. And besides, you're squashing the cakes."

As if he had supersonic hearing, Dan appeared from behind the stacks. "Did I hear the word cakes?"

"You have a one track mind," Shadow told him, and then squinted at his t-shirt, reading the words out loud. "When I think about books, I touch my shelf." She groaned. "Seriously?"

He grinned. "Always."

Harlan looked perplexed and annoyed. "You should be taking this more seriously, Shadow. The man who wants your blood is out there now, planning his next move!"

"And so are we!" She passed the cakes to Dan. "We were coming to see you two anyway, especially you, Dan."

He nodded. "I've found out some stuff, but I'm not sure how helpful it will be." He peered into the paperback bag. "I spot a custard tart. You've done very well."

"Thank you. Now can we move away from The Mysteries of Udolfo so I can drink my coffee in peace?"

Nineteen

While Harlan stopped to speak to Avery, Shadow headed to the kitchen with Dan. As soon as the door was shut, she sat at the table and took a long sip of coffee. "I needed that. It's a bit annoying that Kian is here already and we didn't know."

Dan was getting plates out of the cupboard, and he put them on the table, and then set out the cakes on an oval platter. "You know now! And you're in White Haven. I think that gives you the advantage."

"Only just," Shadow moaned, reaching for a sticky chocolate brownie. "I'd like nothing more than to just fight it out, rather than deal with all of this subterfuge and threats."

Dan sat down opposite her. "But you'll endanger the man who Kian is hiding in. Who is it?"

"Kent Marlowe, a member of the Order of the Midnight Sun." She raised an eyebrow. "Alchemist, magician, astronomer, and other things."

"Really? Since I saw you last, I did as promised and read up on alchemists, and I've heard of the Order. They've been going for years. Very shadowy!"

"Dodgy shadowy?"

"More like secret handshakes, special rites, initiations, and all of that baloney."

"Baloney?"

"Rubbish," Dan explained. "It's an organisation that has levels of secrecy built into it, and you have to achieve certain things to move up the levels."

Shadow chewed her cake, considering his words. "You sound like you don't like them. Do you know them?"

"No, of course not. But it smacks of the Masons. It's like an old boys club, where you get perks for being a part of it. Like avoiding arrest, and getting promotions you don't deserve."

"I think women are in the Order, too."

"Doesn't matter, it's the same principles."

Intriguing. "Do you know what rites they do?"

He swallowed his mouthful of cake. "No idea, I'm afraid—and that's the point. No one does, except for the initiates, and they don't tell anyone. It perpetuates the secrecy and intrigue, and makes everyone feel very important."

"How do you know it's true, then?"

"You can Google it. There are all sorts of articles about them on the net. To be honest, they all share the same basic information, and focus more on the history and old members than current concerns, but they definitely talk about initiation and levels of knowledge. I think their headquarters are in Marylebone, in London."

"Well, I look forward to meeting Kent Marlowe then, when he's no longer possessed. Let's hope he survives."

"I don't want him to die!" Dan looked horrified. "Who knows, I may even like him."

"The witches here have a coven, isn't that the same thing?"

"Not at all. I would imagine Avery has more magic in her little finger than all of those members put together. They don't need initiation rites to make them feel special. They are special."

Shadow hadn't seen this side of Dan before. He was normally so accepting, and yet today he was sceptical. She trusted his judgment, so maybe it was something to consider. Before she could say anything else, Harlan joined them, looking reassured.

"Hey, guys." He slid into a seat and reached for a pastry. "Avery and Sally are keeping watch, which gives us a chance to talk about Kian."

"Did you read Chadwick's research last night?" Shadow asked.

"I did. It seems that there are a few obscure tales attached to him."

"Like what?" Shadow and Dan asked together.

"Like he can summon the dead, and use them for his own bidding."

Dan's eyes widened. "Like a zombie army?"

"Something of the sort."

"Necromancy, then," Shadow said. "We had such sorcerers in our world. They would use the dead to find secrets, hidden treasure, for divination purposes, and other such things."

Dan dipped his pastry in his coffee, looking thoughtful. "There are many instances here, too. Necromancy goes back thousands of years. I must admit, though, I couldn't find out anything about Kian, not even a morsel."

Harlan shrugged. "I'm not surprised. Chadwick's documents are old and obscure, and would have taken him years to find. The references are oblique, and tangled within other tales." He rubbed his stubble. "I have to confess, I'm a bit annoyed with myself, actually. I should have suspected something like this sooner, because Death Magic was one of Chadwick's special interests."

"I bet Gabe would know something about that, too. Necromancy was mentioned in the Old Testament, and Canaan was discussed in my research," Dan suggested, but before he could say anything else, Shadow shot him a look of warning and catching her eye, he clammed up.

Harlan looked between them uneasily. "Is Gabe some kind of Bible aficionado?"

Shadow tried to brush it off. "Sort of. He has many varied interests, all of them sort of Biblical in nature."

Harlan stared at her. "Gabe has Biblical interests?"

She inwardly squirmed. "He's not particularly religious, however. It's just a hobby!" She flashed him her most beaming smile. "Useful for treasure hunting, don't you think?"

"Very," he replied, unconvinced.

Dan leapt in to relieve her. "Back to Kian. He's a fey necromancer, highly regarded, and greatly feared. No wonder they sealed his tomb. They must have been afraid he could come back from the dead."

"No shit," Harlan said dryly. "He has!"

"Because you broke the seal!" Dan pointed out. "You shouldn't mess with tombs!"

"I've been messing with them for a long time, and this has never happened before!" Harlan reached across for another cake. "I need food. I'm getting a headache."

"Can you have a look at these, Dan?" Shadow searched for the photos she'd taken on her phone, and quickly found the images of spirals. "These were everywhere. Are they significant?"

Dan squinted at the screen. "I've seen lots of these shapes—you see them in many megalithic sites. There are some great examples in New Grange. People have been wondering about their significance for years. They may be decorative, or something else."

"What's New Grange?" she asked.

"Another tomb in Ireland. It aligns with the winter solstice, and it's very famous," Dan told her. "The spirals there are very ornate, and it's quite old."

"I agree with you there," Harlan said. "Whatever they meant, it was a great honour to have such a burial."

Shadow looked between them both. "It changes nothing, though. The most important information is that he's a necromancer, which explains the power he has over his own spirit. It won't stop me killing him. Again."

"Are you sure the Empusa's sword will work?" Dan asked.

"I can see him as easily as I can you."

Harlan looked worried. A deep crease divided his forehead, and the cake didn't seem to help. "It doesn't mean you can harm him with it, though. You're assuming a lot."

Shadow's phone buzzed with a text message, and she gratefully picked it up. She hated being questioned. "My lift's here. Must go, boys. Thanks for the update—I'll pass it on to the others. Now that we know he's here, it's time to trap him."

———————◆◇◆———————

As Gabe pulled into the car park at the Kernow Industries warehouse, he saw Caspian's Audi, and he pointed it out to Shadow. "Caspian's here. We'd better update him on the latest."

"Will he care?" she asked. "He's been away for weeks. I'm sure he'll have plenty of his own business to catch up on."

"You'd be surprised what Caspian cares about," he said, exiting the car and locking it.

"You mean Avery?"

"I mean lots of things," he replied enigmatically and then winked, knowing it would infuriate her. She hated not to know everything.

He grinned as she fell into step beside him. He'd learned early on that Shadow was a force of nature who would bulldoze everything in her path if given half a chance, acting first and thinking later. He'd decided to limit those chances, for her and everyone else's safety.

She prodded him for details. "I suppose you mean business concerns?"

"Business, witch stuff, family stuff...you know," he said vaguely.

They passed through the security checkpoint at the entrance to the building, nodding at the guard on duty. Caspian still employed a few guards who'd been with the company for years, and they mostly worked during regular hours, operating the main gate and the second checkpoint into the main building. The other security work, such as monitoring the perimeter and patrolling the grounds, was left to the Nephilim.

Although Gabe was teasing Shadow, during the past few months of working with Caspian, he had come to know him better, and he liked him. Like the Nephilim, he had a strong work ethic and a complicated family. And also like them, he'd had a very difficult relationship with this father, Sebastian. Since Helena, Avery's ghostly ancestor, killed him, it had freed Caspian to become the man he wanted to be, rather than the man his father had tried to shape.

The warehouse was full of crates and boxes of all sizes, and although it looked haphazard, there was a system in place. A few employees were moving crates using a forklift, and making sure to keep out of the way, they headed up the stairs to the mezzanine floor and the two offices that overlooked the whole operation. Barak, Niel, and Nahum were already seated in the security office, monitoring half a dozen screens on the wall, and Gabe raised his hand in greeting, but first he needed to speak to Caspian, so he headed for the bigger office. He could see him through the large window, seated at the computer; he knocked and entered.

"Hey Caspian, welcome back."

Caspian was dressed in his characteristic dark suit with a white shirt, and was perfectly groomed, his dark hair swept back and face clean-shaven—unlike Gabe, whose stubble was now thick. He looked up and smiled. "Gabe, Shadow. It looks like there have been no major issues while I've been away."

"None," Gabe reassured him. "Estelle runs a tight ship."

Caspian's lips set in a thin line. "She certainly does. I hope she hasn't given you any problems?"

Estelle was well known to be prickly and abrupt, and there was no love lost between the siblings. If anything, they seemed to rub each other up even more lately.

"No, I've got used to her, and I think Barak quite likes her prickliness."

Shadow grunted. "I think she's a pain in the ass."

Gabe glared at her, but Caspian looked amused. "I think the feeling's mutual."

Shadow's mouth fell open. "She thinks *I'm* a pain? I don't know why," she said, leaning against the doorframe. "I'm always polite."

Gabe nearly choked. "Liar. You antagonise her deliberately."

A small smile crept across Shadow's face. "Only occasionally."

"You questioned her about an address the other day. It's none of our business!"

"It was just a question!" Shadow went still for a moment. "That reminds me of something..."

She fell silent then, and Gabe looked at her, puzzled, before turning to Caspian. "You should know there are other things going on with us at the moment, in White Haven. It won't affect this business, though."

"What things?" Caspian asked, worried. "Is Avery okay?"

"Avery's fine."

Caspian instantly relaxed, and Gabe realised that whatever feelings Caspian had for Avery were still there. He knew that look, and he'd experienced those feelings, and they would pass, eventually. But Caspian wouldn't thank him for that advice. Instead, Gabe explained about Kian, and he listened closely, nodding and asking questions.

"My family has dabbled in necromancy in the past," Caspian told him, "but nothing recently. A fey necromancer is different though, and potentially more dangerous."

Shadow abruptly interrupted them. "Marylebone! You ship to an address there sometimes. I saw it the other day, and when I asked Estelle about it, she snapped at me."

Caspian looked confused. "We deal with lots of addresses. Why do you care about Marylebone?"

"Dan said the Order of the Midnight Sun is based there, and I remember the name on the package. Do you work with them?"

Caspian shrugged. "I've heard of them, so maybe. But we ship lots of things, some of which come through other companies. Why are you asking about them?"

"Because Kent Marlowe is a member."

"You aren't suggesting that I've got anything to do with this current situation are you?" Caspian asked, a dangerous edge to his voice.

Shadow looked impatient. "No, of course not. But they intrigue me. Do you know any details about them?"

Caspian leaned back in his chair. "Nothing. I'm a witch, not a new-age alchemist. And I'm a business man. I'm not responsible for peoples' orders. We just receive shipments and distribute them."

Gabe shot her a warning look. "Shadow, they have nothing to do with Kian's reappearance—we're responsible for that. What does it matter?"

"It doesn't, I guess. I just like to connect the dots and know how things work."

"Most of our business dealings are with legitimate companies who have nothing to do with the paranormal world. But yes, we do have *other* connections. And shipping is just one of our business arms. There are others," Caspian explained. "We're called 'Kernow Industries' for a reason."

Shadow nodded, "Of course, I'm just curious."

While Gabe talked to Caspian about a few other things, he kept an eye on Shadow. She looked restless, and Gabe knew what that meant. She would be pacing around and getting under his feet for hours, and they had work to do. As much as he didn't want to leave her on her own, he had to admit that she knew how to look after herself.

They left Caspian's office to return to the security office, and he stopped her. "You've got that look in your eye."

"What look?"

"You know what look. You're not paying the slightest bit of attention."

She had the grace to appear marginally guilty. "I'm sorry, Gabe. I can't concentrate right now. I know it's important, but it's driving me mad."

He thrust the keys to the car at her. "Take them and go home. I can go back with the guys. As long as you promise to be careful. No hunting Kian alone!"

She grinned at him as she grabbed them. "As if I would!"

Shadow virtually skipped down the steps, and as Gabe watched her go, he hoped he hadn't just done something really stupid.

The farmhouse was quiet by the time Shadow arrived back there. All of the Nephilim were out. Eli, Ash, and Zee were working for the witches, and the other four were at the warehouse.

There were just a couple of bikes in the courtyard and no signs of intrusion, so it seemed like the perfect afternoon for a ride. She felt restless with excess energy. All of this waiting was frustrating. They knew Kian was a necromancer and potentially dangerous, but despite that, he was a ghost, and she was going to get rid of him. All they needed was his address. If necessary, they could break in and drug Kent, and they could all finish this tonight.

She saddled Kailen up quickly, feeling his impatience, too. He was skittish and needed exercise, and within minutes she was on the moors with the wind in her hair, urging Kailen to ride faster. The fields flew by, and she knew exactly where she was headed. Ravens' Wood. She needed old magic, fey magic, around her.

When she entered the wood, she expected Kailen to settle down. He'd been hard to control on the ride, but if anything that made it more exhilarating. Now, however, it was annoying. "Kailen, calm down," she chided, trying to slow him down.

But he was wilful, pushing beneath the trees as he headed to the middle of the wood. He was following a track she hadn't seen before, which she liked. Ravens' Wood was constantly changing—to her, at least. Paths would appear and then disappear, and just when she expected to come out in one place, she found herself in another. It was a reminder of the Green Man's magic, and the fact that the wood was based on crossroads magic—boundary magic. Did humans find it as bewildering sometimes as she did? Or was it just the fact that she was fey that it misbehaved for her?

Kailen picked up his speed, and she had to duck to miss a branch. She pulled tight on his bridle, trying to slow him, but if anything he sped up, and Shadow had a horrible feeling that something was wrong.

Was Kian in the wood, spooking her horse?

They entered a small clearing and Kailen bucked wildly, throwing her to the ground.

She landed awkwardly in a heap, winded, but dragged herself to her feet. With a hand on the hilt of her dagger she ran to Kailen, concerned that he was injured. But before she could reach him, he collapsed to the ground, unresponsive.

Shadow fell to her knees, stroking his neck. Kailen could not die. He was the one thing she had that she truly cared about. Had he been poisoned? And then she heard a laugh from behind her, just before everything went black.

Twenty

When Gabe arrived at the farmhouse with Nahum and Niel, the place felt empty. There were no lights on in the main building or Shadow's quarters, and Shadow was nowhere in sight.

"This is odd," Gabe said, as he looked through the window of her building. "She should have arrived back hours ago."

It was close to seven o'clock now, the light was fading, and the temperature was falling.

"The car's here. She's probably out riding," Nahum said. "You know how obsessed she is about that. And she was restless earlier—you said so yourself. I'll check the stable."

"Or," Niel pointed out, "she might be asleep on the sofa, in the dark."

Nahum crossed the courtyard to the stable while Niel headed into the farmhouse, Gabe right behind him.

Gabe shook his head. "You know that's unlikely. I'm worried something has happened."

There was no sign of Shadow in the living room, and Niel ran to check the rest of the house. Gabe had a horrible feeling that something wasn't right, but there was no sign of a fight. He stood in the kitchen, looking over the fields beyond. She was out there, somewhere, in trouble. He pulled his phone from his pocket and called her number. It rang and rang before finally going to her voicemail. Damn it.

Nahum joined him in the kitchen. "Kailen is gone," Nahum told him. "She must be in Ravens' Wood, that's her favourite place. But," he hesitated, his face creased with worry, "there's something else."

"What?"

"Kian's bones are gone, too."

"Shit! He's found us!" Gabe was furious with himself. "We underestimated him! I said we shouldn't bring those damn bones here."

"Too late now," Nahum said. "It's done. He must need them to resurrect his body. Anything else missing?"

Before Gabe could answer, the kitchen door flung open and Niel said, "The window in the back door is broken. He must have smashed his way in. I rechecked the living room, and the staff is missing."

"Fuck it!" Gabe said angrily, marching to the living room, the others right behind him. He headed to the table where the grave goods had been spread out and sighed with relief. "At least nothing seems to have taken from here. What the hell does that staff do?"

"He's a necromancer," Nahum reminded him. "Maybe it helps him summon the dead."

"Great, just great! We've made everything so much easier for him by bringing it all here! He must have thought it was his lucky day!"

Nahum and Niel looked completely unconcerned at Gabe's outburst. They'd both seen it happen too many times before.

"On a positive note," Nahum said, pointing at the side table, "the Empusa's sword is where we left it. Shadow must be carrying the other one."

Niel gave a wry smile. "He must have no idea what that can do."

"Unless he has no fear of it," Nahum suggested.

"Hopefully that's one thing on our side," Gabe said, quickly deciding on a plan of action. He strode across the room and picked up the sword. "Shadow isn't answering her phone, so I'm going to Ravens' Wood, and I'll take this with me, just in case."

"You can't go alone," Nahum said, watching as he strapped the sword in its scabbard around his hips. "I'll come with you. For all we know, Kian is in the wood with her right now."

"What do you want me to do?" Niel asked. "I could speak to Harlan, see if he's heard from her."

"Good idea," Gabe said. "He'll know what car Kian now has. If they're not in the wood, with luck we can try and track it down."

Niel looked doubtful. "You really think he has Shadow?"

"I hope I'm wrong, but I don't think I am. If, however, she's still riding around and not answering her phone, I'll kill her." All three headed out of the house, and while Gabe and Nahum went to the car, Niel sat astride one of the bikes.

Gabe yelled, "Be careful! Don't do anything without backup."

Niel just nodded as he pulled the helmet over his head, fired up the engine, and exited the courtyard in a squeal of rubber.

"Are you sure we shouldn't take Stormfall? It might be quicker," Nahum asked, referring to the other horse as he slid into the passenger seat.

"Not once we're under the trees. Besides, I don't want to have to worry about bringing the horse back here if we have to start driving around." Gabe drove quickly, familiar now with the twisting, turning lanes around the house.

"I'll call the guys," Nahum said, pulling his phone out. "Just in case they've heard from Shadow."

But no one had heard from her. It took about ten minutes to reach the edge of the wood, and they parked on the grass verge by one of the pathways that wound beneath the trees, quickly exiting the car and jogging down the track. This area was closest to where Shadow would have entered the wood from the fields on the opposite side of the lane.

"It's not dark enough to fly," Nahum said regretfully.

"I doubt we'd see under the branches anyway," Gabe said. "They're too thick."

In the twilight, flies buzzed, and the birds were noisy as they settled for the evening. Bats were already swooping through the air. They passed a few people walking their dogs, and Gabe smiled and nodded. It wouldn't do to look too alarming at this time of night. He knew their size was scary enough for most people.

Nahum grumbled next to him. "Any idea which direction she may have gone in?"

"Into the middle. She always says that's where it's quieter, and she feels fey magic more."

They came to a junction in the path, and Gabe followed the direction that led further into the wood; it became darker with every footstep.

"I'll phone her," Nahum suggested. "We may hear it." He punched the number in and yelled out, "Shadow! Where are you?"

He waited a beat before calling again, but there was no response, and no sound of a phone either. They carried on, shouting intermittently, and Gabe became increasingly frustrated. *There was no way she'd still be here. There was nothing fun about riding a horse through a wood at night, even for a headstrong fey.*

Then they heard the crack of a branch, and the high-pitched whinnying of a horse, and Gabe headed into the undergrowth as he followed the noises, slapping away branches aggressively before finally coming into a clearing.

Kailen was tied to a tree and he was pulling and sweating, his eyes wild with panic. Gabe ran over, laying his hand on his neck and rubbing gently. "Calm down, it's okay, boy." He turned to Nahum. "Where the hell is Shadow?"

"She'd never leave Kailen willingly," Nahum said, already looking for her. He crouched to poke around in the undergrowth, and then searched in an ever-expanding circle.

"And this isn't our rope, either," Gabe said. He'd already untied Kailen, and he examined the blue nylon cord. "Someone came prepared."

"Kian must have her," Nahum announced, his voice grim. "He must have surprised her. There's no evidence of a fight, and we know she'd have fought if given a chance."

Kailen had calmed down now that Gabe was soothing him, and Gabe examined the ground. "I can't see any blood, either."

Nahum finished investigating the immediate area and joined him. "He either followed her from the house, or followed her once she arrived at the woods."

Gabe shook his head. "There's no way he could have followed her over the fields, not in Kent's body, anyway. She would have seen him."

"Let's face it—it doesn't matter how he got her. Now we just need to find her."

Gabe rubbed his hair, frustrated. "She could still be here, in another clearing."

"Unlikely. It's obvious we would have come looking for her. There's no way he'd stay here. If he's going to start a ritual to get his body back, he needs space and time."

"You're right." Gabe pulled Kailen onto the path. "You ride Kailen home, and I'll drive into town."

"And do what?"

"Hunt for Kian, what else?"

"He could be in *any* house, probably on the outskirts. There are lots of holiday cottages that would fit that bill. We need to narrow it down, Gabe. Once I've secured Kailen, I can take a bike and look, too."

"No, wait at the farmhouse. I'll call you if I need you. You never know, she could arrive at home needing help."

Nahum mounted Kailen, swinging easily up onto his back. He was natural horseman, but Kailen still fretted beneath him. "Something has certainly spooked him. He's normally much calmer than this. I'll call when I get back. Good luck, brother."

Within seconds he'd disappeared into the darkness, and Gabe ran back to the car.

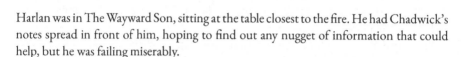

Harlan was in The Wayward Son, sitting at the table closest to the fire. He had Chadwick's notes spread in front of him, hoping to find out any nugget of information that could help, but he was failing miserably.

Now that he knew Kian was a necromancer, many more things made sense. For instance, Chadwick's fascination with him was evident, as he'd said to Shadow and Dan earlier—Death Magic was one of Chadwick's favoured subjects. That's why he had a wall of gruesome masks in his home, and endless books on the subject in his study.

He'd driven around White Haven that morning, hoping to see Kent's car, but he'd found nothing. And knowing what Kian had bought from the shop didn't help, either. Avery told him that the herb ingredients could be used for a number of spells.

A shadow fell across his table as a plated burger and chips was slid in front of him. He looked up at Zee and smiled. "Just in time. I'm starving."

"You're going to need it," Zee said, sitting opposite him. "I've just heard from Niel. He'll be here soon. Shadow's gone missing."

Harlan was already lifting the burger to his mouth, but he stopped, shocked. "Missing? Since when?"

He shrugged. "We're not sure. Lunch, maybe?"

Harlan went to put his burger down, as if he was going to rush out the door right then, but he realised he had no idea where to go. "Shit. Do we think it was Kian?"

"It has to be, but Niel will talk to you. I'd better get back to the bar." He nodded at the plate. "Eat up. There's nowhere to go yet."

Harlan watched him go and took a mouthful of food. The burger was delicious, and just what he needed, but he couldn't enjoy it now. He refused to believe that Shadow was dead. She must be locked away somewhere, injured maybe, but she had to be alive.

He was halfway through his meal when Niel came in. If the situation weren't so dire, Harlan would have laughed, because the room fell silent for the briefest moment as every head swivelled to look at him. He was wearing heavy work jeans and big, black boots with a worn leather jacket, and tucked under his arm was a helmet. His blond hair was shaved at the sides, and he had a decent beard and sideburns. You could just about see the tattoos edging up his neck, and more than one or two women were open-mouthed.

Niel ignored them all, looking for Zee at the bar, who pointed to Harlan. He marched across the room to him and sat, helping himself to a chip. "Harlan, we have a problem."

"So I heard."

"Gabe and Nahum are in the wood right now. Her horse is missing. Have you heard anything?"

"Nothing at all. I didn't even know until Zee told me. But, you know I'll help in any way I can."

"We need an address."

Harlan nodded as he swallowed a mouthful of burger. "I searched most of central White Haven this afternoon, but I think we both know he won't be in the centre of town."

Niel sighed, narrowing his eyes. "Give me a moment. I need a pint."

Harlan watched him head to the bar and talk to Zee, and while he waited he finished eating, his mind racing through their options. They needed help to locate Shadow, but he was reluctant to involve Maggie or Newton. It made him uncomfortable to have the police overlooking their actions, no matter how understanding Maggie was. He hoped she'd been too busy to call Newton.

Within minutes Niel returned, pocketing his phone. "Gabe has found Shadow's horse, but no Shadow. Nahum's gone to wait at the house, and Gabe is coming here to plan our next move."

"Maybe we should ask the witches," Harlan suggested, feeling like they were running out of options and time. "They must have some kind of magic that can help us. Is Alex here?"

"No, he's with Avery." Niel frowned. "I think you need a personal item for one of their finding spells. Shadow told me they've used those spells before with good results."

"I haven't got anything, but you'll have something at the farmhouse, won't you?" Harlan asked, feeling a spark of hope.

"Sure, but that means me running around to find clothing and then witches, and it all takes time!"

A thought struck Harlan. "What about her dressings? Briar was changing them! Her blood will be on them. That would work, right?" He checked his watch. "I know it's late, but she might still be at the shop—it's only a few minutes' walk away!"

"Excellent idea! Monday after work is when they make up new stock," Niel said before draining his glass and slamming it on the table. "I'll call Eli and get them to start preparing the spell."

They rose to their feet, Harlan sweeping the paperwork into his bag, and pulling it over his shoulder. "I'm coming with you."

Twenty-One

S hadow woke up on a cold stone floor, her face pressed against dust and grime. She pulled herself upright, wrestling against her bindings, and cursing all the time at her stupidity.

She could hear Gabe's voice in her head, doing his best I told you so, and even though he was nowhere close, she still wanted to yell at him. She hated that he was right. Her head felt sore, and the room spun, which wasn't helped by trying to sit up. She paused for a moment, breathing deeply in an effort to stop the nausea, and waited for her eyes to focus.

She looked down at her restraints, and found she was wrapped in thick chain that bound her arms to her body. She had very little wiggle room. The room she was imprisoned in was dimly lit and made of thick stone walls, and it smelt damp. She must be in some kind of cellar, and she still had to be in White Haven. The light came from a solitary candle on the floor in the far corner, and as her eyes adjusted to the gloom, she shivered. This was no ordinary cellar. There were markings on the floor, pentagrams and other mystical signs she didn't recognise, and what looked like an altar on the far wall, with an image of the Goddess and Herne the Hunter carved into the stone behind it. Metal lanterns hung overhead, currently unlit, and there was a general air of foreboding.

Her blood chilled. This was a room meant for sacrifice, and as far as she could tell, she was it.

And then a memory hit her that made her feel even worse. Kailen.

Why didn't she listen to Gabe and not go out alone? He would never let her forget this, if she ever got out. She stopped that line of thought straight away. She would get out. It was just a matter of when. The good news was that in his effort to catch her, Kian hadn't been able to prepare properly. The chain was not made of iron, and yes she might be trussed up like a chicken, but she could probably escape from it, given time.

She took a few deep breaths and concentrated. Her knife and the Empusa's sword were in the corner of the room, well out of reach, but at least they were here, and she could feel the small tin tucked inside one of the many pockets in her combat trousers. *Good.* She still had the poisonous paste.

Shadow heard footsteps coming down the stone stairs next to her, and booted feet came into view, until finally Kent, or rather Kian, stood in front of her. He was insignificant in appearance, pale with a slim build, his features regular. Nothing to catch your attention normally, but he had her attention now. He wore a long, woollen robe that fell to the floor, covering Kent's ordinary trousers and shirt, and in his hands were a bowl and a knife.

Kian watched her for a moment. "Shadow, I thought it would take more than smacking you on the head to capture you."

"It's your lucky night, then. Do you want to try again without cheating?"

Kian threw back his head and laughed. "It wasn't cheating, it was smart. Why would I fight a fey if I didn't need to?"

"What did you do to my horse?"

His smile was smug. "I inhabited it, of course. I wasn't sure I could, but it turns out that it was easier than I expected."

"If you've killed him, I will kill you, horribly and painfully."

"All chained up? I don't think so." He smiled at her, but she could see the vague expression behind Kent's gaze, the struggle that his real self was experiencing. "I've found that it is quite fun being able to dip in and out of someone. It makes me incredibly versatile as a ghost. I can leave this unexceptionable body behind, become a horse, or slide through walls to see all sorts of interesting things, and then slip back in again. Poor old Kent doesn't know if he's coming or going. I drugged him earlier and left him sleeping in the wood, ready for when I returned."

She wanted to beg for reassurance that Kailen was all right, but she wouldn't. That would show weakness. And he clearly wasn't going to tell her anything. Bastard. "You'll need more than a chain to defeat me, Kian!"

Kian crouched, his eyes travelling over her body in a way that made Shadow's skin crawl. "I like your arrogance, but I think you'll find that I'm superior to you in every way. For example, I wouldn't have been so stupid as to bring my bones out of the tomb, and have all of my grave goods in one place, especially my staff."

Her eyes narrowed. "You've been in our house."

"You should really have better security, but like I said, I can slip through doors. It was a simple matter to make Kent break in." His face hardened. "But leaving my bones in a messy pile was very disrespectful, Shadow."

"I didn't think you'd need them again! And you're *very disrespectful* to other people's bodies, to be honest!"

"You think you're quite something, don't you, for someone so young?"

"And you have a very high opinion of yourself too, just because you're a necromancer!"

"Never underestimate the dead. They carry all sorts of secrets. They told me about this place!" He spread his hands wide. "This room has known death and sacrifice. There are channels for blood, and there's even a devil's trap! Who do you think this room belongs to?"

Shadow glanced around, looking at the signs and symbols, and realised that the only people she could possibly associate it with were the witches, but they would never use it. Doubt must have entered her eyes, because he laughed.

"Yes, I know about your witches. They have a dark history, for all of their sanctimonious positions now."

She lifted her chin defiantly. "We're not responsible for our ancestors' actions."

"Maybe not, but they benefit from their magic."

She needed to keep him occupied. While he was talking, she wasn't being sliced up. "Where are we?"

His eyes were dark pits, filled with madness and desire. "Old Haven Cemetery—under the Jackson family's mausoleum, actually. It's perfect!"

Shadow was sure that was Reuben's last name, and she tried to keep the shock out of her voice. "How did you find it?"

"Spirits told me. Because I am already one of them, I don't need to raise the dead to hear their secrets. They whisper of this place. And what better place to be for me than surrounded by the dead when I finally resurrect my body."

"You were defeated before, I'll do it again. You're not as superior as you think!"

He reached forward and slapped her, hard. "Watch your tongue, or I'll cut it out!"

Shadow inwardly seethed as her cheek stung and she felt blood trickle down her chin from a cut to the side of her mouth. She wanted to slit his smug throat, but she had to remind herself of the plan. She had to save Kent's body.

She glared at him. "Well done. Feel better now?"

"No. Enough talking. I need your blood, and that is what this bowl and the knife are for. A small incision along your vein should do it." He grinned. "You'll be pleased to know I won't need it all—at least I don't think I will."

"And then what?"

"I complete the ritual to regain my body, and leave this one behind. Although, this man's mind is surprisingly useful." He tapped Kent's head with his finger. "He has all sorts of knowledge tucked inside here."

"You haven't got your own rituals?" Shadow asked, scathingly.

"Of course I have. I'm a necromancer. Death Magic is what I do best. But Kent understands what I need, and he will do my bidding more easily."

They had been right, Shadow thought, *he* had *needed Kent's abilities.*

Kian edged closer. "Now, don't struggle, or I'll do more than slit your arm open."

He reached for her left arm, pulled it onto his lap, and positioned the bowl under it, before slicing the sharp blade into her skin.

The incision burned as her blood welled, but Shadow gritted her teeth, refusing to shout out. He looked at her, almost challenging her to respond, and then squeezed her arm, increasingly the blood flow. The bowl quickly filled, and when he was satisfied, he placed it carefully to the side, pulled a bandage from his pocket, and swiftly wrapped the wound.

"It wouldn't do to have you bleed all over the floor and die on me before I've finished with you."

"How long does your ritual take?"

"Longer than I'd like, but it will be worth it. Rituals require patience, something you do not have."

He stood, picking up the bowl carefully, and although she wanted to kick his legs out from under him, she didn't want to be stabbed. She knew he'd do it, and right now she had to bide her time. He was right; patience did not come naturally to her.

"Gabe will find me." Even as she said it, she doubted her words.

"That big idiot? He's more brawn than brains. By the time he has, it will just be your body that's left." He headed to the altar, where he placed her blood, and Shadow noticed that he staggered as he did so. He wasn't quite as strong as he made it seem. "I'll bring my bones now so we can begin."

Gabe didn't waste time once he left the wood, driving straight into White Haven.

He was about to head to The Wayward Son when Niel phoned, telling him they were at Charming Balms Apothecary. He drove down the main street, noting how busy it still was, even though most of the shops had closed. Instead, the bars and restaurants were filling up, and this would only make life more difficult.

The one thing he wanted to do was fly—he could cover more ground that way. In daylight that was impossible, but it was dark now. He grimaced. The fortunate thing was that most people never looked up unless they had reason to. And he was as silent as a bird. He could glide above them and they'd never know, especially if he stuck to the outskirts. There was no way Kian would be in town. He'd have had to carry Shadow from the car to the site, and that would raise too many questions.

The more he thought about it, the more he wished he hadn't bothered driving at all. He should be flying right now. As soon as he pulled into a spot close to Briar's shop, he called Nahum. "Is she back yet?"

"No. She's definitely in trouble, Gabe."

"Do me a favour. Head out now. Fly around the outskirts. As long as you're high enough, you won't be spotted."

"Will do. I'll call if I see anything."

The lights were still on in Briar's shop, but they were low, just the lights under the shelves and on window displays. He knocked on the door, and within seconds Eli answered, looking grim. Gabe stepped inside, and Eli secured the door behind him, talking to him quietly.

"We're all in the back room," Eli said, nodding in the general direction. "Briar is starting the spell now, but we're not sure how effective it will be for a fey. Harlan's there, too. I can tell he's suspicious about who we are."

"It was inevitable," Gabe admitted, shaking his head, "and seeing as we're going to be working with him a lot more, he'll end up finding out, anyway. If I'm honest, I get sick of hiding it."

"Me too, but even so..." Eli's voice trailed off.

"Eli, I know that more than any of us, you want to leave our past behind, but we are who we are. You're a Nephilim, and you will always be one. I won't ask you to ever do anything you don't want to do, and," he laughed, "let's face it, I couldn't. But Harlan will know sooner rather than later, and Maggie will tell him, too. Newton will have no qualms about informing her."

Eli nodded, exhaling heavily. "Yeah, I know you're right. Anyway, come on through."

When they entered Briar's herb room, they found Niel, Harlan, and Briar bent over a map that was spread out on the counter. Gabe had never been here before, and he admired the ordered workspace and large collection of herbs, creams, and soaps.

Harlan looked up. "Any updates?"

"Nothing. Nahum is searching the outskirts of town for anything suspicious. He'll phone me if he does."

Harlan nodded. "Good. With luck, this spell will work."

Briar was holding a piece of blood-stained bandage in her hands, her eyes dark with worry. "I'm going to start the spell now, but the map is small, and I have no idea how effective this will be for finding a non-human. I have to admit, this isn't my speciality, but it should work."

A silver bowl was on the counter in front of her, and what looked like crushed herbs were in the bottom. She placed the small portion of bandage in it, and with a snap of her fingers, the contents burst into flames. She murmured words quietly, and the smoke that rose up stilled suddenly and then started to wind over the map. It swirled above White Haven's town centre and then moved outwards until it eddied lazily above one point.

Briar frowned, confused. "It looks like Old Haven Church."

"The church on the hill?" Eli asked. "Where the Wild Hunt arrived?"

"And where Shadow arrived. It was drenched in blood magic at one point," Niel reminded them.

"But we cleansed it!" Briar said.

Harlan was already picking his bag up. "He's a necromancer; he'll be surrounded by the dead up there. We have to check it out."

"Do you think this is accurate?" Gabe asked, reluctant to run off if they were heading in the wrong direction. It could cost them valuable time.

Briar looked confident. "It didn't deviate, so I think it is."

"It's all we've got," Niel pointed out, "so let's go."

"I'll help," Briar said immediately. "But we should call Alex. He's best with spirits."

Gabe shook his head. "No. This is our mess, we'll handle it."

"But I can help! Shadow is my friend too," Briar said, annoyed.

Gabe could feel her magic rising, a surprising amount from such a petite body, but the last thing he wanted to do was risk anyone else getting hurt. And he had his pride to consider. "I know you can help, Briar, but you've helped us enough, and I thank you for it. This is our fight. And besides," he grinned, "you know we'll be okay."

She fell silent for a moment, considering him, her mouth set in a firm line. "Actually, I don't know that, but you're stubborn, just like she is."

"And just like you are. You can patch us up if things go wrong. Deal?"

"Deal," she said reluctantly.

Harlan glared at him. "I'm coming. I started this."

Gabe had half a mind to leave him behind too, but maybe Harlan should come and learn exactly who they were. "All right. You're in for a treat."

Twenty-Two

A s Shadow helplessly looked on, Kian placed his remains in the corner of the room, in the area surrounded by the strange sigils carved into the floor.

He took his time, arranging the bones in careful order, his concentration absolute. When he was satisfied, he picked up the bowl of blood, dipped his fingers in it, and rubbed it into the marks. His staff was propped in the corner.

Shadow wriggled, trying to free her arms as quietly as possible. Every chink of the chain seemed loud to her ears, but Kian ignored her. If she could get a hand free, it would loosen the rest, but she knew there was no way she could get out of them quick enough to get to her weapons before he could stop her.

And then she heard another noise, a sort of groaning, or whispering.

She stopped moving, listening intently, and then felt an icy cold sweep over her. She looked up the steps and gritted her teeth in shock. A man was standing at the top, wearing old-fashioned clothing, his flesh half-rotted off his bones, his empty eye sockets staring down.

What had Kian done?

He stood motionless for a moment before turning away, but she could still see the edge of his feet, as if he was waiting for something.

Or guarding something.

Shadow took deep breaths, willing away her fear and annoyance. She was used to fighting, and wasn't scared of anything—usually—but this... At least she had the Empusa's sword, if she could get to it. She hoped the Nephilim had the other one.

A scrape of metal across stone drew her attention, and she saw Kian place the silver bowl back on the altar, and then pick up his staff. He faced the devil's trap and tapped it on the floor rhythmically as he began to chant, his voice low and guttural, and she felt an ice through her veins that had nothing to do with ghosts.

Harlan, Niel, Eli, and Gabe travelled to Old Haven together in Gabe's SUV, and on the way they phoned Nahum to tell him where to meet them.

By the time they pulled up on the car park, gliding in quietly with the lights off and the engine purring, Nahum was already waiting, shirtless.

Harlan blinked, thinking he was seeing things. Why the hell was Nahum shirtless on such a cold night? And where the hell was his car? None of the others looked even remotely surprised, so rather than voice his questions, he shut up.

But there was another car in the parking lot.

"Is that Kent's?" Gabe asked, already opening the door.

"Yep," Harlan confirmed. "I'll get my shotgun out of the back. I think I'm going to need the salt shells." He had insisted on grabbing it from his own car before they left.

Nahum joined them, his voice low. "He's in the mausoleum at the end of the path. I can see a light coming from the entrance, but I haven't got any closer."

Gabe looked shocked. "But that sounds like Reuben's family mausoleum."

"Any particular reason why he'd be in there?" Eli asked.

He groaned. "Reuben found it when he was searching for his family grimoire. He told me about it while we guarded the wood at Samhain. It has an altar and magical signs etched into the floor. It has a devil's trap in there too, and was a place meant for blood sacrifice—from what they could tell, anyway. He was worried the witch would find it."

Harlan's eyes widened with surprise. "Kian is very resourceful, I'll give him that. Any more secrets we should know about?"

"Let's hope not," Gabe said, pulling his shirt off, too. He threw it in the back of the SUV and freed the curved sword from its scabbard. "Can you see Shadow?"

"No, but she has to be with him," Nahum assured him. "He'll keep her close."

"That's what worries me," Gabe answered.

Nahum looked behind him to the dark mass of the church. "We have other problems, too."

"Like what?" Niel asked. He'd left his jacket in the car, and was peeling off his own t-shirt, as was Eli.

Harlan was confused. Was this turning into some bare-knuckle fight? He was pretty proud of his own physique, he kept himself fit with regular gym workouts and boxing, but these guys were enormous.

"He's raised a few bodies," Nahum said, nonchalantly.

"Like actually bodies?" Harlan asked, staring at the church and hoping something wasn't about to attack them. This night was becoming more surprising by the second.

"Yes. The undead have risen."

Harlan shuddered. "Just to be clear, are we talking about zombies here?"

Nahum looked amused. "It's a word I have become familiar with. Yes, I guess that's what they are—zombies."

"A word I have become familiar with." That was an odd thing to say, Harlan mused, but he didn't comment, instead saying, "I'm not sure what's worse, zombies or ghosts. Let's hope that if one bites me, I won't turn into one."

"You fear a zombie apocalypse? I'm familiar with that term too—I've watched the films."

"Well, then you should know that would be a very bad thing," Harlan told him.

Gabe was at the back of his SUV, and he lifted the base of the boot, revealing a collection of weapons, and Gabe, Eli, Nahum, and Niel all armed themselves.

"You wouldn't have something for me, would you?" Harlan asked, thinking a shotgun alone might not be enough.

"Help yourself."

Harlan selected a sharp machete as Gabe asked Nahum, "How many?"

He shrugged. "A small army."

Harlan placed a couple of boxes of shells in his pocket, and loaded the shotgun. "Where are they?"

"Everywhere."

"Can we bypass them?" Eli asked.

"Not really. They're in a tight ring around the tomb."

"They're dead, with decaying bodies," Niel reminded them. "This really shouldn't be a problem."

"We still need a plan," Gabe said. "Shadow is trapped with Kian. We have no idea if she's conscious or not, or even still alive. Our objective is to get in there, quickly."

Nahum glanced at Harlan, and then at Gabe, eyebrows raised. "If we attack from above, we'll have more success."

Gabe didn't hesitate. "Then that's our plan. We circle them, and pick them off one at a time. Whoever gets closest goes into the tomb first. Sound good?" They all nodded, and then Gabe turned to Harlan. "You're about to see something we don't show to everyone. It's a sign of our business relationship, and the level of trust I have in you, and—" he shrugged, "to be honest, we haven't much choice."

He stepped back, and with a shrug of his broad, muscled shoulders, two enormous wings flexed on either side of him. Eli, Niel, and Nahum all followed suit, and despite his best intentions not to appear shocked by anything, Harlan's mouth fell open. They were, for want of a better word, magnificent.

For a second, Harlan couldn't find his voice, and then he croaked, "What are you?"

Gabe grinned as his wings lifted him off the ground. "We are Nephilim."

"And how the hell did you arrive in White Haven? No, wait, let's keep that for another time."

"You okay on the ground? We'll attack from one direction, if you can mop up the rear."

"Sure," Harlan said, trying to sound more confident than he felt.

With an effortless beat of their wings, they headed to the cemetery, and Harlan ran after them.

<hr />

Shadow watched, her breath caught in her throat, as a dark figure rose within the devil's trap.

It contorted, twisted, and finally solidified into a crouched, hunched figure with a grotesque face and body. A demon. It scowled at Kian as it rasped, "Who summons me?"

Kian grinned like a petulant child. "Don't you recognise me, old friend?"

"No. You look like a milk maid, a sop with a backbone so weak I could pull it out with my finger nail."

Kian threw his head back, laughing wildly. "I've missed your wit, you old vagabond." He leaned closer to the circle, which was now bounded by a ring of flames and black, acrid smoke. "Look at me properly!"

The being scowled, and its eyes seemed to slip around its face. "Something lurks beneath your skin," it finally said.

Kian smiled. "I once summoned you to flatten a whole village, remember? They refused their king. We set an example that no one else forgot."

The demon wheezed. "Kian. I thought you had entered the shadow realm."

He straightened, his face grim. "I was afforded no such luxury. I have been between realms, trapped within my tomb, until some fool released me."

Shadow ground her teeth. Fool? She was going to enjoy killing him.

"You must need me for something," the creature said. "Revenge, death, mayhem?"

"Possibly, but for now I want my body."

"You have one."

"It's not mine. I want my own back, and you can get it."

"It is dust."

"My bones are at your feet, and you have the power to regenerate me."

"What's wrong with the one you have?" the demon persisted.

Kian was starting to get annoyed, and Shadow continued to wriggle out of her chains while he was preoccupied.

"It is weak! I am fey, and I demand my own flesh."

"It will come at a price."

"Doesn't it always? I am prepared to pay."

"With what?"

"As many sacrifices as you desire."

"You know the rules. A body for a body."

Kian shot Shadow a look of pure malice. "It's lucky I brought one with me. Will a fey do?"

"A fey will be perfect."

Kian marched over to her, put his hand under her arm and hauled her to her feet; Shadow saw her chance. She whipped her other arm free and punched him, hard, satisfied to see him stumble and fall, and then ran awkwardly to the stairs, the chains still draped around her upper body.

With every step her bonds loosened, but Kian was already on his feet, and he threw himself at her, sending them both crashing to the ground.

Kian straddled her chest, pressing his arm to her throat, but he hadn't managed to trap her arm, and she punched him again, in the ribs and the head, finally rolling over him. Kent wasn't a big man, and he wasn't used to fighting, despite Kian's spirit urging him on.

Shadow punched him again, and his head thudded off the stone, leaving him dazed. She staggered to her feet, desperately trying to shimmy out of the chains.

The room was filling with black smoke from the fire around the devil's trap. Inside the circle, Kian's bones were changing, as flesh started to knit across his skull, and the demon cackled.

A groan distracted her, and she looked up to see the corpse lumbering down the steps. With one final twist of her body, the chains fell to the floor and she launched herself at the sword in the corner, grabbing it firmly.

She turned to face the room, sword raised, trying to see through the smoke. It stung her eyes and burned her throat. The bandage that Kian had wrapped around her arm had torn loose, and blood was dripping from the wound. She ignored it; she could bandage it later.

Kent was groaning as he tried to rise to his feet. Surely Kian would leave the body now? Kent was virtually unresponsive. But, where else would he go? He needed a physical form to catch her, and she hoped that meant he wouldn't try to enter hers—after all, she was about to be sacrificed to a demon.

The corpse was now reaching his rotten hands towards her, and without hesitation, she sliced off his head, and it rolled into the corner. But the headless corpse kept coming, and beyond it were another couple of bodies at the top of the steps.

Great, just great. A demon behind her, and reanimated corpses in front.

Just as she was about to swing her sword again, something seemed to move beneath her feet. She thought it was trick of the light, but it looked as if her blood was running down the channel in the centre of the floor towards the altar at the far end. It seemed as if the channel was actually drawing her blood in from where it had pooled on the ground.

She wiped her arm against her body, trying to stop the flow, but the corpse grabbed for her and she dodged out of the way. Whatever was happening with her blood, the threat from the dead and Kian were more pressing. She lifted her sword, and swung again.

Twenty-Three

G abe circled above the graveyard, watching the scene of destruction below. The ground had cracked open, and the graves were an explosion of earth and rotten wood, as the bodies clambered out of their resting places—because they just kept coming.

Gabe seethed. The dead deserved their rest, not to be used as tools for some mad fey's desire. The corpses were stumbling around the graveyard, and as far as armies went, this one was pretty slow. The group's preference was to avoid them, and they had tried, but as soon as they landed close to the mausoleum, the dead had attacked, clawing and trying to bite the Nephilim. They had been animated by hate and viciousness, and unfortunately when you knocked them down, they kept getting back up again.

Niel and Nahum stood in the centre of them, the swords flashing as they hacked through rotting flesh and bone, body parts flying everywhere. Eli was still flying, swooping down and striking with his blade. Harlan was at the back, and so far he seemed to be holding his own.

Gabe decided it was time to try getting into the mausoleum again and he landed softly, slicing through the corpse immediately in front of him. He picked the others up, throwing them aside. They weighed nothing, unsurprisingly.

He was making decent headway, and barrelled up the steps of the tomb, using his wings to shield himself. The door was shut, and he pushed against it. It didn't budge, but he could see smoke trickling through the gaps around the edges.

He put his shoulder to the door and hit it, hard. It still didn't budge. Gabe glared at it, and steeled himself to try again. If needed, he'd tear the tomb apart, stone by stone.

───◆○◼───

Harlan had seen enough zombie films in his lifetime to know what to expect, but to be honest, this was way worse.

He was covered in spatters of rotten flesh and shards of bone. And he reeked. Well, the corpses reeked. It was all completely disgusting, and he tried not to heave as he fought his way through the mess.

The good thing was that he barely had time to consider how disgusting it was, because it was all he could do to keep moving. He felt something grip his ankle, and he looked down to see a skeletal hand use him to haul itself out of the earth. He slashed at it, careful not to slice his own foot off, and then stamped down hard.

A thumping sound drew his attention, and he saw Gabe at the entrance to the tomb, his shoulder against it as he tried to break the door down.

He renewed his efforts to get to his side. If it was like this outside the tomb, what the hell was happening inside?

Suddenly, another hand pulled his leg sharply out from beneath him, and he fell flat on his back. A corpse jumped on top of him, drooling on his face, as the earth started to give way.

The second corpse's head went flying across the room and landed with a thump before the altar, and a spray of Shadow's blood went with it.

She was carrying the Empusa's sword and her knife now, and she wished she'd thought to pick up her dragonium blade instead. Too late for that now. Two weapons were still better than one. In fact, now that she was finally free of the chains, she was enjoying herself. It felt good to be pitting herself against something other than the Nephilim. With them she had to hold back, but here, there was no need.

Just as she was about to behead the third corpse, Kian lifted himself out of Kent's insensible body and into the corpse in front of her. As she swung, he ducked and tackled her. They landed inches away from the devil's trap, so close that Shadow could feel the heat burning her skin.

Kian was trying to push her head into the fire with his bony hands, and deep within the empty eye sockets she could see a glowing red light. He was stronger now, much stronger, and she felt herself sliding closer to the flames.

Then she heard a loud thumping above her, and a shout.

Gabe.

With renewed enthusiasm, she angled the sword between her and Kian and thrust upward. He howled with pain and momentarily withdrew, allowing her to raise her knee up and kick him away, scrambling out from beneath him.

The corpse fell to the floor as Kian's shade left it, and now she could see him clearly, confusion on his face.

"How have you done that?" he asked.

Shadow held the sword up. "Do you like it? It's my new toy."

She darted towards him, slashing across his stomach, and saw a tear in his body that didn't bleed, but leaked light.

He staggered back again, his hand again clutching his wound. "I'm a ghost. You shouldn't be able to do that! I command the dead, not you!"

"I don't command anything, but I do have a sword from the Underworld. It's calling to you now. Do you hear it?"

The demon interrupted them, rasping his demand. "I need her now, Kian, if you want your body!"

Kian looked his partially reconstructed remains longingly, and then back at Shadow, a calculating expression crossing his face. He would have been handsome once, she could see it, behind the rage and evil that now consumed him.

She shook her head and darted at him, this time slashing across his arms. "Too late, Kian. You're going where you should have gone years ago."

He held his hands up, imploring her. "No! I am fey, like you! We could make a deal!"

She ignored him, and raising her sword once more, she lopped his spectral head from his shoulders, satisfied to see it rolling across the floor before his whole body disappeared.

Immediately, the still-twitching corpses that surrounded her stopped moving, and with an enormous scraping sound from above, she heard Gabe more clearly.

"Shadow, where are you?"

"I'm here," she yelled back, wondering where that exactly was.

Gabe appeared at the top of the steps, the Empusa's other sword in his hand, and he ran towards her, looking over her shoulder to the where the devil's trap was still encircled with flames. Without hesitation he grabbed her, and pulled her close, backing them both against the wall.

"Where's Kian?"

"Dead."

"I'm presuming he called the demon?"

"It certainly wasn't me," she said impatiently.

"How do we get rid of it?"

The demon answered. He was prowling, testing his boundary, but every time he touched it, the flames flared higher. Kian's remains were at his feet, covered in sinew and muscles. "I was promised a body. Give me flesh, and I will go."

Shadow's arm was really stinging now, and what seemed like a lot of her blood was on the floor. She swayed unsteadily, not sure if it was caused by the blood loss or the smoke. Leaving her leaning against the wall, Gabe picked up body parts, throwing them into the trap until the room was empty, but now the smell of burning flesh was worse than the smoke. He addressed the demon. "Take them, and go."

It lifted his snarling face, defiant. "I was promised the fey."

"I have the Empusa's sword," he growled. "If I throw this at you, do you think it will kill you, too?"

Without another word, the demon vanished, taking the bodies with him. With a deafening crack, the devil's trap closed, and the flames extinguished.

Gabe looked at Shadow. "Is it over?"

"I think so."

And then she noticed her blood still running towards the altar on the far wall, and with an insidious whisper, the wall slid apart, revealing another room behind it.

One minute Harlan and the Nephilim were fighting, and the next, the corpses around them collapsed, motionless.

The figure that was pinning Harlan to the ground went limp, and he pushed it off, scrambling away from the churned soil that threatened to swallow him whole. He straightened up, trying to catch his breath, and then joined Niel and Nahum, who were surrounded by a mass of body parts.

"She must have done it," he said. "Kian must be dead."

Nahum surveyed the scene of devastation. "Let's hope so. I'd hate to think this was merely an interlude."

Eli shouted over from where he stood on the steps to the mausoleum. "Gabe's gone in, come on!"

Black smoke drifted through the doorway, and by the time they reached the entrance, Eli was already inside, and Harlan followed him in, hearing Nahum say to Niel. "Stay here, keep watch, and shout if you need us."

The room was full of stone tombs, and Harlan was relieved to see that none of them had opened. Eli had already passed through a door to the side, and was heading down a set of steps towards the sound of Gabe's voice, and Harlan followed, Nahum right behind.

Gabe and Shadow were standing at the back of a creepy chamber, and blood was splattered across the walls and floor. The room was full of occult symbols, and smelled disgusting — the stench of charred flesh and smoke.

"Where did the smoke come from?" Harlan asked, lifting his shirt over his nose.

"A devil's trap," Gabe said, nodding at the corner. "Kian summoned a demon, but I threatened it with the Empusa's sword and it disappeared."

"And where did the blood come from? It's everywhere!"

Shadow was leaning against Gabe, and his arm was cradled around her, holding her up. She held her arm out. "It's mine. Kian cut me. I managed to spread it around while I was fighting."

"Forget the blood! What's with that?" Eli asked, pointing.

On the wall to the rear of the room behind the altar, was an illuminated circle of sigils, and swirling within it was a pool of darkness.

"Shadow's blood has opened something," Gabe said. "Reuben said this place was made for blood sacrifices."

Nahum looked at it warily, clasping his axe. "It's a portal. You must recognise it. It's opening."

"A portal to what?" Harlan asked, alarmed.

"Another realm," Nahum said, glancing at him. "The last time I saw one of those, I ended up here."

"You came out of one?" Harlan's voice rose with surprise. No wonder there wasn't any record of them existing before six months ago.

Eli swore. "No! We cannot let that open. We know the type of things that exist beyond there. What if Kian tries to come back through? We've just got rid of him!"

"Well, I don't know about you, Eli," Gabe said, annoyed, "but I have no idea how to close a bloody portal!"

And then, Harlan felt a cool wind behind him, and hairs lifted on the back of his neck. He whirled around, fearing another corpse was advancing, but he saw nothing. However, Gabe and Shadow obviously did—he could see it on their faces.

"What's happening?" he asked.

"A ghost is here," Gabe said, watching the space in front of him with narrowed eyes.

Immediately, all hands flew to their weapons, but Gabe stopped them. "Wait. I think it's here to help."

The swirling blackness was gaining momentum now, and the signs carved into the wall were bright with a fierce, orange light. It was like gazing into a black hole.

"Someone tell me what's happening!" Harlan said, frustrated.

Gabe thrust the Empusa's sword at him. "See for yourself. I think you'll recognise him."

As soon as the blade was in his hand, Harlan gasped. A man was standing in front of them, of average height and build, with short, dark hair. He had kind eyes, and there was something familiar about him. It took Harlan a few seconds, and then he had it. "He looks like Reuben."

"It's his brother, Gil," Shadow said softly. "He died last year."

"Holy shit."

Gil crossed to the portal, stopping a few feet before it, and drew shapes into the air, and Harlan saw him saying words he couldn't hear. For a few moments, nothing happened, but then the sigils faded, the blackness dissipated, and the wall became just a wall again.

Gil turned towards them, smiled sadly, and then vanished.

Harlan slumped on the steps, exhaustion hitting him like a freight train, but he'd barely sat when a groan disturbed them, and a weak voice said, "Help! Where am I? Harlan, is that you?"

Kent's crumpled body was stirring, his pale face blinking like a mole that had just emerged from his burrow.

He sighed with relief and ran over to help him to his feet. "Kent! Welcome back."

Gabe was looking grim, and dirt and blood were smeared across his face and clothes. "We need to get out of here, and seal this place forever. Come on."

Still supporting Shadow, the Nephilim headed up the steps, Harlan and Kent right behind.

"Harlan, what's going on?" Kent asked, utterly confused.

"I'll tell you later."

Harlan paused at the top of the steps for one final view of the blood-spattered chamber, and then turned his back on it resolutely. Within a few minutes they'd sealed it again, pushing the stone coffin that contained the hidden entrance back into place with a resounding click.

As soon as they were outside the mausoleum, looking at the destroyed cemetery, Harlan felt a wave of guilt wash over him. Body parts were strewn everywhere, and the smell was revolting. "We can't leave it like this. It's horrible!"

Shadow agreed. "Wow! You were busy, boys!"

"We have to put the graves back to how they were," Harlan said, appealing to the others.

"That's not possible," Gabe replied, shaking his head. "The bodies will be all mixed up. But we can at least put them back under the earth. They'll look disturbed, but with luck, nobody will notice for days." He turned to Nahum. "Can you fetch the spades from the house? We'll do it now."

Nahum watched Shadow, who despite her best efforts, was still swaying on her feet, and covered in blood. "You take Shadow home, and we'll handle this. And Harlan, take Kent back to Alex's. He needs a strong drink."

"If I'm honest, I think we all do," Harlan said wearily, still trying to prop Kent up.

Nahum laughed. "Well, ours will have to wait. Get going, Gabe."

"Thanks, Nahum." Gabe passed Harlan his car keys. "Take my car, I'll collect it tomorrow."

He extended his huge wings and picked Shadow up effortlessly. Seconds later, he was soaring over the church, nothing but a patch of darkness on the night sky.

Twenty-Four

Harlan sat across the desk from Mason, sipping his whiskey, and watching Mason's perplexed expression.

It was late afternoon, and Harlan had arrived back in London only an hour or two before. He'd dropped Kent off at his home, updated Maggie, and now all he wanted to do was sleep.

"What do you mean, they're Nephilim?" Mason asked. He still looked pale, even though it was a few days after being possessed by Kian, and although he'd been complaining of headaches, he was focused now. Like a hunter.

"Just what I said. Nephilim, who returned from the dead, last year in White Haven. They have wings. Very big wings."

"How did they get here?"

"Long story, but essentially they came through some type of portal the witches opened. There are seven of them. Shadow lives with them in a farmhouse on the outskirts of the town."

"Do they know you're telling me this?"

"Of course. They're not stupid. And frankly, I wouldn't want to cross them."

Mason downed his whiskey in one gulp and poured himself another. "This changes everything."

Harlan frowned. "It does? Why?"

"I need to contact JD."

"Well, sure, of course he needs to know."

JD was short for J D Mortlake, the head of the Orphic Guild. Harlan had no idea what the initials stood for. Most of the time he lived in his large estate outside of London, but the upper two floors of the Orphic Guild's headquarters were fully furnished for when he wanted to come to town—which was rare. Harlan had only met him a couple of times, because he was also an eccentric recluse.

Mason leaned forward, as serious as Harlan had ever seen him. "Do you know why the Guild was founded?"

"To find occult and arcane items—and to make money from them."

"That's only part of it. JD founded it because he was obsessed with many things, but especially angels—the fallen ones, the Hermetica, and the book of Enoch."

Harlan blinked. "What do you mean, he founded it? It has existed for a hundred years or more!"

"JD is an unusual man."

"I know—I've met him."

"I mean that he's more unusual than you can imagine." Mason looked nervous, and he downed his second shot of whiskey in one go. "I need to call him. He'll want to meet them."

"All of them?" Harlan asked, astonished.

"Just Gabe will do. And Shadow, too. They're valuable assets."

"I'm not sure they'd appreciate being described that way."

But Mason was already picking his phone up, undaunted. "Do me a favour, Harlan. Get them here tomorrow afternoon. They can meet JD then."

Harlan stood, knowing he was dismissed. "How do you know he'll come?'

"I just do. And make sure you come, too."

"What am I supposed to say to them?"

"Tell them it will be worth their time."

------◆◇◆------

Gabe put the phone down and looked at Shadow.

"We've just received another invitation to the Orphic Guild."

She groaned. "Do we have to go?"

"Yes. Give me a chocolate."

Shadow was lying on the sofa wearing pyjamas, her arm bandaged up, and she had a box of chocolates next to her that she was steadily working her way through. The TV was on, and she was watching an old black and white film with the sound on low. She absently picked up a random chocolate and threw it at him. She aimed at his head but he caught it, shooting her an annoyed glance.

She ignored him. "But I really like lying here, and I think I could do it for days." She pointed at the screen. "That's Cary Grant and Katherine Hepburn, and they're trying to raise a lion."

"I think you'll find it's a leopard. They're very different."

"Oh. Never mind. It's funny, sort of. Actually, it's quite ridiculous, but I like it. It's called a screwball comedy."

"That's because it's not supposed to make sense. Like you."

She looked at him, outraged. "I make sense!"

Gabe started laughing, and then found he couldn't stop. "That's what you are. You're a screwball."

"Fuck off!" She threw another chocolate at him.

His hand shot out and caught it again. "That's very fruity language for a screwball!"

"I have more. El and Reuben are very effective teachers! I can throw more than a chocolate, too. You're lucky my knife isn't close by."

Gabe held his hand up in mock surrender. "Well, whether you want to or not, you're coming to London tomorrow, even if I have to carry you there. I smell intrigue."

That grabbed her attention, and she sat up. "What kind of intrigue?"

"I don't know, and neither did Harlan, actually. He said JD Mortlake wants to meet us, and that never happens."

"Who's JD Mortlake, and since when do you call him Harlan? I thought he was Beckett to you."

"I'm calling him Harlan because I've decided I like him."

"So who's JD?"

"The mysterious head of the Orphic Guild, who apparently hardly ever meets people."

"This is because of your giant wings. You've attracted attention."

"Says Little Miss Fey. You're very good at attracting attention, too."

"I know. I can't help it." She stretched luxuriously, revealing a patch of flat stomach and soft skin that gave Gabe ideas he didn't need.

"I don't believe that for one second."

She grinned at him, picked up another chocolate, and threw it so quickly that it smacked off his cheek.

Gabe refused to react. "Happy now?"

"Very. What time do we have to be there?"

"Three. So put on your most polite face, and try not to antagonise him."

⸺◆◯◆⸺

The man who sat opposite Shadow looked very distinguished, and was dressed immaculately.

So this is JD Mortlake, Shadow mused, assessing him intently.

His pale grey suit fitted him perfectly, and beneath it was a crisp white shirt. His hair was a thick, luxurious mass of silver, swept back from his temples, and he had a trim white beard sweeping up his cheeks to his sideburns. But it was his eyes that were arresting. They were pale amber, like fine whiskey, and they were fixed on Gabe as if his life depended on it.

Mason, Harlan, Gabe, Shadow, and JD were sitting in leather chairs around the low table in Mason's office. It was cold today, the sky thick with clouds, and squally. Spatters of rain rattled the windows, and the lamps were on to alleviate the gloom.

There was a tray of coffee in the centre of the table, and its rich smell filled the air, but next to it was a bottle of whiskey, and JD already had a glass poured.

JD leaned forward. "You have no idea what it means to me to meet you."

Gabe smiled awkwardly. "Thank you, but I'm not entirely sure why."

"You're a Nephilim. Isn't that enough?"

"I am what I am."

"You are the son of an immortal being. Your history transcends time. You are history."

Gabe laughed. "I should be history. I cheated time."

"And you have a second chance to use your unique skills."

"I guess that's why we're working with Shadow and your Guild."

JD nodded. "Ah yes, there are more of you, I gather?"

"Seven of us," Gabe said warily.

"Astonishing. How are you finding your new world?"

"It's very different, but we've adapted."

Gabe was being polite, Shadow noted, but cagey too, and she didn't blame him. On their way to London, they had debated what JD might want of them, because he had to want something, beyond what they'd already talked about. Harlan looked just as intrigued, which made Shadow think he didn't have much of a clue about what was going on, either.

JD turned to Shadow. "And you are fey. You cloak your Otherness well."

She shrugged. "My life depends on it." He looked at her so intently that she felt uncomfortable, and her patience was waning. "Is there a purpose to this meeting?"

Her abruptness didn't bother him in the slightest, because a slow smile spread across his face, and he eased back in his chair. "Yes, there is. I formed this organisation for more than grabbing trinkets and baubles for money. I established it because I am obsessed with knowledge, and I know there are more things to discover about this world. Look at you two! You are prime examples of that. I have met fey before, but not for many years. I have most definitely never met a Nephilim.

"However, that does not answer your question. There are things I lost long ago that I want back, and I have been trying to track them down for years. I think you can help me."

Gabe shot a look at Shadow. "Do you think you could expand on that? Everything sounds very mysterious right now."

He nodded. "Of course, but I want you to know that what I am about to tell you, I don't tell many people at all, so I would appreciate your discretion."

"As long we have yours," Shadow said.

"You have. Obviously the other collectors in this organisation know about you, but you have my word it will not go further, unless you give our permission." He raised a well-groomed eyebrow. "Frankly, keeping your real nature a secret is an asset."

Shadow wasn't entirely sure she believed that, but she let it go. She could take care of herself, whatever happened, and so could the Nephilim.

Seeing their nods of agreement, JD took a deep breath and continued. "I have been alive for several centuries. Over five hundred years, to be precise. During my natural lifetime, I discovered the secret of immortality. My passion was alchemy, amongst others, and I have dedicated my life to finding other secrets. My name is John Dee. I was royal magician to Queen Elizabeth the first."

The silence was broken by Harlan's cup crashing back onto the table. "Are you kidding me? You are the John Dee?"

JD looked at Harlan with amusement. "I'm glad you've heard of me."

"Heard of you?" Harlan said, his voice strained. "You're one of the most famous men in history!"

"Not to us," Gabe murmured.

"Trust me," Harlan said. "He is." He turned back to JD. "How did you achieve this?"

"My immortality? By endless experimentation. I ensure there are no photographs of me in any era, and I mostly keep to my Mortlake Estate. Mason keeps me updated as needed, as do a few others. He is aware of my many passions, and he knows about my obsession with angels and Enochian language."

Mason nodded, watching their reactions as he sipped his whiskey.

"What's Enochian language?" Gabe asked, confused.

"The language of the angels."

Gabe's face was pinched with suspicion, and he was paler than Shadow had ever seen him. She had a sudden urge to put her hand on his arm for reassurance, but she didn't. He wouldn't appreciate it.

Gabe recovered quickly, and he shook his head. "I've never heard it called that before."

"Likely not. If I'm honest, I coined the phrase. It's an interesting story that I will share with you one day. But my contact, who I won't name right now, allowed me to compile the language of angels, and since then I've been using it to try to work out the history of the world before the Flood. Your history. Why you were made, your purpose. Our purpose. God's purpose. Hermes Trismesgistus found out these ancient truths and documented them in his Hermetica, the most important of which he inscribed on the Emerald Tablet. It is believed that it survived the Flood, and I have been searching for it ever since. I want you to help me find it."

Gabe folded his arms across his chest. "What you seek is both dangerous and foolish."

JD's eyes widened. "You've heard of it?"

"Of course I have. He was renowned in my time as a dangerous madman, but men sought the tablet even then."

"Did you ever see his Hermetica?"

"No. I'm not sure that it even exists."

Mason had been watching their exchange silently, but now he said, "I thought there were many Hermetic texts?"

JD nodded. "There are, but this particular one is supposedly the key to all. I would like you to help me find it. I also have texts you could help interpret."

Despite Gabe's obvious misgivings, Shadow felt excited. This sounded insane, a rabbit hole down which they would all run headlong and never see the sight of day again. It sounded fun.

Gabe grunted, his face impassive. "I shall consider it. I need to discuss it with my brothers."

"Of course." JD nodded. "I also have an easier request. Many years ago, I entrusted my library to my brother-in-law while I travelled. He betrayed me. When I returned, most of it had gone. Sold." He had looked composed, but now his lips were set in a thin line, and it was clear than even five centuries later, this betrayal burned deep. "I was able to recover some of them immediately, but others remained lost. Over the years, some texts have come to light, and others are now in a library for all to access. I have, with much time and effort, rebuilt it over my long life, but other books are elusive. I want you to help me find them."

"Books about what?" Shadow asked.

"Many things. Mathematics, astronomy, cryptography, ancient history, cartography, alchemy, and other subjects. All with my notes inside." JD looked slightly uncomfortable. "It may involve some underhanded methods."

Harlan poured himself a large whiskey and took a healthy gulp. "Of course, the Orphic Guild is an excellent way to find such things." He frowned at JD. "We've already found some texts. I recall a few years ago a transaction with someone overseas. I had no idea they were for you!"

"Indeed, and that's why you're here too, Harlan. You've been helpful before, and can assist Shadow and Gabe now."

Shadow grinned. "I'm in—for the right price, of course."

"You will be paid very well," JD assured her.

"Excellent. Gabe?"

Gabe drained his coffee and stood. "I agree to the search for texts, but the rest I must discuss with my brothers. I'll be in touch. Are you ready, Shadow?"

She looked at him, surprised by his abruptness, but talking about his past always rattled Gabe, so she nodded and stood, too. After some brief goodbyes, they headed for the door. As they left the room, Shadow saw all three men leaning towards each other, their faces animated, but Harlan looked up, meeting her eyes briefly, and he winked before turning away.

——————◆◇◆——————

That night, Gabe gathered the other six Nephilim, plus Shadow, around a large bonfire in the field next to their house.

Shadow and Gabe had arrived back only an hour or two earlier, and it was close to midnight now. For once, they were all at home. It had been weeks since they'd been together, and the day before, Gabe had arranged cover for Caspian's warehouse.

Gabe's original intention had been to have a party to celebrate Kian's defeat and to burn the remainder of the grave goods, but now it had a second purpose. He wanted to discuss JD's proposal.

He looked around at his brothers and Shadow, grateful for their company. He'd been in a strange mood ever since they'd left London, and he'd brooded on JD's proposal all the way home. Shadow had let him, sensing his reticence to talk. She'd been wrapped in her own thoughts, too. As soon as he'd arrived at the farmhouse, he updated the others on the meeting, and had given them time to think.

"Let's get this over with first," Nahum said. He picked up Kian's rotting leather bag and hurled it into the fire.

Shadow picked up his wooden staff and threw that in, too. The flames turned a dark purple colour and they all stepped back, but moments later they returned to normal, and Shadow breathed a sigh of relief. "Thank Herne for that. I thought he'd left us one final surprise."

"I wouldn't put it past the old bastard," Niel said, as he threw in some of the other items.

They all followed suit, and even the jewellery was thrown in.

"Has anyone commented on the events at Old Haven cemetery yet?" Gabe asked.

"You mean outraged parishioners or the press?" Eli said. "Not yet. Let's hope it's another few days before anyone goes there. The ground should have settled by then."

Barak raised his beer to them. "Well done, guys—and girl, of course!" He nodded at Shadow before downing his drink. "I wish I'd have been there. It sounds like fun."

"I'm fey or woman, thank you," she said archly, and then she grinned at him. "Yes, it was fun. Well, beheading him was. Being trussed up in chains and almost sacrificed to a demon was not."

He grinned back. "I guess not."

Gabe smiled to see them all together, relaxed and teasing each other, but he was too anxious to wait any longer. "What about JD's proposal?"

"I admit, it's intriguing," Zee told him from where he sat in an old wooden chair, nursing his beer. "I'd like to know more about our past. Let's face it—we were pawns, most of the time."

"Most?" Ash scoffed. "More like all! I'm glad to have left it behind."

"But wouldn't you like to know about the reasons behind our making? The events that made us?" Niel asked him. "I'm with Zee. I'm curious. I also think it will be a wild goose chase, but that doesn't mean we shouldn't try."

"Horny fallen angels were the reasons behind our making," Ash said cynically.

Barak looked at Eli, amused. "Something Eli has inherited from his father!"

Eli snorted. "Yeah, like you're a monk!"

Barak threw back his head and laughed, exposing his white teeth, and not denying it, Gabe noted.

"But what if there was more to it?" Nahum suggested, ignoring them both. He poked the fire with a big stick so that the flames roared higher. "We've all heard of Hermes Trismesgistus and his fabled Emerald Tablet. It would be a hell of a search."

"It would be a bloody big tablet, too," Zee pointed out.

Barak had finally stopped laughing and he warmed his hands over the fire. "His history and teachings are layered in mystery. His written works alone—if the rumours are to be believed—are numbered in the thousands. It will be like chasing dreams."

"But who better to chase dreams than us?" Nahum asked, his eyes bright with the thrill of the chase.

"And don't forget there are JD's own lost texts to find," Shadow reminded them. "Hopefully an easier endeavour."

"And of course whatever else comes our way in all of this." Niel grinned, clearly excited by the prospect, and despite Gabe's misgivings, he felt himself warming to the idea.

Ash looked at him. "What about you?"

Gabe considered his words carefully. They were all watching him, and he knew that if he said no, they would honour his decision, but they'd probably resent him for it. Except for Shadow, who'd do what she wanted. She looked amused, but only Nahum really knew how much he'd brooded about their father, and he stood patiently waiting.

"Our past annoys me, as does our fathers' actions and the manner of our passing," he finally said. "There are things I want to know, and this seems to offer us a chance to find out. I'm not sure what good will come of it, but I think we should say yes."

"Yes!" Niel said, punching the air, and with a collective whoop, everyone else chimed in, clinking bottles in celebration.

"For what it's worth," Shadow said, raising her drink to Gabe, "I think you've made the right choice."

"Then let's fly to celebrate!" Gabe said recklessly, eager to shed the trappings of his human body.

Within seconds, the beer had been drained, the empty bottles thrown in the fire, and the Nephilim cast off their shirts and flew into the night, leaving Gabe standing next to Shadow. She looked up at them swooping across the fields, a faint smile on her lips.

"Come here," Gabe said to her softly, not wanting to fly by himself, and sensing that she didn't want to be left alone, either. They were both lonely enough sometimes.

Without hesitation, Shadow stepped into his arms, and he soared into the sky.

Shadow's EDGE

WHITE HAVEN HUNTERS BOOK TWO

TJ GREEN

One

S hadow looked at the house that blazed with light and the driveway filled with cars that spilled onto the road, and then stared at Harlan.

"Are you serious? They're having a party!"

"I did say they were!"

"I presumed it was a small dinner party, not a huge one with hundreds of guests!"

Harlan shifted uncomfortably in the driver's seat, having the grace to look sheepish. "I know this looks difficult, but it's actually easier for you to break in this way. And besides, you're exaggerating. There aren't hundreds!"

"But there are a lot! I could get in trouble with Maggie Milne—again!"

"Of course you won't! You're fey, right? Which means you won't get caught by anyone."

Shadow narrowed her eyes and resisted the urge to wipe the smirk off Harlan's face. She hated it when her own words were used against her. "I like to plan my own methods of breaking and entering, thank you. Methods that involve a little more stealth. I'm not invisible!"

Harlan gave her his most charming smile. "But you are very skilful."

"And you are pushing your luck!"

"But not yours."

Shadow took a deep breath and exhaled slowly, reminding herself that she liked Harlan—most of the time. It was Sunday night, and they were sitting in his rental car on a leafy road on the outskirts of Hope Cove in Devon. His own car was outside the farmhouse in White Haven, because it was so recognisable he hadn't wanted to risk being spotted.

Harlan continued, "It might look like an ordinary house, but as I told you it has a very sophisticated alarm system. It would be a nightmare to disable. This way, we don't have to."

"We?" Shadow turned in her seat to stare at him. "And what are you going to do?"

"I'll wait a little further down the street."

"How nice for you."

"You mean you want me to come with you?" Harlan angled himself towards her, but in the dark confines of the car, all Shadow could see was the hard line of his jaw and his lips curving into a smile.

"Absolutely not. Now remind me, where am I going?"

Harlan had picked her up from White Haven a couple of hours before, and they had talked about the night's plan, as well as the more interesting matter of JD Mortlake, but with the house looking so full, she wanted to make sure she had got things right. She was prepared to fight her way out if necessary, but it would be so much easier not to.

"You need to enter through the back door, next to the kitchen, and if I know Henri, he'll have brought in catering staff. The rear stairs are to the right of the door as you walk in, and they bring you out close to the library that overlooks the garden. The Map is rolled up and stored on a shelf with several other maps, but it will be obvious. He keeps it in a red leather tube-shaped case."

Shadow nodded and gazed back at the house. The well-manicured gravel drive was edged with shrubs, trees, and low lighting, but close to the boundary wall, it was dark. "And you say I should keep to the left?"

"Yes. There's a gate in the wall that leads around to the back of the house."

"Any dogs?"

"A Pekinese called Walter."

"Walter?"

"Henri is a fan of Sir Walter Raleigh. A big fan." Harlan's teeth flashed white in the darkness as he laughed. "At least you won't have to worry about being attacked."

"Great. It will just yap a lot and make me want to throw it over the hedge."

"Walter leads a very cosseted life. I'm sure he will be inside on such a cold night."

"Good." She patted her pockets to make sure she had her tools at hand, and then opened the door, allowing cold air to rush inside. "I should be out within the hour."

"I'll be just down the lane. Good luck."

Halfway out of the car, Shadow paused and asked, "What if the unthinkable happens and I do get caught?"

"You're on your own. I know him, so I can't afford to get involved. Or get The Orphic Guild dragged into it. But you won't. I trust you."

Resisting the urge to say something scathing, she shut the door softly, raced across the road, vaulted over the low wall, and ran beneath the trees. The sound of laughter and music reached the end of the drive, getting louder as she approached the house.

This was their first major job since they had met JD a few weeks before. Since then, Gabe had seen him a couple of times at his Mortlake Estate, telling her that he'd been questioned for hours about his life before the flood, and so far wasn't sure what to make of him. Shadow had spent her time reading up on JD's history. Harlan was right. He was a very famous historical figure with a colourful past, and Shadow didn't know what to make of him, either.

Tonight she was retrieving an old map from a member of the Order of the Midnight Sun, but as yet, she had no idea why because Harlan had been so deliberately cagey. As she drew closer to the house, she saw the catering van that Harlan had predicted, but the driveway was devoid of people, and it was impossible to see into the house, as the curtains were drawn. She felt her way along the wall that provided security between the front and back garden, and quickly found the gate. She depressed the latch and came upon her first problem. The gate was locked.

Shadow stepped back and looked up. The top of the wall was several feet above her head, but it was rustic enough for her to get hand and footholds, so she scrambled up and peered over it, seeing an unlit path running alongside the house. She swung over and dropped to the path. Immediately, a security light went on, and she dived into the borders on the left, flattening herself under shrubs.

Heart hammering in her chest, Shadow waited, feeling the damp, cold earth beneath her, and the tickle of leaves against her cheek. It was early May, and although the days were warmer, the nights were still cold. After several seconds of waiting, no one came running out, so keeping to the boundary wall again, Shadow headed deeper into the garden until she could see the entire back of the house.

At the far side there was a large, paved patio area filled with tables and chairs, and thanks to some outside mood lighting, and the light from the room behind, she saw a few hardy people smoking and chatting, their voices only a low murmur. But this end of the house was quiet. Half a dozen people moved around in what looked to be the kitchen; the back door was a short distance from it, and above it was another security light.

Shadow contemplated her options and decided the best way to enter was to round the corner of the house as if she were part of the catering staff. If anyone looked over from the patio area, they wouldn't question it. She edged back to the house, stepped onto the path that lit up straight away, walked confidently around the corner, and opened the back door without hesitating. She slipped inside and shut it softly behind her.

She found herself in a broad passageway in nearly total darkness. A chink of light escaped through the partially open kitchen door to her left, allowing her to see a line of outdoor shoes, boots, and coats hanging on the wall in front of her. A hallway ran deeper into the house, but to her right was the staircase. Shadow ran up it, pausing halfway to listen for any voices, but it was silent, except for the distant thump of music and laughter, and she continued, only stopping when she reached the landing.

The hall was dim, lit by a lamp on a small table placed under a narrow side window. To her left the passage ran a short distance before turning right into the centre of the house. She followed it past an open doorway, the room beyond in complete darkness. She pushed the door open further, letting her eyes adjust to the light. It was a spare bedroom by the look of it. A bag was on the floor, and the bed was made, so maybe a guest was staying here.

Remembering Harlan's instructions, she hurried onwards, following the corridor until she reached a doorway on her left, and she peered inside the lamp-lit room. Bingo. The study was lined with shelves that were packed with books and files, and a desk sat under a long window that was covered in thick curtains. Shadow shut the door behind her and turned slowly, shaking her head.

The room reminded her of William Chadwick's house. It was stuffed with occult curiosities, a variety of astrolabes, a huge globe of the world, and things she quite honestly didn't recognise. Henri was a member of the Order of the Midnight Sun, so she presumed he'd be some kind of lover of alchemy, science, math, or astronomy—or all of them. But now was not the time to linger.

She scanned the bookshelves looking for the red leather case, but although there were plenty of rolled up scrolls, there was nothing of that description. Damn Herne's hairy balls, and damn Harlan. There were a few cupboards and glass cabinets and she searched them too, again finding nothing, and she turned back to the desk, just spotting the case peeking out from under a jumble of paperwork. Excellent. That must be it. She had just placed her hand on it when she heard the unmistakable sound of the handle turning and the door opening. There was only one place to hide—behind the thick velvet curtains.

Shadow squashed behind them, her back pressed to the cold window, and heard the pad of footsteps across the floor. She peered through a narrow gap in the curtains, seeing a young, petite woman with short, spiky black hair and wearing a catering jacket look around the room. She walked quickly to the table, picked up the red leather case that Shadow had just exposed, and slid the map out to examine it. Seemingly satisfied, she rolled it back up and slid it into a cardboard tube, similar to the one Shadow had strung across her back.

Shadow had a moment of indecision. Should she step out now, overpower the thief, and claim the map, or follow her? She was pretty sure she would win in a fight, but she'd give herself away. And any noise would attract attention. She needed to be patient, and clenching her hands, she waited.

The woman headed to the door again, paused to listen, and then left. Within seconds, Shadow darted after her, following her silently, before coming to a sudden halt partway down the stairs. This time there was no easy exit. The catering staff were packing up their equipment and chatting loudly, and a stack of plastic boxes sat by the open back door. The thief placed the map onto the top of one of the large containers, picked it up, and shouted as she headed outside, "I'll start packing the van."

For a moment Shadow hung back at the bottom of the steps, and when it was clear no one was about to follow her, she cloaked herself in her fey magic and sprinted into the shrubbery. She worked her way to the drive, just in time to see the woman put the box into the back of the van. She froze, back to the wall, relieved to see the mystery woman return to the house, the security light illuminating her short, slim figure. Who are you?

Barely waiting for her to be out of sight, Shadow wrenched the back door of the van open and clambered in, fumbling through the jumble of objects until her fingers closed on the cardboard tube. She grabbed it, swapping it for her own empty one, and then leapt out, just as she heard the front door open and the sound of voices approaching. Shadow didn't hesitate. She ran to the boundary wall and retreated the way she had come, only pausing when she was safely sheltered in the dark corner of the garden next to the footpath.

Harlan was nowhere in sight, but she trusted the fact that he'd be alongside the road somewhere. Taking one last look behind her, she vaulted the wall, and spotting the car idling further along, sauntered to it as if she hadn't got a care in the world.

When she slid inside, the warm air wrapped around her, and Harlan looked at her expectantly. "Got it?"

"Eventually. Go—now."

Two

H arlan focussed on driving down the twisting country lanes, checking his rear view mirror frequently, but no one was pursuing them, and the roads were quiet around the sleepy Devon seaside town.

Shadow looked composed as she leaned back in the passenger seat, the map on her lap. She was dressed in black and her long, slim legs were stretched out into the foot well. Even a close run-in with other thieves didn't faze her, and Harlan rolled his shoulders as he allowed himself to relax. "Are you sure they didn't see you?"

"Positive." A smile played at the corner of her lips. "I was tempted to fight her for it, but I decided stealth was the best option. Have you any idea who she is?"

Harlan grimaced, running through a few options. "Not really. There are several groups that steal for the black market, and a couple are more prominent than most. I know a few of them, but I don't recognise her description. But of course, I don't know them all. They aren't groups we generally associate with." Shadow sniggered next to him, and Harlan gave her a sharp stare. "What?"

"You sound so morally upright, and yet you sent me in there to steal a map from a man you know!" She shook her head with a mocking glance. "Harlan, Harlan, Harlan! I think you're in denial."

Harlan shifted in his seat and clenched the wheel. "Tonight's activity isn't something we do regularly, and for the record, I like Henri and feel very guilty about stealing it. But it's necessary."

"Necessary for what? I've indulged you tonight. I didn't ask questions about this map or why it's important, but someone else wants it—right now! Coincidence? I think not." Her voice was teasing and mischievous. "What's going on, Harlan?"

"Nothing."

"Bullshit."

"You've picked up some very interesting vocabulary."

"I know. It's so that I fit in. And I like swearing. Now, stop changing the subject and tell me what prompted the theft." She crossed her legs and reached for the bottle of water in the drink holder. "We have a long journey back to White Haven, after all."

Harlan fell silent for a moment as he considered how much to tell her. He had deliberately held back information before the theft in case anything went wrong, but now, well, Shadow and the Nephilim were going to get more involved with this, and he had a feeling this was going to get complicated—especially as it seemed others were interested. He gave her a sidelong glance. "Okay, but this is between you, me, and the Nephilim. Don't go running off to the witches with this!"

"How dare you!"

"Dare you my ass. Promise?"

Shadow snorted. "All right."

"The map you have stolen tonight is called The Map of the Seeker. It was made in 1432 and indicates a place in England that allows the worthy a way to talk to angels. But it has long been thought to be fantasy and therefore although beautiful, was considered essentially art and not fact."

"I presume it's been investigated, then?"

"Sure," Harlan nodded. "Extensively at one point, and then it was kind of forgotten, because the actual place was never found, and it was thought to be a hoax perpetrated by the mapmaker himself, Phineas Hammond. I mean, not surprising, right? A place to talk to angels? Henri bought it for its beauty. It's not particularly worth a lot."

"So, what's happened to change that?"

Harlan negotiated the turn onto the main road and sighed. "Phineas was a low-order magician and scryer who could talk to spirits, and he said an angel had contacted him and told him where a worthy man could talk to them directly. But of course it wasn't that simple. The place was in an obscure and hidden temple. There was a ritual to follow to enable the doorway—or whatever you want to call it—to open, and there was also a key that was needed. The final piece. Collectively they are called The Trinity of the Seeker. All the written accounts of it, especially in the fifteenth century, said Phineas had finished making the trinity, but had decided they were too dangerous to keep together, so he separated them."

"If he thought they were that dangerous, why even make it in the first place?" Shadow asked, incredulous.

"I don't think he had much choice—he was compelled by the angel to do it. If I recall correctly, it sent him mad, and he had just enough about to him to break the trinity apart before he died."

"It killed him?"

"Sort of. He kept a diary and records, which by the end were a rambling mess. We must have a copy somewhere," he said thoughtfully.

"And the key? Did he make it, or was he given it?"

Harlan laughed dryly. "No one really knows. Anyway, a few weeks ago, a rare book collector was employed to appraise a private library. The owner had died and the family wanted it catalogued, ready for sale. It was quite the treasure trove, apparently. But he found a document that had been wrongly catalogued for years." He glanced at Shadow, who was watching him with narrowed eyes. "That's not uncommon, by the way. There are probably thousands of documents long thought lost just shoved in a drawer somewhere in the basement of a library or museum. After doing some work on it, the appraiser realised what he'd found. It was The Path of the Seeker."

"Wow. Part of the trinity."

"Yep. It's coming up for auction this week—but no one should know, at the moment. My contact gave me a head's up a few days ago. JD wants it, and he wants the map."

"But obviously someone else knows, too."

Harlan nodded, distracted, his mind once again whirling through the possibilities. "It seems so."

"And JD wants it because of the angel connection."

"Yep."

"Are you saying he actually *spoke* to angels?" Shadow's voice was dripping with scepticism.

"JD or Phineas?"

"Both."

"You know, many people claim to do just that."

"But they don't exist."

"Even though the Nephilim are sons of angels?" he replied, equally scathingly.

Once again he felt Shadow turn to stare at him and he glanced at her, her face brindled with lights from the road. "They are some kind of fey. Not heavenly creatures. Are you seriously telling me you believe in God? Just one! The big guy with the beard in the sky?"

Harlan squirmed. "Not particularly. But there are many Gods and Goddesses and entities we really don't understand. Look at the Empusa! She was Hecate's enforcer in the Underworld. I think what we're arguing about is semantics. You're objecting to me calling them angels, because you want to call them fey. But in the end, we're not denying they exist. Fey or angels? What does it matter what their name is?"

"Because to call them angels suggests they have some kind of heavenly message and righteous role, while fey suggest something far more earthbound—although admittedly Otherworldly."

Harlan's head was already starting to ache, and he wasn't really in the mood for theological or philosophical discussions. "But the Nephilim are something, aren't they?"

"We're all *something*, Harlan! Yes. I agree, there are many Gods and Goddesses—we all remember the mess that ensued at Beltane." She shrugged at his startled glance. "Anyway. Did Phineas speak with an angel, or whatever we want to call it?"

"According to him, yes, through a vision! I have no idea of the angel's name, however."

Shadow groaned. "It sounds too pat. I mean, why tell him? Why wasn't JD told when he talked to angels?"

"I have no idea, Shadow! Do I look like an oracle?"

Shadow drank some water and then asked, "Why does JD care? He speaks to angels already, right? In his Enochian language. What does it matter to him?"

"Ah, that! It turns out JD hasn't spoken to them in years. He was never able to scry effectively, and that's why he had a partner. A man called Kelley who died years ago. Since then, he's had to rely on other mediums, but they've never been as effective—and of course JD hasn't wanted to reveal who he truly is. He thinks the trinity is his way back to them."

"But why? What do they give him? What's the point?"

"Knowledge, Shadow. Haven't you got that yet? That's all that matters to these men. Knowledge and the power it gives them. The key to life itself."

"He found immortality. Hasn't he solved that one?"

Harlan shook his head and laughed softly. "Immortality is just one part of it. It's an addiction—seeking something that is forever just past their fingertips. And to every one of them, knowledge is something slightly different. It's intangible, nebulous, and all the more attractive for it."

"It's a wonder he hasn't gone mad over the years."

"Who? JD? I think he might have, on occasion, and dragged himself back from the brink. Have you been reading about him?"

Shadow nodded. "I have. He's an interesting character."

"That's one way of putting it."

"The map is for JD, then?"

"Yes." Harlan glanced at her. "He wants to find this place—desperately."

"Right," Shadow said, almost audibly rolling her eyes. "And the catering thief? Who is she and who is she stealing it for?"

"Well, those are the million-dollar questions."

Gabe was waiting in the lamp-lit living room at the farmhouse for Shadow to return with Harlan, as Niel, Ash, Barak, and Nahum waited with him.

He'd been nervous all night, ever since she left, and he knew it was stupid because Shadow was more than capable of looking after herself, but nevertheless, he was still worried.

"Gabe, will you relax?" Nahum said from where he sat on the sofa sipping a beer, completely at ease in a loose t-shirt and cotton trousers.

Gabe was standing at the window, looking out on the dark fields behind the house. "I'm trying, and failing."

"We know," Barak said, dryly. "Have a beer."

"I want to keep a clear head, just in case." Gabe glanced at his watch. "They should be here soon." He turned back to the room, unnerved to find his brothers reclining in their respective chairs, ignoring the TV and watching him with amusement. "What?"

"You," Ash said, smirking, "are worried about Shadow. You going to fly in and rescue her?"

"If necessary."

Niel laughed. "How very gallant of you."

"Piss off. All of you."

Barak winked. "Like the feel of her in your arms, brother? Don't think we haven't noticed how you like to take her flying."

He knew they were teasing him, but right now he wanted to punch them. "I can count on one hand the amount of times I've done that, so don't exaggerate!" They all just smiled at him with infuriatingly knowing expressions, and Gabe added, "Besides, she's our business partner. I like to keep her happy."

"Uh-huh," Nahum said. "I bet you do."

Gabe was about to offer a more scathing response when he heard the front door open, and the clatter of footsteps down the hall. He turned toward the door, relieved when Shadow walked in, closely followed by Harlan.

Shadow beamed and waved the cardboard roll. "Success, renegades!" She glanced behind her at Harlan. "I've persuaded him to let us look at it."

Harlan nodded in greeting. "I'd say she threatened more than persuaded me."

"Yeah, she does that," Nahum answered, a smirk still on his face.

Shadow hesitated, looking around the room suspiciously. "What's with you guys? You look...weird!"

"Nothing!" Gabe said hurriedly. "Show us the bounty!"

Shadow headed to the low coffee table, and aided by Nahum, cleared the space and extracted the map. "You're going to like this, boys."

"We will?" Gabe asked. "Why?"

"It's a map that tells you where to speak to angels." Shadow smiled triumphantly as she started to unroll the document.

Gabe exchanged a troubled glance with the others. "It does *what*?"

Harlan held his hands up. "Don't get too excited! It's long been thought to be fantasy."

"Until now," Shadow pointed out. She looked at Gabe, her violet eyes mischievous. "Someone else wanted this, too. I stole it from her."

"Tell us everything," Gabe insisted.

For the next few minutes, Shadow and Harlan told them about their evening, and the Nephilim clustered around the table as Shadow secured the map. She pinned down the edges with nearby objects, revealing a large, detailed drawing of a place called Angel's Rest and the surrounding area. It was fantastical in design, filled with images of mythical beasts, winged creatures, and many symbols.

"Where's this?" Niel asked, studying it intently.

"In the Mendips, which is in the southwest of England," Harlan explained, making himself comfortable on the sofa and taking the beer that Gabe held out to him. "Have you heard of it?"

Nahum shook his head. "No, but that's not surprising. There are lots of places we don't know."

"Fair enough. The Mendips is a huge area, and parts of it are designated nature reserves. It's riddled with limestone caves, gorges, woods, and small villages. There has been mining there in the past. Angel's Rest," he said, nodding to it, "is a village, very picturesque, but otherwise unremarkable, other than being in a place of natural beauty. It still exists, obviously, so we can pinpoint the area where this map covers with reasonable accuracy. But none of it is in proportion." He ran his finger along a craggy line on the map. "Here, for example, is where Ebbor Gorge runs." He shrugged. "And, yes of course, the landscape has changed, but even at the time the map was made it didn't make sense."

Gabe was still standing, his back to the fire as he looked at the map. "I presume the area was explored many times over the years?"

"Absolutely, and nothing was found. The spot right here on the gorge," his finger hovered over a drawing of columns and an apex roof, "is a tiny drawing of a temple, and underneath it says *The Temple of the Seeker*—but it doesn't exist." Gabe drew closer to look, squinting at the tiny, precise lettering as Harlan continued. "Even if it did, there is some kind of path that must be followed in order to allow the seeker to speak to angels." Harlan scratched his head, looking slightly embarrassed. "Everyone thought Phineas had manufactured a hoax. And he wasn't that well-respected as a magician anyway, partly because, I think, he hadn't accrued a huge amount of money and resources, and that goes a long way in the alchemy world."

"You mean he wasn't a gentleman," Gabe said, already knowing how the world of alchemy worked.

"Exactly. And he wasn't thought to be a genuine medium, either."

Ash nodded thoughtfully. "So, the map was ignored and forgotten."

"Yes." Harlan took a sip of his beer. "But, it is beautiful, and very typical of manuscripts of the time."

Shadow had been listening quietly while she examined the map. "There are pictures of angels and fantastical creatures, and even the trees are detailed. I can't believe Henri didn't display this on the wall."

"So Shadow stole this is for JD?" Barak asked, and it was obvious his interest was already stirring.

"Yes," Harlan nodded. "Now that The Path of the Seeker has been found, the second part of the trinity, he is determined to find the temple. As I explained to Shadow, he can no longer talk to angels the way he used to—it frustrates him."

Gabe wasn't surprised. He had spent hours talking to JD on the two occasions he'd met him, and he eventually had revealed he had long since lost the ability to communicate with them. His obsession with angels, however, was baffling, and it had made Gabe rethink his own desire to try to contact his father. He was conflicted about the whole thing. But he said to Harlan, "I take it that you will be buying the document at the auction?"

"Yes—I hope. We have deep pockets for this one. But potentially, considering what happened tonight, someone else will bid strongly for it as well. On the plus side for us, The Orphic Guild is known for our work in the occult world, and it won't seem strange for us to want to buy it."

"Won't the theft of the map make your interest in the second document suspicious?" Nahum asked, looking between Harlan and Shadow. "Henri might suspect you."

"Maybe," Harlan admitted, "but we weren't seen anywhere near Henri's house, so that's in our favour."

"You hope," Gabe said, frowning.

Harlan continued, a brief nod of the head his only concession to that concern. "When news of the auction breaks, Henri might think we're buying it to sell it on for a high price—maybe to him!" He tried to look innocent and wide-eyed. "I had *no idea* that the map was stolen!"

Ash groaned. "Oh, this is so underhanded!"

"Which is why it's so perfect," Shadow said, smiling sweetly.

"Why not approach Henri directly to buy his map?" Gabe asked.

"Because that might have made him suspect we have something," Harlan told him.

Gabe crouched down to examine the map, squashing between Ash and Barak. It was a work of art. It was drawn with incredible skill, and considering the detail of the landscape it was odd that nothing had been found, even if the distances weren't accurate. It made it seem all the more likely it was a hoax—or to be more charitable, a work of fiction and hope.

"Wow," Barak said, looking both surprised and impressed. "So, JD is really going to try to find it. What makes him think he'll be successful now?"

"Because he has you." Harlan looked at them and smiled. "It's likely this place is below ground with an as yet unfound access point. And of course we have to remember that the whole thing sent Phineas mad."

Nahum laughed. "Okay. Now it's getting interesting!"

"Hold on," Shadow said, her hand on Harlan's arm. "JD wants our help with all of this? You didn't say that before!"

He looked sheepish. "I wanted to secure the map first. And we need The Path of the Seeker as well, but it doesn't mean we shouldn't start work on finding the temple."

Niel looked at him, amused. "You called it The Trinity of the Seeker and mentioned a key. Aren't we missing an important part, even supposing we find the temple?"

Harlan leaned against the back of the sofa, and although he looked tired, his eyes danced with excitement. "Yes, we are. But The Path of the Seeker hasn't been seen for *hundreds* of years! To find it changes everything! The trinity has become more tangible—less like a hoax."

"*If* you can buy it," Nahum reminded him. "What if you're outbid? Does that mean we steal that, too?"

Harlan scratched his chin and smiled ruefully. "It might."

Shadow threw her head back and laughed. "I like this. It's more convoluted by the minute."

"However," Harlan added, "I'll be able to examine the document soon, before the auction. I'm hoping it will give us more clues to the key—even if I don't buy it. There'll be photos." He grimaced. "It's unfortunate, but everyone will have access to its contents. But the key has to be out there somewhere."

Gabe drained his beer. "And everyone will have access to copies of the map, surely?"

"Maybe. The current images are poor, and Henri certainly never shared any. And," Harlan laughed, "this isn't treasure we're talking about—it's a gateway to the angels. How many people are really going to be interested in that? Anyway, we have the map now, thanks to Shadow. I'll take it back to London tomorrow. Once I've shown this to JD, we can decide what's next. I'll be in touch about arranging a visit to the site." He looked suddenly uncertain. "Of course, this is presuming you're interested?"

Gabe saw the interest in everyone's eyes, and he answered cautiously. "I think we are."

"Good," Harlan said, rolling the map up. "I'll talk to him and call you tomorrow."

Gabe watched as Shadow stood to see Harlan out, and once they'd left the room, he sank into the closest chair and sighed. "That was unexpected."

Nahum had been gazing into the fire thoughtfully, but now he nodded, suddenly alert. "It was. What do you think?"

"I think it will be a dead end, but I admit I'm curious."

"And we're going to get paid," Ash pointed out, "so why not?"

Niel grunted. "Because I'm not so sure we want the angels—fallen or not—knowing we're here."

"You think that would be a bad thing?" Barak asked, eyes narrowing.

"Don't you?" he replied, ominously.

They looked up as Shadow re-entered the room, and she sat on the sofa, her eyes full of intrigue. "You all look serious!"

Gabe grimaced. "We're debating how likely this is to be true—it sounds like medieval madness."

Shadow peeled off her black leather boots and socks, and sat cross-legged, her elbows on her knees. "I agree, but it is interesting that someone else was trying to steal it. Surely that gives it some merit."

"I think," Nahum said, "that it probably gives the map more value, now that the path has been found. That's all." He cocked his head at her. "You sure you weren't spotted?"

"Very sure. But I'd love to know who the mystery woman is."

"Me too," Gabe mused. "Any whiff of the paranormal about her?"

"Not that I saw." She shrugged. "But I could be wrong."

Barak feigned choking on his beer. "You admit what?"

"It's rare, I know," she said, shrugging his sarcasm off. "But we're in, right?"

Gabe felt his blood already stirring with excitement. "Of course we are."

Three

The Orphic Guild's London office was bathed in spring sunshine when Harlan arrived the next morning. He had opted to drive to the office, rather than risk the tube with his precious cargo.

As he strolled through the front door into the wide reception hall, Robert Smythe, Mason Jacobs's secretary, was coming down the stairs and he narrowed his eyes at Harlan. "There you are! We thought you'd got lost."

Harlan bit back a stinging retort and opted for sarcasm. "I have many abilities, but flying over London traffic isn't one of them. Is Mason free?"

Robert was a prissy man who thought he ruled the London branch just because he was Mason's secretary, and his tone was abrupt with pretty much everyone except for Mason. Harlan was aware that his jeans and leather jacket didn't endear him to Robert either, who was already fussing with the cuffs of his expensive shirt. "Not until eleven. He's in a meeting right now."

Harlan checked his watch. "Excellent. Time for a coffee before I see him. Book me in, will you, just so he knows to expect me." Harlan walked past him and up the stairs to his office, not waiting for a response. Robert brought out the worst in him. He shouted over the banister, "Are Aiden or Olivia here?"

Robert barely bothered to slow down, "Olivia is, Aiden will be here later."

Harlan nodded and continued to his room, noting a new stack of files on his desk, and curious, he checked their contents. All the files were prepared by the small administrative team. It was their job to keep an eye on upcoming auctions and prepare reports for the collectors. They also took phone calls from prospective clients, gathering details of each possible case for the collectors to review. They were divided equally between Olivia, Aiden, and Harlan, except if they were returning clients who were then always referred to the respective collector. Only when they had reviewed the information and sometimes discussed them together did they take them to Mason for the final call. More often than not, he approved their decisions.

The files were a mixture of the usual requests: old occult manuscripts, weapons, jewellery, and magical objects. One caught Harlan's eye. A new client had requested help finding a cursed painting. *Interesting*. He moved it to the top of the pile, and then made himself a coffee from his state of the art espresso machine. While Harlan liked to use the staffroom on the ground floor, sometimes it was easier and quicker to have his machine at hand. Once he'd downed the first cup, he made a second and carried it down the hall to Olivia's office. He knocked and opened the door, peering in cautiously. He grinned when he saw she was free. "Is this a good time to talk?"

Olivia was seated behind her desk going through her own files, and she looked up and smiled. She was a similar age to him, slim and toned, a result of regular workouts that included running, climbing, and boxing.

"You're back! Sure, come on in." Olivia's mid-length, caramel-toned hair had a soft curl to it, and she pushed it away from her face and leaned back, picking up her cup as she did so. "I see you brought your own coffee."

He looked rueful. "It's my second, and I've only just walked through the door. I've been driving for hours and needed a shot of caffeine."

"Of course. You've been in Devon. How did it go?"

"And Cornwall," he reminded her. "I picked Shadow up last night to steal the map and stayed at Alex's flat."

Olivia nodded as she recognised the names. "The witch in White Haven and our fey friend. How did it go?"

"Successfully, but it wasn't without problems. Someone else tried to steal that map, but Shadow beat her to it. I'm trying to work out who it was. Shadow described a young woman with spiky black hair. Any ideas?"

Olivia narrowed her eyes and tapped her cup with her manicured fingers. "It rings a bell. I think I saw her at an auction only a couple of weeks ago."

"An auction for what?" Harlan asked, leaning forward.

"Dark Age grave goods and stone carved idols." Olivia frowned. "I can't be sure, because they weren't sitting together, but there was something about their studied avoidance of each other that made me think she was with Nicoli."

"Damn it," Harlan said, groaning. Andreas Nicoli ran The Order of Lilith, another occult organisation that had far shadier morals than The Orphic Guild, and one of the more prominent groups they competed with. "I hoped it wouldn't be them. Any idea what they were after?" It was always an advantage to know what the opposition was up to.

"No. They brought a couple of very ordinary stone idols, with no valuable occult or paranormal connections that I could discern. However," she said, also leaning forward and putting her now empty cup to the side, "she could be working for someone entirely different, or be a private operator. If she *is* working for Andreas, it's worrying they want the map. That means they'll be bidding for The Path of the Seeker, too."

"If they don't steal it first."

Olivia's eyes widened. "You think they would?"

"I think it's a possibility," Harlan said, running his hand across his chin and realising he really should have shaved that morning. "What the hell day is it?"

Olivia laughed. "Monday. When's your auction?"

"Wednesday night. Good. That doesn't give them a lot of time."

"Which auction house?"

"Burton and Knight."

"Even better," Olivia said, looking relieved. "Nicoli wouldn't dare to piss them off."

She was right about that, Harlan mused. Burton and Knight was a small auction house specialising in the occult. No one working in the paranormal world would want to get on their bad side, or they'd find themselves banned from future auctions. It had happened once before, as far as Harlan knew, to an organisation called The House of Sigils, and they had ended up collapsing. It was a sober reminder to everyone else.

"True," he said brightly. "But I think it will get expensive."

"And if you win, we need to find somewhere very safe to store it."

"But if we lose, we need to steal it."

"Wow." Olivia folded her arms across her chest. "Are we that serious about this?"

"We stole the damn map, Olivia. JD wants this!"

"A map to angels?"

"Yes!" Olivia had no idea who JD really was, and it galled Harlan not to tell her. "But who else would want it so much that they'd be willing to steal for it, too?"

She fell silent for a moment. "I don't know, but Aiden will be in later. We should talk to him."

"Good suggestion. But now," he said, rising to his feet, "I need to see the boss. Catch you later."

He headed to Mason's office, and five minutes later, after Harlan had explained everything, Mason looked very annoyed. "Bloody Nicoli? JD won't like this."

Harlan decided now was the time for his request. "We need to act quickly to find the location. Gabe and Shadow are keen to help. They're just waiting for our permission."

Mason sighed thoughtfully and nodded at the map, still rolled up on his desk. "Will it really be that difficult?"

"Yes. I know you want JD to study it first, but under the circumstances, I don't think we should wait."

"All right. Send them as soon as possible."

"We'll have to book them in somewhere."

"That's fine. Liaise with them and see what they want." Harlan stood, and Mason pushed the map towards him. "Take this with you, and get admin to photocopy it—or scan it—as good a quality as possible, and send it to them. I'll phone JD." But as Harlan was heading out the door, he spoke again. "By the way, I heard from Chadwick's solicitors yesterday. He left us his house in his will."

Harlan paused at the threshold, confused. "William Chadwick left us his house? As in The Orphic Guild?" Chadwick had commissioned them to find the druid Kian's tomb, and had then been possessed by Kian's ghost, and was subsequently killed by Shadow.

Mason was leaning back in his chair, looking solemn. "Yes. It's a stipulation of his will that we leave his collections intact, and has requested that we properly curate them, but we can use the house as a base for anyone we choose. Contractors, for example, who need to stay in town for a couple of nights."

Harlan was momentarily stunned and leaned against the doorframe. "Why us? Why not any relatives?"

Mason shrugged. "I think in many ways we were his family, and I was a good friend, of course." He absently stroked the lapel of his suit jacket. "I am honoured, obviously, and also relieved, if I'm honest. All that work he put into his collection." He shook his head. "It would have been terrible to split it up. I'm going to pick the keys up and visit there later."

"Do you think anyone will contest the will?"

"No, I doubt it. He left enough money to his surviving relative—a nephew, I believe."

Harlan thought of the night that Chadwick died, and felt a wave of regret wash over him. "I'm sorry, Mason. I wish it hadn't happened, and I know Shadow does, too."

Mason brushed his concern away. "It was Kian's fault, not Shadow's." And then he bent over the papers on his desk and Harlan shut the door softly behind him.

Shadow was riding Kailen, her cherished horse, when her phone buzzed in her jacket pocket, and she halted on the rise of the hill overlooking the sea below.

The coast stretched out on either side, the cliffs high in places, and the waves crashing against their feet. She could see the occasional walker on narrow belts of beach, a few others taking the cliff path, and lots of seagulls. One wheeled on the air above her, screeching as she answered. "Hi, Harlan."

"Hey, Shadow. Good news. Mason wants you to go to Angel's Rest as soon as possible. Any chance you can get there today?"

Shadow grinned triumphantly, as Kailen fretted beneath her. "I think so. Gabe is at Caspian's right now, but he's making arrangements to cover security." The Nephilim still worked for the shipping branch of Kernow Industries, but Gabe was planning to leave Barak in charge.

"Good. I thought I'd book you in somewhere close by. Any preferences? We're paying, obviously."

"Some place outside the town, the bigger the better, and at least three bedrooms. Niel will probably come with us."

"Okay. Leave it with me," Harlan said, already sounding distracted. "I'm going to get you a copy of the map, and I'll send it on as soon as it's done. And Shadow, be careful. There are others looking for this, and I'm not sure how ruthless they will be."

Shadow felt a thrill of excitement rush through her. She never felt more alive than when she had opponents. It made her blood sing. "That's no problem at all."

She ended the call and turned Kailen back towards home, urging him to a gallop, and dropping low against him. It was a shame she wouldn't be able to take him with her, but the others would take care of him; all of the Nephilim were excellent riders. When she arrived back home, she spent some time rubbing Kailen down before stabling him, and then she headed inside to shower. By the time she emerged, Harlan had phoned to confirm their accommodation and Gabe had arrived. She could see his SUV in the courtyard.

Shadow's hair was still wet when she walked into the kitchen where he and Niel were chatting at the kitchen table, and her skin was damp from the shower. She'd been so anxious to speak to them she'd barely dried herself. She was hot and barefoot, wearing only a sleeveless t-shirt and her slim fitting jeans. She saw Gabe try not to stare at her figure, which gave her immense satisfaction.

"Heard anything?" Niel asked.

The big, blond Nephilim was cradling a cup of coffee, and he leaned back in his seat, watching Shadow with lively blue eyes. The hair on either side of his head above his ears was shaved, and the rest of it was tied back, making him look more Viking-like than usual.

She helped herself to coffee and dropped into a chair at the end of the table. "I certainly have. Harlan has given us the go-ahead and booked us a place starting today. Are you both ready to go?"

They nodded, and Gabe said, "We've been checking the area. Angel's Rest still seems like a small village, although from what I can recall, there are a few more roads and buildings than on the old map."

"Not surprising though, is it?" Niel said. "Six hundred or so years have passed since its creation."

"Harlan is sending us a copy of the map. How long will it take to get there?" Shadow asked.

"Not long, about three hours," Gabe told her. He checked his watch. "There are a few more things I need to do, but I can be ready in an hour. Does that sound good for you two?" They both nodded, and Gabe rose to his feet. "Good. Let's take weapons, ropes, and other useful supplies. Who knows where we'll end up, or who might be there waiting."

Four

By the time Gabe, Niel, and Shadow arrived at the house that Harlan had booked for them, Gabe was cranky and feeling cramped.

The traffic from Cornwall to the Mendips was heavy, and because they had set out mid-afternoon, they hit lots of commuter traffic, too. Once they'd left the M5 they followed A roads, heading east through Cheddar, and then took a minor road to the house. The Mendips was a designated Area of Outstanding National Beauty and was a popular tourist attraction, for good reason. The route wound through a beautiful landscape, and they had all been quiet as they absorbed their surroundings.

Fortunately, they were outside the holiday season, but Gabe knew the place was popular with walking groups, and potentially that would be an issue. The Mendips was also huge, but the area they were focussed on was in the southeast, near Ebbor Gorge and Wookey Hole. However, the concerns they had talked about on the journey disappeared as he stopped the car at a gated entrance situated on a leafy lane, and gazed at a large, medieval manor house built in warm mellow stone.

"Are you sure that's it?" he said over his shoulder to Shadow, who had been giving him the directions.

"Yes," she answered impatiently. "I know how GPS works."

"But that's enormous!"

Niel was in the passenger seat, and he laughed. "That's Harlan for you. I daresay he'll be staying at some point, and so will JD, and maybe even Mason. I guess they won't want to slum it!"

Gabe whistled softly. "Well, if you're sure." He put the SUV into gear, rolled through the gate, and parked on an immaculate gravel drive.

"I did tell Harlan we needed privacy," Shadow said as she exited the car. "And I think we've got that."

As Gabe shut the door, he looked around at the surrounding high wall and trees. "This place must have cost a fortune."

Niel grabbed their bags from the boot. "How do we get in?"

"There's a key safe around the side," Shadow told him, already crunching across the gravel. "I've got the code. I'll get it."

Gabe took his overnight bag from Niel and hefted a box of food into his arms, and as they walked to the entrance, he said, "This is a good choice. I like that it's so private."

Niel shrugged and grimaced. "Too many trees for my liking—people can hide there."

"But it hides us, too. The first thing I want to do is get our bearings. I want this map narrowed down as much as possible, or we could be here for weeks."

Niel laughed dryly. "More like years."

Shadow rounded the corner of the house with the keys in her hand, and stepping past Gabe onto the double height porch, she let them in and disabled the alarm system. As Gabe followed her inside, his mouth dropped open as he gazed at the immense hall in front of him and the large staircase that swept up to the next floor. "Wow. It's really quite something!"

Shadow smirked. "Best place you've ever stayed?"

Gabe looked at her, amused, as memories of other homes flooded back from millennia ago. "I wouldn't say that. Didn't you know I was royalty in my day?"

She cocked her head as she appraised him. "Royalty? No, I did not!"

"Well, I was—for a while, at least." He walked across the hall and put his bag on the side table. "My palace was made of marble and decorated with priceless silks. I was groomed and oiled, ate only the best food, and hunted on my own lands." He enjoyed watching her surprised expression as her gaze swept from his head to his toes. He looked at Niel, who was sniggering. "And him, too. A palace in a forested land on a mountain ridge, surrounded by snow and ice."

Shadow's gaze slid to Niel, who was still laughing, his arms folded across his chest. A memory flashed into Gabe's mind of Niel wearing his bearskin cloak that he wore in the mountains above Mesopotamia. Despite his northern European appearance, he had been born in the Middle East. His fallen angel father was a white-blond warrior with ice blue eyes and wings the colour of freshly fallen snow. Gabe shook his head to clear his vision. It had been a long time since either of them had seen him.

"Well! Aren't you two full of surprises?" Shadow said, looking marginally annoyed. "I thought you were warriors and mercenaries, not pampered princesses."

Gabe continued to tease her, knowing she was trying to get him to bite. "We were that, too. There's so much more you don't know about us! But, now's not the time. Let's check this place out, find bedrooms, cook, and plan."

———◦○◦———

Half an hour later, after they investigated the house from top to bottom and chose bedrooms, the trio met in the conservatory at the back of the house that connected to the large, well equipped kitchen. It was full of plants, and had a central table surrounded by wicker chairs on a tiled floor. It was light and airy, and late evening sunshine slanted through the windows.

On their way to the Mendips they had stopped and printed the scanned copy of the map that Harlan had sent Shadow. It was good quality with a high resolution, and they had been able to print a large size. They had also bought a detailed map of the surrounding area, and Gabe laid out both side by side, and stood staring at them with his hands on his hips.

"Bollocks. There are differences."

Niel grunted. "Not surprising. Harlan said Hammond's map wasn't geographically correct."

"Where was he from?" Gabe asked, aware there were many more questions he should have asked Harlan and hadn't.

"Hammond? Right here in Angel's Rest," Shadow said, glancing up at him, her violet eyes bright in the fading light. She'd relaxed her glamour, allowing her Otherness to shine through, and she seemed almost ethereal, making Gabe feel like a block of stone in comparison. "But what does that matter?"

"I wondered if he'd drawn this from his vision or from memory, or both." Gabe ran his finger across The Map of the Seeker, tracing lines and hills. "The fantasy images are so detailed, but it's odd the map itself is inaccurate."

"I don't think it's odd," Shadow answered. "Maps are very hard to get right, unless you're a cartographer—vision or not!"

Gabe sighed. "I suppose. Harlan said there were other records, like his diary. They must give some background."

Niel was standing on the other side of Shadow, and he frowned. "What if it's just a product of his fervent imagination?"

Shadow shook her head. "No. Places on it actually exist. Angel's Rest, for example. That's half a mile up the road. And Deerleap Standing Stones. And Ebbor Gorge, of course—the temple is marked partway along it. Although the gorge's shape is different on Hammond's map, it's clear that it's still Ebbor Gorge." She shrugged. "I don't see what the problem is. It's in the gorge, somewhere. And Harlan has thoughtfully booked this house very close to it."

"It doesn't mean it isn't still fantasy," Gabe said. He looked out the windows towards the setting sun. "Let's eat, and then when darkness falls we can fly, Niel. We'll see better from overhead."

"And what will *I* do?" Shadow asked, looking put out.

Gabe grinned at her. "You can stay here and study the map."

She narrowed her eyes at him, and Gabe was pretty sure she'd be doing nothing of the sort, but he winked and headed to the shower, leaving Niel to cook.

———◆○◆———

When it was fully dark out, Gabe and Niel walked onto the lawn at the back of the house, unfurled their wings, and lifted easily into the night.

The moon was waning, covered occasionally by scudding clouds, and Gabe felt his spirits lift as he climbed higher, using the currents to carry him. Below were clusters of lights from the small villages, but large areas were swathed in darkness. He took a moment to orientate himself, noting Angel's Rest below, a short distance from their house that had a few lit windows visible. A little farther up the valley he could see other isolated buildings, and he smiled. This was quite some place. If nothing else, he would enjoy being here. It was important for them to know their new homeland, and he resolved they should travel more often.

For a while he drifted on the wind, enjoying the freedom that flight gave him, and the feeling of power. His strong build gave him advantages over humans, but that was nothing compared to this. His conversation with Shadow earlier had set him thinking, and all evening he'd been mulling on the past and his history, and it had made him restless. He wondered if it had affected Niel, too. Sometimes, it seemed as if the other Nephilim were more comfortable with their present circumstances than he was. But that changed too, depending on his mood. He blinked in an effort to clear his thoughts and focussed on the landscape below.

Gabe's sight had adjusted quickly to the night, and he noted the rugged cliffs, patches of woodland, and wide-open fields that unfurled below him. Dropping lower, he saw the tangled trees that filled the Ebbor Gorge, and he drifted downwards, finally landing on a rocky outcrop overlooking the valley. Within minutes, Niel had joined him.

"There are caves spread below here, did you know?" Niel asked.

Gabe nodded. "I read about them earlier. Many have been explored. There'll be nothing for us to find there, I'm sure."

"True. But potentially the temple will be hidden by some kind of magic, and could be in a cave," Niel reasoned. "It's certainly not above ground."

"Yeah, to hide it in the open would use a lot of power...but angels are powerful!" Gabe pointed down the valley. "Wookey Hole is an attraction now, and so is Cheddar Gorge. Thousands of visitors pour through there, and the caves."

"But back when Hammond drew his map, far fewer people would have been in there—not like today."

"But it can't be in one of the main caves," Gabe said, shaking his head. "The temple is nowhere near them, according to the map. I think, wherever it is, it hasn't been found—for centuries, at least."

"But this whole area has been inhabited for millennia."

"I know. But surely a place where humans can talk to angels must be one that is hard to get to?"

Niel smiled, his teeth white in the fractured moonlight. "You mean you have to earn the right?"

"Of course. When have the fallen or the other angels ever made anything easy?" Gabe flexed his wings as he surveyed the area below him. "The fallen never made it easy for us, and we're their *children*!"

"I must admit," Niel said softly, "that I wonder if they know we're back."

Gabe turned quickly. "What do you mean?"

"They killed us, brother. Drowned us all. Do they know that a handful of us have returned?" Niel's eyes were intense, dark pools. "Here we are, thousands of years later, having made a miraculous escape from the spirit world. You would think they would have detected us somehow."

Gabe considered his words for a moment. "That's an interesting thought, but why would they? We're living quietly. Unobtrusively. You can't find what you're not looking for."

"True. But we're independent right now—and that's what I like. What if this place really exists? What if somewhere beneath our feet is a channel to the angels, and we draw unwanted attention to ourselves? We could make our new life very hard."

Gabe gazed at Niel's hard, angular face and felt the conviction of his words. "What if *they* don't exist anymore?"

Niel barked out a laugh and looked up at the stars spread above. "Oh, I think they're out there somewhere, far less involved in the human world than they used to be. And I think we're below the radar right now, as humans say. I think we should stay that way."

"You're having second thoughts? Already?"

"I'm torn, if I'm honest. I feel as if we're in a void of sorts, out of touch with our roots. But equally, I like the opportunities it affords us."

Gabe nodded, aware that he thought the same, but still...

Niel gripped Gabe's shoulder with his large hand, callused from years of fighting. "Food for thought, friend. I'll see you back at the house." And with that, Niel plunged over the cliff and then rose majestically as his wings caught the uplift, carrying him over the valley below.

Food for thought, indeed.

As soon as Shadow was alone, she strapped her knives to her thighs and ran across the lawn to the bottom of the garden.

She nimbly climbed the high stone perimeter wall and perched on the top, looking at the vista beyond. There was a copse behind the house, and then for a short distance there were open fields, and then a deeper darkness marked the edge of the tree line that ran up into Ebbor Gorge. She dropped down, threading between the trees, fresh air renewing her energy and resolve. After they had eaten, the three of them had examined the map some more, still bewildered at where to start. They would search in daylight, but Shadow also believed that hidden things were more likely to reveal themselves at night. It was fey belief, and one she often found to be true.

She crossed the fields, and once under the trees again, was forced to slow down. There was no path here, and she edged through the thick undergrowth until she finally found a stony trail leading up a narrow gully into the gorge. At this point it was wrong to call them cliffs, but as she progressed they rose in height around her and she paused, listening to the scurry of wildlife, the hoots of owls and the whoosh of bats in flight. But no human noises reached her, and she pressed forward, past crevices leading into the rock, and the scrub trees clinging to the stone. It was an ancient landscape, barely scarred by humans, and the weight of many years was heavy here. There was so much still to find, she was sure. But not tonight. Tonight was just a chance to get a feel for the place, and smiling to herself, she pushed on.

Five

O n Tuesday morning, Harlan found Aiden in the library of The Orphic Guild, bent over a book on a table under the window.

Weak spring light lit up his dark hair, and as he heard Harlan approach, he looked up and smiled. "Harlan! It's been a while. How are you?"

Aiden was the youngest of the three collectors based in the London office, and Harlan estimated he was in his early thirties. Like himself and Olivia, Aiden had been immersed in the paranormal world for years, and was resourceful and clever, but also more cautious. He also spent a lot of time out of the office, and his clothes reflected it. He was wearing old army fatigues today paired with heavy tramping boots, and it looked like he had barely slept.

"I'm fine, I guess, but how are you?" Harlan asked as he sat down in a chair at the table. "If I'm honest, you look like shit."

Aiden laughed, rubbing his hands through his hair. "I know I do. I arrived back later than expected. I grabbed a couple of hours sleep, and then headed in."

Since the last time Harlan had seen him, Aiden had spent weeks in Scotland tracking down treasure in a castle and had then been in York looking for clues to Viking gold.

"Did you have success in York?" Harlan asked.

Aiden held his hand out and wiggled it. "Maybe. I'm here to check a couple of documents and then I'm leaving again. I heard your druid business was tricky."

Harlan rolled his eyes. "Yeah, but we got there eventually. I take it you've heard about Chadwick's death?"

Aiden nodded. "I have, and am sorry to hear it. Our lifelong obsessions don't always turn out the way we want, do they? Anyway, I hear you're on the path of angels now with a fey and seven Nephilim." He grinned. "Sounds like a fairy tale."

"Yeah, well, that remains to be seen. The fey is wayward, and the Nephilim...well, let's just say they're different! And I'm not sure what to think of angels." Harlan leaned forward, his fingers playing idly with the pages of the book in front of him. "I wanted to know if you recognised a description of someone. I discussed it with Liv yesterday. We think she's a new member of Nicoli's team."

Aiden immediately sobered. "Go on."

"Short, slim, black short, spiky hair. Liv thinks she saw her at an auction a few weeks ago."

Aiden thought for a moment. "It doesn't ring a bell, but I'll keep my ear to the ground. I think Nicoli has someone in York, too."

Harlan narrowed his eyes. "Why?"

"Let's just say that I've had a few great ideas, and yet someone is always there before me."

"Lost your touch?" Harlan teased him.

"Not yet, old man. But," Aiden looked out of the window for a moment, his gaze unfocussed, before turning back to Harlan, "I think Nicoli is increasing his operatives. There's nothing I can put my finger on, other than my recent experiences. It's just a feeling."

"You think he's trying to compete with us?"

Aiden shrugged. "Anyone! There are always clients who are willing to try anything to get what they need—and Nicoli is prepared to do that. Maybe he's decided to grow his operation."

Harlan leaned back in the leather chair, hearing it creak beneath him, and his fingers tapped the smooth, varnished wood of the armrest. "I think we're too established to suffer from it, if he is."

"I agree. But competition is bad for auctions, and could make some work more dangerous. Your current job, for example. Tell me about how you saw this mystery woman." Harlan filled him in on the details, and Aiden grunted. "Catering? If it was Nicoli, he must have used that route before if this was such short notice—or, he knew about the path going on sale before you did."

"True," Harlan said, nodding. "I hadn't considered that. You can't just stick someone in a legitimate catering team with no background." He sighed. "Thanks for complicating things, Aiden."

"My pleasure." Aiden pulled the book back to him. "I better get on. I have a train to catch at three. Good luck."

Harlan rose to his feet. "You, too."

— ◆○◆ —

Talking to Aiden had made Harlan restless—and worried.

The Orphic Guild had long known about Andreas Nicoli and The Order of Lilith, and they occasionally competed for occult items, especially in auctions. But this encounter was different, and if Aiden was right, it could happen more often.

Harlan returned to his office and immediately started pacing. He shouldn't leap to conclusions—none of them should—and although he trusted Aiden's judgement, he should explore the other options. As he'd discussed with Olivia yesterday, there were several individuals and collectives that hunted for occult and magical goods, and he was pretty sure the loners wouldn't have teamed up with anyone.

He ran through the obvious single operatives, reconsidering them. There was Jackson Strange, who was strange by nature as well as name. A shaggy-haired, forty-something man who was charming, eccentric, and never to be underestimated. He would never team up with anyone, however. Dana Murphy, an Irish woman with jet-black hair and the bluest eyes, was more ruthless than she looked. She also worked alone, employed by a couple of big museums. He doubted she would team up with anyone, either.

There was someone else he was missing. Harlan paused at the window, looking over the street below, but failing to see anything. Then it came to him. *Samson Randolph. Of course.* He'd met him at a few auctions. His family was originally from Jamaica, but he was third-generation English with a First Class History degree and an endless thirst for knowledge. Harlan shook his head. *No, he wouldn't work with anyone, either.*

Harlan considered the other organisations that were active players in the field. There were The Seekers of the Lost, The Grey Order, The Order of the Chalice and Blade, and The Finders of the Forgotten. Not all of them were based in London, and a couple were family-run affairs that probably couldn't compete for The Trinity of the Seeker. There were potentially others he wasn't familiar with.

That line of thinking brought him back to Nicoli and The Order of Lilith, who would go after anything and everything—much like the guild. Nicoli's organisation had been going for about five years, and he estimated there were maybe three people he employed—depending on need. There was Andreas, of course, a thirty-something Greek man with deep pockets and questionable morals. He had no idea if his employees were full-time or contractors, but he'd seen a few at auctions, clearly stating they worked for Nicoli. There was a big guy with a long beard and red hair whose name he had never learnt. A blonde-haired woman, Gabriella Anderson, who'd bid very high one night to get an obsidian stone with magical properties. And Jensen James, a cocky boy in his twenties who Harlan refused to call a man; he was shifty, watchful, and distinctly untrustworthy.

Harlan ran his finger across his lower lip. Aiden was right. Unless this new woman worked alone, working for Nicoli was the next obvious choice. It might be sensible to find out more about her and what Nicoli was up to—and more importantly, who they were stealing the map for. But what was the best way to do that? He had no idea where Nicoli was based. Was it an office, or his own home? *Shit. Too many questions and not enough answers.* But Harlan knew that whatever was happening, they needed to get ahead of the game, and he needed information to do that. *What contacts did he have that could help?* Burton and Knight Auction House would be the most obvious place, but the auction wasn't until the next evening. He reached for his phone, intending to call Rose Donnelly, his contact there, but maybe that would be a bad idea. He didn't want to give himself away. *Damn it!*

Before he could exasperate himself with more speculation, his phone began to ring, and he picked it, answering impatiently. "Harlan Becket."

"Harlan. Are you all right?" The smooth tones of Mason's voice made him focus.

"Yes, sorry, Mason. Can I help?"

"I just wondered if you had an update for JD? I'm going to see him now."

"Not much at this stage, I'm afraid. Gabe and Shadow are onsite now, but I haven't heard from them. Not surprising, really. They've only just started their search." Harlan was surprised JD hadn't taken possession of the map yesterday, and he couldn't resist saying so.

"He arrived back in the country last night," Mason told him. "So he couldn't. I'm taking it to him now."

"I presume JD's place is secure."

"Very. Don't worry, Harlan. It will be safe there."

Harlan nodded absently. "That's good." He checked his watch. He could be in Angel's Rest in three hours. "I'm heading out too, Mason. I want to see the site in person, but I'll be back for the auction tomorrow. I don't think there's much I can do here before then."

"That's fine. I'll see you soon."

As soon as Mason had hung up, Harlan took a cursory glance around his office, grabbed his overnight bag that he always kept ready, and headed for the door.

Shadow stood in the cave called The Witch's Kitchen and smiled. It was lit up with ghoulish lights of green, pink, and purple, and the cool, damp air made her shiver.

They were at Wookey Hole cave complex, being tourists, and so far Shadow was enjoying herself. When the three of them had woken up that morning, they decided the best way to get a feel for the area was to see what had already been discovered. It was interesting to see how the humans had celebrated these caves, making them an experience for those who would never travel far beneath the earth's surface otherwise. And she'd found out they had actually been used for millennia. Bones had been found going back years, from when man had used caves to shelter in.

"Well, this is something, isn't it?" she said to Gabe, who was also looking around with amusement.

"I guess so."

Gabe's arms were folded across his chest, and he turned slowly as he examined the cavern. Ahead of them was a small boat on an underground stretch of water, and Shadow grimaced at the thought of the dark tunnels that hadn't been discovered yet, or were inaccessible to all but the hardy. There were caves in the Otherworld, especially in Dragon's Hollow, where they mined for precious metals, and the dragons hoarded their gold. She'd had one particularly unpleasant encounter in one of them once, years ago, with a vicious creature that almost killed her. The experience had put her off caves for a long time. While there might not be any dragons here, this was still an unnerving place to be, but at least the lights made her appreciate the unusual beauty.

"You know," Gabe continued, "this place was discovered in about the fifteenth century. I read it."

"Me, too." Shadow considered the heights of The Great Hall, one of the aptly-named caves they had already passed through, and said, "Maybe Phineas Hammond was inspired by them. They could have influenced his visions."

Gabe shook his head, half watching Niel walk around the other part of the cave. "It's too obvious, and too populated."

Shadow looked at him like he'd gone mad. "Now! But not in the fifteenth century. Now it's all lights and experience, and years and years of cave diving and exploration. They're even blasting through to a new cave," she told him, partly impressed and partly horrified at the thought of tons of stone coming down on their heads.

Gabe faced her. "I admit, The Great Hall is impressive, cathedral-like, a fitting place to talk to angels, but I expected to *feel* something, and I didn't. Nothing angelic or divine, or anything of the sort."

"You're right," she reluctantly admitted with a heavy sigh. "This temple will be something different. Come on. I'm cold. Let's get some coffee."

It was only when all three of them were sitting outside Captain Jack's, the restaurant in the Wookey Hole attractions, and Shadow was eating a large slice of cake and Niel and Gabe had burgers, that they discussed their options again.

Niel wiped ketchup from his chin and said, "It's too obvious, too big."

"And it's not where the temple's placed on the map," Gabe added. "But it could be part of the complex. Further in and further up."

Shadow swallowed a mouthful of cake. "As you know, I'm willing to try and do most things, but caving is not one of them."

Gabe pushed his sunglasses on top of his head, and his dark brown eyes looked amused. "Not one of my favourites, either. And besides, from what I can gather, we are much too big to go squeezing through some of these tiny passages that link the caves."

Niel laughed. "Phineas had a *vision*. As far as we know, he never actually came here. Maybe this temple is somewhere in the middle of hundreds of tons of rock. In that case, it can stay there, locked away for eternity. And it's probably a good thing, too."

The day was warm, and Niel had a short-sleeved t-shirt on, revealing his tattoos, and both he and Gabe drew a few curious glances. Shadow could see herself reflected in Niel's sunglasses, unable to see his blue eyes. "Why do you say that?"

"Like I said to Gabe last night, dealing with angels has a cost."

"But what about JD?"

"What about him?" Niel shrugged. "From what we found out, angels did him no favours. For all of his intelligence, which is considerable by the sound of it, he was—is—a brilliant mathematician, he was side-tracked by angels. People lost faith in him. Sounds to me like he was duped by his friend, Kelley, and he ended up losing more than he gained. If he'd never spoken to angels, his life would have been far better for it." Shadow and Gabe exchanged an uneasy glance that Niel saw. "Don't panic, I'm here to help. Just saying, is all."

Gabe's expression was unfathomable. "Niel thinks we may attract the attention of angels, which could cause us problems. And he might be right. They did kill us once."

Shadow leaned back in her chair, considering them both. "It's unlikely they'd send a major flood to kill seven of you though, right? Talk about overreacting!"

Gabe laughed, giving Niel an amused glance. "I think she has a point."

Niel grunted. "There are other ways to kill us."

"I think the angels—if you insist on calling them that—don't give a crap about anything in this reality anymore, so I wouldn't give it a second thought," Shadow told them, suddenly impatient. And then she realised that wasn't a very charitable way to talk about their fathers. She tried to modify her tone. "The important thing—*the thing we're being paid to do*—is the job. And then there's JD. I don't think it's up to us to tell him what he should or shouldn't do. What now?"

Gabe grinned. "Let's go for a drive. I passed over Cheddar Gorge last night; I'd like to see it in the day. You both up for that?"

"You don't want to visit Dinosaur Valley?" Niel asked, feigning surprise.

"Strangely, no," Gabe said, wincing as a group of moms and toddlers settled at the next table, the children already shrieking. He rose to his feet and pulled the car keys from his pocket. "Let's go."

Shadow was only too glad to follow him, and she cast one final glance at the table of small humans, wondering why anyone would want to deal with *that*.

Six

When Harlan arrived at the rental house later that afternoon, he was relieved to find Gabe's SUV on the driveway, and the house looking as good as it did in the photos. He hadn't phoned to warn them he was coming, so it was only as he was close that he realised he might be waiting outside for hours.

Niel answered the door to him, saying, "Oh, it's you! We wondered who'd be calling."

He led the way down the hall, and Harlan dropped his bag at the bottom of the stairs before following him.

"How's it going?" Harlan asked him.

Niel laughed. "How isn't it going would be a better question."

Harlan tried to brush away his concerns. He'd known this wouldn't be easy. Niel led him to a modern, gleaming kitchen that already showed signs of use. A pot was simmering on the hob emitting a mouth-watering smell, and Harlan's stomach rumbled. It was something rich and garlicky. "That smells amazing. What is it?"

"Nothing flash. Spaghetti Bolognese—enough for you, too," Niel reassured him as he headed to the fridge and grabbed some beers. "Want one?"

"Yes, please."

Harlan took the proffered beer and followed Niel to the large conservatory at the back of the house, where the doors to the terrace were open, and a cool breeze carried the promise of rain. The day had turned dark, thick clouds gathering overhead, and consequently the lamps were already on, banishing the gloom. Shadow and Gabe were sitting and talking quietly at the centre table that was covered in maps, along with dirty cups that had been pushed to the side.

They glanced up, smiling in greeting as Harlan and Niel joined them, and Harlan said, "Hey, guys. I hear there's not much progress yet."

Shadow's violet eyes already narrowing. "Did you really think there would be?"

"Calm down, tiger. No, I didn't. It's called a conversation starter."

"Tiger?" Shadow's eyes narrowed even further.

Harlan decided to tease her. "It's an animal. A big cat, known for its viciousness."

"I know what it is," she said coolly.

Gabe sniggered. "If you really want to rile her, call her a screwball."

"Don't you start," she said, flicking her bottle cap at Gabe with startling speed.

He caught it in his large hand just before it hit his face, and he grinned at Harlan. "See what I mean?"

Harlan raised his bottle in salute. "I'll remember that one. Thanks."

Shadow folded her arms and leaned back in her chair. "Have you finished your male bonding? Can we continue?"

Gabe gestured at the maps. "Please, go ahead. We're all ears."

Shadow leaned forward, casting Gabe an annoyed glance. "I believe I was suggesting that we concentrate further up the ridge." She pointed to the old map. "The spot where the temple is marked looks like it could be further into Ebbor Gorge, even though it doesn't really align with modern maps." She turned to Harlan. "While these two flew over it last night, I walked part of it. It's a bit of a scramble, and quite wild in places, but it's possible that there's something in there that has remained undiscovered for years."

"That's what's been worrying me," Harlan admitted. "It's National Trust property. Surely if there was something there, it would have been found by now."

Gabe shook his head. "The trees are thick in places, and it's very rocky. And, it could be hidden by magic."

"The angels like to challenge people," Niel said. "It's not going to reveal itself just like that."

Harlan started to grin. "Of course! Maybe we need The Path of the Seeker first? They might need to be used together!"

"So you mean us searching now is pointless?" Shadow asked, annoyed.

"No, not at all," Harlan said, trying to reassure her, and relieved to see her hands weren't going for her knives that he knew would be hidden somewhere on her body. "I might be wrong. I'm as much in the dark about this as you are."

"And what about the third part of the trinity? The key?" Gabe asked softly. "Without that, we get nowhere."

Harlan sipped his beer thoughtfully. "I know. But I'm hoping that once we find the place, it will become clear what type of key it is, because I don't think it will be what we expect. I'm hoping we'll get clues as to where to go next." Harlan looked out the window at the increasingly gloomy afternoon. "What if we look now? We might beat the rain. I really want to get a feel for this place."

Gabe drained his beer and stood up. "Have you got hiking gear?"

"In my bag."

"Let's go, then."

⸻◦○◦⸻

However, by the time they arrived back at the house two hours later, they were all wet and miserable, and Harlan felt none the wiser.

They had walked partway up the gorge when the rain started, making the rocky path treacherous in spots, but they persevered, clambering up through the narrow, rocky ravine until they came into woodlands. There they'd sheltered for a while, until it became clear the rain wasn't going anywhere. By the time they neared the entrance again, the streams that crossed the track had swollen, and they all got even wetter. Harlan felt guilt ridden and cranky. The walk was his suggestion and the others had agreed gracefully, but he realised it was a waste of time. They hadn't walked far enough, and it was a bigger area than he'd realised—which conversely gave him renewed hope, too. The temple could be there. *No. It had to be there.*

"Damn rain," Gabe grumbled as he shook water off himself like a dog in the hallway of the house. "I'm heading in the shower."

Niel kicked his boots off, going straight to the kitchen. "Food will be ready in thirty minutes, so you all better get a move on!"

Shadow ducked past Gabe and ran up the stairs, yelling, "Ladies first!"

Gabe yelled back. "Since when are you a lady?"

But she'd disappeared already, and Harlan said, "Please tell me there's more than one shower."

Gabe nodded. "Sure there are. But I warn you—she uses a lot of hot water. Nice place, by the way."

Harlan grabbed his bag and walked up the curving staircase next to Gabe. "Thanks. I use this company all the time. Never been here, though."

Gabe grunted as he headed through a door leading off the main corridor. "It's a good choice...defensible."

The door slammed behind him, and Harlan wandered onwards until he found an empty bedroom that overlooked the back of the house. The rain was heavy now, and everything beyond the perimeter of the garden was a misty blur. One thing was for sure—they wouldn't be doing any more exploring that night.

———◆◇◆———

Gabe opened a bottle of red wine, grabbed a couple more beers, placed them and some glasses on a large tray, and carried it into a cosy dining room that led off from the kitchen.

He felt better after his shower, and the smell of Niel's cooking always cheered him up. He'd have liked to return to the conservatory, but it was deafening in there because of the heavy rain, and was now distinctly chilly.

He almost fell over his own feet when he walked in and he caught his breath, hoping that Shadow hadn't noticed as he placed the tray on the table. Her back was to him as she fed the fire that crackled in the grate, and her grace was breathtaking.

She wore loose cotton trousers and a slim-fitting t-shirt, revealing bare arms that looked silky smooth in the light. Her hair was caught up in a messy knot on her head, exposing her slender neck, and he caught a whiff of musk and rose. She finished prodding the fire and rose swiftly to her feet, turning to him with a satisfied smile.

"That's better. A room is not complete without a fire."

"Even in the summer?"

She grinned. "Even in the summer." She shrugged. "Although, I cope with candles. Fire is life."

"I know that. Beer or wine?"

"Wine, please."

He poured her a glass and passed it to her, trying to avoid touching her fingers. They looked beguilingly gentle, but they were lethal killing machines. Not that they worried him too much. He was more concerned about what the feel of her soft skin would do to his scrambled brain right now.

Gabe gestured at the rain. "You know, this will have a nightmare effect on cave systems. Water levels will rise, and some caves will be filled completely with water. What if our temple is the same?"

She took a sip of wine and wandered to the window. "Then we'll be in trouble. But water levels drop quickly—and I don't think our temple will be affected. I think it will be protected, somehow."

"By magic?" Harlan asked, and they both turned to see him walk in and head straight to the fire, warming his hands.

"I think so," Shadow said, watching him. "Or what's the point if it would be inaccessible half the time?"

"Maybe it's part of the challenge," Gabe suggested.

Niel's booming voice filled the room. "I need help with plates!" He appeared in the doorway, carrying a steaming bowl that he placed on the table. "Sit," he commanded to Gabe and Shadow, as Harlan scooted past him to help.

In a few minutes, after pasta and garlic bread had been placed next to the Bolognese sauce and they had all filled their plates, Harlan said, "This is fantastic. Thank you."

Niel smiled. "Cheers. My specialty is breakfast, but this is my other staple."

Gabe laughed. "If you're lucky, Harlan, you might get to try some of Shadow's rabbit stew. That's her specialty."

She looked affronted. "I have several, I'll have you know."

"And what's yours, Gabe?" Harlan asked.

"Barbeque and meat, Middle Eastern-style—koftas, kebabs, that sort of thing."

"Sounds great," Harlan said. "You guys have some sort of cooking roster, then?"

Gabe shrugged. "I wouldn't call it that. We're not all home at the same time. There's lot of midnight cooking, too."

Shadow rolled her eyes. "They eat like horses." She gave Gabe and Niel a sidelong glance. "I think their limbs are hollow."

"You're doing a pretty good job of putting that away," Niel pointed out.

"You're a very good cook."

Niel feigned choking. "Wow. I'm going to remember that one."

They chatted and joked over dinner, the food and alcohol loosening their tongues as they relaxed. When they'd finished eating and had stacked the dishwasher, they moved to the chairs around the fire, and Shadow prodded it back to life again. The rain was falling even harder now, and Niel put some music on, low in the background.

"So, how long are you here for, Harlan?" Gabe asked him, watching as the American stretched his feet towards the fire.

"I head back tomorrow. The auction is tomorrow night." He turned towards them, making himself more comfortable. "Mason delivered the map to JD today, so I'll be interested to see what he thinks of it."

"You think he may have some insight?" Niel asked.

"Maybe. I know Mason will ask me more tomorrow, too. I thought coming here today would help. And I guess it has, sort of."

Niel nodded. "Ground reconnaissance is the best."

"Speaking of which—" Harlan looked at Shadow. She had curled up in the corner of the sofa, as sleek as a cat. "Do you want to come to the auction with me?"

She sat up, suddenly alert. "Why?"

"I think the woman you saw at Henri's will be there. I'm pretty sure I'll recognise her from your description, but I'd like first-hand confirmation."

Gabe felt a stir of worry in his gut. "You think she'll bid?"

Harlan nodded. "I have no doubt. If they wanted the map, they'll want the path."

"Even though we have the map?" Shadow asked, her face flush with intrigue.

"Oh, that won't put them off!"

"Who's them?" Gabe asked.

"I'm not one hundred percent sure, but after chatting to my colleagues, we think a man called Andreas Nicoli is behind this. His organisation is called The Order of Lilith. We cross swords occasionally."

"Lilith?" Niel asked, his eyes narrowing with suspicion and an edge entering his previously relaxed voice.

Gabe felt the worry in his gut turn into a twisted knot of panic. Lilith's name could have an unpredictable affect on Niel.

"Who's she?" Shadow asked.

"Adam's first wife, if you believe the myths," Harlan told her, giving Niel a puzzled glance. "But an unsuitable one. She wouldn't do as she was told."

"Adam—the first man?" Shadow's tone was already laced with contempt, a sign of her disbelief, Gabe knew. "I like her already."

"A demon wife, or witch, depending on what you read," Niel said, his face now turned towards the fire, his gaze distant. "But she was actually none of those things."

Harlan's eyes widened. "You knew her?"

Gabe watched Niel, noting his hands were clenched in his lap, his beer forgotten on the floor, and Gabe answered for them both. "Once. A long time ago. She was a strong woman who was neither demon nor monster, but who wanted to live as she chose. She was demonised for it. She died for it."

"Died for her independence?" Shadow was already bristling with anger.

Niel looked at Harlan and Shadow, seeing the confusion on their faces, and then looked at Gabe. Gabe shrugged. This was Niel's past, not his.

Niel sighed as he came to a decision, heavy and world-weary, and he stared into the flames again. "Lilith was my wife."

Harlan's mouth dropped open, a flood of emotions crossing his face. "Your *what*? I'm sorry I made light of it."

Niel shook his head. "Forget it. You had no idea, and it was a long time ago—even for me."

Shadow was silent, and her eyes burned. Gabe knew she'd be teeming with questions, but she swallowed them, only saying, "I had no idea you were married, Niel."

He smiled sadly. "We were all married once, Shadow. Some of us, many times."

Shadow looked at Gabe. "You were married?"

He felt odd confessing it. "Yes. Just once." Just that simple word brought his memories rushing back. He would dream of her later, he knew it. *But what did it matter that Shadow knew?* She was still staring at him. "Were you? Are you?" he asked her. Shadow never spoke of whom she had left behind.

"No. Marriage is not common for fey, and I was always too busy travelling for a long term relationship." Shadow glanced across at Harlan. "What about you?"

"Me?" Harlan looked incredulous. "I don't think anyone would put up with me. Not long term, anyway." He glanced at Niel, who was still staring into the fire. Harlan seemed anxious to make amends, and it was pretty clear Niel wouldn't say anything else. "Anyway, I was talking about Nicoli's order. They have lots of connections—lots of people who may want the map. They'll be there tomorrow. So will you come?" he asked, looking at Shadow again.

She nodded. "Of course." She settled back into her corner, cradling her glass of wine. "Tell us more."

For the next couple of hours, Harlan chatted about the different occult organisations he knew about and how The Orphic Guild fitted in with the rivalries and characters. It was useful knowledge and Gabe was grateful for it, but he noticed Niel remained quiet, participating with only occasional good grace, and it was clear his thoughts were elsewhere. By ten, Harlan made his excuses and went to bed. Shadow soon followed, leaving Gabe and Niel in companionable silence.

Gabe headed to the kitchen and came back with two glasses of whiskey and the bottle — just in case. He thrust a glass at Niel, and Niel took it from him, a wry smile on his lips.

"I'm fine, Gabe."

"Are you?"

"Of course. It was a long time ago, and her name was bound to come up eventually. It just wasn't how I was expecting it to." He sipped his drink and leaned back in the chair, watching the amber liquid swirl as he turned the glass. "It's odd how you think you've buried your memories, and yet they come back so swiftly, like a knife in the darkness."

Niel wasn't an emotive man. None of them were. But it didn't mean they didn't feel deeply, or love, or mourn lost relationships. It was assumed that anger and violence was their reason for being, but their lives were far more complex than that. Over the last few months they had all mourned in different ways, while simultaneously celebrating their new existence. But Niel hadn't lied earlier. Lilith had been gone for years, even before the flood.

"She was a good woman, Niel," Gabe said softly. "I miss her, too."

"Her death was unjust...unfair. It still burns."

"And it always will." Gabe sipped his drink, enjoying the warmth as it rolled across his tongue and down his throat. "It should. It's a reminder of our limitations—in case we forget."

"I can't forget. I don't want to, not really."

"Then let's drink to memories." Gabe lifted the whiskey bottle and topped their drinks up. "And share a few."

This could be a late night, but that was fine. He'd be up as late as Niel needed him to be.

Seven

S hadow and Harlan were halfway to London when Shadow couldn't contain herself any longer.

"What's the deal with Lilith?"

Harlan glanced at her, before concentrating on the road. The rain was still heavy, and the journey was slow. "That's an excellent question, and one I'm not sure I'm equipped to answer."

Shadow had taken a while to go to sleep the previous night. She'd sat up in bed, the drumming rain a backdrop to the research she'd done on her phone. While she knew that the Nephilim had led rich and full lives prior to the flood, for some reason she never considered wives to be a part of that. *Maybe because she'd never been married herself?*

She said, "I find it hard to believe she really was the first woman for one thing."

Harlan laughed. "You have a hard time believing in creation myths, full stop."

"Don't you?"

"I will admit they seem simplistic. But like most myths, they are there to frame our lives, to give meaning where there was none—especially hundreds and thousands of years ago, when life was complicated and confusing. Don't you have creation myths?"

Shadow shrugged, watching the competent way Harlan threaded through the traffic. "Not like yours. We are fey. We have existed since the dawn of time. Our magic is woven with the elements and the earth. Magic is everywhere for us. But this Lilith—she seems to have significance."

"It's odd, isn't it," Harlan mused, "which names survive time. Who sticks around, who disappears. I think she gets tied up in patriarchy and the church and the rights of women—well, for some people."

"That's what I think, too." Shadow stretched her legs out. "I read about her online last night. The stories are many and varied, too confusing."

"Well, it seems you can have a first-hand account, if you want one."

"I'm not sure Niel will want to talk about her."

"Maybe not right now, but I'm sure he will in time. He seems like a reasonable man."

Shadow nodded. "He is. They all are." She'd wait, and when the time was right, she'd talk to him—and Gabe. They were partners and friends, and she wanted to know more about them. She thought back to her research the night before. "For all that I read, though, I still couldn't get a picture of her."

"For a historical perspective, I think you'd have to talk to theology scholars for that—or a man of God. But only your guys can give you the real deal. Certainly not me." Harlan grinned at her. "Is this the way all of our car journeys are going to go from now on?"

Shadow laughed. "Maybe. I have lots of questions about lots of things." She liked Harlan. He was easy company. And intriguing. Their conversation the previous night had been instructive, and she realised now more than ever that Harlan was deeply embedded in the arcane and magical world, and she appreciated that. "How did you get involved in all this?"

"By 'all this,' do you mean the occult?" he asked.

"Yes."

"Well, that's quite the story, but in a nutshell, I watched too many adventure films and read too many books about the occult, myths, and magic. I fancied myself as a bit of a rogue trader, and ended up making a few finds and some dodgy deals with some very interesting characters. This was in the U.S., of course."

"Which bit?"

"West coast, mainly, but I travelled around. And then I met Olivia, who already worked for The Orphic Guild, while we were both searching for an Incan statue, and I ended up getting a job with them—based in San Francisco, at the time."

"And when did you come to London?" Shadow asked, wondering exactly how dodgy Harlan's past had been.

"Almost ten years ago, when Mason offered me a chance to move here." He flashed a smile at her. "I miss California weather. And what about your past?"

"Ooh." She grimaced. She should have been expecting that. "It was eventful."

He laughed loudly. "I bet. Come on, Shadow, you gotta share something!"

Shadow mentally filtered through her varied jobs, wincing at the memories of some. "I've been a mercenary on occasion—for kings who waged war for land or castles. I've hunted dragon gold, chased and killed murderous creatures, stolen a few things, and searched for a lot of lost treasure." She shrugged. "That type of thing."

"And left family and friends behind?" he asked.

"Yes." She fell silent, thinking of the band of fey that had become her family; the ones she worked with. "I miss them."

"I bet. But you have the Nephilim. That's lucky, right?"

She nodded. "Very." She decided it was time to change the subject, and realising she had no idea what would happen after the auction that evening, she asked, "You asked me to bring my bag. Are we staying in London tonight?"

Harlan nodded. "Yeah, probably best. These things can go on for a few hours, and sometimes there are after-auction drinks. They're good for networking."

"Where will I sleep?"

"If we need to, I'll check you into a hotel, but I think I have a better solution. Remember William Chadwick?"

Shadow squirmed. "The man I killed? Of course." She still felt guilty about that, even though it was her life or his.

"He's left us his house. The Orphic Guild, that is." He grimaced. "Mind you, we only got the keys a few days ago, so it might need airing out."

"You're going to let people stay there?" Shadow remembered the strange Victorian Gothic building with its extensive occult collection and rich decorating. That would be a very interesting place to stay.

"A chosen few. I'm sure you'd make the cut." He cast a sidelong glance at her. "As long as you don't steal anything."

"I can promise that—for you."

"So grateful!"

"S'okay."

"I tell you what. Let's head to the office and see who's around. I have some prep work to do before the auction, and I think you should meet Olivia."

Shadow was about to answer when Harlan's phone rang, and he answered it, the Bluetooth in the car kicking in so that Shadow could hear, too. She recognised Mason's voice.

"Harlan, where are you?"

"On the way back to London now, with Shadow." He glanced across at her. "We're in the car, so she can hear you, too."

"Good. Don't go to the office. Come to JD's estate. I'll send you the address. Any idea when you'll be here?"

"How's one o'clock sound?" Harlan asked after a quick glance at the time. "We should eat some lunch first."

"Don't bother. You can eat here," he said, and then hung up abruptly.

Shadow felt a stir of excitement. "We're going to JD's place? Have you been there before?"

Harlan grinned. "Nope. A first for both of us."

"This home is well off the beaten path," Shadow observed, after it seemed as if they had been driving through the countryside for ages.

"You know," Harlan said, as he negotiated the quiet lanes of Surrey, "JD used to live right by the river in Mortlake, in London. But when he was officially declared dead, it became something else. A Tapestry Works. I imagine that would have been annoying. He had an observatory, I think."

"Not much you can do when you're dead, though," Shadow pointed out as she looked around at the green fields and narrow lanes. "Is that why his house is called Mortlake and he has the same last name?"

"I guess so," Harlan replied, keeping an eye out for the number of the house. "He must have been very fond of the area."

"Seems obsessive," Shadow said, thinking that dwelling on the past was never a good thing. "This place looks expensive."

"Parts of Surrey can be."

They had just driven through a small village, and the houses were becoming sparse as they drove further out. Harlan slowed and he eventually turned onto a drive, finding their way blocked by a large gate and an intercom. He reached out of his window and pressed the button. Shadow saw a camera blink to life, and without needing to speak, the gate swung open and Harlan pulled in.

A house in warm, mellow timbers was at the end of a brick-lined drive, a large garage off to the left. The gardens were a mixture of lawns and borders, and another car was already on the drive.

"That will be Mason," Harlan said, pulling to a halt. "The house is Elizabethan. Not surprising."

"You guys like your big houses," Shadow observed, as she exited the car. It had stopped raining, but heavy clouds were still gathered overhead, looking as if there might be more rain due soon. She stretched as she stood, easing her cramped muscles, and rolled her shoulders before walking to Harlan's side.

"JD certainly does! You know," he said, lowering his voice, "he used to have a lot of money troubles. I guess that with longevity comes wealth—if you invest properly. And there's lots of money in the occult business."

Shadow was taking in the extensive gardens bordered by trees, and the home so isolated from its surroundings. "I guess he likes privacy, too. I wonder how he manages immortality. He must have people he trusts."

"Well, Mason knew, and you're right, there must be others."

"Didn't you say there are other Orphic Guild offices? Maybe they know, too?"

"Excellent point, Shadow." He cocked his head at her, a speculative look in his eyes. "You're not just a pretty face."

She smiled. "But it is disarming, yes?"

"Very." He led the way to the front door, but it was already opening, and an older woman with grey hair cut into a blunt bob stood on the other side, giving them sweeping glances. "Harlan and Shadow, I presume?"

"At your service," Harlan said, extending his hand, and Shadow did the same, surprised by the strength of the woman's grip.

"I'm Anna, JD's assistant. Come in. They're in the map room."

As they stepped inside, Shadow admired the gleaming hall that had a tiled floor and doors leading off on either side. The walls were decorated with a mixture of wooden panelling and wallpaper, and a broad staircase swept grandly to the upper levels. But what was more interesting were the strange sigils, runes, and alchemical shapes carved into the woodwork and the plaster of the ceiling, and she wondered if they protected the house in some way. Oil paintings of figures in old-fashioned clothing, dark and moody, lined the walls, and although Shadow would have liked to examine them closer, Anna was already heading down the hall, and she hurried to follow her. Partway down Anna led them up a small, winding staircase, finally emerging into an attic space, where Shadow looked around, shocked.

The entire back of the roof and walls of the attic had been replaced with glass, and a deck ran out from it onto a flat section of the roof. But the most surprising thing was the large telescope in the middle of the room, pointing skyward.

The remaining walls were covered in maps of the world, old and modern, as well as maps of the night sky, with sections of the universe enlarged and places of significance marked. Hundreds of pictures of planets, moons, and stars jostled for position, and a desk at the far end was surrounded by stacks of paperwork, covering a large area of the floor. On it was a single map, and Shadow could guess which one it was.

Shadow was aware her mouth was hanging open, but she couldn't stop staring, and she noticed that Harlan wasn't doing much better. A cough disturbed her, and she swung around to see JD smiling. "Do you like my map room?"

Shadow laughed. "Sorry. I was being rude. Yes, I do. It's not what I was expecting." She swept her arms wide. "None of this is. You have an observatory!"

"It's very impressive," Harlan added.

JD beamed with pleasure, his chest swelling slightly. He looked the same as the last time she had seen him, but a little less groomed. His white beard and thick head of white hair looked a little more unkempt but he still exuded elegance, intelligence, style, and wit. He wasn't wearing a smart shirt and suit, but was instead in a cotton shirt, full at the sleeves and covered in ink, the cuffs rolled back, and he wore old corduroys and braces. It suited him.

Mason leaned against the edge of the desk, watching with an amused expression. "I'm glad to see I'm not the only one to find this room fascinating," he told them. "Good to see you again, Shadow."

"You too, Mason." Shadow was glad to see Mason hadn't changed. He was as immaculate as when she'd last met him.

"Anna, will you bring coffee and lunch, please?" JD asked.

Anna was waiting at the threshold, and nodded before she left, shutting the door behind her.

"I'm glad you could make it," JD said, heading to the desk. "Mason tells me you've been to the site." He stood over the map, his eyes burning with curiosity, his mouth in a firm line. "I've been aware of this map for some time. I even owned it, at one point."

"You did?" Harlan asked, surprised. "What happened?"

"It was stolen while I was abroad, along with other books I had collected for years." He shot a glance at Shadow. "Some of them I want you to help me recover." He sighed and looked back at the map. "I didn't pursue this because I hunted for the temple at the time, and found nothing. I had presumed that it was a work of fancy."

"But now that The Path of the Seeker is up for auction, that all changes," Harlan said softly.

"It certainly does." JD pulled on soft, white cotton gloves and then ran his finger across the map, finally stopping on the site of the temple. "Back then, Wookey Hole, the village, didn't really exist. There was only a smattering of houses. Wells, the town, was there, of course. There were no roads through the area like there are now. Cheddar Gorge was spectacular, but difficult to get to." He shook his head. "It was hard going, and I toiled for months. Of course I found caves, but nothing that could be a temple. The path could change everything." He looked at Harlan. "You have to get it."

"I plan to," Harlan said decisively. "Shadow is coming, too. It's clear someone else is interested in this. Mason told you about what happened?"

JD nodded. "I don't care what it costs, just buy it."

"It could get very expensive."

JD shrugged. "It doesn't matter. Bring it here as soon as you have it." He gestured to the map again. "Have you found anything yet?"

"No," Shadow said, "but of course we've only just started looking. The map is inaccurate, obviously fantastical, but we'll find it." She sounded sure of herself, but she wasn't. It seemed improbable, but failure wasn't an option.

"Bidding tonight will make us a target," Mason said. "You could be vulnerable to attack by whoever's working against us."

"I think we're equal to it, aren't we, Shadow?" Harlan asked her.

"Of course."

"Have you had an advance look at it yet?" Mason asked Harlan.

"Not yet. Burton and Knight are being cagey and leaving it quite late."

"Is that unusual?" Shadow asked, not entirely sure how auctions worked.

"In order to generate interest in a lot, it's normally well-advertised." Harlan scratched his head, perplexed. "So, yes, this is unusual, and worrying."

The door opened behind them and Anna came in carrying a large tray stacked with food, which she put down on a low table on the other side of the room. "I'll be back with more," she called over her shoulder.

JD peeled his gloves off elegantly. "Excellent. Let's eat."

Eight

Burton and Knight Auction House was situated in an unassuming building in Chelsea. Unlike many other auction houses, it didn't have a large sign over the entrance advertising what it was; instead, there was a small brass plaque next to a door painted shiny black with a medusa's head brass knocker on it.

Its familiarity soothed Harlan as he stepped inside the entrance hall, Shadow next to him. He spent a lot of time there, and he knew many of the staff well. Burton and Knight specialised in the occult and arcane, and it was rare he went elsewhere. Tonight they were in one of the smaller rooms, and Harlan led the way down the corridor, grimacing as he arrived on the threshold. Even though he had purposely arrived early, it was already half full.

They sat at the end of a row at the back of the room as he said, "This will be harder than I originally thought. No sign of the woman yet."

It was more of a statement than a question, but Shadow shook her head. "No."

A couple of people nodded their way, and he nodded back. *This didn't bode well.* There were many objects for sale that night, so with luck, the other bidders would be more interested in those items. After talking with JD and Mason earlier, they'd decided he should bid on a few other objects in an effort to mask their real objective. Some of the lots were an obscure collection from the home of a private collector of medieval objects, and they would fit in with the kind of thing The Orphic Guild would obtain.

Harlan fidgeted in his seat, running his fingers under his collar and adjusting his jacket. He'd dressed in a suit, and the place was overly warm, making him sweat. It didn't help he'd just had a good workout at the guild's gym, followed by a hot shower. Shadow had decided to spend her time strolling the streets of Eaton Place. He was relieved he hadn't needed to entertain her, and she sat next to him now, composed and alert.

He opened the leaflet on his lap, reading through the descriptions of the lots for sale, and pulling his pen from his pocket, he marked a few that he should examine when allowed.

Shadow had been flicking through her own copy with interest, and she now lowered her voice and brought her lips close to his ear. "Are we actually going to be able to look at the path before the bidding opens?"

He nodded and checked his watch. "Any minute now, I hope."

They waited impatiently for a while longer, and then Rose Donnelly, his contact, appeared at the entrance to the adjoining room and addressed the attendees. "The lots are now open for inspection."

Rose Donnelly was a short, plump woman with a porcelain complexion and red hair, and she acknowledged Harlan as she saw him across the room, and then immediately headed through the door.

Harlan left his jacket on the chair, and followed by Shadow, trailed after the growing crowd. Immediately beyond the door was a series of tables, well lit by spotlights, but he ignored them for now, heading to Rose's side.

Her face creased into a frown as he reached her. "Sorry, Harlan. I know you wanted to see this earlier, but it hasn't been possible."

"Why the hell not?" he asked, trying not to lose his cool.

"Things are a little odd right now," she said, lowering her voice. "Who's your friend?"

"Shadow, she's a new contractor," he said, quickly making the introduction. "What do you mean by 'odd?'"

"It seems there are a couple of interested parties, and they're trying to make life awkward." She glanced around as they talked, smiling and nodding at other bidders. "Look, I can't talk, but I suggest you keep on your toes tonight. I think there's more to The Path of the Seeker than originally thought."

"Is it genuine?" he asked quickly, before she walked away.

"Absolutely. We've had it dated and compared it to records of The Map of the Seeker. They are of the same date and hand. Unfortunately," she paused and looked at Harlan suspiciously, "the actual Map of the Seeker has been stolen. We approached Henri Durand for it on Monday. There was quite an uproar, as I'm sure you understand."

Harlan tried to look as shocked as possible, and he felt Shadow still next to him. "Stolen? How?"

"Henri has no idea, but he's quite upset."

"I'm sure he is," Harlan said, smoothing his hand down his tie, and nodding in concern. "Pass on my regards if you see him again."

Rose nodded before walking away, and Harlan started to inspect the lots, examining each one carefully, and making notes in his sales pamphlet. "Keep your eyes peeled, Shadow," he said softly as they progressed.

"I don't need to," she replied. "She's here."

Harlan resisted the urge to jerk his head up and stare. "Where?"

"Where do you think? By the document."

Harlan casually lifted his head and scanned the room, immediately seeing the woman Shadow had described. She was shorter than he had pictured, but her black, spiky hair was immediately recognisable. And it looked as if she was with Jensen James, the cocky young associate of Andreas Nicoli.

Shit.

Trying not to appear rushed, he eventually arrived at The Path of the Seeker, and nodding politely at Jensen he leaned forward to inspect the document, wishing Jensen would piss off. He was aware of their eyes on him as he noted it was a long, one-page manuscript, the paper thick and slightly yellow, but otherwise in remarkably good condition. The title at the top read, *The Second Part of the Trinity of the Seeker. For those who would dare to seek the knowledge of the angels.*

Harlan frowned. This wasn't what he was expecting at all. The document was filled with strange drawings and symbols, very alchemical in nature. Some were laid out in a grid, as well as what appeared to be verse written in Latin. However, the paper matched the map, to the naked eye at least, and Rose said it was genuine. He hoped JD could make more sense of it.

Rather than leave him in peace, Jensen spoke up. "Something you're interested in, Harlan?"

His cocky cockney tone grated on his nerves. "Perhaps." He looked at Jensen coolly. "Are you, Jensen? You look like you're guarding it."

Jensen smirked. "No, mate, just looking, like you." He nodded at Shadow. "You brought a friend?"

Shadow smiled disarmingly, simultaneously releasing a wash of glamour. "I'm Shadow."

Jensen's eyes widened with surprise and he blushed to his roots. "A pleasure."

Suppressing a smile, Harlan nodded at the would-be thief next to him. "Have you brought a friend, too?"

Jensen tore his gaze from Shadow. "This is Mia."

Mia was staring at them both with a suspicious look on her face, but she nodded, remaining mute.

"Well, we must get on," Harlan said, turning his back and returning to their seats in the increasingly crowded room.

"The manuscript wasn't what I was expecting at all," Shadow said, looking worried.

"Me neither. I couldn't make heads or tails of it. I found the words, 'For those who would dare', quite ominous." Harlan scratched his neck. "I have a bad feeling about this. Where's Mia?"

"I can't see her, but Jensen is over there, near the front."

The energy in the room had risen as everyone settled in to bid, and Harlan felt the prickle of nerves and excitement that he always had at the start of an auction, but the feelings generally disappeared when the bidding began.

Another familiar face appeared across the room, and he raised a hand. Olivia headed swiftly to his side, and as she sat down, her silk dress fell in waves around her calves. "Evening, Harlan. Mason suggested I join you tonight." She smiled impishly. "Perhaps he doesn't trust you."

"Funny. Are you my support crew?"

She laughed. "I'm here to keep tabs on the room while you bid."

"That's a good idea." He noticed her eyes slide to Shadow. "Sorry, you two haven't met."

He introduced them, and they greeted one another warmly, and not without a fair degree of curiosity. He realised with a sinking feeling that they were, for all of their physical differences, horribly alike, and were going to get on far too well—probably to his detriment.

Shadow's eyes slid across Olivia's dress, watching as she crossed her legs to show a tanned calf, her Louboutin shoes on full display, the red sole unmistakable.

"I like your shoes," Shadow told her, looking envious. "I normally wear boots, but those are *different!*"

"Thank you. A treat to myself, after finally getting a very nice commission." She leaned across Harlan to get closer to Shadow, and lowered her voice. "They're my third pair."

"I bet you don't wear them in the field," Harlan said, already feeling out gunned.

"Of course not!" She grinned at him. "I'll stick to my steel toecaps for that. So, tell me, where are we at?"

"We have a feeling things aren't going to be that straightforward," he told her.

Shadow lowered her voice. "I still can't see Mia. Does this place have a back door?"

"Two," Olivia answered. "A regular entrance for the staff, and a warehouse door for delivery vans further along, both at the back of the building."

A speculative look crossed Shadow's face and Harlan said, "What are you thinking?"

"I need to be outside."

"You suspect trouble?"

"Don't you? I think I should position myself for an alternative solution."

Olivia grinned. "Oh, I like you. Harlan?"

Harlan inwardly groaned, but knew it was a good idea. "All right. Be careful—and discreet!"

Shadow smiled as she edged past both of them, her eyes as mean as a snake. "Always."

Olivia watched her leave. "She's the fey, right?"

"Right."

"She doesn't look it."

"That's her glamour. It's very effective. When she drops it, it's actually quite unnerving. It's her stealth, however, that's even more unbelievable. She has this knack for disappearing."

Olivia frowned and then smiled. "Really? How very useful."

"Oh yes. And deadly. I suggest we never cross her."

The bang of the gavel interrupted them, and they both turned to the front of the room.

Shadow made her way quickly down the main street, looking for the road that would take her to the back of the building.

After a couple of false starts, she found the one she needed and increased her pace, knowing the auction would be starting imminently. From what Harlan had said, The Path of the Seeker would be auctioned towards the end, so she could have a while to wait, but it would give her a chance to position herself.

The lane was quiet, which wasn't surprising. It was evening, and she imagined most deliveries would take place during normal working hours. Buildings crowded around her on both sides, and overflowing bins and boxes were piled outside most rear entrances. She wrinkled her nose as the smell of rotten food reached her. Some buildings backed directly onto the street, while others had what looked to be rear courtyards. A few vans were parked, pulled in close to walls. There was some activity outside a couple of buildings, and she could hear chatting and music. The kitchens would be here, for the restaurants that lined the street.

It didn't take long for Shadow to find the rear of Burton and Knight. She spotted the warehouse door straight away. It was a large roller door, padlocked to the ground, with a camera and alarm system in place. The normal door to the rear entrance was a short distance away. It was already gloomy in the alley, the light fading rapidly, and she watched and waited across the street, sheltering in the recess of a wall.

Shadow was sure that Mia was up to something. If she wasn't in the auction room, she suspected that she would be finding a way to take the document in case Jensen failed. *Or maybe she was just going to steal it, anyway.* Harlan had told her that thefts were rare from here, but she had a feeling that they were willing to risk the consequences for this. Shadow wondered if Mia would exit this way, or if it would be more likely that she might steal it and stroll out the front door? As far as she could tell, Mia wasn't supernatural, so evading the auction staff would be tricky. *Surely she couldn't hope to steal it from under their noses?*

Shadow ran her finger over her bottom lip, pondering the possibilities, and her gaze drifted up to the windows above. From what Harlan had said, Burton and Knight owned the whole building. A drainpipe ran close to a couple of windows, and if she needed to, she might be able to get in that way. *But no, waiting was the key.* So, she shuffled into a more comfortable position and watched.

It was dark when her phone vibrated in her pocket, and she read a message from Harlan saying that Mia was still nowhere in sight and the auction for the path was about to begin. She put her phone away, and within minutes a loud and persistent alarm rang out, shattering the silence. It was coming from the auction house.

A diversion—it had to be.

Within minutes, the back door burst open and a dozen people exited, pacing and chattering excitedly. In the confusion, a small, petite figure separated herself from the others, and walked quickly down the alley. *Mia.* Shadow followed, hugging the wall as she kept her in sight. Mia was walking briskly, but not fast enough to be suspicious. She could see her short, spiky hair as she passed beneath a light, and Shadow allowed her to reach the far end of the alley, well away from the auction house and the gathering crowd, before she caught up.

Mia was angling to the left, no doubt to head down the network of small lanes. Shadow waited until she was close to the wall and then ran up behind her, throwing her arm around her neck and dragging her to the side. Mia immediately reacted, kicking back as she tried to shake off Shadow, but she threw her against the wall, Mia's face slamming into the brick, and pinned her in place, wondering how best to search her. Mia grunted and her elbow jammed back, catching Shadow in the stomach, and she almost lost her grip. But she was taller and stronger, and although Mia squirmed, she couldn't get free.

Although Shadow wanted to question her, she knew her voice could give her away, and so far Mia hadn't got a good look at her. Besides, she was using her fey magic, which would make her hard to see. Mia took advantage of Shadow's hesitancy and this time she kicked out, catching Shadow in the calf, and Shadow lost patience. She punched

Mia, hard, and the woman went limp. Shadow lowered her to the ground, pulled her behind a large skip, and started to rifle through her coat. But there was nothing within it. Frustrated, she patted her down and then rolled her over, wondering if she'd secured the document to her back. But again, nothing. *Herne's bloody horns.* Mia was groaning, her eyelids flickering, and Shadow debated interrogating her, but it was pointless. She'd either hidden the manuscript, or passed it on. *Jensen. Where was he?*

Leaving Mia, Shadow watched the growing number of people clustered around the back of Burton and Knight. She returned to them, again keeping close to the wall, but there was no sign of Jensen, Olivia, or Harlan. She came to a quick decision and doubled back on herself, running down the alley. Mia had already gone, but Shadow turned left, just as Mia had intended to. She couldn't have gone far.

Shadow reached the end of another narrow road and paused on the corner, spotting Mia's limping figure hurrying down the street on the right as fast as her gait allowed, looking over her shoulder nervously. Shadow pursued her, hoping she would lead her to Jensen. But Mia paused on the corner, beneath a streetlight, and within moments a car pulled up to the kerb, picked her up, and drove away.

Nine

H arlan and Olivia had just sat in Harlan's car when Shadow opened the back door and slid inside.

Harlan turned to look at her, but he could already tell by the set of her shoulders and her bleak stare that things hadn't gone according to plan. "I take it you haven't got it."

"No." Her lips were set in a hard line.

It was an hour after the fire alarm had gone off and Harlan and Olivia had evacuated Burton and Knight. They'd hung around on the pavement waiting for the fire brigade to declare the place safe, hoping that all of Harlan's suspicions were wrong, but within minutes of them getting back inside the building, the staff confirmed that The Path of the Seeker had been stolen. Jensen and Mia were nowhere in sight. The staff were furious, and also profoundly apologetic, but Harlan was still annoyed. His only hope had been Shadow.

"Shit," he said forcefully.

"It was stolen, then?" she asked.

"Of course. That damn alarm was a diversion. What happened?"

"I caught up with Mia, but she didn't have it. She must have passed it to Jensen, or someone else. Or she never had it in the first place, and she was a false trail to start with."

"Damn it!" Harlan smacked the wheel with a clenched fist. "I knew I should have followed that weasel, Jensen, instead!"

Shadow leaned forward, her head between Harlan and Olivia. "She got into a car on the corner of one of the back streets, but I wouldn't recognise it."

"Did she see you?"

Shadow looked at him scornfully. "Of course not. I attacked her from behind, and I didn't say a word."

That was something at least, Harlan reflected.

"It doesn't matter," Olivia said, looking far calmer than Harlan, which infuriated him even further. "We know they're working together, and although we didn't see it get stolen by either of them, we know it has to be them. Let's face it, Jensen disappeared after the fire alarm sounded, and that's highly suspicious. But this means Nicoli is behind it all."

She looked beyond them both to the pub on the corner. "May I suggest a drink? It's not exactly like we need to flee the scene of the crime."

"Great idea," Harlan said, already exiting the car, and within minutes they had bought drinks and found a spot in the cosy pub.

Harlan's fingers drummed on the table with nervous energy. He scanned the room, and satisfied no one was close enough to hear them, especially over the hum of conversation, said, "We need to plan our next move."

"Have you told JD yet?" Shadow asked.

"Of course not. I've barely had a chance to think."

"No need for snarkiness," she told him.

He sighed and rubbed his face, feeling stubble beneath his fingers. "Sorry. I'm frustrated. I really thought we'd gotten the drop on them."

"Me, too." Shadow smiled ruefully. "But, I must say, I'm impressed. When did Jensen disappear?"

"Not until the alarm went," Olivia said. She looked composed and thoughtful, with not a hair out of place. Neither had Shadow, Harlan observed, feeling more unkempt by the second. "I was keeping an eye on him. The bidding for the path had just started, and there were at least another two interested parties."

"Did you recognise them?" Shadow asked.

"I did. One of them was a man who I've seen a couple of times but don't really know. He brought a few items, and I think he was bidding hopefully rather than energetically. He seemed to drop out quickly, but the other man," she raised an eyebrow as she watched Harlan, gauging his reaction, "was Jackson Strange. He arrived late. Did you see him?"

Harlan blinked, and felt even more annoyed. He'd arrived at the auction feeling in control, but now everything had changed. "No. He was bidding on the path, too?"

Olivia nodded. "He arrived just as the auction started and lurked at the back of the room. You were too focussed to see him." She smiled. "But that's why I was there. He put in a couple of bids, and had every intention of keeping going by the look of it, until, of course the alarm went off."

Harlan thought back to the scrambled events when the alarm sounded and they had all hurriedly left the room. "But I didn't see him afterwards, either."

"No." Olivia sipped her gin and tonic thoughtfully. "He obviously didn't hang around—and that might mean something, or it might not!"

Shadow leaned forward, her eyes bright. "Who is Jackson Strange?"

Olivia smiled again. "He's quite the lone wolf, Shadow. Charming, with a dangerous undercurrent of sexiness. He's a hunter of occult objects like the rest of us, but has no known associates."

"Could he be behind the theft?"

Harlan shook his head. "I doubt it. I'm not saying he's not capable of theft, I just don't think he's behind this one."

"Unless they're working together," Shadow suggested.

Harlan looked at Olivia, but she shook her head too, obviously agreeing with him. "It's unlikely," he said to Shadow. "That's why we call him a lone wolf. I've never known him to work with any other hunter."

"So, he either wants it for himself or a private client," Shadow speculated. "And that's means there are three of us after it, but only one of us with the map."

A horrible thought occurred to Harlan, and he mused on it for moment before voicing his concern. "There's a third part to this—the key. I wonder if one of them already has it."

"I must admit, it had crossed my mind," Olivia said. "You should call JD sooner rather than later. What if someone knows he has the map and tries to steal it—tonight!"

"There's no way anyone can know he has it," Harlan reasoned.

"Except for the fact that you were bidding on the path tonight," Shadow told him.

"But that just means we want it, or someone we work for has it, or we have it locked in our offices. There's no reason to think JD has it."

Shadow nodded, seemingly satisfied, and leaned back again, sipping her drink. "So, what now?"

"Well, I have to phone JD, and I'm not looking forward to that."

She waved her hand as if swatting a fly. "But we have to find it and steal it back, right?"

Harlan watched her over the top of his pint, aware that Olivia was smirking. "I suppose that's one possibility."

She snorted. "That's the *only* possibility. We have the map, we need the second part. And frankly, if we find who has the key—if someone has the key—we need to steal that, too."

Olivia laughed. "I knew I liked you! But first things first. Path first, then we'll focus on the key."

"We need both," Shadow persisted. "But, let's start with weasel-face and Mia. Where are Nicoli's offices—The Order of Lilith, is that right?"

"Right. I think it's somewhere in Camden," Olivia said thoughtfully, "but I'm not sure exactly where."

"If you find it, I'll watch it. And then I'll break in."

Harlan laughed, despite his reservations. "You make it sound so easy."

"I'm sure it won't be, but that's part of the fun isn't it?" Shadow finished her drink and wiggled the glass. "Time for another?"

"My round," Harlan said, rising to his feet. "Then we'd better decide where you're going to sleep tonight. And you should call Gabe and let him know what's happening."

Gabe topped his glass of whiskey up and stared at Hammond's map on the table. "What are we missing?"

"An accurate map." Niel's arms were folded across his chest. "You'd think after five hundred or so years, something would have revealed itself."

"Not if it's been hidden well by angels," Gabe reminded him. "They always liked their tricks and fancies."

They were both sitting around the table in the small dining room, the fire blazing and the whiskey bottle in handy reach. It was late now, closing in on midnight, and they had spent the day exploring the area, trying to orientate themselves to the map and work out what some of the more obscure illustrations meant. They had also hiked through Ebbor Gorge again. Fortunately the day had been dry, but the ground was muddy, and the streams were full. After that they had revisited Cheddar Gorge, but after some debate, discounted it.

Niel pulled a bowl of crisps towards him and took a handful. "Maybe this is a good thing," he said softly.

Gabe looked up at him and frowned. "Why?"

"Because I don't think any good can come of it."

"Not even for us?"

Niel swallowed a few crisps, and in the silence of the room, Gabe heard their distinctive crunch. "There were a host of angels, Gabe. Thousands of them. Some minor, many not, but all with a power we can barely conceive of. And some of them fathered us. We know that humanity was seen as something lowly and insignificant by most of them. Beyond their care. Humanity was something that we were made to control—to keep them in their place. The angels were far too embroiled with divinity. You know this, but I need to remind you because I'm wondering *why this temple even exists.*" He tapped the map. "Because for it to exist, it means an angel willed it so. Carved it out of rock and earth. But why? Just because some faithful human could ask him questions? Can you see any of them wanting that?"

Gabe stared at Niel, an uncomfortable prickle of worry crawling beneath his skin. He was absolutely right, but Gabe had been so caught up in wanting to find it, he hadn't really questioned why it should exist. He took another fiery slug of whiskey, enjoying the heat as it coursed down his throat. "It is a good question."

"I know."

"We keep talking about *angels*, but maybe it was the design of one angel, rather than many. Maybe he was curious about humans?"

"I don't buy it," Niel said belligerently. "Say it does exist, out there in the rock somewhere. Why put it *there*? This place, as far as I can gather, has no significance historically."

"Apart from the fact that thousands of people have sheltered within the caves here for millennia. That might be significant."

Niel shrugged. "So, people have sheltered in caves all over the world."

"It is called Angel's Rest," Gabe pointed out. "That must mean something."

"And there's a village called Wookey Hole! I don't think there's a bunch of Wookiees down there!" Niel huffed. "And why give the vision to Phineas Hammond, of all people?"

Gabe shook his head, feeling weary. "Niel, I have no idea. Some people *do* talk to spirits and demons on other planes. I have no idea why some have the gift and others don't!"

"But no angels existed where we were in the spirit world," Niel said forcefully. "Not one! And we were there a long time."

Gabe remembered the swirling chaos of the other dimension with revulsion. "But angels communicate slightly differently. You know that."

Niel nodded, his gaze vague, before becoming argumentative again. "True. But based on our past experience of them, this temple sounds ... suspicious."

"And we also can't forget that JD spoke to angels. They shared reams of information with him."

"But we haven't seen any evidence of that—or rather, you haven't. In the hours you spent with JD, he showed you nothing! And this Enochian language sounds highly suspicious."

He was right, Gabe reflected. *JD was greedy for knowledge, but shared little.* "Despite that," he conceded, "we still have a job to do. And in the event we cannot find the temple after searching as long as is reasonably possible, only then can we stop."

Niel fell silent. Gabe knew what Niel was like when he had something fixed in his mind, and this was well and truly stuck. He'd had misgivings since the start.

Finally, Niel spoke. "All right. But if we find out something more sinister, then we need to really consider whether to continue. Especially once we have The Path of the Seeker. That will hopefully reveal something more useful."

"And the key," Gabe muttered. "Don't forget that." His phone rang, and he saw it was Shadow. He answered, relieved. He hadn't heard from her all day, and he was getting worried. "Hey, Shadow. Success?"

"No," she answered abruptly, before launching into an explanation of what had happened at the auction. He leant back in his chair, rubbing his eyes, and for a moment he thought as Niel did. Maybe this was a good thing? Maybe this was fate? Then she told him she'd be staying in London for another day or so, and he asked, "Where are you staying?"

"With Olivia tonight, Harlan's associate. I'm not sure about tomorrow yet."

"Okay. Don't do anything rash."

He heard the smile in her voice. "When do I ever?"

She hung up, and Gabe pocketed his phone and picked up his whiskey, quickly summarising the conversation for Niel.

Niel groaned. "So now there may be two different parties, as well as us, looking for this?"

"Yep."

"We're missing something."

"Maybe."

Niel pulled the map closer to him, frowning at the page. "These images don't make sense now, but they must mean something. Maybe they signify clues in the landscape?"

"Perhaps. Some look alchemical to me." Gabe pointed. "That signifies water, that fire. But," he added, growing sick of debate, "that's JD's specialty, so hopefully he will decipher it."

"True." Niel pushed the map away, suddenly impatient. "Want to fly again? Have another search?"

"Despite your misgivings?"

"If there is something dodgy about all this, I'd rather we find it than anyone else. We're equipped to deal with it."

Gabe laughed. "Are we? That's good to know."

Niel drained his glass and stood up. "Of course we are. Or more than most. Which is why I'm still in the game."

Ten

S hadow watched Olivia as she prepared coffee and breakfast on Thursday morning in her modern kitchen, and felt suddenly homesick.

She'd slept well, but Shadow missed the chaos of the farmhouse and the banter of the Nephilim. She shook her head, annoyed with herself. It was something she needed to get used to. She could be travelling a lot with this job, and that was a good thing.

Olivia was fun and easy company, and she'd offered Shadow a bed the previous night without hesitating. Shadow had accepted because it was getting late to book into a hotel, and she realised she didn't want the anonymity of a hotel room. Olivia lived in Chelsea, not far from Burton and Knight and the pub where they had drinks and food. Harlan had looked relieved too, and once he'd dropped them off, he promised to be in touch the next morning. And it was a good decision. Olivia's flat was warm and comfortable, decorated with all sorts of interesting objects that Olivia told her she'd bought in many different countries. Photographs of exotic places covered the walls, and Shadow hoped she'd be as well-travelled in this world as she had been in her own.

Olivia placed a cup of coffee in front of her and said, "You look thoughtful. Everything okay?"

"Fine," she answered, picking up the cup and cradling it. "Just contemplating the strange turns my life has taken recently."

Olivia had returned to the counter to collect cereal and toast, and she placed them in the middle of the table, before picking up her own coffee and taking a seat. "I gather you've been here for about six months, is that right?" She gestured to the food in front of them. "Help yourself."

"Thanks, Olivia." Shadow started to butter her toast as she answered. "Yes. I arrived at Samhain. Since then, it's been a bit of a rollercoaster."

"And you live with Gabe?"

"And six others." Shadow frowned. "I presume Harlan or Mason has told you who they are?"

Olivia took a bite of her toast, liberally spread with jam, and nodded. "Nephilim. They sound fascinating."

Shadow laughed. "They are, and they're not. They're like any other men—well, sort of, they're huge — until you remember their past."

"Which makes them useful for this job in particular, I guess."

"Yes," Shadow nodded, as she buttered another piece of toast.

Olivia smiled. "I must admit, I'm quite looking forward to meeting them."

"Well, you seem to be more and more involved in this job, so I'm sure you will." She took a bite of toast and asked, "How did you come to work for The Orphic Guild?"

"Crikey," Olivia said, raising her eyebrows. "It was sort of convoluted. I studied Art History at university, and my passion was the Renaissance. I got a job with a museum as a researcher, and ended up being involved with a very curious collection of objects. It sent me down a rabbit hole of the occult, and I ended up meeting Mason. One thing led to another, and I decided The Orphic Guild had interesting prospects." She grinned. "And I have a passion for adventure. And money."

"Harlan said you worked in San Francisco for a while."

"Yeah, that's where I met him. He was quite the rogue." She winked. "In the nicest of ways!"

"And still is, I think," Shadow said conspiratorially. "So, what's the plan today?"

"I've got a couple of calls to make," Olivia said, topping up her coffee, "and I know Harlan has, too. We both have contacts who may know where Nicoli is based."

"Good. As I said last night, if we find it, I'm happy to watch it all day, if necessary."

"Nicoli is a tricky customer," Olivia warned her. "You've probably gathered that already.""That's okay, so am I."

◆◇◆

It turned out that Nicoli's office was in an old warehouse in Camden. Shadow and Harlan sat in Harlan's car, which he'd parked far down the street, and they hunched in their seats, watching it.

Shadow frowned. "He's obviously not going for the upper class look that The Orphic Guild is."

"I guess not. The Order of Lilith has more threatening overtones though, don't you think?"

She laughed. "I guess so. And therefore, he's looking for a different type of client."

"Oh, I don't know," he said, shrugging. "The occult attracts a certain type of client, whether they are rich or poor, morally upright or not. In the end, depending on how much someone wants something, many are always willing to do something underhanded—including us, as you so rightly pointed out the other night." He turned to look at Shadow with a sly grin.

"It's an interesting line of work," she agreed, remembering the many scrapes she'd got into in the Otherworld. "It seems it doesn't matter what world you live in when it comes to this business." She checked the time on her phone, feeling impatient. "We've been here for over an hour, and no one has gone in or out. Are you sure we shouldn't just march up to the door and rattle our swords?"

Harlan looked at her, clearly intrigued. "What do you mean?"

"Well, rather than subterfuge, we could just accuse him and see what he says."

"Won't that tip our hand?"

"It has already been tipped, surely. You gave that document a very thorough inspection yesterday, and Jensen watched you like a hawk. And then, of course, you started bidding."

Harlan shook his head. "Too soon. It may be that confrontation or negotiation will be needed before this is over, but not just yet."

Shadow's phone buzzed, and she read a text from Gabe asking if she was busy. She called him back immediately. "I'm with Harlan, watching Nicoli's building. How are things there?"

"I'm bored and frustrated," Gabe answered, his voice low and oddly soothing.

She smiled. "Me, too. What do you suggest?"

"We want more details on how Phineas received his vision."

She groaned. "More research? That's not what I had in mind, Gabe."

"Niel has made some very good points, and I want more background. I'm sure Harlan can provide it."

"Hold on." She turned to Harlan. "Gabe wants more info on Phineas's vision. Have you got some?"

"I think so. Well, JD does." Harlan looked puzzled. "Why?"

"Captain Fantastic here has concerns."

"I like that name," Gabe crooned in her ear. "You can call me that more often."

"It was supposed to annoy you," she shot back.

"That's okay, screwball. You can't be right all the time."

Shadow bit back a response, instead turning to Harlan. "Can we get this info to Gabe? It might actually keep him quiet."

"I miss you too, sugar buns," he said, teasing her.

Harlan sniggered. "Did he just call you sugar buns?"

Shadow ignored him. "Gabe, I swear I will have my revenge if you don't shut up, right now."

"Send me the info, then?"

"As soon as I'm not stuck in a car watching The Order of bloody Lilith!" She cut him off and glared at the warehouse.

Harlan suppressed a smirk. "I'll call Mason and get him on that—" And then he stopped and stared, shrinking down in his chair even further. "Shadow, get your head down."

She scooted down, glamouring herself and extending it to Harlan, blurring both of their features. "What?"

"There's a man approaching the warehouse. I know him."

Shadow stared, trying to decide which of the people wandering down the pavement it could be. And then she saw a small, round man head to the entrance of the warehouse. "The little fat man?"

"The very same."

"Who is he?"

"Erskine Hardcastle, necromancer and demon conjuror extraordinaire."

"What? Are you kidding?"

"No." Harlan hadn't taken his eyes off him, and he kept watching until Erskine entered the building. "Well, this changes everything."

Shadow twisted to look at Harlan, still low in her seat. "Why? He's a buyer, like anyone else. Who cares who he is?"

Her glamour still blanketed both of them, and Harlan twisted to look at her, too. "What have you done? I feel weird."

"It's my glamour. I'm going to keep it on us for now. Answer the question."

"He's a well-known user of black magic. He supposedly has a demon at his beck and call, and we refuse to do business with him."

Harlan's normally blasé demeanour had changed dramatically, and for the first time, Shadow saw real concern on his face.

"But you just said that many occult collectors resort to all sorts of things to get what they want. Why refuse him?"

"He's bad news. Rumours of unexplained deaths and mysterious disappearances have dogged his past. He has few friends, and fewer enemies. Most people steer clear of him, and he likes it that way. Fear and intimidation are his friends." Harlan glanced at the road again, and certain that Erskine had gone inside, he straightened up and started the engine. "Time to go."

"But The Path of the Seeker is in there!"

"And that's exactly where it can stay for now. I'm serious, Shadow. We need to find out more before we proceed. I think Gabe's concerns could be legitimate."

Harlan was rattled. *Erskine Hardcastle.* He'd met him a few times, and each encounter had given him the serious creeps. And now, sitting at Mason's desk in his office at The Orphic Guild with Shadow next to him, Harlan knew that Mason was rattled, too.

There was something about Erskine's intense manner and pale, grey eyes that spoke of dark secrets, and power swirled around him. Harlan could never work out if it was actually magic, or just the sheer force of his personality. He had to admit that Erskine had been nothing but polite when he'd met him, usually at the auction rooms and once at a private dinner, but he still didn't like him.

The feeling had been compounded when he tried to manipulate the guild to do business with him, but Mason had smoothly declined citing several good reasons, and they had all breathed a sigh of relief when he exited the building that day. Erskine had never approached them again.

"Damn it," Mason said, immediately standing and pacing around the room. "That is the last name I wanted to hear."

"I can assure you, he was the last person I wanted to see."

"We don't know for sure though, do we, that he went there for The Path of the Seeker?"

"No," Harlan admitted. "He could be there for any other purpose. But it is suspicious timing." He felt compelled to add, "I presume Olivia told you about Jackson?"

"Yes. Something else to worry about." That morning, Mason had been clipped with Harlan, annoyed about the loss of The Path of the Seeker. But now, that annoyance had been pushed well into the background. "What does a demon conjuror want with angels?"

Shadow had been silently watching their exchange as she leaned back in her chair, twirling her dagger and balancing it on the point of her finger. Harlan had tried not be distracted by her dexterity. Still turning it idly between her fingers, she said, "I guess this is why Niel has more questions. He hasn't got a very high opinion of angels. None of them do. They question why such a place would exist."

Mason paused by the window, his eyes also falling to the knife. "They suspect a darker motive?"

"Yes. Have you got what Gabe asked for?"

Mason walked back to the desk, bent down, and opened the bottom drawer, extracting a bundle of papers. "Here are the copies of Hammond's dairies and notes pertaining to the period. The copies are good, the originals not so much. They are not easy reading. I read them a while ago, but not recently—and certainly not today." He handed them to Shadow. "I hope they tell you something of use."

Shadow placed them in the messenger bag on the floor next to her, while Harlan said, "I want to speak to Rose again, from Burton and Knight. She couldn't talk last night, but I'm hoping to get information today. I'm also hoping to get a copy of the path."

Mason frowned. "I thought you said they hadn't released any photos."

"They didn't. But that doesn't mean they haven't got any," he told him. "Of course they'd take pictures."

"I guess the involvement of Erskine would explain the pressure Rose was referring to," Shadow pointed out.

Harlan stood up abruptly, aware that their only option could be taken away at any moment if they didn't get to the auction house quick enough. After all, if Nicoli was willing to steal the path, he'd want to get rid of photos of it. too. "Come on, Shadow. We need to speak to Rose, now." He looked at Mason. "Warn JD. We'll send copies when we get them and then head back to Gabe. And maybe, Shadow, Gabe should call for backup."

Eleven

G abe and Niel sat outside The Witch's Cauldron pub in the centre of Angel's Rest, bathed in bright sunshine.

They had a second pint in front of them, and the remnants of lunch were pushed to the side of the table, but despite that, Gabe felt on edge. He'd just ended the call from Shadow about the necromancer, and he'd updated Niel.

"Gabe, will you relax?" Niel said. "So, there's a necromancer. We've faced worse."

"I can't. We are now involved in some mad race for something that has existed for six hundred years, and all of a sudden, it's hot property! And some of my worry is your fault."

Niel laughed, and its boom disturbed the couple at the next table. He looked at their shocked faces and immediately lowered his voice. "My fault?"

"Yes you, voicing your worries about Hammond's map and vision and the whole Trinity of the Seeker."

"Better to be forewarned than forearmed."

Gabe just groaned. "Oh, shut up."

"Come on, you knew this wouldn't be an easy job. There's no such thing."

"I don't mind hard. What I dislike are the layers of subterfuge."

"You used to thrive on it."

"I was younger then."

Niel fell silent, and Gabe enjoyed the moment's peace as he debated their next steps. They were leaning back in their chairs, the wall of the pub behind them so they had a good view of the street, and both wore sunglasses.

Then Niel spoke softly. "Don't make any sudden movements, but I see a young woman with short, spiky black hair strolling down the high street."

"Are you thinking it could be our thief?"

"Yes. She's small and petite, just like Shadow describes her, and even from here I can see the bruise on her cheek." He gave a short laugh. "Shadow doesn't hold back, does she?"

"Okay. You've convinced me. Whereabouts?"

"She just exited the church."

"The church?" Gabe couldn't keep the disbelief from his voice. "What would she be doing in one of those?"

"Well, maybe she's a believer, Gabe? That happens. There are quite a lot of them. In fact, strictly speaking, we are, too."

"Not in the worshipping sense, we're not," Gabe answered, turning casually to talk to Niel, and looking down the street as he did so. "I see her. Looks like she's got a slight limp, too."

"Has to be her, right?"

"I guess so. I doubt she's here alone. Maybe that skinny Jensen kid Shadow mentioned is here, too."

"Should we follow her?"

"This place is quiet, and we stick out. We'd never pull it off."

"How dare you!" Niel said, looking at Gabe, affronted. "I can be discreet."

"You're the size of a mountain."

Niel shrugged, and the muscles across his shoulder flexed impressively. "It's a gift. Especially to the ladies."

"Don't even suggest attempting to speak to her," Gabe said, trying not to laugh. "I wonder where she's staying. There are lots of holiday cottages here, so I doubt it's far."

"Unless they've got somewhere just outside the town, like us."

"I tell you what," Gabe said, watching discretely as she passed them, heading to the far end of the high street where the antique shop was. "Why don't we visit the church? I want to know what she was looking at."

"Fair enough," Niel said, draining his pint. "Let's hope we don't burst into flames as we walk through the door."

St Thomas Church in Angel's Rest was a solid old building, built of pale grey stone with a tiled roof, surrounded by well-kept lawns and a hedge. It exuded peace, and Gabe couldn't help but feel he was intruding when he stepped inside the stone porch and pushed the heavy door open.

It was small but immaculate, and smelt of furniture polish. It had an arched ceiling, stained glass windows at the far end, narrow windows on either side, lines of wooden pews, a spectacularly ornate pulpit, and an altar. Fortunately, they were alone.

Gabe strolled down the nave, feeling confused. "This is old," he observed. "I wonder if it was here when Hammond was alive."

"It's possible. It's distinctly medieval in design. Maybe it has a connection we haven't figured out yet."

Gabe noted the wooden floor and smooth, plastered walls painted white. Nothing looked mysterious or as if something could be hidden, like in some churches; he thought particularly of the Church of All Souls in White Haven with the sealed chamber below it. "We need to check the date it was built."

Niel was standing by the altar, looking at the stained glass windows behind it. "But nothing appears disturbed in here. Maybe she was in here for personal reasons."

"Come on," Gabe said, "let's check the grounds."

Gabe led the way back outside, and for a few minutes they strolled across the grass and around the small cemetery behind it. He pointed at the tombstones. "Look at those dates—all from the 1430s and onwards. That's Phineas's time."

"So it was here when he was alive! I wonder if he's buried here."

Niel set off across the cemetery with purpose and Gabe searched with him, Niel's shout eventually calling him to his side. In front of him was an old gravestone, covered in lichen, the engraved name faded over time. "There. *Phineas Hammond. Died 1432.*" He stared at Gabe. "That's the year he completed the trinity."

"Interesting," Gabe said, feeling that this was another layer of weirdness. "Let's hope Shadow has got his diary."

------◆◇◆------

Gabe watched Shadow place the bundle of papers and images on the table next to the map, and heard the frustration in Harlan's voice as he said, "They're here already?"

"'Fraid so," Gabe told him, turning to see Harlan's face wrinkle with annoyance. They were in the conservatory again, enjoying the warmth of the afternoon sun. Gabe picked up a page from the stack, glancing at lines of scribbled text. "Well, Mia is. We didn't spot anyone else, but I doubt she's alone. You made good time."

Gabe hadn't expected to see Shadow and Harlan until the evening, so he was surprised when he heard the growl of Harlan's car on the drive later that afternoon.

Harlan thrust his hands in his pockets. "We left as soon as we saw Rose at Burton and Knight. There didn't seem any point in hanging around."

"You got copies of the document?"

"They gave me one copy, but it's a high resolution photo and we made more - some close ups too." He jerked his head to the table. "They're in that pile. We were right about Jensen. He did try to pressure Burton and Knight. He didn't even want them to display the path, but they basically told him to get lost, and conceded only the photos. I'm surprised they even did that. It's an ominous sign."

"Especially after what you told me," Shadow said. She'd finished emptying her messenger bag, and she stared at Harlan accusingly.

"What do you mean?" Gabe asked, looking confusedly between them both.

"Just that Harlan assured me Burton and Knight would never be intimidated, and yet..."

Harlan grimaced. "I feel Erskine's oily touch on this."

Niel had already pulled a chair up to the table to look at the new paperwork, but he said, "Tell us about him."

"I know very little, really. He's in his late thirties, short, round, and has these horrible, pale eyes that seem to look right through you. He appeared in London a few years ago and immediately started bidding on anything relating to demonology."

"Is that a common subject?" Gabe asked, leaning against the table's edge.

"For study? Reasonably so. The medieval period was obsessed with it, the church in particular. That's the type of material that Erskine typically goes for."

"So the fact that he seems to be interested in a document about angels is curious," Gabe noted. He watched Niel shuffle through the new pages, pulling out a couple that caught his eye.

"Very," Harlan agreed. "But the timeframe is right—medieval period, I mean." He started pacing. "I just need to do something to try and get a breakthrough! I feel we're getting nowhere."

"It will come," Gabe told him. "We've only been on this for a few days. I'll grab us a few beers and we'll start searching through the new material. Have you sent JD what you have on the path?"

"Sure. With luck, he'll make more sense of the text than I do."

"Is it that bad?"

Niel interrupted. "See for yourself." He'd extracted the file with the images of The Path of the Seeker and placed it on the table. "I was expecting to see instructions, but there are more diagrams in here than writing!"

"Alchemical symbols," Harlan explained as he pointed some out to Gabe. "It doesn't matter how many times I look at these, they never seem to stick in my brain."

"I can understand why," Gabe said. "But this is where JD excels, right?"

"Correct. He's been immersed in this for centuries."

"I guess we should familiarise ourselves with them anyway," Gabe said. "Although, I doubt they'll make much sense. It's less about identifying the symbols than interpreting them, and that requires a whole other level of understanding." He sighed, feeling like this was getting more complicated by the second. "Do we all want beer?" Everyone nodded, and he left Harlan and Niel talking while Shadow followed him into the kitchen. "How was London?" he asked her.

"Frustrating." She leaned down to a cupboard to grab some snacks, and he couldn't help but take in her curves. He looked away, feeling guilty, and stuck his head in the fridge to cool his thoughts, as she added, "But I met Olivia."

He grabbed four bottles of beer, shut the door, and turned back to her. "What's she like?"

"Cool. I think she'll end up joining us on this. Harlan says she's useful in a fight, and I think we'll have one. There's definitely more to this than we first thought."

Gabe opened a couple of bottles and handed her one, and after he'd sipped his own, he asked, "What did you make of the demon conjuror?"

She leaned against the counter. "He was a long way down the street, so too far away for me to get a feel for him. But Harlan doesn't strike me as a man who scares easily, so there must be substance to his concerns. The church thing sounds odd, too."

"With Mia? Yes, it is."

"Have you called for backup, yet?"

"A couple of hours ago. Nahum is arriving tomorrow, and Ash is on standby."

She sat on the countertop, took another sip of beer, and looked at him speculatively. "What's your demon fighting like?"

Gabe laughed. "That's a good question, and I can honestly say I'm not sure. What's yours like?"

She'd relaxed her glamour again, and her violet eyes glowed with mischief. "I'm not sure, either. They don't exist in my world, and I have yet to come across one here. Didn't you meet one on the other plane?"

It was a place he didn't like to think of, and it felt nightmarish now, like some drug-addled dream of fire, darkness, and chaos. "I did on occasions, but it was different there. They were shapeless, ever-changing things—well, some of them. Others had more substance. But we didn't engage them. They did their thing, and we did ours."

"Which was?" She leaned her elbows on her knees and watched him.

"Well, we didn't go fishing, or to the gym."

She rolled her eyes. "I'm serious. What was it like?"

"I can't describe it, not really." He considered the words he could use, and none of them seemed adequate. "We existed. It was both endless and seemed to last for mere seconds. Like time had no meaning. But I was aware of my brothers—sort of." He shrugged. "It certainly wasn't heavenly, but neither was it like the depictions of hell I have read, either. I was simply nothing."

Shadow teased him. "I'm sure you could never be nothing, Gabe."

He became acutely aware of her physicality, and for a second they just stared at each other, until Niel's shout broke the moment. "Where's my bloody beer?"

Gabe smiled ruefully and pushed away from the counter, grabbing the other two beers as he did so. "You're suggesting we develop a battle plan, then?"

"I'm presuming that a demon conjuror will use his tools to get what he wants. I've got the Empusa's sword, so I'm hoping that has demon-fighting properties, and of course I have my dragonium sword. That metal has many useful qualities, too. Whatever happens will prove interesting."

"Maybe we should have brought a witch with us."

"They're only a phone call away."

Gabe's thoughts immediately flew to Alex. He was the best at this sort of magic, and he'd always offered help where needed. Potentially, if nothing else, he could put up some protection for the house. "Good point. Let's see how the next couple of days go."

Twelve

The sound of the Bee Gees echoed through the ground floor of the house and into the conservatory, and every now and again Harlan heard Shadow singing. Harlan couldn't help but laugh. "Shadow never ceases to surprise me."

Gabe grinned at him. "I know! Who would have thought that she'd be a disco fan?" He shook his head in disbelief. "This is Zee's fault."

"Zee is a fan?" Harlan thought he must be hearing things.

Niel snorted. "No! Zee is responsible for our musical knowledge—well, he, Ash, and Barak—and this particular period was Zee's."

"Does she have the dance moves, too?" Harlan asked, unbidden images filling his mind of Shadow dancing.

Niel and Gabe laughed, and Gabe said, "Oh, yes. Wait until you hear Chaka Khan. Then the dancing really starts!"

"Barak dances with her!" Niel reminded Gabe. "That man has moves!"

"What an interesting household you have," Harlan said, comparing their farmhouse to his own quiet flat and suddenly wishing it was filled with a bit more life.

Niel rolled his eyes. "Never a dull moment." He looked around as Shadow came into the room with more beer. "Having fun in there?"

Shadow smiled broadly. She was barefoot and wearing a t-shirt and skinny jeans, and she danced rather than walked over to them. "Of course! I'm cooking to music. What could be better?"

Niel took a bottle from her outstretched hands. "Thanks for relieving me of that burden."

"My pleasure." She handed the rest of the drinks out and frowned at the paperwork on the table. They had split the work between them; Gabe was studying the map again, and Niel had opted to read through the copies of Hammond's dairies. "Better than doing that. Have you found anything interesting?"

Harlan looked at the images of The Path of the Seeker. "No, actually. It makes less sense now than it did earlier." He could feel a headache beginning and wasn't sure if beer would help, but then again, it was probably just what he needed. "I don't even know why I'm trying. I'm not an alchemist."

Shadow slid into the seat next to him, squinting at it as if it would bite. "Heard from JD?"

"No. But I didn't expect to yet. He'll have his entire library to use for reference. It makes sense that he'd stay at home, rather than come here."

"I've found a few interesting things," Niel said as he leaned back in his chair. "It seems Hammond's vision was spread over weeks. That's not surprising, really. The trinity is so detailed, it couldn't possibly have been given to him in a few hours."

"I doubt it can be interpreted in a few hours, either," Gabe said.

"Maybe not," Harlan admitted. "But the pressure's on now that a few others are involved." He looked at Niel. "Any mention in there of who gave him the vision?"

"Not specifically. Just frequent mentions of the angel who visited his dreams."

A thought suddenly struck Harlan. "Is this difficult for you two? I mean, angels were your fathers!"

Gabe shook his head, but his dark eyes assumed a faraway look. "No. It's intriguing, more than anything. I still have a hard time believing that they—or even just one of them—are giving instructions to humans."

"I'm the first to admit my Bible history is poor, but didn't they used to appear with reasonable frequency in those stories?" Harlan asked.

"I'm not a Bible scholar, either," Gabe said. "I know it exists, and Ash has read bits of it, but it was written well after our time. And the New Testament? Well, that happened a long while after we were killed by the flood."

Niel laughed. "Yeah, we are *old* testament! But, in real life," he sobered quickly, "the angels appeared to a certain chosen few only—and I mean a *few*. Aside from the fallen and their willingness to mate with human women. But they didn't hang around playing happy families."

Harlan rubbed his face, perplexed. "Now my brain really hurts." He stood and walked to the doors to the terrace, needing a break from complicated symbols and the confusion of the past. "It's clouding up again out there. I think we'll get more rain later."

"I hadn't planned on exploring outside tonight, anyway," Gabe said. He stood too, stretching his arms above his head. "We need more direction first. Otherwise, we're just stumbling about blind." He turned to Niel and Shadow. "I can see us returning home for a while until JD can decipher the path."

Harlan nodded. "I guess that makes sense. We can't stay here for weeks doing nothing."

His phone started to ring and he pulled it from his pocket, noting it was an unknown number. "Harlan here."

"Excellent," a cockney voice crowed in his ear. "I've been trying to get you all day."

Immediately, adrenalin flooded Harlan. "How did you get this number, Jensen?"

"That doesn't matter." Harlan was aware that the room had gone silent as the others listened. "What matters is that we need to chat about The Map of the Seeker."

"I don't know what you're talking about."

Jensen laughed. "Bullshit, mate. Why else would you be looking at The Path of the Seeker?"

"It's my job, idiot."

"Let's cut the crap and talk deals. You have the map, we have the path. I'm not sure how you pulled off that particular heist from under our nose, but I'll admit I'm impressed. Why don't we work together?"

"Because you're a sneaky little shit, that's why," Harlan answered, abandoning all pretence. They may as well draw the battle lines now. "And you're working with Erskine Hardcastle."

Jensen fell silent for a second, and Harlan knew he'd surprised him. Good.

When he eventually answered, Jensen's voice was threatening. "Then you know that Erskine always gets what he wants, and you'd do well not to cross him."

"You're not the only one with powerful clients."

"But we have deep pockets, Harlan."

"Your money doesn't interest me," Harlan told him. "Go away, and try to be a good boy." He hung up and turned to find the others staring at him.

"Does he know that we're here?" Gabe asked. "In this house?"

"No idea," Harlan admitted. "And I'm not sure how he got my number, either. But from this moment on, consider us under attack. Jensen pretty much threatened me with Erskine's power."

"In that case, we take it in turns to be on watch tonight," Gabe said, "and we bring all the weapons in from the car."

⚬

Shadow volunteered to take the second watch, and by 2:00am she was wide-awake and standing in the darkness of the living room next to Gabe, looking onto the shadowed drive.

It was raining again, and its steady drumming broke the silence of the night.

"I take it nothing has happened?" she asked Gabe.

His arms were folded across his chest and he shook his head. "Nothing at all. I've been around the perimeter, but it's as quiet as the grave out there. However, that was an hour ago. Let's have another look together before I go to bed. We'll start at the back."

He led the way through the house and into the conservatory, moving quietly despite his size, and had his hand on the door to the garden when Shadow saw movement beneath the trees. She placed her hand on his arm, his muscles like steel beneath her fingers, his skin warm.

"Wait. There, beneath the trees. Something moved."

Gabe paused, drawing them both back from the window and into the deeper darkness of the room. "Are you sure it's not the rain?"

Shadow didn't answer for a moment. She had sharp eyesight, and was pretty sure she hadn't imagined it. And then she saw it again. "To the right, beneath the oak. The shadows look all wrong." Something was creeping along the border, keeping to the shrubs.

"I see it," Gabe said softly, his voice barely audible. "Just one person, I think."

"Mia, perhaps."

"Unless it's an animal. Probably too big."

"I can leave from the front door and make my way around," Shadow whispered, eager to act. "I could get close enough behind to grab whoever it is."

He was unmoving for a moment, and then he looked down at her, uncertain. "You're stealthy, but not as strong as me."

"My blade is my strength." She glared at him, challenging his decision.

"We'd be better off waiting. Cover the window and doors, and then strike when they enter."

"That's passive."

She sensed rather than saw him smile. "Slow down, tiger. It's wet out there. It's harder to fight when you're slipping in mud."

"Spoilsport," she protested, adrenalin already surging through her.

"And besides," he added, "if I wanted to be passive, I'd just turn the lights on and scare them away. But they'd come back another night. I prefer to fight now."

She had palmed her dagger in anticipation, and was watching the garden again, spotting the creeping figure a little closer to the house. "Good. I want to see the fear in their eyes."

"You're scary, you know that?"

She shrugged. "When I need to be."

"Go wake Niel and Harlan. I'll wait here."

She seethed. "An order?"

"A request, you awkward madam!"

He refused to look at her, watching his quarry like a hawk, and although Shadow hated to go, she had to admit his size made him harder to get past.

She turned and ran, but before she'd even reached the bottom of the stairs, she froze. A black silhouette was at the front door, visible through the glass—the distinctive shape of someone tall and skinny. *Jensen?* She waited, and the figure moved to the right towards the windows in the sitting room where they had been only minutes before. Silently, she crept forward, all thought of waking Niel and Harlan forgotten. *How long had she got? And were there more than two of them?*

She followed the direction of the intruder, spotting the quick dart of the silhouette towards the side window, and she made a snap decision. *If there were more, they needed everyone awake.*

She raced up the stairs, barrelling into Niel's room, and he sat up abruptly. She hissed, "Niel! Get up, now!" Within seconds he was on his feet, already in jeans, but his chest was bare. "There are at least two intruders, one front, one back. Get Harlan. I'll be in the front room. And be quiet!"

Shadow didn't wait for a response, instead running back downstairs and approaching the sitting room with stealth and draped in glamour. But those minutes had cost her. The sound of rain was louder in here, and she saw that a side window was open bare inches. She sensed magic. *Was this intruder a witch?*

She dropped to a crouch, hoping the intruder was still in here and that Gabe wasn't being attacked already. But there was no sound from further in the house, and she had surely been too quick for them to get very far. She waited, confident she had melted into the darkness, and within seconds was rewarded when a figure emerged from the dark bulk of the curtains.

It edged across the room, pace quickening as he or she grew bolder, and Shadow saw the distinctive weasel face of Jensen, and the glint of hard steel in his palm. She waited until he passed her and paused in the hall at the bottom of the stairs, and then finally stepped behind him and kicked the small of his back. He crashed forward and landed with a thump on the floor, but in seconds had rolled to his feet, blade flashing. He lunged at her, but Shadow sidestepped and dropped, sweeping her leg out and bringing him to the ground again.

Out of the corner of her eye, she saw another figure emerge from the darkness of the other room across the hall. It wasn't Gabe or Harlan. Deciding to immobilise Jensen first, she smacked his arm on the hall floor and his knife skittered away. But he was wiry, and already trying to get to his feet. She punched him, and he groaned, barely moving. She was already crouching, knife out, but just as she was about to tackle the third intruder, Harlan appeared halfway down the stairs and leapt on the unknown assailant.

And then she heard a scream from the back of the house—a very *female* scream—and realised Gabe was fighting in the conservatory.

The sound galvanised the other two intruders into action.

For the next few minutes there were roars, groans, punches, sickening thuds, and the sound of breaking furniture all around. Shadow pulled her sword out of its scabbard, and with her pulse pounding in her ears and the rush of battle racing through her veins she took on Jensen, as all pretence at silence disappeared. Harlan was holding his own, trading punches, too.

"What the fuck!" Jensen shouted as Shadow's sword missed his throat by inches—deliberately. As much as she wanted to kill him, she reminded herself that the rules were different in this world.

"If you want the map, you weasly-faced little shit," she yelled, "you'll have to do better than this!"

She kept a close eye on his hands, watching for any spark of magic, but there was nothing, other than some fumbling in his pockets, and then trying to grab his knife off the floor.

And then an inhuman growl reached her ears from somewhere in the centre of the house and Jensen froze, his eyes darting nervously, and Shadow froze too, sword outstretched. Harlan and the other figure had also rolled to a stop, and after another unearthly howl, Jensen turned and ran for the open window, the second figure following, and Harlan and Shadow let them go.

"What the hell is that?" Harlan asked, breathless. He wiped the back of his hand across his lips, smearing blood.

"Sounds like a demon to me," Shadow said, quickly unsheathing the Empusa's sword so she was carrying both. She twirled them in her hands, eager to put them to use and not hold back. "Make sure the window is secure, and I suggest you stay here and guard the front entrance. And yell loudly if you need help—although, I think I might be busy."

Shadow sprinted down the hall and through the kitchen, finally sliding to a halt on the threshold of the conservatory. Gabe and Niel were circling a thrashing creature, all fire and smoke with eyes like live coals.

Flames were whipping across the room. Niel stood at the far side, restraining a wriggling and distraught Mia, as Gabe fought the demon. *Was he actually trying to catch it?* No matter. She ran in, feeling the hot lash of flame whip around her leg—and then something else. The dry, rattling creep of a withered hand on impossibly long arms.

She whirled, slicing and cutting at the strange grabbing fingers of the demon, pleased to hear its hiss of pain as her blade found flesh.

But Gabe had grabbed one of the thrashing fire whips, and was hauling the demon closer and closer as he wrapped the whip around his right hand. Her breath caught. His hand must be burning, but he didn't stop, and the creature roared, so loudly that Shadow thought her ears might bleed. Gabe didn't let go, pulling it ever closer, a look of fierce determination on his face as his muscles strained with the effort.

And then Gabe spoke in a language that set her nerves alight. Guttural, gut-wrenching noises that turned her stomach and made her shudder in revulsion.

Everything suddenly stopped.

Mia had fainted, and was hanging limply in Niel's arms. The flames that licked across the demon disappeared, and with another guttural noise that threatened to bring Shadow's dinner back, it seemed to answer Gabe.

Gabe responded, his face wild with fury, as the almost impossible language crawled from his tongue. He released his hold on the creature, and within a second it had vanished, leaving them all in shocked silence.

Thirteen

G abe's right hand and forearm burned with an almost unbearable pain, and he looked down to find that his skin was smoking.

Shadow was at his side in seconds, dragging him through to the kitchen and thrusting his wound under the running cold tap. She yelled, "Harlan, turn the lights on!"

They were still in near total darkness in the kitchen, and aware of noise behind him, he twisted to see Niel carrying Mia's unconscious body into the room and place her gently on the kitchen table. Niel caught his eyes. "I'll secure the building."

Niel turned the lights on as he left, and Gabe blinked at the sudden brightness. His arm still hurt like hell, the searing pain feeling like the burn was smouldering through to the bone, but Shadow's hands were cool and comforting, even more than the icy water that splashed over his skin, and she whispered something soothing, words that felt like a balm to his senses. She seemed like a dream to him.

He watched her as if from a distance, almost like his soul had retreated far away from his body, noting her soft creamy skin, the curve of her neck, and strong yet slim arms and hands, and he suddenly wanted to feel those arms wrapped around him. He swallowed, banishing the thought. *She wouldn't appreciate it.* But then she looked up at him, her captivating eyes full of concern, her lips parted, and he wondered if he was wrong.

For a second she just studied him, and then said softly, "What were you thinking? You could have died!"

He smiled, ridiculously pleased that she was concerned. "I'm still here, though."

"But look at your arm! You might have lost it! I know you're Nephilim, but can you grow limbs back?"

He still hadn't looked away. He couldn't. Her eyes were far prettier than his smoking skin. "I doubt it, but I took a chance. And besides, I heal quickly."

"That was a *demon*! It's no ordinary fire!"

"But I'm no ordinary man."

It was a challenge now. *Who would look away first?* He didn't want to. He wanted to stand here for hours, her cool skin on his, her soft voice a caress.

And then Mia groaned behind them, and reluctantly, they both turned.

Mia blinked and fluttered her lashes, and her head lifted as she looked around. And then alarm flooded through her and she leapt off the table, almost stumbling.

Shadow left his side in an instant. "Not so fast, Mia. We have some questions for you."

She looked wild-eyed at Shadow and whirled around, looking for a way out. But Harlan was already standing in the doorway, his arms across his chest, his face grim. Mia backed away towards the wall, trying to put as much distance between her and them as possible. Gabe, aware his arm was still smoking, stayed put, his arm remaining beneath the running water.

"We won't hurt you," Shadow said. She walked to the table and sat down, gesturing to the chair across from her. "If you answer our questions."

Mia shook her head. "No. I can't."

Her voice was soft, brittle, and Gabe thought she was younger than she looked. And beyond her defiance, she looked terrified. He wondered how much she remembered of the demon.

"They're simple ones," Shadow told her. "Who was the third person who attacked us tonight?"

Mia shook her head. "I don't know who you're talking about."

Shadow shook her head and started to twirl her dagger between her fingers. "Liar. Who was it? We know about you and Jensen, and we know you work for Nicoli and Erskine Hardcastle. Who was the other person?"

She looked nervously between them all, but still didn't speak.

Instead, Harlan did. "It was a man, I know that much." He shrugged when she remained silent. "No matter. I'll find out." He moved into the room, and Mia looked as if she wanted to melt into the wall. "What I *really* want to know is, did you steal The Path of the Seeker?"

"No," she said defiantly.

Harlan grinned. "Lying again? Come on. You have to answer something if you want us to let you go!"

She glared at him, some of her resilience returning. "Yes. Right from under your nose!"

"That's better. How far have you got with finding the place?"

"We haven't got the map. You have it!"

"But you'll have a copy. How far?"

Mia shook her head. "I don't know. I'm not privy to their schemes. I'm just the thief."

Gabe believed her. He wouldn't tell her too much if she worked for him.

Harlan nodded, probably coming to the same conclusion. He watched Shadow's whirling blade, then took another step towards Mia. "Where are you staying?"

"I can't say."

"Where?" His voice hardened.

She hesitated, and then said, "19 Barton Lane."

"With Erskine?"

She nodded.

"And Nicoli?"

"He arrives tomorrow."

"And the key? Do you have it?"

She hesitated again, and Shadow released the blade and it embedded in the wall next to Mia's head.

Mia flinched, her lips pressed close together and her eyes darting between all three of them. "I have no idea. I am just the thief."

Harlan glanced at Shadow and then Gabe, and Gabe knew she'd tell them nothing else. "You can go," he said to Mia. "Don't let me see you here again."

Her eyes widened and she trembled, but nodded silently.

Harlan stepped back, gesturing to the doorway. "I'll let you out of the front door."

Gabe watched as she hurried on shaking legs, but she paused in the doorway, turning to face him. "He has more than one demon."

Gabe nodded. "I know. It told me. I said that if it was sent here again, I would kill it. I trust it's delivering the message to his master right now." He lifted his arm from the water and showed her his smoking flesh. "I'm more than a match for it."

⚫

Ten minutes later, Gabe was sitting at the kitchen table, and Shadow, Niel, and Harlan were sitting with him.

Harlan had seen Mia safely off the property, and then helped Niel finish searching the house. Satisfied that they were secure and the paperwork was still safe in its hiding place, Niel brought the first aid kit in from the SUV, and its contents were now spread before them.

"Good. We have burn gel," Niel said, plucking the packet off the table and opening it.

Gabe's flesh had finally stopped smoking, and the burning pain had dulled, but he could still feel it. He looked at his skin dispassionately. A weal of red, burnt, and peeling skin spiralled around his forearm, and his hand had blackened flesh on it, particularly in a strip on his palm and across the back, where he had gripped the coiled flaming whip and pulled the demon towards him.

Shadow took the gel from Niel. "Let me. Unwrap a dressing."

"Yes, ma'am," Niel muttered, and Gabe suppressed a grin, grateful that he would feel Shadow's cool fingers again.

Harlan was leaning back in the chair, his arms crossed and expression bleak. Day-old stubble covered his chin, and dark circles were visible beneath his eyes. The kettle boiled, and he stirred. "What's that for?"

"Just put it in a jug and then in the fridge," Niel told him. "We need it to clean the wound when we redress it tomorrow."

Harlan nodded and stood. "Sure. And then I need a drink. A proper drink. Who wants one?"

"I wouldn't say no to whiskey," Gabe said, wincing as Shadow gently inspected his wounds.

"Bring the bottle in," Niel suggested.

"Gin for me," Shadow added. "It's in the fridge."

Gabe watched Shadow spread the gel over his skin and immediately felt relief. "That stuff is good."

"Not as good as Briar's balms would be," she said. "I think I'll ask her for a kit for us."

"That's a good idea," Niel agreed. "We should write a list. I'm sure Eli could make a lot of it. He is an apothecary, after all."

Gabe grunted. "I wasn't really anticipating that we'd need field dressings."

"I didn't think you'd try to wrestle a demon," Niel shot back.

Shadow was wrapping a non-stick dressing around his wound. "I didn't think you'd actually let it live!"

Harlan re-entered the kitchen with the whiskey, and he caught the end of the conversation as he placed it on the table. "Yeah. Why was that?"

"I thought that sending it back with a message might be more impressive than killing it," Gabe explained.

In seconds Harlan returned with glasses and Shadow's gin, and he sat down, pouring everyone a hefty measure. "You were showing off?"

Gabe laughed dryly. "Not exactly. It was a warning to Erskine. I thought it might make him back off."

"It's always good to confound your enemy," Niel added. "They won't know what to make of that."

"Maybe," Harlan said, before downing his first shot in one gulp. He slammed the glass down on the table and topped it up straight away. "Damn. That was good. Although, I'm more of a Kentucky Bourbon man."

"Did you see the demon?" Gabe asked Harlan. In all the confusion, he didn't remember spotting Harlan in the conservatory.

"I was making sure our two intruders had gone, but I arrived at the door in time to see you 'talk' to it." He shuddered. "I don't know what I expected a demon to look like, but I am not ashamed to admit that it was pretty terrifying. Want to explain how you can speak demon?"

"I think you know we're adept at languages. Demon language is just another one," Gabe said, watching Shadow finish wrapping the gauze bandage around his arm and securing it. "Admittedly, it's archaic, a language birthed from the Earth itself. Much like the language of the angels."

Shadow picked her gin up. "That was the ugliest language I've ever heard. I thought I was going to throw up."

"Me, too," Harlan agreed. "It's like my whole body rebelled against it."

Gabe nodded. His flesh recoiled from it, too. He'd felt it in the pit of his stomach. "It is not meant for human ears. And I'm not sure you'd even survive hearing the true voice of an angel."

"Why?" Shadow asked. Her hands were cupped around her glass, but she wasn't relaxed. She was poised for action, and her swords were propped on an empty chair within easy reach.

Gabe's injured arm rested lightly on the table, but the fingers of his left hand rubbed the fine grain of the wood as he remembered the last time he had heard an angel speak. It was millennia ago. He looked up to find Niel staring into his whiskey, also lost in his thoughts. He sighed. "They speak the language of fire. It is both exquisitely beautiful and horribly painful."

"Fire!" she said, surprised.

"It is not of this world."

"You told Mia the demon spoke to you. Is that true?" Harlan asked.

"Yes. I really did tell it that I would erase it from existence if I saw it again. And then it couldn't resist boasting that the next time, he would return with more and they would be too powerful to overcome. I told him they would fail, and to tell Erskine that I doubted he would be so brave without his demon servants." He shrugged. "It went."

Shadow frowned. "He really controls them? When they appear? What they do?"

"Yes, through ritual magic."

"Although," Niel added, "it is a fine line that a conjuror walks. If they push too far, or take too few precautions, a demon will strike back. They do not like to be manipulated."

"So, in theory," Harlan said, thoughtfully, "Erskine will be sitting in a room, the demon contained in a circle of protection in front of him. He can summon it and then send it to do his bidding, right?"

Gabe nodded. "I believe so. Or, the conjuror himself is in the circle, protected from the demon that prowls without. Even in our time such men existed."

Harlan rested his elbows on the table, and leaned his chin into his left hand. "So, what does a demon conjuror want with The Trinity of the Seeker? Angels are not demons."

Niel grunted. "That's debatable."

Gabe shook his head, puzzled. "I don't know. But Niel is right. I have read some people's interpretations of angels, and many are wrong. While some angels undoubtedly protected humans, others despised them for being less than them. They were also insanely jealous of their free will. Angels had none. They were there to do the will of their God."

"Which is why some had fallen," Niel added. "Then they were independent. Free to do as they chose. And they created us."

"To control humans," Harlan said. "But if they had fallen, why not influence humanity directly? Why mate with women?"

"Angels do not belong in this world," Niel patiently explained. "They were never made for this existence. The fell to Earth, but were never a part of it. To assume human form and mate with women was difficult, and in the long term they couldn't sustain it. But they still resented humanity's free will. Their mission was control, and we were created to do that."

Gabe's old grievances started to stir in his gut, and he felt his anger rising. "And not all fell by choice. Some were sent to fight the ones who willingly fell, and some of those created us, too. Either way, we were slaves to their will. Until we rebelled."

"Wow." Harlan stared vacantly at the table for a moment as he absorbed the information. "This is too weird. So there was division among the angels."

"Huge division. There were factions, battles, insurrections. Betrayal."

Niel reached for the whiskey bottle and topped his glass up, his face grim. "And that's why I doubt that this temple, or whatever it is, can be good. Fate is stacked against that likelihood. Did you know that after Hammond completed the trinity, he died?"

"Did he?" Shadow asked. "How?"

"I don't know the details, yet," Niel told her. "We found his grave earlier, in the cemetery behind St Thomas's Church in Angel's Rest."

She stared at them all. "That's ominous."

"Yes, it is," Niel agreed. "I'll keep reading tomorrow. I haven't finished his diary yet."

Gabe nodded, rubbing his chin with his good hand. He still hadn't touched his drink, mainly because he thought he needed a clear head, although he was also sure the demon wouldn't return that night. "I'll call Alex tomorrow, see if he can put some protection on the house...something to deter demons. It worries me that Erskine can send them inside the building."

"You also need better weapons," Shadow told them. "The ones you have are not magical. El could strengthen them with properties that do more damage against anything supernatural. My dragonium sword was pretty effective, as good as the Empusa's, and that's because it was forged by fey. Magic is bound into the metal."

"It's a good point," Niel said. "A spell to enhance my axe would be very welcome. And it would be good to have a sword again—a good one."

Shadow leaned forward, animated. "Her friend Dante could make you all swords, or whatever you need, but in the meantime, El can improve what we have." She paused for a moment. "You know, I thought Jensen had used magic to get through the window, but he's not a witch. I'm wondering if he was given a spell to use...something a witch made for him. El told me they'd done something similar for the three ghost hunters."

"Like a one-off spell?" Niel asked, confused.

"I think so."

Gabe sighed. "Great! Magic for hire. That's all we need. All right. I'll ask Alex if El can come with him, to juice up what we have here."

Harlan sighed and stretched. "That sounds good. And now I'm going to bed, because I have a feeling that tomorrow will be another big day."

"You should all go," Niel said, staring at Gabe in particular. "You're injured and need to rest. I'll watch for the rest of the night."

Gabe flexed his arm. "It's feeling better already. I'm hoping it will have healed a lot in twenty-four hours."

"Maybe. But go to bed anyway." Niel grinned. "And I'll reward our success tonight with a big breakfast tomorrow."

Fourteen

Harlan stretched in the large, comfortable bed and realised he could smell bacon. *Such an ordinary, heart-warming smell,* he thought as he blinked the sleep away. Despite the disturbed night, he'd managed to sleep well, finally. But as the events came back to him, he couldn't help but wonder what JD had got them into.

Of all the strange things he'd experienced in his life so far, a Nephilim battling a demon in a conservatory was one of the oddest. And seeing Shadow wielding her sword in the hall was pretty cool, too. He laughed as he recalled Jensen's horrified face, and then sobered quickly. He may be an obnoxious pain in the ass, but even he'd been scared when he heard the demon.

Harlan tried to recall what the other attacker had looked like. It was a man, he was sure of that. Average height and build, reasonably strong, and dark hair—although, in the darkness of the hall, it was hard to tell. He had a good punch, he knew that much. Harlan's ribs and jaw ached from the blows the man had landed. No doubt he was one of Nicoli's team members he hadn't met before. He should have asked Mia what his name was last night, but to be honest, he was more worried about Erskine. With luck, Gabe's message would have either scared him or infuriated him, or both, and that was fine with him.

The scent of bacon soon became stronger, and remembering the Nephilims' huge appetite, he decided he'd better get out of bed before it was all eaten.

Harlan shouldn't have worried. By the time he arrived in the kitchen, showered and shaved, he found Niel setting out a mountain of fresh, crusty bread in the middle of the table, and saw more food on the stove.

"That's a sight for sore eyes," Harlan said as he headed to the counter to make coffee. "Am I the only one up?"

Niel greeted him warmly. "Morning, Harlan! Nope, Shadow is already outside, trying to see where Mia came over the wall. For a little thing, she's pretty resilient."

"You're talking about Mia, right? I wouldn't call Shadow a 'little thing!'"

Niel's laugh filled the kitchen. "Hell, no. She'd have my balls for earrings!"

"Ouch," Harlan said, wincing. "And where's Gabe?"

"Helping." He looked at Harlan and gave a knowing wink.

Harlan almost spilled his coffee in shock. "*Really? Are they—*" His question hung in the air. *Why was he so surprised?* They had chemistry. That was obvious. Maybe he was disappointed. He'd half wondered if he might stand a chance with Shadow himself.

Niel shook his head, a wry smile on his face, as he put bread in the toaster. "No, they are not. Yet. And it's not worth my life to ask."

"Fair enough," Harlan said as he processed the information. Before he could ask anything else, he heard a knock at the front door, and he immediately grabbed a knife from the counter.

"I'm hoping that's Nahum," Niel said, striding across the room and picking his axe up as he headed into the hall. "Stay here and watch the sausages!"

Within moments he heard voices, and then Nahum followed Niel into the kitchen.

Nahum was uncannily like Gabe, even in his mannerisms, and he nodded at Harlan as he picked up a slice of fresh bread and took a bite, mumbling a greeting. "Sorry," he said, once he'd swallowed. "I started early and didn't really eat before I left."

"You heard about the demon?" Harlan asked him.

"Yeah. Courtesy of my brother, at four in the morning."

Niel shrugged. "Gabe's orders."

"It's fine. Where is he?"

"Just coming now," Niel said, pointing out the window.

When Gabe and Shadow entered the room, they were in the middle of an argument, and Shadow was fuming. "Why not? They'd never see me. I can hide better than you, you big-winged idiot."

"Because I say so. What are you going to do if you get spotted and Erskine sends a demon?"

"*In the middle of the street?* Besides, he won't see me! I'm too good." She sounded incredulous, and then she saw Nahum. "Hey, Nahum. Your brother is an idiot."

Nahum just grinned. "I know. But adorable too, right?"

"Since when?" she scoffed, marching to the counter and picking up a slice of crispy bacon.

Niel slapped her hand. "Sit! Or you'll get nothing!"

Harlan saw her hand slide to her knife as she glared at him, and then clearly thought better of it. She stalked to the table and sat down with a thump.

Niel turned to Harlan and whispered, "Sexual tension."

Harlan tried not to laugh and failed, and was rewarded with twin glares from Gabe and Shadow.

"All of you, sit now!" Niel instructed. "Harlan, take the plate of sausages and bacon."

The breakfast was a chaotic, noisy affair, as they caught Nahum up on the events of the night and their progress, or lack of, so far.

"How's your burn?" Harlan asked Gabe.

"It doesn't feel too bad, but I guess we'll see when we change the bandage."

"It can wait 'til later," Shadow told him, gesturing with her fork. "Burn dressings should stay on as long as it's not leaking."

"Ugh," Nahum said, wrinkling his nose. "Leaky wounds. Nice conversation over breakfast."

"Like you have a weak stomach," she shot back.

"By the way," Gabe said, "I phoned Alex once I got up. He'll be here in a few hours, with El."

"And bringing some balms from Briar?" Harlan asked.

"I mentioned it, so hopefully."

Harlan nodded. "It's handy that you have witch friends. There are a couple we use in London on occasion, but I don't know them that well."

"I take it you have resources all over the city?" Nahum asked.

"And beyond."

"Good to know," Nahum said thoughtfully. He turned to Gabe. "So, now I'm here, what do you want me to do?"

"Look at the documents," he answered, "and see if we've missed something, because so far I feel we're wading through treacle."

"And I'll phone JD," Harlan said, pushing his empty plate away and standing up. "He might have news."

<hr />

Harlan's conversation with JD didn't inspire him. In fact, it downright worried him.

He walked into the conservatory to update the others, relieved to see that the room looked better than it had done a few hours earlier.

The demon, and the fight in the hall, had caused damage to furniture and decorative objects that Harlan knew The Orphic Guild would have to pay the bill for, but at least there had been no windows broken. The three Nephilim and Shadow were once again sitting around the table, the paperwork shared between them, and Nahum and Gabe were conferring quietly together.

Harlan joined them at the table. "JD is struggling with the translation, too."

"Why?" Gabe asked, his dark eyes troubled. Harlan noticed he still moved his injured arm gingerly, and that was another worry he added to his list.

"Well, it seems that alchemy hasn't been the top of JD's list for many years now. He's been focussed on astronomy and math—his first love. So, although he has an entire library of alchemical documents, he hasn't really studied them for years." He looked at everyone's shocked faces, and tried to play down their concerns. "I know. To be fair, it sounded like he hadn't slept for days. He's working very hard to decipher the path. Apparently, having the original document is better—something about magic in the paper itself." He shrugged. "Anyway, the upshot is, I have no bad news to share, but JD promises to update us as soon as he can."

"Bollocks," Gabe exclaimed, annoyed. "Let's hope that Erskine is having as many problems."

"I've found something," Niel said, looking up with a frown. "From what I can gather from Hammond's diary—and it's tricky, because his writing is confusing and the account rambling in places—it seems that once he'd finished the trinity, he decided it had to be split up."

"What? Why?" Nahum asked.

Niel barked out a laugh. "He doesn't say! He just rambles about being duped and that the trinity is too dangerous for mortal eyes." He referred to the papers in front of him. "He says, 'My end is nigh, but I will do what I can in the short time I have. I cannot destroy them, he has seen to that, but I will hide them. I am more devious than he thinks.'" He looked up. "He never discloses who he is, or why he knows his end is nigh!"

"Oh, great," Gabe said, sarcastically. "He develops a conscience, but won't tell anyone anything!"

"Better than not having one at all," Shadow pointed out. "And he successfully split these documents up for years. I wonder why he couldn't destroy them?"

They all eyed the map warily, and Niel said, "This could explain why it looks so well preserved."

Without warning, Gabe snatched the map off the table and tried to rip it in half, and Harlan couldn't help but shout, "No! What are you doing?" And then his mouth dropped open as Gabe failed to tear it.

Gabe looked amused. "Well. This is something!"

Harlan's heart was still thumping. "Holy hell, Gabe. That was risky."

Nahum grinned. "Let's try something else." He pulled a lighter from his pocket and held a flame to the corner of the map. Nothing happened.

"Oh, shit. It's not even smoking!" Harlan said. He reached out his hand, and Gabe passed him the map. He ran his fingers over it. *It felt like paper, and it looked like paper...* "What could do this?"

Shadow shrugged. "Magic. Let me try my swords." She walked over to the side of the room where she'd left them, and brought them back to the table. She held the dragonium sword up first. "Spread it on the table again, Harlan."

He eyed her suspiciously, and then reluctantly laid it flat for her. "Just try a corner!"

She nodded, and then chopped the sword down quickly. Sparks flew from where the blade made contact with the paper, and Shadow's arm jerked back in shock. "Ow! I felt that! So, the finest fey metal doesn't work, either!"

By now, all of them had drawn forward and were staring at the map, and Gabe said, "And the Empusa's?"

Shadow tried that too, and the same thing happened.

Gabe leaned back in his chair and ran his hands through his hair, looking frustrated. "Shit. Where the hell does this lead to?" He looked at Niel. "Anything else in that diary?"

He grimaced. "He rambles, and with every entry he sounds more deluded. He mutters about knowledge and the fall of man, and then it gets to the point where I can't decipher his scribbles anymore. And then they end." He squinted at the page, and then referred to another document. "According to this account, which is written by a contemporary, he died only hours after his last entry, and that was only days after he finished the Trinity—The Key of the Seeker, actually."

"The final missing part," Gabe said softly.

"What did he die of?" Nahum asked.

"He died suddenly in his sleep. Heart attack? Aneurism? A curse?" He shrugged. "We'll never know."

Harlan looked at the map in front of him as if magic would ooze out of it and infect the rest of them. "So, whoever caused this to be made, must have killed him."

"It might not have been deliberate," Nahum suggested. "It could have been the accumulation of the pressure of making the trinity. From what Niel is saying, it affected him badly."

"All very mysterious!" Shadow said, smiling impishly.

"I don't know why you're looking so pleased," Gabe said, suddenly annoyed. "This is frustrating!"

She rolled her eyes and tutted. "All good mysteries are! It's a challenge, and I like challenges."

"You're a challenge," he muttered. "Living with some screwball fey. I'm going to age before I should."

She snorted. "Drama queen."

Gabe studiously ignored her, instead turning to Niel. "Good work. Keep searching. Hopefully you'll uncover more useful stuff. See if there's something in the earlier entries that indicates how this all started."

Niel nodded. "Sure thing."

Nahum stood up and walked to the wall of windows that looked onto the back garden. "It's stopped raining again. I'm going to head out and walk the site. I'd like to get a feel for it, in case inspiration strikes."

"I'll come too," Shadow said, rising to her feet. "Now we know that The Order of Lilith is here, we should expect to see them everywhere, and they'll be searching, too."

"Is there anything you want me to do?" Harlan asked, feeling useless.

"Yeah, actually," Gabe said thoughtfully. "I want to know about that church in Angel's Rest—St Thomas's. Mia was in it, therefore it must have significance."

"Sounds good," Harlan agreed. He was happy to do anything that kept him busy and stopped him worrying about fiery demons.

Fifteen

S hadow stood on a crag looking over the narrow gorge, hands on hips, and frowned at the landscape around her. Somewhere beneath her feet was The Temple of the Trinity.

Nahum stood next to her. "I can see why you've been having trouble. It all sort of looks the same."

"I know. Rocks, grass, crags and crevices, and the real possibility that I may break my neck." She turned to look at him, and found that he was grinning. "What?"

"You're as nimble as a goat. It would take more than this to break your neck."

She smiled, secretly pleased. "Well, true. But I'd still rather not have to scramble up and down this slippery ravine."

He nodded to the east. "So that way is the entrance to the large series of caves under here?"

"Yes. It's a tourist attraction. Hundreds of people everywhere, and the caves have been explored for years." She shrugged, perplexed. "I don't understand why anyone would want to wriggle through tiny rock holes just to find caves for pleasure."

"I would imagine that not many people would want to engage in the hunt for dangerous occult items."

"I suppose you're right," she admitted. "To each their own."

He pulled his phone out of his pocket and opened the series of photos he'd taken of the map. "Let's see if we can make any progress." He pointed. "This line here suggests this long ravine to me. Yes, it's out of proportion, but it must be it."

She peered over his arm. "I agree. The stream runs through it, too. I know that sign—it's the elemental sign of water." She indicated the upside down triangle drawn on the map. "There are a few of those. I suspect they're small streams, or a spring, maybe."

Nahum looked at her. "Well, aren't you full of surprises?"

"I read stuff!"

"Well, those signs," he said, enlarging the picture to show her, "are runes. Hammond really did use all sorts of symbols on this. This one means power."

"You're right. He doesn't use one system at all."

"That's interesting, isn't it? Maybe it's significant," Nahum reasoned.

Shadow looked at the view, but her mind was elsewhere. "Angels speak many tongues, is that right?"

"Right, although their own language is that of fire."

She nodded. "Gabe said as much. And you speak many languages too, right?"

"Yes, although signs and symbols are harder for us. They are a type of language, but they have many interpretations." He shrugged. "Like words, I guess!"

"Are there any symbols on there that only you would know?"

Nahum didn't speak for a moment. "It's hard to say. I'm not sure. Not that I've seen so far."

"But you said the map was complex. Those strange, fantastical faces and creatures have shapes within them." An idea was forming, and she didn't like it. Not one bit.

"Yes. We've found runes in faces, alchemical symbols, and elemental signs. The runes certainly indicate strength, power, and wealth, but they don't mark one particular place. Unless that's hidden in more layers of symbols."

"Perhaps the reason this map has so many different symbols is because it was meant for someone who was good at many languages. Like Nephilim."

Nahum's deep blue eyes narrowed with suspicion. "You're suggesting this was made for us?"

"Perhaps. Or it was intended for those who are as clever as you, because they need to have a broad range of knowledge to decipher it—polymaths, magicians, scholars... Whatever is hidden must have great value and is deserving of only the worthy. I think we've said that before. Who is more worthy than the Nephilim? The sons of angels."

"We weren't considered that worthy at the time—well, later we weren't. We were venerated as kings for a while, until the tide turned against us. Literally!"

Shadow knew she was on to something, she could just feel it. "But some thought you worthy! And maybe still did many years after you'd gone." She started pacing. "Maybe an angel thought you might be back and wanted to leave you a gift. Or maybe some of you survived after all, and it was left for them?"

"No!" Nahum said suddenly. "Stop. This is too much!"

"Why? Because of what it implies? The temple exists somewhere beneath us. This is called Angel's Rest! Where did the name come from, Nahum? I talk to Dan a lot! Place names mean something. They retain meaning for years, and although the names modernise over time, they carry a kernel of truth in them. Angel's Rest! I know we've joked about this name, but it must mean something! And you know what else?"

Nahum groaned. "No, and I don't know if I want to."

"Of course you do. After our last encounter with tombs I talked to Dan about them."

"Dan from Happenstance Books?"

"Yes. Tombs were constructed for millennia. As we know, people were buried in them. Some were made to align to the sun at various parts of the day or year." She spread her hands wide. "This could be, too! Or it's specific to you!"

Nahum's tanned olive skin turned paler and his muscular shoulders rose and fell with an enormous sigh. "But we, the Nephilim, don't understand it. We have no idea where to look."

"The wealth sign. Where is it?"

He gave her another long, weary look and then scrolled the photos again, pulling one up and enlarging it. "This place here has wealth and power signs, a rune of victory, and," he paused, "kinship I think."

"Kinship? Where is that particular cluster?"

He looked around, finally pointing across the narrow ravine. "I estimate...there."

"Come on, then."

Half an hour later, after much scrabbling and swearing, Shadow emerged onto a narrow platform of rock, and Nahum scrambled up next to her.

"This would be so much easier with wings," he grumbled.

She smiled at him triumphantly. "Another reason why this is meant for you!"

They were on a narrow lip of stone, surrounded by tumbles of rock, bushes, and stunted trees. Nearby was a fast-flowing stream that was more of a waterfall because of the incline of the hill. The ground fell away beneath their feet, and they were both breathless.

Shadow rested her hand on the stone, warm from the midday sun that peeked through the clouds. She cast aside her glamour, allowing her fully fey self to feel the beat of the earth beneath her skin, and she closed her eyes, breathing deeply. She smiled. Despite the fact that magic was not so obvious in this world, it was still here. And there was something else.

She opened her eyes and found Nahum watching her. "What have you found?"

"You have a distinct signature. You smell different than humans, and your energy is different. It's not obvious, but I can tell because I spend a lot of time with you, and I'm fey."

Nahum rolled his eyes. "Tell me something I don't know."

"Piss off. You need to say something in your language."

"My language?"

"Yes. You must have one. Your original language, not ones you've learnt. Like mine." She greeted him in fey, enjoying the feel of it as it rolled off her tongue.

He smiled. "Give me a few more lines, like tell me what we've been doing this morning!"

"Why?"

"Just do it."

Wondering why, she spoke again, this time for much longer, and when she'd finished, he laughed and answered her, and for a moment she thought she might cry. "You speak fey!"

"All languages, Shadow. But reading or hearing a good sample first helps." He smiled gently, his whole face lighting up. "If you want, we can speak it more often."

Shadow couldn't stop herself, and she burst into tears. Her hands flew to her mouth, and then her eyes. "Sorry. This is stupid of me. It's so nice to hear my own language again. I never thought to ask."

He pulled her close and hugged her, crushing her against his chest. "Sister, just ask, any time."

"Thank you," she mumbled, and then stepped back as he released her. "Now, your turn. Although, obviously, I can't answer."

"Why not? You speak English," he asked genuinely confused.

"The Otherworld was at one point closely aligned with this one, and humans and fey crossed regularly. Human languages have been absorbed into our own. "

Nahum nodded, looked around, and then uttered a string of something unintelligible, but that sounded so musical she felt it deep within her. But before she could comment, the ground rumbled beneath her feet and she almost fell off the ledge. Nahum's hand shot out to grab her, and for a moment they both staggered and then fell to their knees.

"What did I do?" Nahum asked, looking around wildly.

Shadow turned around, still on her knees, wriggled to the edge of the stone shelf, and peered over the side into the dense shrubs beneath. There in the shadows, where the sun hadn't yet penetrated, she saw a deeper blackness. "Nahum, down there! Can you see it? It looks like a narrow opening!"

Lying flat on his stomach next to her, he stared into the undergrowth. "Are you sure that wasn't already there?"

"No," she admitted. "But that looks like a fresh fall of stone, and some shrubs have been ripped from the earth."

He grinned at her. "Have we actually found the entrance?"

"I think we have!" she answered, triumphantly. "What did you say?"

"I said, 'I am here to claim The Trinity of the Seeker. Show me the path, for I am worthy.'"

"Wow. Very dramatic," she said with a smirk.

"I thought the moment called for it." He looked down at the dark entrance. "Should we? It will be a scramble to reach it."

She was already rising to her feet, anxious to explore. "Of course."

Within minutes, after a hair-raising descent that was more of a slide than anything controlled, they both halted in front of a narrow break in the rock, utter blackness beyond it.

"That's going to be a squeeze," Nahum noted, "but I'm not turning back now. Are you sure you want to after all your caving talk earlier?"

"Of course!" she said impatiently. "After you. You opened it, you should have the honours!"

Nahum gingerly stepped inside the narrow cleft, and Shadow followed. Beyond was a passage, the rock pressing closely on either side. They both stood for a moment, letting their eyes adjust to the darkness, and then Nahum continued, sometimes turning sideways to squeeze through the gap. After a few minutes the passageway opened up into a square space, and Shadow stopped, shocked.

This was no rough cave; it was elegantly carved from the rock. The walls were smooth, almost polished, and the ceiling overhead was domed, but more surprising was the doorway etched into the rock in front of them. A series of flowing shapes was carved into the surface, precise and beautiful.

"Can you read that?" Shadow asked.

Nahum was standing in front of the doorway, his hands running over the surface and the edges, and he looked bewildered.

"Nahum, are you all right?"

He glanced at her, never taking his hand from the stone. "It's the language of fire!"

"Angel language! What does it say?"

"'Welcome, Seeker. Say the words and the worthy will enter. Be sure of your intent, for all knowledge lies here. Life lies here. Death lies here. The path to glory awaits.'"

"All knowledge?" she asked, a thrill of excitement and trepidation running through her. "Wow. What does 'say the words' mean?"

He shrugged, finally stepping back from the doorway. "I don't know—maybe the inscription? Maybe it's something from the path? I'm not risking saying anything right now though. We need to come back with the others."

⸺◆⸺

When Shadow and Nahum arrived back and told the others what they had found, Gabe looked at them incredulously. "You found it and left it unguarded?"

They were in the conservatory again, and he glared at Shadow and Nahum, his arms folded across his chest. "What if The Order of Lilith is already there?"

"It's okay, Gabe," Nahum said, trying to reassure him. "We checked that place from various angles, and it's really hard to see."

Shadow's hands were on her hips, and she glared back at him. "We're not idiots! We debated whether I should stay, and I could have. No one would have seen me! But what would be the point? It's well off the track, and there are lots of trees and bushes around it. And besides, it goes nowhere at the moment."

"Yeah," Nahum agreed. "The doorway to whatever lies beyond is sealed shut!"

"But," Gabe said fuming, "The Order of Lilith has the path! They might have deciphered it!"

"We have it, too," Harlan pointed out. "Admittedly in photographic form, and we haven't figured it out."

Gabe took a deep breath and Shadow could see he was trying to calm down, but he still looked at them suspiciously, a myriad of emotions flashing across his face that Shadow couldn't understand. "You're both filthy, too!"

"Herne's horns! Scrambling up and down muddy paths and almost falling off a narrow rocky shelf will do that to you," Shadow shot back. "The whole ravine shook when it opened, and I admit, if not for Nahum's quick reflexes, I'd have fallen to the bottom of it." She patted Nahum's arm. "Your brother's big muscles saved the day."

If anything Gabe looked even crosser, but Nahum and Niel just looked amused.

Gabe narrowed his eyes at Nahum's expression, and ground out, "Sorry. And well done for finding it!"

Niel asked Nahum, "You spoke the old language?"

Nahum nodded. "It was Shadow's idea." Nahum strode over to the table and cleared the other papers off the map. "Shadow pointed out that the symbols are varied—runes of various types, alchemical symbols, elemental symbols, some Greek, some Latin, old English... There is no common language here! But what is common is the fact that we speak many languages—and yes I know, signs and symbols are different. But alchemists, magicians, and many others who are interested in the occult have similar skills to us."

Shadow butted in. "This is a map for the worthy—people who can prove their knowledge!"

"To be worthy of greater knowledge," Niel said, nodding.

"I suggested that maybe this map was potentially made for you," Shadow said, almost tentatively.

"For us?" Gabe questioned, his dark brown eyes boring into hers.

"Maybe. Speaking your language uncovered it." She shrugged. "Potentially another language may have worked, too—or whatever ritual is in The Path of the Seeker."

Harlan nodded, excited. "Multiple entryways, depending on whoever gets there first. But whoever that is has to have the right knowledge and skills! That sounds plausible!"

"And you say it's the language of fire written on the door?" Niel asked.

"Yes," Nahum answered. "Do we want to go back? Now? We deliberately didn't try to trigger anything."

Gabe looked at everyone's expectant faces, and it was clear he was wrestling with what to do, but Harlan spoke first.

"We need to inform JD before we do anything! We are here for him, after all. And, although we might be able to open the door, what if there are more doorways, more tests? We need the path deciphered before we proceed."

"I still want to see it, though," Gabe told them. "Maybe tonight. I presume you can find it in the dark?"

Nahum and Shadow just looked at him, both incredulous, and Shadow bit back a sarcastic comment. "Of course."

"Did you see any sign of Mia or Jensen or anyone?"

"No," Shadow assured him. "A few casual walkers, but no one we recognised. And as we said, the opening is well off the path."

He sighed. "All right. Tonight, then."

A knock at the front door interrupted their conversation, and Niel said, "That must be Alex. I'll go."

Within minutes, El and Alex followed him into the conservatory, carrying a pack each and holdalls. Shadow grinned, heading to El and hugging her. "Sister. It's good to see you! It's been too long."

El was a tall blonde, statuesque and willowy, and Shadow considered her a good friend. There was something about her that resonated with Shadow. Part of it was that her height and build reminded her so much of the fey, but mainly it was El's lack of regard for convention that struck a chord. With her bold makeup and piercings, Shadow admired her free spirit.

"The last time I saw you," Shadow said, "you were dancing around the Beltane fire on the beach!"

El laughed. "I certainly was. All that Beltane magic got under my skin! You were dancing, too!"

"True," Shadow admitted. "That was a good night! It reminded me a little of the Otherworld."

"Where's my hug?" Alex asked, jokingly put out. Alex was tall, with shoulder-length brown hair and permanent stubble on his chin, and was charmingly flirtatious. He now lived with Avery, another witch in White Haven.

"Sorry." She grinned, hugging him, too. "It's good you could both come and help. Being invaded by three intruders and a demon last night was fun, but annoying."

Gabe grunted and shook Alex's hand. "'Fun' is one word for it, I guess. But thank you. I know you must be busy."

Alex shrugged. "I am, but fortunately Zee could cover me. I think he'd rather be here, though."

"By the time we're through with this, we might need him," Gabe admitted.

Alex spun on his heels, looking around. "This is quite some place."

"That's my fault," Harlan said. "JD likes good accommodation."

"Well, there's good, and there's good!" El said, clearly impressed. "This is a big place to protect, but I'm sure we can pull it off!"

"Thank you!" Gabe said, looking relieved.

She nodded at her bag. "We've come prepared. But Alex is your man for demon protection."

Harlan asked, "Are you staying tonight? There's room if you need to."

"No," Alex answered, shaking his head. "We'll leave once it's done—unless you really need us?"

"Hopefully we'll be okay," Nahum told him. "Besides, this thing could go on for weeks. As long as the house is protected, we'll at least be sleeping soundly."

"Mind me asking what you're looking for?" Alex asked, a wry smile on his face. "A bit of background might be helpful."

Niel offered them chairs. "Our manners are shocking! Sit down, guys, and I'll fetch beers and some snacks while everyone explains. You can do your thing later."

While they settled into seats, Shadow asked El, "Did you bring some of Briar's balm?"

"Of course," El said, immediately rummaging in her pack. She produced a glass pot and unscrewed the top, releasing the scent of herbs into the air. "This is a thick cream you need only apply sparingly. She says it's good for all sorts of cuts, but will be really great for your burn, Gabe." She looked at him, concerned. "I can't believe you wrestled a demon!"

Gabe looked sheepish. "I think my adrenalin got the better of me." He glanced at his dressing, which now looked spotted and blood-stained. "I almost bit off more than I could chew. It still hurts a little, if I'm honest."

"I'd offer a healing spell," El said, "but I'm not as skilled as Briar."

He shook his head. "It's okay, I have strong natural healing. I'm sure the cream will be enough."

"Let's do it now," Shadow said decisively, anxious to avoid another long discussion on the trinity. "The others can explain what's going on."

He looked at her, surprised. "I suppose we could. Are you sure?"

"Of course. We'll be done by the time they've finished. I'll get the sterile water and dressings, and meet you in the main bathroom."

Without waiting for an answer, she headed into the kitchen, finding Niel preparing cheese and crackers. "We're going to the bathroom to change Gabe's dressing," she told him, grabbing the water from the fridge while also grabbing a slice of cheese.

"Be gentle with him," Niel said, grinning.

"Aren't I always?"

Gabe was unwinding his dirty bandage by the time Shadow arrived with the water and first aid pack. She wrinkled her nose as the smell of burnt flesh reached her. "Put your old dressing in here," she said holding out a paper bag.

As Gabe held his arm over the long counter next to the sink, Shadow inspected the wound and frowned. "It's healed a bit, Gabe, but it still looks bad!" The burn was still bright red, and blisters had appeared in places. But his hand was worse than his arm, and she lifted it gently, turning it over. The blackened skin had gone, revealing that the burn had bit deep into his skin. "Anyone else would have lost their hand," she told him, looking up to find him watching her. "You're very lucky."

"You don't have to do this. I can manage."

"No, you can't. Not one-handed, and the others are busy. Hold your arm over the sink." She pulled some gauze from the pack and gently cleaned around the wound, flinching as Gabe winced. "Sorry. I'm being as gentle as I can."

"I know." His deep voice was like honey. Seductive. Dangerous.

She tried to focus on the wound and not his closeness. His heat. His corded muscles that felt like steel beneath her fingers. She could hear his breath coming quicker and didn't dare look up. She took her time, making sure his wound was as clean as it could be, and then patted it dry. Only then did she stop and look around to see where Briar's balm was. It was on the other side of the sink, and before she could reach for it, Gabe leaned behind her, his broad chest pressing against her back as he reached for it with his left hand. But he didn't back away. He wrapped his left arm around her, holding the pot in front of her.

"Here you go." His breath was warm so close to her ear, and for a moment, Shadow felt giddy with his nearness.

They were in front of the mirror, and she could see his face in the reflection. As their eyes met, he smiled, slowly, sensuously, still pressed close behind her.

"Thank you." She plucked it from his fingers, trying to ignore the tingle across her own fingers as they touched his briefly.

Trying not to become flustered, because she was pretty sure he was doing this to deliberately provoke her, she took the top off the pot and started to apply the cream. "Hold your hand out."

"I like you being bossy."

She looked into the mirror and saw him smirking. "For someone who likes it, you certainly complain about it a lot!"

"I like a woman who knows what she wants, too."

"Good." She glared at him, trying to suppress her amusement. Frankly, he was looking so pleased with himself, it was ridiculous. "Because this woman needs you to back up—if you want your arm dressed properly without me being squashed like a fly." He shifted back a few inches, and Shadow looked down, forcing herself to concentrate on finishing the dressing, which was doubly difficult with him so close. He felt far too good. *But*, she reminded herself, *he was her partner, and he needed to stay that way.* "You know, I could probably do this quicker if you just stepped back a bit more."

He didn't budge. "I'm in no rush. Tell me what you thought about the temple's entrance."

"It was freakishly precise," she said, continuing to dress his wound. "The walls and roof were smooth as silk, polished, almost sterile. It gave me the creeps, actually, rather than any sense of wonder or awe."

"That's what worries me. JD seems to think this will be wondrous and beautiful, but I think it's more likely to kill us."

Shadow finished wrapping the bandage and secured it, and then turned with difficulty, finding her hips against the counter and Gabe's broad chest in front of her. She ignored his predatory smile and instead said, "Well, maybe you should tell him. He'll listen to you!"

"Maybe, but part of me foolishly wants to see where this leads."

"Because of the link to angels?"

Gabe nodded. "It's tangible—their handiwork is all over it. Inhuman, beautiful, awe-inspiring, but also obscure, confusing, and exasperating. And we haven't even entered the temple yet! I can't walk away now, and despite Niel's concerns, I know he can't, either."

"It seems to me that Nahum is invested, too. And if I'm honest, so am I. And of course so is Harlan." Gabe was silent, thoughtful, but his gaze was distant, and she wondered where his thoughts had fled to. "I've finished your dressing, if you hadn't noticed."

"I noticed. Do you want to go?"

"Don't you?"

"Not particularly. For some strange and inexplicable reason, I'm enjoying myself."

"Oh." Her mouth was dry, and she found it hard to concentrate.

"You didn't answer the question."

"What question?"

He was grinning now, his eyes running across her face and down to her lips. "Do you want me to let you go?"

"Oh. That one." Damn his muscles and smile, and damn her body's reaction to him.

He smiled again, seductively, and the sun glinted in low, capturing them both in golden light. He was like no other man she'd met, and she had the feeling that if she fell for Gabe, she might never recover.

"Yes," she answered, "you probably should."

"Probably? That doesn't sound convincing."

She scowled at him. "Yes. You absolutely should let me go."

"I'm not sure you really mean that." His head lowered, as did his voice, and Shadow inhaled his musky, peppery scent. "Give me one good reason why."

She looked around, pretending confusion. "We seem to be in the bathroom, and we can't stay in here forever."

"That's not a good reason."

Shadow smiled seductively, lifting her face so they were inches apart. *You like teasing, Gabe Malouf? I can tease as well.* "It's the best you're going to get."

For a moment Gabe didn't move, and his lips were so close to hers, she could almost taste him. And then he backed away, still grinning. "All right. Have it your way."

"I will, thank you," she said archly, her heart still pounding, as she passed through the door he held open for her, acutely aware that he watched her like a hawk.

He called after her, amusement filling his voice. "Shall I get the first aid pack?"

She turned and smiled, overly sweet. "That's a good idea. See you downstairs." And yes, she might have exaggerated the sway of her hips as she turned her back on him and continued down the hall.

Sixteen

Gabe spent five minutes pacing his bedroom after Shadow had sashayed down the hall, half regretting his actions, and half wishing he'd just kissed her.

He chided himself. Partners. They were partners.

By the time he arrived at the bottom of the stairs, someone was knocking on the front door. He dropped the first aid pack behind the door, just in case he needed both hands free, and opened it to find an attractive woman in her thirties on the other side, her wavy chestnut hair loose across her shoulders. She wore jeans and boots, a t-shirt, and a worn leather jacket.

She looked up at him and smiled, holding her hand out to shake his. "I'm Olivia James. I work with Harlan. I'm a collector with The Orphic Guild."

He smiled, shook her hand, and welcomed her inside. "Gabe Malouf, at your pleasure. It seems our party is growing in size."

She grinned. "It's not every day you find a missing part of The Trinity of the Seeker."

"I guess not." He glanced down at her overnight bag. "Looks like you're staying for a few days."

She shrugged. "Maybe, maybe not, but I came prepared, just in case."

He gestured to the bottom of the stairs. "You can leave your bag there for now, if that's okay."

"Sure," she nodded, but kept her handbag over her shoulder as she walked with Gabe down the hall.

"Did Harlan ask you to come?" Gabe asked, wondering what Olivia could offer the investigation.

"Not exactly. Mason wanted me here." She winked. "Safety in numbers."

"Well, we're sure getting that!"

Gabe heard the excited chatter of voices before they'd even entered the conservatory, and found the entire group in animated conversation, broken up in twos and threes as they pored over the documents.

"Hey, guys!" he shouted. "We have another visitor. Olivia James, Harlan's colleague, is here."

After a flurry of introductions, and Harlan's pleased but puzzled greeting, Olivia settled in, and Gabe sat next to Alex. Alex was the witch he knew best and had met first. He'd connected with him psychically when the Nephilim were still spirits, and Gabe had been impressed at the strength of his will and power. "What do you think?" he asked quietly so as not to disturb the others.

"Of the trinity, or the protection you want?"

"Both, I guess."

Alex glanced at the papers spread across the table. "Honestly, this temple looks like trouble, and you need to be careful. The whole thing reeks of traps and deception. But, you can look after yourself, I know that." He shrugged, his eyes wary. "However, I'm not sure we can add anything to your understanding of the map or the path. I recognise some runes and elemental signs, but nothing you guys don't already know. Alchemical symbols aren't our thing. But, I always find it's less about translating the meaning of the symbols, and more about interpreting their meaning."

Gabe nodded. "Yeah, you're right. But there are a lot of layers there."

Alex looked genuinely frustrated. "Sorry. But I can certainly protect the house. I'd like to start now."

"Sure," Gabe nodded, already moving his chair back. "Where do you need to go?"

"I'll head outside first. I can ward the building and the garden, and then add protection spells to the ground floor windows and doors."

"Will it keep out demons?"

"I'm doing a general protection spell," Alex explained. "There are obviously a lot of people coming in and out of here. The wards will keep out anything with evil or malicious intent." He frowned. "This Erskine guy worries me. If he decides to throw something really big at you, it may get through without us here to back the spells up, but from what Harlan says, he's a conjuror, not a witch, so that means his powers are limited. They should hold."

Gabe released a big breath, not realising how worried he'd been. "That's great, thanks."

"Any time," Alex said, smiling. "You've helped us out enough. El's brought a couple of blades with her, too."

"Has she? I didn't expect anything so quickly."

"She always has stuff at hand." He looked down the table to where El was chatting to Nahum and Niel. "Hey El, do you want to show the weapons you brought?"

El's eyes widened with surprise. "Of course. I was caught up with the map." She rummaged in the bag at her feet and then pulled out one short sword and one dagger, and laid them on the table. "I had these already," she explained as the table fell quiet to listen. "One of the reasons we're a bit late is because I wanted to add some spells to them before we left—something I needed my forge for."

Nahum picked the dagger up, turning it over in his hands. "Interesting symbols along the blade."

"The symbols and the metal are enhanced with magic. The symbols imbue the dagger with strength and promise an ever-sharp blade. It can never be broken. Whoever wields it will have added agility and speed, and the wisdom to make the right move." She nodded at the sword that Niel was examining. "That has similar spells, but with added dexterity and clarity of thought, and will pierce most armour." She grinned. "Qualities I thought would be useful in a fight."

Niel stood up and carried the sword across the room so that he had plenty of space around him, and started to practice moves. "It's very well-balanced, and surprisingly light."

He looked good, Gabe noted. But then again, Niel had always been graceful in battle, and deadly.

"You could get away with a longer blade," Shadow said thoughtfully. "Your height gives you that advantage."

"True," El agreed. "But try it out. If that's the type of magical weapon you're after, I can make you one more suited to your build. All of you," she added, looking at Nahum and Gabe. "At a good price, too."

"Can you make throwing knives?" Nahum asked, running his finger along the edge of the dagger's blade.

"I can make anything you want. But it will take time, so don't expect them overnight."

Nahum smiled. "I'll keep this for now, if that's okay. I like it. Niel is right. This is well-balanced, too. I can feel the magic running through it."

"Dante, my weapons-maker friend, is very good. I enhance them with magic as we work together. We can make you scabbards for them, too."

"He knows you're a witch?" Harlan asked, surprised.

"He does, but probably not the extent of my power," El explained, looking slightly sheepish. "I like Dante. He's a good friend. The last thing I want to do is freak him out. Although," she laughed, "that would be hard, I think."

Shadow laughed, too. "Having met him, I agree."

"When did you meet him?" Gabe asked, genuinely curious.

Shadow had barely looked at Gabe since he came in, but she met his gaze now. "He helped appraise the Empusa's sword."

Alex stood up, his chair scraping across the floor. "This conversation isn't getting the house protected. You ready, El?"

"Sure. Where to first?"

"Outside," he said, grabbing his bag and steering her towards the doors to the garden. "Before it rains." He looked back over his shoulder, a wry smile on his face. "And we could be some time, so just ignore us, and anything odd you may see us do."

"Interesting," Olivia said after they'd shut the door behind them. "Are those the witches from White Haven, Harlan?"

He nodded. "Two of them." He leaned forward, arms on the table. "You say JD sent you?"

"Mason, really. I'm free this weekend, so he thought you might need backup."

Nahum raised an eyebrow. "Aren't we enough?"

She held her hands up, surrendering. "I'm sure you are. But you're not Orphic Guild employees, and Mason is paranoid."

"Fair enough."

"So, how can I help?" She gestured at the papers. "It looks like you have three things going on here. The map, the path, and the background stuff on Hammond. Is there anything I can focus on?"

"Four things!" Harlan said. "I'm looking into the church in Angel's Rest."

"Well, Olivia," Niel said, placing the sword safely out of the way before walking back to the table. "Nahum and Shadow have found the temple—or the entrance, at least. I'm all over the diaries, so our pressing need right now is The Path of the Seeker. Or, scouting out the house where The Order of Lilith have holed up."

Her eyes widened with surprise. "Whoa! Back up. You've found the temple? How?"

"A little bit of luck and inspiration from moi!" Shadow said, looking pleased with herself.

"And my language abilities!" Nahum reminded her slyly.

"Yeah, and that."

"We're going back tonight," Harlan told her. "I'm presuming you want to come?"

"Of course I do!"

"Just be aware," Gabe warned her, "that we're not planning to go any further. We need to understand what The Path of the Seeker means before we do, or we could be walking into a trap!"

"Sure," she nodded. "But we still have no key, right?"

"Right."

Olivia looked at Harlan. "I've been thinking on why Jackson was at the auction. He can only be interested in the trinity if he has part of it, surely. Or else, why bother?"

"The path on its own is worth getting, Olivia," Harlan reminded her.

"I'm not convinced. Maybe we should call him, see what he knows."

Gabe could feel things slipping away from him. There were already too many people involved, as far as he was concerned. "No. It's too risky, and will give him too much information. I can do without any other threats to make life more complicated."

"But what if he could help?" Olivia said, looking at him belligerently. "We're in a race here. And Nicoli is not to be underestimated. If Jackson has the key, we should try to make a deal."

He laughed. "A deal for what? We don't even know what we're really looking for! And how do you make a deal when JD wants everything?" He looked at Harlan, appealing for support, and felt relieved when he nodded.

"He's right. We need to find the key, because there's every chance Jackson hasn't got it."

Niel laughed. "Guess what, Olivia? Add a fifth line of enquiry. You've just volunteered to help me with the diaries, and figure out where Hammond hid the key."

"In that case, I'm heading out," Gabe said. "I want to stretch my legs and scope out that house, just to see how many are on Nicoli's team." He looked at Nahum and Shadow. "And seeing as you two had so much success earlier, I'll leave you to investigate the path."

───────◆O◆───────

Gabe was glad to be out of the house. He'd been looking at paperwork all day and he felt gritty-eyed. Now he needed to do something, anything.

He also needed space from Shadow. Perhaps distance would bring him to his senses. He was flirting with her like some giddy teenager. Pushing those thoughts to the back of his mind, he set the GPS and followed the directions until he arrived on Barton Lane in the outskirts of Angel's Rest.

The lane curved through a shallow valley, and the further it was from the village, the more spaced out the cottages and houses were. He eventually found the right one, a large stone dwelling behind a hedge. Gabe didn't linger, and he didn't want to park too close, either. There was every likelihood someone would be watching out for them, because he was pretty sure Mia would have confessed to telling them their address. He wondered if she was okay, and hoped she hadn't been punished for being caught.

The valley rose on either side, wooded in places, and he might be able to find a spot to watch up there. He checked the map and decided to turn around and head back to the village, taking another road that wound around the back of the hills. He pulled into a lay-by and hiked up the rise, finally emerging on the top of the ridge in a copse of trees overlooking Barton Lane below.

It took him a few moments to orientate himself, and then he set off, keeping out of sight, until he finally spotted the right house. The ground was damp beneath the trees, but he didn't care. He lay down on his stomach, shuffling forward until he had a good view, pulled out his binoculars, and settled in to watch.

Two hours later, he'd watched Mia and Jensen arrive, dressed in hiking gear, and another man who he didn't recognise, but who Gabe thought could be Harlan's attacker—the mystery third intruder. He was of average height with a muscular build, and had short sandy brown hair; he had returned with bags of what looked like food. Harlan had described Erskine Hardcastle and there was no sign of him, but that didn't mean he wasn't there. Gabe didn't know much about demon conjuring, but from what Alex had told him, the closer you were to where you wanted to send your demon, the better. Pet demon. Gabe rolled his eyes.

Just as Gabe was about to leave, he spotted someone else exiting the house—someone that he hadn't seen before. This man was tall, with a slim and wiry build, deeply tanned skin, and brown hair. He looked like he was from somewhere in the Mediterranean, and Gabe presumed he must be Andreas Nicoli, the head of The Order of Lilith. He paused on the threshold, and Gabe saw a very round man step into the doorway. They exchanged a few words, and then Nicoli turned his back and walked down the drive to his car, a black Mercedes, the other man still talking to him. That was Erskine Hardcastle.

Gabe studied them both, watching the way they interacted, and thought he detected tension. Nicoli appeared brusque, and after a short exchange, he got in his car and left, and Erskine watched him go, a calculating expression on his face. *Interesting.* Erskine finally shut the front door, and Gabe watched the house for another ten minutes, but when there was no more sign of movement, he decided to leave.

Gabe had just got back inside his SUV when his phone rang. "Hey, Harlan. How's it going?"

"I think I've found something interesting about the church. Niel and Nahum think it's bad news."

Gabe froze, his injured hand on the wheel. "Why?"

"I've been reading about the stained glass windows and the images they depict. They're all original, restored over the years, and apparently the angel in the central panel is holding a book."

Gabe tried to remember the images he'd seen when he was there with Niel. He honestly hadn't studied them closely. "I have a vague recollection of an angel, but there are always angels in stained glass windows."

"This one is the Angel Raziel. He is holding his Book of Knowledge."

Gabe slumped back in his seat, no longer seeing the lane in front of him. "Raziel? Are you sure?"

"That's what it says on this website I've found."

"And he's holding a book?"

"I believe it's actually called *The Book of Raziel the Angel*."

"*Sefer Raziel HaMalakh,*" Gabe said softly, his mind whirring with possibilities. "The book he gave to Adam."

Harlan fell silent, and Gabe knew he had a million questions he wanted to ask, but to his credit, all Harlan said was, "Nahum said it is the book that leads to Eden."

Gabe closed his eyes, and the heat and dust of an afternoon millennia earlier flooded back to him. He had been tasked to find that book, and had searched for decades, before he finally admitted defeat. *But now...*

"I'm going to the church," he said, abruptly ending the call.

Clouds were once again thick overhead when Gabe drove down Angel's Rest's main street. He found a parking spot a short distance from St Thomas's Church, and he was so distracted by Harlan's news he almost didn't notice the Mercedes parked a few cars down from him. Nicoli.

He paused, his mouth dry, not from the prospect of seeing Nicoli who may also be in the church, but of the images the stained glass might contain. He looked at the church sitting quietly, encompassed by smooth green grass, the tiny graveyard behind it, and the enormous yew tree by the lichgate, and wondered why he had thought the church so peaceful. Now he found it ominous.

He crossed the lane quickly and walked up the path before his courage failed him, but when he pushed open the heavy door, he found himself alone. The church was dim, the stained glass windows at the far end the one patch of colour, but even they were dull because of the impending rain. But in the centre panel, the Angel Raziel seemed to emit his own light. *Or was that his paranoia?*

Gabe looked around the nave carefully before he advanced, ensuring he really was alone, and then walked up the centre aisle, his footsteps loud in the hushed place. He paused in front of the altar, studying the angel. The design was large, his face serene, his wings partially folded behind him. *The wings were always so small,* Gabe thought, too small. An attempt to humanise, make them appear kindly, protective, approachable, while the reality was all too different. Raziel was holding a large, open book, yellow splinters of glass radiating from its open pages, and he stared into the church, his eyes on the pews; Gabe felt pinned beneath his gaze. Raziel held the book out as if offering it to him. A temptation.

Gabe sat on the front pew, his face impassive, but his mind was anything but. It churned with memories, stories, possibilities, and the growing certainty that the temple was something to flee. Raziel had the old God's ear. He was privy to every secret, every plan, every order. He heard everything, and recorded everything, and his book was considered a book of magic—straight from the old God's mouth. And he had given it to Adam and Eve to find their way back to Eden, or so Christian history said.

Such childish stories, Gabe thought. *Such simplifications.* Adam was not the first man, and Eve was not created from his rib. The old God had not made him from clay, or placed him in a heavenly garden that they were expelled from because Eve had been swayed by the angel Lucifer. *Utter drivel.* Adam was a man like any other, but blessed with intelligence, drive, and the need to succeed, and so was his wife. But the Gods disliked intelligence when it led them away from worship and towards independence. The Book of Knowledge, as it was so simplistically called, was the gift of life itself. Gabe looked up at the three stained glass panes again. The panel to the left of Raziel was of the traditional image of Adam and Eve, naked except for fig leaves, walking in the Garden of Eden. Lush leaves and flowers filled the image so that the figures were barely visible. The panel on the right was made of glass in varying shades of blue depicting huge waves, and lost within them was a boat. *Noah's Ark and the flood.* Within the waves were floundering figures—animals, men, women.

His blood thundered in his ears so loudly he didn't hear the door open behind him.

Only when footsteps echoed around the church did he turn. The man he presumed to be Andreas Nicoli walked halfway down the aisle and stopped, staring at Gabe. He looked from him to the stained glass and said, "They are quite something, aren't they?"

Nicoli's voice was authoritative, but he spoke quietly, calmly, and Gabe heard the Greek accent through the faultless English.

Gabe turned to face him fully. "They are."

Nicoli scanned the panels before finally appraising Gabe. He stared at his bandaged hand. "You must be the man who questioned Mia."

"And you're the man who sent her, and the other two intruders. And let's not forget the demon. Andreas Nicoli, I believe."

Nicoli smiled, tilting his head as he shrugged. "I am, but I did not send the demon."

"I know. It was sent by Erskine Hardcastle. Don't send them again, or they won't walk out of there. Demon included."

"Mia told me of your fight." He narrowed his eyes, and Gabe knew he was trying to work out who he was. What he was. "Not many men could do that."

Gabe smiled. "I'm gifted."

Nicoli folded his arms and leaned his hip against the edge of the pew next to him. "You have my name. I know you work with Harlan Beckett and The Orphic Guild. What is yours?"

"Gabe Malouf."

"Well, Gabe Malouf, you have something we want. I am willing to pay for it. Anything. Our pockets are deep."

"What would that be?" Gabe asked, playing dumb.

"Time is too short for games. You have The Map of the Seeker. I don't know quite how you pulled it off, but you stole it from us."

"I don't think so. It was owned by Henri Durand."

Nicoli laughed. "You're splitting hairs. Mia had it. You stole it. Somehow. There's a woman on your team." He tapped his nose. "My instincts suggest it's her."

"Talking of stealing," Gabe said, ignoring his probe. "You stole The Path of the Seeker, in the middle of the auction. Not convinced your pockets were deep enough?"

He didn't answer, instead saying, "Let's deal. I'll make you an offer; take the map off your hands."

"I'm in no position to make deals. It isn't mine. Besides, why do you need it? You must have photos."

"We want the original."

"What do you think the trinity leads to?" Gabe asked, watching Nicoli closely.

"The same thing that you do." Nicoli glanced up to the image behind Gabe. "This place is called Angel's Rest for a reason. Raziel's book lies in that temple, and it contains the knowledge of a God. It's not a path for the unworthy."

"What makes you think I'm unworthy? If anyone is unworthy, it is your demon conjuror. They aren't popular with angels."

Nicoli laughed, a broad grin spreading across his face before he sobered quickly. "Take my offer to Harlan. I'll give you twenty-four hours."

"Or what?"

"We come and get it."

Gabe walked up to Andreas, so he was inches away, and he looked down at him, pleased that the man had to lift his head to meet his eyes. "Or perhaps we'll steal yours."

And then he walked away, feeling Nicoli's eyes on his back until the door slammed shut behind him.

Seventeen

Harlan needed fresh air. The conservatory felt small, hemmed in, and too full of people after the conversation he'd just had.

He walked outside to the paved patio area overlooking the garden and sat in a wooden chair, sheltered beneath the overhanging eaves. The late afternoon had turned still. The wind had dropped, and thick clouds pressed on the land, muting all sound. Rain was due, lots of it. And maybe thunder. Alex and El were walking slowly around the perimeter of the garden, one on either side, and he watched them slowly arrive at the rear boundary together. They joined hands, and although Harlan couldn't hear them, it looked as if they were saying something—a spell, no doubt. He wasn't sure quite what happened next, but he felt a ripple of power flow around him, something comforting, like he was being wrapped in a soft, warm blanket. He smiled. The protection spell. Then they turned and headed back to the house.

Harlan looked across at the conservatory, an impressive structure of high-arched windows and brick, glowing with yellow lamplight. Shadow, Nahum, Niel, and Olivia were still in there, and he watched them talking animatedly, still clustered around the table. Harlan took a deep breath and ran his hands through his hair, trying to sort through his jumbled thoughts and emotions, but in the end he kept circling back to Raziel, the Keeper of Secrets, who disobeyed his God to share forbidden knowledge.

As soon as he'd read about that, he knew it was what The Trinity of the Seeker led to, and the others agreed. He laughed to himself, feeling half deranged. When he'd taken on this hunt for angels, he hadn't really understood the potential implications. It seemed distant, vague, and unlikely to produce much. Now it felt very real, but at the same time, just as unlikely. He'd been unnerved by Nahum and Niel's response, plus Gabe's curtness on the phone, and he suspected there was more to learn. But for now, he needed to call JD.

He picked up within moments, sounding distracted, and Harlan decided to cut to the point. "Hey JD, it's Harlan, I have news. Lots of news, actually."

"Ah, Harlan! Have you? So have I! You first."

"We've found the entrance to the temple, but the way onward is sealed."

"You have? That's excellent! How?" JD's was suddenly focussed.

"Hold on, we have other news. We think we know what the trinity leads to—what the temple houses—and it's not just the opportunity to communicate with an angel. It's something different. We think it is storing the angel Raziel's Book of Knowledge."

There was silence, and Harlan thought the line had gone dead. "JD?"

"I'm here. What makes you think that?"

Harlan sighed and relayed what he'd read about the church. "It seems a logical assumption to make."

"Yes, yes it does," JD said hesitantly, as if he still had some doubts. "Actually, that makes my interpretation of the path a little easier."

"Why? What's your news?"

"The path is what we thought—a passage to the inner temple, with instructions and tests. I think I have deciphered some, but others still tease me, and the ultimate test is unclear. But actually, knowing that this could lead to Raziel's book..." He went silent again, and Harlan could hear him shuffling papers. When he finally spoke, his voice was filled with steely determination. "This is the pinnacle of all prizes. We have to get in there."

"When do you think you can come down, JD?"

"Not yet. I'm not ready. Is there any news of the key?"

"No."

"Are you guarding the entrance?" JD asked.

"It's well hidden. But we have competitors. Nicoli is here. I don't think they are any further ahead of us, though."

"I cannot work any quicker!"

"I know," Harlan said, trying to sound calm. "But if we don't have the key—whatever the hell that is—then it's all pointless, anyway. And I'm not sure Nicoli has it, either. Although, he might." Harlan's head hurt. "Maybe he's had it all along." *But where did that leave Jackson Strange?*

"Focus on the key," JD instructed, "and before you go, tell me about the entrance to the temple."

By the time Harlan ended the call, his head felt like a vice, but before he could move indoors, his phone rang; it was an unknown number. He answered cautiously, but he knew the voice on the other end. It was Jackson Strange.

"Hi, Harlan. I have a proposal. Can I come and see you? It's important."

He sighed and made the arrangements, and when he re-entered the conservatory a few minutes later, Shadow and Niel had disappeared, and he could smell food cooking and hear music coming from the kitchen. Nahum and Olivia were talking quietly, leaning close. Harlan groaned inwardly. He recognised that look on Olivia's face. She was flirting, and it looked like Nahum was enjoying it.

"Hi, guys," he said as he entered. "We have a new proposition to consider. Jackson Strange will be here this evening to offer a partnership."

Olivia's eyebrows shot up, and she leaned back in her chair. "Really? He's got the key, hasn't he?"

"He didn't say as much, but I think he does."

She grinned. "I feel smug. I knew it!"

Nahum frowned. "Do you trust him?"

"More than I trust Nicoli," Harlan said as he sat at the table with them.

"Any idea who Jackson's working for?" Olivia asked.

"No. He said very little, other than that he wanted to meet us. So, I gave him the address and he'll be here in a few hours."

"He's still in London?"

"I don't know! Maybe. He could be in Wales, for all I know." He rubbed his face. "I need a beer, and more than anything, I need to clear my head." He looked up again, abruptly. "And JD is close to working out the path. Sorry, I should have mentioned that first."

"Wow," Olivia said, wide-eyed. "We might actually do this!"

Nahum stood, rolling his shoulders with the athletic grace that all the Nephilim had. "Yeah, we might, and I'm not sure what I think about that. But, I need a shower. I'm still covered in dirt from earlier. And I think I need to clear my head, too. See you later."

When they were alone, Olivia looked at Harlan slyly. "I like these guys!"

"You're so predictable."

"Piss off. They're big and handsome, and I'm single. I can look!"

"Don't think I didn't notice that flirting."

She fluttered her lashes. "I'm playing nice with our new colleagues." Her fingers drummed on the table, and she leaned forward, suddenly serious. "This thing is feeling very real, and if I'm honest, a bit intimidating."

"Intimidating? That's one word for it. As far as occult and magical objects go, this has to be one of the biggest finds!"

"In *Christian* history. Although, maybe the Ark of the Covenant would be bigger."

"Funny."

"Why funny?" Olivia shrugged. "If this book is real, and the temple, then anything is on the table. And besides, we've found some pretty incredible things over the years."

Harlan shook his head. "Not like this." He lowered his voice. "I'm not sure of the wisdom of this, and I was hoping JD might get cold feet."

"Why would he? Imagine what we could sell it for!"

"JD doesn't want to sell it. He wants to own it."

"Really?" Olivia asked, puzzled. "Finding and selling it would make us one of the biggest occult finders on the planet!"

Harlan knew he needed to tread carefully. Olivia had no idea who JD really was. "What do you know about JD?"

"That he owns this business and is interested in the occult, just like us. I met him once, years ago. Interesting man. Very dapper. He must be well into his eighties now."

And then some. "Yeah, I met him a few weeks ago, and once since. He's old, but looks fit. And he's determined. This kind of thing is very much his personal obsession. You know how some of these people get."

"Sure. They're why we make a lot of money."

"Well, trust me, once he gets this, it will never see the market."

"Does he have a vault to keep this book in?" Olivia looked incredulous. "Because if this gets out, everyone will want it, and it will be all over the news. JD will have a big, fat target on his head. We might actually break the Internet. Religious enthusiasts will be coming out of the woodwork. And museums! They'll demand this should be on public display!"

"They can demand all they want. If it ain't for sale, it ain't for sale," Harlan drawled. "And besides, we're good at keeping things quiet—so are Nicoli and Strange. It's what we do, Olivia! Discretion is our first, middle, and last name."

She took a sharp intake of breath. "Oh, my God. I know who will want it!"

He wondered if Olivia had been drinking, because she looked decidedly excitable. *Maybe she was drunk on Nahum? She looked like she'd been inhaling him earlier...* "Who?"

"The Catholic Church! The Vatican! They'll think it belongs to them, anyway! They'll want to squirrel it away in their massive library, and it will never see the light of day again."

Harlan blinked as Olivia's words sank in. "Oh, shit. I never even thought of them."

"Who else knows about this?"

He shrugged. "Lots of people have known about the trinity for years. The site has been searched for before, when The Map of the Seeker first surfaced in the fifteenth century, and then again during the nineteenth century when this kind of thing became very popular again. Then interest waned, as it does, and it disappeared into obscurity. Hammond was dismissed as a crackpot."

"No, not the site as the place to talk to angels," she said impatiently, "but Raziel's book. This is brand new, right?"

"I guess so. But, the stained glass image in the church is Raziel. You'd have thought someone would have connected that information to the trinity before now."

"Not necessarily. If you're looking in the wrong direction, things don't always align." Olivia started to gather all the papers together, dropping them into ordered piles. "Nahum is right. We all need a breather from this. I'm going to find myself a bedroom, grab a beer, and have a shower, too."

"So you're staying, then?" Harlan asked.

"Of course I bloody am."

Harlan glanced at the tense faces in the conservatory and checked his watch again. Where was Jackson?

Gabe was outside sparring with Nahum and Shadow, and the clash of swords was quite unnerving. And mesmerising. It was a good distraction, while the rest of them tried to read and relax. It still hadn't rained, and the air was getting stickier, as if a storm was imminent.

Gabe had almost growled at Harlan when he told him that Strange was visiting. "You invited *someone else*?"

"If we want to complete the trinity, we need the key," Harlan had told him, squaring up to Gabe, while at the same time trying to be reasonable.

Gabe glared at him, but Harlan refused to back down. This was his gig, and JD was his employer. Gabe didn't have a choice, despite his obvious wish to be in charge and everyone else's natural deference to him. *Tough luck.* Eventually Gabe just nodded, grabbed the sword, and headed outside to work off his anger issues. Alex and El had stayed long enough to have a meal with them and complete their spells, but then they'd left, though Harlan could feel their magic still. He'd thought Gabe was being overprotective earlier, but now he was glad for it.

"He'll calm down," Niel said, and Harlan looked around, surprised. Niel was reclining on a daybed in the corner of the conservatory, a book open on his stomach. "Gabe, I mean. He has a complicated history with the book."

"So you said earlier. Is he going to share it?"

"He will when he's ready."

Olivia looked up from her phone where she'd been scrolling for the last half an hour. "Did you know Raziel?"

"I knew of him. He had a reputation, even amongst the fallen."

Olivia twisted in her chair to look at him. "Why?"

"He was one of the most powerful angels. Enigmatic, secretive. Everything you'd expect from the one who had the old God's ear. And to give the book that contained the mightiest of secrets away to Adam...well, let's just say that his betrayal sent ripples through all worlds."

"To Adam?" Olivia cocked an eyebrow and looked at Harlan. "I can't even believe I'm having this discussion."

Niel smiled, and propped himself up so he could talk with more comfort. "He wasn't what you think. He actually wasn't the first man to be created. But he was the first man to question his existence and the word of the old God. His wife, too. Raziel decided he should have full knowledge, not bits and pieces. The other angels were horrified, and took the book back. They threw it into the ocean. The old one retrieved it, and then it was stolen again." Niel closed his eyes briefly. "It caused a fight. But that is Gabe's story to tell."

A loud knock at the front door made Harlan jump, interrupting their conversation. "It's Jackson. Get the others in, Olivia."

Eighteen

S hadow lounged in a chair in the corner of the conservatory, idly playing with her dagger as she watched Jackson Strange enter the room.

He was about the same height as Harlan, and looked slightly unkempt with his shaggy mane of hair streaked with grey. He seemed to lope in rather than walk, his gait fluid and easy. He wore a long, loose black coat over faded jeans and a t-shirt, and scuffed trainers; he grinned as he surveyed the group spread around the conservatory. "Well, this is quite the reception." He nodded at Olivia. "Good to see you, Liv. So you're involved in this, too?"

She laughed. "Wild horses couldn't keep me away."

Harlan made the introductions, and the Nephilim all shook his hand, but Shadow stayed put, greeting him from her seat. She enjoyed watching the exchange. Jackson was clearly very comfortable with himself, completed unfazed by Gabe, Nahum, and Niel, and he sat at the table looking composed.

Although Olivia seemed relaxed, no one else did, and Gabe was still brooding. He'd fought more aggressively than she'd ever experienced from him, which was fine, but bruising. Their sparring had required her full concentration, and by the time they'd finished, all three of them were out of breath. At least it had banished thoughts of the trinity from her head for a while.

"So," Harlan started, "what brings you here, Jackson?"

"I know you're looking for The Temple of the Trinity—I saw you at the auction. I also suspect that you have the map, and that Nicoli has the path. That auction theft has his sticky fingerprints all over it. I have the key."

"Really? Because it's been missing a long time," Harlan said sceptically.

"So was The Path of the Seeker." Jackson frowned. "I wouldn't come here, otherwise...I haven't got time to make empty promises."

"Show it to us, then," Gabe said from where he was seated on a long bench beneath the window.

Jackson smiled as he looked across to him. "I haven't brought it with me. I'm not a fool. But I will bring it with me when you find the entrance."

"And what do you want in return?" Harlan asked.

"I want to come with you when you enter the temple."

Harlan gave a short laugh. "You're presuming we'll find it, then."

Jackson shrugged. "It's only a matter of time. You're here now and have been for days, and so is Nicoli. I have the feeling neither of you will stop until it's been found. Eventually, all things reveal their secrets, and this one is due." He tapped the table impatiently, and his eyes narrowed. "This is the first time in hundreds of years when all three items are present at the same time. We can't let this opportunity pass!"

"Who are you working with?" Olivia asked.

"No one. At the end of a job many years ago, I found something that led me to The Key of the Seeker. " He rubbed his chin with his hand. "It was tricky to get, but I managed it, and I've been sitting on it ever since."

"Why didn't you sell it?" Harlan asked, still suspicious.

"I didn't know where the other two parts were, and without them it seemed pointless. Besides, there was something about the whole thing that attracted me. It seemed too interesting to sell." Strange looked around them all, assessing their interest.

Shadow had only one question. "Why didn't you go to Nicoli with this?"

"Because he's an untrustworthy bastard, and he's working with Erskine." He looked puzzled for a moment, and then his expression cleared. "You were at the auction the other night! I thought I recognised you. You left just as I arrived."

She nodded, and decided to keep it vague. "I had other business."

Jackson smirked. "I bet you did. Maybe Nicoli wasn't the one who stole the path after all."

"It wasn't me," she assured him.

"That's a shame, in many respects," Jackson said, "because from what I've read, you need the original manuscript to access the Inner Temple."

"Where did you read that?" Harlan asked.

"Same place I found clues to getting the key. It didn't spell it out as such, but it was suggested in the layers of meaning. I can't remember the exact wording right now." The tension in the room thickened as everyone shuffled and cast worried glances at each other, and Jackson finally said, "Yeah, I didn't think you had it." He stood up. "Look, I don't expect you to answer me right now. Talk it over. You have my number, Harlan. But you won't enter the temple without the key, and you won't get that unless I come with you. Besides," he stared at Harlan, "you have no reason to doubt me. I may operate alone most of the time, but you know you can trust me. I'll see myself out."

He turned and left, and despite his assurance, Niel followed him.

"Bollocks!" Gabe said, standing and pacing in the thickening gloom. "That's just what we didn't need."

"It's what I expected," Olivia said, watching him. "I had a gut instinct."

"I didn't want anyone else involved!" Gabe stopped suddenly and clenched his fists. "I have a very bad feeling about this temple."

There was one lamp on in the corner, and it cast Gabe's features into harsh relief. There was no sign of his teasing manner from earlier that afternoon, and Shadow could feel her arm aching from where they'd clashed swords. They all needed to know why he was so rattled. "Gabe, I think you need to tell us what you know about Raziel."

He glared at her. "I think that would be a bad idea."

A flare of anger raced through her and she stood up, hands on her hips. "Herne's hairy balls! We are all in this together, and we are all going into that temple! The more we know, the better. Two people in this room have no paranormal skills, and will be vulnerable to whatever may happen in there. I'd suggest they stay here, but I know that won't happen!"

"Absolutely not!" Olivia said, looking horrified.

"And in case you've forgotten, Gabe, this is not your show. It's JD's," Harlan said forcefully.

"He's right," Nahum agreed in his usual reasonable tone. "And so is Shadow. They don't need details, Gabe, but they need something."

Niel arrived back in the doorway and leaned against the frame, an expression of resignation on his face. "I know what you blame yourself for, Gabe, but you weren't responsible."

Gabe was silent, a myriad of emotions sweeping across his face, and Shadow wanted to reassure him in some way, but now wasn't the time. He eventually came to a decision, sitting heavily on the window seat again. "Before we even existed, Raziel gave away The Book of Knowledge. We called it *Sefer Raziel HaMalakh*. The book was given to Adam and Eve—well that's your name for them, not ours. But it was seen as a great betrayal. The book has been called the first grimoire. It contains powerful magic about life, elemental magic, words that commanded the rain, the sun, the earth, the seas—the basic matter of life. I'm not talking about The Creation, as you call it," he warned, looking particularly at Harlan and Olivia, who watched him with fierce concentration. "Life *evolved*—it was not created. But the book did contain powerful, raw magic, base spells from which all others derive."

"Why the hell would you give away something so powerful?" Harlan asked, finally finding his voice.

"That's the big question," Nahum said softly. "It was supposedly an act of charity. And a reward to the couple who questioned their existence."

"Anyway," Gabe continued, "the book was stolen back by a couple of angels who decided humans were not worthy of such information. They cast it into the sea, but the old God wanted it back. It was too important to lose. He rescued it and hid it, forgiving Raziel for his betrayal, because after all, he was his favourite. But it didn't end there. Raziel quarrelled with the old one, stole the book again, and war broke out in the Otherworld—Heaven, as you call it. It raged. And that's when angels started to fall to Earth. They left the Otherworld by the thousands, fleeing to this realm, and eventually we were created."

Olivia exhaled heavily. "Wow. And the book?"

"Still missing. Along with Raziel. The magic that was in that book found its way everywhere—and we're not entirely sure how. By Adam and Eve, though they had it only for a short time? By Raziel himself? By another human who deciphered it and shared it? By the book itself?" He shrugged. "Regardless of the means, pockets of knowledge sprang up, elemental magic took flight, and man began to take control of his destiny."

"And women?" Olivia asked, tongue in cheek.

Shadow laughed as Gabe smiled. "And women."

"Are you serious?" Harlan asked, looking around as if someone would announce it was a huge joke. "This is amazing! Alex and El should have heard this! You're talking about the first witches!"

"I'm glad they're not here," Gabe said. "I'm happy to share this with them, but I don't want them inside the temple—if we ever get there."

"Why not?" Shadow asked, annoyed on their behalf. "They could be useful. They wield magic better than any of us. I can't manipulate it like they do."

"No," Gabe said, shaking his head firmly. "This isn't about fighting magic with magic. This is about dealing with Raziel and whatever is in there. And there are too many people involved already."

Although the room was now very dim, Shadow could see enough to know that Gabe was adamant, his face set in stone, and Shadow wasn't entirely sure he'd made the right decision. Two powerful witches had just walked out the door when the group might need them most. "But that can't be all," she said, watching Gabe. "There's something else, isn't there?"

He stared at her, his dark eyes full of sorrow and guilt. "Yes, there's more. The Book of Knowledge caused many problems long before we were born, and long after. Many of us believe that one of the reasons we were created was to control the effects that The Book of Knowledge had on humanity. Eventually, I was tasked with finding it. I failed." He sighed. "And I believe that my failure caused the flood."

"I disagree," Niel said forcefully. He was still standing in the doorway, barely visible in the gloom. "The flood would have happened anyway. Our God was vengeful, and angry about many things—humanity's independence, the loss of the book, Raziel's betrayal—and whatever else was pissing him off at the time!"

"Agreed," Nahum said. "You should not blame yourself. Even if you *had* found the book, the flood would have happened. They had determined to start anew."

"But essentially the flood failed, didn't it?" Shadow said, feeling a stir of pleasure at the Gods being thwarted. "Magic survived."

Olivia stared at her. "You think the flood was about destroying magic?"

"Maybe." Shadow laughed suddenly at the idea. "What a ridiculous notion. Magic is everywhere! My race wields it naturally, to varying degrees. To think you could erase it…"

"Not erase it entirely," Gabe told her, "just remove it from man's ability. Well, that's one theory, anyway."

Harlan stirred. "This doesn't answer what we're going to do about Jackson. I think we need to accept his help."

Gabe stood up. "I guess we do, but first I want to see the entrance to the temple myself." He glanced outside. "Rain is coming, and it's dark enough now. With luck, we won't run into The Order of Lilith."

"And if we do?" Nahum asked.

"We make sure they don't follow us," Gabe said firmly.

Nineteen

G abe followed Nahum and Shadow as they led the group through the dark ravine to the entrance of the temple, and he was grateful they were both so adept at working at night.

For the Nephilim and Shadow, the going was straightforward, but Harlan and Olivia struggled, stumbling on the uneven path, even with their head torches in place to keep their hands free. Gabe had tried to persuade them not to come, but his pleas were useless. He had been tempted to fly to the entrance, but in the end decided that accompanying the humans on foot was probably the safest option.

Gabe had asked Niel to hang behind to make sure they weren't being followed, and he had lost sight of him some time back. Niel could hide himself easily despite his size.

"There," Nahum said, suddenly stopping and pointing halfway up a steep, rocky hillside covered in trees and bushes. "It's hidden behind the scrub."

"Bloody hell," Olivia exclaimed. "I'm not a mountain goat!"

"I did warn you," Gabe said, annoyed.

Olivia just glared at him, although it was hard to see her expression with the torch on her forehead. "Don't worry. I can make it. It was a joke!"

Nahum said, "I can help you if you struggle. And so can Gabe, when he stops worrying." He shot him a look that warned him to play nice, and Gabe acknowledged it with an almost imperceptible nod.

He knew he was being unreasonably grumpy, but with every step that brought them closer to the temple, he felt the weight of those expectations years ago, and he'd decided that it didn't matter how much JD wanted this book, he was going to find a way to destroy it. There was no way he was letting it loose in the world. Maybe he was being as judgemental as the old God, but he had first-hand experience of cataclysmic vengeance, and could do without experiencing it again. But he hadn't even voiced that to Nahum or Niel yet.

Shadow was already scrambling up the slope, sure-footed and nimble, barely needing the stunted bushes to pull herself up, and Harlan scrambled after her. "Shadow, wait at the entrance," Gabe instructed. "Don't say or do anything!"

As he'd grown to expect, she completely failed to answer him, and he bit back his annoyance.

Olivia set off too, Nahum following, but Gabe waited, wondering if Niel was close. He listened for a moment, but only the scrape of sliding rock disturbed the silence, and Gabe ground his teeth, wishing Harlan could be quieter. Then he felt a rush of air, and in seconds Niel landed next to him, furling his wings behind him.

"Anything out there?" Gabe asked.

"Nothing. We're all alone—not surprisingly. It's going to rain." He looked up the slope. "The entrance is up there, then?"

"Yep. Can you keep watch?"

"Sure. I'll settle on the ledge above. I should be able to see most of the ravine from there."

"I'll get Nahum to relieve you later. I want your opinion of what we've found so far."

Niel nodded, and in seconds had soared above, and Gabe saw Olivia gasp and look around before focusing on the climb again. Satisfied with Niel's report, Gabe headed up too, and within a few minutes they were all precariously balanced outside the long, narrow crack in the rock face.

"I'll lead the way," Shadow said, already sliding through the gap. "It's single file, but the anteroom is big enough for all of us."

They all filed in, shuffling awkwardly along the narrow passage, the press of rock tight on either side, but any discomfort fled as soon as Gabe reached the first chamber. The smooth, polished walls were like glass, and Harlan and Olivia's torches bounced off them, the walls acting like a mirror.

"Holy shit!" Harlan exclaimed, turning slowly. "It's impossible to make rock this smooth without machinery."

"Not if you're an angel," Gabe said, overawed despite his reservations.

"If this is what the antechamber's like, the inside should be unbelievable," Harlan continued. He walked over to the door set in the rock, and examined the inscription, careful not to touch it.

Gabe headed to Harlan's side, a deep dread filling the pit of his stomach. "That's the language of fire. The language of angels. " He stared at the script faultlessly etched into the surface, elegant and powerful.

Olivia looked at Nahum and Gabe. "You understand it?"

Despite their unusual situation, Nahum looked calm and self-assured; when he answered, his voice was filled with wonder, and something else. Regret, perhaps. "We do. I have not seen it for many years."

Gabe read the inscription carefully, the words translating easily, just like breathing to him. "'Welcome, Seeker. Say the words and the worthy will enter. Be sure of your intent, for all knowledge lies here. Life lies here. Death lies here. The path to glory awaits." He turned to Nahum. "Your translation is the same?"

Nahum nodded.

Harlan had his phone in his hand. "I need to take pictures to show JD. But it seems obvious to me—you need to say the line in that language to make it open."

"It seems the most likely suggestion," Gabe agreed. He looked up at the domed roof, and then examined the floor below. The room was immaculately constructed, with no sign of tool marks. "I haven't seen work like this for years."

Shadow frowned. She had been quiet, pacing around with her sword in her hand, but now she asked, "When was that?"

"Our father used to see me occasionally in one of these chambers. He carved it in seconds out of hillsides, just like this, but on the edge of the desert. It was like scooping water from a bowl." His tone grew impatient. "It was meant to impress me. Remind me of my place. I guess it worked."

Nahum nodded. "I had almost forgotten that. He did it so effortlessly."

"Remind us we were nothing compared to him?"

Nahum gave a short laugh. "I meant the cave, but I guess both applied."

"In fact, it was in a place like this when I was tasked with finding the book," Gabe said dryly. "How apt I am so close now." Gabe had been honoured with the request at the time. It felt like a vindication of his worth; it was only later it had felt like a death sentence. It had come at a time when he hadn't seen his father for years, a time when the Nephilim had shaken off their fathers' commands, so this request was memorable in many ways. He was annoyed with himself for even accepting it.

Who was he kidding? He had no choice.

Nahum took another look around and then said, "I'll get Niel."

While they waited, Olivia took photos too, snapping the entrance and antechamber from every angle. Gabe eyed the doorway suspiciously. This felt more like a tomb than a temple. They could all die in here. There was one thing he was sure of. This temple would become far more convoluted and complicated before it gave up The Book of Knowledge.

Harlan needed to see JD. Talking on the phone wasn't an option. JD was evasive and easily side-tracked, and while that was understandable considering the task at hand, it was still frustrating.

He announced his plan at breakfast the next day, and nobody argued with him. There was nothing for Harlan to do at the house, and Olivia had been happy enough to stay. And everyone was as tense as he was, too. Standing in the antechamber of the temple last night, Harlan had thought how tempting it was to walk straight in. It may be that the Nephilim's knowledge would be great enough they didn't need JD, but they weren't sure. And besides, JD wanted to be there.

Part of Harlan's intention today was to bring JD back with him. If Nicoli found the entrance too, they might not have the luxury of waiting for much longer. And then there was the added worry that they might need the original Path of the Seeker upon entrance.

By the time Harlan knocked on JD's door, it was late morning, and Anna answered, surprised to see him.

"You didn't ring," she said by way of welcome. Harlan wondered exactly what she did as JD's assistant. He assumed she helped to research and catalogue his library, and maybe searched for new acquisitions, but maybe not.

"I didn't see the point," he said as he brushed past her into the hall. "I have some things to show him." Harlan frowned at her expression. "I presumed it would be fine."

She shrugged, her face impassive. "He tends not to like unexpected guests, but I guess under the circumstances..."

She turned and led him up the main stairs to a room at the back of the house. *Actually*, Harlan estimated, *it was the only room at the back of the house*. It encompassed half a dozen windows that were shrouded in thick curtains; the rest of the walls were lined with shelves, all packed with books. This was JD's library. Harlan presumed the curtains were to protect his collection from sunlight. It felt stuffy, even more so considering the muggy day that hadn't been alleviated by the overnight rainfall.

JD was seated at an enormous table in the middle of the room. Overhead lights on long chains hung over it, low and intimate, and books were spread across its surface. JD was busy making notes, and it was only when Anna coughed gently that he looked up, surprised. "Anna, I told you not to disturb—" He faltered. "Harlan? What are you doing here?"

"I'm sorry to come unannounced," Harlan said, striding in, "but I have photos of the temple's antechamber. I decided to show you in person."

Harlan had stopped on the journey to print the photos so they could be studied in a reasonable size, and he pulled them out of the envelope and handed them over, sitting next to JD as he did so. It was only when he was so close that he realised how exhausted JD looked. "JD, are you all right?"

"Tired. I have only had about three hours sleep a night since I started deciphering the path."

"If that," Anne said disapprovingly, as she picked up an empty plate from next to JD's elbow. "He's eating all his meals in here." She looked at Harlan accusingly, and he wondered what the hell he should say. It wasn't his fault JD was up all night. But she marched off, calling, "I'll bring coffee," before shutting the door behind her.

"Don't mind her," JD said, flicking through the photos. "She worries, and frankly I'd starve without her." His eyebrows rose expressively as he examined them one by one. "The language of fire! I have never seen it outside of my own library."

Harlan was shocked. "You've seen it before! How?"

JD looked impatient. "The angels taught me it!"

Harlan felt like a fool. He'd assumed JD's conversations with angels were useless ramblings. "Can you read it?"

"I will be able to, with time. But the Nephilim have translated it, I presume?"

"Yes," Harlan said, pulling himself together. "We think saying the words out loud will open the door, but obviously we need The Path of the Seeker deciphered before you can go any further."

JD didn't speak for a moment, but when he looked up, his eyes were wide. "This place looks inhuman."

"It's carved by an angel, JD. Look, I hate to rush you, and I know you've had the document for only a few days, but are you making headway? We need to act quickly, before Nicoli does. It would take an act of violence to keep his group out of the temple, and although the Nephilim and Shadow are more than capable, we don't want things to get ugly."

"I'm close, very close, but there are still a couple of symbols that confuse me." He looked distractedly away, a frown furrowing his brow.

"Can you bring your research with you? Continue it at the house? I really can't express strongly enough the need for us to act quickly here. This is a race against time."

"It's been there for hundreds of years," JD tutted absently, frowning once again at the documents in front of him.

"But no one knew where it was! And we think this is Raziel's book. *The Book*." Harlan watched JD, half wondering if he'd fully absorbed everything he'd told him. "And Jackson Strange thinks we need the original path. Did I mention that?"

JD looked at him, annoyed. "No! No wonder I'm struggling." He searched through the jumble of texts on the desk, finally plucking a piece of paper from beneath a book. "This symbol here means 'within'—within the page, the paper?"

Harlan looked surprised. "You think Jackson is right?"

"It makes sense." JD looked at him, and it felt as if his pale brown eyes that had seen so much, and that had already deciphered the means to immortality, were looking straight through him. "Tell Gabe to take it."

Harlan's mouth dropped open. "You want him to steal it? From Nicoli and Erskine?"

"Yes."

"But there could be terrible consequences—Erskine conjures demons. He sent one two nights ago. He could send one here!"

JD rolled his eyes, a strangely teenage gesture in such an old man. "This house is well protected, and besides, I have dealt with demons before. Don't worry about that. But you're right. I need to come with you." JD's gaze swept over the table. "There are a few books I will bring, but that's all."

In seconds, JD had gone from absent-minded to very decisive, and Harlan stumbled over his words. "Er, okay. Good. And what about Strange? He says he has the key, but wants to be involved before he hands it over."

"I suppose you had better say yes, then. But I want to see that key before we go inside the temple—just to make sure. I have my own theories about The Key of the Seeker." His eyes glittered with excitement, and a fair degree of ruthlessness. "It wouldn't do to go in there with the wrong one."

Twenty

S hadow ended a call with Harlan, a thrill of excitement already racing through her, and shouted to Gabe and Nahum, trying to stop their fight.

They were in the garden behind the house, and bored by inactivity, Nahum and Gabe were sparring with swords again. It had rained heavily overnight, and they were both wet and grass-stained from where they'd rolled on the ground. They were so absorbed in their fight that they didn't hear her, and Shadow felt the clash of metal in her bones. They grunted and shouted, and every now and then threw a taunt at the other, trying to provoke a miss-step; but they were equally good, combative, and unwilling to lose any advantage.

Shadow shouted again. "Harlan phoned! We have a job to do. Stop fighting!"

This time they heard her, and they reluctantly broke apart to stare at her.

"Did you say job?" Gabe asked, wiping his brow with the back of his hand and smearing more dirt over it in the process.

"Yes. JD wants us to steal The Path of the Seeker. It seems that Jackson might have been right about needing the original."

Nahum's chest was still heaving, and sweat gathered in a v down his t-shirt. "Now? In the daylight?"

"He just said the sooner the better. We should go watch the house, see who's in." She wrinkled her nose. "But you two need to shower first. You're sweaty!" She looked at Gabe's hand, and then up at his amused eyes. "I presume your hand is feeling better?"

He transferred the sword to his left hand and flexed his fingers, the bandage wrinkled and dirty. She noticed before that he fought using both hands, but he was naturally right-handed and consequently favoured that one. "Yep. Feels much better. Briar's balm is good."

"Good. I'll redress it as soon as you get out of the shower, and we'll make a plan for the break-in." She'd assumed charge and knew it would needle Gabe, but that was okay. It didn't work to always let him get his own way. Turning away, she led the way back to the house, Gabe and Nahum falling into step behind her. "Did you say you found a spot on the hill to watch their house, Gabe?"

"I did, on the hillside opposite. You want a lookout?"

Shadow entered the conservatory, spotting Olivia still searching through Hammond's papers. Niel was in the ravine, watching in case The Order of Lilith found the entrance. "Yes. I think Olivia should be up there."

She looked up as she heard her name. "Up where?"

"Harlan has just phoned. JD wants us to steal the original path. I think you should be our lookout."

Olivia leaned back in her chair, her hands behind her head. "Does he? JD's got more balls than I expected."

"Maybe it's because he isn't the one doing the stealing!" Shadow pointed out. "You found anything interesting in there?" She gestured at the papers.

Olivia nodded. "These are fascinating. This poor man was clearly tormented by his visions. There was nothing beautiful or heavenly about them! It sounds like he got barely any sleep for weeks while he completed the trinity. He lost weight, argued with everyone, and became a semi-recluse. It sounds like torture! And I agree with Niel—he must have hidden the key somewhere close to where he lived."

"Why?" Nahum asked.

"Because he was too ill to have travelled far." Olivia's eyes slid across Nahum's muscular chest before she looked at his face, and she clearly tried to focus. "He lived not far from here. I don't know if that's why he was picked for receiving the vision. I mean, was the temple here for thousands of years beforehand? Or was it made at the same time as the visions? You said creating such a thing was easy for angels."

Gabe pulled a chair out and sat down. "I said a single chamber would be easy. I doubt whatever is beyond that door is so simple."

Nahum exhaled heavily. "Why here, in England? I'd have thought it would be somewhere in the Middle East, in Mesopotamia or Babylon."

"We may never know that," Gabe said, shrugging.

Shadow leaned against the table, absently picking up pieces of paper. "Maybe there are entrances all over the world. Perhaps this is just a portal?"

Gabe's head whipped around to look at her. "A what?"

"A portal to the place that stores the book." She stared at him, wondering why she hadn't thought of this sooner, because as soon as it popped into her head, it seemed natural.

"Stored between worlds?" Gabe voice rose, incredulous.

"Maybe. Or stored in one place in this world. " Shadow immediately started to doubt herself. "I suppose it does sound odd."

Nahum groaned and stared at Gabe. "Actually, that sounds just about right. Raziel would have no idea who would have survived the flood, or where anyone would have lived, but he was determined to preserve his book. He created a place to store it in, but with multiple entrances."

"And then after the flood," Gabe said, his voice low as the suggestion's implications reverberated around them, "when civilisation was secure, he left clues to those entrances. Different clues in different countries."

"Different visions," Olivia echoed, her gaze distant. "Different visionaries."

Gabe laughed, almost maniacally. "That's one hell of a conspiracy theory."

But there was something else pricking at Shadow. "How many people can speak the language of fire? Surely no one except for you?"

"JD might. Other alchemists might. JD called it Enochian—I've never heard of that, but maybe it's the same thing?" He looked puzzled. "I thought it would be something we'd talk about, but we haven't yet."

Olivia tapped the papers in front of her. "Communicating with angels or spirits has been a thing many have claimed to be able to do, but surely few really have. What if some of those were chosen to be instructed in the language, like JD? What's the point of hiding a book, guarded by the language of fire, if no one can speak it or read it? The book would be truly lost."

"Either that," Shadow said, "or it was intended for Nephilim all along. Raziel hoped you'd survive, and this would be your gift."

"Or our curse," Nahum said, his voice grim. "Shower time, and then we leave. With luck, most of The Order of Lilith are out searching for the site. Let's get this over with."

———◆———

Shadow, Gabe, and Nahum had made sure Olivia was positioned on the hillside opposite the house, and then Gabe had parked his SUV at the side of the quiet lane, a few doors down from the house that Nicoli's team were staying in.

They were trying to look as unobtrusive as possible while they waited for Olivia's update, which was frankly ridiculous, Shadow noted. It was broad daylight. If any of The Order of Lilith walked up the lane towards them right now, they would be easily spotted.

"It doesn't matter if they see us. We say we've come to talk. Easy," Gabe said, shrugging.

"We want to steal it, not chat," Shadow said scathingly, annoyed at his *laissez-faire* attitude. "And let's face it, if we do steal it, they will know exactly who's taken it."

Nahum grinned. "So? They'll try to steal it back and fail."

Shadow scowled at him. "Never underestimate your opponent. You should know better than that."

"I don't underestimate us! We have advantages they don't."

"They have a demon!"

"Now, now children," Gabe said as his phone rang. "Olivia."

He turned away to take the call as Shadow said, "We need a back entrance. Many of these houses look quiet. We could jump over a few fences and get into the back garden. Well, I could, anyway," she said in response to Nahum's sceptical expression.

He just shook his head. "Not in the daytime! Our new employer should be better educated as to the best time to do break-ins."

Shadow looked up and down the lane. "This is the best time! There's no one here. It's Saturday. Many people are out on daytrips or shopping. And I bet Nicoli's team is off looking for the entrance!"

Gabe ended the call. "Olivia says there are no cars on the drive, and no sign of anyone in the house. Nahum, you sit behind the wheel. Shadow and I will head inside. Edge a bit closer in a few minutes, in case we need a quick getaway. Sound good?"

"Sounds good."

Shadow and Gabe set off down the lane as Nahum swapped seats. When they reached the end of the drive they turned straight into it, confidently walking up to the house, and then to the side gate.

Shadow scanned the windows. Nothing moved. They both turned to survey the houses around them, but again, everything was quiet, so in seconds Gabe boosted Shadow over the gate and then followed, landing softly next to her. They waited for a moment, listening carefully, and then proceeded down the path to the side door. Gabe pulled skeleton keys from his pocket and quickly manipulated the lock, but although the lock opened, the door wouldn't budge.

"Damn it," he whispered. "There must be bolts securing the door."

"We need to get through a window," Shadow suggested, stepping back and looking up. None of them were open, so she carried on around the house, checking each window as she passed. "Everything's secure."

"Up there," Gabe said, pointing up to where a window had been left ajar. "They must have thought that would be safe. I can reach it."

"Only if you fly. But it's broad daylight!" Shadow inspected the wall. "There's a drain pipe, but it's not close, and there are no hand holds."

Gabe turned his back to the building and surveyed the garden and the neighbours. "I can't see anyone or hear anyone, Shadow. That's our way in. Give me a minute, and I'll open the door."

"Someone could be sleeping in there!"

"Trust me," he said, winking.

Seconds later he had pulled his t-shirt off, revealing sculpted muscles across his whole upper body, and his wings unfolded majestically. Despite vowing to herself not to stare, Shadow couldn't help it. She had never seen Gabe's wings in daylight, and they were breathtaking. She could see the colours in the feathers properly—shades of bronze, copper, and brown, all slightly darker on the underside.

"You shouldn't have to hide them. They are too beautiful."

Gabe smiled, despite the tenseness of their situation. "No one's called them that in a long time."

She wondered who had. His wife, she presumed, and for a second she envied their intimacy. "I want to run my fingers through them." The admission was out before she could stop it.

Gabe's smile broadened in to a lazy, seductive grin. "Another time." And then he stepped away from her, flew up to the window, and unlocked it easily. In a heartbeat his wings had vanished, and he was clambering through it.

For anxious seconds she waited, hoping not to hear shouts or fighting, but all was silent, and then she heard the door unlock and it swung open. She pushed his t-shirt at him and entered the room, quickly shutting the door behind her. "Anything?" she asked quietly as he dressed.

"I've had a quick look in the upstairs rooms, but there's no one here. There are papers and books in the sitting room. That seems to be their base."

"You focus there," Shadow said, "I'll double check the house."

Leaving Gabe searching through the research material, Shadow methodically worked her way around the ground floor, checking any bags or papers she came across, and finding a few photocopies of documents with notes made on them. She headed upstairs, knowing Gabe would have given them a cursory search only. The bedrooms all showed signs of someone sleeping in them—five rooms, so at least five people. Books were in a couple of bedrooms, novels mainly, and bags were half emptied, clothes strewn across the floor and other furniture. Shadow sniffed and frowned at the smell of unwashed clothes. At least the Nephilim were clean.

She found Mia's room next. It had to be hers; she was the only female in the group, and then found the one she thought was Erskine's. There were a collection of books about black magic, demons, angels, and a large Bible with numerous bookmarks sticking out of it. She flicked through it idly, but she certainly hadn't got the time to read it all. She considered taking it, and then decided against it. She needed to head back to Gabe and see if he'd had any success.

⚬

Niel was lying flat on his stomach on the narrow ledge of rock above the entrance to the temple, hidden behind a screen of bushes, watching Nicoli's team toil up the gorge.

They had worked their way up the narrow track over the last couple of hours, investigating thoroughly, and concentrating on the right hand side of the gorge, which was logical. That was the side it was marked on the map. They nodded politely as hikers passed them, pausing their search until they were out of sight. The day was still overcast, the air close, and although so far it hadn't rained, it was still hard going. He lost sight of them on occasions, but they always re-appeared a little closer.

Nicoli was leading the party, referring constantly to what Niel could only assume was the map. Erskine was easy to spot. He was short and fat and was clearly struggling with the trek, waddling more than walking, but to be fair, it hadn't stopped him. He clutched a leather bag close to his chest, and every now and again he pulled a document out of it. Niel suspected it was The Path of the Seeker, but as he couldn't be sure, he hadn't rang Gabe about it.

They finally paused below him, and Niel had a horrible, sinking feeling that they would find the entrance. They were well equipped too, carrying rope and heavy packs, and he had no doubt if they did find the entrance, they would attempt to enter the temple. There was a lot of pointing going on, and he heard raised voices. Eventually Jensen, the skinny man, started up the slope, directed by Erskine. His voice carried to Niel, high-pitched and mean, as he yelled instructions to Jensen. "No, higher. Naamah told me it was halfway up a steep slope. I feel sure we're close." *Naamah? His demon, perhaps.* Erskine shot a look of loathing at Nicoli. "I told you we should have started farther up the ravine. We've wasted hours."

Nicoli held on to his patience. "We searched here the other day and found nothing. It was logical to start at the beginning again."

Jensen's laboured breathing grew louder as he drew closer, and Niel could smell his fear; he didn't like Erskine. He was sure none of them did. Erskine stood slightly apart from the rest, only the tall Greek man willing to speak to him during their search. Mia looked mutinous but wary, and the other man, who they still had no name for, looked distinctly annoyed. They were not a happy team, and Niel was sure that could work to their advantage.

Jensen was getting closer, poking behind bushes and stunted trees, and although Niel was tempted to intervene, he knew it was pointless. To stop them discovering the entrance would mean killing them, or injuring them, and he wasn't about to do that.

Niel had discussed his options that morning with Gabe and Nahum before he left, just in case this happened, but they all felt they were on a collision course that couldn't be avoided. Fate was moving in odd ways, pushing them together in this crazy race. He knew why Gabe was worried. Raziel's book was powerful and had caused so much bloodshed and arguments in the past, it wasn't hard to imagine the destruction it might bring now. And Gabe had undoubtedly suffered at the time, having been unwillingly dragged into a search and lifestyle he had long abandoned.

A shout disturbed his thoughts. Jensen. He was lost to view now, but he heard him yell, "I found an opening in the rock!"

Shit.

Erskine punched the air with unconcealed greed and started his slow, laborious climb. Niel unhappily accepted the inevitable. It was time to call Gabe.

Twenty-One

When Gabe received Niel's call, he responded quickly, anxious to get there as soon as possible. When he and the others reached the spot in the ravine below the entrance, they found Niel with the unconscious unknown member of The Order of Lilith. The man was lying on the slope as if he was asleep, and Niel stood over him, waiting impatiently.

"How did that happen?" Gabe jerked his head at the man.

"They left him watching. I decided he needed to be out of the way." Niel held his hand up. "Don't worry, he'll be fine. It was just a small punch, and I only did it when I knew you were close."

"Good. Are all the others in there?" Gabe asked.

"Yep. You made good time."

Shadow grimaced. "Even so, they've been in there for almost an hour. They must have progressed beyond the first door. We need to get in there. Now."

Gabe noted her determined expression. Shadow wasn't scared; in fact, he doubted much scared her at all, and that headstrong determination worried him. But she was right. The drive hadn't been long, but they'd had to run up the valley, and that had taken time.

"I guess we'll soon find out, won't we," Nahum said, eager to head up the rocky slope.

"Hold on," Niel cut in, stretching out his arm to stop him. "What exactly are we going to do when we get in there?"

"If I'm honest," Gabe answered warily, "I'm not sure."

"They were well equipped," Niel told them. "And they haven't come out—I'm sure of that. Are we really prepared to go in after them?"

Nahum stepped close to Gabe, gripping his shoulder. "This is one of those times when we just follow our gut."

Gabe stared at the man he trusted above all others and knew he was right. "All right. If they've entered, we enter."

"Even without The Path of the Seeker?" Olivia asked, looking shocked. "They could be well ahead now, and without guidance, it could prove disastrous for us."

Gabe was filled with doubt about their next steps too, but he needed Olivia to understand. "Like Nahum said, this is one of those times where we have to run on instinct—unless you want them to get the book before us."

"Of course not!"

"Maybe we just snatch the path out of Erskine's grubby little hands," Shadow suggested, her violet eyes glittering.

Gabe held Shadow's gaze, staring her down. "We'll assess the situation. If the opportunity is right, then yes—but no jumping ahead and compromising our safety." He knew what she was like when she had an idea in her head, and he needed her to focus. "Besides, unless they have the key, I think they are in limbo, too. Whatever happens, we stay calm." He looked at them each in turn, and they all nodded, Shadow more reluctantly than the others. "Let's go."

Niel lifted the unconscious man like he was a sack of potatoes, flinging him over his shoulder as he scrambled up the slope, seemingly unimpeded by his burden, and the others scrambled next to him. They slowed when they reached the entrance to the temple, Shadow approaching first in her unnervingly graceful silence. She listened, nodded, and slipped inside. Gabe turned to Niel and with a wordless gesture, told him to remain outside, and then he followed the others.

To Gabe's ears, every slide of clothing or shoes along the rock seemed loud, but there were no shouts from up ahead, or any other sounds at all. When they finally stepped into the antechamber, they found it completely empty.

"Fuck it!" Gabe said, looking around. He'd been hoping they would find them here, still puzzling how to open the door. "They must have gone in."

Nahum examined the door etched into the rock. "This looks different now. Turn your light off, Liv." When it was fully dark again, Nahum pointed at the edges of the door. "There's a faint light there. See it?"

He was right. An almost imperceptible orange light seeped around the door, and the letters held remnants of the same colour.

Olivia groaned. "They really have gone through it."

"We have to follow," Shadow said, her voice filled with steely resolve. "Erskine must have mastered the language of fire."

"But he hasn't got the key," Olivia reminded them.

"Unless Jackson was lying and he made a better deal later," Nahum suggested.

"But he wasn't with them!" she pointed out.

"Maybe," Nahum countered "they stole it from him. Or maybe the demon got to him."

Gabe was debating their options as he asked, "Have you heard from Jackson today, Olivia?"

She shook her head and her eyes widened. "Shit. I hope he's okay."

"One of you two has to say the words and let us in," Shadow said, her sword in her hand.

Gabe blinked. Where the hell had that come from?

"We are wasting time," she persisted.

Nahum nodded at Gabe. "She's right. We have to follow them."

"And if they're stuck there? We could be, too—some weird angel purgatory." Gabe rubbed his eyes. "I don't want that for any of us." He looked at Olivia's worried face. "You don't have to come," he told her. "You can stay with Niel."

She squared her shoulders. "If I don't go, I'll never forgive myself."

Shadow raised her voice. "Gabe! Do it."

"Wait!" Gabe raised his hands, fearing once they entered, there was no going back. "I've studied our copy of the path and remember some of it. Does anyone else?"

Olivia nodded. "I was comparing it to the map and some of Hammond's rambling diary. I can remember bits of it, but not all, and it didn't make much sense to me."

Nahum nodded, too. "Same here. I remember parts of it."

"Shadow?" Gabe asked, starting to feel slightly more positive.

She shrugged. "A little."

He sighed. "Let's hope a little knowledge goes a long way. And more than anything, let's hope Erskine has the key. Nahum, go let Niel know. We'll wait."

Gabe stepped in front of the door, pulling El's sword from the scabbard he had strapped to him, and he was thankful for the feel of the cold steel in his hands. He silently rehearsed the words, the old language feeling odd because he hadn't spoken it for so long, and his heart thumped uncomfortably in his chest. Everything about this screamed danger, but he had to do this. To turn away now, knowing that Erskine could get the book, was impossible.

When Nahum reappeared at his side, he was carrying El's dagger. "Ready?"

"Ready."

Gabe spoke the inscribed words, feeling the power in them. They rumbled around the chamber, and the stone trembled. The script etched into the rock burst into flames, as did the entire outline of the doorway, and the doors swung wide silently.

Gabe eyes widened at the sight. A passageway lay beyond the doors. The walls along its entire length were inscribed with the language of fire. Every single word blazed with light, reflecting off the shiny black granite it was etched into. He heard Olivia's sharp intake of breath, sensed Nahum's grim determination and Shadow's eager curiosity, and swallowing his own reluctance, he gripped his sword tighter and stepped through the door.

Harlan was halfway back to Angel's Rest, with JD next to him, when his phone rang and Niel gave him the news. He nearly crashed the car.

"They've done *what*?"

He listened as Niel patiently related the events, but his calmness did nothing to alleviate his own panic. His driving slowed as he absorbed the news. "We're not ready, Niel."

"You'd better get ready. It's happening now, whether you like it or not. And call Jackson. We need the key."

When he hung up, JD was already glaring at him. "They had no right to go in. I expected better of Gabe. I trusted him."

"To be fair, they really had no choice, JD. Nicoli was already ahead." He put his foot down, driving faster than the speeding limit, but he didn't care. "If you want a shot at this book, Gabe, Shadow, and the rest of their crew are it." He glanced at him, but JD was staring resolutely ahead, his lips set in a thin line, and Harlan lost patience, despite the fact that JD was his boss, and immortal to boot. "They are risking their lives, JD. They're in there without the path or the key. The consequences could be deadly! You should be grateful, not sulking." He felt JD's hard stare but he concentrated on driving, not giving a shit about what JD thought. "Olivia is with them. She could die. I happen to like Olivia, a lot. I like the others, too. This isn't some walk in the park they started without us."

JD was silent for a few minutes more, and then he said stiffly, "Sorry. I'm very anxious, and sleep-deprived."

"Then I suggest you sleep now, because once we get to Angel's Rest, we won't stop."

"I can't possibly sleep now!"

"Well, in that case, do something useful and finish deciphering the path!"

"I've tried."

"Try harder! I need to phone Jackson."

The conversation with Jackson was straightforward, and Harlan didn't mince words. "Meet me at the house with the key."

"Slow down," Jackson remonstrated. "I need some assurances first."

"I can assure you that potentially people could die imminently, and you will never see the book or get any future favours from me unless you meet me at the house. That good enough?" He ended the call abruptly.

JD looked at him, intrigued. "That was unexpected."

"Yeah, well, there's a whole lot more to me than meets the eye."

They completed the rest of the journey in silence.

The first thing Harlan did when they arrived at the house was call Niel while he paced around the conservatory. "Any change?"

Niel, normally upbeat and optimistic, had never sounded so despondent. "It's been over an hour, and there's been no movement from inside. Nicoli's team has been in for over two hours. I'm anxious to get in there, Harlan. Tell me you're close."

"I'm at the house with JD, waiting for Jackson. I'll be with you as soon as we have the key." He lowered his voice and headed to the far end of the room, out of JD's hearing. JD was rifling through paperwork, making space for his own, and Harlan could tell he was already lost within his own thoughts and unlikely to hear him anyway. "Look, JD hasn't deciphered all of the document. We're missing key information. I'm not sure if Gabe told you, but we need the original."

"Too late for that," Niel said. "The original Path of the Seeker is in there with Erskine, but it's good to hear that Jackson still has the key—I think. However, I might have someone who can help."

Harlan frowned. "Who?"

"Nicoli's unknown soldier is currently lying unconscious at my feet. I think it's time to wake him up."

Shadow was right behind Gabe when he stepped through the door, and she tried not to let her awe get in the way of concentrating on the way ahead.

The illuminated script blazed on either side, but gave off no heat, despite the curling flames that flickered relentlessly. And it was utterly silent, except for their muted footfalls. Olivia was behind her, with Nahum at the rear, and as soon as Nahum stepped beyond the threshold, the door swung shut behind them, leaving no sign of where it had been.

"How the hell do we get out again?" Olivia asked, her voice unsteady.

"With our wits and by the skin of our teeth," Gabe said, as he set off down the corridor.

The corridor was uniform, as carefully constructed as the antechamber, and the far end was in darkness. They kept close together, walking slowly and wary of traps.

"Gabe, what does the script say?" Shadow asked.

"'Prepare yourself for The Path. Only the worthy will succeed.'"

"We'll be fine, then. I was born worthy!" she declared, trying to feel as confident as she sounded. This place felt completely alien to her.

"Maybe you shouldn't test that statement just yet," he answered, shooting her an annoyed look over his shoulder.

The corridor ended with a door made of shiny black stone, this one etched with a symbol, and again there was no handle.

"The symbol for water," Shadow said, immediately recognising the upside-down triangle.

"How do we open it?" Olivia asked. "The language of fire again?"

Gabe shrugged. "Let's try," and he quickly uttered a phrase.

A seam appeared down the middle of the panel forming two doors, which promptly swung open. Immediately afterward, ice-cold spray hit them, and a fine mist filled the space ahead.

Shadow blinked, droplets of water already obscuring her vision and soaking through her clothing. She tried to discern what lay ahead, but it was impossible to see anything through the spray. Gabe glanced at them uneasily, and then walked through the door, the rest of them hard on his heels.

The door sealed shut behind them, and for a moment the mist cleared, allowing them to see that four passageways lay ahead. Their walls streamed with water that pooled on the ground, already submerging the path. The walls were so high it was impossible to see the top, and so narrow that the Nephilim couldn't extend their wings in the space.

"Is this some kind of water maze?" Olivia asked, already shivering in the cold.

"Perhaps." Nahum nodded at the floor. "Look, the water is already rising. We need to move, now."

"But to which entrance?" Gabe asked. "We pick the wrong one and we're dead."

"Wait," Shadow said, trying to think of what she'd seen on The Path of the Seeker. "The elements have orders. I think water is the second one. We need to take the second path."

"Are you sure?" Gabe asked, his shirt already drenched with spray, and he slicked his hair away from his eyes.

"Yes—the order is earth, water, air, fire. If this relates to that, then it's the second path." The others looked uncertainly at each other, and Shadow asked, "Have you got a better idea? Or any suggestions at all?"

They shook their heads, and Shadow shouldered Gabe out of the way. "After me, then."

The water was icy, and within seconds Shadow was drenched. She gritted her teeth to stop them from chattering and forged ahead, trying not to lose her footing on the slick surface. For the most part, the way was flat, but it snaked left and right, and was completely disorientating. It was impossible to see the end, and every now and then she stumbled on hidden steps and slopes. They had walked only a short distance when the water was up to their knees, and then thighs, and she still had no idea how close they were to the end when it became waist deep, the current pulling with every step.

Gabe tapped her on the shoulder, shouting to be heard above the fall of water. "Are you sure you're right?"

"Yes, but even if I'm not it's too late now!"

"Shadow!"

"It's a test—of faith in my decision, as well as knowledge. I'm right." She glanced behind Gabe and saw Nahum and Olivia white-faced and shivering, and she quickly continued.

By the time the next door appeared, the water was up to her chest, and she struggled against the current. As soon as she stepped onto the narrow platform, the others staggering after her, the water ebbed away, leaving them all trembling and exhausted.

Olivia nodded at the door, and with a shaking voice asked, "What's etched on this one?"

It wasn't a symbol; instead, it was another word in flowing script.

"'Fire,'" Nahum said grimly before attempting a smile. "At least we'll warm up."

Twenty-Two

N iel shook the man lying prone on the ground, noting the bruise already swelling on his chin. He'd hit him with a quick jab and he dropped quickly, and despite their situation, Niel smiled. He hadn't lost his touch.

"Hey, wake up!"

The man stirred, blinked, groaned, and then his eyes widened and he sat up, trying to edge away. "Who the hell are you?"

"Your new best friend. Tell me what you know about The Path of the Seeker."

The man's eyes clouded. "I don't know anything about that damned thing." He was English, from somewhere in the north of the country, Niel estimated. His hair was cut very short, he had a thick, muscular build, and he looked like he'd been in a few fights. His nose had clearly been broken and never fixed, he had a scar across his neck, and he looked belligerent.

"Don't lie," Niel said, leaning close. "You work with Nicoli and the demon conjuror. What do you know about the path?"

"I know they're going to beat you to the temple. You're with Harlan's team." His mouth twisted into a smile, revealing missing teeth. "They're in there now—with the document. You're too late."

"I know they're in there, you idiot. I watched you. Two hours later and they're not out yet. Tell me what's hidden in the document."

"No idea what you're saying." He stared at Niel, challenging him, and despite Niel's size, he could tell he was spoiling for a fight. Niel was inclined to give him one.

"You will tell me what's hidden in that document, or I will take you in there with me, and you can tell me there—when we're potentially on the verge of death. Your choice."

"I don't know anything."

Niel tried to decide if he was telling the truth, or really had no idea. He had been in the house, privy to the discussions and research, and although he looked like a thug, that didn't mean he wouldn't have heard something useful.

Niel lifted him up by his jacket and pinned him to the wall of rock next to the entrance, his arm across his throat, thankful they were screened from the ravine below.

The man's eyes widened with shock at finding his feet off the floor, but he recovered quickly, squirming in his grasp.

"I don't believe you," Niel said. "I think you're a lying little shit, and if my friends die because of you, I will kill you."

"I don't give a shit about your friends!" the man ground out, struggling for breath.

He lifted his foot and kicked at Niel, striking his legs. Niel dropped him and he fell awkwardly, and Niel straddled him, pinning his flailing limbs easily. He leaned into him, inches from his face, and despite the man's belligerence, he could smell his fear now.

"I've decided you're coming in there with me."

"I am not going in there with that demonic idiot!"

"Tell me what's in the document."

"Screw you!"

Niel considered him for a brief moment longer and then punched him. The man's head hit the rock and he passed out again.

Bollocks. He really was going to have to carry him in there. Niel was pretty sure that if they ended up near death, he'd give up the information quick enough. And if not, then at least Niel would have the pleasure of them both dying together.

Harlan studied the key in Jackson's outstretched hand.

It was not a normal key. It was constructed from jade that had been carved into an octagon the size of his palm, and was made out of several interlocking pieces. It was ornate, decorative marks all over it, and a single sigil was etched into the centre.

"You can pick it up," Jackson said, sounding amused. "It won't bite."

"I know that!" Harlan grasped it, surprised at its weight. "Is something in the middle of it? It's heavy for its size."

Jackson shrugged. "I don't think so, but to be honest, I haven't taken it apart. It looks as if it breaks into separate pieces, but I confess that it has defeated me."

JD was standing next to Harlan, glasses perched on the end of his nose as he watched him handle it. "May I?"

He handed it to JD, who walked to the closest lamp and held it close, turning it over in his hands. He murmured to himself, and then marched over to his notes on the path, turned his back on them, and sat down.

Astonished, Harlan said, "Er, JD, we really need to go."

"Not yet. I'm not ready!" he said impatiently.

"But our team is in there—"

"Then shut up and let me concentrate!" JD shot back.

Harlan bit back his impatience and glared at Jackson, who had a wry smile on his face. "Something funny?"

Jackson immediately sobered up. "I guess not." He stuck his hands in his pockets and walked to the conservatory windows, looking out at the deepening gloom before turning back to Harlan. "What happened?"

Harlan sighed and joined him, keeping his voice low. "Nicoli's team found the entrance and Gabe followed them in, leaving Niel outside. I asked Niel to check the antechamber, and it's empty. They must have crossed the threshold and the door has shut behind them. That was nearly three hours ago."

"Shit. That's a long time. Who was with him?"

"Shadow, Olivia, and Nahum."

"Niel's the big blond man, right?"

"Right." Harlan looked out the window, but he wasn't focusing on the view. "I'm worried sick. Anything could be happening in there. They could be injured, or even dead."

"You say Liv is in there?"

"Yes, and although I don't know the others well, I'd say she's in good hands."

"Olivia is pretty capable herself," Jackson reminded him.

"This is something else though, isn't it?" Harlan said, not looking forward to having to go after them.

A rumble of thunder carried across the hills and Jackson groaned. "Shit. We don't need a storm now, as well as everything else."

"You're still planning on coming?"

Jackson sighed. "Are we really going to do this?"

Harlan shook his head. "No. I just wanted to see if you really wanted to go. I wouldn't if I didn't have to."

"You're nuts, then. This could be one of the biggest finds ever! Angels, Old Testament stuff, all in those hills! You'd want to miss that?"

"Actually, yes. I'm not a believer. That alone will make me 'unworthy.'"

"Just think, you might become a believer after this."

"I wouldn't count on it. Don't get me wrong—I believe in the old Gods and supernatural stuff. How could I not in this job? But it doesn't make me want to worship them."

JD broke into their conversation. "This isn't the key."

Both men spun around to face him, ready to protest.

"I've had that for years, JD," Jackson said, marching over to the table. "The documents I found talked about this being The Key of Angels, and it referred to Raziel. That's what this is about, isn't it? Raziel's Book of Knowledge."

Harlan looked at him, surprised. "You know that?"

"I suspected as much."

"Shut up, both of you. Yes it's a key, but not the key we want," JD remonstrated. "Where did you find it?"

"In a small church in Rome dedicated to St Thomas, hidden within the stonework. It took some getting out, too."

JD banged his hand on the table. "Bloody Rome! Use your brain, you lumpish, onion-eyed pumpion!"

"What did you just call me?" Jackson asked, more bewildered than annoyed, and Harlan realised he'd just witnessed a Shakespearean insult.

"For God's sake!" JD continued. "This is an *English* series of clues given to an *English* visionary right here in Angel's Rest! What on Earth made you think that *this* key would fit *this* trinity?"

"The clues in the paper I found all referred to The Key of the Trinity! This is it!"

"This is *one* of them, you yeasty clotpole!" JD clutched his hair and paced the room, incensed.

Harlan ignored the ripe insults that were now coming thick and fast, and that he had no idea JD would ever be the type of man to utter, and instead asked, "What do you mean, *one* of them?"

JD marched over to the table, picked his notes up, and shook them under Harlan's nose. "This is one of many trinities spread across the world! This is the key to a different entrance, you blazing nincompoop!"

Harlan's hand shot out and grasped JD's arm, hard, shocking him into silence. "There are *multiple* trinities?"

"Yes!"

"Why didn't you tell me?"

"You didn't need to know. We found *this* one!"

"Had you told me this, I would have questioned Jackson, not assumed. Didn't that strike you as important?"

"You know, I'm still standing here," Jackson pointed out. He picked his key up, examining it with fresh eyes. "Other trinities? Wow. So where is the key to this one?"

JD wrested his arm from Harlan's grasp. "I have no idea."

"Holy shit," Harlan said, his mind spinning in a million different directions. "They are in there alone, they don't have the path, and now we haven't got the key. This is a disaster! They could all die!"

"You don't know that!" JD said, annoyed. "If anything, it means Erskine does have the key! What is clear is that we won't get The Book of Knowledge."

Harlan was seething. "My friends are worth more than this bloody book!" And it was suddenly very clear to him that despite his short acquaintance with Shadow, Gabe, and the others, that he did consider them friends and he liked them a lot. "And can I remind you that Gabe was someone you wanted very much to meet." He didn't want to say Nephilim with Jackson there, but hoped the reminder would jolt JD to his senses.

"He's not the only one, is he?" JD said churlishly, turning away quickly and refusing to look at Harlan.

"You are unbelievable!" If Harlan was quick-witted enough to think of a Shakespearean insult he would hurl one, but right now he needed to find the key. "What made you realise Jackson's key is wrong?"

"At the end of the document—The Path of the Seeker—there is a reference to angelic music leading to glory. I think the key is something musical."

Harlan looked at him, stunned. "And that's it? That's completely vague!"

"That's all I have!" JD said crossly.

"Damn it!" Harlan said loudly, making JD flinch. "I need to speak to Niel."

He turned his back on Jackson and JD, phoned Niel, and walked to the window, seeing a flicker of lightning in the distance. As soon as Niel answered he updated him with the situation, and he could almost feel Niel's fury radiating down the phone.

"Harlan, my brothers and insane sister are in there!"

"I know. Listen, I was in London this morning, but Olivia said she was going to read Hammond's dairies again. Did she find anything of interest? Anything at all?"

The line went silent, and Harlan heard thunder rumble again in the distance.

Niel finally responded. "Nahum updated me on the latest before he went in. He said Olivia had pointed out that Hammond was too ill to travel too far to hide the key anywhere, and suggested that it had been hidden here, somewhere in Angel's Rest. I guess she presumed, like all of us, that it had been found years ago, and that's how Jackson obtained it. Anyway, in the diaries he talks about St Thomas's Church and how it was near completion. He knew some of the craftsmen who were working on it, and spoke of visiting it. It could be there, or it could be where he lived."

"Which is where?"

"I'm not entirely sure, but I think it's on Crofter's Lane—one of the cottages." Harlan could hear the frustration in Niel's voice. "I'm so annoyed with myself for not thinking about the key more. I got side-tracked when I heard Jackson had it!"

"We all did. Don't be too hard on yourself. Look, if you had to choose between the two options—house or church—which would you pick?"

"Church. Home seems too obvious, too close. And the church has more places to hide it."

"It would be somewhere very permanent, surely. Something stone, walls, carvings..." Harlan thought of where Jackson had found his key. "Okay, I'm going to head there now and start looking, although this feels like insanity."

"Thanks, Harlan. And hey, there's one thing I do recall about the key."

"Yes?"

"Hammond said it would deliver the voice of the angels—I assumed he meant the words in the book, but it might not be that."

"Voice? That's sounds similar to something JD has just said. Okay, gotta go."

"Keep me informed."

"I will—and sit tight. Shelter inside if you have to because it's going to rain, just don't go in. I promise I'll be there as soon as possible!"

He ended the call and turned to find the others watching him. "Jackson, you're coming with me. JD, work on the document, because I'm going to find this damn key and then we're going in."

Twenty-Three

G abe surveyed the chamber that lay before them, unable to stop his mouth from dropping open in surprise.

This chamber was vastly different to the one before. For a start it was hot, and for that he was thankful. The icy cold water seemed to have penetrated his bones, and his muscles ached in a way that they hadn't for centuries. Poor Olivia was blue, and she was currently jumping up and down trying to thaw out. Shadow had fared better, and she was already assessing the landscape before them.

They stood on the edge of a desert, the rolling red sand dunes stretching to a wall of sandstone in the distance, illuminated by an unknown light. It was beautiful, in an unearthly, unexpected kind of way.

"How the hell can a desert be underground?" Shadow asked.

Gabe grunted. "How the hell is any of this here? By Raziel's crazy idea of a challenge. Son of a bitch." Then he grinned, already peeling his wet t-shirt and jacket off. "On the plus side, we can fly."

Olivia's eyes widened with surprise, and probably some admiration, he noted. "Fly? Oh, wow!"

He unfurled his wings, as did Nahum, and Gabe felt his strength return. His wings always enhanced his abilities—his senses were keener, he was quicker, stronger, and more agile, even if he wasn't flying. As his wings lifted and rustled, heat flooded through him, and he assessed the way ahead.

"There's got to be a catch," Nahum said, his dagger already drawn. "That sand could hide anything. What did you say the Realm of Fire had in your world, Shadow?"

"Djinn."

"As in, Aladdin?" Olivia asked, looking out expectantly, as if one would suddenly appear.

"I have no idea what Aladdin is," Shadow confessed. "But deserts also have dragons."

"Dragons!"

"And they are mean!" She wielded her sword. "This sword is pure dragonium, made from their flesh."

Gabe wondered if she was pulling his leg. "How can you make a sword from dragons?"

"In my world, dragons are part gems and priceless metals, and when they die their body transforms. It's quite an industry—if you can kill one."

Gabe stared at the desert again. "Let's get this over with. Shadow." He beckoned to her, and she stepped within his arms. Nahum did the same with Olivia. Within seconds, they were all travelling over the hot sand.

Thermal air caressed his skin, carrying them for a short distance, and for a while Gabe thought they'd be fine. And then with an ear-splitting screech, a dragon rose from the desert below, intercepting them, and in his haste to swerve and pull his sword free, Shadow wriggled from his grasp and plummeted to the sand below.

The rumbling of thunder was growing ever closer by the time Harlan arrived at the church with Jackson.

The main door was locked and they sheltered under the porch, Harlan grateful for the failing light and impending storm that had kept pedestrians off the lane. He patted his pockets looking for the lock picks he had taken from his car, but Jackson already had his in hand and was working the lock.

It was now close to five o'clock, and Harlan was wired on adrenalin, which was fortunate because driving to London and back in such a short span of time was tiring. He'd grabbed a simple sandwich before leaving, aware he was starving. He watched Jackson's quick, sure movements and said, "Thanks for coming. You didn't have to help me with this."

Jackson concentrated on the lock, but he said, "Two of us will be quicker. I like Liv too, and hate to think I might never see her again."

Harlan wondered how true that was, and couldn't resist adding, "And of course, there's the added bonus of finding the book."

Jackson shot him an amused look. "Now is not the time to doubt my reasons for helping."

"It's the perfect time! We are essentially rivals in this."

Jackson stopped and straightened, his shaggy hair falling over his brow. "Do I need to worry about my safety now? Because I can assure you, I have no intention of killing you to get this thing!"

"I'm not a killer," Harlan said evenly. "I'm just like you—an occult collector. Just want to make sure you don't leave me high and dry in there."

"I won't. I think we both need to worry about Nicoli more than each other. Can I trust your team?"

"Yes. Although, JD is worrying me right now." JD's ominous comment about Gabe still rattled him. The last thing he needed was to find out JD was a ruthless bastard.

"The comment about there being more of them? Yeah, sounded disturbing. What does that mean?"

Harlan shook his head. "I can't say, but let's agree to keep an eye on JD, too."

Jackson resumed picking the lock. "It concerns me that you don't trust your boss. I've not heard much about him. He keeps a low profile for a bigwig."

"Yeah. Turns out his ego isn't all that low profile."

The lock clicked and Jackson slipped inside, and with one final look at the lane, Harlan followed him, passing through the small entrance hall to the nave. The church's interior was cold, gloomy, and utterly silent. The smell of polish and dust hung in the air, and Harlan wondered where to start.

As well as the stained glass windows at the end, there were three narrow windows on either side of the nave, and Harlan imagined that on a sunny day the light would flood over the rows of pews that ran to the altar.

Jackson had already started to examine the walls and floor on his left. "Didn't you say Gabe ran into Nicoli in here?"

"Yes, and noticed Mia leaving it a few days ago."

"Are you sure they haven't already found the key?" Jackson asked, repeating the question he had raised in the car. "They wouldn't have gone into the temple otherwise!"

"I honestly don't know! My initial thoughts were that they went in, like Gabe did, not knowing if they'd be stuck in there, and just wanted to explore what they could. And of course I assumed you had the key. But now—" he raised his shoulders in a shrug, "I don't know. If we presume they have it, then we're wasting time here. But if they haven't got it yet then they are stuck in there, and we have to find it to stand any kind of chance of getting all of them out!"

Jackson straightened up and scanned the room. "Nothing looks obviously disturbed or broken, but let's be logical. Hammond knew some of the craftsmen. He could have asked them to help him hide the key in the pews, the decorative woodwork, the altar, the pulpit, maybe even the floor. He could have hidden any part of the trinity in here. He could even have hidden them in some stone work."

"Damn it!" Harlan exclaimed as the possibilities overwhelmed him. "We've left it too late to find now. It's impossible!"

"It is with that attitude!"

Harlan needed to get his shit together, quickly. Logic was needed, not panic. He pulled the photocopies of the documents covered with Niel and Olivia's notes out of his pack. Just holding them helped him focus. "JD said something about angelic music and the key being the sound of God, and Niel mentioned the voice of an angel." He marched down to the altar and scanned the papers, looking for Niel's notes in the weak light coming through the stained glass windows. "Here it is. There's some garbled reference to hearing the music of God that will reveal all knowledge. 'When angels sing, the heavens part and the radiance of God will bathe us in glory.'" He looked up at the angel in the stained glass above him. "What makes music?"

Jackson was standing at the pulpit, an ornate wooden structure, frowning as he scanned the nave. "There isn't an organ in here, there's no place for a choir, and only the parishioners would make music as they sang. "

"But look how many pews there are!" Harlan said, hoping they didn't need to examine every single one.

"It could be hidden in a place not associated with music," Jackson pointed out. "Hammond was hiding this forever, he hoped. Wouldn't you hide the key somewhere obscure, rather than obvious?"

"Maybe. But he was also delirious and confused. Who knows what he was thinking at that stage? And it's impossible to know what was already built at that time." Harlan strode to the middle of the aisle, turning slowly and hoping inspiration would strike. And then his gaze settled on the pulpit again, and Jackson elevated several feet above him, framed within the ornate structure—unusually so, for such a simple church. "The vicar is the voice of God in here. Well, His messenger, at least. That pulpit is fairly dramatic for a country church."

"That's true," Jackson agreed. His voice carried easily, almost booming across the nave. "But medieval pulpits could be grandiose." However, Jackson had already started to tap the wooden structure, and now he fished his flashlight out to examine it.

Harlan continued to study it from a distance, examining the area that presented itself to the parishioners. The pulpit was divided into six painted panels in a hexagonal shape, filled with detailed pictures and surrounded by carvings. The paint had faded and the images were worn in places, but the colours were bold—blue, red, and yellow, some embellished with gold. One contained the Virgin Mary, carrying the baby Jesus, and three panels referenced three different angels, dark starry skies above them radiating with light. Another depicted Noah's Ark, flailing in high seas just like on the stained glass window, and the sixth... Harlan frowned. It was hard to see from where he was standing in the middle of the aisle. It was in deep shadow, on the far side of the pulpit, and he walked towards it, hearing Jackson still tapping away.

When he reached it, he paused, and his breath caught in his throat. The image was of an open book, shrouded in smoke and darkness, the edges curling with fire. No wonder he couldn't see it from a distance. It was still hard to make out the image from close up. Harlan ran his fingers over the panel, feeling the imperfections beneath his fingers, and then concentrated on the intricate carvings that framed it. He tapped, prodded, pushed, and then sighed. Nothing was happening.

"What have you found?" Jackson asked.

Harlan looked up to find him peering down on him. "Nothing. You?"

"Nothing. Yet." His head receded and the tapping started again, as a rumble of thunder echoed around the church.

Harlan inwardly groaned. *If rain started, would the temple be flooded? Or would it be protected by Raziel?* He pushed the thoughts to the back of his mind and continued to explore the panels, finally hearing a hollow *thunk* when he reached the image of the flood. His heart raced, and he kept tapping, trying to narrow down the area.

Jackson shouted again. "You've found something?"

"It sounds different, can you hear it?"

In seconds Jackson was at his side, shining his light on the panel, and the old varnish reflected a dull glow. "The flood. Interesting."

"Very. According to a source I have, the flood might have been sent to destroy Raziel's book."

"Really? You know it's the same book that Solomon was reported to have had at one point?"

Harlan nodded, his face close to the panel, finally seeing the carved animals, tiny and precise, that framed the image. He applied pressure to them, hoping to feel them depress. And then he spotted a snake, curling around something. A book. Harlan's mouth went dry and he applied pressure, light at first and then harder, and with a satisfying *click*, the carving sank back into the frame. He heard Jackson inhale, saying, "Holy shit," but he didn't look at him, focussing instead on the wafer-thin black line that became visible along the edge of the panel.

He hardly dared to look away, but he needed something to angle into the tiny gap. Luckily, Jackson had already anticipated his need, and a small knife appeared in front of his face. He took it wordlessly and pried the panel backwards.

It opened slowly, stiff from lack of use, but inside was empty space. Harlan, unable to hide his disappointment, cried out, "No!"

"Shit," Jackson said forcefully, and he reached in, feeling around carefully. "Nothing. Maybe this was where The Path of the Trinity was initially hidden."

Harlan was silent, frustration flooding through him, and he staggered back to the front pew, looking up at the pulpit absently, his torch flashing wildly before settling on an area of carving. When Harlan eventually focussed on it, he frowned. Cherubs were carved above the panels, a whole row of them, all blowing on tiny pipes, but in this odd light, one looked slightly different. Most of them held fluted horns, but one had a normal flute that was longer than the others.

He stood up abruptly. "Jackson. Look at that cherub."

"Which one?"

"The one my torch is on, you idiot. Look at the pipe between his lips. It's different than the others!"

"So it is," Jackson said softly, already stretching up on his tip-toes, but he was inches too short to reach it. "It's too high."

They both looked around for a chair or a stool, but neither was in sight, and then tried to move the pews, but they were fixed to the floor.

"I could try to lift you," Jackson said, frowning. "But I'm not known for my gym workouts."

"I'm not sure I could lift you, either," Harlan admitted, frowning at Jackson's long, lean build. "But, I could dangle from the pulpit, if you hold my legs."

The platform where the vicar delivered his sermon was several feet above the cherubs, and would be difficult to access from there too, but Harlan was sure he could lean over with Jackson's help.

"Let's do it," Jackson said, leading the way. In moments, Harlan was upside down, his legs on the wooden lectern as he supported himself to slide down the carved pulpit. He had discarded his jacket, and clutched the small knife in his teeth, his flashlight in his left hand. It was precarious, but Jackson's weight on his legs reassured him, and once he was eye level with the cherub, he took the knife from his mouth and studied the instrument.

"It has holes in it!" Harlan shouted. "I think it really is a working pipe." After examining it well with his light, he thrust the flashlight in his belt, hoping it wouldn't dislodge and crash to the floor, and then tried to pry the pipe free. "It's stuck. Glue, I think."

"Use the bloody knife then," Jackson said impatiently.

"I don't want to damage it!"

"It can't be destroyed, remember!"

"True," Harlan mumbled, feeling like a fool. He prodded at the pipe gently, and then when that didn't work, he became more aggressive, whittling the blade between the cherub's hands and the instrument. It was horribly awkward, the space tight, especially upside down, but eventually the pipe slid free. "Haul me up!"

With much fumbling and swearing Harlan regained his feet, both of them looking at what appeared to be an inconsequential wooden flute, unadorned except for three small holes.

Jackson laughed. "Is that what produces the music of the Gods?"

Harlan was just able to make out his bewildered expression in the dark church. "I don't know! Is this it? The key is a simple flute? Or have I just damaged a cherub for no reason?"

"Blow it."

Harlan just looked at him.

"I'm serious. See if it plays! If it doesn't, we're back to square one."

"What if I summon the wrath of God?"

"Then we know it works." Jackson's eyes filled with humour.

Feeling like an idiot, Harlan lifted the pipe to his lips and blew, and the clearest, sweetest tone filled the church, lifting the hairs on Harlan's arms. Ominously, as soon as the notes died away, an enormous crack of thunder sounded overhead, a flash of lightning lit the nave, the pulpit shuddered, and Jackson and Harlan both staggered as the building shook.

"There you go," Jackson said confidently. "The wrath of God. Let's rock and roll."

Gabe hadn't fought so hard in years.

The dragon that attacked them was huge, its wingspan three times the size of theirs, and although Gabe tried to coordinate his attack with Nahum, it was difficult when they couldn't even get close.

But it was also fun.

Shadow had landed safely, and he could see her below, a moving spot on the ground, Olivia nearby, as they made their way to a ruined building.

Gabe had no wish to kill the dragon, or even injure it; he just wanted to get past it. But the dragon had no intention of letting them, and they couldn't get close enough to inflict any kind of damage.

He shouted to Nahum, "Should we fight it on land?"

"I don't think we'd gain anything," he yelled back as he twisted gracefully to avoid a stream of fire.

The dragon turned his sharp, angular head to Gabe, fixed him with his sulphurous yellow gaze and roared fire, and any other questions Gabe had disappeared as he fought for his life.

Shadow stumbled across the burning hot sand, her clothes already dry from the furnace-like heat, finally reaching the shade of a ruined fort, half buried in the dunes.

But shade from what? She shielded her eyes, looking up to an orange sky, but there was no discernible sun, no obvious source of heat. *This place was nuts.* But it also reminded her of the Realm of Fire that she'd visited once. It was a vast expanse of desert, dunes, searing wind, an occasional oasis, and a string of volcanoes spewing lava.

The cities were hewn from red desert granite and sandstone, their streets narrow and dug deep into the earth, sheltered from the burning sun. She had hunted for a fey who had killed others and would do so again. He'd hidden in the small fey population that traded in the markets there, occasional partners with the djinn, but she'd caught him eventually.

Now, as she examined the walls, she saw script carved into the rock. A flurry of activity distracted her, and Olivia stumbled through the remnants of a doorway, breathing heavily.

"Are you okay?" Shadow asked, noting her flushed, sweating face.

"Depends what you mean by okay? I'm not freezing anymore, and there's a bloody great dragon above us, but yeah, I'm fine."

"Good," Shadow said, not having time to chat. "These are runes. Any idea what they say? It's certainly not fey script."

Olivia studied them, running her hand across the stone to brush loose sand and dust away, coughing as she did so. "They're Futhark runes."

"They are *what*?"

"A type of writing, used across Europe and originating from old Norse." Olivia wiped her sweaty face with the back of her hand. "Not really sure why they're here, but I can have a crack at deciphering them. When you're a collector you pick up a few things."

A roar sounded overhead, closer than was comfortable, and Shadow grabbed Olivia, flattening them to the ground as a wave of flame flashed over them.

Olivia quickly regained her feet, studying the runes again. "It says something about commanding the dragon to help...no wait, to command passage."

Shadow frowned. "Is there a dragon language?"

"I have no idea! This is your world, not mine!"

Your world. That was an interesting observation. Shadow brushed the comment away, recalling a story that her friend Bloodmoon had told her once about the Wolf Mage, and with a sudden revelation she yelled, "Gabe! Nahum!"

Olivia joined in, and within a few moments that felt more like hours, Nahum dived down and landed next to them, streaked with blood and sweat, and smelling of burnt feathers. "What?"

"Dragons have a language," Shadow said quickly. "You need to command passage."

"What?"

Olivia pointed at the wall. "Command passage—*go!*"

Twenty-Four

By the time Harlan, JD, and Jackson met up with Niel, it was fully dark, and the storm was upon them.

Wind howled up the ravine, lightning flashed overhead, and thunder echoed around them, bouncing off the rocks and shaking the valley floor. And there was rain, torrential rain. The streams had filled, and the night seemed full of water cascading down stony gullies. Harlan half pushed and half pulled JD up the steep slope to the temple's entrance, grateful when Niel appeared and hauled them both up.

They slid through the narrow cleft like wet fish, and finally stopped in the antechamber, panting and dripping water everywhere.

"I was beginning to think you'd never make it," Niel said, worry etching lines into his face. "You have the key?"

Harlan fished it out of his pocket. "It's a pipe."

Niel took it, turning it over carefully. "You have got to be kidding me."

"No. That's it," Harlan said, still incredulous. "It plays—but don't do it here. Who knows what you'll trigger!"

"Fair enough." Niel handed it back and as Harlan tucked it safely into his pocket, Niel turned to JD, who looked distinctly grumpy for a man who desperately wanted to be here. "Are you ready?"

JD grimaced. "Not really, but I'll probably manage."

Niel could barely conceal his annoyance. "My friends went in there hours ago, with only a few weapons. You've got the path, the key, and plenty of other crap in those bags, so you'd better manage!"

Jackson had been silent, shaking water from his coat and watching the exchange, but hearing a groan he turned and frowned at the rumpled figure in the corner. "Is that Jimmy Wilson?"

"You know him?" Niel asked. "Not a friend, I hope."

Jackson gave a dry laugh. "No. He's a sneaky, second-rate thief. Why is he here?"

"He's with Nicoli. I figured he must have heard about what's hidden within the paper the path is written on." He glanced at JD. "We need to know that, right?"

JD nodded, "Yes, I think so."

Jackson looked at Jimmy thoughtfully. "I wouldn't trust him. Did he hit his head or something?"

"Yes. With my fist." Niel scooped him up and flung him over his shoulder. "JD, I'm going to say the words now...or do you want to? You need to speak the language of fire."

JD looked around him at the perfectly uniform room carved by Raziel's hand, appearing overwhelmed. Then he squared his shoulders, licked his lips and positioned himself in front of the door. "I'll do it."

• ◦ •

A fierce wind blew up from a seemingly bottomless abyss in front of Shadow and the others, and not for the first time during the journey that seemed to threaten death at every turn, Shadow questioned why she was here.

"Because the Gods themselves couldn't have stopped you, you headstrong madam!" Gabe shouted over the howling gale.

"I was curious, and honestly didn't know what to expect," she shouted back.

"I did try to warn you."

"Bullshit. You didn't have a clue, either."

This was the fourth chamber they had entered, and each had been distinctly different to the one before, but this area must be the fourth and final element. They had passed through the earth element with relative ease, thanks to Shadow. So far, each chamber led to another, offering no other choices as to their route ahead. They had only had to conquer each element to pass. *Only!* She chided herself. *Like that had been easy.* Now that they were here, it seemed logical—the four elements were the basic building blocks of magic. In her world, different beings were associated with each. She was from the Realm of Earth, but water elementals lived in the Realm of Water, djinn and dragons lived in the Realm of Fire, and sylphs lived in the Realm of Air. Having Nephilim with them was a distinct advantage in every area.

"You're just going to fly us over, right?" Olivia asked, trying to secure her hair back as the wind whipped it around her face.

Shadow sheltered behind a rocky outcrop, pulling the others with her, and the wind abated, allowing her to hear more clearly. The door they had entered through had sealed shut behind them, just like all the others. This chamber, however, was more naturalistic than the proceeding ones; well, everything except for the unceasing gale. Streams of water ran down the uneven rock face that was mottled with moss, and enormous stalactites hung above them.

Nahum looked uncertain. "It's a strong wind. If we get caught in a vortex, it will be tricky."

"But how would Nicoli's team have crossed?" Gabe asked. "They can't fly!"

"Maybe Erskine used his demon in some way," Olivia suggested. "Or a spirit? He's a conjuror—he could have summoned either."

Shadow frowned at Olivia. "Something you said to me earlier makes me think these tests are tailored for us. Why would we be encountering things from my world? Dragons in a desert? Really?"

"You think each team is facing something different?" Gabe asked.

"Maybe." She shrugged. "I don't know. Perhaps in some chambers. The important thing right now is how we cross this."

"There must be a way of communicating with the element," Gabe said, "as we did with the dragon."

"I think it's just about strength," Nahum mused. "I'm going to fly high—test the wind up there." He nodded to the roof of the cavern, lost in darkness, and without waiting for comment, extended his wings and flew away.

For a short while Nahum seemed to struggle, meeting resistance at every point, until halfway along he soared across the cavern, his wings finally able to open fully. In moments he was back with them, grinning. "There's a tunnel of utter calm. But," his face fell, "there's a body down there, on a narrow shelf. It's impossible to get closer, but I think it's Jensen."

Olivia's hands flew to her mouth. "No! Poor Jensen. He was annoying as hell, but this is no place to die."

"I'm amazed no one has died before now," Gabe said. "Maybe they have and we just haven't found them. Anyway, Shadow?" He held his arms open. "Allow me."

The flight across the cavern was undeniably terrifying, but also exhilarating, and Nahum was right. Jensen's crumpled body lay on a ledge far below. As they drew closer to the end of the cave, it was clear there was no door. Instead there was an opening high in the rock and they flew through it, passing through some kind of shimmering veil, into a chamber of breathtaking magnificence.

Gabe and Nahum flew to ground level and landed on a short platform, and they looked around them, jaws dropping, as Gabe muttered, "Bollocks."

This chamber, like the antechamber, was made from polished granite of some sort. It was dark, speckled with a substance that sparkled in the unseen light source that mimicked moonlight. A series of graceful bridges soared across water, and at the far side of the vast chamber was The Temple of the Trinity—all towering columns, gilded symbols, braziers spitting fire, and an enormous statue of an angel holding an open book.

"Herne's horns. Are we in the final room?" Shadow asked, already deeply suspicious. It felt too quiet, too calm, as if something was just waiting to pounce. And there was no way out; the opening high above them had sealed.

"Seems so." Gabe gripped his blade, his eyes darting everywhere. "Where's Erskine?"

"Perhaps he's dead," Olivia whispered.

"There!" Nahum pointed to a solitary figure on a broad column that stood alone, surrounded by water. "Is that Nicoli? How the hell did he get to that?"

"Perhaps the bridges move," Olivia suggested, "and it left him stranded."

"You've been watching too many tomb-raiding games," Nahum said, laughing.

"You wait!" Olivia replied darkly.

Shadow squinted at the distant platform. "Where are Erskine and Mia?"

"Erskine's on the steps of the temple," Gabe said. His wings were still visible, and he flexed them. "I need to stop him. He's not getting that book."

"But where's Mia?" Shadow asked, feeling a weird sort of responsibility for her. Having fought with her and interrogated her in the kitchen, she was no longer a faceless enemy.

"I can't see her at all," Olivia said, worried. "I don't think that bodes well. Perhaps we should rescue Nicoli," she suggested, looking at Nahum hopefully.

He shook his head, "Sorry, not yet. He can stay exactly where he is—out of the way."

Gabe was already rising into the air, but Shadow tugged at his arm. "Wait. If he hasn't got the key, he can't get any further."

"Then what's in his hand?"

"It could be anything; we haven't got a good view. And besides, if either of you fly, they will all know what you are!"

"Too late for that," Nahum pointed out. "We flew in, and our wings are pretty obvious."

Gabe exchanged a worried glance with his brother. "We can't let Erskine get this book. It's too powerful, especially in the wrong hands."

"I doubt if you could just fly there, Gabe," Shadow said. "That's too easy—you might trigger something. And besides, we need to stick together. Harlan and Niel could be here any minute with the key."

"She's right," Nahum told him. "Let's have a good think about this before we proceed. It's been one chaotic path to get here. We don't want to mess it up now. And if Miss Headstrong advises patience, that must mean something!"

Shadow swallowed her tart reply, just grateful Nahum agreed.

Gabe finally nodded. "I'll wait...for a while."

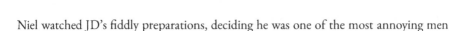

Niel watched JD's fiddly preparations, deciding he was one of the most annoying men he'd ever met.

He caught Harlan's eye, and had the feeling from his tight-lipped expression that he agreed. He pressed his hand to his temple and said, "JD. Can't you do this any faster?"

"No." JD clenched his jaw and continued to lay out a collection of dried herbs, a silver dish, and a collection of jars containing liquids. "We need to conquer earth. I believe that if I concoct the right mixture, I can use to it to open our pathway ahead. Patience is a virtue. Besides," JD shot Niel and Harlan an impatient look, "you have tried and failed. And this is how I interpret the path."

Niel sighed heavily. *JD was right.* They had entered this chamber fifteen minutes ago, and found an impenetrable wall of thick, green plants blocking their way. They'd tried to push through, squeeze through, and hack through, and had failed every time, the plants impervious. And there was no way Niel could fly, either. There was no airspace at all.

He pulled Harlan and Jackson aside, leaving a now conscious Jimmy to lean sullenly against the wall. "I guess JD is right, unless you have other suggestions?"

Jackson shook his head. "I'm amazed we made it this far. Water traps and fire chambers are primitive, but effective. And JD has got the instructions."

"This is not what I expected," Harlan admitted. "I thought the tests would be esoteric, or mystical, and instead I feel we're in the Chrystal Maze."

Niel nodded at JD. "That looks mystical."

"Alchemical, actually," Jackson said. "I have no idea what he's doing, but let's hope it works."

"I'm beginning to wish I hadn't brought Jimmy," Niel confessed. Jimmy was conscious because Jackson said he would keep an eye on him, and so far Jimmy was compliant. But then again, he had to be, or he'd be stuck there.

"He may help us yet," Jackson said, looking at Jimmy thoughtfully.

"How do you know him?"

"I've worked in London for years doing this business. He crops up from time to time, often associated with Nicoli, but also with Occult Acquisitions, and The Grey Order."

"Who are they?" Niel asked, puzzled.

Harlan explained, "Other arcane organisations. Well, Occult Acquisitions is a shop, actually—well worth checking out."

"Dodgy, obviously," Jackson said with a wry smile, "but we all are in this business."

Niel wasn't sure what he thought of Jackson, especially after that admission. His first impression was that he was trustworthy, and he was certainly helpful, and hadn't been fazed by this insane angelic obstacle course, but as he'd thoughtfully reminded him, this was a dodgy business.

The scent of smoke drew his attention. JD was carrying his smoking bowl of herbs across the edge of the dense plants, intoning something under his breath, and with a rustle and a swirl of wind, a path opened through the greenery and JD turned to them, victorious. "Gentlemen, follow me."

Twenty-Five

G abe examined the chamber analytically, noting the complex span of bridges that crossed the large lake in a confusing web, and tentatively walked to the edge of the long platform, hoping he wouldn't trigger anything.

"This must be what The Path of the Seeker is really useful for," he suggested to the others. "There can be only one true way across, and if we pick the wrong one, we're screwed." He scratched his jaw. "I suspect that if I try to fly, I'll fail."

Nahum nodded. "I think you're right. There are seven bridges leaving this platform. We have to choose the right one."

Olivia was crouching next to the start of the bridge to Gabe's left. "This one has markings on it—a symbol etched into the stone."

"And this one," Shadow called, further along to his right. "Runes, maybe. Or alchemical symbols? I don't recognise any of them."

Nahum kneeled next to Olivia, quickly calling Gabe over. "I recognise this. Isn't this Samael's sign?"

Gabe frowned at the complex sigil etched into the rock, and his heart sank. "Yes, I think so, although it has been long since I saw it."

"Samael?" Shadow asked.

"The Angel of Death," Nahum said, already hurrying to the next bridge. "Gabriel's sigil is on this one."

Gabe groaned. *This was worse than he thought. Bloody Gabriel.* The angel who had sent Gabe on this quest in the first place.

Shadow nudged him. "The Angel of Death? There really is one?"

"Sure. He reaps souls—or used to. Not entirely sure what he gets up to now."

"You don't need help for your spirit to cross to the Otherworld," Shadow said, annoyed. "What did he do?"

"Don't ask." The Angel of Death did far worse things.

"And Gabriel?" Olivia asked.

"The Angel of Destruction—but he was also a messenger," Nahum told her bleakly.

Gabe looked at Olivia, confused. "I thought you liked all of this stuff. Shouldn't you know this?"

Olivia pushed her hair off her face, frowning. "This is Christian theology. I spend my time on other belief systems."

"Never thought of myself as a *system* before," Gabe told her, not feeling entirely sure whether he was happy about that, angry, or couldn't care less.

Olivia's startled expression told him she hadn't really considered that either, but Nahum interrupted both of them as he called out the other names. "Raphael, Sachiel, Hanael, Cassiel, and Michael. Some archangels, others not."

"What's the difference with an archangel?" Shadow asked.

"They are the more powerful than the others; the old God's princes, I suppose you could call them."

"Why these angels out of thousands?" Olivia asked.

Nahum re-joined them. "No idea. Whatever pattern these make, I don't know it."

A shout broke their concentration, and Gabe looked up, seeing Nicoli waving furiously, almost jumping up and down as he tried to attract their attention.

"What's going on?" Shadow asked, her hands moving instinctively to her blades.

"It's Erskine," Gabe said. He'd been keeping an eye on his slow progress. He'd stopped at the small fires burning across the temple, dropping something into each one before progressing, and he had now reached the feet of the statue that dwarfed him. "He's using the key. Damn it!"

A red mist of rage descended as memories of Gabe's last encounter with Gabriel clouded his thoughts, and despite everyone's warning, he flexed his wings and rose into the air, trying to fly to the temple. But it was as if he'd hit an invisible wall. A force smacked him backwards, sending him crashing into the wall and tumbling to the floor. Winded, he staggered to his feet to see Erskine twist something into a mechanism at the base of the angel.

An enormous boom echoed across the chamber and the placid water erupted in a series of geysers, blocking their view of the temple. The platform rocked, his companions stumbled, and with horror, Gabe watched as Shadow fell into the water.

⸺◆⸺

By the time Harlan and the others reached the Chamber of Wind, as JD called it, he was exhausted and mentally drained.

This place was a nightmare. Despite JD being able to clear the path through the Chamber of Earth, the ground had been uneven, and every time Harlan had stumbled, the vegetation threatened to swallow him, as if the reaching fingers of the plants wanted to pull him into their depths. His skin crawled, and adrenalin was making him shake. What he needed was a big shot of bourbon. What he had was water. The good news was that they had, in general, progressed quickly.

Glancing at his companions, all sheltering from the unceasing wind behind a rocky spur, he noted that only JD and Niel looked unfazed by the entire experience. Niel watched JD with suspicion, and JD had a fanatical gleam in his eye. Jackson and Jimmy looked as over the whole thing as he did.

Jackson pulled him aside, his lips close to his ear so he could be heard over the wind. "JD looks like he's lost the plot."

"He's our only way through this. We have to trust him."

"So why don't you look more confident?"

"It's not his abilities to get us through this that I doubt. It's his intentions once we get there."

"And Niel?"

"I trust him."

Jackson looked at Niel speculatively. "He's a big guy. There's something about him. And his brothers." He stared at Harlan. "Anything I should know?"

"Er, no. They're just regular guys." Harlan tried to look as honest as he could and knew he'd failed.

"Liar." Jackson smiled.

Harlan decided to avoid this uncomfortable conversation and stepped closer to JD and Niel, who were now arguing. "Is there a problem?"

Niel looked angry. "I offered to fly. JD said it will cheat *The Path*."

"Your secret will be out," Harlan said.

"Right now, I don't care. My brothers are through there—I hope. How else did they cross? Unless they're down there somewhere, dead." He gestured to the pit before them, his face bleak.

"You think there's a way through?"

"There has to be!"

JD was scanning the document again, his fingers shaking as he traced the page. "What conquers wind?"

"Flight," Niel answered abruptly.

"No! It doesn't conquer it, it uses it!"

"Exactly, you exasperating man!"

JD's eyes blazed with fury. "In the system of magic that I designed—aided by the angels—air is the Eastern Watchtower. It is governed by the archangel Raphael, and his angel Chassan. I must summon them for our passage!"

JD rummaged in his bag producing a rolled up cloth, which he proceeded to lay on the hard, earthen ground, securing it with rocks. Once unrolled, Harlan saw the cloth had a large, complex geometric design drawn on it. JD then pulled a dagger out, engraved with magical signs, and kneeling next to it, started to chant.

Niel turned away, impatiently scanning the cave, and Harlan knew he wanted to fly.

An almighty boom rocked them all off their feet, and Harlan winced as he collided into the rock wall, smacking his head and landing in a tangled heap next to Jackson and Jimmy. JD was sprawled on his stomach, but Niel was still standing, his enormous wings now unfolded, bracing him.

Harlan ignored Jackson and Jimmy's shocked faces and instead scrambled to his feet. The howl of the wind had increased, and at the far side of the cave he saw a flash of white light.

What the hell was going on?

Shadow couldn't breathe. A vortex of water sucked her downward, and she twisted and turned in the current, struggling to break free. It was icy cold, her limbs were already numb, and she was utterly blind. It was pitch black in the water. She was dying.

Bloody determination swiftly kicked in. She was not going to die in a hole in the ground. *This is not what the Raven King had seen for her future, surely.* If that was the case, she may as well have died at the hands of the Empusa, or Kian. She was fey, powerful with earth magic, and she was going to use it. She might be surrounded by water, but beyond that was earth and rock and she instinctively felt for them. In seconds, the element responded.

Power flooded through her as she struggled against the current, and she surged towards the far, distant light. When she finally broke the surface, her lungs screaming for air, it was to find the chamber in tumult. The water was rolling across the bridges and crashing against the columns, and the platform she'd fallen from had disappeared behind the high waves. And then a surge of water lifted her, throwing her against a bridge, and she crawled onto it, gripping it fiercely.

Finally, the rising water started to abate, and she rolled onto her back, blinking at the vast expanse of starlight that glittered above her. *Herne's balls. What had happened? Where was Gabe?*

Standing on trembling legs, she finally saw Gabe, Nahum, and Olivia staring across the chamber, searching for her. She shouted, shocked at how hoarse her voice sounded, and waved, and then saw Gabe point at her, relief washing over his face. His eyes were boring into hers even from this distance. For seconds she found she couldn't look away, thinking how warm she'd be in Gabe's strong embrace, and then she blinked. *That kind of thinking wouldn't do at all.*

Shadow turned slowly, taking in her new perspective on the cavern. Nicoli was a short distance away, clinging to the top of the column, drenched and looking terrified, but he was alive. She was closer to the temple now, too, and she examined it properly. It was far bigger than she'd realised—supersized, even—to dwarf those who tried to claim the book. Its clean lines and absolute symmetry were intimidating, alien in its Otherworldly manner, and as someone who understood the Otherworld, that was saying something. It spoke of the absolute power of the Gods—and the angel Raziel. His statue was immense, wings folded behind him but visible above his shoulders, the tips curling around his ankles. She looked up at his grave face carved in stone, and felt the weight of his pitiless regard. At his bare feet was the crumpled body of Erskine, his papers strewn around him. He'd had the wrong key, and a surge of hope rose within Shadow.

And then she realised something else. The bridge she was on was connected to the temple, admittedly by interconnecting with another two, but it was passable. *Dare she try to get there?* Gabe had been knocked back, but maybe her earth magic had brought her this far for a reason.

Shadow looked across at Gabe, who was shouting something, but he was too far away to hear clearly. *Was it encouragement, or a warning?* It didn't matter which. She was sick of being here, and she wanted to end this mad quest. She clutched her sword that she'd managed to hold on to, took a deep breath, and marched along the slippery surface that gleamed in the muted light with its remnants of water.

Niel had taken matters into his own hands. JD's rituals took time, time they hadn't got. Niel watched from above as JD stood as close to the abyss as he could get, his hands raised, appealing to the angels for help.

Niel shook his head, doubting that they would come to their rescue. Unlike JD, he had a very negative view of them, like all the Nephilim. Angels were selfish, capricious creatures, obsessed with their own immortality, and they had all learned years ago, not to place any trust in them, especially their own fathers. And perhaps, if he was honest, Niel didn't want them to appear. As he'd said to Gabe only days before, the angels didn't know of their existence, and that's the way it should remain.

Niel focussed on finding passage through the wind, but it drove him back at every point. It tugged on his wings, trying to pull him down, or force him into the rocks. But if his brothers had made it, so could he.

Then something odd happened.

A presence arrived—something powerful, but formless—and as Niel hovered on the edge of the abyss, he felt the rush of wings and smelled something he hadn't for centuries. A pungent combination of blossoms and honey, with an undercurrent of smoke. And just like that the wind dropped, leaving an eerie silence in its wake. A bridge appeared below him, gossamer thin and fragile as a cloud, and JD stepped onto it, triumphantly leading the others across the abyss.

Harlan paused to look up at him, but Niel just nodded, unable to move. He hung in the air, his wings beating gently to keep him in place, and he felt a breath across his cheek and a presence that was unmistakably angelic. Two words echoed through Niel's mind, flooding his thoughts with unbidden images of the past and his palace in the Zagros Mountains.

Welcome back.

Twenty-Six

G abe watched helplessly as Shadow approached the temple, his heart in his mouth, and only Nahum's restraining hand stopped him from flying again.

"Whatever is happening, brother, she is meant to be there."

"It's a trick! It has to be," Gabe argued, not taking his eyes from her. So far her progress was sure but steady, as she took her time negotiating the bridges.

"There's one good thing," Olivia said, trying to smile. "At least Erskine failed."

Nahum nodded. "True. Odd, though. He must have thought he had the right key."

"Well, Shadow has *no* key," Gabe pointed out, "so what will happen to her? Erskine is in a heap on the floor, probably dead."

"She's like a cat," Nahum said, reassuring him. "She must have nine lives. She was underwater for a long time before she was spat out. Give her some credit, Gabe."

Gabe finally looked at Nahum. "It's not Shadow's abilities I doubt."

A hushed whisper carrying a breeze sounded behind them, and all three spun around, weapons raised. But to Gabe's utmost relief, JD was stepping through a shimmering white veil that filled a break in the rock, and Harlan, Jackson, Niel, and Nicoli's unknown team member were behind him.

Despite his worry about Shadow, Gabe grinned. "You made it!"

JD preened. "Of course I did, I summoned—" His voice faltered as he stared at his surroundings. "Well. We're here. The final chamber."

"And time is running out," Gabe said. "Shadow is over there, on her own, without the key. We need to get over there—now!"

JD collected himself, his glazed expression transforming into a fierce, intelligent stare. "What do we know so far?"

Nahum took over, and accompanied by Olivia, directed JD to the bridges, leaving Gabe to update the others. "What have you brought him for?" He gestured to Nicoli's teammate.

Niel grunted. "That's Jimmy. I thought he might know what was hidden within the paper the document is written on, but now I'm not so sure."

However, Jimmy, sullen, moody, and looking more like a truculent teenager than a grown man, said, "Actually, I did hear something, but it doesn't make sense to me."

"And you only thought to tell us now?" Jackson said, exasperated.

"You didn't need my help before, but," he swallowed, "I just want to get out of here—alive."

"Join the club," Harlan muttered. "You'd better go with JD, tell him what you know. And don't fuck up!"

Jimmy just nodded, mute, and walked across the platform to join the others.

Gabe was puzzled. They hadn't been that long in the final chamber when the others had caught up. "Did you follow us in quickly?" he asked Niel.

He shook his head, "Not at all. We entered hours after you. Harlan had to find the key first. Why?"

"Because we only got here a short while before you did."

Niel shrugged. "It must be some weird kind of angel ability to compress time. Talking of angels," he grabbed Gabe's elbow, steering him away for privacy. "Have you felt one yet?"

"One what?" Gabe asked, confused, and still side-tracked by Shadow. He angled himself so he could continue to watch her.

"An angel, you idiot!"

"No. Should I have?"

"Well, we are in a temple designed by one—and I just did!"

That grabbed his attention, and he stared at Niel, trying to work out if he was joking. "Where?"

"In the Chamber of Wind. I felt Chassan, Raphael's right hand man. JD summoned him."

Several things rushed through Gabe's mind, not the least of which was JD's unexpected ability to summon an angel after years of claiming he hadn't spoken to one in centuries, and his own belief that he never really had. But his foremost concern was Chassan. "Did he see you?"

"Of course he bloody saw me!" Niel tapped his own head. "And spoke to me, in here. Which means Raphael will know already." Niel closed his eyes briefly, and when he opened them again his blue eyes looked resigned. "Whatever anonymity we had before is gone. Whatever life we thought we'd forged, is over."

"You don't know that."

"Gabe, who are you kidding?"

"We are few. We're no threat, and we're of no use."

But Niel's mouth was set in a stubborn line, and Gabe had a horrible feeling Niel might have been right all along. He was glad for Nahum's shout. "We're ready!"

They all clustered behind JD, who was gripping his grubby copy of The Path of the Seeker and taking deep breaths, his eyes focussed on the temple.

"What's the plan?" Gabe asked, noting Shadow was still on the final bridge.

JD snapped his head around, suddenly aware of his presence. "The angels all have correspondences—many, in fact, complex and interwoven. But these particular seven angels correspond to planets, in this instance." He gestured to the cavern roof above. "We need to navigate our way across; the temple is the sun. I will use those to guide us."

Those? Gabe realised that the sparkles he had thought were part of the finish of the cavern were actually constellations.

JD continued. "I suspect there will be more angel and planetary markings as we progress. Follow me closely." He frowned with annoyance. "There are too many of you here."

"Well, we're all coming with you, like it or not," Harlan told him as he looked around the chamber with distaste. "Let's get on with it."

Shadow finally reached the broad temple stairs and after a moment's pause, stepped onto the first, relieved that there was no earth-shattering rumble to throw her back into the water.

The steps were high, each rise reaching to her waist, making them impossible to climb easily. However, she was nimble, and she pulled herself onto them gracefully. *Seven steps,* she noted. *Seven bridges.* She wasn't sure what that meant, but she ascended to the temple proper, taking stock of her surroundings.

It was even more breathtaking close up. The columns were white, smooth and unadorned, and the floor was made of polished milky white marble that reflected the rosy glow of the fires burning within the braziers. She stepped beyond the first column, noting that the temple extended far back into the cavern, its recesses dark. She had assumed that the angel's statue was at the back of the temple, but there was so much more beyond it. Something glinted in those shadows—maybe gold? She shivered. *How long had this place stood here? It was incredible.*

Shadow was wracked with indecision. She didn't have the key, and yet she had been allowed to arrive here, and she had no idea why. *Because she was fey?* Gripping her dragonium sword in one hand and the Empusa's in the other, she headed to the base of the statue and crouched next to Erskine's inert body.

He was undoubtedly dead.

He lay on his back, staring vacantly up at the gilded roof high above them. His skin was a peculiar bluish-black colour, and his eyes were bloodshot. There was no visible sign of how he had died, and Shadow could only surmise it was because the angel had willed it. Tumbled to the side was an ornate iron key, and she tentatively picked it up. The false key. She tucked it into her jacket pocket and stood to examine the statue.

It towered above her; the only things on her eye level were his feet and the tips of his wings that curled around his ankles, every feather detailed, precise, and flecked with gold and silver.

Between the angel's feet, set into the sweep of his clothing, was a carved panel, filled with symbols she didn't understand, and what looked like numerous keyholes of varied shapes and sizes. *Did they need more than one key?*

One more thing to worry about.

It was clear there was nothing she could do until the others arrived. Shadow turned around, looking to see where her team was, pleasantly surprised to find that they were closer than she expected — almost halfway over. The party clustered together as JD paused at the junction of several bridges.

She had time to explore the rest of the temple, so turning her back on the advancing group, Shadow headed into the temple's depths.

Harlan hated this, which surprised him. He thought he'd love exploring this temple and navigating the path, but it was not what he'd expected. This jumble of collected symbols and sigils, angels and correspondences, was esoteric and frustrating and way beyond his abilities. Give him a regular tomb, any day.

As annoying as JD was, Harlan had to admit that he was brilliant. He led them confidently across the network of bridges with their carved symbols, studying them before gazing at the constellations and planets above—not that he could see that they were planets. It was only JD who insisted they were. It was gratifying to know Harlan wasn't alone in his confusion. Every now and then JD would confer with Jimmy, and then having made his decision, advance a little further. Harlan had had his doubts about Jimmy, but he was glad to be proved wrong—at least for now.

Olivia was next to him, her normally clear brow furrowed with worry, and he lowered his voice, saying, "We're nearly there. Cheer up."

"Yeah, but what then?"

"Let's just cross one bridge at a time," Harlan said, and then grinned. "Excuse the pun. JD is doing well, though."

Olivia nodded. "We have a theory that the tests are tailored somehow to whoever the seeker is."

"That's interesting. What made you think that?"

"We faced a dragon in the Chamber of Fire. Did you?"

"No! Are you serious?"

"Yes. Shadow said they exist in her world, in the Realm of Fire. Weird, yes?"

"Very," Harlan agreed, now even more overawed with The Trinity of the Seeker.

They all shuffled forward again as JD led them onto the next bridge, finally bringing them within close range of Nicoli, whose natural swagger had vanished. He shouted over, "Check the document carefully! Erskine misread it at this juncture, and I ended up here!"

JD faced him. "Misread how?"

"I'm not sure, something about a reversed sign?" He looked frustrated. "I don't know! It was something about Venus and Mars."

"How do we know you're not trying to kill us?" Gabe asked suspiciously.

"Because you're my only way out!" Nicoli snapped. "You think I want to be stuck on this column forever?"

JD nodded and scrutinised the document, while Harlan asked, "How did you get stranded there?"

"Our misstep caused the bridge to disappear, and we ended up in the water. I managed to scramble here, Erskine made it onto the right bridge, and Mia…" He shrugged, his face bleak. "Didn't make it. I'm really hoping you can get me off here."

"We'll try," Harlan said, not wanting to leave anyone behind, even the slippery, untrustworthy Nicoli. "Although, I have no idea how. You don't want to swim for it?"

Nicoli shook his head. "It looks calm, but there's a fierce current below the surface. I'm not risking it again. Unless, of course, I think I'll be stuck here forever. I'm not there yet."

Harlan nodded, and seeing JD about to step on the next bridge hurried to join the team, terrified he'd be stranded, too. Niel was sticking close to Jimmy, shepherding him at every turn. If Jimmy had any thoughts to betray them he was given no opportunity, although that was unlikely to happen until he was in the temple. Harlan figured all bets were off at that stage.

Shadow waited for her sight to adjust to the gloom behind the statue. There were only a couple of braziers here, but what little light they gave illuminated a collection of objects. *No, weapons.*

Swords, spears, armour, shields, helmets, daggers... All manner of them jumbled together in a heap, like in a dragon's lair. She knelt to better see them, noting their fine engravings and superior quality. They weren't quite as good as fey made weapons, but they were close. *What were they doing here?*

Leaving them, she headed to the back wall, also made of smooth, polished granite, and what appeared to be a door set into it, flush with its surroundings. *Was this their way out?* At the moment it was sealed shut. Then she noticed the strange, fluted striations in the rock on either side of the chamber, all of varying shapes and sizes that stretched far overhead. It was familiar to her, for some strange reason.

However, there was one thing she couldn't see, and that was Raziel's book. She presumed that only the key would reveal it. A clatter of footsteps behind her sent her running to the front of the temple. The others had arrived.

Gabe reached the top of the stairs first, and relief swept across his face when he saw her. He strode towards her, and then stopped abruptly, clenching his hands, and Shadow waited too, stopping her ridiculous urge to hug him.

"Shadow. You're okay."

"Just about, after my near death by drowning. Any mishaps on the bridge?"

"None." He glanced behind him to the others clambering up behind him. "JD knows his stuff. He summoned an angel; they know we're here."

She knew he meant the Nephilim. "That was inevitable," Shadow said softly, seeing the worry on his face. "It might mean nothing."

"It might mean everything."

"Come on you two," Nahum said as he reached Gabe's side, his tone light, but his eyes watchful. "It's key time."

Twenty-Seven

Gabe studied the statue of Raziel, craning to see his face far above him.

It was impressive, cold in its beauty, and Gabe wanted nothing more than to see it crumble before him. All of his rage at how they'd been betrayed, double-crossed, and used flooded back. And now that damn book—his final charge from Gabriel—was within his grasp. Shadow stood close by, and his brothers were on either side; he took strength from them all. He only wished his other brothers were here, too. Then he changed his mind. No. He was glad they were out of it. He just hoped he'd live to see them again.

His gaze fell to Erskine's dead body that they had moved to the side of the statue, and despite the fact that he'd sent a demon to attack them, he felt sorry that he died here. Then he watched JD, who had now put his papers away, and was instead studying the panel carved into the stone between Raziel's feet.

"What's the deal with the key?" Gabe asked. "How come Erskine had one?"

Harlan laughed, somewhat bitterly. "Turns out, JD's been holding out on us. There are entry points to this temple across the world, and that means multiple maps, paths and keys. Erskine had the wrong one." He jerked his head at Jackson. "And so does he."

"What?" Gabe had thought this was his worst nightmare, but that news topped it. He glanced at Nahum, who shut his eyes at the news. "I don't understand. How does that even work?"

Niel shrugged. "We're not entirely sure. We only found out once you'd entered. Things happened pretty quickly when JD arrived and Jackson told him where he found his key."

Jackson was leaning against the closest column nonchalantly, but his eyes darted everywhere. When he heard his name, he looked sheepish. "Yeah. I found it in Rome. Stupid me. I didn't know."

Harlan added, "Thanks to Niel and Olivia, we realised our key was in St Thomas's Church. I think we found it more by dumb luck than judgement."

"Not true," Jackson corrected him. "We found it because we're smart!"

Gabe remembered the strange, shimmering veil that seemed to be between the Chamber of Wind and the temple. "That veil we passed through—does that have something to do with it?"

"I have no idea," Niel said, baffled.

Jackson shouted, "Hey, Jimmy. Don't stray so far!"

Jimmy was edging to the rear of the statue, but at Jackson's voice he froze, looking mutinous and as if he was about to argue, but seeing everyone staring at him, he crossed his arms and waited.

"Where's the key?" JD barked at Harlan.

Harlan's eyes widened. "'Please' is always polite, JD." He withdrew a simple flute from his pocket and handed it over. "I don't think there's a place for you to stick that." His tone made Gabe think there was somewhere specific he wanted to stick it, and it was nowhere pleasant. "You need to play it. I'm just not sure where."

"A flute is the key?" Gabe strode over, and despite JD's sullen protest, took it from him. In the relief at seeing Niel and Harlan arrive, he hadn't thought to ask about it. "Are you serious?"

"Well, I hope so," Harlan said, "or we're screwed." He frowned at Gabe. "What?"

Gabe faltered. "I guess nothing. It's just not what I expected."

"Can I suggest we get on with it?" Jackson said. "Someone just blow the damn thing. It's clear there's nothing else to do."

JD held his hand out, and Gabe handed it back. "Go ahead, then."

JD raised it to his lips, hesitated, and then blew softly into the pipe. The sound that filled the air was pure and sweet, raising the hairs on Gabe's arm. But as the notes fell away and nothing happened, everyone looked bewildered.

"Why isn't it working?" JD demanded, searching their faces for answers, but none of them had anything to offer.

And then Jackson laughed. "Maybe we're supposed to stick it in Raziel's mouth!" His laughter died as they all stepped back to look up at Raziel's impassive face. "It was a joke. There would be a ladder up his middle, right? Or his back? Or some weird mechanism that would carry us up there?"

"There probably is, somewhere," Harlan said, scanning their surroundings.

"Or a Nephilim could fly it there," Shadow suggested, staring at Gabe. "I've just realised what I saw at the back of the temple."

"There's something behind there?" Niel asked.

"Weapons—lots of them. And weird hollow pipes in the stone walls. It's like an organ...a church organ, or something of the sort."

Uneremoniously, Niel grabbed the flute from JD's hands, thrust it at Gabe and said, "Go. I'll check the back."

Without waiting for anyone's approval, Gabe extended his wings and soared upwards, and the closer he got to Raziel's head, the more he felt as if he was in there, somewhere, lurking behind the icy facade. He passed the open book, held in outstretched hands, carved in marble, the visible pages inscribed with gilded letters, and finally hovered before Raziel's face and his blank eyes. But his lips were pursed, a small hole in the centre, and Gabe held his palm over it, feeling a rush of wind. Gabe studied the flute in his fingers. It was tiny in comparison to the lips, but the game was progressing now and he had to try. And besides, it was the only way to get out of here.

He positioned the instrument and carefully inserted it, feeling it slot into place. Immediately a soft, low tone filled the air, deeper than when JD had played it. The tone quickly changed as it resonated, becoming unearthly, haunting even, and soon it filled the air as accompanying notes rose across the chamber.

The air shifted, turbulence swirling around him, and as shouts reached his ears, he knew he had set something in motion.

<hr />

As soon as the swell of music started, several things happened at once, and Shadow wasn't sure which way to turn first.

The panel between Raziel's feet crashed to the floor, revealing a chamber beyond, and JD, narrowly avoiding being crushed, scooted inside. At the same time, Jimmy started to scream, his hands clutched to his ears, and ran, almost drunkenly, towards the temple steps and the water below.

For an instant they all froze, and then Harlan and Olivia took off after Jimmy, and Jackson, seemingly mesmerised by the temple itself, prowled around the columns, exploring the space. Shadow, however, followed JD, Nahum right behind her.

The interior of the inner chamber was hot and dark, illuminated only by candles that flickered in the hundreds in the surprisingly large space. In the centre, on an enormous stone table, was a thick tome bound in leather. It lay open, its pages humming with power that she could feel across the room, and as Shadow drew nearer she saw that the archaic script inscribed on the pages glowed with a fiery light.

Nahum was close to her, a reassuring presence, and he lowered his lips to her ear. "The oldest grimoire."

Shadow turned to him, seeing his eyes were fixed firmly on JD, who stood before it. "Have you seen this before?"

"Never."

"Are we going to take it with us?"

"Well, that's the question, isn't it?" Nahum answered, finally meeting her eyes. "Gabe thinks not, and I agree with him. It's brought nothing but disaster."

"Not true," she countered. "It enabled mankind to master magic, and gave them freedom."

JD heard them, and spun around, furious. "Of course we're taking it with us! I haven't come all this way for nothing!" He turned his back and stepped forward, holding his hands above the book reverentially, as if scared to touch it. "Just imagine the secrets that it holds!"

Gabe's voice boomed from behind them. "Those secrets have killed countless people. Don't touch it—it will do you no good."

If JD heard him he gave no sign of it, instead laying his hands either side of the book, and resting his fingers gently on the pages. Within seconds, he was transfixed.

"JD!" Shadow shouted, stepping to his side, alarmed. The pages of the book were moving as if flicked by an unseen hand, and JD stared with unfocussed eyes. Whatever he could see wasn't in front of him.

Gabe was beside her in seconds, and laid his hand on her arm. Shadow had never seen him look more furious—or more desolate. "Don't touch him!"

"What's going on, Gabe? Isn't this what we're here for?"

"Yes and no." He finally focussed on her. "This is our chance to destroy it forever. It's what Gabriel wanted."

"So why doesn't Gabriel destroy it himself? Why do you have to?"

"Because," Nahum said, circling the table and watching JD, "he hasn't been able to get near it. This place has protected it—shielded it from everyone."

Shadow was incredibly confused. "But they're supernatural beings! Surely he can see through this facade!"

"Not if Raziel has been hiding it!" Gabe told her. His lips tightened. "Recording the old God's magic was Raziel's life's work. He was both generous and foolish. You can't give away this kind of knowledge and not expect repercussions!"

"But you said the knowledge in this had freed people. That it enabled them to master their own destiny—shape their world. It gave us witches and an understanding of elemental magic!" Shadow stared at Gabe and Nahum, perplexed. "That's good!"

"Of course it is," Gabe replied, anguished. "I'm all for freedom and independence! But if it gets out again, there could be another disaster; another flood, or volcanic explosion, or worldwide tornados! The old God may stop at *nothing*! Do you want that on your conscience?"

Shadow reeled at his suggestions. *Could that really happen? Were the old Gods still that powerful?* "But Gods care nothing for us! We are *nothing* to them."

"We are something once our knowledge begins to rival theirs."

While they talked, JD was still transfixed by the book, its pages moving faster and faster.

"The book is filling his mind with knowledge," Nahum said. "We have to stop it—now, before we condemn him to being a hunted man. And then find a way to get out of here!"

"Did you suspect this would happen?" Shadow asked, suddenly angry. "Did you warn JD?"

"I didn't know what to expect," Gabe answered. "But yes, I warned him."

JD was shaking now, his eyes rolling back in his head, and Shadow couldn't even imagine what incredible secrets might be flooding through his brain. "Stop him!"

"How?" Nahum asked. "We could be caught in whatever is happening to him."

"Break his grip!" Shadow lunged at JD, but Gabe caught her around the waist before she could get close, pulling her back, and it was impossible to break free.

Shadow shouldn't care what happened to JD, not really, but she did. She thought of Chadwick pursuing his life's dream, and Kian killing him when he found it. She did not want that to happen this time. She had enough blood on her hands already, even though this wasn't really her fault. And then she had another thought.

Still squirming in Gabe's tight hold, she said, "Think about what you've just said—power to rival a God! What if this knowledge turns him into some kind of demi-god with a power he was never meant to wield, and he tries to kill us all?"

That got Nahum's attention, and he wrapped his powerful arms around JD, trying to wrestle him away from the book. But JD was immovable and Nahum cried out, thrown backwards by an unseen force. "Shit! Any other ideas?" he said, regaining his feet.

Gabe finally let Shadow go and she glared at him, but he was already striding around the room, eyes darting everywhere.

"What are you looking for?" she asked.

"Something to use! He must have a weakness, or the book does!"

Slightly mollified that Gabe was taking her suggestion seriously, she and Nahum joined his search. Above the table hung a gilded metal chandelier, a simple circle studded with candles that hung from the roof by chains, and she had an idea.

She jumped on to the stone table behind the book, and shouted, "Gabe, Nahum, one of you help me grab this and pull me backwards! I'm going to swing into him!"

Nahum darted behind her, lifting her higher, and she caught the light by the tips of her fingers until she had a good grip.

"Now!" she instructed.

Nahum grabbed her feet and pulled her back as far as he could, and then pushed her. The momentum wasn't enough—yet. Shadow pulled her knees up to her chest so she cleared JD's head, and then swung back and forth, again and again. When she finally had enough speed, she angled her feet towards JD, and hoped she wouldn't end up falling onto the book instead. She let go and flew forwards, ramming her feet into JD's chest, and they both crashed onto the floor, the collision knocking JD's head hard against the stone, and winding her.

"Herne's horns! Have I killed him?" she gasped, struggling to untangle herself.

Gabe crouched next to her, feeling for JD's pulse and then despite the situation, laughed. "No. He's just unconscious, but he'll have a serious headache! And maybe a few broken ribs." He pulled her to her feet and looked at her with a mixture of admiration and annoyance. "You crazy woman!"

She grinned smugly. "I know. I'm a genius!"

"Certainly one of your more interesting ideas," Nahum said. He bent down and picked JD up, throwing him over his shoulder. "Now what?"

They all swung around to look at the book. The pages were still turning as if by an unseen hand, and power was building in the chamber.

"Take JD and try to find a way out of here, and find Niel," Gabe instructed. "I'm going to find a way to destroy this. And little Miss Fey here is going to help me."

Twenty-Eight

Harlan raced after Jimmy, Olivia right behind him, but he was a good distance ahead of them, running like he was possessed.

"What the hell's got into him?" Olivia yelled.

"Something with this damn music!" Harlan shouted, watching with horror as Jimmy jumped down the first step, and then stumbled to his knees before quickly righting himself again. His hands were still clutching his head, and his screams filled the chamber, mixing with the haunting music that resounded around the temple like a horror film.

Harlan bounded down the stairs, his knees jarring painfully. "Jimmy, stop!" But he doubted Jimmy could hear anything. Fortunately, Harlan was getting closer. Just as Jimmy reached the final step and was mere feet away from leaping into the water, Harlan tackled him from above, and they both landed heavily, Harlan feeling his knee crunch into the unyielding floor.

The adrenalin kept the pain at bay, and up close he saw that Jimmy's eyes were wild, and spit flecked his jaw. Jimmy tried to wrestle away, straining to reach the water like it gave off a Siren call, and Harlan didn't hesitate. He punched him, knocking him out cold, and then rolled to the side; his knee felt like it was on fire.

Olivia scooted next to him as he clutched his knee. "Harlan! Are you okay?"

"No. My fucking knee is killing me! Check Jimmy!"

"What's to check? He's unconscious!"

"At least he's not going to drown!" Harlan sat up, the pain in his knee ebbing slightly, and caught sight of Nicoli waving wildly. "Shit. Nicoli is still stranded."

Olivia stood and hauled Harlan to his feet. "I'll go and find Niel or Nahum. Perhaps they'll rescue him. We'll need them to carry Jimmy, too." She studied the steep rise of stairs, frowning. "There's no way I can help lift him up there."

Harlan looked around, frustrated. "This is a shitshow! What were we thinking? I can't concentrate with that god-awful music."

"Heathen! I think some would call it *uplifting*."

"Do you?"

"I might if I didn't think I was going to die here." She set off up the stairs. "Be back soon!"

———————◄○►————————

Niel couldn't believe his eyes. *These were Nephilim weapons.* He bent and picked up a shield, scarred in battle. He recognised the emblem on it—*the House of Tiril*—the mark of one of the fallen. He picked up another—the *House of Baraquel.* One after another, he saw other names, Haures, Exael, Tumael, and he dropped them like they burned.

What were these doing here? Was this a warning to them? Was Raziel screwing with them? Or were they gifts?

Trying to order his chaotic mind, which wasn't easy with the increasingly powerful music vibrating in the air around him, he walked away, examining instead the back of the temple. The doorway that Shadow had mentioned was here, still impassable. But there was no writing on this one. No command to utter. However, this had to be their way out, and it must be triggered by something else. But who knows how deep they had travelled, and how long it would take to get out of there?

He paced the perimeter, looking for anything else of significance, but other than the fluted columns hollowed out of the rock and the pile of weapons, there was nothing.

A shout distracted him. It was Olivia, and she reached his side, breathless. "Can you rescue Nicoli? He's stranded on that column! And then we need help with Jimmy."

"What's he done?" Niel asked, already striding to the front of the temple.

"He went mad—tried to throw himself in the water. It's something to do with the music. Harlan knocked him out."

"Again? The guy's going to have concussion!"

"You started it!" she said. "It was the only way to stop him."

Niel winced with guilt. It was his fault Jimmy was here, but they had needed him. "Can't you and Harlan move him?"

"Harlan smashed his knee, and I can't haul them both up those steps!"

Niel nodded. "Okay. I'll get Nicoli first."

While they talked, Nahum emerged from the inner chamber, JD slung across his shoulder, and he collected Jackson en route, still pacing around the columns. Niel and Olivia intercepted him.

"What happened to JD?" Olivia asked, looking horrified.

"Shadow," Nahum replied bluntly. "It was for his own good. They're trying to decide what to do with the book now."

Jackson looked bewildered. "I think this music is getting to me. This place is surreal!"

This was worrying. The music seemed to be affecting everyone differently. "Go with Nahum," Niel said, concerned. "I think that would be safest."

"Sounds good," Nahum said, adjusting JD's weight.

Niel jerked his head to the rear of the temple. "Wait back there; I'll get the others. The exit is that way—if we can figure out a way to open the door. I'll be with you soon."

Nahum and Olivia nodded, and Niel extended his wings and flew to Nicoli.

Gabe stared at the book, hyperaware of the power flooding from it. "JD's touch must have activated it, or something of the sort."

Shadow nodded, also watching the turning pages. "It probably hasn't been handled for hundreds of years." Her face wrinkled with distaste. "We can't destroy it! It would be wrong. I don't even think we could. The Trinity of the Seeker couldn't be destroyed!"

She was right, Gabe reflected. Destroying a book written by an angel would be impossible. *But...* "We haven't even tried!" He glanced at the dragonium sword in her hand and remembering his own, pulled it from his scabbard. "I'm going to attempt it."

Shadow's violet eyes were wide as she appealed to him. "Gabe! No!"

"Shadow! The old God sent a flood and drowned everyone because he couldn't get it back! Because I couldn't get it back!"

He marched over to the book and without hesitation, brought the sword down with enormous force.

A white light flashed, jolted up his arm, and sent him flying back into the wall, half landing on Shadow, and she pushed him off. "Get off, you big lump! I told you so! Have you damaged the sword?"

He looked at her, disgruntled. "No. It's fine. My arm, however, feels like it's been electrified." He struggled to his feet, and pulled her with him. "I guess you're right."

"So you're saying we leave it here, then?" She looked relieved. "Good. We've got the clues to get here. We can hide them again. No one will ever know. It will be stuck here for eternity!"

Gabe folded his arms across his chest. "You're forgetting the other ways to get here! There are other trinities out there."

"How does that even work? Different countries? Different routes?"

"Raziel left opportunities to get here from all over the world! Sneaky bastard." The scale of Raziel's planning really was impressive. "You're from the Otherworld, Shadow. You understand magic. This chamber had some kind of veil over it when we first entered here. I think it's in a special portal all on its own. It's the only thing that makes sense." He suddenly knew what he had to do. "We need to destroy the temple."

She looked at him like he was nuts. "We can't even destroy the book!"

"Do me a favour. Go see what's happening out there. See if there's something we can do. I'll wait here."

She stepped close to him, pinning him beneath her suspicious stare. "Don't do anything stupid."

Shadow grimaced as she left the chamber between Raziel's feet. The music in the temple was louder, and everything seemed to tremble—the floor, the walls, and even the water was disturbed, ripples rolling across its surface. Power was building.

They had unleashed something.

She raced around the statue, finding the others clustered by the door set into the rock. Niel was standing over JD and Jimmy, both unconscious. *Probably for the best*, she reflected. Even unconscious, Jimmy looked tortured, his face contorted. Harlan was leaning on Olivia, wincing, Nahum was examining the door, and Nicoli and Jackson were conferring quietly. They shot Shadow a suspicious look as she approached.

"I hope you're not debating doing something stupid," she said, repeating her concern to Gabe, her hand automatically going to her blades.

"Seeing as I've just saved Nicoli's life," Niel pointed out, glaring at him, "he better not be."

"Actually," Nicoli answered, glancing nervously at Niel's wings that were still visible, "I have no intention of crossing you. I'm not insane." He lifted his chin, defiantly. "We're talking about how to open that door. We're supposed to leave with the book. That means the book triggers the exit."

Nahum groaned. "Please don't say that."

"It makes sense," Jackson reasoned, thrusting his hands in his pockets. "That is the purpose of being here, after all—to find the damn thing."

"Look at JD," Shadow said, jerking her head at him. "He laid his hands on it and it possessed him. The flood of knowledge it imparted was huge!"

"And knocked him unconscious?" Harlan asked, bewildered.

"No, that was me," she admitted sheepishly. "But it was the only way of separating him from the book."

"Wait," Jackson said thoughtfully. "JD couldn't control it?"

"It seemed not. I mean, he did for a while, and then something happened and he was lost."

Nahum nodded. "She's right. And I've just said a few phrases in the language of fire to try and open this door, and none of them have worked. I even tried fey, and several ancient languages."

Jackson frowned. "Hey guys, I don't know JD well, but he clearly knows his stuff. He navigated us through this madness, summoned an angel, and led us across the bridges. He's a very clever guy! If he can't handle the knowledge in the book, how can anyone else?" He stared at the Nephilim. "Just who was it that handled this book first time round?"

Nahum answered, glancing warily at Niel. "Adam and Eve. But they were human."

"Not regular humans though, right? From what you said before, they were the first to question their existence. They had longevity in life, as did their children. They must have had some Otherworldly qualities that allowed them to handle the book?"

"No," Niel said, shaking his head vigorously. "They were human—that's all. But they were also chosen by Raziel. From what I heard, he gifted their entire line. Maybe he strengthened them in some way to enable them to absorb this knowledge."

Nahum nodded. "That's true. I hadn't even thought about that. It happened before our time."

"And then the magic leaked out into society," Shadow said, remembering her conversation with Gabe. "Humans learned how to manipulate it. Maybe JD tried to absorb too much, too soon."

"Well, I don't think one of us humans should risk it," Olivia said. Her natural buoyancy and enthusiasm had gone, and now she looked tired. "I don't want to die down here. One of you needs to get the book."

"We cannot return it to the world. It's too dangerous," Niel insisted. "We came here to stop this from happening, not enable it!"

Nicoli laughed bitterly. "It's too late! Events have been set in motion now! Look at this place. We have to leave!"

"And damn the consequences?" Nahum said, rounding on him angrily. "This book brought about mankind's destruction!"

"And liberated it!" Harlan said quickly. "Don't forget that."

If Nahum heard him, he didn't show it. He was still glaring at Nicoli. "No one asked you to come here! You came because someone paid you a lot of money. You didn't give a shit about the consequences then!"

Nicoli clenched his fists and shouted, "I had no idea what they were!"

"Do your fucking homework!"

Shadow had never seen Nahum look so angry.

Olivia stepped between them, pushing them apart. "Stop it! This is not the time for macho posturing. No one wants to die down here! Get the damn book, and open the door. Let's think about what we do with it after!"

Nahum took a deep breath and nodded at Shadow. She ran back to Gabe, finding him pacing the chamber.

"Progress?" he asked hopefully.

"None. And the atmosphere is ugly—Nahum and Nicoli nearly had a fight."

"Nahum? Not Niel?" Gabe asked, shocked.

"Yep. We think we need Raziel's book to open the door. It's the trigger, and the door is our only way out."

His face fell. *"No."*

"Gabe," she pleaded, "see reason. We need to leave. You can't hear it in here, but the weird music is getting louder out there, and the whole place is shaking. Time is running out! We need to leave—now!" She crossed her arms. "If you don't pick it up, I will."

Tight-lipped he turned, braced himself, and quickly slammed the cover shut and picked the book up. He went white, shaking slightly.

"Gabe, what's happening?"

"Nothing. I'm okay."

"You don't look okay."

"I can feel its power, that's all." With that, his jaw clenched, he left the chamber, with Shadow running behind him.

Twenty-Nine

A s soon as Gabe stepped out of the inner chamber, the entire temple rocked as if a bomb had exploded beneath it, and the smooth granite walls that had emitted only starlight were suddenly covered in the blazing script of the language of fire.

"Herne's hairy bollocks!" Shadow exclaimed next to him. "What have we done?"

"Something terrible," he answered darkly.

The water was rising in the pool, waves rolling across the bridges, and in the seconds they stood there, they cracked and fell into the churning depths. The book was thrumming with power, and Gabe felt it pulsing through his arms and chest. This might be what Raziel wanted, but it wasn't good. He had cursed Gabriel at the time for asking him to find this book. He had raged, in fact, furious that his life had been dragged back to the service of angels—and not the fallen ones. At least they had an earthy humour, and a liking for humans.

But now, feeling the book and the power it held, Gabe knew he couldn't let it return to the world. He didn't even trust the witches with it. But equally, he couldn't let everyone die down here. Once again he berated himself for letting so many people come along on this mad search. If it was just himself and JD, he'd willingly die down here, and he'd be prepared to sacrifice JD, too. But that wasn't an option.

He ran to the rear of the temple, Shadow beside him, and with every step they took, the chamber shook even more, chunks of rock crashing around them. Even the statue was shaking. He did a double-take as he passed the weapons on the floor, but he kept running until he reached the others, clustered around their exit. Nahum was carrying JD, and Niel was carrying Jimmy. Everyone looked terrified.

As Gabe skidded to a halt, script appeared on the door; he looked at Nahum and Niel, taking a deep breath. "Are we sure about this?

"Yes. Do it," Nahum said, and he saw everyone's relief as he spoke.

Gabe faced the door and uttered the words of command. The door swung wide, revealing a passageway ahead, script blazing along its walls and illuminating their way. With the barest moment's pause, Nahum led the way out.

Harlan's knee was throbbing, and adrenalin was the only thing that kept him going.

He let the others go before him, worried he would hold them up, but Shadow pushed him ahead. "Go on. Gabe and I will go last."

"But I can't run properly!"

"It's fine. I'm not going to leave you behind!" She pushed him, and he limped down the long passageway.

The ground still shook, even out there, and he heard the crashing of masonry over the haunting music that continued to resound around them. And then he passed through something, the veil that that kept the temple suspended somewhere in time and space. The well-lit passage disappeared, and he was suddenly stumbling through darkness, the ground uneven beneath him. He fumbled for his flashlight, relieved when it switched on. He could just about see Olivia up ahead and heard her shout, "Harlan, come on!"

"I'm coming as quickly as I can!"

It was only then he realised that the ground had stopped rumbling, and the sound of the unearthly music and the destruction of the temple had disappeared, leaving an eerie silence in its wake. When he looked around, he found that Shadow and Gabe were no longer there, either.

Shadow was just about to follow Harlan through the veil that protected the temple from the world when she heard Gabe's footsteps slow.

She stopped and turned. "What are you doing?"

"I'm staying here. Go."

"No." She crossed her arms, resolute.

His face was impassive, and he clutched the book to his chest. "This cannot leave here. The rest of you are safe. Go without me."

"You'll die here."

"I told you that I'm prepared to do that."

Shadow's pulse sounded in her ears and she felt dizzy. The thought of never seeing Gabe again was horrible. "I won't leave you. There's got to be another way."

"There isn't. You can see what this book can do. It had its place—once. But not now." His fingers tightened on the leather bound tome, his knuckles whitening, as if she would wrest it from him, and his dark eyes were hard.

She stepped closer to him, feeling his heat. "You don't want to do this. You've got your life back now. It's just beginning!"

"They know we're back. Our life will never be what we want it to be."

"You don't know that! You're letting Niel get to you," she said, growing angry. "And you can't leave your brothers!"

Gabe's eyes softened as he appealed to her. "By keeping the book here, I'll have earned them some freedom. We'll have paid our dues. Now go."

She started to panic. *He really meant it.* "Leave it here, in this passageway, and we'll pass through the veil—we're close enough! That would work." She stumbled as the ground shook. "Look around you. Everything is being destroyed."

"I don't know that. Leaving it here may stop the destruction. The temple may right itself." His eyes were full of regret, and her heart ached. "I can't risk that. Go. Please."

Shadow took another step towards him, tentatively, as if he might flee. "That's illogical. The same applies if you stay with it! The book will survive, but you won't! It has to cross that threshold!"

"*No.*"

"You are the most exasperating man I have ever known!"

"I'm not a man."

"You are a shit!"

He smiled and reached out a hand to stroke her cheek, and his touch was like a brand on her skin. "I'll miss you, too."

Another rumble resounded around them, and the smooth, granite surface of the walls began to crack. For a second Gabe staggered, and Shadow saw her chance. She whipped out her knife and stabbed his bandaged hand that was holding the book, and he cried out in shock, releasing it. She grabbed it, turned, and ran.

"You'd better come get it, Gabe!"

And then she plunged through the veil.

Cursing Shadow as his wounded hand throbbed, Gabe stumbled after her.

She was his friend, his partner, and he never thought she would betray him. *Never.* But now... The veil flickered, and Gabe threw himself through it, landing on the other side with a crash, and found himself in a rough-hewn stone passage. Water was pouring down the walls and along the ground, and he saw Shadow up ahead. She stopped, looked behind her, grinned, and then took off again, and with a roar, he followed.

"I am going to kill you!" he yelled.

"You've got to catch me first!"

And that was the problem. She effortlessly negotiated the way ahead, and he lost sight of her on occasion. There was no sign of the others, and he hoped they were far ahead by now. *How long was this path? How far underground where they?*

The path widened, and Gabe soon arrived at the entrance to a large cavern. It was deafening. Water roared around them, pouring down the walls and thundering into a churning lake below. The stone lip that ran around the edge was uneven and slippery, and at the far side he saw his other companions racing along a narrow ledge, disappearing into another dark passageway. The cavern narrowed at that point, and the lake plunged into a shallow cave at the base.

Shadow was moving quickly, and she had virtually caught up to Harlan at the rear. Gabe started running, and then wondered why. *He could fly. This place was big enough.* He pulled his clothes off, extended his wings, and sailed off the ledge, the spray splashing over him. It was freezing in here but he ignored it, getting ever closer to Shadow.

She paused, as if waiting for him, and for a second he couldn't work out what she was doing. She was above the highest fall of the cave, the water racing below her. Craggy rocks jutted from the slippery walls, and she started clambering down them. He swooped towards her, but just as he got close, she dropped like a stone into the churning water below.

And then something very ominous happened. The entire chamber shook, as if there was an earthquake. But he hadn't got time to question it.

He folded his wings away and dived in after her.

The water was icy, and it felt as if a hand reached into his chest and squeezed his heart. For a second he couldn't see anything, and he flailed in the current. Then he spotted her, almost crushed beneath the flow of water against the bank of the lake. She wriggled into a gap, and disappeared.

The current was insanely strong, and it took all of his strength to reach her. She had slipped inside a skinny cleft of rock, and there was no way he could follow her. The only part of her still visible was her foot, and he grabbed it and hauled her out. But she wasn't carrying the book anymore, and he was running out of air. So was she.

He pulled her in front of him, pressing her against the rock walls to prevent her from being swept away, and then gripping the rocks tightly, hauled them both to the surface, taking huge breaths of air when they finally reached it.

When he'd got his breath back, he yelled, "What the hell are you doing?"

"What does it look like, you big, winged idiot?" she asked. "I'm hiding the book!"

Gabe blinked with surprise. "What?"

"You didn't actually think I was going to let it get to the surface, did you?" She stared at him, annoyed. Her hair was plastered to her head, and her skin looked almost blue. "No one will find it here. I wedged it in there, tight, and shoved a rock in front of it. It's gone, Gabe!"

He fell over his words. "But it might break free, or someone may find it!"

"Look around! The cavern is collapsing. Will you stop arguing with me for once? Let's get out of here."

For once? Cheeky madam. She was the one that argued, not him!

Shadow started to clamber up the slippery walls to the rocky ledge above, and for a second Gabe hesitated, looking at the icy pool and debating just how secure the book was. Then a massive chunk of rock splashed into the water, almost taking him with it, and he realised she was right.

It was time to leave.

Niel hustled the others along the path. If they didn't get out of here soon, they would drown or be trapped down here forever. Fortunately, the ground was rising steeply now, and with renewed energy everyone was running, slipping, falling, and then running again.

Fresh air streamed around him, and a patch of pale grey light appeared far ahead, as Nahum shouted, "Come on, we're nearly there!"

Jimmy was still over Niel's shoulder, groaning on occasions as he regained consciousness, but Niel had ignored him, he'd been so set on their escape. He paused and looked behind him, seeing Olivia running back to grab Harlan. She ducked under his arm, helping him limp towards their exit.

But there was still no sign of Gabe or Shadow.

"Where are they?" Niel asked, scared to hear the answer.

"They're behind us," Harlan said, "somewhere."

Niel nodded, wanting to run back, but instead he pressed on, finally emerging on a shallow hillside strewn with rocks. He put Jimmy down, noting the others were standing around, taking deep breaths and looking relieved at being alive.

It was still raining, but only a fine drizzle now, and he estimated it must be close to dawn. He sought Nahum out, and found him standing over JD, trying to rouse him.

"Nahum, I'm going back in. Gabe and Shadow are still in there."

"What?" Nahum straightened quickly. "How far back?"

"I last saw them in the cavern," Harlan explained, grimacing as he leaned heavily on Olivia. "But it was collapsing." As he spoke, the land shuddered beneath them, and the ground cracked. "What now?"

"Run!" Niel urged them. "All of you, go! This whole place is going to collapse."

Nahum paled. "JD is still out."

"Go, brother. See that they all get away." He looked beyond Nahum, seeing that Jackson supported the other side of Harlan, and was virtually frog marching him up the rise to the fields beyond. Nicoli had grabbed Jimmy and was helping him to do the same. "Take JD."

Niel had backed towards the entrance, ready to re-enter, and Nahum was about to argue, when something hit Niel from behind, knocking him off his feet, and he heard Shadow say, "Get out of the way, you big lump! Are you trying to kill me?"

He lay flat on his back, staring up at her irate expression, and then grinned as Gabe emerged behind her. "You're here!"

Shadow grinned back at him, her hands on her hips, soaked to the bone. "Of course I am! You can't get rid of me that easily."

Gabe was behind her, a wry smile on his face, and there was no sign of the book.

"Where is it?" Niel asked.

"Gone, but," Gabe said, swaying as the ground shook beneath them, "I suggest we discuss this another time."

He pulled Niel to his feet, Nahum grabbed JD, and they all ran to catch up with the others.

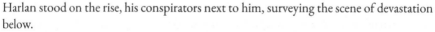

Harlan stood on the rise, his conspirators next to him, surveying the scene of devastation below.

A whole chunk of the hill they had emerged from had collapsed, forming a narrow ravine. In places, small openings were visible, but water poured from many of them, as underground streams found their way to the surface. Somewhere under all of that was the cavern. He wouldn't be surprised if there was another collapse eventually, but for now he was just happy to get his breath and rest his aching knee.

"So," Niel asked Gabe. "What did you do with it?"

Gabe looked at Shadow, amused. "Maybe you should ask Shadow, not me."

She shrugged, nonchalantly. "I hid it, in the cavern's pool, in a place I doubt anyone will ever find. Especially now."

"You did what?" JD was rousing, a mixture of fury and disbelief on his face.

Shadow looked at him, utterly unconcerned. "It's too dangerous for this world. Gabe was right. No one should ever get their hands on Raziel's book. It almost killed you."

He glared at her. "It did not!" He struggled to his feet, and Olivia helped him, but he almost brushed her off he was so cross. "I remember it...fragments, at least. It's still here." He tapped his head. "Unbelievable knowledge! Like a glimpse into another world."

"Good. You got something out of it, then." Her face hardened. "Mia, Jensen, and Erskine are all dead." She jabbed him in the chest, and he winced. "And so would you be if it wasn't for us. Be grateful for what you have."

"You still work for me!" he said, squaring up to her.

Harlan tried not to cheer as Shadow's knife suddenly appeared beneath JD's chin. "Say that again, you miserable little man, and I'll show you exactly what I think of that statement. I am fey. I work for who I choose."

Wow. She was impressive. Shadow had dropped her glamour, and her Otherness was arresting. And JD had it coming. He really had been irritating. He noticed Nicoli looking at Shadow with new appreciation, and intense speculation. That didn't bode well.

Gabe, however, laid a restraining hand on her arm, and said to JD, "I wouldn't test that threat." He held his hand out, showing his blood-stained bandage. "She stabbed me—and she likes me. I'm not sure what she thinks of you. Best not to risk it."

JD's face twisted with emotion but he remained mute, and he shifted his glare from Shadow to Gabe. "She needs a leash."

Gabe leaned in close. "Watch your mouth." He stepped back and took a deep breath. "Come on guys, home time." He looked around, narrowed his eyes, and then pointed across the hills. "That way."

Olivia murmured, "Bloody Hell," as she ducked under Harlan's arm again. "Come on old man, I'll help."

"Not so old, thank you! This injury was caused by an act of bravery." He glanced over his shoulder at Jimmy. "At least Jimmy looks okay now."

Jackson had fallen into step beside them. "Yeah, what was that about? The music was odd, and really got inside my skull, but not like Jimmy." He called over to him. "Your head okay?"

Jimmy shrugged. "I've got a splitting headache...not sure if that's from the punch or the hideous noise. Either way, I'm glad to be out of there."

"Yeah, sorry about the punch," Harlan said. "It was the only way to stop you from jumping into the water."

"I'm not sorry," Niel admitted.

Jimmy shot him an annoyed look. "I was only doing my job!"

Nicoli gave his slippery smile. Despite being soaking wet and covered in mud, he still managed to look charmingly ruthless. "My instructions. It's just business. I'm sure we'll have the pleasure again."

"I can't wait!" Niel said dryly.

"I couldn't help but notice—" Nicoli pointed to Niel's shoulders. "You appear to have wings that have now somehow disappeared!"

"Ah, those! Yes, they are useful."

"Care to explain?"

"No." And grinning broadly, Niel turned away, leaving Nicoli looking perplexed.

"Is JD keeping up?" Harlan asked Olivia, worried. "Best not to lose him now."

"He's behind us, with Nahum." She lowered her voice. "Things might be tricky at work for a while. I'm hoping this won't get us fired."

"We'll be just fine. And besides, I know too much for him to get rid of me that easily." Seeing Olivia's puzzled face, Harlan realised he'd said more than he should have, so he shut up and concentrated on hobbling to the car.

Thirty

H arlan sat in front of Mason's large antique desk, Olivia next to him, and tried not to show his annoyance.

It was early on Sunday afternoon, and Mason had called them into the office to discuss the events of the previous few hours. Harlan had showered at the house in Angel's Rest, so he was at least clean, but he was also exhausted and wanted to go to bed. He had really hoped this conversation could wait. At least Olivia had taken JD home, which was a good thing, because he was so annoyed with him, he could barely look at him. Apparently, the feeling was mutual.

Mason grimaced. "As I'm sure you know, JD is extremely unhappy about the outcome of The Trinity of the Seeker. I am annoyed for him." He glared at both of them as if he was the headmaster and they were schoolchildren. "I would like some assurances that this won't happen again."

Harlan exchanged a glance with Olivia, noting she was as furious as he was, and said, "Mason, you have no idea what happened in that temple. It was insanity! We're talking old school mojo, angels, the oldest grimoire known to man, and unbelievable power! We did the world a favour!"

Mason shuffled uncomfortably. "Be that as it may, JD wanted that book, and we are here to enable his acquisitions—"

Olivia broke in, cutting him off. "And damn the consequences? I don't think so, Mason." She leaned forward, gripping the table. "Half of Nicoli's team died in there! Erskine Hardcastle—the notorious necromancer—is dead! Did you want us to let JD die, too?"

Mason sat back, chastened. "Of course not."

"Then you have to trust us, your agents in the field, to make the right decisions," she said. "JD was not in the right mind to make a rational choice."

Harlan backed her up. "Nicoli and Jackson Strange also agreed—and that's saying something."

"And that's another thing," Mason said, firing up again. "Since when do we work with the opposition? Especially The Order of Lilith!"

"We weren't working with Nicoli," Harlan said scathingly. "He got in there first! Jackson was helping us because he had the key...or thought he did. Anyway," he shrugged, "he was very helpful in the end. I wouldn't have found the right key without him. Like Olivia said, you have to trust your field agents. We know what we're doing, Mason."

"Actually," Olivia said, weighing in, "I'm not very impressed with JD's attitude!"

"What?" Mason said, surprised. "What do you mean?"

"He seemed to suggest that Gabe was replaceable. I don't like that kind of thinking. No one is expendable here—not me, not Harlan, not Gabe, not Shadow. We are not his tools to be discarded when they no longer suit, or when better options come along." She banged the table. "As my immediate manager, I expect you to look after my interests, too—not just JD's. Do you understand?"

"I'm with her," Harlan said, wishing he'd thought to say exactly that.

Mason clenched his jaw. "You can be sure I take your safety seriously."

"Good! Remind JD of that!" Olivia stood abruptly. "Now, I am very tired and need my bed."

Harlan stood with her, deciding to capitalise on Mason's discomfort. "Yeah, this meeting is over, Mason. See you tomorrow."

And without another word, and leaving Mason fuming, they exited the office, Olivia slamming the door behind her.

⁃◄◇►⁃

Shadow had never been more grateful to be home, and she looked around at her brothers lounging in the living room with a big smile on her face. *Well, they all felt like brothers, except for Gabe. She wasn't entirely sure what he was.*

He sat next to her, his brooding presence magnetic, and she tried not to touch him. She could still feel his hand on her cheek. Every time their skin brushed she felt sparks, and she wasn't sure that was a good thing.

The farmhouse was warm and comfortable, music was playing, and for once, they were not killing each other in a simulated game; they were chatting instead. Zee and Ash had cooked, and they were eating informally, a delicious spread of Middle Eastern and Mediterranean food laid out on platters on the coffee table in front of the fire.

They had left Angel's Rest early that morning. The trek back to the cars at the bottom of the gorge had taken well over an hour, as they'd had to skirt the newly collapsed area. It was already on the news, blamed on unusual earthquake activity and something about sinkholes. They had parted ways fairly amicably with Nicoli and Jimmy, although Jimmy had barely spoken a word. Nicoli, a sly smile on his handsome face, had told her he'd be in touch, and she just nodded. He could get in touch all he wanted; he wasn't getting anything from her.

Once back at the rented manor house, Jackson had kissed Olivia and Shadow's hands with exaggerated manners, thanked them profusely for the entertainment, and quickly left. Olivia had then bandaged up Harlan's swollen knee, and both had given JD a wide berth. In fact, they all had. JD was still fuming, and Shadow couldn't decide what to make of him. Yes, he was a clever man, and a skilled alchemist. He *was* over 500 years old, after all. But, he was also annoying, fussy, and pretentious. They had packed up all of the information on The Trinity of the Seeker for JD to take back to his estate, and then left Olivia and Harlan to close up the house after promising to call them soon.

"Penny for your thoughts," Gabe said, nudging her gently.

She smiled. "Just thinking about today. It's been a weird one."

"That's one word for it," he said, watching her in a way that brought goose bumps to her skin. "You stabbed me in my already injured hand!"

"For your own good."

Barak heard her and gave his big booming laugh. "Shadow! You have some nerve."

"It's true." She turned away, glad for an excuse to break Gabe's stare. "If it wasn't for me, Gabe would still be in that temple."

She reached forward and topped up her plate, feeling the shift in mood. Underneath the relief at Gabe, Shadow, Niel, and Nahum being home again, there was worry.

Nahum was shaking his head. "I can't believe you were going to do that, Gabe."

Gabe just shrugged. "I felt it was the only option."

"Fortunately, I made him see sense," Shadow said, pleased with herself. "Even though I did nearly drown trying to hide the damn thing."

"Well," Eli said brightly, "I am very grateful for your headstrong nature and willingness to stab anything that stands in your way. Even if you are a pain in the ass most of the time."

He was sitting on the floor cushion in front of her and she smacked him across the head. "You're lucky I know that you don't mean that!"

"Yeah, right," he grumbled.

"Seriously though, guys," Zee said, "did you really feel Chassan, Niel?"

Niel nodded. "Yes. JD summoned an angel to help cross the Chamber of Wind, and he appeared... Well, was present. I didn't see him. And at least it wasn't Raphael."

"Who's Raphael?" Shadow asked.

"He's an archangel," Niel explained to her. "Archangels are more powerful, and highly unlikely to appear in this realm. It doesn't suit them. Chassan is a lesser angel."

"But even so," Eli said, looking horrified. "For any of them to appear is major!"

"Did he say anything?" Zee persisted.

"Just, 'welcome back.'"

The room fell silent, and Zee rubbed his face wearily. "What does that mean? *Hi, great to see you, we'll leave you to it! Enjoy your life.* Or," he lowered his voice, making it sound more ominous, "*Hi, you unimportant worm, you'll be hearing from us!*"

"I don't know!" Niel said, frustrated. "It was non-committal!"

"So, it could mean anything," Barak concluded. "And Raziel? Was he there?"

Gabe answered that. "I didn't sense him, even when I carried his book. The whole place felt like it was set on automation. But surely he'll know his book is gone?"

"I'm not convinced," Nahum said. "That temple could have existed for a very long time—since well before Hammond's time. He may have put his book there and then got distracted!"

"With what? His laundry?" Niel asked sarcastically. "This is his big project. How likely is it he'd have forgotten about it?"

"Maybe he has other stuff brewing?" Gabe suggested thoughtfully. "Or maybe we'll wake up one day and find he's set the lesser angels on us."

"Any sign of the fallen?" Ash asked quietly. He'd been sitting and watching them, as was his way, Shadow reflected, taking it all in. But he'd hit the crux of the matter. Their fathers.

"No," Gabe said firmly. "Other than Chassan, there were no other angels present. Not even Gabriel, who set me off on this search in the first place. If he ever finds out what happened today, I expect a pardon!"

"Hold on," Shadow said, trying to work out all of the angels and their allegiances. "If Chassan was summoned to help you cross, that means he would know about the book. Why would he want to help?"

"Because the angels took sides," Ash explained. "Some thought The Book of Knowledge should be used by those who were worthy and clever enough to deserve it. Chassan was one of them. Most did not. It caused a war, remember, the war that led to the fallen."

"So, several angels might have known about the trinity," Shadow reasoned.

"Yes." Ash nodded.

"And were the fallen for the book, or against it?"

"There was a mix of opinions," Gabe said. "The war triggered many things, and not all fell because of Raziel's book. From what I can gather, many stayed with divided opinions, too. It's...complicated."

Shadow nodded, still confused. "Seems so."

"And what about JD?" Barak asked, reaching for his beer. "Sounds like he wasn't exactly pleased?"

"He was furious," Nahum conceded. "All the way to the car he brooded and tutted. Muttering about magic that underpins the world and being denied his history." He rolled his eyes. "What a strange man."

"You could argue that it's a noble pursuit," Ash pointed out. "Men like him have furthered everyone's knowledge."

"It's not that," Nahum said. "It's him. He's so fussy! So exacting!"

"You don't learn the secret to immortality by being sloppy," Shadow said. "His house is fascinating. Despite his odd ways, I think I like him."

Niel laughed at that statement. "You held a knife to his throat and called him a miserable little man!"

Shadow winced, recalling her flare of annoyance. "Well, he said that he employed me! I really don't like that assessment of our relationship. He offers a job, and I choose whether to take it or not. That's different."

"Too right, sister!" Zee said, raising his beer in salute. "And as far as future jobs go, anything else on the horizon?"

"Not yet," Gabe answered. "Although, I'm keen to avoid tombs for a while—and angels, if at all possible."

"And what if they come to us?" Ash asked.

Gabe shrugged, an expression of grim determination on his face. "Then we deal with it, on our terms, because I'm not prepared to lose our independence. Not now. Not ever."

Shadow watched him, hoping he was right, but fearing that the future might prove more complicated than they had all hoped.

Whatever happened, she'd be with them all the way.

DARK STAR

WHITE HAVEN HUNTERS BOOK THREE

TJ GREEN

One

S hadow studied Caldwell Fleet, the Grand Adept of The Order of the Midnight Sun, and decided he was more pompous than JD, and that was saying something.

She leaned against the wall of the large reception room in the order's Marylebone headquarters, watching him talk to Gabe and Harlan, and wondered how much power he may have. Probably no natural magic, likely to be more of a ritual magician than anything else.

He looked to be in his early forties, slim and of average height, but fine-featured, with high cheekbones and sharp, appraising eyes. He was currently draped in his ornate ceremonial robes, no doubt to impress them with his position and influence, and his thick curly hair with a widow's peak was swept back from his face, revealing a tight expression.

"I'm sure you can understand my reticence to share too many details about this object," he said to Gabe and Harlan. "It's quite rare, and I would like to get it back as quickly as possible."

Harlan's expression was just as tight. "If you're hiring us to find this stolen object, then we really do need some details, Caldwell."

"I understand that! But of course, I expect complete confidentiality."

"And you already know that we provide that," Harlan said impatiently. "Can we get to the point, please?"

Caldwell stood abruptly and turned his back on them. He walked to the empty fireplace that dominated the room, tapping his fingers on the marble surface, while Harlan and Gabe exchanged annoyed glances.

It was close to nine o'clock on Friday evening a week before the summer solstice, and Shadow, Gabe, Niel, and Nahum had driven to London that afternoon at Harlan's urgent request, after he'd been contacted by Caldwell. Gabe hadn't been entirely sure of what they might face, so he'd opted to bring Niel and Nahum just in case. But things were tricky in White Haven right now, and Shadow was worried about her friends. However, she couldn't pass on the job either, and knew it wasn't anything that the other Nephilim couldn't handle. Niel and Nahum were outside, checking for access points and generally surveying the area and the layout, leaving the three of them to attend the meeting conducted on luxurious upholstered chairs that were arranged in a cluster in the centre of the rapidly darkening room. Their only light was from low lamps, adding a suitably gloomy atmosphere to the whole proceeding.

As one, Gabe and Harlan stood too, and Harlan said, "I think we should leave until you've had time to think about what you want. But just so you know, you will be billed for this evening, including transport. These guys have travelled a long way to see you."

Caldwell whirled around. "No, stay! Sorry. This is the first time we have had such a theft, and to be quite honest, it's a bit of a shock. This place," his arms encompassed the room and the building, "is alarmed, so I'm still trying to work out how it happened." He strode back to them, gesturing them to sit again as he also resumed his seat, and then looked up at Shadow uncertainly. "Would you like to join us?"

"No, thank you." She'd been sitting enough in the car on the way here, and had no wish to sit any more. Besides, being outside of the group allowed her to inspect the room while they talked. Aware she sounded rude, she smiled in her most charming manner and said, "Carry on, please."

Caldwell's gaze swept across her coolly and then returned to Harlan and Gabe. "The object in question is an astrolabe that was made in the thirteenth century. It is extremely beautiful, and its design makes it quite expensive, but there is another reason for its importance." He paused and cleared his throat. "Its design incorporates the latitude and longitude of Europe, and points the way to our place of origin."

"The origin of your order? Don't you know that?" Gabe asked, confused. "And why would anyone else be interested?"

Caldwell straightened his shoulders. "We do not know specifics, and therefore it's very important to us. We had humble beginnings, but we quickly grew in stature."

"Hold on a minute," Harlan said, clearly confused. "I thought your order was founded in the sixteenth century?"

"Ah, that." Caldwell gave a small shrug as if that was of no consequence. "We used another name originally, and it was changed in the 1500s for various reasons. We disassociated ourselves from the original identity as our goals changed."

Harlan narrowed his eyes at Caldwell, but Gabe pursued the original question. "But that doesn't explain why someone else would be so interested in your origins...unless it's a rival organisation seeking to annoy you. Or," he stared at Caldwell, "there's something hidden there? Something valuable."

Shadow had been listening while her gaze idled on the huge oil paintings covering the walls, detailing previous Grand Adepts all wearing ceremonial robes, occult symbols worked into the images. But she now walked around the room's perimeter to where she could see Caldwell's face.

His intense eyes stared back at Harlan and Gabe until he finally said, "It is rumoured that a great treasure can be found there."

Shadow perked up. Now that sounded more interesting.

Harlan leaned forward in his seat. "What do you mean, rumoured? You don't know?"

Caldwell licked his lips. "No. Books on the origin of our order suggest there may be treasure, but it is veiled in mystery. As is the astrolabe, which was a recent acquisition, and long searched for by us. We found it only months ago, thanks to one of our scholars.

The time is approaching when we can use the astrolabe to pinpoint the place. Someone obviously knows that and seeks to get there before us. You must get it back."

"Is this a solstice thing?" Gabe asked. "Because that's only a week away."

"No, it's not, but it is a planetary thing. Sorry." He shuffled, his eyes dropping to his hands before quickly looking up again. "It's called a large planet parade, in fact, and it occurs next week—*before* the solstice. I realise this is short notice."

"What the hell is a large planetary parade?" Harlan asked, alarmed.

"It's when five planets line up in a section of the night sky. The more planets in a line, the rarer it is," Caldwell explained. "We need to read from this alignment."

Gabe stifled a curse. "What happens if we miss the deadline?"

"We lose our chance for years—and of course, whoever has it could find the place first."

"So," Harlan said, his American drawl becoming more drawn out, "you're saying this is one of those aligning-of-the-stars moments, hence the timeframe."

"Exactly."

Gabe stood and started pacing, his huge build dwarfed by the large reception room. Thick carpet muffled his footfall, and the lamps threw his shadow across the room. "You better be able to tell us something about who stole it, or we're going to run out of steam on this pretty quickly."

"I can tell you they are an accomplished thief," Caldwell said, rising to his feet too and striding across the room to the door. "I take it you're willing to help?"

Gabe looked over to Shadow, a question in his eyes, and she nodded. "Yes," he answered, "provided we have something to go on!"

"Follow me."

Caldwell led them back into the round hall that was at the centre of the eighteenth-century building, through a door at the rear, and into a long, winding passage that eventually led to stairs leading downwards. While they walked, Shadow inspected her surroundings, noting the opulence of the reception was not repeated in these back rooms. Although the mouldings were fine, the decor was far more pedestrian.

At the bottom of the stairs was a sturdy wooden door with a keypad next to it that Caldwell tapped a number on, and the noise of locks clicking preceded the door swinging inwards into a dimly lit room. Thick black carpet was underfoot, the walls were painted a matte black, and on the far side was a large safe door set into the wall.

"This is our securest room, where we keep our most prized treasures."

Harlan whistled. "Is that a walk-in safe?"

Caldwell nodded. "It is. There's just one room beyond there, and that's where the astrolabe was stolen from."

"You said the building has an alarm?" Shadow asked, already examining the safe door.

"It does. Plus, there's the keypad to this door, and that state-of-the-art safe door to which only three of us know the code—and I trust them with my life!" Caldwell folded his arms across his chest. "And yet nothing was set off! We're not even sure of the exact time the theft occurred."

"When did you last enter the safe?" Harlan asked, watching Shadow and Gabe prowl the room.

"Monday evening when the astrolabe was put back in there after our Senior Adepts meeting, and then this morning when we discovered the theft."

Shadow extended her fey magic, ignoring their conversation while she tried to detect anything unusual, and felt rather than saw Gabe move next to her.

"Feel anything?"

She ignored him for a moment, passing her hand over the safe door, and then dropped to her hands and knees to examine the carpet. He crouched next to her, and she finally looked at him and said softly, "Wild magic. Shifter magic."

"*Shifter?*" His eyes widened and he inhaled deeply, as if he would smell it, too. "I don't sense a thing."

She closed her eyes, feeling for it again. It was subtle, had almost faded completely, but she just about caught it. "Definitely. It reminds me of Hunter's magic." She sprang to her feet and turned to Caldwell. "You need to open the safe."

He broke off from his conversation with Harlan and turned to her, outraged. "I'll do no such thing! That is private."

She shrugged and made as if to walk out. "Then we can't help you."

"But you said you would!" He drew himself up to his full height and blocked her exit. "We had an agreement."

Her knife was in her hand in seconds, her blade at his throat. "Don't ever block my way."

He swallowed and moved aside, apologising swiftly. "I'm sorry. We're desperate."

Tempting though it was to slap him for his cheek, she put her knife away. "We said *if* we had something to work on. I need to see inside the safe, to see if what I sense out here will be clearer in there."

Caldwell looked at Harlan for guidance. He nodded and said, "They're good. I suggest you trust them."

Clenching his jaw, Caldwell marched across the floor, and shielding the safe, swiftly entered the code before pulling the enormous door wide. He stood back, silently watching Shadow stride past him, Gabe waiting on the threshold.

The safe itself was a long, narrow room, lined with shelves that were filled with several old books, rolled scrolls, and locked boxes. It was temperature-controlled, and therefore cool and dry. Several silver and gold goblets and candlesticks were also there, as well as some more unusual curios that Shadow barely glanced at. "Where was the astrolabe?"

"Down the far end," Caldwell instructed.

Shadow prowled deeper inside, cursing the thermostat that dispelled interesting smells and clues, but the scent of shifter was strong in there, especially on the shelf where the astrolabe had been. It was hard to say if it was a wolf-shifter, but she definitely scented the magic that indicated a being that could change form. Unfortunately, there were no other clues at all.

She strode back out again, addressing Caldwell. "Your thief was a shifter. Have you managed to annoy one lately?"

"A *what?*" he said, alarmed. He turned pale, a bead of sweat appearing on his upper lip.

"A shifter. A being that changes form." She studied his discomfort. *Maybe he'd never heard of one.* She spun, inspecting the room again, but only saw a small ventilation grill high in the wall. "I think it came into this antechamber through that and then opened the safe. I presume once it was inside it could leave by an easier route, perhaps, without setting your alarm off."

All three men were looking at her, surprised.

"What kind of shifter are we talking?" Harlan asked.

She shrugged. "I don't know, but something that can shift into more than just one form, I think. But there's nothing else here that I can detect. Gabe?"

He shook his head, too. "No. But that's something to go on. Are you sure you don't know any shifters?" he asked Caldwell. "Someone you've upset, or may know about your supposed treasure?"

"No. Our members are human. Respectable!"

"Well, that's not very nice," Shadow told him. "I know some lovely shifters." She exuded a flutter of glamour and saw Caldwell blink with confusion. "We accept the job, with a payment upfront for expenses, but we will need photos and details of the astrolabe. I'm sure it will be a pleasure working with you."

Two

Gabe eyed his partner across the table, noting her easy, nonchalant confidence that was incredibly sexy, and she smiled back at him triumphantly, saying, "Remind me again of how lucky you are to have me."

"I'd rather I didn't." He sipped his pint, holding her gaze and refusing to back down. "You're lucky I put up with you."

Gabe, Shadow, Nahum, Harlan, and Niel were seated in a small pub a short distance from the headquarters of The Order of the Midnight Sun, talking through their options.

"Shut up, both of you," Nahum said, amused. "You've accepted the job, so I'm hoping you have more than just shifter magic to go on."

"Not yet, but we will," Shadow answered Nahum, not looking in the least bit concerned that they had so little information.

"Know any shifter thieves?" Niel asked Harlan.

He huffed. "No! I don't know any shifters at all. I know they exist, and that there's a community of them in London, but I don't know where they are." He sipped his pint and eyed them all over the rim of his glass. "I need to ask Maggie."

Gabe shook his head, recalling the conversation with Caldwell. "He doesn't want the police involved."

"I'm not involving them! But Maggie will know the community, or a few individuals at least. It's her job to know. I won't tell her anything about the theft, obviously."

"She has a nose for trouble," Shadow said uneasily. "She'll suspect something."

"She can suspect all she likes. I won't tell her a thing!" Harlan laughed. "If anything, she'll be glad to keep out of it. She's probably busy enough."

Nahum caught Gabe's eye. "Sounds like a plan. Once we know where to look, we can start asking more questions."

Gabe had a feeling this was going to get messy, but Nahum was right, and so was Harlan; they needed more to get started. "Agreed. But just because they're a shifter community, doesn't mean they harbour thieves. It could be an outsider."

"But," Niel argued, "it's likely they will have heard something." He turned to Shadow. "Did you pick up anything outside the building?"

"No. It's been too long, and there are too many other distractions. I could barely pick it up inside."

Harlan nudged his pint aside and rested his folded arms on the table. "What exactly are you 'picking up?'"

"Magical energy. I don't have a superhuman nose, so it's not scent I detect, but I can feel magic, and shifters have their own signature."

Gabe nodded, thinking of the wolf-shifter who was dating Briar, the witch in White Haven, but who lived in Cumbria with his pack. "Like Hunter, who you think has a kind of fey blood."

"Sure." She leaned back. "There are a few types of shifters in my world—birds, deer, bears and wolves, mainly, but there are others. Hunter is *not* fey—there's no doubt about that—but his ability to shift gives him a fey quality."

"Interesting," Harlan said, intrigued. "So, he's like a hybrid?"

Shadow wrinkled her nose. "No, not really. More likely that he—and his kind—are diluted. A remnant of fey-shifters that probably bred with humans forever ago and have changed over hundreds of years." Her eyes widened. "Hunter has a good nose...he would be able to scent another shifter really well!"

Gabe could see where this was going, and held up his hand. "Slow down! Let's see where we get first. We can think about Hunter if we need help."

"I take it," Harlan said, "that you guys can't pick up this 'signature?'"

Niel shook his head. "That's not what we do, I'm afraid."

Shadow winked and looked smug. "That's why they have *me*!"

Niel grabbed a crisp from the packet on the table and threw one at her. She caught it and popped it in her mouth with a crunch and a grin.

"So, tell me, Little Miss Fey," he said with a raised eyebrow, "what about shifters who take multiple forms?"

She chewed and swallowed. "There are very few who can take multiple forms. We call them chimera-shifters. It will make life harder, certainly, but if we get his—or her—magical scent, we should be able to track it. Or at least trace its movements."

"I presume," Nahum said, "that this shifter was also hired. I can't see why a shifter would be interested in the origin of The Midnight Sun. Which reminds me, tell me more about this astrolabe."

Gabe reached into his jacket pocket and extracted the bundle of folded papers that Caldwell had given them. "This is it." He selected a few and spread them on the table, and everyone leaned closer to look at the photos and schematics. "It's made of brass, but inlaid with silver and rose gold, and has tiny black pearls along the limb," he pointed to the engraved rim around the astrolabe. "The pin in the centre has a pearl set in it. It's called the Dark Star Astrolabe."

"Dark Star?" Nahum asked, leaning closer. "That's intriguing. I've read about these things. They seem complicated."

Harlan grunted. "That's because they are. Although, they are a brilliant invention. I believe they were created in the east before they became widely used across Europe in the twelfth century and onwards. They made travel easier. From what I know, these things are like the modern smart phone...they have up to a thousand uses." Everyone looked at him expectantly, and he shrugged. "Don't ask me what! My knowledge is basic, at best—although, I have bid for a few in the past." Harlan pointed at the picture closest to him. "This thing, the ornate plate with the squiggly pointers, is called a rete, and it aligns with the plate underneath, which has a fixed latitude and points to stars. It allows you to find your way by fixing on constellations. You can use it with the sun, too. And that's it! I have no idea how you use it, or how these guys could use it to find their place of origin."

Gabe stared at the page, not really seeing it, but thinking of their job ahead. "It was made specifically for the order—that seems clear. But that doesn't concern us, and we don't need to use it. We just need to find it before the end of the week."

"Because?" Niel asked, not privy to their earlier discussion.

"A rare planetary parade is occurring soon," Shadow answered, "and they need to fix on it for their directions. If they miss the opportunity, that's it for years!"

"Bloody typical," Niel groaned. "Did he say where they need to read it?"

"No," Gabe admitted, intrigued more than he cared to admit. *What was so mysterious about the origins of the order, and was there really any treasure?* "But we don't need to know." He said that more to remind himself than anyone else. He drained his pint. "So, you'll contact Maggie tomorrow, Harlan?"

"Yep, and I'll be in touch. You guys still happy to stay at Chadwick House?" He looked uncertain, which wasn't surprising. "It's all clean and aired out. I think you're the first people to stay there since Chadwick died."

Shadow finished her drink, too. "Is it still filled with his stuff?"

"Of course, but we have created a couple more bedrooms." He shrugged. "It meant rearranging some of his collections, but essentially we have honoured the conditions of his will. You'll have access to his extensive library, too. And—" he shot Shadow an accusatory glare. "*Nothing* goes missing! We know what's there."

She looked affronted, and Gabe tried not to smirk. "How dare you! I wouldn't steal from you!"

"Yeah, right," he muttered into the dregs of his pint.

Gabe stood, his chair scraping across the floor as he stretched. He'd never been to Chadwick's house before, so was suddenly anxious to see it. And the lure of a whiskey before bed sounded great. "Come on guys, let's get moving."

——◆O◆——

Harlan steeled himself to call Maggie 'ball-breaker' Milne on Saturday morning.

He'd had a fitful night's sleep worrying about shifters and where this search might lead them, and also what Mason might say. What he hadn't told Shadow and the Nephilim was that he hadn't run Caldwell's request past Mason like he would normally do. His relationship with him was tricky at present, mainly because of JD.

After the experience with JD the previous month, when he'd found out exactly how fickle and untrustworthy he was—and to be honest, downright annoying—Harlan couldn't help but question what he knew about Mason, especially as he realised how close they were. Harlan might have known Mason for years, but recently, every interaction he'd had with him had felt edgy, and Olivia had reported the same issue. If anything, Olivia had been angrier than him, demanding Mason looked after their interests, and consequently he and Olivia were prone to having secret meetings down the pub. Although, it would be fair to say that nothing untoward had happened, and life at the guild had pretty much continued as it had before. Jobs came in, he attended auctions, followed up acquisitions he could handle alone, and brought in others when needed.

This job had come when Caldwell phoned Harlan directly. It seemed that Kent Marlowe had been impressed with Gabe and Shadow, and Harlan too, after the affair with Kian. Harlan had decided that it would be too subversive not to include the guild, but he just quietly got on with it, including booking Chadwick House for the team. He knew he was risking Mason's wrath, but at the end of the day, the guild would still get paid. Now that the job was going ahead, he debated whether he should come clean to Mason, but for some reason that he couldn't pinpoint, he decided to keep it quiet. If Mason went looking through the records he'd find it, but Harlan would worry about that later.

Maggie's phone rang several times before she answered with a clipped, "Hey Harlan, I presume you have some new shit to land on my doorstep."

"Actually, no. And good morning to you, too!"

"Whatever. What do you want? I've got a fucking vampire tearing through the East End, and I need to get moving."

"I need to know where to find shifters in London."

"What the fuck for?"

Everything Maggie said suggested she took every word as a personal affront. It was exhausting. "Because I think one has committed a theft, and I need to find it."

"A theft where?"

"It's a private matter...and I thought you were busy?"

"All right," she grumbled. "Wimbledon, like the bloody Wombles."

"Wimbledon? The shifters are rich?" For some reason, Harlan had presumed they'd be short of cash.

"I don't bloody know! But it's close to the common and Richmond Park. I figure they like green spaces."

"Have you got someone we can talk to? A contact?"

She sighed, impatient to get moving, he could tell. "Maverick Hale. He's annoying but useful, and likes to keep the pack clean."

"Wolf-shifter?"

"And Alpha. He's got the usual swagger. Thinks he's a fucking rock star. I'll text you his number."

"Thanks, Maggie. I really appreciate this."

"You owe me."

She hung up on him and Harlan sighed. That actually went better than he'd thought. And he had a number. Maverick Hale. *What sort of name was that?* He wasn't lying when he said he didn't know any shifters. He knew many people who used The Orphic Guild for business, and while they were a diverse bunch, shifters hadn't been part of them...not that he knew of, anyway. Rather than second-guess himself, he called straight away, but the phone rang and rang and eventually went to voicemail. Reluctant to leave a message, he hung up and decided to try again later.

Harlan made another coffee and then decided to search the Internet for any reference to Maverick, and was pleased to find an early hit. *No wonder Maggie called him a rock star*. He owned a club in Wimbledon called Storm Moon. Harlan sniggered. *Seriously*? It was a live music venue that looked to be a mix of the dark, edgy, and up-market—a potent combination—and it was just off the High Street, not far from the Ivy Restaurant.

Harlan leaned back in his chair, sipping his drink. *A nightclub made sense*. Shifters were generally night creatures, and it would be the perfect business, and a chance for Maverick to employ some of his pack. No wonder Maverick wasn't answering his phone now. He probably kept very late hours. Harlan stared at the image of its respectable façade on the search page and decided that if he didn't answer his phone, they could visit there that night. He'd update Gabe and Shadow, and then head to the gym.

Three

S hadow studied the pictures of the astrolabe that were spread across the table, marvelling at its intricacy and beauty.

"This really is magnificent," she murmured, more to herself than anyone else.

She was sitting with the three Nephilim in the kitchen at Chadwick House after having just finished Niel's usual breakfast spread, and they were debating what to do with their day.

Nahum pulled one of the pictures towards him, looking puzzled. "It's ingenious, even if I don't have a clue how it works. But Ash would be good with this. He has an analytical mind."

Shadow nodded. "You're right."

"But," Gabe reminded them, "we don't need to know how it works. We just need to find it."

Shadow frowned at him. "But I like to know how things work."

"Not the dishwasher, you don't," Niel shot back.

"Sod off. I'm a racehorse, not a carthorse!"

Gabe laughed. "Where do you get these stupid sayings from?"

"It's not stupid," she said, her ire rising as she looked at him sitting there so infuriatingly collected and calm. "It's true. Aren't you the slightest bit curious about this?"

"Slightly," he admitted with a shrug. "But it's unnecessary. We need to focus on who the shifter is, who hired him, and where he's gone now."

"And potentially what they've stolen it for," Nahum said. "Because that could indicate where they've gone with it. I mean, if they intend to find the origin of the order and the potential treasure there, they may already have a lead."

Shadow huffed, looking at Nahum like he was an idiot. "The clue is in there!" She tapped the image. "Only to be revealed on the day of the planetary alignment. They can't know where to go yet!"

He stared at her. "I mean, that they have clearly done some research, so they must know *something*!"

Niel leaned on the table, his hand rubbing over the shaved hair on the side of his head. "This could be an inside job. If Caldwell has kept this quiet, who else would know about it? It sounds like they've been searching for it for a while, and only found it recently."

Gabe gazed into the middle distance, tapping his mug. "Maybe we should clarify that. Which leads to the next questions. Where did they find it, who found it, and who brought it here? There's a trail, and trails aren't clean. Information could have leaked at any point."

Shadow eyed Gabe, impressed at his logic. He was looking good this morning. His black t-shirt fit his sculpted muscles perfectly, the colour making his olive skin glow, and his dark eyes had taken on that intensity which, she reluctantly admitted, gave her an unwilling shiver. He turned that intense gaze on her sometimes, a smoulder of desire behind them that filled her mind with thoughts of how those hands would feel on her bare skin. She blinked away her thoughts and focussed on the job.

"We need to ask Caldwell more questions," she mused.

Niel grunted. "I'm not sure we'll get answers."

Shadow considered what Harlan had asked the night before. "Remember when Harlan was confused about the date of the order's origins, and Caldwell said they'd had another name? I wonder what that was. Why would you change your name?"

"Caldwell gave a reasonable explanation," Nahum pointed out, "but it's worth investigating." He looked around the table. "This house has a study. Maybe there's something in there. And Chadwick collected ancient stuff, right? He might have an astrolabe. I'd like to see one, properly, just to get a feel for it."

"Good suggestion," Shadow said, eager to do something. "I'll search the house."

"Why don't we all take a tour?" Gabe suggested, rising to his feet. "I didn't get to see much of the place last night, and I'd like to explore it fully."

They quickly cleared the breakfast things away and headed into the dining room, where the first thing Shadow saw was the hole her knife had made in the wall. She walked over to it, running her fingers across it, before turning to survey the room.

"It's hard to believe the last time I was in here I was being attacked by Kian."

Gabe swung around to look at her. "That was here?"

"Yep." She pointed to the sofa that was next to the fireplace, now cold and empty in the summer. "I dived behind that. We were sitting at this table when Harlan and Mason fell unconscious." She was standing next to the polished walnut table, its elegance belying the violence of that night. She pointed to the large, wooden head on the coffee table. "And that's what I threw at him, too."

Niel laughed as he walked around the room, picking things up and placing them down again in idle curiosity. "I bet he didn't expect that."

"No, I don't think he did. And then of course he scarpered down the hall, and I gave chase."

The room looked like it had that night. The furniture was antique and occasionally ostentatious, and the decor was rich and challenging to the eye, although in the bright light of day it lacked the power of the candlelit evening. It was odd being back here again, but also good. Her place with the Nephilim seemed certain now, assured, as was her friendship with Harlan. Time had changed things for the better.

She left the room, checking on the living room briefly before entering what had been the drawing room but was now another room displaying Chadwick's occult collections.

It allowed a room upstairs to become a bedroom, and The Orphic Guild had converted the attic, too.

Nahum was behind her, and he said, "This place is interesting! He's got all sorts of stuff." He peered into a glass case. "Is that a poppet?"

She went to his side, looking at the rudimentary cotton doll that had been hand-sewn with crosses for eyes. It was old, yellowed with age. "He must have a witchcraft collection. Look, old rune stones and amulets," she said, pointing out other shelves.

"Is that a withered hand?" he asked, heading to another cabinet and pointing out the shrunken yellow skin wrapped around bones. "That's disgusting." He grinned at her. "Let's hope it's not cursed. You might find it creeping across your pillow at night."

She glared at him. "Funny. *You* might find it around your throat. Oh, wait, that will probably be me!"

He lowered his voice. "Gabe better not find you creeping in my bedroom. He'd get very upset."

She looked at his cheeky expression, and despite her best intentions, felt herself flush. "I'm sure Gabe doesn't care where I go at night."

He laughed. "Pull the other one. Come on, sweet sister, this is not finding an astrolabe."

"Did I hear my name?" Gabe asked, appearing silently behind them.

"Nope. Vanity, vanity," Shadow said aloofly, and then headed to the rooms that were linked with the double doors. Hearing them behind her, she said, "This is where I was almost pinned beneath the cage, were it not for my lightning-fast reflexes."

"And this," Gabe said, casting her a withering glance as he marched across the room to a collection on a low shelf, "is an astrolabe." He picked up the ornate, bronze disc that was the size of a side-plate, and headed to the large bay window so he could see it in the light. "It's bigger than I thought. Heavy."

Niel had joined them, and he said, "I looked them up this morning. That ring on the top is to hang it so you get the most accurate reading. It's made up of several different layers, all pinned in the centre."

"Are they all this size?"

Niel shrugged. "I think they vary. They are portable, after all." He pointed at the ornate, curly bronze squiggles. "These point to stars, but it can be used in the day, too."

Shadow leaned against the window frame. "So, the Dark Star Astrolabe has a specific purpose, whereas this one can be used to find your way anywhere within a certain latitude."

"It seems so," Niel agreed. He checked his watch. "I'm heading up to the study, see what I can find up there. A couple of hours should see us through to lunch."

"Good plan," Gabe said, still carrying the astrolabe. "I'll bring this with me, see if I can work it out." He looked at Shadow. "Don't pout. Come and help."

"Dusty books? Ugh!" She gestured out the window. "It's beautiful out there! We should go out."

He stared at her with his implacable gaze. "Are you part of the team or not?"

"Spoilsport," she said, reluctantly following them up the stairs. "You owe me a pint."

Harlan finally managed to speak to Maverick Hale at about three that afternoon, and he didn't sound as he'd expected. His voice was smooth, almost a purr, whereas he'd been expecting a growl.

"Mr Hale, my name is Harlan Beckett and I've been given your name by Maggie Milne." He deliberately left out her title, but he was pretty sure Maverick would know her name.

Maverick paused before answering. "Maggie? That can only mean trouble."

"I hope not for you," Harlan said swiftly. "But I gather you're the Alpha of the local pack, and I need your advice about a shifter."

"She told you what I am?" he asked, a dangerous edge to his voice.

"I work in the occult world. Your secret is safe with me."

"It better be. One of *my* shifters?"

"We don't think so. A rare object has been stolen, and my colleague thinks a shifter is responsible, but it's not a wolf-shifter. We need a lead and thought you could help."

He laughed dryly. "We are not the only pack in London."

Harlan faltered for a moment, and then pushed on. "Obviously you're the only one Maggie trusts enough to send me to."

"Sorry; she misled you. I can't help."

"What if this brings trouble to your door?"

"We can deal with trouble. And besides, why should it? You said it's not a wolf-shifter."

Harlan was losing him; he was clearly on the verge of ending the call. "But you own a bar. Surely you have all sorts of people hanging out there. And you live in the paranormal world. One of your pack may know something."

"What is it you do, Mr Beckett?"

"I'm a collector for The Orphic Guild. Occult acquisitions. I have many contacts, and we're good at what we do."

"I've heard of you, although I have never had need of your services before. If I help you now, perhaps I'll get a better deal if I do need you in the future?"

"Of course," Harlan said eagerly. Deals were part of the game.

"Then come to the club tonight at ten. I'll leave your name at the entrance." And then he hung up, leaving Harlan murmuring his thanks into the dial tone.

Gabe was back at The Order of the Midnight Sun on his own.

He'd left the others to while away the afternoon while he questioned Caldwell. Despite the fact that Caldwell had engaged their services, he hadn't seemed that keen to speak to Gabe again, which was curious.

The front door was locked to the public, but a casually dressed man admitted him to the reception room and then left him to wait alone. Gabe could have asked his questions over the phone, but he wanted to see Caldwell's expression. He could get a better feel for his responses that way. He walked around the room while he waited, noting the large oil paintings, the heavy furniture, and the rich silks and brocades that on close inspection were worn in places, their colours faded. Maybe they were short of money and needed this treasure—if it even existed. Or maybe it wasn't a monetary treasure, but another type of treasure entirely.

His thoughts were broken when Caldwell came in, this time wearing ordinary jeans and a t-shirt—no ornate robes today. His plain attire removed some of his mystique, making him look smaller, too.

Caldwell crossed the room quickly, shaking his hand as he asked, "Have you found anything?"

Gabe shook his head. "In so few hours? No. But we have a line of inquiry." *Bloody hell*, Gabe thought, *I sound like the police.* "My team were talking this morning, and realised we had more questions."

Caldwell sat, inviting him to do the same. "Of course. What do you need to know?"

"First of all, how many people here know about the astrolabe?"

"All of our Inner Temple. That's only twenty-one people."

"And they are what you called the Senior Adepts, correct? The ones who met on Monday night?"

"Yes. They are utterly loyal, and privy to our innermost secrets." He looked affronted. "They would never betray us!"

Gabe wasn't so sure of that, but he continued, "And the three of you who hold the code combinations are part of that group?"

"Yes. Myself, the Major Adept, and the Secretary of the order. All of us have been members for decades."

"And the rest of the Inner Temple?"

"Many for years, others are more recent, but all have earned their place."

"How do they do that?"

Caldwell laughed. "That's a secret. There are tests to undergo, rituals I cannot divulge."

"Okay. How many others belong to the order?"

"I couldn't say exactly off the top of my head, but close to a hundred." Gabe must have looked shocked, because Caldwell said, "They are spread across the country. Not all live in London. We have many initiation levels, and some members who have been with us for years only progress a short way, while others can progress rapidly depending on their...abilities."

Herne's horns. It already sounded like mumbo jumbo, but Gabe kept his face carefully neutral. "And you're sure no one else would know about the astrolabe?"

"No one." He shook his head decisively, his curly hair bouncing as he did so.

"It might be that I need the names of those in the Inner Temple."

Caldwell stuttered. "Not a chance."

"Well, we'll see how we get on, won't we?" Gabe answered calmly. "Who found the astrolabe, and who was part of the search?"

"Again, it was a member of our Inner Temple—he was unaided. One of our greatest scholars and researchers who has made it virtually his life's work. He found it in France, in the south."

"And I presume he brought it here with him, in his luggage?"

"Er, no actually." Caldwell looked downright uncomfortable now, and he cleared his throat. "He feared it would be seized by customs, so arranged another method for its shipment."

Gabe's lips twitched with amusement. "He stole it, then?"

Caldwell's eyes dropped to the floor. "I didn't ask for details."

"Of course you didn't. Was it stolen from a private residence? Because potentially," he said, forestalling any lies, "they sent someone to get it back."

"The adept in question assures us he was discreet."

"Maybe he wasn't as discreet as he thought." Gabe groaned. This was getting more complicated by the minute. "And how did he ship the astrolabe?"

"He used Kernow Shipping. They are also very discreet."

Gabe froze. "Kernow Shipping, based in Cornwall?"

"You know them?"

"Sort of." At least Gabe should be able to access the records. Gabe was wearing an old, worn leather jacket, and he reached into an inner pocket for a pen and paper. "I need the dates of shipment, and ports. And also the address it was stolen from."

Caldwell jutted his chin out. "I told you, I can't get that."

Gabe settled back comfortably in his chair. "And I'm not leaving until you do."

Nahum, his two brothers, Shadow, and Harlan were in the beer garden of the Dog & Fox Pub & Hotel in Wimbledon, and had already finished a hearty pub meal. They were now sipping drinks and sharing news, while keeping a watchful eye on the comings and goings along the High Street.

It was a warm summer evening, and to Nahum it seemed as if the entirety of Wimbledon was outside. The beer garden was packed, and the street bustled with people who strolled up and down and in and out of the various bars and restaurants. There was a thrum of activity, a bustle of energy that made the place seem exciting, a very different feel to the seaside charm of White Haven. Nahum had lived in many cities in his lifetime, and he enjoyed their energy and the mix of characters that lived in them. London was no different, and he felt comfortable there.

Nahum turned his attention to the table, and particularly to Gabe and Shadow, trying to hide his amusement. They were sitting next to each other, as they often did, a studied indifference to their features that belied the chemistry between them. The air almost crackled around them sometimes—much to the amusement of himself and his brothers. They argued, fought, teased, and slid each other sly glances that they thought no one else would see. They were trying very hard not to admit it, but they were clearly attracted to each other, and he knew that only the business was keeping them apart. Neither wanted to wreck what was clearly turning into a profitable and entertaining enterprise. *Well, that and their mutual stubbornness.* He had known Gabe his entire life, and hadn't seen him like this with a woman for a very long time. *Then again, why should he wish for the entertainment to be over?* They were all running side bets on how long it would take for them to get together. Which reminded him—he should let Harlan in on the bet.

Harlan was proving to be a worthwhile ally. He had great contacts, a good work ethic, and a strong moral code, all of which meant the Nephilim respected him. And he had a great sense of humour, thank the Gods.

Harlan was looking at Gabe, incredulous about his visit to Caldwell. His mouth gaped open, his pint suspended halfway to his mouth. "Caldwell actually gave you the information? Just like that?"

"No! Stupid bastard thought I was going to go and that he could somehow talk me out of needing to know who they stole the astrolabe from." Gabe too looked incredulous. "What an idiot! What about me looks like someone could force me to leave?" Gabe threw his shoulders back and spread his hands out. "I pointed out that he had employed me, so he'd better run along and do as I asked."

Niel laughed and slapped his shoulder. "I always knew your stubbornness would be an asset."

Niel had shaved the sides of his head again, taking the long hair left into a high ponytail. His good looks were attracting his fair share of attention, especially paired with his booming laugh.

Nahum leaned his elbows on the table, wishing he'd met Caldwell. "It is odd that he would not want you to have as much information as possible. Sounds like he's in denial."

"It sounds," Shadow suggested, "that he wants to keep the image of the order as above reproach."

Gabe nodded. "I suspect that by the time this is over, he'll have trouble smoothing over the cracks. I think they're broke, too. In the cold light of day, that place isn't nearly so impressive."

"So," Harlan pressed, "who did they steal the astrolabe from?"

"A house in Nice, in the south of France. I have the address, but I haven't looked it up yet. It's owned by a Madame Raphael Charbonneau." He shrugged. "I don't know anything about her, either. But at least we have a name now."

"She may have nothing to do with the theft at all," Niel pointed out.

"True, but it's something to bear in mind." Gabe took a deep breath. "It was sent from Marseilles using Kernow Shipping, which is great for us, because it means we can get shipping details—like who booked it in."

Shadow laughed. "Like the thief, you mean?"

"Exactly," he said, meeting her eyes. "It will help us build up a picture. I've already asked Barak to look into it."

Harlan nodded enthusiastically. "Fantastic. I agree. The more we know, the better. Did you find out the order's old name?"

"No. And to be honest, it isn't my most pressing question right now." Gabe gave an easy smile. "But I will find out."

Harlan sipped his pint, nodding thoughtfully. "I take it you couldn't find their history in Chadwick's study?"

"No," Nahum answered, remembering how daunting that room was. "But we have time to look. That room is pretty chaotic."

"Yeah." Harlan looked sheepish. "It's been catalogued in a very basic fashion, but not organised. We haven't had time. Their history is something I can look into, and let you concentrate on the rest."

"Fair enough," Nahum told him. "You had success, though. Well done."

Harlan looked to the roundabout a little further down the road and nodded. "Storm Moon is down the street across from here—Church Road—in a very unassuming building. It opened at eight, and there's a band on at nine. A rock band, I think."

"I take it you've scoped it out?" Shadow asked, already looking like she wanted to jump out of her seat and leave.

"Only briefly. It looks like there's a bar on the ground floor and the club below ground. There's a big parking lot to the side, and around the back, too." He shrugged. "I didn't go in, but it looks flashy and edgy from the pictures on the net."

"I suggest," Gabe said, "that Niel and Nahum stay outside and check the exits, and we three will go in. That okay with you?"

Nahum and Niel nodded. They were used to running surveillance, although Nahum would love to look inside the club.

Gabe turned to Shadow. "Do you think you can pick up a distinct magical energy in there?"

"Maybe. It depends on how many shifters are around. I can certainly detect them now."

"You can?" Harlan asked, looking uncomfortably around him. "Are they close?"

"At the table in the corner, I think. Far enough away they shouldn't be able to listen—although they have exceptionally good hearing."

"But there's a lot of background noise," Niel said, angling his body casually so that he could look behind him. "I see them. The half a dozen in the corner."

Shadow nodded, and Nahum glanced around too, seeing four men and two women, all enjoying drinks and food. They looked harmless enough, and he said, "I'm sure they're just enjoying their Saturday night like everyone else here." He turned back to the others. "I think the club will be packed tonight. And frankly, the thief may have no connection there at all. Or they will be long gone."

"Unless they live here," Gabe suggested. "Once the goods were passed on, there's no need to run."

Niel drained his pint. "At this point, there are numerous ways this could go, and it's all pointless speculation. Let's have another drink and see what transpires later."

Four

Storm Moon was much bigger than Shadow anticipated. They entered the bar through sturdy wooden double doors that led into an ornate foyer where one heavily muscled bouncer, unsurprisingly a shifter, gave them a cursory glance before they headed through the next door into the ground floor bar.

Harlan, Shadow, and Gabe all paused just inside the threshold to get their bearings. The windows were blacked out, and the lighting was low. The long bar that ran across the far side of the room was topped with polished copper, and the back of the bar was mirrored and lined with rows and rows of spirits. The walls were covered with dark-patterned, opulent wallpaper, the floor space was filled with tables, and around the sides were cushioned booths upholstered in teal velvet. The light gleamed off the polished tables, many of which were already taken, and there was a cheerful, chatty atmosphere. An area in the middle of the right-side wall was free of side booths, creating a clear section that housed a door that had *Storm Moon Club* on it in gilt letters.

"Nice place." Harlan said, taking it in slowly. "Should we go down there already?" He nodded at the door.

"May as well," Gabe said, leading the way.

As they crossed the floor, Shadow felt a few curious gazes fall on them, and detected a few shifters in the room, especially behind the bar, but far more of the customers there were normal humans.

Gabe opened the door, revealing a staircase leading down to a reception area with a cloakroom combined with a ticket office. Again the decor was dark, illuminated only by low lights. A couple of staff stood behind the counter, one taking coats from two young girls, and another large bouncer guarded an ornate door. *There was clearly no expense spared here*, Shadow noted, *as even the reception areas were designed to impress.*

Harlan addressed the young woman behind the ticket counter who was casually dressed in jeans and a black t-shirt. "Maverick Hale is expecting me, and I have two colleagues with me."

Her eyes raked over them. "Let me check with Maverick." She turned her back as she picked up the phone.

The bouncer studied them too, and Shadow detected his shifter magic. She leaned against the wall, aware of where her blades were in case she needed to pull them quickly, and stared back. Gabe stood with hands thrust into his pockets, relaxed but alert. As usual, she was fully aware of his heat and physicality, and wasn't sure whether it was comforting her or distracting her.

The bouncer was tall and lean, his eyes watchful, and he carried himself with an easy grace, but he wasn't threatening. He opened the door for the two girls who had just checked their coats, greeting them warmly, and making Shadow think they were regulars as they passed through, giggling.

The call the woman made was brief, and she turned back to them with renewed curiosity. "That's fine, you can all go through, on the house. Head across the floor to the passageway and up the stairs on the right."

Harlan murmured his thanks and led the way inside.

The loud music assaulted them immediately. The club was full, a crowd of seething people standing in front of the stage on their right, situated at the rear of the building. A rock band was playing, clad in leather, jeans, and t-shirts, and the dull thud of the bass guitar and drums resounded through the floor and equally through Shadow. She smiled as she looked around, the energy infectious.

Shadow hadn't been to a live music venue since she'd arrived here, and she knew she'd missed out. The room was large, and as well as the crowd in front of the stage, there were a few booths and tables by the bar at the other end of the room, but not many, and all of them were taken. Opposite, across the dance floor, was the passageway the woman had told them about. Harlan was already heading to it, but Shadow took her time to follow, taking stock of the room, and so did Gabe.

Gabe nudged her and lowered his voice to her ear. "Are there lots of shifters around?"

"A fair few, though less than normal people." She nodded to the bar. "Most of the staff are shifters, and the two bouncers."

"I expected as much," he said, and then steered her behind Harlan, who waited at the entrance to the narrow passage. At the far end of it was a door marked *Exit*.

As instructed, there was a shallow set of stairs at the rear heading up to a narrow landing and a door. Smaller rooms were on their left, filled with low seating and tables, half-full at present, and it was quieter here, allowing the customers to chat.

"Anything feel off?" Harlan asked Gabe and Shadow.

"Not to me," Gabe said, glancing around and looking relaxed, which was deceiving. He was absolutely on full alert.

"It feels fine," Shadow agreed. "Just a lot of people having a good time."

"Good. Let's hope it stays that way," Harlan said, heading to the landing.

At his knock, the door that was marked *Office* was opened by another tall shifter with blond hair and astute eyes, dressed in what seemed to be their uniform of black jeans and a t-shirt with the Storm Moon logo on the front, and he stepped back, allowing them entry. As soon as the door shut behind them, the noise vanished, leaving them in a soundproofed room overlooking the club. A desk was at the far end next to a couple of filing cabinets, and a seating area was at the other, along with a small self-serve bar in the corner. A large window, which Shadow hadn't noticed from the main room, looked out over the club. A couple of staff stood looking through it, while a man worked at the desk. All three stared at them as they entered.

The man behind the desk leaned back, his eyes wary, a smile playing across his lips as he studied all of them. "You must be Harlan Beckett and *colleagues*. I'm Maverick Hale." He stood and walked around his desk to meet them, shaking their hands with a firm grip.

"Thanks for your time, Maverick," Harlan said, introducing them.

Maverick appeared to be in his late thirties and was tall and lean with the athletic build of many shifters, and now Shadow knew what Maggie had meant when she'd sarcastically called him a rock star. He oozed self-confidence. His black t-shirt clung to his broad shoulders and powerful deltoids, and his thick, shoulder-length hair, which was a dirty-blond colour, had a slight curl to it. Shadow realised that Maverick was supremely aware of his power, but he didn't try to overwhelm them, as many Alphas might. She liked that about him. He reminded her of Gabe in that respect. It was Gabe he studied most, perhaps because of his build and height. His eyes narrowed as he greeted him, and Shadow was pretty sure he detected something different that he couldn't quite place.

Maverick gestured them to sit in the lounge area and headed to the bar. "Drinks? Whiskey, gin?" He smiled at Harlan. "Bourbon?"

"You read my mind," Harlan said, taking a seat.

"It was the accent that suggested it," he admitted, pouring his shot, and then getting a whiskey for Gabe and gin and tonic for Shadow.

Rather than sit, Shadow accepted her drink and stood at the window looking down to the club, saying, "I didn't see this window from the other side."

"You're not supposed to," Maverick told her. "It's a one-way mirror with a non-reflective surface on the other side, so it blends in with the wall in the dark. It's useful for my security team to keep an eye on things." He gestured to the two people who had returned to surveilling the club—one man, one woman—but didn't introduce them. He sat down, sipping his whiskey. "You think I can help you find a shifter?"

Harlan nodded. "A chimera-shifter who was responsible for a theft on Thursday night. We were hoping that he—or she—might have passed through here."

Maverick swirled his drink, the ice clinking against the glass. "A chimera-shifter? I presume you mean a shifter that can change into many forms?" At Harlan's nod, he continued, "That's an interesting name for them, but we call them therian-shifters. And how do you know it's a therian?"

Harlan glanced at Shadow, a questioning look in his eyes, and she said, "Because I could tell. It's one of my skills."

"Care to share?" he asked, meeting her eyes.

"Not really. But I can tell that you, your man on the door—" she gestured to the man who had let them in and now leaned against the wall watching their exchange, "and the woman are wolf-shifters, but the other man—" she pointed to the burly man who had been looking through the window but now stared at Shadow, "is human." He grinned and returned to surveilling the club, and Shadow said, "I also know most of your bar staff and bouncers are shifters, but most of your clientele is human. Although, I would need a good look around to say for sure."

"Consider me impressed," Maverick said, raising his glass in salute. "And you can tell the difference in types of shifters?"

She kept it brief. "Yes. You all have a certain *quality*."

Maverick watched her for a few more seconds, his amber eyes warm like the whiskey he swirled in his glass, and Shadow felt his magic flare. But her glamour was firmly in place and she waited until he nodded and addressed Harlan and Gabe. "You can see how busy my club is. Sometimes less than savoury characters pass through here, but in general it's a safe place for the supernatural people of this world. However, I don't keep track of everyone. We are open to all, as long as they don't cause trouble."

"But you are the only pack in the area, and shifters like to be together. It's natural you might have heard something," Harlan suggested.

"Wolf-shifters like to be together...on the whole. There are loners. Therian-shifters are very different creatures altogether. Have you ever met one?" They all shook their heads, Shadow unwilling to admit she knew them only in her own world, and he shrugged. "Trust me. Much like their ability to change form, they are slippery at best, downright troublemakers at worse. All indulge in some kind of crime, most petty, but not all. So, if I'm honest, it doesn't surprise me that your thief is a therian."

Gabe leaned forward, speaking for the first time. "Is there a community of therian-shifters around here?"

Maverick laughed. "They don't even trust each other." He dropped his smile, becoming serious. "You're going to a lot of trouble to find this guy. What did he steal?"

Now it was Harlan's turn to laugh. "I'm not telling you that, but rest assured it is expensive and precious to the people who hired us. And if I'm honest, we don't know exactly what it can do, so I think it's safer back with the people it belongs to."

Not exactly true, Shadow thought, *but close enough*. Suddenly, the thought of the astrolabe in the hands of a rogue shifter and whoever had hired him made her feel very uncomfortable.

After another moment of studied concentration, she presumed Maverick came to the same conclusion. He looked over to the woman who was as tall as Shadow, dressed in black leather from head to toe with long, tawny hair and green eyes. "Domino is my head of security, and Grey, next to her, is her second. She, more than anyone, knows of the comings and goings here, and the wider community. Tell them what you've heard, Dom."

She leaned against the glass, arms folded across her chest. "A therian-shifter called Blaze came sauntering into the bar on Wednesday night. Edric was on the door that night and questioned him before letting him in—just casually. He's been here before, and generally causes us no problems, but he has a dubious reputation, like all of his kind. He said he was down here on a job and all he wanted was a drink, so he let him in." She nodded behind them. "He sat in one of the smaller rooms for a few hours, drinking and chatting up girls. He's good looking—if you like dodgy, bad boys." Domino did not look impressed. "Anyway, one of those girls he chatted up is actually one of ours who we pay to circulate to get information." She smirked. "We like to know what trouble may land on our door, and this is one way of keeping tabs. Apparently, he was staying close by, although the job was across the river. He didn't specify what it was and she didn't push. He just said it was tricky and needed his particular expertise." Domino rolled her eyes. "He looked very pleased with himself. Bragging impresses some people."

Harlan looked excited. "Across the river sounds promising. It could be our guy. Any idea where he was staying? And why here? Wouldn't he want to be closer to the job?"

Domino shrugged. "He didn't say. But, if I remember correctly, there's bad blood between Blaze and the North London Pack. And maybe he likes to keep his distance from the job, too."

"Maggie said they weren't as amenable as you guys," Harlan admitted.

Maverick advised, "Unless you like drug dealers, lowlifes, and brawlers, it's best to avoid them."

"Are they the ones based in North Finchley?" Harlan asked.

Maverick gave a tight smile. "Yes. A good distance from here, fortunately. We don't get on."

"This guy, Blaze," Gabe said, drawing them back to the shifter in question. "From where up north?"

"Yorkshire, if I recall," Domino told him. "In his mid-thirties I'd guess, average height, slim build, longish dark hair."

"That's great, thank you," Harlan said. "Have you seen him since then? Or did your girl get an address?"

"No address, but you can talk to her if you like. She's working tonight." She looked at Maverick, who nodded, and then turned to her second. "Grey, can you fetch her?"

Grey's long stride carried him across the room, and while they waited, Maverick topped up their drinks. Shadow watched the dance floor, hearing the other three continue to chat. She filtered them out, concentrating on the scene below her.

The band had finished their set and were clearing their instruments from the stage. Another raised area opposite that she hadn't noticed when they walked in was where the DJ was set up, and from the dancing she could see below, it looked as though he had taken over from the band.

Domino was still studying the club, and Shadow said, "Do you have a band on every Saturday?"

She nodded. "And Tuesdays and Thursdays, most weeks. It's a popular venue for both established and smaller bands."

"All rock?"

"Mainly, but the DJ does 80s nights, too. That's always fun."

From the expression on her face, Shadow assumed she was not an '80s music fan. "Do you ever have disco nights?"

Domino looked sharply at her. "Don't tell me you're a fan?"

"I'm partial to Donna Summer and the Bee Gees." She shrugged. "Weird, I know, but what can I say?"

A broad smile spread across Domino's face. "Well, I'd pay to see you on the dance floor dancing to that!"

Shadow lowered her voice and moved closer. "How did you come to lead security here?"

"I earned it through hard work and a gift for diplomacy. And I fight well too, which helps."

"And do you really see only a little trouble here?"

"Really!" Domino nodded to the mass of people below. "This place is about fun and security for those in the paranormal world."

"And how come you have a human as part of your team?" Shadow asked, genuinely curious.

Domino studied her. "The worlds mix, as you well know. Grey was here one night as a patron when there was an incident. He's ex-Forces and leapt in to help, and managed to impress me and the boss. We felt it was a good idea to have humans on our staff, too. It adds perspective, and it has worked out well. What's your story?"

"Essentially, I was looking for new work, too and fell in with these guys."

Domino looked her up and down and inhaled. "There's something different about you."

Shadow smiled. "Not really." *Time to change the subject.* "Do you know Blaze?"

Her face hardened. "Only slightly. Arrogant shit, but there's no doubt he's good at what he does. He may be from up north, but he gets around a lot."

Their conversation was interrupted by the arrival of Grey and a pretty, young, dark-haired woman dressed in black—a fitted short-sleeved top, short skirt, and high-heeled ankle boots. Her arms were tattooed, and she reminded Shadow of El because of her makeup, piercings, and jewellery.

"Ah, Jet," Maverick said, gesturing to a seat. "Come and join us. Drink?"

She grinned at him as she sat, her bangles clinking together. "I better not if I want to stay sharp. Maybe in another hour."

"Trouble?"

"Just some interesting arrivals I want to chat with."

He gestured to his visitors and introduced them. "Tell them what you remember about your conversation with Blaze the other night."

She groaned and laughed. "He was at his most charming, which meant he was also at his most smug."

"You've spoken to him before?" Gabe asked.

Her eyes ran over Gabe, assessing him. "Sure, several times. I've worked here for a few years now and he's down every few months on one job or another. Sometimes he's here with other girls, but if not, we catch up."

"Sounds like you have a pretty good relationship with him. He tells you stuff."

"Depends how much alcohol he's had and how big his ego is, but generally, yes."

"Even though you work here?"

She smiled. "He might suspect it, but it doesn't bother him."

"I gather he said his job was over the river," Gabe asked. "Did he say where?"

"He said he had to acquire something from a bunch of old men with God complexes. I asked him if he was stealing from a cathedral and he laughed his head off! Said it was more old school than that." Jet huffed. "I thought he was pissed, because it made no sense to me."

Shadow took a seat. This was sounding more promising. Harlan placed his empty glass down on the table and leaned forward. "Did he say who employed him, or where he was delivering it to?"

She shook her head. "No. Even when he's had a few drinks he never says that."

Shadow had another idea. "If he's down here regularly, he'll have friends here. Is there anyone he sees in the club?"

Jet's gaze became distant for a moment, and then she focussed quickly. "Yes. There are a couple of guys I see him talking to. Neither are shifters, and I don't know how they know him, but they seem reasonably friendly."

"You don't know them?" Maverick asked her.

She shook her head. "No—just a passing 'hi' and 'bye.' But one of them is in here tonight. I saw him about an hour ago with a girl, watching the gig."

Gabe stood immediately. "Show me."

They all headed to the window and looked down on the dance floor below. It was more crowded now, and groups congregated together in front of the bar, chatting, and that's where Jet pointed after scrutinising the club.

"That's him. He's short-ish, talking to a blonde woman in jeans at the corner of the bar. Scruffy guy."

"We need to talk to him," Gabe said, watching him. "Got a name?"

Jet smirked. "Typhoo."

That stopped Gabe in his tracks. "*What*?"

"As in Typhoo Tea?" She looked at him quizzically, waiting for the penny to drop. "Tea-leaf—thief—it's his nickname."

Grey sniggered as Gabe rolled his eyes. "Are you serious?"

"Yes—it's a Cockney thing."

"Fuck's sake," Gabe muttered, as Harlan and Shadow exchanged amused glances.

"Don't cause trouble in my club," Maverick warned them, his amber eyes starting to glow.

"No trouble. We just want to talk," Gabe said, wide-eyed with innocence. Shadow almost snorted. *As if anyone would believe that.* "Any other exits I should know about, just in case he decides to run—other than the one outside your office?"

Maverick's lips pursed, but he couldn't hide his amusement. "One behind the bar—but he can't get to that. And one next to the stage door."

Harlan shook Maverick's hand. "Thanks for your help. I appreciate it."

"Good rates at The Orphic Guild then, should I need you?" Maverick asked smoothly.

"Of course."

Gabe was already striding to the door, Shadow next to him. She threw a smile over her shoulder and found everyone watching them. "Next time."

Five

Gabe already had a plan, and he addressed Shadow first. "Call my brothers. Make sure the rear exit is covered. Position yourself close by because you'll be quickest to follow him—especially if he heads to the main exit. And keep out of sight!"

"And me?" Harlan asked, rolling his shoulders.

"With me. Let's try the nice approach first. But if he runs, let him. We don't want to make a scene here." He'd found he liked Maverick and his club, and didn't want to piss him off and get himself banned. Although, from the amusement on Maverick's face, he had a feeling they would be watching from the window above, like he was here to provide entertainment. *This was no time to fuck up.*

Shadow gave him a knowing smile, and for a second he felt a stab of desire that he quickly quenched. She was at her sexiest when she hunted, but now was not the time. He saw her reach for her phone in the quiet of the corridor, and he made his way slowly to Typhoo, aware of Harlan keeping pace. He loved these moments of pursuit when everything was so unpredictable. Gabe was pretty sure he would run, but he had every faith that they would get Typhoo outside. He groaned. Even saying that stupid name in his head felt ridiculous.

Typhoo was still at the corner of the bar, talking animatedly to a short blonde woman, and Jet was right. He was scruffy. There was clearly no dress code at Storm Moon, because although many chose to dress up, Typhoo wore old jeans, trainers, and a worn Motley Crew t-shirt. *Ugh. Bad rock.* Gabe hated him already.

Gabe approached him casually, Harlan circling to his other side, and Gabe leaned in and raised his voice. It was quieter here by the bar, but the music was still too loud for comfortable conversation. "Typhoo, I need a word."

Typhoo's head jerked up, his eyes narrowing with suspicion. "Who the fuck are you?"

"I have a question about Blaze."

Typhoo stepped away from the blonde woman, who was watching with equal suspicion and dislike, and glared at Gabe, not in the slightest bit intimidated by his size. "You didn't answer my question. Who are you?"

"You don't need my name," Gabe told him, aware of the looks they were getting. "I understand you saw Blaze this week, and I just need to know where he is."

Typhoo took his time looking Gabe up and down before settling on his face again, arms crossed. "I ain't telling you nuffin'."

Gabe leaned in, nose to nose. "It sounds like you have something to hide, Typhoo. I can assure you that it's in your best interest to tell me what you know."

"Or what?"

Good question. Typhoo clearly felt very confident in the bar surrounded by a crowd, and obviously didn't expect Gabe to do anything in such a respectable place, and he was right. "You have to leave at some point, Typhoo, and me and my friends will be watching and waiting. It's much easier if you just tell me where Blaze is." He shrugged. "That's all I want."

At the mention of friends, Typhoo looked around uneasily, finally noticing Harlan. Then, unexpectedly quickly, he threw his pint at Gabe, punched Harlan, shouldered through them in the confusion, and ran. With lightning-quick reflexes Gabe ducked, though beer still landed on him, and he saw Harlan stagger from the punch, his hand on his jaw. But Gabe was triumphant. Typhoo had done exactly as he wanted. Ignoring the stares from the people immediately around them, he turned his attention to the blonde woman, but she had vanished.

No matter. They made their way through the crowd, most of them completely unaware of the altercation, and because of his height Gabe was able to see Typhoo weaving towards the rear exit by the stage. He couldn't see Shadow, but that didn't mean she wasn't there. He phoned Nahum, telling him where to watch, and then pushed through the exit door, finding that it led to a small courtyard area and a broad set of stairs heading up to the car park.

The rear stage doors also led to the courtyard, and a few band members were lurking outside it, smoking, their attention drawn to the sound of shouts from above. Gabe and Harlan raced upwards, and as they reached ground level, saw that Nahum and Niel had pinned Typhoo to the ground, and that Shadow was standing over them.

She looked at Gabe and Harlan, hands on her hips. "He's a slippery little shit."

"I can see that." Despite Niel and Nahum's strength, Typhoo was wriggling like an eel, yelling curses, and although the area was deserted except for cars and the band's van, it still felt too public. Gabe pointed to the rear of the car park where low-branched leafy trees provided some privacy. "Take him over there."

Niel and Nahum hauled him to his feet, and because he was still yelling, Niel gave him a quick punch. Typhoo's head flew back and he fell silent. They lifted him clear off the ground and carried him to the corner.

"Did you have to punch him?" Gabe remonstrated, watching Typhoo's dazed expression and blood trickling from his nose.

"He was yelling!" Niel pointed out. "Do you want the police around here?"

"Fair point," Gabe grumbled. "I guess it will soften him up."

Harlan grimaced. "I can't see him talking. He's belligerent."

Shadow already had her blades drawn. "I'm sure he will, eventually."

Harlan looked at her, alarmed. "Nothing serious, I hope."

"That depends on him."

Nahum sniffed the air and frowned at Gabe. "You smell of beer."

Gabe glanced down at his stained t-shirt, feeling the dampness on his skin. "He threw his bloody pint at me."

"Better that than a punch!" Harlan said ruefully, rubbing his chin again. "He was quick."

"Admirable, really. Not too quick for me, though," Shadow said, tongue in cheek and earning two fingers from Harlan.

Typhoo was still being held up by Niel and Nahum, but his head sagged down. Avoiding the blood, Gabe took his chin in his hand and lifted his head. "Wakey wakey, Typhoo. I have questions."

"Fuck off," he said, groggily, and Niel sniggered.

"Tell me where to find Blaze and we'll let you go," Gabe repeated. "That's all I want—an address!"

"Who the fuck are you?" Typhoo demanded, finally focussing and glaring at all of them, blood and spit running down his chin.

"Blaze has stolen something from some very powerful men, and they have hired us to get it back." Despite the flecks of blood that threatened to hit Gabe's face, he leaned closer, deciding to layer the threat. "This could get Blaze killed. He has no idea what he's messing with, and neither do the people who have hired him. If you value your friend's life, you'll help us."

"Blaze has been involved in dodgy shit his whole life. He can take care of himself."

Gabe eased back, shaking his head. "I'm not sure he can, with this."

Typhoo swallowed, his eyes nervous, but he remained silent. Gabe nodded at Nahum. "Release one arm, let him clean himself up."

Nahum let him go, and immediately Typhoo grabbed his t-shirt and used it to wipe his face, sniffing loudly.

"We're not the police and we're not the enemy," Gabe continued. "We're his guardian angels. Tell me where to find him."

Shadow was still playing with her blades, twirling them in her hands, and Typhoo watched them uncertainly. "All right. He's been stayin' at a small hotel, but he's not there now. He left yesterday, heading to the drop off point." He shuffled nervously. "He hadn't worked for these guys before, but he said they had a lot of money and he was getting paid well."

"That's good," Gabe said, nodding encouragingly. "Did he say a name, or tell you where the drop off point was?"

"Something about Black Cronos. Another bunch of posh nobs, apparently, but he'd only met one guy."

Harlan had gone very still, his face becoming pale. "Black Cronos? Are you sure?"

"Yeah! I'm not an idiot," Typhoo complained, wiping his arm across his still bloody nose. "He kept making jokes about a God of chaos and disorder."

Harlan exhaled and stepped back a pace. "Yeah, that's him. And the drop off point?"

"Oxford. That other bloody posh nobs place."

"It's a big city, Typhoo. Narrow it down."

"I didn't ask for a bleeding address, did I?" Typhoo answered belligerently. "What am I? His mother?"

Gabe studied his shifty face, convinced he knew more than he was saying. "He's your mate, and mates talk. Where is he staying?"

At his extended silence, Shadow placed her knife against his throat, the blade tickling his skin as fey glamour rolled off her. Typhoo's eyes widened and then swam as if he'd been drugged. Shadow's voice was like honey. "He's in danger, and that means that you are too, so tell me where he's staying, or I'll gut you like a pig."

Typhoo's voice when he finally answered was barely more than a squeak. "The Griffin Inn. He's used it before and he knows the owner."

"Well done," Shadow said, stepping back. "That wasn't so hard, was it?"

Gabe nodded, satisfied. "That's all we need. Let him go." Once free, Typhoo ran across the car park, disappearing into the darkness along the edge of the road as Gabe said, "He'll phone Blaze as soon as he gets a chance, so that means we need to go to Oxford tonight." He turned to find the others watching him expectantly. Well, all except for Harlan, who looked preoccupied. Gabe quickly came to a decision. "I'll go to Oxford with Shadow tonight, but you three stay here. Nahum and Niel, I want you to keep watching the order. I want to know what members are in the Inner Temple—or whatever the hell they call themselves."

Nahum frowned. "That's going to be very hard. Is it worth it?"

"Yes! Someone is leaking information out of the inner circle, and I want to know who! Even if Caldwell Fleet is in denial about it."

"But," Niel reminded him, "it could be that Madame Charbonneau found out who stole the astrolabe. She could be behind it."

"She might," Gabe acknowledged, "but I want to cover all bases. While our primary job is to find the astrolabe, the more we know, the better. I don't want to find us on the end of a double-cross. In fact, we should be careful about what we share of our investigation to Caldwell, because we don't know who he's telling."

"Good suggestion," Shadow agreed.

"Who's looking into the Madame?" Niel asked.

"Barak, which leaves Harlan free to follow up on the origins of The Midnight Sun."

"And Black Cronos?" Nahum asked.

"I'll do that, too," Harlan said, finally seeming to focus. "I know that name and I can't think of why, so leave it with me. Unless, of course, you happen to come across something."

Gabe headed towards his SUV, pulling his keys from his pocket, and the others followed. "If we find the astrolabe tonight, we'll be back in Cornwall tomorrow."

"Sure," Shadow said, snorting with laughter, "and Herne wears tinsel at Yule."

Six

S hadow looked out of the window as they drove along the main road into Oxford, the landscape silent around them. She was already excited to be visiting a new city.

It was close to two in the morning. As soon as they had dropped the others off, she and Gabe had grabbed their bags and driven straight here, the roads quiet at this hour, and they had made good time. It was rare for them to spend so many hours alone, and it had felt strange at first, both uncomfortably aware of each other. Gabe radiated strength, and she was acutely aware of every move he made. She couldn't help but notice his strong hands gripping the wheel, and she thought of the way they had felt on her skin in the bathroom in Angel's Rest, and the way his corded muscles had felt beneath her fingers. Banishing those thoughts, she had fallen into safe talk about the case, and then she had looked up Oxford, telling him that it was an old city that housed one of the oldest universities in the world—a suitable place for a meeting to pass on a mysteriously occult object.

"What do you think will be at the place where the order's origins lie?" she asked him.

"Probably a bunch of old stones and nothing else."

"You think they're chasing ghosts?"

He shook his head. "I don't know. The cynic in me says yes, but the fact that the astrolabe has now been stolen twice in recent months mean there has to be more to this. Maybe something alchemical, knowing what these guys are like."

Personally, Shadow hoped it would be old treasure or arcane weapons, because that would be more interesting than old documents and buildings, but she had to admit that Gabe's alchemical suggestion was the more likely assumption.

They passed through the leafy outskirts of the city, and Gabe asked, "How far now?"

"A bit further along yet, in the centre," she instructed, checking the directions on her phone. "Just keep going on this road. I must admit, I didn't expect we'd be leaving London so soon."

"Or me, if I'm honest, but an early lead is a bonus." Gabe glanced at her, the streetlights illuminating half of his face. "You don't think this will be over tonight though, do you?"

"No. This has the feel of something dark and twisty, and I think tonight will just add to that."

"It will be good if you can pick up Blaze's magic. We might be able to track his movements from his hotel."

"I think I'll have trouble. Besides, he might have already left," she reminded him. "He was only coming to drop off the astrolabe."

He grunted. "He seems like a party person. I reckon he'd stick around to socialise on a Saturday night."

"True," Shadow answered thoughtfully. "We always liked to celebrate a win."

"We?" he asked, shooting her a quizzical glance.

"My team back in the Otherworld. Every successful job was celebrated, as soon as we'd split the money."

"And how many were there of you?"

"Four of us. Me, Bloodmoon, who's another fey, Cheloc, a satyr, and Rowan, an Aerikeen."

"What's one of those?"

"A bird-shifter." It was odd talking about her old team; it gave her a pang of homesickness, and she hoped that they were all okay. She'd mentioned them before, but no one had asked for details then. It was almost like an unspoken pact that they didn't discuss the old days, because she really didn't ask the Nephilim too many questions about the past, either. But here, the dark, quiet confines of the car invited confidences. "He was handy for break-ins."

Gabe smirked. "Of course. And the satyr?"

"A good fighter, utterly loyal, with the best connections in the business. And he loved gambling—was good at it, too."

"And Bloodmoon?"

She smiled at the memory of him. "Charming, handsome, excellent swordsman, great horseman, and very funny."

"More than a friend?"

"No. Just a very good one. Although, he was an outrageous flirt." She stared through the windscreen, the Oxford streets suddenly replaced with memories of her team. "I wonder what they're doing now. I wonder if they miss me."

"Of course they do, Little Miss Fey," Gabe teased. "In fact, I wonder if they get anything done at all without you."

"Well, that's true," she said breezily, shooting him a grateful glance. Sometimes Gabe was unexpectedly kind. *No, she shouldn't think 'unexpected'—he was always kind.* It was an admirable quality. She focussed on the present, deciding now was not the time to ask Gabe about his wife. She wanted a whiskey in hand before broaching that topic, and needed him to be more relaxed than he was now. She brought the conversation back to Blaze and checked her phone again. "Take the next left," she instructed.

He turned onto a road leading into the city centre, where it was much livelier. Young people exited nightclubs and pubs, the sounds of laughter and shouting filling the air.

"This place is busier than I expected," she said, watching a group stumble down the street, obviously drunk.

"It's a city, and it's full of students—and students like drinking."

She checked the GPS. "Take the second right, and the hotel should be on the left."

In another couple of minutes, Gabe passed an elegant, eighteenth century building with The Griffin Inn displayed on a sign swinging above its entrance. He cruised down the street, turned, and then found a spot to park.

After studying the hotel, Gabe suggested, "We should check in here. It looks good. And I think there's a car park around the back."

Shadow nodded. "Well, most hotels have around the clock reception, so we should be okay. And it is convenient."

"Plus, it gives us a good reason to nose around."

"It looks pricey, though. I hope Harlan doesn't object."

"It's the order who are paying, and they want their astrolabe back." He gave her a lazy smile, and Shadow's stomach flipped. "Besides, we're worth it."

"I am, you mean," she said flippantly, and gave him her cheesiest grin as he started to scowl. She scooted out of the seat and grabbed her bag from the boot. "Check us in then, oh great leader."

"You always like to push it, don't you?" he grumbled, grabbing his own bag and following her.

When they entered the hotel, they found a couple of staff seated behind the counter at the rear of the lobby. While Gabe went to check them in, Shadow strolled around, noting that the interior of the building was all cream wooden panelling, polished floors, and tasteful furniture, and Shadow could already feel the power of wealth creeping up on her. It was a good feeling. She liked money. It meant you could stay in nice places and eat good food. And she liked that money meant she didn't need to worry about the tedious stuff...like bills.

What surprised her was that Blaze was staying here. His friend, Typhoo, didn't look that well-groomed, but she assumed that Blaze's acquaintances must be broad. So far, though, she could not detect any shifter magic, which was frustrating.

Gabe joined her. "Anything?"

"Not yet."

"Well, I've got us two rooms on the third floor, so let's drop our bags off and do some snooping. Of course," he said, as they entered the lift, "he might have already left, if Typhoo got hold of him."

"Maybe Typhoo hasn't got his number. I wouldn't give it out if he was just my casual friend who I bumped into in a club occasionally."

Gabe nodded. "Good point. You sure you're not too tired to search tonight?"

"Oh, no. Night hunts are the best."

Gabe gave her a slow smile as they exited the lift and walked to their rooms. Unnervingly, Gabe's room was right next to hers, and she could hear him moving around as she dumped her bag and used the bathroom. This *thing* between them hadn't abated since they'd returned from Angel's Rest, although they both ignored whatever it was. It was easier when they were at home with the others around them, but there was something about staying somewhere else that just stirred up her blood—and his, too. She could tell. He had that glint in his eye again.

She took a deep breath in and out, cursing her hormones, and then went to meet him in the corridor as arranged. "Okay, where to first?"

"Let's prowl the corridors, starting with this one."

They found nothing on their own floor, or the second, but on the first floor Shadow paused as she detected the faint swirl of shifter magic. She walked along the dimly lit corridors slowly, pausing outside each room, until she reached the end. "I think he's on this floor, but I can't tell which room. And I don't know if the magic is fresh or not, either."

"So, he's either in bed or out somewhere, and without barging into every room, there's no way to know." Gabe looked pleased anyway. "But at least we have *something*. I noticed there's a bar and restaurant at the back on the ground floor, but it's closed now, so he definitely won't be there."

"That's a shame," she said, realising she was hungry and thirsty. "I could do with a drink."

Gabe steered her towards the stairs. "Let's head out and find a bar, then. Even at this hour, I'm sure we'll find something."

Since their arrival, the centre of town had quieted again, and Shadow feared they'd be too late to find anything open until Gabe searched on his phone, finally leading them down a narrow side street to a place called Plush Oxford.

"This is the only place open now. Cocktails, beer, wine, and bar food. This work for you?"

They were standing in front of another fine, eighteenth century building where a set of steps led down to a door.

"It's set under the brick arches of the medieval city." He grinned at her. "And it's a gay bar, but it doesn't bother me. They're all-inclusive."

"As long as they have food, I don't care either," Shadow said, following him down the stairs.

Once they'd paid their way inside, they heard the loud thud of music, and Shadow found they were in a warren of corridors with rooms set on either side, as well as a large dance floor still heaving with people. They managed to find a table in the bar under the stone arches that formed the roof, and Shadow eyed the eclectic groups of people around her while Gabe brought cocktails.

"Herne's horns," she said when he returned with margaritas. "I love this place!"

"Two clubs in one night," he said, laughing. "I thought my clubbing days were behind me."

"You went clubbing in ancient Mesopotamia?"

"Not quite like this. But obviously there were late night bars, music, revelry, drinking, dancing—"

"And food?" she broke in hopefully.

"Chips are on the way—lots of them."

She chinked his glass. "Thank you. If Blaze is still in Oxford and not in bed, then there's a good chance he's here. As soon as we've eaten, I'll scout the place, and see if I can feel him."

"And we have a sketchy description of him," Gabe reminded her.

After they had eaten their food and started on the next cocktail—she'd decided they were too good for just one—she detected shifter magic. "He's here," she said softly, scanning the room as casually as she could. Not that it was really an issue. Everyone was so busy letting loose, they weren't really watching their table.

In seconds she saw him leaning across the bar as he ordered a drink, exactly as Domino had described him. He was tall and slim, his shoulder-length brown hair curling slightly on his shoulders. It was warm in the club, and he only wore a t-shirt with his jeans, revealing a Celtic-style tattoo on his forearm, but a messenger bag was slung over his shoulder, and it looked heavy.

"Far end of the bar, with a bulky bag."

"I see him," Gabe said, trying to hide his excitement. "I think he's brought it in with him."

"And he's buying two drinks, too," Shadow noted. "Is he handing it off in here? There must be better places!" she said, incredulous. She was always a fan of secluded places for dodgy exchanges herself, but there was no accounting for taste.

"Maybe he's killing time until the meet up."

"I'll follow him back to his seat," Shadow suggested, "on the pre-text of heading to the ladies."

As soon as Blaze left the room, she followed him at a distance, watching him weave through the crowd before finally ducking into a dark side room, where he sat next to a young woman with long, dark hair. Unfortunately, her back was to the door and Shadow couldn't see her face, but he seemed to settle in, draping his arm around her shoulder, and she returned to Gabe.

"He's with a woman, but I don't think she's the one. They're too intimate."

"We need to watch them. We're too far away here." Gabe picked up his drink and stood, grabbing her hand. "Time to play."

"What are you doing?" she asked, glancing at his hand and then staring at him pointedly.

"We're going to find a nice seat and get cosy."

"We're going to do *what*?"

"This is no time to argue. Just remember, I'm irresistible, and you can't keep your eyes off me. Or your hands."

He looked insufferably amused with himself and she narrowed her eyes at him, his heat already radiating up her arm.

"You have got to be kidding me!"

"If you don't move right now, I'm going to kiss you."

"I'll stab you first."

He leaned in closer, his head bending and his lips closing in on hers. Barely thinking about what she was doing, she turned and dragged him with her, almost feeling his amusement. *Bastard.*

She pulled him along the corridor. The club was beginning to empty, but those who were still there were glassy-eyed and raucous, and several couples were clasped in close embraces. Feeling hot at the thought of getting close to Gabe, she pulled him into the low-lit room and onto the squashy leather sofa just inside the door. It gave them a good view of Blaze, who was busy flirting with the unknown woman.

Gabe pinned her in the corner of the sofa, his arm already across the back of the seat and curling protectively around her shoulders, pulling her to him. His eyes drifted over her lips.

"Well, this is nice."

The heat he radiated was almost overwhelming, and it took all of her willpower not to sink into his arms. Unwillingly she stared at his lips, noting how full they were, and thought how very good they'd probably taste. Keeping a smile pasted to her face, she said, "I'm glad you think this is funny, when the reality is that I'm in the middle of my very own hash-tag Me Too moment."

His smile spread as he put his lips next to her ear, his warm breath making her giddy. "Really? Because I can hear your heart pounding right now, and I don't think it's with fear."

He planted feather-light kisses along her neck as her eyes closed, her breathing becoming shallow. *Herne's horns.* That felt way better than she'd imagined, and she'd imagined it plenty.

She forced her eyes open. "You really should stop that."

"Then say it like you mean it," he murmured through his kisses that were now melting her insides. His hand slipped into her hair as he stroked the base of her neck.

"I'm trying to focus on Blaze," she hissed, watching him kiss the mystery woman across the room.

"Trying? So I'm putting you off, then? That's good to know."

The one good thing she had to admit was that no one was taking the slightest bit of notice of them—least of all, Blaze. The woman was almost straddling him now, and Shadow closed her own eyes again, swimming in the heady scent of Gabe. He smelt of a peppery spice, warm and inviting.

Focus, she chastised herself. When she next opened her eyes, the woman was pulling away from Blaze, and he looked like Shadow felt—drugged. She couldn't see his face, but he seemed to loll against the back of the sofa. *Something was wrong.* She could feel it. And now that she was closer to them, the woman felt all wrong, too.

"What's going on?" Gabe mumbled, lifting his head to look at her. His back was to Blaze, but he didn't look around. "You've become tense."

The woman eased back slowly, her hand reaching towards the messenger bag that was wedged behind Blaze. "Shit. I think she's the one. And she's done something to Blaze."

As Shadow spoke, the woman turned, giving Shadow the briefest glimpse of black eyes—flat and far from human—and as she swung around even more, Shadow grabbed Gabe's head, her hands in his thick hair, and pulled him in for a long kiss. He leaned against her, pinning her to the back of the sofa, his lips exploring her own. For a second, she almost forgot what was happening, but then she felt the woman walk past. Waiting for a beat, she then pushed Gabe away.

Blaze was insensible on the sofa. In fact, from here he looked dead. Shadow again moved Gabe off her and pulled him out of the room. "Fuck it. She's gone!"

"She can't have gone far," he said, following her down the corridor.

They spotted the woman heading through the exit and hurried after her, emerging onto the street where a few people loitered by the entrance. They hurried to the deserted entrance of the lane, the woman already ahead on the main road. Gabe began pulling his t-shirt off, and he thrust it at her, his wings expanding.

"I'll follow from above—and be careful."

Shadow glanced back anxiously at the club entrance, but they were out of view for now. "But what's the plan? Are we aiming to just take it from her—presuming the astrolabe is in the bag—or find out where she's taking it?"

"Part of me wants to know who's behind this, but that's not really our job," he said, clearly anxious to get moving. "Let's wait until she's somewhere quiet, and just take it."

She grabbed his arm. "I don't know what she is, but she's *not* human."

He nodded and then soared upwards, leaving Shadow to follow on foot.

Seven

Harlan woke in the middle of the night after a poor sleep that had been disturbed by dreams of shifters and the information they had found out from Typhoo.

He lay on his back, staring up at the ceiling and thinking about what Black Cronos was. He had brooded all the way to his flat, sitting in the back of Gabe's SUV in the dark, watching the lights of London flow past like a river. Gabe and the others had asked him a few questions, but he'd batted them off, telling them he needed to think. He had heard of Black Cronos years and years ago, but the mention was more of a rumour than anything substantial, something mysterious and ephemeral. However, the name was also so unusual it had stuck with him. He wondered if Olivia knew anything, or Mason. Or even JD might, but for obvious reasons he didn't want to involve either of the latter.

Harlan's mind was too busy to go back to sleep, so he rolled out of bed and headed to the kitchen to make coffee, and then took it to his small office and library. A few months before, he had found a collection of documents and notes in the guild's library, and had been so intrigued with them that he made copies for his own reference. It was these he wanted to read now. The notes had been amassed by the collectors who had gone before him. There was intelligence on rival organisations, such as The Order of Lilith and others like it. It included members both past and present, structure, headquarters, and whatever was known about them. He was sure he'd read the name in these. They now stored the files on the computer too, but he liked to handle the old, paper ones. It was as if they stored impressions in the pages that a computer failed to impart.

After the job at Angel's Rest, Harlan had added his own notes to the file for The Order of Lilith, updating their address and the members who had died. He hadn't seen Nicoli since. After the theft of the astrolabe he'd wondered if Nicoli was behind this problem, but it hadn't seemed the right fit for him somehow, and he was glad his gut feeling had been proven right. He paused, remembering Jensen's broken body in the Chamber of Air, and the fact that Mia's body had been lost forever, and shuddered. The Temple of the Trinity had not been what he expected, and he hoped this particular investigation wasn't going to play out the same way.

He checked his watch as he settled in his chair. Gabe and Shadow would be in Oxford now, and he wondered if they were still up and whether they'd had any success. It was better that they followed their lead quickly, which meant he needed to find answers quickly, too. He opened the file, and settled in to read.

⚬

Gabe hovered high over the lane, watching the mysterious woman move swiftly through the centre of town.

The streets were empty now, but it didn't make her easier to keep track of. She was like Shadow; she blended into the darkness, and even under streetlights seemed to look insubstantial. He couldn't even see Shadow now, but he presumed she was maintaining a safe distance in her own pursuit.

Shadow said she wasn't human, so what did that make her? Another shifter, or something else? And how had she killed Blaze? One swift look was all it took to see that he was dead. Soon enough, someone would find him as the club closed, and then all Hell would break loose.

They should have stopped it. But then again, how? They couldn't make a scene in the club; that would have got them into all sorts of trouble. And why couldn't he tell there was something different about her? Probably because he was enjoying himself too much with Shadow. Even now, he could feel Shadow's soft skin. He was an utter fool.

Instead of getting lost in those thoughts, he concentrated on the scene below. The colleges of Oxford jostled around shops and lanes, their old buildings imparting a weight of ages. There were so many churches, squares, and cloistered grounds it was bewildering. The woman turned into the leafy garden of a church, and he realised this was their chance. He soared downwards, dropping on her from above, and pinned her to the ground, facedown, the bag squashed beneath them.

The woman was slender but strong, and she twisted beneath him as she tried to throw him off, but he lay across her and attempted to pull the bag out from under her. She bucked, unbalancing him, and just as he wondered where Shadow was, she arrived.

"Grab the bag," he said, still restraining the struggling woman.

But as Shadow leaned in, the woman turned and looked Gabe full in the face. He gasped, almost releasing her in shock. The woman's eyes were utterly black, and as she stared into his, he felt as if she was staring into his soul, feeling a tug deep within him.

Shocked and disorientated, he lost his grip and she wriggled free, but Shadow didn't hesitate. She punched her, and as the woman fell back, Shadow grabbed the bag, wrenching it from her grasp. She threw it over her shoulder, and pulling her two knives out, circled the woman.

The thief dropped and rolled, kicking at Shadow. She dodged her easily, and Gabe lunged at the woman. But she was like a wraith, and again she stared at him, exerting her strange power, and he felt his breath catch in his chest.

The sound of sirens broke up their fight, and police cars streamed past, their blue and red lights playing across the gravestones. All of them dropped to the ground in an effort to stay hidden, and by the time Shadow and Gabe stood again, the thief had vanished.

Shadow whirled around. "Where has she gone?"

Gabe scanned the area, but there was no sign of her. "I have no idea, and I daren't fly again. Did she hurt you?"

"No, and I still have the bag." She peered inside it and grinned. "And the astrolabe."

"Good." He retrieved his t-shirt and put it on again. "We need to get off the streets. They must have found Blaze, and strolling around at this hour won't look good."

"But the woman?"

"Let her go. We have what we came for."

Shadow looked disappointed. "So it's over already?"

He shook his head. "I don't think we should drop this just yet. I want to know more about this Dark Star, and why someone is prepared to kill for it. Don't you?"

She lifted her chin, her eyes firing with excitement. "Absolutely."

Harlan rubbed his hand across his face and muttered to himself. "Damn it!"

He was still sitting in his library, and the previous hour had flown by. He'd found the references to Black Cronos, and admittedly although they didn't tell him much, they said enough to know the group needed to worry.

The first record that mentioned Black Cronos was made in 1894 by Rosamund Fairchild, a collector for The Orphic Guild's Rome branch. She was outmanoeuvred for an artefact called the Handmaid's Chalice, a suitably intriguing object that promised that whoever drank from it could bewitch anyone they chose. It was also intriguing that a woman was a prominent collector at that time. Harlan imagined she must have had independent wealth and enough status to allow her to travel where she chose. Maybe she was married to an enlightened man, or perhaps she was a rich widow. Whatever her background, it seemed she spoke fluent Italian and had helped set up the branch.

Rosamund had recorded the encounter in a flowing script, noting that she had been followed for weeks by a shadowy figure who she struggled to lose. She had finally found the chalice in an old palace in Florence, after searching for it for months for an unnamed client, and within days it had been stolen from a secure location and her pursuer vanished. During that time the Rome branch's director had received a note from Black Cronos, telling them to stop their search or there would be consequences. They hadn't, and other than being trailed, Rosamund had been unharmed. Harlan rolled his eyes at the suitably Machiavellian threats. Rosamund went on to say that they had never found out anything else about them.

Then during the chaos of the First World War there had been another mention of Black Cronos in London, the entry made by another collector named Peter Shelley. The guild had been threatened, again by letter, to stop searching for a collection of papers. Peter had ignored it and was then attacked one night and badly beaten, but he couldn't identify his attacker, and he never found the papers. And then the same thing happened again just before the Second World War, a threat this time to stop searching for an old diary.

Three letters, all sent to the director. That was weird. Had The Orphic Guild sufficiently threatened them to warrant such a warning? And why bother to warn at all?

Harlan flicked through the few remaining documents, pleased to see the letters themselves had been kept. Initially, he was disappointed. There were no clues as to who had written them, obviously, revealing no name other than Black Cronos, and they certainly gave no indication of where the organisation was based. *Or maybe it was an individual? Possibly even a family affair?* But then laying them out side by side, Harlan had a shock. The handwriting was identical. He blinked as he spread them out. Three letters, sent between 1894 and 1937. Not too long of a period, so potentially the same person would have been alive then and working for the organisation the entire time.

Damn it. He needed to see the original documents, and that meant going to the guild, but that would have to wait until later. He was exhausted and needed more sleep. Before retiring again, his phone rang, startling him in the silence of his flat. "Gabe. Is everything okay?"

"We have the astrolabe, but it wasn't secured without difficulties," he said, updating Harlan on their encounter. "The thief was not entirely human, but I don't know what exactly she was."

"She killed Blaze?" Harlan asked, shocked. "With a kiss?"

"Looked that way." Gabe sounded rattled, and that was unusual. "I'll explain more tomorrow. But, I wanted you to know that we have it. We'll get some sleep and return to London later today. I also want you to know that we are going to continue to look into this, even though the job is over."

"Excellent, I think we should, too." Harlan stared at the papers in front of him, deciding to wait to tell Gabe what he had found out. "I need to head to the guild later this morning. What if I catch up with you this afternoon at Chadwick House? Say, three o'clock?"

"Perfect," he said, ending the call.

Harlan couldn't believe it. *Blaze was dead.* As awful as that was, it also made things far more complicated. They had fulfilled their obligations to Caldwell, but like Gabe, Harlan wanted to know more about Black Cronos and this strange woman. If they were prepared to kill Blaze, the likelihood was they would try to get the astrolabe again. They could hand over the Dark Star and be out of it, but he had the feeling all of their lives could be at risk—including the members of the order—and that didn't sit easy on his conscience.

The one person who may know more about all of this was JD, and he was also the one person Harlan did not want to speak to. He gazed out of the window, not really seeing the faint approach of dawn as he debated what to do. He'd sleep on it, and then make a decision.

———◆◇◆———

Barak stared at the computer screen, his eyes aching. This was the first time since Gabe had asked that he'd had a chance to examine the inventory, but Sundays were generally quieter at the warehouse in Harecombe, so he took advantage of it.

It was mid-morning, and he was the only Nephilim here today. He'd told his brothers to have the day off, feeling he'd get more done alone. The security team was covering the gate and perimeter, and there was only a skeleton crew in today, so he was determined to find the information he needed.

He'd filtered the shipments by port and date, and found one large shipment on the date in question, but it was composed of lots of companies, as well as individuals. He ran down the list, knowing many of the companies now and able to dismiss some easily. He was focussing more on individuals, but without a name to go on, he was looking for final addresses.

He groaned. He'd thought this would be easy, but it was turning out to be tedious and he blinked, his eyes dry. He absently sipped his coffee as he scrolled, almost spilling it in shock when he saw The Order of the Midnight Sun listed as an address. He clicked on the details of the package. All shipped goods should be itemised, and this one was no different. Several objects were listed, but not one of them was an astrolabe, and they all had proof of purchase. He frowned. *That couldn't be right.* He shook his head, amused. They must have covered their tracks, hiding it within the other items—most likely the nineteenth century statue that was listed and was of no significant value. On arrival in port, all goods had to clear customs, and most of the time it was a formality. Drugs or guns were the most commonly smuggled items, but hidden antiquities were also big business. Barak knew that Caspian ran a legitimate business, but that he also had occult customers. Not surprising, considering he was a witch. But it was unlikely Caspian or any other member of his family would know the details of particular shipments.

Barak scrolled down the page, looking to see who had sent it, and grinned in triumph. Aubrey Cavendish. *Let's hope it isn't an alias,* he mused. Just to be sure, he checked the dates on either side, and once satisfied that no other shipments had been made to the order, he checked the arrival date, finding it had arrived two days later in the large port of Falmouth. It had been collected by hand from their office, and signed for by the same person, an ornate, fanciful signature.

He leaned back in his chair, thoughtful. Cavendish was taking no chances. Normally, items like this would be posted by courier once they had arrived. He phoned Gabe, passing on the information, and frowned when Gabe updated him on their overnight activities. "It's over, then?"

"No, because this bothers me, and I can't just drop it," Gabe told him. "Will you do me another favour, please?"

"Sure."

"See if you can find out what The Order of the Midnight Sun used to be called—pre-fifteenth century—and see if you can find out anything about a Madame Raphael Charbonneau. Harlan will do some research too, but he's focussing on Black Cronos for now."

"You think this astrolabe is more significant than we've been led to believe?"

"Maybe even more than the order suspects. But at least there aren't any angels involved."

Once the call ended, Barak stared at the screen, thinking about angels and their previous assignment, The Book of Raziel. Shadow had buried it under rock and water, and he wondered if that would be enough. The old God had once been so incensed at its loss that he plucked it from the ocean, so it being buried beneath an avalanche of rock was no guarantee it wouldn't be found again. And Raziel also had an obsession with the book—enough to build an entire temple to it.

Over the last few weeks, they'd all wondered if the search for The Temple of the Seeker was really over. *Did Raziel know his book had been found and his temple destroyed? And if he didn't, why not?* He'd spent a lot of time making it, laying clues, sending innocent men insane with the burden of his demands. Surely he wasn't about to just let it go. Maybe the war between the angels had raged long after their deaths, and had long-lasting consequences. Niel's encounter with Chassan, one of the angels of air, had been alarming, too. He *knew* the Nephilim were back. *Didn't it matter? Did no one care?* It seemed they had all been watching over their shoulders, waiting for a summons or a visitation that they desperately hoped would not come, because the consequences could be disastrous.

Barak rather liked this life, although he was itching to leave the security job, as good as Caspian had been to them. He wanted to be with the others, searching for occult goods and exploring their new world. He shrugged it off, though. Gabe had given him a job to do, so he should get on with it.

He had just started a basic search for information on the order when he heard the door below bang open and then footsteps on the stairs leading to the offices. He went to the inner office window, surprised to see Estelle, and he headed to the door to speak to her.

"Hey, Estelle. What are you doing here on a Sunday?"

"Trying to find peace and quiet, and failing," she said, glaring at him.

He ignored her jibe as she walked past him to the office that was normally occupied by Dean Ellis, the warehouse manager. She looked as good and as pissed off as usual, except that she was dressed casually today. She was wearing a fitted t-shirt and yoga pants that hugged every curve, and her hair was caught up in a loose knot, revealing the dip of her shoulder and the nape of her neck, and he swallowed. *Herne's horns, she looked good.* Barak should have found her aggressive manner off-putting, but he didn't. Beneath that tough-bitch exterior, he detected vulnerability. And then as she slammed the door behind her, he winced. *Maybe he was delusional. Or maybe it was the thought of her soft skin and long hair falling over him that gave him such idiotic thoughts.*

He leaned on the door frame, contemplating his actions. Ever since the beginning of the week she'd been meaner than usual, and somehow, more brittle, too. It had coincided with Caspian's attack by spirits, and he wondered if that had shaken her, or if it was just a coincidence. Although Caspian had been recuperating with Reuben, she had spent more time here than at her main office—and Dean was complaining. Taking his life in his hands, Barak headed to the office, knocked, and opened the door.

"What's going on, Estelle?"

She was busy arranging her phone and bag and switching on the computer, and she glanced up at him, narrowing her eyes. "Nothing. Just paperwork and a couple of shipments I want to check. I won't be here next week."

"Why not?"

She leaned her elbows on the table and met his eyes. "What business is it of yours?"

"Because something is wrong. You're always a miserable cow, but this week you're even worse. What's happened?"

Her hands clenched and he felt her magic build as she spat, "I beg your pardon! Did you just call me a miserable cow?"

Barak knew he shouldn't provoke a powerful witch, but actually, he realised, that's exactly what he wanted to do. He had a reasonable working relationship with her normally, and she had a good sense of humour when she relaxed. But most of the time, she was uptight. Constrained. Sad.

"You are and you know you are, and that worries me, Estelle." He opened his arms wide, knowing, if he was honest, that it displayed his huge, muscled chest to her often-admiring eyes. "You are rich and powerful in the business world, a skilled witch, an intelligent, beautiful woman with impeccable taste, and yet you are so fucking miserable that I just don't get it!" She sat in stunned silence, looking at him as he advanced into the room. "It's pretty clear to me that you hate your life, which begs the question—why don't you change it? You could do anything!"

Estelle's mouth trembled, her face went white, and her eyes filled with tears for the briefest moment before she blinked them away. "How dare you. Get out!"

He refused to stop or break eye contact with her. "Why are you lying to yourself? What does it achieve? If I've learnt anything in my life, it's that you have to do what makes you happy, or life is long and hard. And what's the point of that?" Her folded arms trembled across her chest, and he knew his time was limited. "I wondered if you were worried about Caspian, but you hate him, too. What a dysfunctional mess your family is—and that's saying something, considering what my family dynamics were like."

Without warning, she struck him with a bolt of energy, blasting him out of the door and over the railing that edged the walkway above the warehouse. Instinctively, he flexed his wings and they shot out from his shoulders, shredding his t-shirt, and he hovered in the air, cursing himself for not preparing for this, but mostly admiring her speed and power.

Estelle was already running to the door, her hands raised, looking as if she was about to hit him again, and then she stalled as the realisation of what she'd done spread across her face. He glanced below him, relieved to see no one was there. With luck, the staff were all outside.

Barak flew back to the walkway, landed softly in front of her, and then folded his wings behind him. "Feel better now? You're lucky I'm Nephilim, or you could have killed me."

She glared at him. "You shouldn't have provoked me, then. You know what I am."

"And you should have better control over yourself. Working with you is like working with a lit stick of dynamite." Barak was suddenly furious with himself. His provocation had risked exposing both of them, and for what purpose? *To get a rise out of Estelle? He'd done that, but what the hell had that achieved?* He turned his back on her, marching into his office and grabbing a spare t-shirt from the cupboard in the corner where they kept some company stock. He pulled it on, and when he turned around, she was standing in the doorway, watching him.

"I've never seen your wings before," she said, her dark eyes openly curious.

"Just ask, in future." He glanced at the security screens showing activity around the warehouse, and saw the handful of staff clustered outside smoking or drinking coffee, and he sighed. *They'd got away with their little tiff.* He sat in front of the computer, pulling up the search screen again, and then stared at her. "You're right. I shouldn't have provoked you, but sometimes you're exasperating. And I meant it. No one should be as sad and angry as you all the time. But I won't bother you again." He looked back at the screen, ignoring Estelle, and trying to clear his head.

Nevertheless, she was still in the doorway, her expression contrite. "I'm sorry, Barak. I lashed out, stupidly. It's just the second time this week that I've been on the receiving end of verbal abuse, and I was over it. Did I hurt you?"

"Does it look like it?" he asked. "You've just ruined a perfectly good t-shirt, that's all." Then he frowned. "And it wasn't abuse. Well, it wasn't meant to be."

"I can assure you that it was the first time." Barak was itching to ask what had happened, but he wouldn't push again. She continued, "What are you doing?"

"If I told you I was doing research for Gabe rather than working, would it earn me another blast in the chest?"

"No. What kind of research?"

"He's working a case with Harlan, for The Order of the Midnight Sun, and he needs some more background on them."

She walked into the office, perching on one of the chairs. "Why have they hired you?"

"Someone stole an astrolabe from them, a very important one, apparently. It was shipped through here originally, from France." His lips twitched. "They stole it from some French woman."

Estelle laughed, finally relaxing. "Karma, then."

"Maybe. But Gabe and Shadow stole it back again last night."

"That quick? Impressive. Go on," she said, suitably intrigued. "Tell me more."

He filled her in on the background and what they'd found so far. "Do you know much about the order?"

"Nope. But," she picked up her chair and put it next to him, hustling him along, "I'll help you look."

She batted his hand off the mouse and he wrested back again, amused. "I thought you had work to do?"

"This sounds far more interesting. Or don't you want my help?" Her eyes held his with a clear challenge.

"Far be it for me to question your wishes," he said, starting the search again, and thinking what an interesting few hours this was proving to be.

Eight

Shadow sipped her coffee, half slumped over on a table in the hotel's dining room, watching Gabe eat a late, large breakfast.

They had made it before the breakfast buffet closed, both trying to get as much sleep as they could before they travelled back to London. Even so, she was gritty-eyed. She and Gabe had ended up sleeping in the same room, but there were no romantic entanglements, despite the fact that she remembered every second of his lips on hers. It was purely for security.

Gabe had taken first watch while she grabbed a couple of hours of sleep, and then she took the second, wary of any movement along the corridor or on the street outside. But they were undisturbed, which was a relief. They had travelled back to the hotel quickly after their encounter with the thief, cautious of being followed, but no doubt the thief was as keen to keep off the streets as they were.

Before going to bed, she and Gabe had examined the astrolabe, curious as to what had caused so much excitement. But beautiful though it was, it gave away nothing of the secrets it might reveal. Now it sat on the table between them, wrapped in a bag.

"Have you phoned Caldwell yet?" she asked Gabe.

"No," he mumbled through a mouthful of food. "I'll do it when we get to London."

"You don't want to give it back, do you?"

"No, but I will." He put his knife and fork down, his breakfast finished, and picked up his cup. "I just want a few more answers first."

"We're thieves. It's no business of ours what he does with it, or what's there. That's the first rule of business. We fulfil our contract and move on."

Gabe frowned. "But a few hours ago, you said you didn't want to drop it and were enthusiastic to know more. What's changed?"

"Sleep and the cold light of day. Don't get me wrong—I'm curious. But if we overly involve ourselves in our jobs, we'll get caught up in crap that has nothing to do with us."

His expression softened. "I know that. But this is our business to shape as we choose. I will give the astrolabe back, but I just want to do a bit more digging."

"It's like you're marshalling an army. You've got half the Nephilim on this."

"We're not quite an army. Besides, I used to be good at it."

"I'm more worried about the woman. What was she?"

Gabe rubbed his chest. "I felt her here, like those weird eyes were trying to pull my very being out. Did you?"

"I felt something, but she wasn't really staring at me like she was you. When she stood up after she killed Blaze, I glimpsed them then and they looked soulless." She shuddered. "I'm not easily spooked, but I had the feeling that if she saw me watching her last night, all would be lost." She laughed. "Sounds dramatic, right?"

"So you kissed me."

This was the first time they had spoken about that, and she held his gaze. "Yes. You started it, and it was a ruse."

"You threw yourself into it very convincingly."

"So did you, Mr I-think-I'll-smother-your-neck-with-kisses."

His slow, sexy smile spread across his face, and once again she could feel those kisses on her neck. *Maybe this is why they hadn't mentioned it in the bedroom. The hotel restaurant was safe ground.* "Do you want me to promise not to do it again?"

That was the last thing she wanted, but she said, "Yes, I think that's an excellent idea."

Gabe continued to smirk. "Sorry, I can't. Who knows when we may need it as cover?"

"True," she acknowledged, deciding to tease him. "And I may have to do the same thing with any of your brothers, too. Or even Harlan. Who knows what weird situations we might get into?"

Shadow watched his expression tighten, her own smirk hidden behind her drink. And then he smirked, too. "You're right. I may have to do the same with Olivia. It's a useful tactic."

She couldn't help but grin. "Excellent. That's that sorted. So now what?" She lowered her cup and leaned forwards. "Do you think Black Cronos could be based in Oxford? Maybe we should stick around."

"Even if they are, it will be a waste of time. We have no leads, and if that woman is still in town, I don't want to give her a chance to steal the astrolabe again." He shook his head. "No, we need to leave, and hope that the others find us a clue. Besides, Blaze's death is all over the news now. I do not wish to be questioned by the police if we've been caught on one of the club's cameras, do you?"

The thought of being questioned again filled Shadow with dread. "No. You're right. Let's get out of here, and I'll give some thought as to what kind of creature our attacker could be."

—◆—

It was late morning on Sunday, and Niel shuffled in his seat at the café that was across the road from The Midnight Sun's headquarters in Marylebone. "There has got to be a better way of finding out about the members of the order."

"Like what?" Nahum asked, eyes fixed firmly on the front of the building. "We can't break in because it's alarmed."

"But what is this telling us?" Niel argued. "We can see who's going in and out, but we have no idea who they are or what their role is. It's a waste of time."

"We're getting photos," Nahum reminded him. "They could be useful."

"But we have the astrolabe!" Gabe had updated them earlier. "We'll give it back to them later, and then we can go home."

Nahum shot him a long look. "You're nuts if you think this is over already."

"But it should be. We were asked to find it, and we have. Whoever this mystery woman is doesn't concern us."

Nahum glanced around to make sure they weren't being overheard. "Blaze's death is all over the news. She was prepared to kill for that thing—and eliminated him no doubt to stop him from identifying them. They'll try again. And Gabe is onto something. We should be worried about what the astrolabe will lead to."

"I guess you're right," Niel agreed, sensing they were going to investigate the Dark Star Astrolabe regardless, and realising the reason for his ill temper. "I'm hungry."

"You're always hungry, and we're in a café!"

Niel lowered his voice, unwilling to insult the owners. "I've drank enough of their dodgy coffee, and frankly, the sandwiches just don't cut it. I want a proper lunch."

"It's not even lunchtime yet. And a sandwich *is* a proper lunch."

"It's really not." And then another thought struck him. "Didn't Caldwell tell Gabe that they had a Senior Adepts meeting on a Monday night? That's when we need to be here...if Gabe wants us to continue this stupid stake out. He may have changed his mind by the time he returns."

"He hadn't three hours ago! But that's very true, brother. And according to Caldwell, the Inner Temple are the only ones who know about the astrolabe."

"Good! That means we can come back here tomorrow evening and watch them all then. We'll get photos, and maybe Harlan can help us identify them...which leaves this afternoon completely free!"

Nahum frowned, which Niel knew he would. As Gabe's right-hand man, he hated to cut corners. "I still feel we should do something useful."

Niel cut him off before he could even start to argue. "Pub, now. Then we'll discuss options."

Half an hour later, with pints on the table and both of them halfway through a Sunday roast, Niel was feeling much more affable. "That's better," he said, poised for another bite. "This is excellent."

"Try not to inhale it," Nahum told him. "Although, I agree. This was a great idea."

Niel glanced around while he ate and felt it was only the fact that they'd arrived before the lunch rush that they'd found a table at all. They were seated in a traditional English pub that was very busy. The air resounded with chatter, and the music playing in the background meant they could talk easily without fear of being overheard. "Go on, then," he said. "What do you want to do this afternoon?"

"We're not far from The British Museum. It's a short tube ride or walk from here, and I gather they have some info in there on JD, and lots of displays of ancient civilisations. I think it's a good idea to see some of that. No one trusts JD, and I want to read and see something about him—something from his past. And," Nahum wiped his chin with his napkin, "they have a collection of astrolabes, and more importantly, statues from ancient Egypt, Mesopotamia, and Iran—Persia, to us."

Niel's curiosity flared. Since they had passed through the portal, he and his brothers had looked up the history that had passed since their time, but their research had only been online or in books. Here was a chance to see the past, up close and personal. "That's a brilliant idea. Although," he hesitated, "it could get very weird."

Nahum's blue eyes fixed on him, suddenly serious. "I know. I don't know whether to expect good memories or bad ones, but we're too close to pass up the chance."

Niel had been intending to have another pint, but now any such plans were forgotten. "I agree. Let's go."

⬥

Harlan arrived at the guild at midday, exhilarated after his bike ride through London and grateful for the fresh air, which had finally banished the fug caused by his late night. He let himself in through the back door and stood for a moment, listening.

It was quiet, the normal hum of chatter from the offices missing on the weekends, and the air devoid of the smell of coffee or food that often wafted from the staff kitchen. With luck, Mason wouldn't be here either, and certainly not Robert, the officious idiot who was Mason's secretary. Harlan walked straight upstairs, stopping by his office to grab another espresso, and then headed to the library on the second floor.

The warm scents of vanilla and old books enveloped him, and placing his coffee on a table under the window, he browsed the section that contained the originals of the papers he had looked through a few hours before, quickly extracting the letters and placing them on the table. He pulled one page out of its plastic sheet, feeling the quality of the paper, and holding it up to the light was disappointed to find no watermarks or any other interesting features. He searched the others with the same results and sighed, muttering under his breath. *What had he expected? A map?*

A thump overhead made him look up, alarmed. It came from the office and living area set aside for JD. *Had someone broken in, or was JD here?* Quickly re-shelving the papers, he exited the library and headed for the stairs. The lower floors were still silent; the only sound was the traffic, still constant in London, despite it being a weekend.

The stairs that led to JD's flat were at the end of the corridor, and much narrower than the grand sweep that led up to the first two floors. He crept up their carpeted surface, paused on the shallow landing, and listened. He could still hear shuffling and more thumps, and trying the handle, found the door was open. *Should he knock and warn the intruder? Or was it JD, and he'd give him the shock of his life if he crept in unannounced?* He'd prefer the latter.

Harlan slipped inside and found himself in a small reception room decorated with antique furniture. There were doors on each side, all partially open, and a corridor lay ahead, leading deeper into the flat. One door led to a bathroom and the other a large bedroom, but both were empty.

He edged down the corridor and realised the sounds he heard were coming from the door at the end. For a second, he thought of Gabe's warning about the mystery woman who didn't seem human, but then threw the door open regardless, leaping in and hoping to take whoever it was off-guard.

But instead of meeting an intruder, he heard a shriek and saw JD whirl around. "You idiot nincompoop! What the hell do you think you're doing?"

"Sorry, JD," Harlan said, scanning the opulently decorated room. "I heard noises up here, and thought you were an intruder."

JD was pale and had backed up to the wall behind him, a hand on his heart, his sharp features tight with anger and shock. "What are you even doing here today?"

"Research. What about you?"

A sly look crept across his face. "The same."

"Well, I apologise for interrupting you." Harlan went to leave, and then hesitated. He really needed help, and JD wasn't the enemy, as much as he'd been annoyed by his attitude in Angel's Rest. *His very dangerous attitude*, he reminded himself. *JD was not to be underestimated*. "Can you spare me some time? I have questions about one of my cases."

JD nodded, and taking a seat at a table, gestured to another chair for Harlan. "Of course."

"We were asked by The Order of the Midnight Sun to retrieve an object for them. It seems it was stolen by Black Cronos. I wondered if you'd heard of them?"

"Black Cronos?" JD's voice rose with alarm. "They're back?"

"Er, it seems so. You're familiar with them?"

"Of course I'm bloody familiar with them," JD said irritably. "They've threatened us in the past."

Harlan nodded. "I found the letters downstairs. Did you ever find out anything about them?"

"Nothing conclusive," he said blandly. "I have no idea where they are based, or who their members are, and besides, the last we heard from them was before the war. What did they steal?"

"The Dark Star Astrolabe. Apparently, it—"

But Harlan couldn't finish his answer, because JD stood so quickly that his chair crashed to the floor. "The *what*? It has been found?"

Harlan looked up at him, shocked. "You know it?"

"It points to the seat of a daring alchemical experiment that ended in disaster."

"I thought it pointed to the origins of The Order of the Midnight Sun?"

"Ha! Is that what they told you?" he marched across the room. "Dissembling fly-bitten giglets! Churlish beetle-brained gudgeons! No wonder Black Cronos stole it!"

Harlan's head was spinning. "Why would they steal it?"

"Because it's their origin, too!"

"*What*? But you just said it had nothing to do with origins! I don't understand."

JD didn't bother explaining. "Who has the astrolabe now?"

"Well, we do, actually. Gabe and Shadow retrieved it last night."

A smile spread across JD's face. "We bested Black Cronos."

"Apparently so. Their thief wasn't quite human...but then again, neither are ours."

"They must bring it here!"

"We have to return it to Caldwell."

"That simpering, half-witted fool." JD's eyes were hard. "He hasn't got the balls for this."

"Whether you think he has or not," Harlan said, knowing he was risking JD's considerable wrath, "it belongs to them."

"I don't care. I want it."

Harlan rolled his eyes. "That's tough, JD. You can't have everything!"

JD banged the table. "*I* tracked it down over two hundred years ago and then it disappeared, right under my nose. I will *not* be thwarted again!"

"Maybe you're not meant to have it," Harlan said, suddenly furious. "We have to give it back, even if they stole it," he added, suddenly wondering who it really did belong to. "Our reputation is based on delivering the goods to those who hired us. We cannot change that now, just because you want it. This is your company, your reputation, your money on the line."

"And therefore, I can risk all of that if I so choose." JD drew himself up and peered down his nose at Harlan. "And as my employee, you will do as I ask."

Shit. And this is why he shouldn't have come to JD. "What will you do with it?"

"Do exactly what they want to do. Find the Dark Star."

"What possible interest can it have for you? It's *their* place of origin!"

"Oh, no," JD said, shaking his head. "The Dark Star is a person. Or was. Bring it here now. Phone them."

"What?" Harlan's head was spinning. "What do you mean, a person? You're talking in riddles. And how do you know it's Black Cronos's origins, too? You said you didn't know anything about them!"

JD glared at him. "Stop questioning me and do as I say."

Harlan had no idea where Shadow and Gabe were right now, but he needed time to think. "They're travelling at the moment, and won't arrive until later."

"Tonight then, up here, at seven. And don't be late."

JD turned his back on Harlan, dismissing him, and Harlan strode out of the suite of rooms, slamming the door behind him, and not caring that JD knew he was angry. *The jumped-up little shit.*

As soon as Harlan was safely in the privacy of his office, he called Olivia. "I've just had a disturbing encounter with JD."

"What's that old git done now?" Olivia's admiration of JD seemed to be over.

"He wants the latest occult object I've been charged to find. Actually, he demanded it," he added, remembering his tone. "I can't do it, Liv. It's not his, but if I don't comply I risk my job."

"Then you need to seek support from Mason. He's the director. Surely, he'll see your point. Our reputation depends on our honesty and integrity."

"I know. I told JD that, but he didn't seem to care."

Olivia muttered under her breath. "Can I ask what it is?"

"Sure," he said, filling her in on the job so far.

"You're right. JD has no say on this. You need to stand your ground, and I'll stand by you. Do you want me with you when you speak to Mason?"

Harlan leaned back in his chair and lifted his feet on to his desk. "No. I don't want to drag you into this. But thanks. I knew I shouldn't have told him, but I needed to find out about Black Cronos, and that was a bust. Shit!" He was angry with himself, knowing he should have trusted his instincts not to tell JD.

"What will you do now?" Olivia asked, her kind tone unable to calm him down.

"I'll meet Gabe as planned, and then contact Caldwell and hand it over. JD can go screw himself."

Nine

"Find anything good yet, Estelle? I feel like we've been at this for ages," Barak said grumpily.

Estelle leaned forward and tapped the computer screen. "This is interesting. It's an article on a website about old occult organisations, and it suggests that The Order of the Midnight Sun began in France."

Barak had stood to stretch his legs and make them coffee, checking the security screens as he did so. Satisfied that all was quiet, he faced her. "France? Does it give a name?"

She was still staring at the computer, absorbed in their research. "Yes, it was called Seekers of the Morning Star. *Chercheurs de l'étoile du matin*. According to this, it was comprised of a small group of men dedicated to unlocking the secrets of celestial bodies and harnessing their power for immortality and knowledge."

Barak snorted. "Nothing new there, then. Does it list any names?"

Estelle shook her head. "No. It says their members were shrouded in secrecy, with only the name itself surviving. For a while they released a few documents, alchemical of course, and there was conjecture about the membership. A landowner in Aquitaine was the most speculated about." She leaned back to look at him. "It was an area in the southwest of France, long since renamed."

"Ah, fallen empires and all that," he said, waiting for the kettle to boil.

"Something of the sort." She smiled, softening her austere features, and reminding Barak how attractive she could be when she wasn't so waspish. Oblivious to his thoughts, she turned back to the article. "Apparently, something happened and the group split."

"How do they know that?"

"Good question." She frowned and fell silent as she continued to read, and Barak made their drinks and carried them to the desk, settling in beside her.

The site she was looking at was crowded with alchemical symbols and heraldic signs and he exhaled slowly, trying not to get too excited. They had found all sorts of articles over the previous few hours, and most of them said the same thing, more or less. They talked about The Order of the Midnight Sun during the last century, and speculated on the famous figures that may have been members—a couple of prime ministers, some notorious celebrities, and members of the aristocracy. But the further these articles looked back in time, the more speculative they became.

"Do you think they tried to hide their origins?" he asked Estelle.

She absently picked up her drink. "Maybe. It's hard to know, really. History is for the winners, and the real stories or people involved are often relegated to footnotes."

"Like us?" He smiled at her.

"You're hardly a footnote. But yes," she conceded, "I know what you mean."

"We *are* a footnote," he argued, unwilling to drop it. "We're barely mentioned. We're like a fairy tale in the Bible."

"Like I said, history is for winners." She was watching him closely. "And you weren't winners, not in the end."

"No. But we were for a long time, and will be again." He nodded at the screen, happy to have Estelle scrutinise it for him as he enjoyed her closeness. "What else does that say?"

"There's brief mention of a catastrophe, and then the group split in two."

"What kind of catastrophe?"

She shrugged. "It doesn't say."

"And after the spilt?"

"It seems that some of their ex-members lay low for years, shedding their dark past and reforming under the name Seekers of Enlightenment, before finally emerging as The Order of the Midnight Sun in the sixteenth century."

"And the other half?"

"They continued on the quest they had started. A couple of names are mentioned for them too, as if they went through numerous iterations." She leaned forward to study the article again. "Hades' Path, The Dawn Star, and that's it. It suggests their organisation became ever darker, more nebulous." And then she jerked up right in shock. "It also says the Dark Star Astrolabe is attributed to them! You need to read this."

Barak leaned forward too, squinting at the screen. "'The group was believed to have lost its way in their obsession to unravel their past. There are many mysteries about them, but one in particular still has the power to draw our attention—the Dark Star Astrolabe—rumoured to have been made in the thirteenth century, but long lost to time and memory. Where is it, and what does it point to? And who will have the courage to follow its directions? Those who spoke of it do so with dread, for at its end is a monster.' What the hell..." he murmured. "A monster?"

Estelle was looking at him with an expression he had never seen on her face before. *Excitement.* "This is brilliant."

"This is insane! It's mumbo jumbo, at best."

"Why?" she asked, suddenly annoyed. "You can't possibly scoff at this."

He rubbed his face, bewildered. "No, you're right. Let's print this out and see what else we can find."

Nahum looked at the Assyrian statue of a winged lion that towered over him in the British Museum and felt a shudder of recognition. This was more than he was expecting. *So much more.*

He took a step back, feeling suddenly hot, and decided he needed to find Niel. He had left him in the Mesopotamian rooms, lost in his memories, but it was unlikely he was still there, surely.

Nahum made his way upstairs and through the galleries, feeling dizzy as the past assailed him. Many things there were from after his existence, but they were recognisable enough, their roots being found in his own time. But other things were far too close. The Assyrian lion hunts, the Canaanites, the Egyptians, the Levant, so many names... But here, fragments of their existence were right in front of him.

Almost blindly, he stumbled along, and finally found Niel in a long room staring at the Assyrian reliefs from Nineveh. He moved to his side, Niel transfixed on the images in front of him. Nahum nudged him gently. "Niel, are you all right?"

"No. I'm not." Niel turned to face him, his face pale. "This is weird."

Nahum smiled weakly. "It's unnerving, that's for sure."

"We need to bring our brothers here." Niel turned away to study the panels again, moving slowly through the room. "I'm amazed at what has survived."

"Maybe we're not out of time after all."

"Oh, we're out of time, all right. I remember commissioning things like this to be carved. The work it took, the skill, the conditions. Brother, I need a drink."

"Not yet you don't," Nahum said, steering him out of the room. "Let's look at something more modern. We came here for JD, after all."

"Right now, JD seems insignificant."

"But he's not. He's our occasional employer, and immortal, too."

Niel shook his head, his stride matching Nahum's as they headed for the galleries housing the modern displays. "These ancient remains remind me who we really are. We shouldn't be taking instructions from him! He should be grovelling at our feet."

Nahum looked at him sharply, alarmed by his tone, and grabbed his arm, pulling him to a stop. "There'll be no grovelling, Niel. We don't do that anymore."

"But you know what I mean." Niel's blue eyes stared into his own. "JD has no power over us."

"I know that, and so do our brothers. But this isn't about us exerting our authority or ancient bloodline. This is about us forging our way in the world. And potentially, JD may have just lived a bit longer than we did. And he's a lot more familiar with the past five hundred years than us!"

"So why are we focussing on the more recent past when we could be utilising what we do know?"

Nahum paused, feeling ambushed. "Because at the moment, that's where the money is. And I guess because our own time is too long ago."

"And yet..." Niel spread his arms out, almost knocking over a bystander. "It's not. It's *here!*"

"Dug out from the earth after painstaking archaeological digs. And how much has been lost? 99.9 percent of it, that's what! This is amazing, I agree, but let's be honest, Niel. Most of our history is just dust. Let's enjoy the glimpse we're getting of it and appreciate it for what it is." Nahum stared him down, knowing that Niel could be bloody-minded and belligerent sometimes, and thankful that most of the time he wasn't. "You're shocked, like I am. That's all. It's doing strange things to my head, too."

They stared at each other for another moment, and then Niel nodded. "Yeah, I'm in shock. But still..."

"Come and look at JD's stuff, and let's find some astrolabes." Nahum urged him along, desperate to move to more modern displays. He agreed that they should bring their brothers here, but what would they think? Some days being here seemed easy, when the past felt at a distance. But now, it felt like it might swallow him whole. And last month's encounter with The Book of Raziel didn't help, either.

When they finally arrived in the gallery containing JD's belongings, Nahum led them to his obsidian mirror. "It doesn't look much, does it?"

"No, but it is an old Aztec relic," Niel said, and then nodded to the wax disc next to the other objects. "And that's his Seal of God. The design given to him by Uriel, *apparently*."

"Don't you believe him?"

"Do you?" Niel asked sceptically.

"He's a wily old devil, but he did summon Chassan," Nahum reminded him.

"Like I'd forget," Niel mumbled. "At least *he* hasn't contacted me." Niel looked around the room. "Come on, let's find some astrolabes, see if someone can give us a lesson on using one, and then we can head home. I've had my fill of history for one day."

Gabe and Shadow were back in London by early afternoon, and once inside Chadwick House, Shadow headed to the kitchen to prepare a late lunch, while Gabe went to the study with the astrolabe. He'd just spoken to Barak and was disturbed by his news. He eyed the astrolabe with distaste. The object was getting more bizarre by the minute.

The rete, which depicted the celestial hemisphere, was ornate and delicate, each tip representing a star. There appeared to be a couple of plates layered in the disc, but he had no intention of dismantling it to investigate further. The centre pin that connected them all together had a large, black pearl in the centre, and its lustre shone in the sun. *Was it supposed to represent a dark star, whatever that was?* He shook his head, confused, and placed the astrolabe on the table just as Nahum and Niel arrived, both looking preoccupied.

"What's happened?" he asked them as Nahum threw himself in a chair. "You look spooked."

Niel just grunted and carried the astrolabe to the window to examine it in better light, but Nahum said, "We went to the British Museum and had an interesting encounter with our past." He updated him on what they'd seen, and for the first time in 24 hours, Gabe's thoughts left their current case.

"Really? Was it that weird?"

"Weirder, brother. But, having said that, I think you should go. We all should." He lowered his voice. "It made Niel cranky."

"I can hear you!" Niel called across the room. "And yes, I am cranky. I'm not apologising for it, either."

Nahum rolled his eyes at Gabe and he smiled. They all knew what Niel could be like. "I am intrigued," Gabe admitted, "but not right now. Why weren't you watching the order?"

"Waste of time. There was hardly anyone going in, and we decided we'd be better off going tomorrow night," Nahum said, explaining their reasoning. "But we did manage to get some basic instructions on how astrolabes work. They're complicated things, clever, very sophisticated for their time. I know we don't need to know how to use it, but—" he shrugged. "It felt like something we should do."

"Fair enough. But I'm handing that thing over later today. I'll call Caldwell as soon as I've spoken to Harlan." He checked his watch. "And that should be any minute now."

For the next short while they talked about what had happened in Oxford, until Shadow arrived in the room with sandwiches and drinks on a tray, Harlan next to her.

Harlan looked flustered, and Gabe's heart sank. "Is something wrong?"

"Just JD being his usual, belligerent self," Harlan said. He didn't sit, instead picking up the astrolabe that Niel had placed on the table again and examining it. "So, this is what's causing all our problems?"

"It is," Gabe said nodding. "It's beautiful, isn't it?"

"And a little different from the astrolabes we've been examining, including Chadwick's," Niel added. "The jewel on the disc is unusual, but from our admittedly brief instructions, it seems it would work the same way."

Harlan grunted. "As long as Caldwell is happy, I don't care. I just want it out of my hands."

"What problems are you having?" Shadow asked. She was sitting at the large table covered in paperwork with her lunch in front of her, and seemed none the worse from the late night.

For a moment, Harlan didn't answer, instead running his fingers across the engraved metalwork of the disc, seemingly lost in thought. Watching him now, it was clear to Gabe that Harlan had experienced just as disturbed a night as the rest of them. His eyes had dark shadows beneath them, stubble grazed his jaw, and his lips were tight. He seemed to be wrestling with something. Finally, he said, "JD wants me to double-cross Caldwell and deliver this to him."

Silence fell as Gabe looked at his companions' incredulous expressions, and then he laughed. "Over my dead body! I don't break deals."

Harlan grinned, finally meeting his eyes. "Neither do I, so I'm glad to hear you say that. But he did give me some interesting news."

"So has Barak," Gabe confessed, not having told his brothers Barak's information yet. "I'll start. You might want a seat."

For a few minutes they exchanged information, and by the time they'd finished, the mood had darkened.

"Can I suggest that we don't waste time, and pass this on right now?" Harlan said. "I don't want to be ambushed in this house by your mysterious attacker, or JD. Shall I call Caldwell?"

Gabe nodded. "I think we should go fully armed, too. Tell him we'll be there within the hour."

Their journey through London was relatively quick, and once again, Shadow, Harlan, and Gabe went inside the order's headquarters as Niel and Nahum waited outside, watching the building. But this time, Aubrey Cavendish was with Caldwell, the man who'd orchestrated the theft from France. He was a big, middle-aged man, soft around the edges with a paunch that indicated good living, and a very unlikely thief, Gabe decided. *Maybe he'd engaged someone else in France, or perhaps he had hidden skills.*

Caldwell grasped the astrolabe to his chest, his eyes wide. "I can't believe you found it so soon!"

"Speed was the key, and some luck," Gabe confessed. "But you need to be careful. Some powerful people want that, and I would guess they'll try again."

Aubrey prised the astrolabe from Caldwell's hands, scanning it quickly. "Is it damaged?"

"I don't think so," Shadow said, "but we did have to fight to get it."

"A fight?" Caldwell asked, alarmed. "With who?"

"Someone who was not fully human," Gabe explained, eyeing their worried expressions, but it was important they knew what they were up against. He described their encounter, noting that both Caldwell and Aubrey had gone very still, Caldwell fumbling for the chair behind him and sitting heavily.

Harlan cut in. "We believe Black Cronos is behind this. It was a name given to us by the thief's contact."

"Impossible!" Aubrey said immediately, his face flushing. "They do not exist."

"But you have heard of them?" Harlan looked amused. "Because I'll be honest, we had to do some digging to find anything on them. It seems they've been around a long time."

Aubrey and Caldwell exchanged nervous glances, and then Caldwell said, "They existed once, but a very long time ago. Your source is wrong."

"And the woman who had the ability to kill with a kiss?" Shadow asked. "If it wasn't Black Cronos, who employed her?"

"That really doesn't matter," Caldwell said, standing abruptly. "Thank you for your time and excellent service. I will arrange payment immediately, and I shall certainly use you again, should I need to."

So that was it, Gabe thought, experiencing a weird mixture of relief and disappointment. And then his phone rang. It was Nahum. "A black van has just pulled up outside, and I can see five people so far, including a woman, surrounding the building. This is not a social call. Me and Niel will try to stop them."

Gabe turned to Shadow, who was already holding her two daggers, poised for action. "Check the hallway. They've come for the astrolabe."

"*What?*" Aubrey said, already backing away as Shadow left the room. "Who?"

"Four men, one woman, and maybe more. Is there anyone else in the building?"

Caldwell shook his head. "No, it's just us."

"Good," Gabe said, immensely relieved he didn't have to worry about protecting anyone else. "Harlan, stick with these guys and leave the fighting to us."

Then a scream resonated down the hall that was abruptly cut off, and Gabe ran to the door.

Ten

Shadow spun away from the man she had just stabbed and who had fallen dead at her feet, covered in blood, just in time to dodge the attack of another man who had entered the reception hall from a doorway at the rear.

He was lean and stealthy, and like her, carried two sharp daggers. In seconds they were engaged in deadly combat. Shadow was aware of another figure approaching from the stairway, but Gabe ran to help, yelling, "Harlan, get them to the safe room!"

They fought side by side, Shadow swiftly dodging the whirling knives of her attacker. He was good. *Inhumanly good.* She felt his knife slice her arm, and she knew she'd need every ounce of her skill to defeat him.

The man's eyes were dark, and the longer they fought, the darker and more intense they became, just like the woman from the previous night. She could feel his immense concentration as he tried to back her into a corner. She dropped suddenly, rolling to the side before regaining her feet, able to slash his side with a long, deep cut before he rounded on her, a low, inhuman growl in his throat. Gabe seemed to be having a similar struggle, and she could hear his sword clashing with his opponent.

A strangled cry came from another room, and out of the corner of her eye she saw Niel stride through a doorway, whirling two swords at the same time as he aimed for their side. And then something dropped down from above, sending Niel crashing into a wall. It was chaotic, and the fight was messy. All of the furniture in the hall was upended, and the sounds of splintering wood and shattered porcelain mixed with the clash of swords and grunts of aggression.

Shadow finally managed to thrust her blade between her opponent's ribs, watching him slide to the floor, eyes wide, before the life passed out of them. She ran to Harlan's side as he hurried Caldwell and Aubrey to the door that led to the passageway and the safe room below. But they had barely walked a few feet down the hallway when the woman from the night before appeared at the top of the rear stairs, her dark eyes glowing with malevolence.

Herne's bloody horns. How many of them were there, and where the hell was Nahum?

Nahum was engaged in his own battle in the alley behind the building. Two huge men faced him, both with full beards and bearing unusual weapons. One carried a short sword with an oddly shaped blade, the other carried a double-bit axe, both sides wickedly sharp, and in the dull light of the alley, Nahum could see strange engraving on the blades.

But that's all he could take note of, because the men struck quickly, clearly intending to kill him.

Nahum was suddenly glad of the sparring he did regularly with Shadow and his brothers, because he needed strength and agility now more than ever. As the axe head missed his own by mere inches, he realised he needed his wings, and damn the consequences. One man feinted to the right, trying to draw his attention, but his wings punched through his shirt, shredding it, and he used them to crush the man against the wall, throwing him with such force that the man's skull cracked and he fell, lifeless, to the ground. His remaining opponent roared with fury, his eyes bloodshot with a berserker rage, throwing himself at Nahum.

Nahum lifted effortlessly above him, grabbed the man around the neck, and hauled him off his feet. He twisted and writhed as Nahum flew higher, hoping the alley would protect him from prying eyes. His opponent flung his arm back, swiping wildly with his axe, and in an effort to dodge it, Nahum dropped him. With a strangled cry he fell to the ground, the sound cut short with a sickening crunch.

Nahum dropped to the ground, and ensuring there was no one else outside, ran through the damaged back door, across a large kitchen, and into the hallway beyond, where he saw Shadow fighting furiously with a dark-haired woman. Nahum knew who she was. Her black eyes and athleticism marked her as the woman Gabe and Shadow had fought the night before. It was unlikely she had followed them, but it was obvious that she and her companions had decided to stake out the order's headquarters.

Caldwell and Aubrey were cowering in the hall as Harlan pushed them back towards the kitchen. He eyed Nahum with relief. "I'm trying to get them to the safe room, but we're blocked." He nodded behind him. "Gabe and Niel are back that way."

Nahum didn't speak, his eyes still on Shadow and the mystery woman. Shadow ducked and rolled, striking out at the woman's legs, and Nahum took his chance. He pulled one of his throwing daggers from where it was strapped to his forearm and threw it at the woman's throat. But like she had a sixth sense, she turned, and it caught her in the shoulder. While evading Shadow, she pulled the blade free and hurled it back towards Nahum. Nahum was vaguely aware of the others dropping to the floor behind him, but the knife landed in the wall, and he grabbed it once more.

Cornered and desperate, the woman ran to another doorway, and Shadow raced after her. Nahum seized the opportunity, and hauling Harlan to his feet, asked, "Where's the safe room?"

Harlan was already leading the way. "Down here, bottom of the stairs."

Nahum checked behind them to make sure they weren't being followed, and then ran in front of Harlan, ensuring their path was safe and the room secure.

"Are you sure there's no other way in?" he asked him as he scanned the small room, noting the large safe door opposite.

"Not unless you count the air ducts."

"Good. Lock the door, and we'll come get you when it's safe."

Harlan looked as if he were about to protest, but instead just nodded.

Nahum raced back up the stairs, pausing as he considered which way to go. *Should he help Shadow, or his brothers?* Deciding that Shadow could cope admirably on her own with one opponent, and not knowing how many his brothers might be facing, he ran to the main reception hall, but both Gabe and Niel were standing over the bodies of their dead assailants, breathing heavily.

Gabe frowned. "You're covered in blood."

He glanced down, noting the blood spatter across his ripped t-shirt. "I'm surprised there's not more. So are you two. I don't think our attackers were fully human."

"Neither do I," Niel said, crouching to turn over the man at his feet. "Their eyes look odd."

"Let me guess, matte black, shark eyes?" Nahum asked.

"Something of the sort."

"Not this one," Gabe said, pointing to the man at the bottom of the stairs. "His eyes turned silvery. How many did you face, Nahum?"

"Two—brothers, by the look of them. Both huge, with matching beards. Both expert fighters."

Gabe examined the man in the corner of the room. "These were, too. Shadow killed this one. Is she okay?"

"Of course I am," she said, entering the room. Shadow looked none the worse for her encounter, although her hair had fallen loose from its knot on her head, and coils of it tumbled down her back. "Although, I lost the woman. She got out through a rear window and made it to a van on the street before I could catch up to her." She nodded to the dead men on the floor. "What are they?"

"Enhanced humans?" Gabe suggested.

"Or weird shifters?" Niel countered.

"Either way, they were strong," Shadow said. She looked at Nahum. "I take it the two huge guys out back are your work?"

"They are. Anybody else out there?"

She shook her head. "Not that I could see, but we should check the perimeter, just in case."

She had voiced Nahum's next plan, and he said, "I agree. Come with me, Shadow. Let's make sure they're all gone."

"We'll check in here," Gabe said, and he and Niel left the reception area together, leaving Nahum and Shadow to exit through the rear again.

"Did you see them arrive?" Shadow asked Nahum, as he edged down the alleyway.

"We noticed a large black van on the road, blacked out windows, very suspicious. We kept an eye on it, and noticed someone exit and head to a side window. Then the others exited and walked around the back. That's when me and Niel spilt up, and I called Gabe."

They had reached the end of the alley now, and Nahum looked around the corner and then headed to the road, checking for unusual activity. "There's nothing going on out here, and the van isn't in sight."

Shadow stood next to him, surveying the street, thoughtful. "So, we killed five, and one escaped. The woman headed to the passenger door, which means they had a driver who wasn't involved. Unfortunately, I didn't get a look at whoever it was. Did you?"

"No. I didn't have time. My priority was getting in here," Nahum said, annoyed with himself.

Shadow exhaled heavily. "We're going to have to call Maggie Milne, aren't we?"

Despite the situation, Nahum laughed at her bleak expression. "Yes, we are. But we acted in self-defence, and to protect others. Let's hope she's okay with that."

They circled around the front of the building for good measure, but the road was quiet, and the late afternoon light was dim as clouds thickened overhead. Nahum sighed, satisfied. "I think we're good for now, but we shouldn't linger. For all we know, they've gone for backup."

"They won't come near the place with police here," Shadow said. "But I agree. They'll surely try again. And Caldwell may not be so lucky next time."

<hr />

Harlan studied Caldwell, who sat on the floor of the safe room in obvious shock. His hand was clutching his head, pushing his hair back off his face as he stared at Harlan.

"Were all those people sent to get the astrolabe?"

"It seems so. You're lucky we were here, because you would have been dead by now. Although," he frowned as he thought through the sequence of events, "they would have known we were here. They must have wanted to kill us all. That's why they sent so many. They underestimated us."

In fact, Harlan had to admit to himself, *if he'd been without the Nephilim and Shadow, he might be dead, too.* He'd felt useless as he'd snuck past Gabe and the others. They moved so quickly they were a blur, and when he'd seen the woman waiting at the top of the stairs, his heart almost failed him. He owed them all his life.

Aubrey looked a little more composed, clutching the astrolabe as he took deep, calming breaths. "I thought the rumours that surrounded this thing were exaggerated, but maybe I'm wrong."

"*Maybe?*" Harlan snorted with scorn. "That thing must lead to something pretty special. You gonna hire an army to keep it safe? Because those people meant business."

Caldwell looked up, sharply. "You think they'll be back?"

"Of course! It's a miracle you still have it. And," he added thinking quickly, "you should tell all of your members to stay away from here for a good week, maybe longer. You don't want to risk your members being kidnapped for blackmail purposes."

"Shit." Caldwell's head dropped onto his knees. "I had no idea we would be risking so much for this thing."

"Well, I suggest you give it more thought, because clearly there's a lot at stake. Of course, if it's all too much, you could always hand it over."

"*What?*" Aubrey was apoplectic. "After all I've done to get it? I don't think so! This is ours!"

"Well, Black Cronos thinks it's theirs." Harlan looked between them both. "Who's right?"

"We are!" they said mutinously.

Harlan sat down too, leaning back against the wall, the soft carpet comfortably warm beneath him. The attack had certainly made up his mind. He was not giving the astrolabe to JD, and he was going to have to face the consequences. *Perhaps JD would be glad of it when he found out about the attack.* Harlan groaned to himself. *Who was he kidding? JD would be furious.*

<hr />

When Gabe was satisfied that the building was secure, everyone gathered again in the reception room off the main hall. He'd left Nahum and Niel covering the front and rear doors, and he could hear Harlan out in the hall talking to Maggie Milne.

He felt sorry for Caldwell and Aubrey, who still looked shocked. "You need to take the astrolabe and hide it somewhere, and you should keep away from this building. They'll try again."

Caldwell rubbed his face as he paced the room. "But what are we supposed to do?"

Gabe shot Shadow an impatient look. She was leaning against the wall, watching nonchalantly, but he knew she was listening for any signs of attack. She raised an eyebrow, amused, and said, "Caldwell, you *stole* this. You must have expected repercussions."

"Not like this, I didn't." He rounded on Aubrey. "You said you were discreet!"

He looked affronted, drawing himself up to his full height. "I was! No one knew I took it."

"Wrong!" Gabe said dryly. "*Someone* knew! Either Madame Charbonneau knew and has tracked you down. Or you have a leak...which I suggested the first time."

"No one would betray us!" Caldwell insisted. "I trust the Inner Temple implicitly." He might have sounded sure, but a flicker of doubt crossed his face.

"It could be a newer member?" Gabe suggested. "Or an older member, perhaps, who feels they been passed over for something?"

Aubrey and Caldwell exchanged questioning glances, but simultaneously shook their heads.

"No," Aubrey answered. "I've known these people for many years, and they're as committed to this action as us. It has to be someone else."

"Madame Charbonneau, then?" Gabe persisted. "You were seen leaving the house, or perhaps left a clue behind."

Aubrey looked like a petulant child. "No. I planned the theft well, and knew exactly where I was going."

"If you don't mind me saying, you don't exactly look like a thief, or strike me as being nimble."

"Well, you are clearly misjudging me!" Aubrey shot back, suddenly furious.

"Enough!" Caldwell shouted. "Whatever happened, we must deal with it."

"Yes, you must," Gabe said. "But we'll be leaving as soon as we've spoken to Maggie Milne, so make sure your plan is a good one."

Harlan's head was already pounding, and as Maggie started to shout, he felt it start to escalate.

"Five fucking dead bodies!" she yelled. "What the fuck is the matter with you guys?"

"They attacked us," Harlan pointed out, trying to stay calm. "If we, er—well, actually they—" he pointed to Gabe, Shadow, Niel, and Nahum who all stood in the reception room looking amused but trying to hide it, "hadn't killed them, *we* would be dead! And we're pretty sure they're not human."

"How do you know that? Did you *ask* them before you left their entrails all over the bloody floor?"

"It was the way they moved," Gabe said, his voice low. "They were too fast, too agile, too hard to kill."

Maggie rounded on him, looking him up and down scathingly. "Too hard to kill? What are you, a fucking assassin? Do you kill a lot?" There was a dangerous edge to her voice.

"Once, I did, but not anymore," Gabe said evenly.

Maggie's eyes slid to Shadow. "I knew I'd be meeting up with *you* again!"

"And once again, it's a true pleasure," Shadow said, her violet eyes mischievous. "Like Harlan said, we acted in self-defence!"

"Think it's a fucking game, don't you, with your smirks and cockiness? Well, it's bloody not! You have killed five people."

"Two escaped," Shadow pointed out blithely.

"That doesn't count!" she yelled. She looked at Nahum and Niel, quiet up to now, although covered in blood, and Nahum still wearing the remnants of his t-shirt. "And you two! I presume you're toeing the party line?"

"We had no choice," Nahum said calmly. "They arrived intending to kill all of us. They were heavily armed, organised, deadly, and competent, but they underestimated us. Harlan is right. We'd be dead if they weren't."

Maggie fell silent for a moment, and then turned back to Shadow. "Did you get a number plate?"

"No."

"I did," Niel said quietly. "I made sure to before I ran inside."

Maggie's attention swung back to him. "Good. You did something useful, then. Who did you say these guys worked for again?"

"Black Cronos—we think," Harlan told her. "Heard of them?"

"Nope, but you can be sure I'll be looking into them." She glared at Caldwell and Aubrey. "I'll need full statements off you two, as well, so you all need to stay put. My SOCO team is on the way, and they are very used to the paranormal, so we'll be able to find out whether they're human or not. And," she jabbed a finger at the Nephilim and Shadow, "that means you, too! I want statements, fingerprints, DNA, the works."

Maggie strode out of the room banging the door behind her, but leaving a constable in the corner of the room.

Gabe glared at Harlan. "Fingerprints? DNA?"

"Those are the rules, Gabe. Maggie will treat you better than anyone else."

Nahum nodded. "We have to expect this, Gabe. Harlan is right. It's the world we live in."

"The rules in the paranormal world are muddier than most," Harlan added. "Fortunately for us."

"I've made a decision," Caldwell said suddenly. He was sitting on the worn sofa, and had been quietly talking to Aubrey. "I would like to retain your services."

"My services?" Harlan asked. "Or Gabe's?"

"Don't you work together?" Aubrey said, confused.

Harlan saw his chance to distance himself from this, and therefore keep JD at arm's length from the astrolabe too. "Sometimes, but you can work with Gabe and Shadow's team directly. You don't need my help." He turned to look at the Nephilim and Shadow, hoping he'd said the right thing.

Gabe nodded. "Yes, you can employ us directly. But to do what?"

"Be our bodyguards. Help protect the astrolabe."

Gabe looked at his companions, who answered with nods or shrugs, and he said, "Okay. But not here. We keep you on safe ground, somewhere Black Cronos won't know. But I want full disclosure. No secrets. You must share everything you know."

Without hesitation, Caldwell said, "Deal. Where?"

"Cornwall. We leave tonight."

Eleven

Harlan was not looking forward to his conversation with JD. It didn't help that he'd had to delay it either, because of the interviews at the order's headquarters, and it was now well past eight that night.

He was relieved that Caldwell had asked Gabe for help. Without it, Harlan wasn't sure they'd have lasted until morning. He had reservations about his own safety too, but hopefully Black Cronos wouldn't know of his involvement—yet. He'd taken a long, circuitous route to the guild as a precaution, and pulling up outside, he saw the lone light on in the upper flat. With a sigh, he entered around the back, as he'd done earlier that day. He'd worked out what he was going to say on the way here, but he knew it wouldn't make any difference. JD would still be very angry.

JD was pacing in front of the unlit fireplace when Harlan entered the apartment, and he looked up eagerly, his eyes traveling across Harlan's body. "Where is it?"

"I haven't got it."

"Why not?" JD's hands were on his hips. "I've waited for hours!"

"Because we were attacked this afternoon, and only just escaped with our lives. I wasn't about to wrest the astrolabe from Caldwell at that point. It's theirs, and I wasn't about to risk my life to bring it here, either."

JD almost snarled, his hands clenched into fists. "Your life is worth *nothing* compared to that!"

Harlan looked at him, astonished. "It is to me!"

"You are employed by me, and my wishes should override everything!"

"Even my life? Are you insane?" Harlan strode across the room, wanting to shake some sense into JD, but in the end he just stood over him, satisfied at seeing him step back. "You risked everything for immortality, and still do to accumulate knowledge. How dare you think my life is yours to risk, too! I choose what risks I take. And like I said this morning, I don't back out on deals and double-cross my clients, and neither do Gabe and Shadow."

"It's a fine time to earn a conscience," JD said scathingly. "Where is it now?"

"Somewhere you won't find it. Caldwell has retained Gabe's services privately to protect them. It's out of my hands now." He stepped back, suddenly needing to put more distance between him and JD.

JD looked feral and half-mad as his eyes narrowed, a calculating look sweeping across his face. "They've gone to Cornwall, haven't they? I have their address."

"You think you can take an astrolabe from Gabe and his team? You're madder than you look." A sudden certainty struck Harlan. "You know much more about the Dark Star Astrolabe than you're letting on. What does it lead to?"

JD tutted. "Oh, no. You haven't earned the right to that knowledge. The order has no idea what they're dealing with."

Was he bluffing? Harlan wasn't sure, but he decided to brazen it out. "It's theirs! I'm pretty sure they know what it leads to, and they certainly know the risks now. And none of it has anything to do with you. I'm leaving, JD. This is over. Let it go."

Harlan turned and headed to the door, but on the threshold, JD called, "It is far from over, and if you think I'm letting it go, then you don't know me at all."

Harlan stared at him, suddenly spooked by JD's tone and the vicious look on his face, but he resolutely turned and left, not slowing until he was on his bike and well away from the guild. It was only then that he allowed himself to slow down and think about what JD had said, as the cool evening air washed over him. *You don't know me at all.*

He was right. None of them did, expect for maybe Mason, and he doubted he did, either. JD's obvious age made him seem fragile, physically incapable of acts of violence, but it didn't make him any less unpredictable or dangerous. He had five hundred years of knowledge stacked up...mystical, powerful knowledge. He had mastered immortality. And he summoned an angel at Angel's Rest when he led Gabe to believe he hadn't summoned them for years. He'd been prepared to risk Gabe's life, and had told Harlan much the same. *Your life is worth nothing.* When JD had fixed those sharp, hazel eyes on him, he felt a shudder of apprehension run through him. *What else could JD do? And had he just made an enemy of a man with dubious morals and unknown powers?*

Harlan tried to calm himself down. He was tired, and JD was angry. Everything would be fine. However, he knew a few charms and amulets that could offer protection, and he decided once he got home, he was going to ward his flat and himself. Then he'd warn Gabe, and tomorrow he would see Mason.

Niel was relieved to be home. The drive to Cornwall had put them all on edge, wary of further attack.

It hadn't helped that they'd needed to return to Chadwick House for their bags, as well as wait for Caldwell and Aubrey to pack and make arrangements for the headquarters, even though it was now going to be sealed for days while the paranormal division combed it for evidence.

He and Nahum were in Aubrey's car with Aubrey and Caldwell, following Gabe who travelled ahead with Shadow. When they pulled into the farmhouse's courtyard, it was after midnight and the lights were on. Their brothers were still up.

Barak flung the door open to greet them, ushering them inside quickly before locking them in. "Finally! I was getting worried."

"Just a tedious number of interviews and being fingerprinted," Niel told him as the others trudged ahead of them into the kitchen.

His eyes widened with surprise. "Really? That's shit."

"That's what happens when you kill a bunch of supernatural dudes in London."

Barak grinned. "Wow. You did have fun. I don't know if I'd say as much fun as me, but..."

Niel halted at the bottom of the stairs. "Why? What did you get up to?"

"I had the very lovely Estelle Faversham help me research our little problem." His white teeth gleamed within his wide grin. "Research has never been so good."

"You're a sneaky shit," Niel said grudgingly. "Although, Estelle wouldn't be my preferred assistant."

"Admittedly she did throw me halfway across the warehouse floor, but it was worth it."

"And?" Niel asked, wondering what else Barak had got up to with her.

"And nothing, brother. We just helped each other. I was being charming, of course."

"You obviously weren't when she threw you across the warehouse."

"I like to feel that honesty is part of my charm."

Gabe appeared at the door to the kitchen. "When you two have finished gossiping, we're having a meeting in the living room."

Niel nodded. "Be with you in five. Just moving a few things into Nahum's room—we let Barak know en route." They had agreed on the journey to bunk together, letting Caldwell and Aubrey share Niel's room until they could come up with a better solution.

"Great idea," Gabe said, looking relieved. "I was about to decide on that." He headed back into the kitchen, leaving Barak and Niel alone.

"I've already put the extra mattresses and bedding in both of your rooms," Barak said. "I presumed you didn't want to share Nahum's bed?"

"No bloody thank you," Niel said with feeling.

Barak laughed and then lowered his voice. "Any bets coming home to roost yet?"

Niel knew exactly what bets he was referring to. "Hard to say. They spent a night together in Oxford, and I'm pretty sure something happened. I'm just not sure what exactly. They are both being a little aloof."

Barak gave him a knowing grin. "Ah. We'll discuss it another time, then. Want a beer?"

"Always. Is there any food?"

"Of course—but don't rush."

Niel spent a few minutes moving his belongings into Nahum's room, eyeing the camping bed with distaste, but he'd slept on worse. The Nephilim had been lucky when they found the farmhouse to rent. It was big, with plenty of space for everyone, which meant when they needed peace and quiet and privacy, they could get it. Even so, living with his brothers could try his patience sometimes. At least Nahum was quieter than most.

As he left his room with his belongings, Nahum appeared with Caldwell and Aubrey. "This is where you'll be staying for now," Nahum explained as they looked around with relief.

"Are you two okay?" Niel asked, thinking the last few hours had taken their toll on them both. No one had really spoken in the car, and he'd presumed they'd been in shock. "That was a bad few hours in London."

Caldwell dropped his bag on the floor and sat on the bed. "To be honest, I don't think I've absorbed it all yet. And I can't get the image of the dead bodies and all the blood out of my head."

"If it's any consolation, it wasn't pleasant for us, either."

Aubrey was standing by the window, looking through the blinds at the moors beyond. He turned, his eyes bleak. Wary, even. "You were very good at it."

Nahum shuffled uncomfortably beside him. "We're warriors. It's what we did for years, but we do it less now. We don't kill for pleasure."

"No, of course not." Aubrey nodded and swallowed. "I'm not suggesting you did."

Niel tried to put himself in their shoes, and thought that actually moving in with a bunch of men you hardly knew who were very good at killing people was probably terrifying—even though they had just saved your life. "You can trust us. You're under our protection now. Take a few minutes, use the bathroom, get settled in, and then join us downstairs."

------◄O►------

Gabe waited until everyone had settled down and had their fill of food and drink before he turned the subject to more serious matters.

His brothers had already been asking questions about what had happened in London, and although he'd given them some details, he wanted to talk to them together. Unexpectedly, they were all at home. It seemed that while he'd been away, the problem with the vengeful spirits who had attacked Caspian and the other witches had been resolved. Well, partially. Ash had told him that a couple of the Cornwall witches were involved and had disappeared. It seemed Caspian had granted them all the night off in thanks for their help with the issue, and had covered security at the warehouse with his other men.

"I think it's because we'll be called on more often in coming weeks," Ash had confessed quietly. "We could well be dragged into a witch war."

"Seriously?" Gabe asked, alarmed. "Can't the White Haven witches cope?"

Ash had shrugged. "I think they are all shocked that another witch could have been involved in the attack, and fear that this could get ugly. But yes, they can cope. I think Caspian is just being cautious."

Gabe ran his hands through his hair, wishing he'd showered, but that would have to wait. "Well, we might not be able to help, because I think this job is going to get ugly, too."

Ash was now asking their new arrivals all sorts of questions. Of all of them he was the most intellectual, and Gabe knew he'd be fascinated with the astrolabe. Zee and Eli were also watching and listening, and he presumed Barak had filled them in on his investigations already. Barak was now keeping watch outside for the arrival of any unwanted visitors, and Shadow, still streaked with blood, sat next to Ash while he chatted to Aubrey and Caldwell. Gabe was relieved to see that with some tapas and drink inside them, they were finally starting to look more relaxed.

And what the hell was he going to do about Shadow? Neither had discussed the night at the club beyond their brief chat at breakfast. The kiss. Nuzzling her neck. That had been good...too good. And he knew she felt the same, despite her protestations. But they were engaged in a wary dance, both worried about ruining a good thing. Because what they had right now *was* a good thing. He allowed himself a smile. *But it could be better.* Shadow must have felt him look at her, because she glanced up at him, a questioning look in her eye. He refused to break contact first. She gave him a slow smile before turning away again.

They all needed to sleep, but there were a couple of things he had to know first. Gabe cleared his throat and tapped his half-empty beer bottle. "We need to talk about some important things before we sleep tonight." The idle chatter stopped, and everyone looked at him. "Caldwell, you said you'd be honest about the astrolabe and your order's origins. Now is the time to share."

"Are you sure this can't wait until morning?" he asked.

"No. If by some miracle Black Cronos finds us and attacks again tonight, I at least think we should know why. I'll tell you what Barak has found out, and then you can fill in the gaps."

He summarised Barak's findings, and Caldwell grimaced. "It's mostly accurate, but sketchy. And if I'm honest, our knowledge of the order's past is, too. It seems to have been deliberately obscured." He took a deep breath. "We have heard of Black Cronos, of course. Although Aubrey is right in saying that we didn't think it existed any more. No one has heard mention of them for years, least of all us. But, yes, it could be argued they have a claim to the astrolabe, just as we do. Several hundred years ago, both of our organisations were one, and as Barak suggests, a terrible accident happened. An alchemical experiment went wrong."

"What type of experiment?" Ash asked.

"We are not entirely sure, but think it had to do with the transmutation of the soul," Aubrey explained. "There are no written details of the experiment itself, you understand, just the consequences."

Ash propped his chin on his hands, elbows on knees. "But the transmutation of the soul is one of the seven hermetic principles. It's what many alchemists strive for."

Zee snorted, looking at Ash with incredulity. "Seriously? You know about this stuff?"

"I made it my business when we became involved with JD," Ash explained. "It's been my bedtime reading."

Gabe had no idea of what Ash had been up to, and looked at him in surprise, but Aubrey appeared excited. "You understand it, then?"

Ash shrugged, understated as ever. "I understand the basic philosophy of it, that's all."

Aubrey looked slightly disappointed, but he carried on regardless. "Well, you're right, of course. It is one of the principles, but not all alchemists focus on it. It is considered the highest principle, but also the hardest to achieve. But apparently, our order found the way. Or thought we did."

Gabe stopped him. "Hold on. So you admit your order and Black Cronos at one point were one organisation. Barak's research was correct?"

"We were one until that fateful moment when everything changed," Caldwell said.

Zee butted in. "Wait! Explain this transmutation business. What does it mean?"

"Essentially," Aubrey began patiently, "it is about the soul transcending the base materialness of our body and becoming one with the universe. It is about truly understanding the mysteries of life—the assimilation of the masculine and feminine principle."

A brief silence fell as everyone struggled to understand Aubrey's explanation, and Gabe was relieved he wasn't the only one baffled by alchemy. It looked as if Zee was about to complain, but Gabe shot him a look and he clamped his mouth shut.

Instead, Shadow asked, "Is this about immortality?"

Caldwell answered emphatically, "No. It's about knowledge. About understanding how our world works."

"You're all obsessed with *knowledge*," she observed.

She made 'knowledge' sound like a dirty word, but Gabe knew what she meant. Some men went too far, but others, well...they had made the world a better place.

"So," Gabe continued, "the experiment. Someone was about to do *what*? Conjoin with the universe?"

"We believe so. To achieve the highest state of being. To find the divine within us, and without."

The divine? That didn't bode well, but he didn't voice it. "Okay. And what went wrong?"

"We don't know," Aubrey declared, shrugging.

"According to Barak, they created a monster."

Caldwell winced. "An unfortunate term."

"Isn't it just? What happened?"

"The subject—" Caldwell started.

"The *person*, you mean?" Gabe corrected, his voice hard.

"Yes, the person—well, er," he stumbled over his words, confused. "We think it was more than just their soul that was affected. We think it was their mind, too."

Niel snorted. "Like they went mad? Were possessed? What?"

"We have no idea!" Caldwell could see their sceptical faces, and he persisted. "Seriously, we don't! According to our history, the room was sealed. The experiment was never talked about again. That's what led to the division in our order. Our half vowed it would never attempt it again. The other half said that a result was within our grasp, and we had to keep trying. They went their way, and we went ours."

"So, you have no written history anywhere?" Ash asked.

"Nothing." Aubrey shook his head vigorously. *Too vigorously.*

Gabe felt like they were going around in circles, and he was too tired and too worried about the possibility of being attacked again. "So why is your order, that has so distanced itself from that murky failure at transmutation, interested in where it happened now?"

"Well, some time ago," Caldwell explained, looking ever more shifty, "our order—in particular the Inner Temple—decided that we had strayed too far from the basic principles of alchemy, and that the form had become diluted."

Aubrey nodded. "To put it bluntly, we were all show and no action. Theory, but no practical application. So, we've been trying again, focussing all our energies on this project for the last year. We want to achieve something tangible."

"You want to build on the past," Gabe said, suddenly understanding.

"Yes! We need to understand what went wrong and do it right. We know of no better way than going back to the place of that fateful experiment." Aubrey leaned forward, a fervent light in his eyes that alarmed Gabe. "There could be records there."

"But you saw the members of Black Cronos—if that's who they are," Nahum remonstrated. "They were supernaturally strong. Their eyes were *odd*. What if they progressed their own experiments, and are some sort of weird, transmuted hybrid species? They obviously want the astrolabe, too. They *made* it!"

"And we have it," Aubrey said confidently. "We need to keep ahead of them, that's all."

"That's all?" Gabe said, trying to contain his anger. "We almost died earlier!"

"But you're better than them!" Caldwell pointed out. "We can do this! We can push alchemy forward, as it hasn't been for years!"

"Hasn't been pushed by *you*," Ash pointed out. "I think there are others who have never stopped. Potentially, you have just entered a race that you are so far behind in, you can't possibly win."

"But if we don't try, we'll never know," Aubrey said, smiling softly. "I stole this because," he grabbed the astrolabe again, holding it aloft, "it will take us to our destiny."

Twelve

Harlan had suffered through another poor night's sleep. He had tossed and turned, worrying about the attack and its possible repercussions, his fight with JD, and was nervous that every noise in the dark heralded someone breaking into his flat.

He was behaving like a frail idiot, and after a shower he decided to tackle Mason head-on. However, it seemed that Mason had the same idea, because when he walked through the door of the guild that morning, Smythe seemed to be hovering in the entrance hall, fussing with a huge display of flowers.

"Ah! You're here," he said in his usual insufferable superior tone and a barely-disguised look of glee on his face. "Head straight to Mason's office, please."

"Sure. I'll just take my coat off first and get a coffee," Harlan drawled nonchalantly as he headed up the stairs, refusing to look alarmed.

"But he said—"

Harlan cut him off. "I'm not at school, Robert. I'll be with him in five minutes." He smiled, a challenge in his eyes. "Let him know please, won't you?"

Robert didn't dignify that with a response. Instead, he turned and headed down the hall, his heels clicking with his disapproval. Harlan spent the next few minutes drinking his strong coffee and debating on the tone Mason was going to take, and how he would deal with it. When he thought he'd made Mason wait as long as he could, he swallowed the dregs of his coffee and marched down the hall.

"Harlan." Mason's voice was sharp as he looked up from the papers he'd been scrutinising on his huge, antique desk. The sun behind him made his hair glow in a halo of angelic light he didn't deserve. "JD tells me there was a problem yesterday." He vaguely gestured for him to sit, but Harlan remained standing.

"Yes, there was. JD seemed to think it was okay to renege on a job and double-cross our clients. That's not how we do business, Mason."

Mason blinked, the only sign of his surprise at Harlan's tone. "I agree that it put you in an awkward position, but JD does own this company."

"But he doesn't own *me*."

Mason leaned back in his chair, his eyes hard. "He employs you."

"The company employs me, and we have rules. Our reputation would be on the line. *My* reputation. I'm good at my job, Mason. Our clients trust me. Do you really want me to compromise that?"

And that was the question, Harlan mused, because Mason was both uncomfortable and furious as Harlan reminded him of something Mason had constantly used as his mantra. "The client comes first."

"I know exactly what we'd be risking, but," Mason smiled, an icy glitter in his eyes, "we are no long working for them, are we? They have employed Gabe directly now, correct?"

Fuck it. Harlan had a horrible feeling he'd made a terrible mistake in distancing himself from the job, but he brazened it out. "Correct. We don't act as bodyguards."

"Excellent, then we won't be acting against our clients, will we? JD wants you to retrieve the astrolabe. As soon as possible. He says it's in Cornwall."

Harlan laughed at the preposterous suggestion. "You want me to wrest the astrolabe from seven Nephilim and one fey? Are you insane? And besides, we use them for jobs! They'd never work with us again—and I don't think I need to remind you of how good they are and how much we need them. They found the astrolabe within forty-eight hours. That's quite simply amazing."

Mason stared at Harlan. "That's exactly what I want you to do. And I suggest that you do it discreetly, so that we can continue to work with them in the future."

"You want me to betray our friends."

"Our contractors, not friends." A dangerous edge entered Mason's tone. "You need to consider where your loyalties lie."

Harlan folded his arms across his chest, a white-hot fury starting to build within. "And *you* need to consider where our morals lie."

"We have none, and neither do you when it suits you. Steal back the astrolabe!"

"No! The fact is, more than anything, that I am simply not skilled enough to overcome the Nephilim and Shadow and their phenomenal abilities. I won't do it! Or do you want me to die?"

"But that's the beauty of this. You won't die! They won't kill you!"

"No! Because should I actually be successful, they'll also know where to come looking for it if they suspect me. *And I will have betrayed them!*" Harlan's anger was being replaced by incredulity at the idiotic plan. "This is moronic! JD would be better off trying to come to a compromise with the order."

"But he doesn't trust them or Gabe, actually. Not after he double-crossed him with The Book of Raziel."

"Saved his life, you mean?"

Mason cleared his throat, smiling. "Well, that conversation went as I expected it to, so it's fortunate I already have a second plan in motion."

"*What?*" Harlan was struggling to keep track. He felt like he was in a hall of mirrors. "Have I just been subjected to some kind of test?"

"Yes. And I can say that you both impressed me with your logic, and disappointed me with your loyalty. You were, obviously, my first choice, but I sensed this outcome. So, I have already employed an old, valued contractor who is a very skilled thief. This thief will secure the astrolabe, and you won't be compromised." He nodded a sharp dismissal. "You can go now."

"Wait. Someone's going to steal the astrolabe? Now? *Who?*"

"I'm not that stupid, Harlan. You just go about your business. I presume you have other cases?"

"Er, yes, several," he said, recalling the stack of files on his desk he needed to follow up on.

"Good. Then you needn't worry about this any further. And of course, I thank you in advance for your discretion. You will, of course, say nothing."

Mason then studied the papers on his desk, ignoring Harlan, and just like that he was dismissed. *Just*, he thought, cursing his cockiness with Robert, *like a schoolboy from the principal's office.*

⸻◆⸻

The clang of Shadow's sword against Nahum's shuddered up her arm and through her body, making her feel thrillingly alive.

Nahum was getting quicker and more deadly as they fought aggressively, kicking up dust whilst they whirled around the barn. The early morning sun sliced through the open barn doors, carrying in birdsong, and for a while, Shadow tried to forget about the astrolabe and the strange, not-quite-humans who had attacked them.

Nahum grunted as he fought, although it wasn't from being tired—he was barely breaking a sweat. It was more the effort he put into each move. Shadow, however, was silent. She had heard it made her fighting all the more unnerving, and apart from the odd thud as she landed on the ground, she didn't speak and her feet moved silently across the floor. With a dramatic whirl of his blade, Nahum sought to block her in the corner, but she swung out of the way in an unexpected turn of speed, before finally flicking his sword out of his hand and bringing her blade under his throat.

"Pretty good, Nahum. You've been practicing."

"Not enough," he grimaced. "If I'm to beat you."

She grinned. "I wasn't holding back by much. You're getting faster."

He groaned. "You were holding back?"

"Only a little. I'm fey—that makes me very fast."

"Yeah, yeah! Maybe I should use my wings next time." He grabbed his towel off the bench and wiped the dust and sweat off his face and neck.

"That's actually a good idea. It would add another dimension to our fight, and give me an extra challenge. And I'd like to see how you use your wings in combat, too."

"Please tell me I gave you a reasonable fight, though."

"You did," she reassured him, and not just to massage his vanity. She grabbed her own towel and patted her face and arms, swiping off dirt as she did so. "I'm genuinely impressed. Eli and Zee need to practice more, though. Especially now. They could be dragged into this fight."

"With Black Cronos, you mean?" Nahum sighed, placing his sword down and flexing his wrists. "Zee will, but Eli will only do the bare minimum. But you know that."

"Yes, but he can't choose who he is. I'd hate to see him injured. Will you speak to him? He won't listen to me."

"Gabe already has. But he *can* fight, you know."

"I do know. I've seen him." She'd watched him sparring with Niel a few weeks ago, and was relieved to see that despite his natural aversion to violence, he was quite skilled in combat. "But he doesn't practice as much as he should. Yesterday, we were attacked out of the blue. I feel we got lucky."

He nodded, resigned. "It's only a matter of time before they find us again."

"Perhaps we should find them first."

Nahum looked intrigued. "How?"

"Maggie. Niel gave her the van's number. She must have found out something about the owner by now." Shadow became excited at her suggestion. She'd made it idly, but now it seemed an excellent idea. She'd always rather be on the offensive. "I'll call her."

"She wanted that registration so *she* could find them, not us. She won't just give it to you."

Shadow threw her towel on the bench and started to pace. The fight had given her more energy, not less, and she needed to expend it doing something useful. "Maybe we should go back to Oxford. They must have wanted Blaze to go there for a reason."

Nahum shrugged. "And that reason could be because it's neutral ground. It's a pointless trip without a lead."

Shadow glared at him. "Why do you have to be so logical?"

"Because it saves a lot of time—and we haven't got much of it, either!"

"True. But Caldwell and Aubrey must know more than they're letting on."

"I agree." He raised his brows above his startlingly blue eyes, and Shadow thought if she hadn't already got this ridiculous thing going on with Gabe—because yes, it *was* a thing—she could easily fall for Nahum. He was calm, charming, handsome, and not half as annoying as Gabe. But she shoved that thought quickly away as he said, "Perhaps they're holding back. You know, safeguarding their privacy. They must have some idea where to go. Especially Aubrey!"

"You're right. If they know of an area we should be searching, we should make our way there quickly. Although," she paused, thoughtful, "perhaps Black Cronos has already narrowed it down, and will be there before us?"

Shadow's phone started buzzing on the bench, and she picked it up, noting it was an unknown number. "This is weird," she murmured. "Hello?"

The connection was poor, and the voice faint, but she heard Harlan say, "Shadow? Is that you?"

"Of course it's me! Where are you?"

"In a phone booth, so I'm making this quick. Mason has hired someone to steal the astrolabe. He knows you're in Cornwall. You need to either leave or prepare to defend yourself, now!"

"What do you mean, steal it?" She was staring at Nahum as she spoke, and he froze, watching her.

"Look, I'm betraying the guild by telling you this, and Mason will kill me if he finds out. I'm in Leicester Square and I'll get a burner phone soon. But just listen to me. Get out of there quickly! Gotta go."

He rang off, and Shadow pocketed her phone. "Practice is over. We need to speak to Gabe."

Nahum placed his sword in the scabbard that Shadow insisted he wore while they practiced, grabbed his towel, and, while Shadow headed into the main house to find Gabe, Nahum looked up to the roof of the outbuildings, pleased to see Ash sitting up there, leaning against a chimney. He flew up and sat cross-legged next to him.

Ash was leaning back against the warm stone of the chimney, relaxed but watchful. The sun had burnished his natural olive skin, giving him a golden glow. It also made his cheekbones look sharper, and highlighted his intelligent, pale brown eyes that gleamed in the light. His long hair was tied high on his head, and Nahum thought that when men talked about Greek Gods, they had probably envisaged someone who looked like Ash.

"Anyone approaching?" he asked Ash.

He shook his head. "Nothing. It's calm and quiet." He grinned. "It's a relief, after the noise of the house."

Nahum nodded and looked at the view. He had sat up here many times himself, often at night, enjoying watching the lights of houses spread across the moors, the cars travelling along the lanes, and White Haven, though most of which was hidden in the fold of the valley. Sometimes he could see the moonlight glinting off the sea, but at other times it was a swell of endless grey. In the day, however, it was easier to discern the rise and fall of the land, the gentle curves as one field rolled into another, the distant trees of Ravens' Wood, and the castle on the cliff. It was a beautiful, sunny June day and the sea sparkled, calm and flat to the distant horizon. Nahum wished he could ride Stormfall to the woods. Maybe he could later, once they had made plans.

Ash was watching him. "Are you seeking respite after your fight with Shadow?"

Nahum laughed. "A little, perhaps. She's so fast it's bewildering. She's told me to use my wings next time to add *fun* to the fight." He raised his eyebrows. "I still think I'd lose! But actually, I have news, too. We have more trouble. JD has decided he wants the astrolabe. He's sent someone to get it."

Ash muttered a curse in ancient Greek. "He has the obsessive nature of a true fanatic, which makes him a dangerous man. I've been reading about him."

"You've been reading about lots of things."

Ash shrugged. "Alchemy interests me, and I found it began a long time before JD came along—in the East. In JD's time, before his immortality, he was a very ambitious man. History suggests he could have been a professor at various universities. He made maps, you know. Cartography and mathematics were his specialties before he became obsessed with angels. He was held in high esteem by Queen Mary, and then Queen Elizabeth. I think his obsessions derailed a potentially excellent academic life. Not that I should criticise, of course. He still achieved a huge amount." Ash's gaze was distant. "You can't switch off that life. He must have continued to write and publish under other names after his 'death.'"

"Perhaps he did," Nahum agreed. "I'm sure there's a wealth of things we don't know about JD. I wonder what he wants this astrolabe for?"

"To build on the knowledge of the experiment, I'm sure, just like the others."

Ash frowned as he stared across the valley, and Nahum followed his eye line. "Have you seen something?"

"I thought I did, but it's just birds."

Nahum saw a flock of birds on the field scatter into the air, disturbed by a farmer. He sighed, wishing he could stay with Ash, but he had to find out what their plans would be. "I'll leave you to it. I suspect we'll be leaving soon."

"So be it, brother," Ash said, settling himself back against the brick once more.

Niel was preparing food in the kitchen when Shadow strode in, bristling with purpose and smeared with dust after sparring with Nahum.

In typical Shadow fashion, she was abrupt. "There's more trouble coming. Where is Gabe?"

Niel stopped chopping vegetables and looked up, alarmed. "He's in the cellar. What do you mean, more trouble?"

She ignored him, striding out of the room, and biting back his annoyance with her peremptory manner, Niel followed her downstairs.

The cellar was the place where Shadow had been held captive after they had captured her in Old Haven Church woods. Since then the iron cage had been dismantled, and the cellar was just a big, empty space used for storage. But that morning, Gabe had taken an old wooden table and chairs down there, and Aubrey and Caldwell had set up their books and research.

Shadow marched in, interrupting their conversation, and Niel leaned against the door frame, watching the animated discussion within as Shadow related Harlan's phone call.

"We should leave," Shadow argued. "What if Black Cronos tracks us here, and both parties arrive at the same time? I mean, I like our chances, but why risk it?"

"But we know this place," Gabe said. "We're on high ground, we can see people coming, and all of the Nephilim are here. Plus, the witches."

Caldwell and Aubrey looked startled and watched the exchange avidly.

"But we're sitting ducks!" Shadow protested.

Gabe rubbed his face, exasperated. "You say Harlan doesn't know who Mason has sent?"

"No. Just an old and valued contractor. It sounds like one person, but they may bring support. And we have no idea if they are human or not. And the likelihood is that Black Cronos will send a lot more people this time!"

"If they have more!" Niel argued.

Shadow shot him an impatient look. "Oh, come on. They'll have more! I suspect they have a lot of resources at their disposal, which is why they will find us here sooner rather than later." She rounded on Caldwell and Aubrey. "You two must have some idea where this astrolabe leads. That's where we should go!"

"Er," Caldwell stammered, glancing nervously at Aubrey, who looked at the floor. "Not really."

"Bullshit," she exclaimed. "Yesterday you admitted that you'd been studying this for a long time."

"And," Gabe added, "you promised us full disclosure. I promised to protect you, but if you lie, I'm out, and you're on your own."

Aubrey groaned. "Yes, okay. You have to understand that we've been very secretive about this. It's hard to share so much now."

"But someone hasn't been secretive, and that's why we're in this mess," Gabe reminded him. "However, we'll come back to your mole later. Where now?"

"We think the place of the original experiment, the place that has been sealed for centuries, is in France, in what was old Aquitaine."

"Which is where?" Niel asked, feeling excited at the prospect of leaving England.

"The southwest, bordering the Atlantic and Pyrenees, and in what now comprises the Dordogne and a few other places."

Gabe nodded, his arms folded across his chest. "The place where the order was thought to have originated."

"Yes." Aubrey pulled a map from under the papers on the table, spread it out, and pointed to an area. "Here is Bordeaux, the capital of the region, and we believe the place is close by. There are fields, woods, and a wide range of *châteaus* there, though many now are vineyards and visitor attractions."

"And Madame Charbonneau?" Gabe asked, eyes narrowing. "Where does she fit into this?"

"She lives much further south, close to Nice," Aubrey said, "and is not connected to these events."

Shadow gave a short, dry laugh. "So then why did she have the astrolabe?"

Aubrey had been hunched over the map, deep in thought, but now he straightened. "She's a rich antiquarian living on an old estate. She used to collect all sorts of things, not just occult objects. A decade or so ago she was a regular visitor to auction rooms, and has pretty much neglected her estate for her passion. Now," he shrugged, "she is old, pretty much housebound. It was sad to see how she now lives. The house is falling apart around her."

Niel felt a stir of distaste for Aubrey. His soft exterior belied the sharp brain and ruthless ambition to steal from an old woman, and he couldn't help but say, "Why didn't you just buy it from her?"

Aubrey looked at him in surprise. "We couldn't risk her not selling it to us."

"How did you track it down?" Gabe asked.

Caldwell had been thumbing through an old book while they talked, but now he gave a delighted laugh. "That was pure luck! We'd been searching for months through old catalogues of astrolabe sales going back decades, in the hope of finding ours, and stumbled upon the records for an auction in France years ago. The image was grainy, but it was enough to give us hope."

Aubrey nodded. "I did my homework, found out everything I could about her. I crossed my fingers and hoped she hadn't sold it, and then flew over to investigate. It was like the Gods willed it to be. There was hardly any security, and only a couple of staff." He shrugged. "I picked my moment and was able to hide in the house long enough to search for it. I found it in one of her rooms." Aubrey shook his head at the memory, his gaze distant. "Such a beautiful place, falling into ruin."

Shadow seemed utterly concerned about the theft and picked up the Dark Star Astrolabe that lay on the table, gleaming with intrigue under the light. "Are you sure it's the right one?"

"Yes, absolutely." Aubrey started leafing through an old leather-bound manuscript. "This diary belonged to one of our members in the eighteenth century. He'd conducted his own research, and based on papers he found, drew this image of it. Unfortunately, those original papers have long disappeared."

He showed them the drawing that had been carefully and skillfully drawn in ink, and it was clear it was the same as the one Shadow now held. Niel was confused. Something wasn't right, and clearly Gabe thought the same, because he froze.

"You two have plans you haven't told me about," Gabe accused them. "You must be planning to go to France. Why haven't you discussed this with me?"

"Er, well," Caldwell stuttered, "we thought you probably didn't need to know, and that we could just go."

"*Just go*? I bring you here—to my home—to keep you safe, and you don't think to say that you'll be going in...when, a day or two?"

Aubrey looked at him coolly. "We assumed that we were in danger here, but that once we got on a plane, we'd be safe. We have a secure place in France to go to, arrangements we made weeks ago. It's there that we shall read the astrolabe on the assigned date."

"You were going to do a midnight flit?" Gabe asked sarcastically.

"I don't know what the issue is!" Caldwell said, rising to his feet, his fine features haughty. "We thought the less we divulged, the better."

Gabe lowered his face to Caldwell's so that they were inches apart. "And in the meantime, I'm pulling *my* men from other jobs to cover you, and making plans for the next few days, and you're not even going to be here? You ungrateful shits!"

Aubrey leapt to his feet too, laying a restraining hand on Caldwell's arm. "No, not ungrateful at all! We are extremely appreciative of your protection, but equally, this is a very delicate situation. The search for something that had been lost for a long time! And of course we were going to tell you. We wouldn't just go in the middle of the night!"

Gabe rounded on him too, his fists clenched. "You don't think they would follow you there?"

"It is a secure location!" Caldwell repeated. "Only our Inner Temple know of it."

"And one of the members of which have betrayed you!"

"No!"

"You are deluded!"

Niel hadn't seen Gabe look so angry in years, but he wouldn't step in. Gabe could control his temper, and he wouldn't touch either of them, despite his menacing presence.

"Fine!" Gabe was continuing. "You get on that plane and hole up in your secret location, and you'll see just how trustworthy your Inner Temple is!"

Before anyone could say anything else, a shout disturbed them, and Niel headed to the door, yelling, "We're here! What's the matter?"

Nahum appeared at the top of the stairs, a towel around his waist and his hair still wet. "Ash has spotted a large van on the lane heading into White Haven. I think we may have company."

Thirteen

G abe stood on the roof next to Ash, following the direction of his pointed finger. "They were on that road, heading into White Haven." Ash's golden eyes were suspicious. "It could just be a random black van, but then again..."

Gabe nodded, trying to subdue his fury from the conversation he'd just had. "Best to be prepared. Although, if it is them, surely they won't attack in broad daylight?"

"But that is both the advantage and disadvantage of being here. We're isolated."

Gabe considered their options, and the more he did, the more he realised he didn't want to run. "This is our home. If just a few of us flee, we'll leave the ones who remain behind vulnerable. I won't do it. We'll fight them off—make a stand."

Ash nodded. "I agree. Zee is still here, so we're only missing Eli and Barak."

"And we have plenty of weapons," Gabe said, thinking of the stash of swords, daggers, and axes they had, the crossbow they had recently acquired, as well as Shadow's long bow, and the couple of shotguns. He hated using guns, but had been persuaded to get them by Niel. "We could lock Aubrey and Caldwell in the cellar and keep one of us in that corridor to protect them, and then position the rest of us around the house."

"They're bound to split up. Probably approach over the fields."

Gabe nodded, taking a couple of deep breaths to calm down. He needed to put his annoyance with Aubrey and Caldwell aside, and focus.

"What's happened?" Ash asked. "You look furious."

"Bloody Aubrey and Caldwell are planning to go to France, and they didn't even bother to tell me! What is it about alchemists and their bloody secrets?"

"France?" Ash asked, confused. "Why?"

Gabe quickly summarised their conversation and saw disappointment sweep over Ash's face. "Damn it. I really wanted to be involved with this one."

"Depending on what happens tonight, we still might be. They'd be mad to continue this alone." He took another deep breath, trying to filter through his emotions. "I'm disappointed, too. I'll talk to them later."

"Would you consider me? It interests me, and I think I could be useful."

Ash looked eager, and he knew some of the other Nephilim were keen to be involved in their new line of work. Depending on what they earned on this job, maybe they should consider leaving Caspian's employment at the end of the year. That would free them up to take on new jobs, too. There was no doubt that having to cover Caspian's warehouse was starting to become a pain, but he also felt loyalty to Caspian for offering them work in the first place. The same applied to Eli, Ash, and Zee, all of whom worked for the witches, though he knew Eli would want to remain working with Briar.

Gabe nodded. "Sure, if we're still involved. I'll see if Barak wants to come, too. Niel can cover the warehouse instead. It's only fair. Although," Gabe grimaced, "I'll miss his cooking."

Ash grinned. "We'll work it out. Thanks Gabe, I'm really looking forward to this."

"Let's just hope that we can get through the next twenty-four hours, or we won't be going anywhere."

Leaving Ash on lookout, Gabe flew down to the courtyard and walked the perimeter. They had several outbuildings, the barn being the biggest. Next to it was the stable, although both horses had been put out in the fields to graze. Shadow and Nahum were the best on horseback, and Kailen and Stormfall were battle-hardened. Using them both would certainly be an advantage. There was also the building where Shadow lived, and a storage room next door. His SUV and Nahum's car were generally in the courtyard if they weren't stored in the barn, as were the bikes the other Nephilim used. A couple of his brothers could potentially hide in the buildings.

He called Eli on the way back to the house, just to make him aware of their circumstances, and Eli promised to call them if he saw anything odd in White Haven. Then he called Barak and updated him, too.

"There's a chance we might be going to France—if Caldwell comes to his senses. I'm wondering if you want to come, if we can sort everything out soon enough?"

"Are you serious?" Barak asked, sounding excited. "Did you read my mind, or something? I'd love to come. But who'll cover here? There'll be night shifts to consider."

"Leave it with me," Gabe said, sighing. "I'll see if I can work something out with Caspian."

Zee was in the kitchen when Gabe entered. He was making coffee and wiggled a mug at Gabe. "Want one?"

"Please. Make it strong."

"Where is everyone?"

"In the cellar, probably. Come on down with me while I update the group."

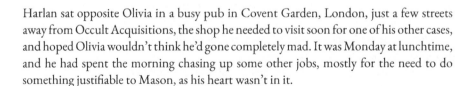

Harlan sat opposite Olivia in a busy pub in Covent Garden, London, just a few streets away from Occult Acquisitions, the shop he needed to visit soon for one of his other cases, and hoped Olivia wouldn't think he'd gone completely mad. It was Monday at lunchtime, and he had spent the morning chasing up some other jobs, mostly for the need to do something justifiable to Mason, as his heart wasn't in it.

Olivia eyed the burner phone that sat between them on the table. "Is that really necessary?"

"Yes! For all I know, Mason can trace my calls, and I don't want them to know that I'm helping Gabe." He stared at her bewildered expression, and his heart sank. "Shit. You think I'm doing the wrong thing, don't you?"

Olivia was in her hunter attire, as Harlan liked to call it. She was wearing old jeans, boots, and a t-shirt, her leather jacket thrown across the back of her chair, and her hair was loose around her shoulders. She was, however, still wearing makeup, and managed to pull off glamorous charm, despite her clothes. She gave him a sad smile. "No, I'm sorry to say. I think you are doing exactly the right thing. I don't trust JD or Mason anymore after Angel's Rest." She pushed her white wine away, rested her elbows on the table, and dropped her face into her cupped hands. "I hate this situation, and that you've been dropped in it. But I'm not entirely sure what I can do to help."

Relief swept through Harlan. "You don't need to do a thing. I'm just glad you see my point. I thought maybe I'd lost the plot. But—" He paused, looking at her hopefully.

"Always a 'but,'" she said, resigned but still smiling. "Go on."

"I want to know who Mason has sent after the astrolabe."

She gave a short laugh. "Ha! That might be tricky, but I'll try. I can head in there soon on the pretext of grabbing some files, and if I can't manage today, I'll try tomorrow. I reckon I can worm something out of Smythe." She smirked. "He can't help but let out how much he's privy to things."

"True, plus he likes you."

"As much as he likes anyone, which isn't much at all. I need to leave London for a few days after that."

"A case?"

Olivia nodded. "In Nottingham." She sipped her wine for a moment, and then said, "Mason didn't threaten you, did he? Or JD?"

"No, but I gotta admit, this whole thing is making me uneasy." He considered the maniacal gleam in JD's eyes, and the sneaky look in Mason's. "I don't trust them anymore. But equally, I'm good at my job, so I don't think Mason will fire me. I think I just need to lie low for a few days and let this play out."

"Okay, but if you need me, just call. I'm on your side, Harlan."

Harlan smiled and squeezed her hand. Maybe he should tell her who JD was. *It could be safer for Olivia in the long run.* If she was putting her neck on the line for him, she deserved the whole truth. "Thanks Liv. Let's get some lunch, because I have something else I need to tell you."

———◇———

Barak had just finished eating his lunchtime burger when he heard Estelle's voice resonate across the warehouse and through his door. In minutes, she appeared in his doorway. She leaned against the frame nonchalantly, today dressed in a slim-fitting skirt and silk shirt. He missed her yoga leggings.

"Have you got news about the astrolabe?" she asked him.

Barak brushed the breadcrumbs from his chin and nodded. "Apparently the order was holding out on us. They have an approximate address for where they think this mysterious chamber is...somewhere in old Aquitaine, in France. They're heading there in a day or two."

"Around Bordeaux!" She sidled into the room and sat opposite him, intrigued. "So, what now?"

He grinned, unable to contain his excitement. "We might be going—if we can get flights. And if Gabe can persuade Caldwell that they still need us. He thinks they'll be out of danger once they leave the country."

"Idiots. Wait, we?" she asked, frowning.

"Yup! I'm going, too. Niel will cover here, but I think Gabe is going to try to make arrangements to cover him too, just in case he's needed." He ran his hand across the stubble of his shaved hair. "I can't wait, to be honest. I want to see more of the world—as lovely as Cornwall has been. And you, of course," he teased her.

Her eyes widened with surprise and then she suppressed a smile, a slight flush gracing her cheeks. "You're such a flirt, Barak."

"I know. But I mean it. Miss me?"

"You wish!" But she smiled as she said it, and Barak's pulse quickened.

"The only thing is, if Gabe *can* persuade them to let us accompany them, he's reluctant to use their accommodation. He's pretty sure one of their Inner Temple members has compromised them. But the possibility of securing new accommodation now is unlikely." He was aware as he was saying it that the Witches Council had just endured their own betrayal, and hoped that it had nothing to do with Estelle. He knew she hated them.

Estelle leaned forward. "You know, I might be able to help you find somewhere to stay in that area, if you're struggling."

"Really?" He leaned across the desk, catching the scent of her musky perfume. "How?"

"As you know, we have an office in Marseilles, and my Uncle Max lives close by. He has a lot of friends, rich friends, with old, rambling *maison de campagnes, châteaus,* and maybe some *gîtes*—although, they will be small."

"You really think you can get one for us?"

"There's no harm in trying, is there?" She leaned forward, too, and he felt the heat radiate from her skin, mere inches across the table from him. "But there'll be a catch."

Of course there would be. "Go on."

"I want to come, too. Caspian is back, and to be honest, I need a break from him."

"I knew something was going on between you two. What happened?"

Her eyes hardened. "I don't need to explain."

"Come on," he coaxed, his voice dropping as did his eyes to her lips. "Indulge me. I need to give Gabe a reasonable explanation as to why you want to come."

"The fact that I will find the house as a favour should be reason enough!"

"Not for Gabe."

Estelle propped her chin on her hand and looked him straight in the eye, weighing up her response. Finally, she said, "We had an argument, an unpleasant one, and he used his magic on me. I'm not sure I'll ever forgive him for that."

He raised an eyebrow. "What did you do to provoke him?"

"You think *I* provoked *him*?" Her voice rose with anger.

"Yes! I know you, and I know Caspian. He's a very reasonable man, whereas you are a firecracker. My ripped t-shirt in the bin is witness to that." He watched a range of emotions race across Estelle's face. "What did you do?"

"We argued about the White Haven witches and that stupid Witches Council, and that's all I'm prepared to say. Things got ugly."

She'd needled him about Avery. "They're his friends, Estelle. Good friends, and I like them, too. They're decent people. You should cut Caspian some slack. He could have died last week. I was there, remember? Alex saved his life."

She withdrew, easing back in her chair. "Well, he's fine now, and is back in the office tomorrow, but I need some space. And I'm due a holiday, and beautiful, sunny France will suit me perfectly. Is that enough to satisfy Gabe?"

"We'll see. Why don't you rustle up a place now and I'll let Gabe know that you're our knight in shining armour? I guess having a witch around will be handy, too. I presume you are prepared to fight with us, should it be needed? Black Cronos is a dangerous adversary."

She stood abruptly and walked to the door. "Of course I will. My anger with Caspian still burns right here." She tapped her heart. "I can't wait to let off some steam." She gave him a smile that didn't quite reach her eyes, and then gracefully exited.

For a few moments, Barak didn't move as he considered her words. As much as he wanted to, could he really trust Estelle, or was she bewitching him with her beauty and intelligence? Was he sex-starved enough to want to believe anything of her? Or, more to the point, did he really think he could melt her icy demeanour?

By the Gods, he was willing to give it a try.

He grinned and picked up his phone. *Time to tell Gabe the good news.*

———◆O◆———

Shadow couldn't believe her ears. "Resting Bitch Face has offered to help...and wants to come with us? Is this your idea of a joke?"

"No! I'm serious!" Gabe said, glancing up from the array of weapons spread across the kitchen table.

"But Caldwell doesn't want us there! Have you forgotten that?"

Gabe straightened up. "We need to persuade them to let us come."

"Why?" Shadow asked, annoyed. "The man is an idiot! They both are! Let them die. I believe it's called Darwinism."

Gabe sighed. "Shadow! That's mean."

"Don't pretend you weren't annoyed with him. You were furious!"

"Yes, I was. I hate being lied to, but I also understand that this is their big secret, and they've never dealt with anything like this before." His shoulders dropped as he appealed to her. "That's why people like them need people like us."

Shadow hated being lied to, as well. It made her feel stupid, like she'd been double-crossed. "Who cares! They had their chance. How can we trust them?"

"They're not bad people, they're just out of their depth. Besides, if we get attacked again, which I sincerely hope we don't, I think they'll be begging for our protection." He smiled, triumphant. "And that means staying in a place of our choosing."

"Hence, Resting Bitch Face to the rescue."

Gabe tried and failed to subdue a smile. "We need a place to stay, and she can help. Nahum has been looking for accommodation, just in case, and they're all booked! We're screwed without her."

"And screwed *with* her!" She groaned and threw her dagger at the wall, embedding it deep in the plaster next to the doorframe, and causing Nahum, who was entering, to flinch.

"Herne's balls, Shadow. Watch where you're throwing that!" Nahum pulled the blade out, crossed the room, and handed it back to her, saying, "I like my face just the way it is."

"I was aiming at the wall, idiot, and I don't miss." She swiped it out of his hand and slid it into the sheath strapped to her thigh, fuming. *Living with Estelle would be a nightmare.* Shadow's hands clenched just at the thought of her superior manner.

"Besides," Gabe was adding in his calmest and most annoyingly diplomatic tone, "a witch will be a useful addition to our skill set."

Shadow marched to the window and glared at the fields beyond, taking deep breaths as she willed herself to be calm. She would have to try very hard not to sink a knife into Estelle's throat, and she wasn't sure her patience would be equal to it. *Maybe she could engineer an accident...*

"Stop it right now," Gabe instructed her, causing her to whirl around to face him. He was glaring at her and tapping his head. "I can hear those little cogs squeaking around, making malevolent plans. Just don't. I rely on you. Don't let me down."

Shadow was about to argue some more, but that comment brought her up short. He'd never told her he relied on her before. She knew it, but it was something else to hear it. And that was the trouble with Gabe. He knew how to push her buttons. Every single one.

"Fine," she ground out between clenched teeth, trying not to show how pleasing his comment was. "I shall do my utmost to be polite. But if she starts something—"

"I fully expect you to rise above it. Can we move on?"

"I suppose so."

Nahum cleared his throat, causing both to turn to him. He was watching them with a broad smirk across his face. "I have news, if you're interested."

Gabe nodded. "Go right ahead."

"On the presumption that we can talk them around, I've booked flights for eight of us, at nine-thirty in the morning the day after tomorrow, taking us from Newquay Airport to London, and then Bordeaux Airport directly. Us three, Aubrey, Caldwell, and Ash, Barak, and," he grinned at Shadow, "Bitch Face."

She glowered at him. "Please don't gloat. It's unbecoming."

Nahum sniggered. "So is sulking."

Gabe ignored their bickering. "Couldn't get flights any sooner?"

"Nope. All booked. It might mean we have a tricky day or so fending off Black Cronos."

"Not if we can make a big enough impression today," Gabe said thoughtfully. "If that's even who Ash spotted."

Shadow shook her head. "It will be JD's thief we have to worry about first. Although, I'm sure a thief won't be much of a threat to us."

"Let's hope you're right," Gabe said, staring vacantly out of the window for a moment. "Would you two take the horses out and check the fields and beyond? I can't shake the feeling that someone's out there, watching us."

Desperate to get out and do something other than skulk around the house, Shadow said, "It will be my pleasure. Ready, Nahum?"

"Right with you, sister."

Fourteen

Barak was stacking the dishwasher and doing pointless busywork after their evening meal in an effort to stop worrying. Dusk was falling, and Shadow and Nahum had been gone ten minutes, out to survey the land again. As he waited, Barak had that horrible nervous sensation, like the silence before a storm.

He had left the warehouse late that afternoon, swapping places with Niel, who had grumbled about it for a while, before insisting that it was fine. Barak knew it wasn't, and that he desperately wanted to join them. He hoped there'd be a way for that to happen.

A shout rang out across the courtyard and Barak froze, just as an arrow broke the kitchen window and embedded into the wall behind him. In seconds he'd dropped to the floor, listening for a beat, before grabbing the axe from the table.

Gabe shouted, "Barak! Are you okay?"

"I'm fine!" he shouted back, risking a peek out of the window. But although no one was in view, another arrow zinged through the window, and glass rained down upon his head. "Someone must be beyond the hedge at the back of the field!" His heart was hammering as he thought of Zee, who was now on the roof instead of Ash. "Can you see Zee?"

Gabe appeared at the doorway in a low crouch. "No. I was in the cellar. But I've secured Aubrey and Caldwell down there, and Ash is on the rear corridor."

Another crash of glass indicated they were now targeting Ash, too.

Before either of them could call out, Ash yelled, "I can see him! He's in the long grass in front of the far hedge. Shit—he's covering for about three others who are headed this way."

"Stay put," Gabe instructed Ash and beckoned for Barak to follow him.

Eli had been in the living room, but he joined them in the corridor, a sword already in his hand. "Where do you want me, Gabe?"

"We'll head to the courtyard, see if we can fan out around the house."

Barak grabbed the shotgun before racing to the front of the house that overlooked the courtyard, crouching below one of the windows. He lifted his head in time to see a bloom of debris fly up from the chimney that Zee had been next to, an arrow embedding into the brick. But there was no sign of Zee.

"Who's got the crossbow?" Niel asked.

Gabe looked grim. "Zee, but where the hell is he?"

"Sounds like he saw the shooter first, so hopefully he's on the ground," Barak reasoned. "And if there's only one of them with a bow and arrow, then we should be protected back here." He stood against the wall and peeked around the window frame, but the courtyard was deserted, and there was still no Zee. "I'm heading to the barn."

"I'll go to the right," Eli said, gripping his sword.

Gabe was on the phone to Shadow, summoning her home, as Barak pulled the door open and sprinted across the courtyard, making the barn door just as an arrow whizzed by his head and landed in the barn wall.

A second shooter.

Twilight was falling quickly now, the half-light making it harder to see, but as Barak dropped and rolled, bringing his shotgun up, he saw a figure beyond the gate, holding close to the wall. Barak was too far away to do much damage with the shotgun, but he fired regardless, and the figure vanished. Eli had made it to the empty building next to Shadow's, and he disappeared through the door safely.

But a splintering crash from behind had Barak diving to the ground, and before he could shoot, a heavy-set man was on him, a blade flashing, and he was fighting for his life.

———— ◆◇◆ ————

Gabe cursed the attackers, though he was relieved to know that Shadow and Nahum were on their way back. *How had they got so close when Zee was on watch? And why the hell hadn't Shadow or Nahum seen them?*

They must have some paranormal stealth the group was unaware of. At least Zee had spotted their shooter, and had hopefully made it to safety.

With Niel in the barn and Eli in the storeroom, Gabe crept around the rear of Shadow's room. As he rounded the corner, he saw a sudden movement to his right and a strong arm snaked around his neck, choking him and trying to drag Gabe to the ground. He had a second's shock that someone had the strength to do that before he fought back, throwing his whole body backwards and cracking his attacker against the wall. The grip loosened, allowing Gabe to turn and punch. With a sickening crunch he felt his opponent's cheek break, but it didn't slow him down, and in seconds they were both rolling across the ground, trading punches.

The man was as big as Gabe, hugely muscled with the dead-eyed gaze of the men they had encountered before. He wrapped his huge hands around Gabe's neck and squeezed, but Gabe's wings unfurled, lifting them both. The man's eyes widened with surprise as his grip slackened, and Gabe pushed him against the wall, wary of flying too high. But within seconds an arrow landed in the man's chest and dropping him, Gabe spun around to see Zee at the corner of the building.

Zee just nodded, and then crept around the side of the building, his crossbow raised. Gabe headed the other way. A shout, the clash of swords, and the boom of the shotgun broke the silence, but before Gabe could respond, the black-clad woman who'd escaped from the order's headquarters emerged from the long grass of the fields and tackled him to the ground, her lips closing on his.

Eli edged to the grimy window at the far end of the empty building, dodging around some old farm machinery that had been rusting for years.

The shadows were dark in here, contorting into strange shapes, and he took a moment to ensure the skittering noises he could hear were just mice and nothing else. They really should get cats...he'd been telling Gabe so for months. Eli advanced slowly in a half-crouch, his sword at the ready, but also wishing he'd grabbed another weapon. He passed a large wrench on a battered work bench, and picking it up, peered through the window to the lane beyond the gate.

Like all the Nephilim, his eyesight was keen, but the grimy window both afforded him protection and obscured his view. He waited for long moments, ignoring the fighting he could hear outside, and focussed on the hedge edging the lane. Within moments he was rewarded, as another three figures sidled out of the darkness. All three were lean and stealthy, and in the dim light he could see the glint of steel in their hands, and caught a glimpse of a long bow behind the shoulders of one of them. Only one was heading towards him, and there was no way Eli could attack quietly. There was no door at this end, and the window was sealed shut. Deciding speed was his best option, he waited patiently until the man was close and then leapt through the window, glass shattering everywhere as he tackled him to the ground. With two quick slashes of his sword, the man lay dead at his feet, and he ran towards the next at the outskirts of the barn, and who was already turning to face him. But Eli's speed had given him the upper hand, and after virtually gutting his opponent, he turned to chase down the third.

Unfortunately, there were another two advancing on him, and Eli realised there were still more lurking in the shadows. Just as he was squaring up to face his opponents, he heard the whisper of an arrow in flight and he dived down, the arrow catching the top of his shoulder and spinning him around. His sword fell from his hand, but he still had the wrench...and his wings.

Eli unfurled his wings as he stood and used them like a shield, batting away a couple of arrows before his opponents were on him. He felt his blood rush as it hadn't in years, and he couldn't suppress a grin. Fighting with a wrench was inelegant, but it would have to do.

Desperate though Shadow was to return as quickly as possible to help Gabe and his brothers, she slowed her approach as she reached the edge of the fields bordering their own and slipped from Kailen's back in the deep shadows of a huge oak, leaving him in the hollow on the other side, well out of sight.

It wasn't fully dark yet, but the twilight was confusing. *Their enemies had picked a good time*, Shadow mused, *when the light was at its most deceptive*. But she couldn't work out why they hadn't seen them approach. She could only surmise that once she and Nahum left they had moved swiftly, and there was only so much ground they could both cover effectively.

Shadow scrambled up the tree to find a good viewpoint, and then melted into the dark as she attuned her senses to her surroundings. She heard the scuttle of small mammals and the swoop of the bats before they wheeled into view. The birds were settling too, the air full of their evening song.

And then she saw them—half a dozen figures, making their way swiftly through the long grass in the field where the horses grazed, and heading towards the house. By the hedge, one man was already dead; she could see the arrow in his chest and his spread-eagled pose, but another was taking pot-shots at the house to offer cover for the others. Then another figure popped up by corner of the house, dispatching a bolt that embedded deep in the shooter's chest, killing him instantly. She grinned as she realised it was one of her brothers.

The other attackers immediately dived into the grass, and Shadow realised this was the perfect spot for a sniper. She readied her bow, and moving from left to right, released her arrows in quick succession and with deadly accuracy, each earning a head shot. She waited, wondering if more would emerge. They clearly had a plan, but they had made a mistake letting her and Nahum go alive.

Shadow focussed on where she knew the lanes bordered the far end of the field, and spotted the tell-tale swish of the tall grass, indicating someone's steady progression towards the corner of the house. As good a shot though she was, the distance was too far for accuracy. She dropped to the ground, deciding to advance on foot. Tempting though it was to charge in on Kailen, in this case, stealth was her friend.

Nahum was on the moors when he received the call from Shadow, and he raced over the rugged landscape, his body low against Stormfall.

The trees were stunted from the relentless wind that blew at this elevation during the winter months, the land rising and falling and silvered with streams. He paused on a rise to study the farmhouse a short distance away, and despite the twilight, his superior eyesight meant he could see the dozen intruding figures at various points around the house, some very close and others further back, as if they were planning a wave of attacks.

He urged Stormfall forward at a trot, the thick heather masking his approach. Like Shadow, Stormfall was silent when he needed to be, and faster than any horse Nahum had ever been on. He decided to strike quickly by sweeping around the back of them, and when he was close enough, he let Stormfall race. Withdrawing his sword, Nahum charged the first man down, trampling him underfoot. He killed the next two with his sword, and then was almost unseated when a few figures rose out of the murky twilight, previously unseen. But Stormfall didn't scare easily, and Nahum wheeled him around, the horse responsive to Nahum's every need. Nahum felt the burning slice of a blade along his leg, but ignored it as he cut another figure down and then turned towards the farmhouse, deciding to charge into the courtyard.

Ash had already killed three enemies—two men and one woman—all who moved with the swift efficiency of practiced killers. Fighting in the tight confines of the rear corridor wasn't the easiest, but it hampered his opponents too, and now with all three dead at his feet as well as the shooter in the field, Ash hoped this was nearly over.

But a sound from the end of the corridor made him withdraw to the top of the cellar stairs. He risked peering around the corner, and an arrow embedded into the plaster, mere inches from his face. *Great. Now they were in the house. What the hell where his brothers doing?*

A flurry of arrows kept him pinned in position, and Ash realised he was a sitting duck. He considered retreating to the cellar with the others when crossbow bolts suddenly flew from the other direction. Ash heard a thud and then a shout.

"It's Zee! Ash? Niel? Are you there?"

"Yes, brother. I'm coming out, don't shoot!"

Zee marched towards him, his face grim. "They have sent many to attack us, all well-trained." He kept out of view of the window, but glanced towards the fields. "I think Shadow is out there. She shot the others in the field, so I'm heading upstairs to see if I can pick off some more. Are you okay here?"

Ash nodded, gesturing at the cuts on his arms and legs. "Superficial only. You carry on."

"Shout if you need me."

Ash watched Zee round the corner and settled in at the top of the stairs again. It was full dark outside now, and all the lights were off in the house. So far, there was no other movement on this side of the house, and he hoped his other brothers were coping at the front.

Zee swept the house on his way upstairs, ensuring the area remained secure.

Stepping over the dead man, he saw that the front door was partially open, another man dead on the threshold, and shattered glass lined the hall, but there were no other intruders inside. Zee raced upstairs, positioning himself at the landing window overlooking the courtyard, and witnessed mayhem below.

His brothers were fighting furiously. Eli was at the gate, Nahum was mounted on horseback, sweeping through the courtyard like the Angel of Death, Barak was just visible inside the barn doors, a shadowy blur of action, and Gabe was below him, fending off a woman. A few men had broken away from Nahum's fury and one ran at Gabe, the others heading for the open doorway. Zee raised his crossbow and began to shoot.

Gabe felt the assassin's icy lips press against his own, her hands gripping him like steel. Before she could begin to do whatever it was she had done to Blaze, he flew up and threw her off, watching her land spread-eagled below.

Her eyes blazed with fury, alleviating for a moment their blackness, and Gabe soared down, sword outstretched as she leapt to her feet, pulling a rapier out of nowhere. For the next few minutes Gabe fought furiously, the woman's lightning-quick reflexes equal to Shadow's. Her quick, darting glance behind him had him whirling around, but a flurry of bolts rained down, some finding their mark in the men behind him, the others thudding into the earth. The woman ran off, and Gabe gave chase through the fields beyond the outbuildings.

Gabe decided to risk flight, hoping the enemy shooters were dead, and soared upwards, easily keeping pace with the woman. To his left he could see a handful of figures fleeing too, all converging on a copse of trees just beyond the next field, Nahum already racing after them. He glanced back towards the woman below and blinked. She had disappeared completely. He dropped lower, searching anxiously as he skimmed over the treetops. He peered through the leafy branches, trying to see the ground below. Nothing moved and all was silent, except for the haunting screeches of a barn owl.

Glancing behind him, he saw the fighting seemed to have stopped, a slew of bodies littering their land, and for a horrible moment, he wondered where Shadow was, until he saw her racing across the far field on Kailen.

He sighed, debating if he should search for the woman on foot, but had the feeling he would not find her. *Good. Let her take back news of what they had faced.* Maybe Black Cronos would think twice about attacking again. They had lost many men today, and with luck, someone would still be alive for questioning.

Fifteen

S hadow studied the muscular man lying on the barn floor and knew he wouldn't live much longer.

He'd been fighting with Barak, who had inflicted a deep stomach wound, and he was now bleeding out, his blood soaking into the dry, dusty ground that absorbed it like a sponge. Eli crouched next to him, pressing a bundle of cloth into his gaping wound to try to staunch the bleeding, but it wasn't from any expectation they would save him. It was only so that they could question him for longer.

Gabe crouched next to him, watching him dispassionately. "How many more are there of you?"

The man's eyes flickered as he fought to focus. "Too many. You won't win."

"The woman with the long, black hair," he said abruptly. "Who is she?"

The man gave a croaking laugh. "There are many women who fight with us."

"You know who I mean." Gabe gripped his shoulders and shook him. "Who is she?"

"The Silencer of Souls." He met Gabe's eyes. "She takes all, in the end."

"How?"

"I am a soldier. It is not for me to know."

Gabe tried a different tack. "What is so important about the Dark Star?"

"I am a soldier. It is not for me to know," he repeated.

"We have killed all of you!" Gabe said, his voice rising with incredulity. "You must know what you fight for!"

A smile played on his lips as his gaze swam. "You don't." The man had just enough about him to look at the others. His eyes were cold as they swept over Shadow who stood at his feet, Eli who was still trying to slow the bleeding, and Barak and Zee who were at the barn door, half watching the courtyard beyond. Nahum was outside, somewhere, and Ash was still guarding Caldwell and Aubrey. "You will all die in the end," he told them, and then his head lolled to the side as the life slipped from his eyes.

"Shit." Gabe rose to his feet, rubbing his face absently. "This was a bloodbath, and we still know nothing."

"Not true," Shadow said. "We know they're a much bigger group than we ever suspected, that they're organised, well-funded, and—" she stared at the man at her feet, "that they aren't quite human."

"But we suspected that anyway," Gabe said, his eyes skimming over her. "Are you injured? You're covered in blood."

She glanced down, surprised to see how much there was on her clothes. "I chased down a few stragglers at the end of the field and slit their throats. It's a very bloody way to die."

"Did you see any transport? A sign of any way at all that they approached us so quietly?"

"No, none. I suspect they made their way by foot, slowly, sheltering carefully before moving on again."

Barak grunted. "They did their homework. They knew we'd have a good view across the fields. And they are freakishly stealthy."

Gabe looked over at him, nodding. "I suspect that one of the places they sheltered was the copse of trees I just flew over. I think tomorrow we should see if they've left any clues behind."

"They won't have," Shadow said confidently. "They're too good. But," she added, noting Gabe's jaw muscles clench, "I'll look anyway."

Eli was searching the man's clothes, and then studied his face, peering into his eyes. "Look, his eyes are changing from black to brown. It's as if his humanity is returning. And his tattoos," he added, startled. "They're fading, too."

He had curious tattoos on his forearms and chest, just visible beneath his ripped t-shirt and the smeared blood. "I think they're magical," Shadow said, thinking of similar spell work she'd seen in her own world. "They imbue strength and agility in their recipient."

"But why are they fading now?" Barak asked, leaving the doorway and joining them. Like the rest of them, he was bloodied and sweaty, his clothes torn.

"Perhaps in death, the spell breaks." She shrugged. "It's just a guess."

"The Silencer of Souls has tattoos, too," Gabe mused. "What the hell kind of name is that, anyway?"

"An ominous one," Zee called over. "What are we going to do about these bodies, Gabe? We can't leave them on the fields."

"We collect them all, bring them here. And then we need to tell Newton."

"*Here*? Newton?" Shadow's hands settled on her hips. "Are you mad?"

"What in Herne's horns am I supposed to do, Shadow?" Gabe looked drained, and his dark eyes stood out against his pale face. He didn't look well at all.

"Are you injured?" she asked, changing the subject.

"No, why?"

"You look...weird."

Eli stood and stared at Gabe. "She's right. Are you sure you're not injured?"

Worry passed across Gabe's face. "I had an encounter with The Silencer of Souls. She kissed me, briefly." His hands passed over his lips. "She was like ice. But I threw her off." He shook his head as if to try and focus. "I'm fine."

"Liar!" In seconds Shadow was next to him, one hand gripping his arm, the other touching his face. "Your skin is cold. What else do you feel?"

"I guess I feel a little weak, but it will pass. I'm Nephilim. I heal quickly."

"Eli," she said, turning to him. "Is there something we can give him? A herbal drink to strengthen him? Do we need Briar?"

Eli pulled her back. "It might be some kind of poison. But yes, I can handle that."

"What if she's started to extract his soul?" she asked, alarmed, and then realising she sounded shrill, tried to calm herself down.

Gabe answered impatiently, "Maybe she did! I don't know what her weird kiss can do, but honestly, I'll be fine."

Eli propelled Gabe toward the barn door. "Let's go to the house. I have my kit there, and some goodies from Briar. And then you need to rest." He eyed the others. "I'll find Nahum. Can the rest of you start the clearing up?" But he didn't wait for an answer, and it was a mark of just how unwell Gabe was feeling that he followed Eli without question. On his way out the door, Eli shouted, "And come see me when you're done! You're *all* injured!"

There was silence for a moment as Barak, Zee, and Shadow looked at each other uneasily. Finally, Zee said, "He'll be fine. He's strong, and Eli is good. But I think it's lucky we're wearing protective gear." He indicated his black vest and thick leather gloves that all the Nephilim wore. Shadow had her own lightweight, fey-made armour on.

"But unfortunate that they were wearing it, too," Barak pointed out. He lifted the shattered breastplate that the dead man had been wearing. "This made my job so much harder."

Shadow surveyed the half a dozen men and women who lay dead around them, all similarly attired, and all with horrific, bloody injuries. Barak's axe had done a lot of damage, and outside, in the courtyard and surrounding fields, the fallen would have similar injuries inflicted from their swords, daggers, arrows and cross-bolts. It was carnage. *Newton would be furious.*

"Let's collect the bodies and then I'll call Newton. But," she asked Zee, who still held the crossbow, "can you patrol? We shouldn't just assume they're gone."

"Sure. I'll head up to the roof again, as long as you two promise to stay together."

Barak was already dragging the fallen over to the far wall of the barn, but now he straightened, wielding his axe once more. "Agreed. Come on, sister."

Harlan stared at the ceiling, watching the play of lights from the streetlights and occasional car that passed at this late hour.

He recalled Olivia's shocked expression as she learned the truth about JD, and then her anger quickly followed. "You've known for *months* and didn't tell me? You bastard!"

"Liv, please! I was sworn to secrecy. But honestly, I wanted to tell you! And I have now," he added, pleading with her.

She'd glared at him, and then sighed. "I guess I'd have done the same in your position." She sipped her wine, her hands unsteady for a moment. "Wow. I knew JD was odd, but I didn't expect him to be—" she lowered her voice and leaned forward, "*immortal*!"

"I know. I think I've underestimated him."

Olivia picked at her food while they talked, asking, "Do you think he's as powerful as your witch friends?"

"More so in some ways, I guess. And infinitely less trustworthy."

And that's what kept bothering Harlan now, hours later at two in the morning, alone in his flat. He couldn't help but wonder, how untrustworthy was JD, and should Harlan even be here in his flat, although warded with amulets and charms? Could JD summon a demon or an avenging angel to attack him? Harlan had money. Maybe he should book into a hotel.

He still had questions, and despite Mason's instructions, he wasn't dropping this. *Who were Black Cronos, and who was the thief JD had hired?* Olivia had said she would call when she found something out, but so far he'd heard nothing. And he needed to know more about the Dark Star. He'd heard nothing at all from Gabe or Shadow, either.

Then he heard a faint, almost imperceptible noise from somewhere in his flat, and he sat bolt upright in bed. *Shit! Was someone here?* He sat quietly, trying to ignore the loud pounding of his heartbeat, and thought he detected a shuffling noise. He slid out of bed and padded silently across the room wearing only his shorts, then waited behind the door, wishing he had a weapon. *Should he try to surprise them, or scare them off by flicking on the light? If it was Black Cronos, surprise would be best.*

Crouching, he edged into the hall, where he could see his lounge and study. His breath caught in his throat as he saw someone next to the study window, rifling through his paperwork, a light playing across the desk. *Someone was in his freaking flat!*

Harlan crept forward to get a better view, and then incredulity set in as he recognised the figure. *Time for some fun.* He yelled, "Freeze or I'll shoot you! I've already called the police!"

The figure stumbled backwards. "Don't shoot! It's me, Jackson!" He turned his small flashlight on his face, showing his eyes, wide with alarm.

Harlan flicked the hall light on. "I know it's you, you thieving shit! What the fuck are you doing in my apartment?"

Jackson leaned against the desk looking sheepish. "Sorry, Harlan. I'm in a bit of bother. You haven't really phoned the police, have you?"

Harlan groaned at the typical English understatement. "Of course I haven't. I'm not telepathic. What do you mean by *bother*?"

Jackson looked as rumpled and nonchalant as ever, now that his shock had worn off. "Couldn't we chat in a more civilised manner? Over a drink, perhaps?"

"You break into my flat and expect me to be civilised?" And then seeing Jackson's chagrined expression, he groaned. "Yes, all right. I need one anyway, after that scare. You nearly gave me a heart attack."

He waved Jackson through to the lounge, pulled a t-shirt on, and then after flicking on a couple of lamps, poured them both bourbon.

Jackson prowled around with his drink, looking with curiosity at Harlan's collected objects displayed on shelves and in bookcases. "This is a nice place." He gave him an appraising glance. "You've done well for yourself."

Harlan downed his first shot, poured a second, and then sat on his sofa. "Thanks. I'm sure you have, too. We're in a lucrative business."

Jackson raised his glass in salute. "But you've done better than most."

"Well, I guess I'm good, and The Orphic Guild pays well. But rather than this bullshit chat, why don't you tell me what you broke in for? And," he added as another thought struck him, "how you got past my amulets and charms."

Jackson rolled his eyes and sat in the armchair. "Amulets and charms are not meant to stop people from breaking in, Harlan, you should know that. They're more to ward off ill intent, and you could argue they have worked. It's only me!"

"But you could have phoned!" Harlan adopted a mock English accent. "Hey Harlan, I'm in a spot of bother. Would you mind helping a chap out? I'd be awfully grateful."

Jackson looked unimpressed. "No one has spoken like that in fifty years!"

"Er, you were the one who said, 'spot of bother.'"

"I'm self-effacing, that's what us Brits do, but I said *a bit of bother*, not the rest."

Now that he had a chance to study Jackson better, he could actually see that he seemed a bit edgier than normal, despite his banter, and Harlan stopped teasing. "What were you searching for?"

Jackson sipped his drink and then said, "News flies in this world, you know that, so it shouldn't be a surprise to know that everyone has heard about the attack on The Order of the Midnight Sun."

Harlan shrugged. "Not surprising at all. There were bodies everywhere, and we had to call the police."

"But rumour has it that it's because of the Dark Star."

"Well, bully for you," he replied, keeping his face carefully schooled. "Because I'd never heard of it, so I'm amazed you have."

Jackson leaned back, rolling his glass between his hands. "I admit, I hadn't. But one of my regular clients has. We caught up for a drink yesterday, and he told me to stay clear of it. Said it's bad news."

"From what I've heard so far, I'd agree. But why did you break in?"

"It's Black Cronos I'm interested in, not Dark Star—although, I realise that right now they come as a pair." Jackson had become very serious, all trace of humour erased from his face. "I hoped to find some current information on them, without alerting you to my interest."

"They're bad news too, Jackson. From the glimpse I had of them yesterday, they aren't quite human. They're fast, deadly, and honestly, if the Nephilim hadn't been there, I would be dead right now. So would Aubrey and Caldwell. You should stay away from them."

"I can't." Jackson stood abruptly after draining his glass. "Would you mind if I topped up?"

"Go ahead."

Harlan watched Jackson pour another shot and then pace back and forth. He waited, knowing that Jackson was wrestling with something. Moments later, he seemed to come to a decision, and he sat again.

"It's ominous that they're back," Jackson told him, "because all news of them disappeared after World War II. They caused trouble searching for occult goods. Not for the Nazis, you understand, but themselves. They screwed everyone. They compromised enemy lines. I know this because my grandfather was part of a team sent to find them. He disappeared, and was never seen again."

The room seemed to shrink around them, utter blackness beyond the pool of warm, orange lamplight. Jackson's face was cast in harsh lines, and he suddenly appeared much older.

"How can you possibly know that?" Harlan asked, a sense of doom approaching. "That would have been top-secret information."

"Because I sometimes work for the government. That sort of thing runs in my family. The fact that I also work in the occult business is not chance. It's fate. And that's why I mostly work alone."

Harlan's mouth dropped open, and he had to make a conscious effort to grip his glass. "Are you a spy?"

A flicker of a smile crossed Jackson's face. "Not exactly. But the government wants all news of Black Cronos. Anything I can find, however small. The hunt is on for them—again."

"Should you even be telling me this?" Harlan's gaze flicked to the main entry as if someone was about to kick down the door.

"I can tell who I deem helpful and trustworthy enough." Jackson grinned. "And I've decided you are."

Sixteen

N ahum turned over another fallen enemy that he'd found halfway in the hedge, finding her throat cut. *One of Shadow's kills.* Nahum sighed as he thought of his own victims. He hadn't killed so many people in years, and he knew he'd have to kill more before this was over.

Ash must have heard him, because he called over, "Weary, brother?"

"Weary of killing. Black Cronos is like a small army."

"A well-equipped and well-trained army. It doesn't feel like a group of alchemists to me."

"No, they don't," Nahum agreed. He rolled his shoulders, feeling the deep ache in his muscles, and winced. "I think I'm covered in bruises."

"At least we're not dead."

It was the early hours of the morning, and Nahum and Ash had been working their way steadily along the farthest field from their house, while Barak and Shadow concentrated on the other direction. Eli and Gabe were in the house, trying to reassure Caldwell and Aubrey. They were, understandably, terrified. Nahum and Ash had flown back and forth in pairs, refusing to leave each other alone.

The moon was riding high now, throwing its silvery light across the fields, and the long grass around them swayed in a gentle breeze that blew in from the sea. The light also, unfortunately, highlighted the dark pools of thick, congealed blood splattered across the fallen.

"We must have faced almost two dozen, by my reckoning," Nahum said, running through the numbers. "That's a lot of people."

"And still that woman escaped." Ash chewed at his lower lip. "I'd love to know what it is she does."

"Her manner of killing, you mean? Yes, me too."

Ash made slow progress as he searched the boundary where the shadows were darkest. "I suspect their tattoos have been magically enhanced with some kind of ritual. Maybe they came out of an alchemical breakthrough?"

"Or it's just plain old magic. The witches have magically enhanced tattoos."

"How do you know that?"

"El told me a few months ago."

"But I bet theirs don't disappear after death," Ash pointed out. He grunted as he pulled another man from the hedge and slung him over his shoulder. "Surely we're nearly done now. I need a shower."

"Just that corner left," Nahum said, pointing over his shoulder. He hauled the dead woman up, wondering how she had become embroiled in Black Cronos. "Come on, let's gets rid of these two and finish up. I stink of death."

Eli watched Gabe drink another draught of his herbal tonic, satisfied that he appeared brighter now, and started to dress his own wound. He had sustained a deep cut across his left forearm, but the wound was clean thanks to their opponents' sharp blades; he was lucky it hadn't gone deeper.

Eli had set up his herbs, balms, and poultices on the long cabinet at the back of their lounge. The fire was blazing, even though the night was warm, and Aubrey and Caldwell sat before it, clenching a glass of whiskey each. They talked quietly, the astrolabe and their books on the coffee table, while Gabe stared at the flames.

Eli washed his wound with a cloth he'd dipped into a bowl of warm, herb-scented water, and once it was dressed, pulled his shirt off and cleaned his other cuts, noting the bruises blooming over his skin. He studied his face in the mirror on the wall, tentatively probing the graze across his check from where he crashed onto the ground earlier, and knew Briar would have a thousand questions for him tomorrow. As would Isabel, the woman he had been sleeping with on and off for months. *Well, one of them.* Eli refused to be tied down. It made him feel suffocated. But he was very clear on his attitude with his women. They knew he wasn't interested in being exclusive, and they either accepted it or walked away. He smiled thinking of Isabel's warm hands, and wondered if the bruises would appal her or excite her. *It was hard to know. She might enjoy ministering to his injuries.*

He pulled his t-shirt on and walked over to Gabe, crouching in front of him. His colour looked better, but he still seemed shaken, which was unusual. Gabe was generally stoic, calm, and organised, and they all took his leadership for granted. Welcomed it, even. Well, Eli did; he had no wish to order his brothers around and make the decisions. "Gabe, are you okay?"

Gabe focussed. "Yes, I just feel a little weird, that's all. I'm sure it will pass."

"You say the woman is a called 'The Silencer of Souls?'" Caldwell asked.

Startled, Gabe turned to him, as if he'd forgotten the others were there. "Yes. I still don't know what she is, but she's not fully human. She'd have easily killed you."

Caldwell looked contrite, and Eli knew what was coming. "I'm sorry we doubted you. I honestly didn't think they'd find us here, or that there would be so many."

Eli had taken them to the barn earlier to see the dead being laid out. He hadn't wanted to, but Aubrey insisted, as if he needed proof that they hadn't made the attack up—even though they'd certainly heard the fight from the cellar, and the house was a mess of shattered windows, floors covered in broken glass. They had both staggered back to the living room in shock.

Caldwell continued. "We have reconsidered our options, and agree that it would be best if you accompanied us to France."

There was no flash of victory from Gabe, just a grim nod. "Good."

Aubrey hurried on. "Not that we doubt our Senior Adepts, of course, but clearly Black Cronos have means of finding us we didn't anticipate."

"Regardless of your trust in your colleagues, in order for you to retain our services, I want a full list of every single member of your Inner Temple, and anyone else you've told."

"There really is no need," Aubrey started to say, but Gabe held his hand up.

"There is *every* need. I want every name, particularly those who know that you are here. And we will go to a new location in France. One of my choosing, that you tell no one about."

Caldwell spluttered, "But we have made plans—"

"They're changing. Those are my terms. Understood?"

They were obviously uncomfortable with Gabe's requests, but Eli knew Gabe was right, and so did they. With visible reluctance, they nodded.

"Good," Gabe said. "Write the list right now, and then we'll go through it, one by one."

The sound of an engine in the courtyard had all of them looking up, alarmed, but Eli realised it would be Newton, or Zee would surely have alerted them.

Eli stood, placing his hand on Gabe's shoulder as he made a move to stand. "You stay here, I'll go and see what's happening."

Gabe nodded his agreement, and Eli knew that he had to be feeling worse than he was admitting, or else he'd argue. Eli picked up his sword, just in case, and walked up the hall, the glass crunching under his boots. Newton's BMW was in the courtyard, and Eli suppressed a grin as he saw him already arguing with Shadow.

Newton's hands were on his hips. "Please tell me this is a joke!"

"Look at me, Newton," she protested. "I'm covered in blood, and it's some stupid hour of the night. Of course it's not a joke."

Newton looked up at Eli's approach, his eyes sweeping across his injuries. "Bloody hell. I thought you lot were invincible."

"I wish, but we do injure, as anyone does. We just heal quicker." Newton looked tired, and his hair was sticking up from where he'd run his fingers through it. "I'm sorry, Newton. I know you've had a rough week. When is Inez's funeral?"

Newton closed his eyes briefly. "Today. You better show me what's going on."

Shadow's eyes flitted beyond Eli to the door, and Eli knew who she was looking for. "Gabe is fine. Resting. Where's Nahum?"

"In the barn, which is where you need to be, Newton."

Eli followed them inside. It was better lit now, the floor swept of debris. Although, large pools of congealed blood still marred the floor, and the stench of it now, hours later, was sharp. Worse was the line of bodies laid out on the far side.

Newton gasped. "Jesus Christ! What the hell has happened here?"

Nahum and Barak were talking, but broke off as they saw Newton, and Nahum said, "We were attacked by an organisation called Black Cronos."

He quickly summarised the events of the previous few days, watching Newton examine the bodies while he listened. He shook his head occasionally as he processed the story, and when Nahum had brought him up to date, Newton straightened, already reaching for his phone. "You know I'm going to have to call my team in on this. All of these bodies have to go to the morgue and get processed properly."

"And us?" Barak asked. "This was a coordinated attack, and we were defending ourselves."

"I know, but I can't pretend this didn't happen. You'll have to make statements, but under the circumstances, that will be all. But these guys," he gestured at the dead, "worry me. Will they come back? Will White Haven be at risk?"

"They might come back for us," Nahum said, "but I don't think you need to worry about White Haven."

"I suspect that after this," Eli added, "they will rethink their strategy. They took a big hit today when they underestimated us. But," he said, trying to reassure Newton, "some of us will be leaving soon for France." He caught Nahum's questioning glance. "They've just requested our help—not surprisingly." He addressed Newton again. "If they're watching our movements, they'll know it's pointless to come here again."

Newton nodded. "They'll follow you though, and you won't be able to take your weapons with you. Have you considered that?"

This was something they had discussed at length, and now there was talk of someone driving to France and carrying all the weapons in Gabe's SUV, hidden somehow. Nahum nodded wearily. "We'll think of something."

"What does this astrolabe lead to that they want it so badly?" Newton asked.

Shadow was examining the bodies again, still clad in her armour. "We have too many theories and no real answers, unfortunately. But, knowing whether these are human or not would be good."

"Didn't you say that Maggie had taken the bodies in London?" Newton asked, frowning. "She might have results already."

"Could you find out for us?" Nahum asked. "I doubt she'll tell us, but she will surely tell you."

"Potentially we'll be working together on this," Newton said thoughtfully. "All right. Let's get started, because I want the bulk of it finished before the funeral this afternoon, and at a more reasonable hour I'll call Maggie." He rubbed his face. "Christ. I'm exhausted. This is all I need with rogue witches on the loose."

Having seen first-hand what mayhem Mariah and Zane, the two witches from the Witches Council had caused, Eli had every sympathy for Newton. "I'll still be here, with Zee and maybe Niel. We'll help if you need us."

Newton met his eyes gratefully, a faint smile on his face. "Thanks Eli, I appreciate that." He took a deep breath and punched a number into his phone. "Let's get this show on the road."

Harlan regarded Jackson, and suddenly he didn't seem the same diffident, affable occult hunter at all. There was an edge to him he'd never seen before.

"I wish I could tell you more," Harlan said after recounting their fight, "but the only other information I have on them is from years ago."

Jackson nodded. "Could I see it anyway?"

"Sure. Wait here." Harlan fetched the papers from his study, glancing nervously out of the window as he did so. He half-expected to see a figure loitering on the street, watching him like in some film *noir*, but was relieved to see that the road was deserted. Cursing himself for being jumpy, he passed the folder to Jackson and took a seat again. "I copied these records from the guild."

Jackson studied the pages for a few moments. "Old letters." He looked up. "The same handwriting, too."

"I noticed, but that might mean nothing other than they have long-serving, loyal staff."

"Could JD tell you more?"

Harlan cleared his throat. "We're not on good terms right now, but when I mentioned their name, he had definitely heard of them. He seemed surprised to learn they were back." Harlan leaned forward, sitting on the edge of his chair. "I presume you know they have the same origin as the order, but they went their separate ways."

Jackson nodded, still examining the papers. "We do. They've meddled in many things since then, and have accumulated a lot of money. But," he stared at Harlan again, "this is the first time they have been so openly aggressive in years. This is our chance to hunt them down and destroy them for good."

"*Destroy* them? That seems extreme!"

"You witnessed them the other day. You know what they're capable of. That's only a sample of their power. And it's not just in the UK. They have a presence everywhere. They may have been dormant here, but our European friends have reported their activities over the past few decades."

"What about in the U.S.?"

"They have no presence there yet, as far as we know."

"So, you have no idea where they're based?"

Jackson sipped his drink again. "None whatsoever. Any leads we think we have simply disappear into the ether." He tapped the folder. "How did you get the astrolabe back?"

"Good detective work...and some luck." He recounted their trip to Storm Moon and what they found out from Blaze's friend.

"You met Maverick Hale? He's an interesting character."

"You know him?"

Jackson wiggled his hand. "A little. I wonder if there is a Cronos presence in Oxford?" He was talking more to himself than Harlan. "I'll mention it to my contact."

"How high up is your contact?" Harlan asked.

Jackson winked. "High enough, but you won't have heard of him. Like anything paranormal, it sits under a covert operation. Hopefully though we'll learn something from the post-mortems."

Harlan blinked with surprise. "They work with Maggie and her team?"

"Hell no!" Jackson recoiled in horror. "She's not discreet enough! But the division accesses her reports and her SOCO team's findings. Most of the stuff she follows up on we have no interest in."

"We, hmm? So, you're involved with them more than you're letting on, Jackson."

"On occasions," he reiterated. He stood, shrugging on his long raincoat that he wore regardless of the weather. "Can I take these documents? I'll bring them back."

"Sure. But soon, please."

"Just give me a few hours. If you hear anything else at all, please let me know—no matter how small. And I suggest you get out of here."

Harlan stood too, walking him to the door. "I was debating that same thing. I'm jumpy as hell."

Jackson's clear eyes were troubled. "I have no doubt they would use you as leverage to get to the astrolabe, so make yourself scarce. And leave your toys behind," he added, referring to Harlan's bike and car. "They're very recognisable."

With that he slipped out, and Harlan started to pack.

Gabe was glad to see the farmhouse returned to normal by late Tuesday afternoon. He watched the last of the SOCO team drive out of the courtyard, taking all sorts of samples with them. Newton and Moore had left hours before, as had the dead once the coroner had arrived.

He had berated them for moving the bodies, but Gabe had stood his ground, arguing that they were trying to prevent panic if a passing walker found the bodies. They had all given statements, and although Gabe knew it was for the best, they all felt scrutinised and judged, and quite nervous, despite Newton's reassurance that they wouldn't be arrested. Gabe spotted Shadow emerging from her room in the outbuilding, looking refreshed after her shower, something he had yet to do.

"You should get some sleep," she suggested, walking over to join him. Her hair was still damp, looking darker than normal, and she combed it out with her fingers as she talked. "Are you feeling better?"

He nodded. "Whatever was in Eli's herbal tonic was really good, although," he rubbed his fingers across his lips. "I can still feel her touch. It's like an ice burn."

Shadow studied his face. "You'll be glad to know they look fine."

"Care to test them?"

She laughed. "Not right now, thanks."

"Later, then?"

She shot him a warning glance. "Partners don't snog!"

"Who says?"

"I do!"

"The rule you broke the other night!"

"For the cause, as you well know. And you started it." She walked into the house, swinging her hips in a way that made Gabe's loins ache, and he followed her in, deciding to change the subject while he felt he was ahead.

"Any sign of JD's thief?"

"No." She headed to the fridge and grabbed a couple of beers. "But that's not surprising after last night's debacle." She popped the caps off and handed him one. "But they might try tonight."

"They'll have to be invisible to get in. I spoke to Caspian, and he's going to manage at the warehouse without us for a few days, which means we can have a couple of lookouts tonight."

Shadow leaned against the counter. "Everyone will burn out if we're not careful."

"That's why most people are in bed right now, except for Eli. He's patrolling. Niel and Zee will be our lookouts tonight. The rest of us can sleep, and then catch the flight tomorrow."

"Niel is gutted he's not coming."

Gabe sank into a kitchen chair, his tiredness mixing with his guilt. Niel was loving their occult work, but he needed to keep the other Nephilim motivated and involved, too. "I know, but to be honest, the way we're going, he'll be joining us anyway. I guess I just want to ensure the remaining guys will be safe once we leave."

"Maybe he could follow with the weapons. *If* we can hide them well enough."

"That will be his first job when he gets up. He's going to take my SUV apart. Or," he said, voicing something he'd been mulling over, "he could fly."

Shadow looked surprised. "That's a long way!"

"It is, but we've travelled such a distance before. And it will be easy enough to do over the course of one night. He can stop and rest a couple of times, especially before he crosses the channel."

"Even carrying a big bag of weapons?"

"Yep. We'll work out some way of strapping a bag to him."

Shadow sat opposite him. "That would solve our problem. Maybe a few of you could have flown."

"I'd considered it, but there's a lot more air traffic now. And besides," he flashed her a grin, "I wanted to see what a plane was like."

She smiled at his admission, and for a moment her company was so easy and relaxed it made Gabe think that anything was possible between them. "Me too," she admitted. "Another new experience to savour in our strange, new world. Anyway, it sounds like you and Niel will be busy later, so I'll cook."

"Rabbit stew?" he teased.

"I can manage more than that!"

"I know. Thanks, Shadow. For everything. The fact you killed half a dozen of them last night really helped."

"I think you'll find it was closer to ten. I am fey." She sipped her beer, looking smug.

Gabe groaned. "Will you ever stop saying that?"

"I doubt it."

He hoped she didn't. It infuriated him and amused him equally. "You heard that Caldwell and Aubrey gave me the list of their Inner Temple last night?"

She nodded. "What are you going to do with it?"

"We went through them all, one by one, and there are a couple that strike me as suspicious. I think we should give their names to Harlan and ask him to follow them up."

"How?" She looked incredulous. "I know he has connections, but that might be a stretch, even for him."

"We haven't got time, and I think it's important. Black Cronos found us too quickly! I don't care how good their resources are."

"True. Where's the list? I'll call him."

He dug into his pocket, extracted the folded piece of paper, and handed it to her. "I've asterisked the couple I suspect. One's a newer member, and the other is the secretary —one of the members who had the codes to the lock and safe. And an eager beaver, according to Aubrey at least. One of the more fervent ones." A wave of tiredness washed over him, and he stood, leaving half his beer in the bottle. "I need to shower and sleep. So should you. You may be fey, but you're not invincible."

"I grabbed a couple of hours, post-interview." She glanced around the kitchen and grimaced at the mess. "I'll call Harlan first, and then before I cook, I'll get rid of the glass."

The mess from the shattered windows had been partially swept up by Aubrey and Caldwell who had helped with some of the clean-up, anxious to do something useful after they had taken shelter in the cellar.

Gabe checked his watch. "Shit. The glaziers are coming in the next hour or so."

"Good. I'll supervise them." She nodded at the door. "Go. By the time you wake up, the place will be almost back to normal."

"Oh, and warn Harlan that he could be in danger."

She waved him away with a flick of her hand. "Consider it done."

Seventeen

Harlan checked into the Mandarin Oriental in Hyde Park, central London, a hotel that combined a satisfying mix of the old and new, equipped with restaurants, a gym, swimming pool, and bars. He had debated whether a small boutique hotel would be better, or even a basic hostel, but then decided the anonymity of a big hotel with lots of staff and security would be safer—for everyone. And besides, who was he kidding? He hated basic hotels. *They sucked.*

For added protection, he had booked in under a pseudonym, a name he had used rarely, but for which he had a credit card and passport, all completely separate from anything he used for The Orphic Guild. It was a precaution he'd taken years ago following a few hairy moments with previous hunts, and now seemed the perfect time to use it again. Today he was Bradley Harris, a suitably common name that didn't stick out.

Following a phone call on his burner phone with Shadow, where he learned the details of their horrendous night, he debated whether he should follow them to France using his current cover, but then he'd considered his conversation with Jackson Strange, and the list Shadow had entrusted to him. He decided that for now, he'd stay put. He still had his other cases that were keeping him busy, and needed to visit the office to show good faith—and hopefully see Olivia.

He examined the list he'd written down, recognising a couple of names that he suspected were high up in the order: Henri Durand and Kent Marlowe. The two names that Gabe was suspicious of were unfamiliar to him, but, he noticed with a smile, there were a couple of lesser nobility and one celebrity whose names he did recognise. *No wonder Caldwell had been reluctant to hand it over.* He considered sharing this information with Jackson, but he hadn't discussed that particular development with Gabe or Shadow yet.

He decided he'd think on it, and by the time he arrived at the guild, it was after four in the afternoon. He entered his office without anyone seeing him.

As soon as he sat down, Olivia called him, not giving him time to even greet her before she spoke. "You're here! I'm coming to see you."

In seconds she was in his office, still dressed in her fatigues, and she marched purposefully to his desk and sat down. "I stopped by your place at six this morning and you weren't there. You had me worried!"

"Six! Why were you there so early?"

"I've been worrying about everything after our conversation yesterday, and I just wanted to see that you were okay."

He smiled. "That's very sweet of you, but why didn't you call?"

She shrugged. "I don't know. I guess I was worried you were someplace where a phone might compromise you."

He rolled his eyes and walked to his espresso machine. "Drama queen. I was sleeping elsewhere, and then spent the day chasing leads on my cases."

She looked at him surprised. "Sleeping *where*? With a woman you haven't told me about? Harlan!"

"No, dummy! A hotel room, where I had the best night's sleep I've had in days. Well, the best early hours of the morning's sleep. I moved in the middle of the night and slept in."

She was on her feet and at his side instantly. "Did something happen?"

He'd decided not to tell Olivia about Jackson's visit. That would betray his trust, and possibly put Olivia in danger. The less she knew, the better. He'd decided to stick to the basic truth. "I got paranoid about Black Cronos, and," he lowered his voice and switched on his machine, the rumble helping to cover his voice, "I'm also a bit paranoid about you-know-who."

Olivia nodded and leaned against the wall. "I get that. It's a sensible move."

Harlan passed her a cup of coffee and started to prepare his own. "And I'm not going to tell you where I'm staying, either."

"Okay, well, just stay safe. These guys sound terrifying, to be honest." Olivia put her cup down and rolled up her long-sleeved cotton top, looking at him wide-eyed. She pointed to her inner forearm, close to the elbow where something was written, all the time continuing to talk. "I'm heading out in an hour, to Nottingham on that case I mentioned, so I just wanted to check in with you, really." She mouthed at him. "*JD's thief.*"

Harlan squinted at the tiny lettering as Olivia continued to chat, and although the ink was smudged, he made out the name, *Mouse*. He lifted his head abruptly, staring at her. He mouthed back, "*Are you kidding me?*"

She shook her head, and then raised her voice. "Anyway, I better get on, I have a couple of calls to make before I go." She downed her last mouthful of coffee and then walked across the room, opening the door as she called back. "You take care, Harlan, and let me know if can help with the case in the East End."

"Yeah, sure, but I'll be fine."

Olivia flashed him a beaming smile, murmured, "Afternoon, Mason. Can't stay, see you in a few days," and then she was gone, leaving Mason in her place.

Harlan sipped his drink, schooled his face into pleasant affability, and said, "Hey, Mason. Can I help you with something?"

Mason stepped inside, his sharp eyes darting everywhere. "Harlan. You've been gone a few hours. Are you okay?"

Harlan frowned, and had the horrible feeling that Mason had been following him—or was trying to. "I'm out of this office more than I'm in it, so why are you worried?"

Mason adjusted his silk tie. "Concerned about Black Cronos, of course, especially after Sunday."

"Oh." Harlan was still standing by his coffee machine, but he walked back to his chair with his drink, refusing to ask Mason if he wanted one. "No need. I've been following up leads for the Ouija board my client is after. I've narrowed it down to a couple of places."

"The East End job?"

"No, that's another one. The strange mirror with those unnerving properties, remember?" Mason had background on most of their cases, and he was aiming to bewilder him with a few of them. "Some little antique shop unearthed it, and we're researching its history. It's dark, very dark." He sipped his coffee. "I dropped in to grab another couple of files, so don't expect to see me much over the next day or so."

Mason moved idly around the room, touching Harlan's books and other objects, before asking, "No news from Gabe, then?"

"None. That's not my job anymore. Should I have heard something?" He was damned if he'd tell him about the huge attack on the farmhouse last night. Besides, Mason might already know.

"No, of course not. Glad to see you're staying out of the Dark Star business."

Harlan decided to have a little fun with him. "Your thief has retrieved it, then?"

"Not yet," Mason said, clenching his jaw. "There were some unexpected difficulties yesterday. But," he smiled icily, "it is a small delay only."

So, Mouse's attack had been thwarted by Black Cronos after all. Good. "Well, whoever it is will need some luck, but as you instructed, this is JD's business now." Harlan stood up, grabbed the large leather bag he used to carry paperwork, and started to gather some files and books together. "Is that all, Mason, because I have an evening appointment I need to keep."

"Yes, of course." Mason walked to the door. "I presume we can find you at your flat, should I need you?"

Harlan inwardly groaned at Mason's hideous subtlety and decided to mess with him a little more. "No, I've checked into a hotel until this Black Cronos business is over—personal safety, you understand."

Mason nodded, fake concern all over his face. "Of course. And where would that be?"

"I couldn't possibly tell you. It might endanger you, too. If for some reason they try to get to me through you, it means that even under torture you couldn't give me away." He shrugged. "I figure this way you could sincerely say you don't know. Obviously, let's hope it never comes to that!" Mason froze, his mouth working, but it was obvious he had no argument to that, and Harlan added, "Of course, my phone is always on if you need to talk."

"Excellent. In that case, I shall leave you to it."

In the minutes that followed Mason's exit, Harlan worked quickly, gathering anything he may need, as he had no intention of returning to his office for a while. He had no idea what might happen next, but he wanted to keep his distance from Mason and JD, and if they were trying to follow him with some hired unknown, the less he was here, the better. He had a circuitous route away from the office planned that would be even more confusing with rush hour, and the tubes would be packed. And then, once everything was safely in his hotel room, he needed to call Shadow, and then meet with Jackson.

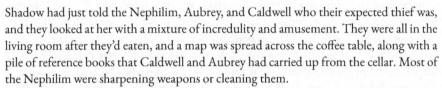

Shadow had just told the Nephilim, Aubrey, and Caldwell who their expected thief was, and they looked at her with a mixture of incredulity and amusement. They were all in the living room after they'd eaten, and a map was spread across the coffee table, along with a pile of reference books that Caldwell and Aubrey had carried up from the cellar. Most of the Nephilim were sharpening weapons or cleaning them.

"Mouse?" Niel questioned, glancing her way as he sharpened his axe blade. "Should I be scared? That's a dumb name."

"I believe," Shadow said impatiently, "that she is so named because of her ability to get in anywhere—just like a mouse."

Ash nodded. "It's an excellent name. Mice are derided. People call them timid, but did you know that a mouse is highly adaptable to new environments, can squeeze through tiny places, is incredibly fast, can climb very high walls, and cross wires and power lines? That suggests to me," he said, reaching for another book from the table, "that Mouse will be a formidable thief."

"Well, thank you, David Attenborough," Barak groaned, "but I refuse to be intimidated by a mouse."

"Speaking of which," Niel said rising to his feet and hefting his axe, "I need to get on watch. As do you, Zee."

Zee groaned as he stood and stretched. "True. I'm sure Eli is wondering where we are."

Gabe was polishing his sword until it gleamed, but he set it aside and looked at Niel. "Are you happy with the bag arrangement?" Gabe and Niel had spent some time packing a large overnight bag with their various weapons and trialling it for flight.

"Sure," Niel nodded. "I can carry it easily, and strapped to my chest it will provide protection, too."

"All right. I'll phone you once we get to France, anyway."

"Are you sure you don't want me to go tonight? I'm happy to spend a few hours in France before you get there."

"Not on your own. And we can manage without weapons for a while. Plus, there'll be a few of us," Gabe pointed out. He walked over to examine the map and frowned. "It's a long way. Almost six hundred miles. I'm not sure you should do it in one go."

Niel paused in the doorway. "It'll be fine. I'm planning to rest on this side of the channel for a while before completing the final leg."

Gabe nodded, looking relieved. "Good."

"Well, I for one am not happy at having to travel without my daggers," Shadow protested as Niel and Zee left the room. "Planes sound stupid."

"Stupid or not, those are the rules," Nahum said, amused. "Don't you trust your bare hands?"

She looked at him disdainfully. "My hands are deadly with or without a blade, thank you. However, I feel naked without them." In fact, Shadow couldn't remember a time when she didn't carry her daggers at all times, strapped to her thighs, normally. Even when she was resting at home, like now, they were always close by. "Although, I am looking forward to trying plane travel. We have nothing like it in the Otherworld."

Nahum laughed. "Something new for all of us, except Estelle. It's a good job we have her to help us navigate the airport." He addressed Barak. "I presume she's told Caspian her plans?"

Barak nodded, although he looked worried, which was unusual for him. He was unconcerned about most things. "I have to say that I'm worried we're leaving Caspian a bit vulnerable." He reached for his beer and sipped it. "He's only just recovered from being attacked by those pirate spirits, and the two witches who were behind the whole thing have disappeared. I feel like we're running out on him when he needs us most."

"I agree," Ash said, "but the White Haven witches are closer to him now than before, so he's not alone. And they have the Witches Council behind them. He'll be fine." He leaned forward and tapped the map. "We need to focus on this."

"Very true," Caldwell said, speaking for the first time in a while. He'd been absorbed with reading a manuscript, and had been talking quietly with Aubrey. "We've studied this record before, but now that we have the astrolabe we've examined it again, and we're fairly confident that the reading we take based on the parade of planets will lead us directly to the chamber. Unfortunately, it won't be pinpoint-accurate, but it will be close."

Shadow was confused. "You had doubts?"

"Yes." Caldwell picked up the astrolabe and took out the central pin to dismantle its layers. "Traditionally, astrolabes have many plates to enable the user to choose the one suitable for the area that they are travelling in. This astrolabe only has two plates. The general European area, and France." All the Nephilim were watching now, their activities paused. "We were worried that the France plate would not be detailed enough, and we'd need another one, but now I think it will be accurate enough."

Aubrey nodded excitedly. "We just may need to do a bit of hunting at the site." He lifted one of the plates, turning it over in his hands, and the rose gold metal gleamed in the firelight. "This is an extremely detailed plate for all of France. Obviously, the places on here have slightly different names now—after all, this was made several centuries ago—but it should be easy enough to cross-match. Besides, place names or not, the directions will reveal all."

Ash frowned. "Do you think there will be other things to achieve once we're there?"

"Perhaps," Caldwell said, wiggling the manuscript. "The language on this is obscure. We can understand it, but it seems sort of like gibberish."

"Perhaps it's something Black Cronos will understand better," Nahum suggested, perplexed. "It was one of their members that designed it in the first place."

"Maybe," Ash mused, reaching forward to take the paper from Caldwell's grasp. "But maybe not. Let me study it for a while."

"Any further details about the Dark Star itself?" Gabe asked.

"None, other than vague references to the failed experiment. It's all quite ominous," Aubrey sighed. "And I must admit that after yesterday's attack, I am very worried about what we're going to find."

"It's not too late to change your mind," Gabe told him.

Aubrey shook his head. "Yes, it is. We haven't gone this far to give up now. The future of our order and all of our plans relies on this. We're not backing out."

"Neither will Black Cronos," Gabe asked softly. "So you'd better be prepared for a fight."

———◆◇◆———

Harlan sipped his pint and checked his watch. Jackson Strange was late, and worry ate away at him.

He glanced around the small, crowded pub that was situated opposite the tube station in Covent Garden, full of people who'd come in for an after-work drink on Tuesday evening. He'd chosen this place deliberately. It was convenient to get to, and very popular. That meant that no one would overhear them, and it offered decent anonymity.

He glanced up as the door to the street opened, bringing in fresh evening air, and sighed with relief as Jackson entered. Harlan raised his hand, and Jackson nodded and headed to the bar, finally arriving at the table with his pint of Guinness.

"You were worrying me," Harlan admitted as Jackson sat. He looked flushed, his eyes bright, and Harlan hoped this boded good news.

Jackson took a long drink, and then brushed the foamy head from his lips. "Sorry, I got caught up in a meeting, and took a circuitous route to get here. Did you take my advice?"

Harlan nodded. "I'm staying in a large hotel."

"Good, because what I discovered today makes me very nervous."

Harlan had been about to sip his beer, but now he put it down. "Shit. What?"

"I told my superiors about Oxford, and it ties into some other knowledge they have. They've had their eye on a professor in one of the colleges for a while, but have nothing conclusive on him."

"So, what makes them suspect him?" Harlan asked, puzzled.

"His specialty is medieval alchemy for a start, and he lectures on alchemy masters—Ibn Sina, Artephius, Roger Bacon, Johann Georg Faust, John Dee, Elias Ashmole, and the Count of St Germain, amongst others." Harlan froze at the mention of JD's name, but Jackson didn't seem to notice, as he was too busy glancing at the menu. "He also comes from a rich family with all the right connections." Jackson looked up at him and smiled. "You get a nose for these sorts of things, and he hits all the markers."

"What's his name?"

"Stefan Hope-Robbins. They don't think he's the big guy, but they believe he is high up in Black Cronos. The fact that Gabe and Shadow tracked Blaze there has added weight to that."

"Wow." Harlan sipped his pint, thinking how insanely cloak-and-dagger all of this sounded. "Have they got any leads on the woman who killed Blaze?"

Jackson put the menu down, rested his elbows on the table, and knitted his fingers together. "Did you see any of that footage?"

"No. Did the club release video?"

Jackson nodded. "There was nothing inside the club, but there was some footage recorded from outside the entrance. It was blurry, all the images unreadable. But this is

England, and there are cameras everywhere. They caught sight of the woman with long, black hair heading through the town, but again, anything too close became fuzzy."

"She was able to destroy the images?"

"It seems so. Or it was your friends. I know Shadow and Gabe fought her. Some wildly blurry images of that were caught, too."

Harlan felt his breath catch in his throat, and wondered if they had even considered that. "They don't have clear images of them, then?"

"No. Although," he looked amused, "it looked as if someone had landed from a height."

Harlan gripped his pint glass. "Gabe."

"Don't worry. Like I said, everything was blurry. Shadow is fey, isn't she? She should have magic that could do that, even if she used it unconsciously."

Harlan didn't answer, instead asking, "Did you tell your friends about them?"

"Sorry, but I had to. But they're not interested in them...yet. However, they think they know who the woman is."

"Ah," Harlan said, feeling guilty. "My guys know, too. Shadow told me they questioned one of the men before he died. Who do you think she is?"

Jackson took a long sip of his Guinness as if to fortify himself. "She's called The Silencer of Souls, because of the way she kills."

"Yep, that's what Shadow said. Does she kill a lot?"

Jackson regarded him steadily. "Unfortunately, yes. She has left other victims behind, but in less crowded circumstances. All they ever catch is a glimpse of her, and then she's gone. This was in Europe, you understand, not the UK."

"And she really kills them with a kiss?" Harlan asked, horrified.

"Yes, but the mechanism of it is unknown."

Harlan's mouth grew dry, and he sipped his pint again, feeling horribly out of his depth. "This is not what I expected, Jackson. Not at all. I know our job can be dangerous, but this feels next level."

"It does to me, too, if I'm honest." Jackson ran his hands through his hair, leaving it ruffled. "I also have the autopsy results back, courtesy of my *friends*, too. They are all human."

"The men who attacked us? Impossible. They were too...*different*."

Jackson shrugged, apologetic. "Maybe they were just well-trained."

Harlan considered their strange eyes. "No. I'm sure there was something inhuman about them."

"Nothing that an autopsy picked up—at least not yet. There are some tests they're waiting on. Toxicology, for example."

"By the Gods! I was hoping for good news, and instead you bring me shit."

Jackson gave a dry laugh. "You were kidding yourself. Why would I have good news? This search has been going on for decades. They can't swoop in on them in mere hours!" He glanced down at the menu. "I'm starving. Do you want anything?"

Harlan had read the menu while he waited. "Yeah, the steak. Rare, please." He put some cash on the table. "Pay with that."

"My treat," Jackson said. "I have a favour to ask."

Harlan groaned, wondering what new level of Hell his life was about to descend to while Jackson placed their order, and as soon as he sat down again, he said, "Well, don't keep me hanging."

"Your friends killed many men and women yesterday in Cornwall. It was quite the bloodbath."

"I know, Shadow told me." Harlan felt guilty he hadn't been there to help, and also relieved he was left out of it. "I'm just glad they're okay."

"They've impressed my superiors."

Jackson was looking at him calmly, but his words seemed weighted with import. "That's bad, isn't it?"

Jackson smiled ruefully. "Depends how you look at it. And it depends on the outcome of the Dark Star investigation. If Gabe, Shadow, and their team end up on top, my superiors would like an introduction. They will be the only ones who've been up close and personal to Black Cronos in years who have lived to tell the tale. They'd consider them useful allies."

"I get it. If they die, well...never mind, but if they win, they're recruited into the fight?"

"Sort of. Do you think they'd be interested?"

"They might be. Depends on the pay and conditions." Harlan thought they'd probably jump at the chance, especially Shadow, but he could be wrong. *Best to be cautious.* "They do work for us too, remember?"

"But Dark Star is a private gig, right?"

"Well, it is now."

Jackson studied him for a moment. "Why did you pull back from this one?"

"The order wanted them to be bodyguards," he answered warily. "The guild doesn't do that."

"It was nothing to do with JD, then?"

Now Harlan was really alarmed. "No! It was my decision."

"Just checking if you were under any pressure at all. You did say you were on bad terms now."

Harlan was increasingly aware he had no idea who these mysterious friends were of Jackson's, or who they really worked for. He believed Jackson to be trustworthy. Although now it seemed he was some kind of part-time spy, but what did he really know? He had no idea who he should trust, and was it really better to trust in the devil you knew? At least he had history with Mason and The Orphic Guild, and he trusted Olivia and Aiden implicitly, and Shadow and the boys. The list was in his pocket, ready to discuss with Jackson, but he decided to keep it to himself, for now.

"No," he said firmly. "No pressure at all. We're on bad terms because JD was such a shit a few weeks ago, over the trinity. I just thought it was best to continue with my other cases and let them pick up the bodyguard business. All I'm doing now is protecting myself from further attacks by Black Cronos...just in case they recognised me on Sunday."

"That's good, then," Jackson said breezily as took the letters he'd borrowed from his inner pocket and slid them across the table. "And thanks for these. There are a few things I need to do now, but nothing to involve you, you'll be pleased to know."

"I have a question," Harlan asked as he scooped the papers up and put them in his messenger bag. "If they consider Black Cronos so dangerous, and the Dark Star something to be avoided, why aren't they trying to stop them from reaching it?"

"I'm not privy to all of their decision making," Jackson pointed out. "They might be. I suspect they're tracking your friends, at least. And where they go, Black Cronos will follow. Perhaps you should warn them, just in case."

Harlan nodded his agreement, deciding he needed to call Shadow as soon as his dinner was over, but before he could comment, they were interrupted by one of the bar staff bringing them their food, and they paused until he left the table. When they spoke again, Jackson changed the subject with a grin.

"I have some gossip about Andreas Nicoli, if you're interested."

Harlan laughed, happy to have a reprieve from the mysterious intrigue, but part of him couldn't help but be disappointed Jackson didn't need him, or wonder if he knew something about JD he wasn't letting on.

Shit. His life was so complicated.

Eighteen

Niel was sitting in the lee of the chimneys on the main farmhouse, trying not to shuffle with discomfort, and thinking longingly of his bed.

The fields around him were dark, lit only by the occasional flash of moonlight when the clouds cleared enough to let it through. *Rain was coming.* He could smell it on the air and feel the dampness intensifying. The ever-changing light made his lookout job difficult, despite his good eyesight. The hedges whispered with night creatures, the trees swayed in the strengthening sea breeze, and the scream of the foxes and screech of the barn owl blocked out more subtle sounds. *They sensed the rain, too.*

But it was beautiful, and Niel felt a calm ease over him. He glanced behind him, around the chimney, and stared at the dark roof of the outbuilding to his rear, reassured when he spotted Zee sitting motionless. Zee was facing the other direction, covering the gate and fields beyond, the crossbow resting on his lap. Niel returned to his own view, scanning the fields.

Unbidden, a memory came to him of a night like this, with scudding clouds and glancing moonlight. A night he had spent in a loggia with Lilith. A night of love and laughter. It seemed like a jewel now. Something to be polished and examined from a thousand different angles, and yet he would never see into the heart of it. He could only feel that. Ever since Harlan had mentioned her name in passing at Angel's Rest, these memories had returned more and more frequently, a bittersweet reminder of what had once been.

Lilith, and his life with her, had been complicated. Her life was far longer than her first husband's had been, and that was due to the magic of The Book of Raziel that had leaked into society. Magic she had accessed through private groups, studying in the depth of night, mastering secrets meant for the Gods alone to exact a revenge she never carried out. She was called a witch, amongst other names, for a reason. And Niel was still haunted by the memory of the angel, Chassan, his breath on his cheek, his unspoken welcome that resonated through his head. The weight of the memories felt as if it could crush him sometimes.

A tapping noise through his earpiece was a welcome break from his thoughts. *Zee had spotted something*. Niel tapped in response to acknowledge the message, and scanned his surroundings again, sweeping left to right. For a few moments he saw nothing, and then as the moon disappeared beneath the clouds again, he noticed a slow, almost imperceptible movement through the long grass bordering the hedge, moving ever close to the house.

Niel didn't move a muscle, refusing to break eye contact, and was rewarded when he made out the slim, creeping figure, arms and legs materialising out of the blackness.

Zee tapped five times in rapid succession. *He was on the move*.

Niel scanned the fields again, ensuring this wasn't part of another coordinated attack. Reassured, he then turned back to where the figure had gained ground, fully in the shadow of the house now. Niel crept forward on hands and knees just below the shallow apex, his head down until he reached the edge, sheltered by the final chimney. He spotted Zee to the left, crouching behind an old, crumbling wall. He had descended silently from the other roof. Niel was impressed; he hadn't heard a thing.

Niel focussed on Zee stalking the unknown attacker, and then he was on him or her, Zee's strong hands immobilising the figure completely. Not even a cry escaped.

Niel extended his wings and dropped behind them, folding his wings away again before moving into view. Zee had caught a woman. She was lithe and petite, dressed totally in black. She was wriggling and kicking but Zee had his arm wrapped around her, lifting her off the ground. His hand was over her mouth, and to Niel he said softly, "Let's take her to the barn."

Her eyes widened with alarm, but Niel raised his fingers to his mouth, shushing her. "We won't harm you. Calm down."

Neither he nor Zee wanted to alert the others, preferring to let them sleep, so they carried the woman to the far side of the barn, well away from the house, before speaking to her.

Zee still had a firm grip on her, and Niel quickly patted her down. She was wearing slim-fitting trousers and a top, with a balaclava on her head, revealing only almond-shaped eyes. "No weapons. Just lock picks," he told Zee. He met the woman's terrified, yet angry gaze. "Mouse, I presume?" She immediately froze. "We're going to release you now. No screaming, please." He lifted his sword for good measure. "Or you'll feel this."

Zee lowered her to the floor, and then took his hand from her mouth. As soon as she was free, she backed away, her eyes darting everywhere before finally settling on them both.

"What now?" Her voice was low but firm, with no hint of the unease she must be feeling.

"Good question," Zee said, amused. He folded his arms across his chest. "It depends on you. Are you Mouse? I suggest you be honest with us."

"How do you know the name?" she immediately countered, her chin up.

"We have good intel. Your name?" Zee insisted.

"That's one of them," she admitted, a hint of amusement in her eyes. "You're very quiet for big men. Both of you. I didn't see you or hear you."

"Good," Niel said, warming to her, even though she was trying to steal from them. "Nice to know we haven't lost our touch." He glanced at Zee. "Perhaps we should check for backup?" Zee nodded, and without another word left the barn. Niel stepped back, thinking Mouse might be more amenable with more space between them. "What do you want, Mouse?"

"You know what I want. The Dark Star Astrolabe."

"You can't have it. Tell JD his actions are dishonourable to his colleagues."

Her eyes lifted and he knew she was smiling. "Not JD."

"Mason, then. How were you going to deliver it?"

"Does it matter?"

"I guess not. Leave it be, Mouse."

"And that's it? You're letting me go?"

"Yes. If you'd threatened me with violence, I might have been provoked to do something else. But you didn't, and we don't kill mere thieves. Go, but I suggest you be careful. You're not the only one after the astrolabe."

"I know that." Her eyes darkened and her stance stiffened. "I watched them last night—for a while. I almost stumbled into the middle of it before running for my life. You killed many."

"Then you know *exactly* what we're capable of." Niel stepped back again, allowing her to access the open doorway. "Don't come back here, Mouse. We might not be so accommodating next time."

She walked past him, as quick as her name, but paused at the door to look back at him. "Last night there were more in the lane beyond here, way across the fields. I saw them as I was fleeing, but they didn't see me. A man with white-blond hair seemed to be coordinating them."

Niel crossed the barn, pausing when he was a few feet away. "How old was he?"

"Hard to say. Mid-forties perhaps? Hard-faced, fit. Furious. I suspect he will strike again."

"How many others with him?"

"Three that I saw. They were in a big, black van."

Niel wondered what had prompted her to share her news. "Thank you. I appreciate it."

"What's your name? You have mine."

He smiled. "Othniel, but everyone calls me Niel."

She nodded. "Stay safe, Niel, and perhaps we will meet again."

"Will you try again?" he asked, unwilling for her to leave so soon.

"I don't like to fail, but it depends on my instructions," she said softly. "Good luck."

She slipped out the door, and Niel realised that he had no idea of her real name, what colour her hair was, what shape her mouth was, or whether she really was as pretty as her beautiful eyes suggested. He flew back to the roof to finish his watch with many more things to ponder on.

<hr/>

Harlan walked nonchalantly up a side street in Islington, walking straight past the address he had for Barnaby Armstrong, the Secretary of the order and member of the Inner Temple. Harlan had met him once, briefly, and remembered him being a short, gaunt individual with a pale face and serious gaze. He gave the building a casual glance as he sauntered past, but it was quiet, with only a couple of lights visible.

He'd been circling the street for the last half hour after exiting Highbury and Islington Tube Station, and nothing seemed unusual. There were no lurking black vans with darkened windows, or shady characters that looked abnormally dangerous, and he was certain he wasn't being followed. He paused in the darkest part of the road between the streetlamps, and wondered what the hell he thought he was going to find. Short of knocking on the door and marching in to ask questions, how could he know whether this man might have betrayed the order? Harlan's specialty was the paranormal and occult, not identifying dodgy people with an axe to grind.

The area was respectable, and the address in question was a narrow townhouse that Harlan suspected was split into flats. He should have a dog with him, under the pretext of taking it for a walk, or Olivia, pretending to be having a romantic late-night stroll. That was much more preferable. Or his car for a stakeout, if it wasn't so damned recognisable.

Harlan walked up the street again and then around, finally returning ten minutes later to find the street still quiet. Impatient, he checked his list. The next suspect didn't live too far from here, easily accessible by foot, so lifting his jacket collar, he hurried onwards, passing a few people leaving the pub on the corner, and mixing in with them for a short while.

But it was when these people thinned out and their chatter faded that Harlan thought he heard footsteps behind him. Footsteps that didn't veer off, quicken, or slow down, just remained steady. *Was he being paranoid, or was he being followed?* If he looked around now, he'd alert whoever it was to the fact that Harlan knew.

There was a corner ahead, and as soon as Harlan rounded it and was out of view, he sprinted and turned right onto the road he knew led to Upper Street, the main road through Islington that went back to the tube. A figure manifested on his left, dark and huge, but he kept going, his footsteps drowning out everything else as he pounded along to the main street and turned left, running straight into a group of people smoking outside a pub.

He muttered his apologies and immediately slowed to a fast trot, glancing behind him. A broad-shouldered man dressed in black emerged from the side street, staring intensely at Harlan, but there were lots of people milling around pubs, restaurants, and the KFC, offering Harlan a brief respite. A green space at the front of Union Church was dark with shadows and the rustling of summer leaves. Keeping to the other side of the road, he saw another man emerge ahead, and Harlan knew he was screwed. The man stood between him and the tube station.

And then he spotted a black cab depositing a couple of people on the sidewalk and ran, catching the door just as it was closing, and narrowly beating someone else to it. He slid inside, and as the cabbie pulled out, looked out of the window. The two figures watched him from the pavement, one of them already on the phone.

"Where to, mate?" The driver asked, his eyes on the road.

"The Mandarin Oriental." He'd half wondered if he should have the driver take him somewhere else, but there were so many black cabs around that he felt relatively safe. And besides, he wanted to be inside his hotel room, drinking a stiff bourbon without delay.

Harlan debated his options. He wasn't suited to surveillance, not with these threatening guys around. But perhaps it meant he was on the right track with Barnaby. He might not have seen anyone, but they had been there, somewhere. Either that or he'd been followed all along, and he was pretty sure that wasn't the case. Despite his reservations, he pulled his phone from his pocket, and when Jackson answered, he couldn't hide his relief.

"Thank the Gods. I need your help."

Gabe exited the airport in the bright blue of midday Bordeaux and gasped. "Herne's horns! This is *hot*!"

Estelle was next to him in a sleeveless blouse and jeans, and she threw back her head so that her hair cascaded down her back, closing her eyes as she looked towards the sun. "It's glorious, isn't it?"

Shadow rolled her eyes, and Gabe shot her a warning glance while he answered Estelle. "It is! Is it always like this?"

"Far more often than the UK!" Estelle surveyed the group as they took in their surroundings. "How did you find your first flights?"

"Like being trapped in a tin can," Nahum grumbled. "I much prefer how we do it."

Barak shrugged, his huge shoulders straining against his shirt. "It was a bit snug for my liking."

Estelle laughed, and Gabe realised he'd never seen her look so relaxed. "That's because you're all enormous—well, except for Shadow. They design seats for the average human, not giants."

"I enjoyed it," Ash said, fixing his sunglasses over his eyes. "As new experiences go, it could be worse. But I am anxious to be out of the airport."

"Me too," Aubrey said, shuffling uncomfortably with his briefcase clutched in his hand. It contained the astrolabe, and he hadn't wanted to relinquish it to anyone else, despite Gabe's protestations.

Estelle swung one set of keys that she'd collected from inside the terminal. Gabe had the other. "Let's get the hire cars and get out of here." She led the way across the car park to where the rental cars were kept beyond the visitor parking, and stopped in front of a couple of silver SUVs. "These are ours—they should do nicely. Who's going with who?"

He and Nahum had chatted about this earlier, and Gabe was keen to keep Shadow from Estelle, and Aubrey and Caldwell separated for safety reasons. "I'll take Shadow, Aubrey and Nahum, if you take Barak, Ash and Caldwell."

"Sure. You've got the address, so if you get lost, I'll see you there."

"I'm planning to follow you all the way," Gabe reassured her as they loaded their bags into the car. "How far is it?"

"About thirty or forty minutes. It's deep in the countryside, reasonably isolated, and surrounded by vineyards. It's perfect."

After one last sweep of the carpark where nothing looked untoward, Gabe slid into the driver's seat and started the engine. "You've got the address, Nahum?"

Nahum was in the passenger seat, and he lifted his phone. "Programmed in, just in case."

Aubrey was in the back, and Gabe caught his wary expression in the rear-view mirror. "Are you okay, Aubrey?"

He looked up, startled. "I'm fine. Just paranoid that we've been followed."

"I think they're regrouping," Shadow said, looking out the window with an eager curiosity. "And licking their wounds. We'll have a brief reprieve."

"And they will be planning another attack, no doubt," Nahum put in. "That's what Mouse suggested to Niel, anyway."

"Maybe. But if I were them, I'd try stealth next," she said thoughtfully.

Gabe thought about Niel and Zee's encounter with Mouse while he followed Estelle's car. "At least we don't have Mouse to worry about, although she might have been on the plane, for all we know." He glanced at Nahum. "Can we get a description from Harlan? Niel gave us nothing except 'almond-shaped eyes.'"

Shadow grunted. "Niel really should have taken her balaclava off. Idiot. And I already asked Harlan. She's petite, and that's about all I could get from him, because her appearance changes all the time. But he did say she was of Asian descent."

Gabe felt compelled to defend Niel. "They stopped her, that's the most important thing. And she shared information she didn't need to. Niel obviously made an impression." And clearly, so had she. Niel had that look on his face when he talked about her. He was intrigued, and Niel loved a mysterious woman.

Nahum nodded his agreement. "They did well to catch her. But let's not forget that according to Harlan, we might have a government organisation following us, too."

Gabe hated to feel hemmed in, and right now, he felt like he was suffocating. "It's ridiculous. I feel as if everyone is watching us!"

Nahum smiled. "It makes me feel very important. Three groups are after us, and we're one step ahead."

"I'd like half a dozen steps ahead, please!" Gabe glanced in the rear-view mirror at Aubrey, debating whether now would be a good time to tell him about Harlan's encounter with Black Cronos while investigating Barnaby Armstrong's address. *But maybe not.* Perhaps the less he knew at this stage, the better. And besides, they might learn more from Jackson later today.

Aubrey's voice was quiet but confident as he said, "If we make it to the reading, we'll be going directly to the chamber. They'll be too late."

"One more day to go," Gabe mused. "A lot could happen before then."

Shadow gave a dry laugh. "Let's hope this *château* is more castle than manor house."

Gabe nodded his agreement; otherwise, the coming days would feel like a lifetime.

They fell silent, admiring their surroundings as Gabe followed Estelle off the main roads and onto quiet lanes, meandering through villages, past fields, old stone houses, and vineyards. Gabe was aware of the subtle differences between this area and England. The design of the buildings for a start, never mind the French road signs, which didn't really register with him as he translated them automatically. It was more the feel of the place, and a change in the air itself. He was so absorbed that the time passed quickly, and it was with surprise when they turned up a long drive edged by stone walls, and finally swept into an immaculate courtyard surrounded by a variety of outbuildings with red stone roofs and slender columns. It was very different to their own courtyard at home.

The *château* itself was built of buttery yellow stone covered in ivy, a mix of square and round turrets with gothic arches and square windows, a sign of how it had been added to over the centuries, all of it charming and soothing to the eye. Lush planting edged the buildings, vibrant with summer flowers, and as Gabe exited the car, he was assaulted by their heady perfume. The whole place exuded a serene calm, but despite that, Gabe was worried.

Nahum echoed his thoughts when he said, "This place will be a nightmare to defend."

"I agree," Shadow said, walking around the car to stand next to Gabe. She surveyed the place with her hands on her hips, her eyes narrowing against the glare of sunshine. "It's beautiful, but there are so many places someone could hide!"

"Complaining already?" Estelle said, eyeing Shadow with distaste as she joined them. She had parked the other car against the far gate that looked over a tree-filled park that bordered the property.

Gabe felt a stab of worry as Shadow cast a withering glance at Estelle. "I am merely agreeing with Nahum that it will be hard to defend. But," she said, clenching her jaw, "it is a stunning place. Thank you for finding it for us, Estelle."

A shocked silence fell over the group, and Barak's lips twitched with humour. He was behind Estelle and Shadow, so neither of them could see him, and Gabe fought back his own grin, swiftly saying, "Really beautiful, Estelle. But there *are* a lot of outbuildings that could hide Mouse, should she ever find us here. And of course, there's Black Cronos."

Estelle looked slightly mollified. "Don't worry. I can set up good defensive spells for us when we get settled. Let's head inside."

For the next half an hour they explored the quirky building, assigning rooms and unpacking, and Gabe was even more disturbed. The layout was bewildering; corridors and staircases twisted back and forth on each other, as different levels revealed themselves. And everything was beautiful and expensive. He daren't think how much breakages would set them back. They needed to set up patrols immediately, no matter how good Estelle's defensive spells were.

They met up again at a long, wooden table on a sheltered terrace, climbing plants softening the stonework and scrambling through the beams overhead, jugs of lemon-scented water set out for refreshment. Aubrey and Caldwell had lost the slightly haunted look they had carried since the night of the attack, but Gabe knew this was no time to get complacent.

"We need to scout the outbuildings and the perimeter," he said to the group. "I want us to know this place intimately. Our lives may depend on it."

"I'll cover that," Barak volunteered immediately.

"I'd like to study these manuscripts some more," Ash said. "See if we can work out a few more details about the Dark Star chamber. I still feel like we'll be stumbling in blind once we uncover the location." He looked apologetically at Caldwell and Aubrey. "Sorry, guys. I know you've been working hard on this, but we still know so little!"

They shot each other uneasy glances, but nodded their consent, and Gabe hoped they weren't concealing something.

Nahum's chair scraped back as he said, "I'm with you, Barak. Shadow?"

"Coming, too," she said, rising swiftly to her feet.

"In that case," Estelle said, calmly, "I will start my spells. Is someone going to buy food?"

"I can do that," Ash volunteered, "before I hit the books."

"Then I'll search the house," Gabe said, checking his watch. "Let's meet here again in about four hours."

Nineteen

It was mid-afternoon when Harlan received a call from Jackson, just as he'd the left the tube station in Soho, and he sheltered in an alleyway.

"Everything okay, Jackson?" Harlan asked, as he registered Jackson's hurried tone.

"Stefan Hope-Robbins, the professor I was telling you about, has left Oxford, and is heading to France. Bordeaux, to be precise. And he was with a woman with long, black hair."

Harlan sagged against the wall. "Shit. The Silencer of Souls?"

"We think so."

"I need to tell Gabe," Harlan said, his mind racing through the possibilities. "It could be a place they'd be going to anyway. The trail seems to lead there."

"Unless the potential leak, Barnaby Armstrong, has already shared their location," Jackson suggested. "Can you check with Gabe, see if Aubrey or Caldwell had been keeping in touch with him?"

Harlan closed his eyes briefly. This is what they'd been worried about, but Caldwell was still adamant there was no mole. "Yes, of course. I'll call him now."

"I have a favour to ask you, actually," Jackson said. "I'm heading to Bordeaux too, and wondered if you'd keep an eye on the order. Update me if you hear any news? Or news from JD."

When Harlan had caught up with Jackson again the previous night, and had finally come clean about the list, he'd also thought he should share about JD wanting the astrolabe, too. It wasn't as if he'd told him anything about who JD really was, but he was starting to cling to Jackson like he was a life raft in the ocean, and reasonably full disclosure seemed important. But being asked to keep an eye on the order seemed risky. He had no wish to meet Black Cronos again. "Me? Haven't you got guys who do this?"

"It's not MI6, Harlan. It's a small division." Jackson sounded both impatient and amused.

"But they're on to me," he pointed out, feeling Jackson was playing fast and loose with his life.

Jackson fell silent for a moment, and then said, "Yes, fair enough. Just any info on JD then, and the call to Gabe."

Harlan sighed with relief. "Okay. I'll call Gabe now."

For a few moments, in the silence that followed the call, Harlan wondered if he'd gone mad, and then chided himself. He had wanted to be more involved, so here was his chance. He called Gabe quickly, taking advantage of the quiet alley, noting only a sole kitchen worker ducking out of a bar's back door to smoke a cigarette, and when Gabe picked up, he relayed Jackson's news, and asked him about the possible issue with Barnaby.

"But look, Gabe, the fact that Black Cronos members were at Barnaby's last night might just mean they are following all key players, just in case one of them can lead them to you guys. We shouldn't jump to conclusions."

Gabe swore loudly and promised to call him back, leaving Harlan loitering uncomfortably for a few minutes, but when he did return the call, he had news.

"That stupid oaf Aubrey confessed that he has been talking to bloody Barnaby Armstrong! Thank fuck I didn't tell him the address. He swears he hasn't called since we've arrived. I've taken his bloody phone anyway—and Caldwell's."

"Shit." Harlan leaned against the alley wall. "Barnaby is sounding more and more suspicious. Just out of curiosity, who's the other Senior Adept who has the codes, and why aren't I checking him out?"

"It's Henri Durand, and seeing as he's in Devon, I thought it might be tricky. However, I haven't completely ruled him out," Gabe said.

"No, best not to," Harlan mused. "But I can't see Henri being the mole." Another thought struck him. "Are you sure you can trust Aubrey and Caldwell? One of those two could be secretly working for Black Cronos."

"Don't make me even more paranoid," Gabe remonstrated.

"Are you sure they haven't spoken to anyone else in the order?"

"Aubrey swears only Barnaby, and that Barnaby would have told no one. But—"

"Yeah, yeah, he could be lying, too. I must go, Gabe, but I'll pass this on to Jackson."

Ash had situated himself at the wooden table under the vine-covered shelter with a selection of books. He had a view of the vineyards from here, and the small park with the trees to the right. He could see his brothers and Shadow in the distance, and didn't envy them being out in the full sun for so long.

Aubrey and Caldwell were at the other end of the table, looking mutinous after Gabe had thundered through there an hour ago, asking questions about Barnaby. Both of them had fiercely defended him, but now, after hushed conversations, they were looking very worried. Caldwell had raked his hands through his mane of hair and looked like a bewildered puppy that couldn't find his toy. Aubrey, however, seemed to be flushed with both annoyance and the temperature. Unlike Ash, who had spent his entire life in the heat of the Mediterranean and the Middle East, he was sure the two Englishmen weren't so used to it.

Ash sipped his water and decided to keep out of their disagreement. He returned to the text in front of him. This particular book was a couple of hundred years old, written by a member of the order who was piecing their history together. It seemed that every hundred years or so, one of them did. *An effort to reclaim and reinterpret their past glories.* It was written in ink in mostly legible writing, but portions of it were scrawled, suggesting the pressure of time, or maybe the flow of ideas. Also, sections appeared to be copied from more historic texts, and were written in old French. Neither Aubrey nor Caldwell had understood it well, and Ash had offered to try.

The truth was that once he studied it, he translated it easily, but it was less the words than the message within them that was confusing. Ash was pretty sure that the text had been copied from a much older document, written much closer to the time of the order's beginnings, when it had just split from Seekers of the Morning Star.

A name made him pause. *Mithra, the ancient God of Persia, now called Iran.* The document referred to a chamber of worship beneath a hill, sealed to contain the power within. He searched the text again, wondering if he'd got it wrong. *Or had the scribe copied the original text inaccurately? And what had this got to do with the large planetary alignment that was starting tonight, but would be at its most accurate tomorrow when Aubrey and Caldwell were planning to read the astrolabe?*

Mithra was an old and powerful God who had gone through many incarnations. He was powerful in Ash's time; his places of worship spread far and wide, especially in Persia, and he knew from his reading that he had been popular with the Romans, who called him Mithras. He was a Sun God, and was rumoured to be the inspiration for Jesus Christ. His birthday—or day of rebirth—fell on the winter solstice. From what he could remember about Mithras, he was linked with bulls. According to some histories, a bull was sacrificed to him, or Mithras killed the bull himself. But he was sure that was a later addition by the Romans. He'd also been adopted by various groups, particularly soldiers, and because of that association, he was also linked to Mars, the God of War—one of the planets in the planetary alignment.

Ash sat back in his seat, both bewildered and excited. The Romans had marched through many countries, sweeping up religions, adopting them under their fold, and spreading their own. They were generous like that, and it was sensible, because they were accepted more easily. There could be old Mithraic chambers close by, long sealed shut, their secrets shuttered. *Was it one of these that the Seekers of the Morning Star had used? Alchemical experiments that toyed with an ancient Sun God?*

"Focus," Ash muttered to himself, looking again at the French scrawl, and he settled in once more.

Shadow had volunteered to cook once they had completed their inspection of the *château*, and was pleased that Barak had offered to help.

She watched him through the open window as he set up the barbecue at the end of the terrace, not far from the long table where Ash, Aubrey, and Caldwell were still studying. He lit the briquettes with a flourish while she prepared everything in the cavernous kitchen. Ash had brought a mountain of meat from the local supermarket earlier that afternoon, plenty of salad, and fresh, crusty bread. It would have felt like a party if only the threat of attack wasn't hanging over them.

When Barak re-entered the kitchen, he frowned at Shadow. "What's with Gabe? He looks furious!"

"I believe he found out that Aubrey had been speaking to Barnaby, the Secretary. Ash told me when I took them some beers."

"Seriously? Despite our warning?"

She rolled her eyes and started to chop the salad with relish. "Yes. Although, he insists he hasn't given the address."

Barak shook his head as he reached into the fridge and pulled out half a dozen steaks and pieces of chicken. "I know it's nice to have confidence in your friends, but it does seem stupid—all things considered."

Shadow had been considering what they were going to do if—*once*, she corrected herself—they found the chamber, and she voiced her concerns now. "I get the impression that this isn't just about finding the chamber. It's also about enacting the alchemical experiments. Is that something they do when we open it? Or can they just come back and take their time after that?"

"Providing Black Cronos doesn't swoop in and seal it off, you mean?"

"Or JD? Yes, absolutely. Because," she dumped the chopped onions, tomatoes, and cucumber into a bowl, "wouldn't that mean they need their Inner Temple?"

Barak stared at her, perturbed. "That's a good point. But surely the time scale for using the astrolabe is just finding the damn place. Once they find it, they can do what they want with it. And don't forget, our flights are booked to take us back home in a few days."

Shadow nodded and turned back to her preparations. "Good. But maybe we should clarify that, because by that reasoning, they could stay here for ages, and they might want to move to the first place they reserved. They surely can't expect us to guard them for months." As she spoke, Shadow felt a rush of magic sweep up and around her, and saw Estelle walking outside, her hands raised and her lips muttering. "Did you feel that?" she asked Barak.

He nodded as he watched Estelle's progress. "I know you're not a fan, Shadow, but I think she's useful to have around."

She smiled at him, noting his admiring glance. "Sure, Barak. But she probably doesn't glare at you as much as she does me!"

He gave his familiar, booming laugh. "I wouldn't say that! You heard about how she blasted me across the warehouse the other day?"

Shadow watched his big grin, amused. She knew he liked Estelle, for some unfathomable reason. "Is this a type of mating ritual for you? A sort of trial by combat?"

Barak laughed even more and then winked at her. "Maybe, Shadow. I think I'm thawing her frosty exterior."

"Yeah, well, let's hope one of your valuable assets doesn't get frostbite!" She glanced at his groin meaningfully, pleased she could tease him. She liked the fact that he didn't dissemble, and was planning to be open about his pursuit. It would also give her some entertainment over the next few days.

He had a wicked glint in his eye as he stepped closer, lowering his voice. "So, seeing as we're sharing intimacies, I'm going to address the elephant in the room. What's happening with you and Gabe?"

"That is a ridiculous saying. And nothing is happening!"

Barak shook his head. "Don't come that with me. You two have got a thing. He watches you, you watch him. There's this—" he wiggled his hand, "*heat* between you. What happened in Oxford?"

She scowled at him, her fingers itching to fly to her knives. "*Nothing* happened!"

"Really?"

"Has he said something?"

He grinned again. "So, something *did* happen!"

"Nothing happened," she repeated, loftily. "And if you repeat such slander, you'll find my knife somewhere unpleasant."

Barak backed off, arms raised in surrender, but still looking hideously pleased with himself. "Suit yourself. But I know Gabe, and I know what I see. And for the record, I approve."

He turned around and marched to the fridge to get another beer, leaving Shadow seething.

"For the record, I don't need your approval!"

"Good for you. Beer?"

"Yes!" She snatched it from his outstretched hand, wondering how she'd let Barak get the better of her. But she couldn't stay mad at him. He was too funny. "Are we going to get on with the food before we all die of starvation?"

"Yes ma'am!" He scooped up the meat with one arm, his beer in the other hand, and led the way outside, heading to the BBQ to prod the charcoal.

Shadow followed him with a large bowl of salad and the bread, and once she'd placed everything on the table, she surveyed their surroundings. The sun was sinking into the west, but it was still hot outside, the heat lying heavy across the landscape, with no breath of wind. The cicadas were deafening, but the heat was delicious. The other Nephilim were gathering, settling into seats around the table, and Ash, Aubrey, and Caldwell put aside their books.

Gabe emerged from the house, still brooding, and he drew her away to the edge of the terrace. He looked good, his skin already darkening from the sun. His sunglasses were pushed back on his head, and he scanned the grounds before looking at her.

"You've heard about Aubrey talking to Barnaby, their bloody Secretary?"

She nodded. "He's either an idiot, or ridiculously trusting."

"Or he's been working for Black Cronos all along."

Shadow considered his words and then shook her head. "It doesn't make sense. Why would they launch a full-on attack when he already has the astrolabe? No, he's just an idiot." She turned to watch them all chatting easily around the table. "And they looked too terrified the other night."

Gabe nodded, relieved. "Good. One less thing to worry about. Any news from Harlan?"

"No, but I imagine he's following up on a lot right now. What do you think of Jackson's involvement?"

"Unexpected! It seems everyone has secrets."

Shadow's gaze fell on Estelle, who was walking through the park towards them. She must be completing her protection spells, because her arms were still raised. "I wonder if she has any. I just hope she hasn't been working against El and the others."

"Estelle may be headstrong, but I doubt she's that devious. The trouble is," Gabe said, suddenly amused, "that you two are very alike!"

For a second, Shadow couldn't get her words out. "I am *nothing* like her!"

"Occasionally superior, brimming with self-confidence, scathing of lesser mortals, impatient, wilful, and very skilled. Am I wrong?"

"I haven't got a resting bitch face!"

His eyes travelled across her face, heat building in his eyes again, and she swallowed. "True. And generally, you are very positive, unlike the very unhappy Estelle."

Mollified, she changed the subject. "Have you heard from our brothers back home?"

"It's all quiet, fortunately. Neither Zee nor Eli have seen anything unusual in White Haven, and Niel says the farmhouse is quiet." His eyes settled on the horizon. "They're coming here. They'll have their own intel."

"We'll have to keep one step ahead," Shadow reminded him. "Come on. Let's get a beer."

Twenty

Harlan had spent a hot and sweaty afternoon tramping around Soho and had just emerged from the shower after an evening dip in the hotel swimming pool, when his regular phone rang. He wrapped a towel around his waist, quickly drying his hands before picking it up.

He frowned when he saw the overseas number. "Hello? Harlan speaking."

A voice with a French accent but excellent English addressed him. "Harlan, thank the Gods someone has answered. It's Jean, from the Paris branch. We met a couple of years ago."

Harlan had a sudden recollection of a slender man with light brown hair. "I remember. The hexed ring case. How are you?" He tried to sound relaxed, but he was anything but. He put the phone on speaker and continued to dry off.

"I'm good, very good, but look—we've had trouble booking JD the place he wanted in Bordeaux, and we've arranged something else. The only thing is, I can't get hold of him, or Mason. Or even that Smythe man. Can you contact them?"

Shit. JD was going to France. "Maybe they're on the flight and they can't answer?"

"*Non, non.* He should have arrived hours ago. If they are heading to the wrong place, they won't get in. I've left messages, and now I'm starting to get worried."

Several options raced through Harlan's mind, none of them good. "Was Mason traveling with him?"

"I think so. He turned down any offer of help from our agents."

"Mason hasn't been on a job in years!" Harlan said, incredulous. "Are you sure?"

"I am sure of nothing, *mon ami.* But we had a group call, and Mason said he would visit the Paris office, all being well, before he flew home. Of course, his plans may have changed, *oui*?"

Harlan rubbed the towel through his hair, raking it dry. "Did he tell you what his plans were? I mean, I suspect it's some new acquisition." He was intentionally cagey. "He mentioned something to me before he left, but I've been working on another case."

"He said he was researching the origins of an old order. He didn't say what."

Harlan should have known he wouldn't give up, regardless of whether he had the astrolabe. *Had Mouse travelled there, too? And did he know where Gabe was?* "I can try his number, but I have the same one you do."

"Fantastic, thank you. And of course, if I hear from him, I will let you know."

"Do me a favour, Jean. Send me the two addresses—the old one and the new one. I may be able to track him down with the help of some friends."

"*Certainement.* I'll text them." He paused, and then added, "Was this dangerous? He didn't indicate it was."

"Possibly," Harlan said, unwilling to mention Black Cronos by name. "I'll see what I can find out. But in the meantime, don't send anyone after them, okay? Leave both houses well alone."

As soon as he ended the call, he stood motionless, wondering what to do. Perhaps Black Cronos had kidnapped them. Maybe it was some blackmail attempt—a plot to swap JD and Mason for the astrolabe?

His phone beeped with addresses. Time to phone JD. And then, perhaps, Gabe.

Having eaten his fill of barbequed meats and salad, Gabe finally started to relax. He felt more confident now that Estelle had extended a powerful wall of protection around them, and that they had checked the house and grounds thoroughly. Even if that idiot, Aubrey, had revealed the new address to Barnaby, he'd be surprised if Black Cronos could get through. Unless, of course, they had a witch of their own, or other magic in hand.

He leaned back in the comfortable wicker chair, sipping his beer, and studied the collection of individuals around the table. They all seemed relatively relaxed with each other. Although Aubrey and Caldwell were opposite each other, they chatted easily enough to Nahum and Barak who sat next to them. Estelle sat next to Nahum, in easy conversation with him and Caldwell, and Shadow was next to Barak, half-listening to his conversation with Aubrey while twirling her knife. She and Estelle were civil with each other, but neither directly engaged the other in conversation, Gabe noticed. Gabe was at the end of the table, opposite Ash.

"Have you had a productive afternoon?" Gabe asked him.

Ash pushed his plate away, nodding. "I have. I think I have an idea as to the type of chamber we're looking for, but I haven't discussed it with Aubrey or Caldwell yet." His voice was low, but they were chatting so animatedly at the other end of the table, they couldn't hear him anyway. "I think this has to do with Mithras."

Gabe leaned forward, puzzled. "That name sounds familiar."

"He was around in our time. A Persian God whose worship ended up spreading far and wide."

Gabe nodded as his memories flooded back. "I recall he was called a Sun God."

"Amongst others." Ash glanced at Aubrey and Caldwell again. "It may be that they know this. In fact, they must, considering the amount of research they've done on it, but they haven't mentioned it yet. Perhaps they think we don't need to know."

"Is it a problem?"

"Hard to say." Ash pulled a hair tie from around his wrist and bound his hair up on his head. "I have not experienced this heat in a while. It feels good."

Gabe smiled. "It does. It makes me miss home...our old home, that is. But go on. Why haven't you talked to them about it?"

"I wanted to be sure of my facts first, and having done some more reading, I'm fairly convinced this astrolabe will lead us to a Mithraic chamber."

Gabe held his hand up. "Before you go on, should we discuss this with everyone?" He nodded, and Gabe resisted the urge to ask more questions. He tapped his glass, calling everyone's attention. "Ash has some news. Things to confirm with the order, too."

"Is there a problem?" Aubrey asked straight away.

"Perhaps," Ash said cautiously. The low sunlight was slanting in now, casting long golden rays across the terrace, and it seemed to Gabe that a stir of unease rippled around them, disturbing the calm. "I've translated that French passage you were having trouble with, and well, to be honest, it sent me down a rabbit-hole, as you say. This chamber that is at the end of our search—it's Mithraic, isn't it?"

Aubrey and Caldwell exchanged a wary glance, and Aubrey said, "We think so. Nothing that is alluded to directly, except for in the passage you read. The name crops up a couple of times."

"Hold on," Shadow said, confused. "Explain Mithraic."

"Mithra, who was later known as Mithras," Ash began, "was an ancient God of Persia. In fact, he was also called Mehr in the early days. He was a Zoroastrian angelic divinity."

"Angels again," Shadow said, shooting them an uneasy look.

"He wasn't one, though," Ash assured her. "It was because he was associated with light and truth, as many angels were."

"I've heard of Zoroastrianism," Estelle said. "It's one of the world's oldest religions, isn't it?"

Ash nodded. "Based on the teachings of the prophet Zoroaster." Excitement filled his eyes as he warmed to his subject. "The religion is the forerunner of many other religious systems, including Judaism, Christianity, and Islam. It was based on good winning over evil, judgement at death, and a type of heaven and hell. It's very old. That's why some believe that Mithra was the inspiration for Jesus Christ."

Estelle rolled her eyes. "No surprise there. Christianity was cobbled together from all sorts of religions. Most of them pagan."

Nahum smiled. "You could argue that the old Gods have many different names. They reinvent themselves for new generations, for new theories and philosophies."

"But," Ash continued, "Mithraism changed over time. Its history is long and very complex. Eventually, it was adopted by the Romans. He was particularly worshipped by soldiers."

"But, by the sound of it, he was a force for good?" Shadow asked.

"Absolutely," Ash agreed. "Mithraism became a Roman mystery religion, which essentially means their rites were private, belonging only to initiates, much like—" he gestured to the end of the table, "private orders, like The Order of the Midnight Sun."

"But we are not a religious group," Caldwell pointed out testily. "We are an organisation devoted to alchemy, philosophy, astronomy, mathematics, and many other things."

"But you seek knowledge," Barak rumbled out with his deep voice. "The power to unlock the universe and the secrets to life itself. It is a type of religion, as well as science."

Caldwell's lips tightened into a thin line. "Not at all."

"Maybe not for you now," Ash conceded, "but for your predecessors, maybe? Merely small degrees of separation. I am Greek, and our most powerful mystery religions were the Eleusinian Mysteries, veiled in secrecy. And then there was Isis later on, a female deity, and another religion that rivalled Christianity." He shrugged. "There is nothing new in this world, not really."

"What's this leading to?" Shadow asked.

Ash gestured around him. "There are probably several Mithraic chambers hidden in this area. Some may be long destroyed, but others could just be sealed. I think the order's ancestors found one and used it for their experiments. All places of worship carry power to be used—if you know how."

Estelle steepled her fingers, putting them under her chin. "Interesting. You think the alchemists found a source of power to explore. Or exploit."

He nodded, a frown crossing his face. "And it went horribly wrong. Somehow." He looked sharply at Aubrey and Caldwell again. "And of course, symbolically Mithras was linked to a few things, one of them being Mars, the God of War. I thought it an interesting link to the planetary alignment tomorrow. Perhaps it's Mars that the reading is taken from."

"We thought the same thing," Aubrey said, nodding. "But we could take readings off them all, just to be sure."

Ash tapped the old book that was at the end of the table, well away from the food, and drew it closer. "Once you have taken the reading, I presume you wish to go straight there?"

"Of course!"

Gabe grunted, thinking this was bearing a horrible resemblance to the search for The Temple of the Trinity. "You assume it will be so easy! That the directions will lead us straight there. But what if it's still hidden? Or directs us to an inhabited *château*?"

"The astrolabe is the key," Aubrey said confidently. "All will be revealed."

"I was talking to Shadow earlier," Barak said, thoughtfully. "We wondered, if we do find the chamber, what then? Surely you can't be planning to do some kind of experiment straight away?"

Aubrey looked relieved to be asked something else. "No, of course not. This is all about finding the chamber. Once it's found, our Senior Adepts will join us here. We will explore it fully. We hope to find more details on the experiments performed in there. As I told you," he looked at Gabe and Shadow, "those will be the building blocks on which to base our own research."

Shadow sipped her beer and gave Gabe an amused, sidelong glance before turning back to him. "And the Dark Star? The monster within? What if he's still there? And if he's not, how do you keep it safe from Black Cronos?"

Caldwell cleared his throat. "We wish to keep it hidden. Only we will have the coordinates."

"And you'll be on the run forever from your enemies? Of course. Sounds so logical." Her voice dripped with sarcasm.

Gabe sighed. *Shadow was right. This problem would not be resolved easily.* His phone rang then and he left the table, taking his beer with him and glad to be stretching his legs. He walked over to the end of the terrace and watched the countryside disappear into a hazy purple twilight.

"Hey Harlan, how it's going?"

"Very badly. JD is in France, and he's disappeared."

Gabe listened to Harlan with increasing worry. He felt like a noose was tightening around them, and when he headed back to the table, his expression must have said volumes, because Nahum asked, "What now?"

"I have two addresses that we need to explore. JD and Mason are here in France, somewhere, but neither of them is answering their phones. And we know The Silencer of Souls is here, with some bloody professor. It doesn't sound good," he said, relating what Harlan had shared.

"JD from The Orphic Guild?" Caldwell said, shocked. "Is he here for the astrolabe, too?"

Gabe felt sorry for him. "It seems so."

"But, does that mean that Harlan..." he stuttered, his eyes wide.

"This has nothing to do with Harlan. This is all JD," Gabe assured him quickly. "Harlan is a man of his word. JD, however, wants *that*!" He nodded to the astrolabe that sat at the head of the table, its jewels winking in the candlelight that someone had recently lit.

"What professor?" Aubrey asked, seemingly unconcerned about JD.

Gabe mentally fumbled for the name. "Stefan Hope-something, from Oxford."

Aubrey jerked so violently that he knocked his wine glass over. It shattered, wine pouring over the edge and onto the ground. Everyone jumped in shock as Barak grabbed a napkin and mopped it up. Gabe however didn't budge, staring intensely at Aubrey who had gone horribly pale.

"Do you know him?" Gabe asked, fearing he already knew the answer.

"Stefan Hope-Robbins. He was a member of our order many years ago, but it ended badly. He sought...*darker* things. Was willing to risk more than we were happy to do. It brought a darkness over us. Things became ugly when we asked him to leave."

Caldwell's hand rested on the astrolabe protectively. "Please tell me he doesn't want this."

"It seems he does. He travels with The Silencer of Souls. He's with Black Cronos."

Caldwell's voice was barely audible as he addressed Aubrey. "His experiments, do you think..."

Aubrey looked horrified. "He found a way!"

The table had fallen silent, watching them both with rapt fascination.

Gabe could feel his anger building again. "Found a way to do what?"

"Harness the power of the universe to change humans into..." He stuttered over his words again. "Well, super-beings."

"*What*?" Gabe said, now furious. He glowered at Aubrey from the opposite end of the table. "And you didn't think to mention this when we were attacked by those enhanced humans the other night? *Twice!*"

"I honestly didn't put them together. I thought Stefan was a madman, and that it was a dangerous obsession that would never work. And it was years ago!"

Gabe realised he was clenching his hands and he took a deep breath. "Well, it clearly bloody has!"

Ash spoke calmly, gesturing for Gabe to sit. "This is not the time for a deep, involved discussion on how he may have achieved this, but give us the basics."

Aubrey pulled himself together. "Alchemy is about distilling the essence of things, harnessing the power of the planets and stars, and using their correspondence at the proper times. Using celestial beings to guide us, with transformation and transmutation. Stefan was particularly interested in how they could transform the soul. Make it different. He looked at all the planets and thought their power could be harnessed, particularly Mars and Mercury—the warlike and the mercurial."

Gabe heard someone utter a dry laugh, and with a shock, realised it was him. "Can you hear yourself? Mars? *Mithras*?" He stood abruptly again. "I haven't got time for this. We need to search for JD. Barak, Nahum—you're with me. Ash," he looked at him, appealing. "Try and understand this for me, please. Shadow and Estelle, you two need to stay here, make sure this place remains protected."

"*Me?*" Shadow protested. "I want to come with you!"

"I need you here, while Ash works with Aubrey and Caldwell." His face softened, knowing part of her really didn't want to be with Estelle. "And I need to know this place will be secure upon our return. I trust you to do this. Both of you." He encompassed Estelle with that statement.

Shadow and Estelle exchanged wary glances, but nodded anyway, murmuring their assent.

Barak and Nahum were already standing, striding to the corner of the terrace. "You realise we have no weapons, yet," Barak pointed out.

Gabe stood next to him, gazing out across the now dark sky. "We'll just have to manage."

Twenty-One

H arlan knocked on the door to Smythe's flat for the third time and glanced uneasily at Jackson.

"He could be out. It is only nine o'clock, after all."

"But why hasn't he answered his phone all evening?"

"Maybe he's in a busy pub, or out on a date," Harlan reasoned, trying to recall what he knew about Smythe's private life. "Although, he never seemed the social kind, if I'm honest. Or maybe that was just with me." Harlan pressed his ear to the door. "I can't hear anything."

Robert Smythe lived on the third floor of an elegant Art Deco apartment building, which suited Smythe perfectly. It was in a quiet residential area, and the whole place seemed hushed. Harlan had returned to the guild to raid the office personnel files to get his address.

Jackson was already preparing his lock picks. "Come on, let's get in there before we're spotted loitering."

Harlan hoped his ominous feelings wouldn't be proven correct. If JD and Mason had been kidnapped or even killed, there was only one person who would have known all of their movements, and that was Smythe. The lock clicked, and Jackson cautiously opened the door. They slipped inside, pausing in the small, square hall. The living room was on their right, illuminated by the streetlights from the uncovered windows.

Harlan called, "Robert, it's me, Harlan."

He pushed the lounge door open wider and stepped inside, scanning the room, and with horror saw a figure lying in the centre. As his eyes adjusted to the light, Harlan hurried to his side, confirming the body was Robert Smythe.

"I'll look into the other rooms," Jackson said, "while you check him."

Harlan didn't need to examine him to see he was dead. His sightless eyes stared at the ceiling, a horrible blue-grey tinge to his skin. But what was worse were the spidery black lines that had spread across his face and down his neck. He was still wearing his suit, and Harlan could even see the lines appearing on his hands below the cuffs.

Harlan stepped back, his mouth suddenly dry. *Robert was dead. Snooty, precious Robert.* Harlan hadn't liked his snide ways, but now he felt guilty for every horrible thought he'd had about him. *And what the hell had killed him?* It had to be someone from Black Cronos. But there had been no struggle. The flat, or in here at least, looked immaculate and undisturbed.

Jackson re-entered the room, swiftly crossing to Harlan's side. "It's clear. We're alone."

"Smythe is dead. He's covered in these tiny black lines I've never seen before."

Jackson crouched and flashed his torch across his features. "Perhaps it's poison. Or something sucked the life out of him."

"Have you ever seen this before?"

Jackson stood again, his expression bleak as his eyes swept the room. "No. There's no sign of a fight, nothing untoward at all. The other rooms are the same."

"Perhaps he knew his attacker?"

"They could have overpowered him too quickly."

Harlan stepped well away from Robert's body, pulling his phone from his pocket. "I'll call Maggie...again."

Jackson shook his head. "No. Leave it to me. I'll call my contacts first."

"Why? What will they do? I do not want trouble with Maggie!"

"You won't have any, trust me."

Jackson's voice was low as he made the call, and Harlan wondered what they should do now. He needed to update Shadow, again. And he needed to break the news to the guild staff. They would be devastated, and scared. Harlan closed his eyes for a moment, wondering if Black Cronos had caught up to him, could he have died by similar means?

As Jackson ended his call, Harlan's eyes flew open. "Did you say The Silencer of Souls was with the professor earlier today?"

Jackson nodded. "Yes, why?"

"I guess I thought she might have done this, with her weird kiss. But if Smythe was at work all day, it couldn't have been her. They must have attacked as soon as he arrived home." Harlan frowned as he considered the timeline. "Jean said they had been calling all of them all afternoon."

"Perhaps he finished work early," Jackson suggested. "He might have taken leave, seeing as Mason had left."

"This is my fault."

"Of course it's not!"

"It is. They must have known who I was from Sunday's attack."

"Not necessarily. JD has clearly been making his own enquiries. And Black Cronos has threatened your organisation before. For all you know, JD has knocked heads with them in the past for this very thing."

"I guess so," Harlan said reluctantly, still unable to shed his guilt.

Jackson started to pace again, checking his watch. "My contact will be here within the hour. Until then, we wait."

"I get to meet him? Or her?"

"Her. As far as Robert's killer goes, I'm sure they have other assassins with other interesting means of killing. In fact, I know they do."

"How?"

"As I said before, Black Cronos has been around for years. All manner of curious deaths have been left in their wake. Some like this, strange black spider webs on their body. Others are just left dead through no obvious means. Some were killed violently, but we couldn't identify any obvious weapon that was used. It's like they have manufactured weapons we haven't seen yet. No knife edges or shapes to understand."

Harlan flashed back to the fight at The Midnight Sun's headquarters in Marylebone. "When I saw them fighting the Nephilim and Shadow, they had unusual silver blades, and one seemed to pull it out of thin air. I thought at first that my eyes were deceiving me—they moved so fast! But maybe you're right. They are new, unknown weapons."

Jackson looked as if he were going to respond, but instead simply said, "Let's wait for Layla."

Nahum circled next to Barak and Gabe, basking in the warm currents of air. If it wasn't for the current task, Nahum felt he could do this for hours, the pleasure of spreading his wings was so great.

But soon they would land. Below them was the country house that JD should have been heading to, but that Jean, the guild member from the Paris branch, couldn't book. It was situated at the edge of a French village, lights on in many of the houses and their gardens, their residents enjoying the balmy evening air. There were lights in the house below too, and a couple of cars on the drive.

He flew close to Gabe. "It must be a holiday rental. They might have nothing to do with JD's disappearance. And he's hardly likely to have kicked them out, no matter how odd he can be."

"Probably not, but we have to be sure."

"Let me land. You watch with Barak."

Nahum dropped to the ground, landing in a dark corner of the garden, and folded his wings away. Blade in hand, he edged across the grass to the side of the house, feeling guilty as he peeked through the windows, uncovered by blinds or curtains. Most of the rooms were lit. In the kitchen he spied an older couple clearing plates and stacking dishes, and when he edged to the side of the patio, he heard voices from a younger couple, with two children close by. He circled all the way around the house, as much as he was able, peering into bedrooms and other areas, but saw only the belongings of a family with kids.

Sighing, he took to the air again, quickly reaching his brothers. "No JD or Mason. Just a family."

Without speaking, Gabe turned and rose higher, leading them to the place JD was expected. They hovered above another big, stone-built house, but this one stood on extensive grounds, a little to the east of where the Nephilim were staying.

"It's in complete darkness," Gabe observed. "No lights, no cars."

"He's not here," Barak said. "And I checked the roads around the last place. There's no evidence of an accident. Black Cronos must have intercepted them."

"But how?" Nahum asked. "It's not like he advertised their whereabouts."

"Smythe hasn't answered his phone," Gabe reminded them. As he spoke, his phone rang, and he answered quickly. "Harlan. We've had no luck so far. I'm above the new place right now."

He fell silent, his lips tightening as he listened, and within moments had rung off. "Smythe is dead. Which means JD and Mason were picked up somewhere between the airport and here. Let's sweep the area and then head home. I have a feeling we won't find them tonight." He nodded to the landscape below them. "Black Cronos is already here, holed up somewhere. My guess is, we won't hear from them until we've used the astrolabe tomorrow night."

While they talked, hovering high above the building, Nahum had been idly surveying the grounds, and now he saw a figure close to the walls of the house. "Wait. I think there's someone down there. The east side, by the terrace."

As he pointed, another figure strolled to join the other. They flew lower to get a better look, and saw the familiar black clothing and protective vests of Black Cronos.

"Lookouts," Barak said. He looked eagerly at the others. "They suspected that someone would come looking for JD and Mason. We shouldn't disappoint them."

A spark of interest flared in Gabe's eyes. "It could be a trap. More may be waiting under the trees. And they had a bow and arrow last time."

"But if we can pick a few off, there will be less to worry about," Nahum pointed out, his blood stirring at the prospect of battle.

"All right," Gabe said reluctantly. "We go down quickly, swoop in and out, and if they are too many, we retreat. There's no point risking our lives on this. They won't underestimate us again, so this could be tricky."

Barak grinned. "But we're better than them."

"I see more now." Nahum pointed to the driveway, where his sharp eyes could see three figures clustered together. "I'll take them."

"I'll take the others," Gabe said. "Barak, hold back, and attack whoever comes running."

He nodded his agreement, and in seconds Nahum was plummeting to the ground, his wings arrowed behind him. He was on the group in seconds, and he lifted one, throwing him into a tree, used his wings to sweep another against a high stone wall, and ran at the third, tackling him to the ground in one swift movement. None of them seemed to be expecting an attack, and they were certainly not looking above them.

Nahum pressed his arm against the man's throat, pinning him to the ground, while keeping a wary eye on the other two, but both had fallen, insensible, to the ground. "Where have you taken JD?" he hissed.

The man wasn't tall, but he was lithe and strong, the corded muscles of his neck apparent as he strained under Nahum's grip. A strange, silvery light appeared in his eyes as he unexpectedly grinned. The light grew and Nahum blinked, dazzled, and then the man reared up, throwing Nahum off as if he weighed nothing. Nahum rolled, quickly regaining his feet, and cursing himself for loosening his grip. *But his eyes...*

His opponent had his fists together, and as he swept them apart, a long silver staff appeared in them. With devastating speed, he whipped across the space between them, sweeping it under Nahum's legs, and he jumped to avoid it. This man was not like the others they had met, and Nahum realised this would be a test for him. *A test he had to win.*

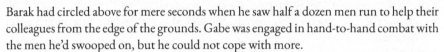

Barak had circled above for mere seconds when he saw half a dozen men run to help their colleagues from the edge of the grounds. Gabe was engaged in hand-to-hand combat with the men he'd swooped on, but he could not cope with more.

Angling himself low over the ground, Barak soared over their heads, picking up a man in each hand and lifting them high. They twisted furiously, one of them slashing a blade, but Barak dropped them into the trees, satisfied as they crashed through branches to the ground. He swooped in again, but this time arrows were flying around him. He turned and spun mid-air, as graceful as a bird of prey, and continued to pick the men off, the occasional arrow glancing off his wings. He felt one penetrate his shoulder, but ignored it as he flashed towards the area where the shooter was. It was a woman, and her aim was good. She followed his movements despite his speed, one arrow catching his rib cage, another embedding in his thigh before he was finally on her, and with one swift movement, he pulled the arrow from his thigh and stabbed her in the neck. The blood bubbled out as she choked and fell to the ground. He picked up the bow and quiver, aware that his thigh and shoulder were aching with a toxic heaviness.

He flew high again, scanning the area, but it was a struggle. He looked at the arrows' tips, wondering if they were poisoned, but saw nothing obvious. Below him, there was no other movement. Gabe was standing over two dead bodies, and Nahum was limping to his side. Satisfied there were no other attackers, Barak landed next to them, noting that they looked bruised and weary from their exertions.

"We need to go," Barak said abruptly. He was feeling odd. "I think I've been poisoned." Blood was pouring from his thigh wound, and his ribs burned where the arrow had grazed him. "Have I still got an arrow in my shoulder?"

Nahum searched behind his wings. "Yes. Brace yourself." With a wrenching sensation, the arrow was finally out, and Barak felt a flush of sweat race across his skin.

Gabe's hand flew out to steady him, his dark eyes serious. "We need to get you home. Can you still fly?"

He nodded. "It's not far, but perhaps you should stick close. And we should take these." Barak held out the bow and remaining arrows. "Don't touch the tips."

Gabe nodded, taking them from his hands. "Let's go."

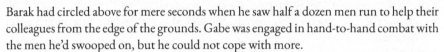

Harlan watched Dr Layla Morgan examine Robert's lifeless body with gloved hands. At her instructions, once she had given the room a cursory examination, they shut the curtains and put the overhead lights on, allowing them to see the full, shocking image of Robert's skin.

It was like something from a horror film. Robert's eyes were already covered in a filmy grey, and Layla had closed them before proceeding to examine his body. The black, spidery tracks fragmented his skin like broken pottery, and Harlan still wasn't sure whether he'd been poisoned, or if something odder had occurred.

The light also allowed him to watch Layla. Jackson had introduced them, and she had shaken his hand with a surprisingly strong grip. She was closing on sixty, Harlan estimated, a tiny birdlike woman with sharp pale blue eyes, and greying hair that still held traces of rich chestnut. She was dressed expensively, and looked as if she'd been interrupted at an evening event.

"Well," Jackson prompted her. "What's the verdict?"

"Bag." She stood and peeled her gloves off in one swift motion before dropping them into the plastic bag Jackson held out for her. It was practised, smooth, and Harlan wondered how often they had both done this. "Iron, Mars's metal of choice. I spy a pin-prick on his neck."

Harlan thought he was hearing things. "What do you mean, Mars? The God? Or the planet?"

"I have been studying Black Cronos and their death-dealing for years," she said, fixing Harlan with her piercing gaze. "They use their alchemy differently to many others. They utilise the planets and their corresponding metals as weapons. Over the years they have become more sophisticated. More deadly."

Harlan must still have looked baffled—he knew he felt it—because Jackson explained, "Alchemical correspondences. Planets, metals, astronomical timing, plants, grids, experiments...all of that." He shrugged. "Sorry. I'm no alchemist, so I can't give you details."

"I wouldn't understand this even if you did!" Harlan confessed. "How do you know about that, though?" He gestured to Robert.

Layla's lips tightened. "I know Jackson has explained our role, especially our fascination with Black Cronos. Their wartime exploits—Second World War, you understand—were horrendous, almost as bad as the Nazis. We suspect, however, it has been going on much longer. I'm referring to human experimentation, of course."

"Of course," Harlan said, nodding weakly. *What the hell had he gotten himself into?* "And now?"

"Still happening. We suspect that they recruit some voluntarily, and others...well, the vulnerable go missing every day, don't they?"

Layla was so matter of fact about it all. It was chilling. But then again, she dealt with it far more often than he did, and would have needed to find a way to deal with it.

Harlan tried to joke. "It sounds like something from a horror film. Are they making some sort of super-army?"

Layla gave him a thin smile. "Not quite. I don't think they have such lofty ambitions as to take over the world, but they are subverting and manipulating matter for their own ends."

"And you honestly have no idea where they're based?" Harlan asked, incredulous.

"No. For all the men and women that you saw at the order's headquarters and that were at your friend's farmhouse, they are actually not a big organisation. We're pretty certain of that. The man that we think is at the heart of it all moves regularly. The rest are scattered to the winds, converging when they need to. Like now."

"And the way they're converging in France," Jackson echoed.

Layla walked over to her leather bag that she'd left on a chair and pulled her phone out. "I need to call the team in."

"What about JD and Mason?" Harlan asked, hoping they hadn't already met the same fate as Robert.

"Ah, yes." Layla stared at him again. "JD. He's been interested in this for a *long* time." Her words were weighted, her gaze speculative.

Herne's horns. She knew all about him. Harlan glanced at Jackson, and saw an awareness behind his eyes too, as he added, "A *very* long time."

They were wondering if he knew. He laughed, almost maniacally. "Holy shit. You know who he really is. How long have you known?"

A broad smile spread across Layla's face, making her look suddenly younger. "A few decades."

"And you?" he asked, turning to Jackson.

"Two or three years. You?"

"A few months only. He told me himself."

Layla sat elegantly in the chair, still watching him. "Well, this makes life easier. Do you know how the secret service came to be?"

Harlan frowned. "No, why?"

"It was invented by John Dee for Queen Elizabeth I in order to help her build her empire—which, by the way, was his idea, too. He's always been bold in his thinking. He has an inquisitive, questing mind. Avaricious, almost."

"Holy shit!" Harlan repeated. "Are you telling me that he's one of you?"

Layla laughed. "No. Absolutely not. JD does not work well with others. I suppose you've noticed that?"

"Of course I have. He's infuriating!"

"But," she added, "he steps up, occasionally. Unexpectedly, too. Like now."

Harlan felt his mouth drop open. "Are you telling me that him wanting the astrolabe was for *you*?"

"Not for us. But it was to stop Black Cronos."

Harlan felt dizzy. And an idiot. "He's been liaising with you?"

"Ha! Nothing so useful. He's working on his own, but did think to inform us—ever so briefly." She rolled her eyes. "But he knows where the astrolabe could lead to. How the rumoured early experiments could enhance Black Cronos's current ones." Layla shook her head, sighing deeply. "They might even release an old monster, if the fragments of stories are true."

Harlan sat in the nearest chair, his legs growing weak. "I guess JD knows all this because of his age, right? His immersion in the occult world?"

"That and the fact he saw the results of their experiments first-hand during the Second World War. He was an ally then, for a while."

"Why the hell didn't he explain this to me?" Harlan appealed to both of them, knowing they couldn't really answer him. "I've suspected him of being a nut-job, and now it seems he's acting out of some kind of hero complex!"

Jackson shrugged. "You said it yourself. He's odd. Maybe he was trying to protect you?"

Harlan somehow doubted that, but didn't voice it. "But he's gone with Mason, of all people. He hasn't been in the field for years! He was terrible at it!" Harlan leapt to his feet, his path clear. "I have to get out there. Where the fuck are they?"

"Glad you said that," Jackson said, smiling. "I'm booked on an early flight. Want to come?"

"Yes, of course! But—" Harlan's gaze flew to Smythe. He felt responsible. "Who will deal with this, and tell the guild?"

"Leave that to me," Layla said softly as she picked up her phone.

Twenty-Two

S hadow had never seen Barak look so ill. His burnished black skin was grey, and a film of sweat covered his entire body.

Gabe had landed with him cradled in his arms after Barak had become so weak that he almost fell from the sky. He now lay unconscious on the big dining room table inside the house, his wings still folded beneath him, acting as a giant bed of feathers. The glossy, jet-black plumage shot through with blue had lost its shine, too. Shadow felt sick with worry; in fact, she was terrified they would lose him.

Gabe, Nahum, and Caldwell stood close to her, as serious as she had ever seen them, and her heart went out to his brothers. They watched Estelle and Aubrey as they tended to Barak's injuries, Ash helping them in his calm, collected way. They had already dressed his shoulder wound, cleaning out a sticky yellow substance that smelled foul. Now Estelle cleaned the graze along his ribs, while Aubrey tended the deep thigh wound. Estelle's lips moved rapidly as she worked, much as Briar's did when she used healing magic, although she had confessed it was not her best skill. Fortunately, they had travelled with a first aid kit filled with Briar's medicinal balms, as well as the herbal provisions that Eli had packed.

"This is my fault," Gabe muttered, eyes fixed on Barak.

"No, it's not. It was Barak who suggested this," Nahum said immediately, "and I backed him up."

"I sanctioned it!" Gabe rounded on Nahum. "And I asked Barak to mop up the extras."

"And he did it willingly!" Nahum shot back. "As any of us would."

Ash raised his voice, glaring at them. "Not now, and not here!"

Shadow took Gabe's arm, needing fresh air, and knowing he did, too. Besides, she should be on watch. "Come with me."

"But—"

"But nothing," she said, giving him no room to argue and propelling him out the door.

She led him to the terrace, and they leaned on the railing, looking out over the vineyards and the land around them. The cicadas had quieted, finally, and an almost full moon bathed the landscape with its silver light. But she knew Gabe wasn't really seeing it. He looked to the far horizon, but his gaze was inward.

"He's strong," she told him, more to reassure herself than him. "He'll pull through. Especially with Estelle's magic and Briar and Eli's balms."

Shadow had spent an uneasy few hours with Estelle while the three Nephilim were out. Ash had been deep in conversation with Aubrey and Caldwell, leaving her and Estelle alone. They had cleared the remnants of dinner together, awkwardly polite, before Shadow had patrolled the grounds, confident they were secure because she could feel Estelle's powerful protection spell. To Estelle's credit, she had looked as distressed as the rest of them at Barak's condition, pushing the others out of the way to help him.

"You were right," Shadow conceded. "It was worth bringing Estelle."

Gabe nodded but didn't look around. "If he dies, I will never forgive myself."

"His enhanced healing will flush the toxins out...or whatever they were."

"We're fighting something we don't even understand." He finally looked at her, his dark eyes questioning. "It's like some battle that's been raging for centuries, under the cover of darkness. Or maybe *battle* isn't the right word."

"It is, of a sort. A battle for knowledge. Advancement."

He tried to laugh. "Enhancing humans with alchemy? It sounds insane!"

"Alchemy is science, that's what I understand. And science enhances everything. They're just approaching it a different way." Shadow glanced away, the weight of his gaze feeling suddenly intimate.

Gabe gripped the railing, his arms tense as he stared over the fields again. "They pulled strange weapons on us, again. I'm trying to imagine how this will play out tomorrow, and I can't see what we should do."

"I'm sure it will become apparent once we're there."

She studied his broad shoulders and powerful arms, his sculpted chest that was visible beneath his t-shirt, and was once again aware of his heat. His thick, dark hair was swept off his face, revealing his square chin covered in dark stubble, and she wanted to comfort him, caress him, hold him. *What if she were to die tomorrow? Or Gabe?* Her heart faltered at the thought. To remain here without him was unthinkable. And they were out here, alone, serenaded with soft moonlight on a balmy night.

Without thinking it through, she slipped under his arms that gripped the rail and faced him. He looked down at her, startled, and she lifted her hands to his cheeks, pulling him to her lips with a sudden hunger. Desire raced through her, and it felt as if every nerve ending was on fire. His lips were soft but firm, exploring her mouth with deepening passion. His arms were suddenly around her, one hand in her hair, the other pulling her close, and she mirrored his actions, revelling in his heat that threatened to consume them both. He lifted her up, seating her on the wooden rail, and she wrapped her legs around his waist, pulling him closer. Time seemed suspended, everything else disappearing as Shadow realised everything felt right. When they finally eased apart, she was shocked by the longing in his eyes.

His voice was husky. "Come to my bed, now."

"But, Gabe..." Why was she hesitating? Was it because Barak was clinging to life? Or was it because their relationship would be changed forever?

"What?" he murmured, burying his face in her neck, and covering it with kisses as his hands slid down her back. She felt breathless, giddy with desire. "I know you want this as much as I do."

She tried to be rational, but Herne's horns, it was hard. "But what if it all goes wrong?"

He lifted his head to stare at her again, his face inches from her own, his passion encompassing her so completely she couldn't think straight. His voice was almost a growl. "It won't go wrong, because it's us."

And with that, she was lost. He grabbed her hand, pulling her to the stairs and up to his room.

Ash watched Barak's motionless body, and squeezed his eyes shut. For now, they had done as much as they could do. He debated appealing to their fathers for help, and then swiftly rejected it.

"I'll watch him," Estelle said, her clipped voice firm and decisive.

Ash's eyes flew open. "You've done enough. You used a lot of magic. You probably need to sleep."

She regarded him coolly, arrogantly even. "I'm strong enough to sustain my magic."

"It wasn't an insult, Estelle. I'm trying to be considerate." He wanted to throw something at her, but instead clenched his fists. "And he's my brother."

"And he's my friend!" Her eyes were burning now, fierce with intent.

Ash noticed she wasn't touching Barak at all, but she was sitting close, her hand resting on the blanket they had thrown over him to keep him warm. They were still in the dining room, but Barak was now on a bed they had made on the floor, his head resting on a pillow, his wings still beneath him. Despite the summer night, they had the fire burning low, too. Estelle had thrown on a bundle of herbs, and their fresh healing smells alleviated the heavy atmosphere in the room.

They were also alone. Nahum and the others had headed to bed, or to the shower, in Nahum's case—he was covered in blood—and Ash had no idea where Shadow or Gabe were.

Estelle was still glaring at him, and he needed to back off. Something was going on with these two, more than he realised. "Okay. As long as you're sure."

Her shoulders dropped as she took a deep breath, releasing it slowly. "I'm sure. You should sleep, too. You've been busy all day."

Ash's mind was whirling with his earlier discussions, and now the worry about Barak. He wasn't sure he could sleep. Or if he even wanted to. "Why don't I make us some tea? Or something stronger?"

"Tea would be good, thank you."

He nodded and walked to the kitchen, the silence of the house falling around him. With only a low light on, he boiled the kettle and made a pot of tea, placing a mug, milk, and sugar on a tray. But he did not want tea. He needed something stronger. Something to take the edge off the evening. He took the tray to Estelle, saying, "I'm on the terrace if you need me."

He retraced his steps, picked up a bottle of local red wine and a couple of glasses, and took them out to the terrace where he sat at the long table looking out into the night.

It wasn't long before Nahum joined him, dressed in more casual clothes. "Good thinking," he said, helping himself to a glass. "Estelle told me you were here."

"I'm too wound up to sleep."

"Me too, but Aubrey and Caldwell have gone to bed. And," Nahum gave him a wry smile, "so have Gabe and Shadow."

Ash nodded, absently. "Good." And then he realised what Nahum meant and his eyes widened. "Hold on! Do you mean *together*?"

Nahum laughed. "Yep. That's the only thing that's made me smile all night. They don't know I saw them, though. I happened to follow them up the stairs, but frankly, they were oblivious." He took a sip of wine. "About time, too."

"The risk of imminent death always heightens one's emotions." Ash sipped too, appreciating the rich, full flavours. "Who won the bet?"

Nahum grinned. "Niel keeps tally. We'll ask him when he gets here. He should be on his way. Let's hope nothing happens to him," he added.

"He'll be fine. And so will Barak."

"Is that just wishful thinking?" All humour had left Nahum's face.

"Partly. But Barak is strong—and stubborn, just like his fallen father." Barak's father had been one of the strongest of the fallen angels, and fiercely loyal to Lucifer Morningstar who had triggered the fall. Conviction had burned in his eyes, along with a fervent loathing of the old God.

"Stubbornness is nothing though if the poison is too strong." Nahum shifted in his seat, alert with curiosity. "What did you find out from Aubrey and Caldwell?"

Ash grunted with frustration. "Alchemy has to be one of the weirdest, most complicated esoteric fields of study I've ever come across. They speak in our language, but it is almost incomprehensible!" He was frustrated just thinking about his discussion. "I've read books on it and had long conversation with two experts—two *Adepts*—but I am baffled. No wonder it takes years to be conversant with its laws and correspondences."

Nahum looked puzzled. "But I thought you were familiar with it from our old days, before the flood."

"The Emerald Tablet of Hermes Trismegistus triggered all of it, but I took little notice then. We had other things to occupy us."

"But the super-humans, what's with that?"

"Essentially, it's as Aubrey said earlier. Harnessing the power of planets, using their alignment in the sky and other astronomical correspondences and their associations with metals. Long experiments, with essences and applications."

"And they must have utilised those things to make weapons, too," Nahum said. He shook his head. "These people and their weapons make me feel old-fashioned."

Ash smiled. "There's something to be said for age and experience, though, brother."

"JD would understand it, surely," Nahum said, topping up his drink. "He's an expert."

"Perhaps that's why he wants the astrolabe. After all, he cracked immortality." Tiredness started to creep up on Ash, the quiet conversation and fine wine working its magic, but he filled up his glass again, enjoying talking to Nahum without anyone to disturb them. "Do you think we should leave a watch?"

"I'll ask Estelle," Nahum said. "But if she's still confident in her magic, perhaps we should all sleep tonight. I doubt we will get much rest tomorrow. But in the meantime," he said, smiling mischievously, "tell me what you think of Barak and Estelle."

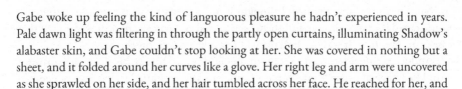

Gabe woke up feeling the kind of languorous pleasure he hadn't experienced in years. Pale dawn light was filtering in through the partly open curtains, illuminating Shadow's alabaster skin, and Gabe couldn't stop looking at her. She was covered in nothing but a sheet, and it folded around her curves like a glove. Her right leg and arm were uncovered as she sprawled on her side, and her hair tumbled across her face. He reached for her, and then paused.

Barak.

He must have survived the night, or they would have been woken. The house was quiet, at peace. A good sign. And Barak was strong. Soon Gabe would have to get up and face the day, make decisions, but now was for pleasure. He rolled over, snaking his arm around Shadow's waist, and pulled her into him, curling around her protectively.

Last night had been more than he could have dreamed—and he'd dreamed of it plenty. Shadow complimented him in every way, and she was as fiery as he had expected. They ignited passion in each other. She stirred, and he pulled her closer, his cheek resting against her hair and then his lips nuzzled her neck. His desire was already stirring.

She wriggled in his arms, and turned to face him, her violet eyes luminous in this light, her fey otherness breathtaking. She blinked and her eyes widened, and Gabe knew she was flooded with memories of their night. For a horrible moment he thought she would pull away, her defences up, but then she smiled, pulling him closer, and her eyes said everything. She threaded her hands through his hair, lifted her leg over his hip, and kissed him, and he could think of nothing but her.

Nahum eased the door of the dining room open with his elbow, juggling two coffees, and saw Estelle stir in the half-light, her long dark hair loose as she sat upright. She had lain next to Barak all night.

"How is he?" Nahum asked softly, handing her a drink.

"Better. His breathing is easier, and his colour is good."

"Good." Nahum sat on a chair, sipping his drink and enjoying the rush of caffeine. "Did you sleep?"

"A little. I kept the fire going and repeated a few spells, and I dozed in between." She paused to sip her coffee, and stared at Nahum with a puzzled expression on her face. "Something odd happened in the night."

Nahum's thoughts immediately flew to an intruder. "Did you hear something?"

"No. With Barak. I felt him getting hot, and thought at first we were too close to the fire, but something seemed to ignite beneath his skin—like flames! He glowed. It started in his chest and then radiated out to his limbs, even through his feathers."

She pushed back her hair, and Nahum thought how much better she looked without that permanent tight-lipped frown of disapproval she always wore—her resting bitch face. He subdued a smirk, focussing instead on what she'd seen.

"It wasn't something you'd done?"

"No! I'll admit I was terrified. I thought it was a new level of the poison working. I nearly raised the whole house! But then," she looked at Barak again, confused, "I felt this ease come over him. It was like he'd burned away the poison somehow."

A sudden memory returned to Nahum, and he slumped back in his chair with surprise. "Ah. His father did that. I saw him do it once to a man injured in battle. I remember it because it was such a generous, unexpected gesture from one of the fallen. He laid his hands on him, and it was like a fire raged beneath his skin, healing every single cut." Nahum laughed with delight. "It must be inherited. He healed himself!"

"It certainly took him a while!" Estelle protested. "The poison must have overwhelmed his system really quickly." She smiled. "Our actions bought him time."

Nahum looked at his brother with new appreciation. "Maybe this event has unlocked a healing skill. These correspondences apparently link with angels. I remember JD saying so. I wonder if the poison responded to something that has to do with his angel father?"

"That's a very interesting idea, Nahum."

They were silent for a moment, considering what that meant, when Barak stirred and groaned, his eyes fluttering open. He lifted his head, trying to focus. "Where the hell am I?"

"Welcome back, brother. You certainly know how to give us all a fright."

He sat up, dwarfing Estelle next to him. "Welcome back from what?"

"Poison," Estelle explained. "Courtesy of Black Cronos, remember?"

Barak looked at her, his bed, the fire, and finally, his wings. "What in Herne's horns happened last night?"

Nahum smiled and rose to his feet, his heart light. "I'll let Estelle explain, and get started on breakfast. I'm hoping Niel is here somewhere, asleep."

"Oh, yes he is!" Estelle announced, looking apologetic. "He arrived just before dawn and found himself a room."

"Good," Nahum said, sighing with relief. He was glad to know Niel was safe, and that they now had weapons. "I was a bit worried, if I'm honest."

"He made good time—said the weather was calm and clear."

"Good, I'll leave him to sleep."

Barak had been listening, and he still looked confused. "Is Gabe okay? My memories aren't all there yet."

"Don't you worry about Gabe. He's *just fine!*" Nahum said enigmatically, and left them to catch up.

"So," Barak said, stretching his arms out and wincing as he felt the pull in his shoulder, "it seems you need to fill the gaps in my failing memory."

Estelle had edged away from him to give him room, but not too far, and she sipped her coffee, watching him over the rim. "You really can't remember?"

"No. I mean, I remember we went to look for JD's place, but after that…"

"You had a fight with some Black Cronos members and got shot with poisoned arrows. Does that jog your memory?"

His head felt woolly and confused as he struggled to remember the events, and then it struck him. *The woman with the bow and her impressive accuracy.* "Yes. I was hit while I was flying. Nahum spotted them lurking around the place JD should have been."

"It was a trap, and you ploughed right into it."

He rolled his eyes. "You are always so combative! Of course it was a trap, we knew that, but also saw it as a chance to take a few of them out. And we certainly did," he said smugly.

"So nice to know I spent my whole night looking after you, and you don't seem to care that you nearly died."

"I do care! I didn't want to die! I didn't want to be injured, either. Hold on," he said, as her words filtered through his foggy brain. He took in her lack of makeup, t-shirt and yoga pants, and her mass of tumbling hair that he wanted to run his hands through. "Are you saying you slept with me?" He patted the blanket next to him, still feeling its warmth. "Right here."

"Guilty," she teased, batting her eyelashes. "Does that make you feel a little vulnerable? I promise I did not take advantage of you."

Her eyes swept across his bare chest and down his body, and he realised he'd been cut out of his jeans, and that all he was wearing were his boxer shorts under the blanket. "I would be more than happy for you to take advantage of me, but I must insist I be awake to fully appreciate it. Deal?"

He couldn't contain his grin as she stared him right in the eye and said, "If you have to play by the rules, then I suppose so."

"Oh, Estelle," he said as a rush of early morning desire told him everything seemed to be working properly, and also made him grateful for the blanket. "You are a very naughty girl."

"Naughty *woman*, actually. Now, if you can possibly get your mind out of the gutter," she said, sipping her coffee demurely, "do you think you can explain why you seemed to internally combust last night?"

He did not appreciate the change in subject. "I did *what*?"

"You seemed to have this rush of fire just under your skin, about two to three hours ago. It started in your chest and spread everywhere. Nahum said your father did similar things. Has that happened before?"

"I don't think so!" He placed his hand on his chest as if he would feel different. "Where, here?"

"Yep. It sort of blossomed outwards." She explained their thoughts on the poison and alchemy.

All sorts of memories flooded back to Barak. His father was huge, a giant amongst the angels, and a fierce warrior. He didn't show compassion often, but Nahum was right, every now and again he healed using his hands, a flash of fire that flared from his fingers.

"I've never knowingly used it, but maybe it's been latent in me all along." He stared at his hands, willing them to produce fire, but nothing happened. "I can't do it now."

Estelle studied him, puzzled. "Maybe it only happens when your body is in stress, or perhaps you just need to practice. But I'm a fire witch, so maybe I can help you."

"Well, that sounds like fun."

"Oh, does it?" she laughed, rising to her feet. "I'm a hard task master."

"I'm fine with that. Where are you going?" he protested, enjoying their quiet intimacy.

"I need a shower, and so do you."

"Is that an invite?"

"You're incorrigible," she said as she walked to the door. "No. But I'll see you later, over breakfast."

She smiled as she left him, and Barak realised he felt better than he had in years. He was pretty sure it was Estelle's doing too, rather than his father's power. It was certainly time for a shower...a cold one.

Twenty-Three

Niel had only taken a cursory look around the *château* when he arrived. He hadn't flown so far in a long time, and he was more tired than he expected, so for a few hours he'd slept well. Now he followed the sound of voices to the long, covered terrace at the back of the house, and discovered a few people gathered around the table. Covered dishes and jugs of coffee had been placed down the centre, and the remnants of breakfast on used plates indicated he was the last to arrive.

"This is where you all are! Morning all! Wow. What a place!" For a moment he simply took in the view of the vineyards, appreciating the warmth that promised a hot day, as the others greeted him. He sat next to Nahum and poured himself coffee, glad that it was still warm.

"I thought I'd let you sleep," Nahum told him, "but everything should still be hot."

"I could eat it cold, I'm so hungry," Niel confessed, already filling his plate. He looked up at Barak, who was still not his normal self. "I'm glad to see you looking better. You were out cold when I arrived!"

Barak gave him a wry smile. "You've heard I had a run in with a strange poison, I take it?"

Niel nodded to Estelle, who sat next to Barak. She looked tired, but there was something different about her that Niel couldn't place. "Estelle gave me a brief rundown."

"Yeah, my body did an odd thing I need to think about," he said, distractedly topping up his coffee.

"But everyone else is okay?" he said, glancing around the table.

"We're fine," Gabe and Shadow said together, almost too quickly.

Niel frowned, thinking they both looked furtive—flushed, even—but despite that, Gabe radiated a calm Niel hadn't seen in months. Shadow, however, could barely meet his eyes.

Oh. He paused, his fork partway to his mouth, and then catching Shadow's scowl, he shovelled food in quickly and turned away. Nahum and Ash were both looking at him with barely concealed smirks that told him to shut up and move on. *So, it had finally happened. About time, too.*

Struggling to hide his own amusement, he spoke quickly. "Great! So, what's the plan today?"

"Harlan will be arriving in a few hours," Nahum said. "He's bringing Jackson, and he sounded excited."

"Jackson?" Niel grunted. "Why him? Not that I mind, obviously."

"More weird connections, I gather."

Ash sighed. "Let's hope they provide a way through this mess. JD has gone missing, along with Mason."

Niel paused. "Really? How—and why?"

"He's not answering his phone," Nahum explained. "Although, he could be sneaking around and lying low."

Aubrey and Caldwell hadn't spoken yet. As usual, they were sitting close together, looking furtive and worried, but then Caldwell said, "Everything is gathering. I can feel it. The planets are aligning, and so are the players."

Aubrey nodded. "It's like a portent. When we take the reading tonight, we need to be ready to act quickly."

"You can't read it in the day?" Niel asked.

"No. After further discussion, and some thorough reasoning with Ash, we will take the reading from Mars. Once we have our new destination, we have to head to the place itself."

"And Black Cronos?" Niel studied the faces around the table. "They're here, obviously. Surely they can't follow us?"

Nahum grimaced. "Unfortunately, we're worried that they have JD and will use him for leverage."

"But we don't know that yet," Gabe remonstrated. "When Harlan arrives, we can pool our knowledge. Until then, we should use the day to rest, plan for all eventualities, and check our weapons. If we fail tonight, Black Cronos wins, and who knows what that could mean."

—◆◇◆—

When Harlan arrived at the *château* in the late morning with Jackson, he felt alert, excited, and more alive than he had in days. He felt, in fact, like a spy—especially when he left his very expensive hotel and was picked up a by a sleek black Audi to be taken to the airport.

As he and Jackson passed through the gates of the property in their rental car, a wave of power passed over them, and Jackson, who was driving, grunted. "Now *that's* a protection spell."

"You don't have to keep insulting my charms and amulets," Harlan told him.

"I'm just saying it was good!"

"If they're protection spells, how come we're getting in?"

"Something to do with us not having malevolent intent, or something of the sort, I guess."

Harlan had barely time to think about that when they swept into a grand courtyard overshadowed by magnificent architecture, and Nahum stepped out from under a shaded loggia, his scabbard and sword strapped around his waist, the hilt glinting in the light.

"Good to see you," he greeted them, as Harlan exited the car.

"You too, I think," Harlan said, shaking his hand. "I'm glad to see this place seems secure. I wasn't sure what we'd find."

"Oh, we're settled and safe here, for now." Nahum turned to Jackson. "Good to see you, too. I'm looking forward to hearing your news."

"The calm before the storm," Jackson said wryly.

Nahum gave a hollow laugh. "Caldwell said something similar this morning. Something about everything aligning." Nahum led them inside the house, asking, "Any news from JD?"

Harlan's anxiety that he'd finally contained flared again. "No, even though Jackson's contacts have been trying to trace his phone. He's a wily old fox. Part of me is hoping he's gone underground and turned it off. It might still be likely, if it weren't for Smythe."

"Yeah, sorry to hear about that," Nahum said, his bright blue eyes flashing with sorrow. "Look, I'll take you to your rooms upstairs where you can freshen up, and then come and join us on the terrace. We've been virtually living out there. We're going through strategies for tonight, and it would be good to get your opinion. And of course, share your news."

Nahum led them through the warren of rooms and staircases, finally depositing them in ornately decorated bedrooms on the same hall. Harlan headed straight to the shower, sluicing off the grime from the journey, and then joined the others outside.

It was a hive of activity. A telescope had been set up at the end of the terrace, and Aubrey, Caldwell, and Ash were clustered around it. Books were sprawled across the long wooden table, and a laptop was at the far end. Barak, Gabe, Shadow, Niel, Nahum, and a woman he'd never met with long, dark hair were all sparring in a patch of shade in a grassy area below the terrace. All the Nephilim wore cotton pants only, their bare chests covered in sweat. Shadow wore jeans and a t-shirt, looking nimble and lithe next to the well-muscled Nephilim, and the other woman looked like she was dressed in yoga gear. She must be Caspian's sister, Estelle. He'd heard a little about her. She had no weapons, just her forbidding magic that she was using to fight with. Flashes of fire and bolts of energy flew from her hands, making everyone work hard to duck them or counter them.

He leaned on the railing watching them all for a moment, unnoticed. Shadow was battling Nahum and Gabe, while Niel and Barak fought Estelle, but it seemed to Harlan that Barak wasn't fighting with quite as much vigour as the others, and they seemed to be treating him gently.

"They like their practice," Jackson observed, leaning on the rail next to him. "I think it's too bloody hot!"

Jackson had finally taken off his long coat, and just wore his jeans, t-shirt, and scuffed sneakers.

"I really don't think they care. Look at them! They make me feel inadequate."

Jackson grinned. "They make me feel safe." He gestured to his regular-sized biceps. "I'm not really the workout kind. I have to rely on my wits."

"I think we'll need wits, luck, strength, and anything else we can use tonight."

He heard a shout of greeting, and saw Gabe waving. In minutes, all of them were trooping back to the terrace, using towels to wipe the sweat off themselves.

"I gather you two have some things to share," Gabe said, slinging the towel around his shoulders.

Harlan cast a sideways glance at Jackson. "Yeah, *someone's* got some interesting connections."

Jackson shrugged nonchalantly. "It's just one of those things." His gaze slid over the table, to the kitchen. "Shall I get drinks?"

Niel waved him off. "Sit, please. I'll get everything."

Despite their half-dressed, sweaty state, the Nephilim and the two women sat around the table, looking at Harlan and Jackson with interest.

"Have you met Estelle?" Nahum asked. He quickly made the introductions, and Estelle nodded briefly, her cool gaze sweeping over them.

Niel returned, handing out beers and placing down jugs of water, and as Shadow opened a bottle, she asked, "What's with JD?"

Harlan grimaced. "We have a horrible feeling that he's been kidnapped, him and Mason. He landed in Bordeaux, we know that for sure, but he's since gone missing."

"And still no response?"

"Nothing. Half of me wants to think he's keeping his head down somewhere, but I believe that's wishful thinking."

Ash, Caldwell, and Aubrey joined the group, and Caldwell said, "We have all the cards right now. We have the astrolabe and will read it tonight, from here. Unless they've found out somehow where we are, they can't follow us." He looked triumphant. "They've lost. Tonight, we'll go into the chamber."

Ash shot an impatient look at Caldwell. "But if they have JD and his life is threatened, we'll be forced to compromise. They'll kill them if we don't, and I will not have that on my conscience."

Aubrey and Caldwell looked as if they might protest, but Jackson stepped in. "Actually, we want them there, so them having a bargaining chip works in our favour."

A chorus of *whats*, *hows*, and *whys* rung out around the table, and Jackson raised his hand.

"Hear me out. I work for a division of the government on occasions—the Paranormal Interests Division—and ever since World War II they have been looking for Black Cronos, which we believe to be a small but well-funded group, dangerous, and often without scruples. You've seen that for yourself. This is our chance to catch the ringleader and hopefully stop them for good."

"*If* he—or she—is there," Gabe said.

"We think they will be. The Dark Star chamber is a big deal. It contains secrets hidden for centuries. He'll be there."

Aubrey looked pale. "Please don't tell me it's Stefan Hope-Robbins."

Jackson shook his head. "No. We think it's a man called Toto Dax. He comes from a long line of alchemists and occult dealers, but has a small group of alchemy experts as part of his group—Hope-Robbins being one of them."

"Toto Dax!" Niel exclaimed. "Is that for real?"

Jackson laughed. "Maybe not. We suspect he has several names."

Niel's arms were crossed over his broad chest. "Is he a guy with white-blond hair?"

Jackson looked at him wide-eyed. "Yes, why?"

"Mouse saw him on our back lanes on the night we were attacked at home, supervising the few survivors."

"He was in Cornwall? Wow!" Jackson ran his hands through his tangled hair, a gleam of excitement in his eyes. "For him to be so close shows how much this means to him. He's hardly ever spotted. He must be here now, too."

Nahum looked puzzled. "If you want to catch him, does this mean you have backup?"

"Of a sort." Jackson looked shifty. "The PID doesn't have any military support, not since the war. They are primarily an intelligence-gathering organisation. There's a witch who has done work for them in the past, me of course, and they've used The Orphic Guild before too, JD included. They also access police paranormal divisions, so we're more like the link for a few things."

Harlan listened, noting the word 'we' was used a lot, and a few things Jackson had already told him dropped into place. They were the link to the paranormal SOCO team and their results, Maggie's findings, Newton's, and probably other police divisions he'd never heard of. Harlan knew the occult world ran far and wide, but he'd still never really considered a government agency existed, which was stupid.

Jackson was continuing, "We only get really involved if we determine there's a big risk—and this is one. We'd like to utilise your skills, and want you to catch him for us."

Gabe gave a dry laugh. "Will you pay us?"

"Of course. I have a small unit on standby that can transport him, or anyone else you capture, out of the country. But, as I say, we're not military and don't want to involve them, either." He sighed. "They have a tendency to take over things."

"But we get to keep access to the chamber?" Aubrey asked, frowning.

Jackson's gaze swung to him. "It depends on what you want to do with it. I'm hoping you're not planning on making your own super-humans or monsters?"

Caldwell spluttered. "No! This is about transmutation of the soul for a higher purpose!"

"Potentially yes, then. You get to keep access."

Harlan watched Jackson's coolly measured response, but knew from the conversations he'd had that it wouldn't be that easy. Jackson had already told him that if the place looked too dangerous, they were going to destroy it. Or seize it for PID. Right now, Harlan wasn't sure which way it was going to go.

Caldwell was now bristling with annoyance. "This is not on! This is *our* origin. Our find! Aubrey did all the hard work in locating the astrolabe, and I don't see why someone should be swooping in and taking it from us! Our order has plans."

"I appreciate that," Jackson said smoothly, "but don't forget that a monster is rumoured to be lurking in this chamber. Safety is paramount."

Harlan realised Jackson had all the smooth, calm, competent assuredness of a man used to getting his own way. He had a quiet strength about him, Harlan had always known that, but now cast in this new light of working with the government, Harlan decided that he was probably far more involved than he was letting on. He hadn't elaborated on his grandfather's disappearance, but had intimated it was a family business. *In which case, where did his parents fit into this?*

Harlan sipped his beer, watching the interactions between everyone sitting around the table, and thought that the next twenty-four were going to prove very interesting indeed.

Shadow took a deep breath, inhaling the scented, balmy air. She looked up at the rising, waxing moon and the night sky that was blanketed with stars, the planets lined up amongst them. She tried to remember which was which after Ash's explanations, but all she could think of were the stars back home which looked completely different to here.

She turned to watch Aubrey and Caldwell's preparations. The time was approaching, and Aubrey was currently looking through the telescope and then at the astrolabe that Caldwell was shining a torch onto.

The Nephilim were in the house, finalising weapons and discussing tactics with Harlan and Jackson, but Shadow had left them to it. She would fight the same way she always had, and if they managed to capture Toto or Hope-Robbins that was fine, but she wouldn't worry about killing them, either.

Shadow also wanted to keep her distance from Gabe. She found that she wanted to keep touching him; he was like a magnet. All day he had been glancing at her, touching her arm and the small of her back, and her body had yearned for him. His touch had branded her skin, and now, closing her eyes, she remembered every moment of their night together, like some glorious, drug-addled dream. And this afternoon, of course, when they had managed to sneak off to shower and find some time alone.

She knew her brothers had found out. They all looked at them both in that knowing way. None of them had commented yet, but that was just a matter of time. And that was okay. She had nothing to be ashamed of. As Gabe had whispered last night—it was inevitable.

An excited burst of chatter made her look back at Caldwell and Aubrey. They were lining up the astrolabe, referring to their notes as they did so. Aubrey made a few final adjustments as Caldwell gesticulated. They seemed to be bickering. Shadow could not understand what they were doing, but after several minutes, Aubrey emitted a small whoop and high-fived Caldwell.

"You've done it?" she asked, strolling to their side.

Aubrey was beaming. "Yes. For good measure we read from all the planets, but this Mithras link makes Mars seem the perfect match." He tapped the astrolabe. "We have the coordinates."

He bustled over to the table where the detailed map of the area was secured with candles, and Caldwell shone the torch on it while Aubrey measured. He jammed his finger on the spot. "Here, next to the sea."

Shadow squinted at the map. "And we are where?"

Caldwell pointed, "Here. So about half an hour's drive." He too was frowning at the map. "It's on the grounds of an old estate, *Château de Porge*."

He pulled out his phone and tapped it while Shadow studied the map. The building was situated on a rise in an area of green, but it was impossible to see how big it was.

"As I thought," Caldwell said. "It's a ruin, a shell of a building with extensive grounds." He was already heading indoors, saying, "I'll tell the others."

"We'll need to search," Aubrey said. "The chamber could be anywhere."

Shadow huffed. "Another bloody search for an underground room. *Great.*"

He looked at her, confused. "Another?"

"Just our last two jobs, but I guess that's the nature of this business, isn't it?" She straightened up. "We need to leave. Is there anything else you must take?"

"We have our bags prepared." Aubrey swallowed, looking nervous. "We have our ritual equipment, as well as torches, our reference books, and we'll take the astrolabe, of course."

She watched him dispassionately. He was an odd man, full of bluster, large, pompous, undeniably intelligent, and willing to risk everything for the Dark Star, including stealing for it. And his near miss with death—twice—hadn't fazed him, either. *Very curious.*

Everyone followed Caldwell outside, and while most clustered around the map, Ash headed to the telescope with Caldwell to look at the planets.

"Are you sure of the coordinates?" Harlan asked, a frown creasing his brow.

"Very sure. It's not some random place on the map—it's an old *château*. It could well have been owned by one of the members back then!" He looked uncertain. "I can of course check the other coordinates…we read from all the planets, but they'll be close."

Jackson nodded, his shaggy hair falling around his eyes. "Do it anyway."

Gabe glanced at her, but before he could speak his phone rang, and everyone froze. He answered it quickly. "Gabe here."

He grimaced and mouthed, *Black Cronos.* "What do you want?"

Shadow could hear a tinny voice but not what was said, especially when Gabe paced, his shoulders hunching. They had already discussed their options, so what Gabe said wasn't a surprise.

"I need to speak to him and Mason first… JD, keep a cool head, we'll meet soon—Mason, I'm afraid it's true." Gabe's lips tightened, and Shadow heard the tinny voice again. "We will meet you there, and go in together… Okay, then kill them and you will find nothing." Gabe's voice was hard, unyielding, and there was a pause as the person he spoke to considered his words. Shadow wouldn't doubt him. Gabe sounded as mean as a warrior sylph, and they would cut your throat just as soon as look at you. He continued, "I've met him a few times, and he was prepared to let me die last time. I'm returning the favour… It's called compromise, and I guess a question of faith—in your men and mine… *No.* I'll text it when I know we're close… Because I don't trust you."

He ended the call, his lips twisting in a crooked smile. "Mason and JD are alive, and both are furious—especially Mason when he heard that Robert was dead."

"You spoke to Toto?" Jackson asked.

"That's who he said he was. Smooth and oily." Gabe checked his watch and then the map. "We can be out of here in five minutes. We'll fly, obviously, and I'll take Shadow. Flight should take us ten minutes or so. I want to do some homework and check the site before we call them. The rest will follow in the car. Agreed?" He looked at Estelle, who seemed as if she might complain, and Shadow couldn't help but feel pleased she wouldn't fly with them. "I want someone with strong magic to protect the humans. Okay?"

Estelle had changed out of her yoga clothes and was now dressed in jeans and dark outerwear like everyone else. She lifted her chin. "Okay."

"I still don't like it!" Aubrey said, and it was clear he thought victory was about to be snatched from him.

"Nobody likes it," Harlan drawled, obviously impatient. "But we play with the cards we're dealt. Let's get out of here."

Twenty-Four

G abe circled over the *Château de Porge* ruins, Shadow in his arms, dropping lower and lower. Gabe's brothers were close, checking out the lanes below the ridge and the sprawl of lightly wooded grounds.

"See anyone?" he asked her.

She squirmed in his arms. "No one. It's isolated, isn't it?"

"Good. It needs to be, considering what may happen here later."

From the air they could see broken towers that were set into the steep ground that fell away to the sea, the fallen stones silvered in the moonlight. A rudimentary path ran up from the road below, and the remnants of other buildings were visible, long lines of stone crossing back and forth over the flat part of the grounds. He landed on the highest point, next to the remains of an old wall, the arched window framing the starlight. Before releasing Shadow he kissed her, pressing her back against the stone wall before letting her go reluctantly. She looked amused but pleased, and within seconds she'd drawn both her swords, and he followed suit. Her long bow was across her back too, which had made her more difficult to carry, but he didn't care. She'd faced him this time, wrapping her legs around his waist, her cheek pressed to his chest. It was gloriously distracting, but now he banished those thoughts from his mind and focussed on the task at hand.

Gabe stared over the low wall, noting the steep sides of the grassy hill that became more acute as it reached the cliff edge. Below, the surf roared against the rocks. A fall here would kill a mortal, and it was unlikely anyone could sneak up that way. He wondered how close Black Cronos was. They could take up to an hour to get there, but he doubted they'd be so lucky.

Within minutes his brothers landed next to him, all similarly dressed in military-style combat clothing, including protective vests strapped around their chests. None of them liked wearing them, but Black Cronos was too formidable not to take every precaution around. Barak had seemed none the worse for his injuries as the day progressed, and had looked annoyed at the suggestion of being left behind. They couldn't afford to anyway; he needed them all.

Barak was already surveilling the grounds. "It's impressive...and big. Did Caldwell and Aubrey narrow down the area here?"

"Of course they bloody didn't," Niel grumbled, swinging his axe to limber up. "But if it's a chamber, then it should be beneath a tower, surely?"

"Not necessarily," Ash said. "Mithraic chambers were often in the countryside, in natural caves or old tombs."

"Are there any clues at all?" Niel asked.

Ash smirked. "I have been researching *châteaus* in this area with Aubrey and Caldwell, as I'm sure Black Cronos has, too. A *château*, ruined or not, was always the most likely location when you considered the members of the group. They were rich landowners, for the most part. Unfortunately, this area has lots of crumbling *châteaus*, but this one caught our eye because of its great age and the grounds. It is one of only a few that are this old. I have an idea where to look."

"Lead the way, then," Nahum said, sweeping his arm out.

"I suppose I should call Toto," Gabe grumbled, pulling his phone free as he followed Ash. "I don't want him to get too upset and trigger-happy."

"Did JD and Mason sound okay?" Shadow asked, eyes narrowing.

"Mad as hell. I think JD's ego is bruised, but Mason," Gabe recalled the shake in his voice. "He was very upset about Smythe. And upset means unpredictable, which I don't like."

"It's Mason," she said scathingly as she fell into step beside him. "He's hardly a gun-toting, axe-wielding murderer."

"Nothing wrong with axe-wielding," Niel said, swinging his own through the air with a whoosh once more.

Gabe fell back a pace while he dialled, and Toto answered quickly. He didn't even let Gabe speak. "The address?"

"*Château de Porge.* It's on the coast."

"I know exactly where it is. Do not go into the chamber without us," he said, ringing off abruptly.

"Arrogant prick! We haven't even found it yet," Gabe muttered as he caught up to the others who were now some distance away from the main buildings, standing in the remnants of a stone tower.

"I think it's either beneath us, or in one of the other stone towers," Ash was explaining. "Or over there." He pointed to a stand of trees. "There is a stone circle in the centre. I checked when I flew over. It's almost completely overgrown now, but a stone circle suggests a place of worship."

Nahum nodded, clearly excited. "Beneath there would have held significance. Let's split up. I'll take a spade to the circle."

They had brought digging tools with them, and the car that the others were traveling in had a pick and other tools, too.

"I'm with you," Barak said. "Anyone else?"

"I'll come," Shadow volunteered. "I like your odds."

She winked at Gabe and set off with the others, leaving Gabe to start digging with Ash and Niel.

They both looked at him, amused. "Don't worry, brother," Ash said, patting his shoulder. "She only has eyes for you."

Gabe stared at them. He'd been expecting this all day. "Don't start!"

"Start what?"

"You know what! Don't think I haven't caught your smirks!"

"We're pleased for you, Gabe!" Niel said, already stomping over the heavy-set, cracked stone slabs and listening for any difference in noise. "Quite honestly, I'm glad it's finally happened. Your testosterone was close to exploding."

"Shut up!" Gabe said, wanting to throttle both of them. "It is out of bounds!"

Nahum threw back his head, laughing loudly, and an owl hooted close by. "It is *so* not out of bounds! Now, come and help us, and stop looking so bloody enraged."

Shadow studied the stone circle that was overgrown with weeds and dappled with moonlight. It was chilly beneath the trees and she shivered, sensing something evil lurking in the air.

"I think you're right, Nahum. This is the place."

He whipped around. "What makes you say that?"

"I can feel something dark here. Something unnatural."

She crouched and placed her hands on the earth, expanding her fey senses. She already picked up more wild earth energies than the others, except perhaps Briar, the earth witch, but if she became quiet and focussed, letting her senses open wide, she could pick up so much more. *Yes, she felt a displacement of energy here, and it was old.*

Taking a deep breath and holding that sensation within her, she stood again and walked across the centre of the circle. The stones were tall, misshapen, and crooked, and although the trees closed in around them, the circle itself was undisturbed, except for long grass. To the east the stones looked slightly different, and she realised they made an entrance, two of them slightly taller than the others. At their feet was a long piece of stone that she presumed had fallen from the roughly squared-off tops.

"Look," she said, striding over. "This would have been the ceremonial entrance."

Barak stood next to her. "I feel it, too. It's like the air is weighted."

Shadow turned abruptly, walking out of the circle and into the trees, expanding her awareness beneath her feet. The earth felt less dense, and she sensed air beneath her. When she looked up, Nahum and Barak were watching her.

"Well?" Nahum asked.

"I think there's a passage directly below us."

Barak's voice rose in excitement. "Where's the entrance?"

Shadow didn't answer, pacing deeper into the woods where she lost the feeling for a moment. She changed direction, retraced her steps, and tried again, keeping her alignment with the eastern gate. And then she felt the stirring of something far below her.

Nahum and Barak had followed her, watching her silently, and she lifted her head, triumphant.

"Here."

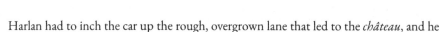

Harlan had to inch the car up the rough, overgrown lane that led to the *château*, and he had barely progressed when he saw lights behind him in the distance.

"Damn it. I think Black Cronos is here already."

"Nothing we can do about that," Jackson said. "Keep going."

"I could blast a fire ball or two at them," Estelle suggested.

Harlan caught her eye in the rear-view mirror. "Save it until we have JD and Mason safely with us."

Harlan now knew why Shadow couldn't stand Estelle. She was a prickly individual, her face prone to setting in stern, uncompromising lines, and although Shadow was wilful, there was a lightness to her that Estelle didn't have.

She continued to speak, her voice clipped. "They will try to kill us, you know that, once we are inside. They will want this for themselves."

"We know," Jackson answered, refusing to be riled. "But we remain on alert at all times." He twisted in his seat to look at her. "At some point we'll all be fighting for our lives, but until then, we wait."

"And your extraction team?" Caldwell asked, his voice tight with tension.

"They're close. Don't worry about that."

Harlan concentrated on the final part of the drive, his mind whirring over the term 'extraction team.' It sounded ridiculous.

An area of rough grass was at the top of the rutted lane, and Harlan pulled well to the side. As soon as they parked, Harlan and Jackson armed themselves with shotguns, while Aubrey and Caldwell gathered their bags. Estelle needed nothing, and sparks of magic were already firing in her hands.

Harlan was relieved to see Gabe and Ash approaching, fully armed, and said, "I saw lights behind us—Black Cronos is close. Have you found anything?"

"Shadow thinks she has discovered the entrance. They're digging now." Gabe gestured behind him. "In the stand of trees over there. I've decided that when we enter, I'm leaving Shadow, Niel, and Nahum outside, on watch."

"I think that's wise," Jackson said, loading his shotgun and pocketing some extra shells. "I presume we're sticking to the plan and waiting for them to act?"

Gabe nodded. "I think they'll wait until we're all inside the chamber. He'll want to know we're in the right place before they jump us."

"We should pre-empt them!" Estelle said scathingly. "All this playing at being gentlemen is ridiculous. We all know how it will end." She returned to her earlier argument. "As soon as JD and Mason are safe, we kill them instead. Well," she shrugged, "maybe not *kill*. Incapacitate, certainly."

"I'm glad you said that," Jackson said sharply. "If we kill them while defending ourselves, that's one thing, but we are *not* killing them in cold blood. That's not what we do—nor are we sanctioned to do! I'm not 007, and the paranormal division does not condone that type of behaviour. And," he added forcefully, "we want Toto alive! This—" he waved the shotgun around, "is a last resort."

"I hate to say this," Harlan said, "but I'll think you'll be using that whether you want to or not."

The rumble of engines disturbed their conversation as two large black vans pulled up beside them, and Harlan realised that for all their planning, Black Cronos could exit right now and kill them all, agreement or not, and he took some deep breaths to steady himself. He glanced nervously at the ruins around them, hoping there were no other members of Black Cronos creeping up the hillside.

The passenger door to the first black van opened, and a man with carefully combed, white-blond hair exited the car. For a moment, he didn't speak as his deep-set eyes swept over them, the look of the obsessive about him. And then he smiled, a shark's smirk that didn't reach his eyes, and that if anything made him look even more deadly.

"So, here we all are at last." His voice was smooth, and he frowned as he took in Gabe and Ash. Instead, he addressed Caldwell. "I see you have brought your formidable bodyguards with you."

Caldwell stepped forward, a challenge in his eyes. "Of course. We have as much claim to this as you."

"I suppose you think that, but our forefathers made the astrolabe after your half abandoned the enterprise."

"But we were there at the time of the great experiment. There is no reason we cannot work together."

Another man exited from the driver's side, and Caldwell took a sharp intake of breath. "Stefan. I wondered if you'd come."

"As I wondered if you would." Stefan was of average height and build with unruly brown hair, round glasses perched on his nose. He wore corduroy trousers and a tweed jacket, the very epitome of a professor, and Harlan found it hard to believe he was involved in such an enterprise. But he looked at them coldly, his expression aloof. "You rejected my ideas once."

"We have different ideas as to how this knowledge should be used," Caldwell said, squaring his shoulders.

Harlan was impressed. He didn't think Caldwell had it in him.

Caldwell studied the man with the pale hair. "I presume you are Toto Dax?"

"The very same."

"You seem to be leading this."

"Perhaps." He gave another cold smile. "Have you found the chamber?"

"First things first," Gabe said, interrupting them. "Where are JD and Mason?"

Dax gestured brusquely to Hope-Robbins, and he slid the side door of the van open, revealing JD and Mason inside, their mouths gagged and their hands and feet tied. Two men sat on either side of them, and with a flutter of fear, Harlan saw The Silencer of Souls, too.

"Let them go," Gabe said, "and then I'll lead the way."

Toto gave a dry laugh. "We really don't need you to lead the way. We could kill you all right now. I have brought my own team."

His words triggered approximately a dozen men and women to exit from the second van, and The Silencer of Souls joined them.

"You've tried that before," Gabe pointed out, unperturbed. "It won't go any better for you now."

Toto's lips twitched with amusement. "Mason will remain here, with his guards. Should I not return safely, we will kill him. JD, however—" he looked at him with interest, "may have something to contribute, so he can come, as long as he behaves."

The men cut the ties binding JD, and with a worried glance at Mason, he stumbled out of the van, grasping to loosen his gag as Harlan stepped forward to help him keep his balance. Both were usually dapper, especially Mason. He took pride in his well-made suits. Now he looked grubby and unkempt, but he met Harlan's eyes with a steely determination before the door slid shut, hiding him from view once more.

JD virtually shook Harlan off as he rounded on Toto. "You are an animal! You do not deserve to find the Dark Star chamber."

Toto leaned in close, his voice a low snarl. "Oh, yes I do, and when we find what's in there, you'll *all* regret coming along."

<hr />

Nahum looked at the ornately carved stone slab that was set into the earth, wondering what they would find beneath it. It had taken some digging, but eventually they found the entrance about half a metre below the surface. Once they had brushed the soil away, they could see it was etched with strange symbols, and they had left it closed for the alchemists to see.

Both groups clustered around it, and he eyed Black Cronos warily. *So many guards didn't bode well.* The Silencer of Souls looked as sleek and deadly as a black panther. She was self-contained, looking at no one except Toto and Gabe, whom she regarded with a slow smile. If she affected Gabe in any way after their last encounter, he didn't show it, and Gabe met her stare with a wry smile of his own. Only Niel and Shadow were missing from the crowd. They had withdrawn into the trees, circling the perimeter, and watching from a distance.

All the alchemists dropped to their knees to examine the symbols, a fervent light behind their eyes, and for a few moments at least, it seemed that their animosity had been forgotten.

"Fascinating," JD muttered. "The entrance faces east as is befitting for a Sun God. See the ancient signs for Mithras etched in the surface?"

"And symbols of the stars and the planets," Aubrey said, nodding along enthusiastically.

Toto smiled like a shark again. "And the symbol for a journey."

Nahum took the opportunity to speak quietly to Gabe. "Where's Mason?"

"In one of the vans by the *château* ruins. As soon as you have the chance, free him."

He nodded, and Gabe turned his attention to the alchemists. "Are there symbols that warn of what we may face? Clues to a path?"

JD stood and brushed earth from his trousers. "No. This is an ornate entrance only."

"But it does carry a warning," Caldwell said, rising too, and looking unconcerned at his announcement. "It says only those who seek the truth shall be victorious." He straightened his shoulders. "And seeing as I do, I do not fear that statement."

Toto regarded him through slitted lids. "We shall see, won't we?" His subtle undertones conveyed that he knew much more than anyone else did, unless he was just very good at trying to undermine them. He gave a mock bow to Caldwell. "Perhaps you should lead the way."

Caldwell looked at him suspiciously, perhaps wondering as Nahum was, if they were sacrificial lambs, but he merely nodded and shouldered his bag, and then addressed Gabe and Nahum. "Let's remove the slab, then. It can tell us nothing more."

The slab was one huge square of stone, easily two metres across, and Nahum picked up the crowbar they had brought with them—they had come prepared for anything—and angled it beneath the slab. Gabe positioned himself, ready to lift the raised edge, as did two brawny members of Black Cronos.

It took a few moments to position the crowbar correctly; the stone was thick, and Nahum needed to slide the bar down the side until he felt it catch underneath. Then he levered it up, allowing Gabe and the other two men to flip it over, where it crashed to the ground with a judder. Stale air erupted out around them.

Gabe shouldered past Caldwell, saying, "Let us go first. It's what you're paying us for." Caldwell looked as if he might protest, but then stepped back as Gabe added, "Nahum, make sure this entrance remains open."

Nahum nodded, and Toto grimaced before speaking to one of his own men. "You stay with him."

Nahum eyed the man who positioned himself on the other side of the entrance. He was easily as tall as Nahum, his dark hair shaved close to his scalp, and he planted his feet firmly, crossing his arms over his chest as he stared back.

This could prove interesting.

Twenty-Five

T he steps below Gabe's feet were littered with soil and small stones that crunched as he went, the only sound breaking the silence. His torch flashed across the stone walls and he inhaled deeply, and then promptly wished he hadn't. The air smelled foul, was tainted somehow by something cloying beyond the scents of earth and cold stone.

The steps were wide enough that Ash could walk next to him, and Gabe murmured, "What in Herne's balls is that smell?"

"Smells like death. Not quite the shining glory of the Temple of the Trinity, is it?"

"Not really, but I prefer this one, despite the smell, if I'm honest." Gabe was more than happy to have no angel involvement here, fallen or otherwise.

They proceeded slowly, making sure the steps were firm and there were no hidden traps. He'd experienced those before—stairs falling away into a pit of spikes, or into deep holes with water far below. But everything felt stable, as it should, really, if it was a regular place of...what? Worship? Or just experiments with time, matter, and whatever else alchemists did.

He glanced behind him and saw that Caldwell and Toto were merely steps behind them, the others following in a procession—a weird, unholy alliance. *For now.*

The steps travelled deep into the earth, and they finally came to a halt on a stone landing with two enormous wooden doors in front of them. Again, symbols were carved into them—signs for air, water, fire, earth, sigils of protection, the large image of a bull, a stylised sun, and several strange patterns that he couldn't quite recognise—but more ominous were the thick iron bars that crossed the wood, and the heavy beam that slotted into brackets, sealing the door shut. However, he stepped aside, allowing Caldwell and Toto to approach it together.

"The Bull of Mithras. It is the Mithraic Temple!" Caldwell said, almost breathless. He glanced at Ash. "We were right."

"And the constellation of Lyra—the lyre of Orpheus," Toto said, his hands running across the patterns that Gabe hadn't recognised. He nodded, as if he expected as much. "To reference a journey to the Underworld, perhaps. And that one," he pointed to another cluster of carvings, "Virgo. Linked to Persephone."

Gabe could have kicked himself. Star constellations, of course, and they both referenced the Underworld.

JD hustled next to them. "References to Mithras and Orpheus? Odd."

"Not really," Toto said dismissively. "Many organisations combined different beliefs. Our order sought knowledge. Were willing to travel where others would not. I think it's time we enter."

Gabe hefted the thick beam out of the brackets and placed it to the side, and then he and Ash pulled the great doors open, allowing another wave of stale air to billow around them. A short passageway was visible ahead, the walls lined with old-fashioned torches wedged into brackets. They progressed down it quickly, and the torches flared to life as someone lit them. They arrived at another set of double doors at the end, again sealed with a thick beam.

Gabe stared at the alchemists' eager faces. "Are you sure you want to go in? These are very big doors, and must be sealed for a reason."

"Of course we're sure," Toto said impatiently. "You hardly think I'm going to change my mind now?"

It was the response he'd expected, and to be honest, despite the dangers, he was curious to see what lay beyond. He laid the beam to one side again and opened the doors to reveal a large chamber before them. Stone benches ran along either side, and in the centre was a statue of a man slaying a bull.

"The Mithraic chamber," Caldwell said, pushing past Gabe in his haste to get inside. There were more torches in here, and they flared to life as Estelle threw balls of fire at them, filling the chamber with a rich, golden glow.

But Gabe was looking beyond the statue to the wall at the end. "This can't just be it."

Ash shuffled through the gathering of men to Gabe's side, ignoring the excited chatter of the alchemists. "I agree. The Order of the Morning Star must have used this as their entrance."

Gabe and Ash clambered onto the stone benches to squeeze past the others, and Estelle joined them, her gaze sweeping along the end wall constructed of hefty blocks of stone. She pointed to an area on the right. "That section isn't as well finished. Look at the crumbling mortar."

"It's a later addition, put up hurriedly, I suspect," Ash said, running his fingers along it.

They started tapping, and found it had a hollow sound to it. By now, the chamber had quieted again, and Caldwell and Toto were right behind them.

"Break it down," Toto said, his eyes gleaming.

"Allow me," Estelle said, raising her hands and releasing a blast of power at the wall.

A rumble resounded around the chamber as a section of rocks flew backwards. A wave of dust rose into the air, and instinctively they all stepped back, shielding their faces. But when the dust settled, it was clear there was a large space beyond.

The Silencer of Souls grabbed a torch from the wall and thrust it at Toto, her gaze raking over Gabe as she did so, and for a moment, he could feel her cold lips on his again; he vowed if he had the chance later, he would kill her. Toto, however, took no notice of the look that passed between them, almost absently taking the torch as he stepped over the debris, and interestingly, Caldwell let him go first.

Shadow heard the blast and felt a rumble beneath her. Alarmed, she jumped down from the tree branch where she'd been surveying the almost pitch-black land beyond the edge of the grove, tangled with shrub and brambles. She readied her bow, wondering what the noise meant.

Niel materialized out of the shadows. "It's too soon," he reassured her. "They'll have barely got in."

"That's what worries me. What if the entrance is booby trapped?"

"I guess it's a possibility."

She glared at him. "You're supposed to be reassuring me!"

He grinned. "Oops. Worried about lover boy?"

"What did you say?" she asked, aiming an arrow at Niel's chest in a split second.

Niel stepped back, hands raised. "Just teasing. You can take a joke, right?"

"And just what is so funny about me and Gabe?" *Bollocks. She'd vowed not to rise to their taunts or confess anything, and what had she just done?* She lowered her bow with a sigh. "Don't you dare start."

"I'm just glad you two have finally...well, whatever. All that sexual tension was starting to affect me."

"Really? I'm so sorry," she said, her voice dripping with sarcasm. "It wasn't exactly easy for me!"

"But you could have acted sooner."

She floundered for words. "Well, I was worried about the business—and stuff."

"It's fine. It gave us time to place some bets," he said, grinning broadly.

She raised her bow again before he could blink. "You did *what*?"

"It was just some fun. You should be pleased I'm telling you! Now you know."

"I should shoot your balls!"

"Will it make you feel better if I tell you we've got bets on Barak and Estelle now?"

She lowered her bow and mimed gagging. "You have? Does that mean it might actually happen?"

"That's what the bet is about. Care to wager a yes or no or a tentative date?"

Suddenly, Shadow felt much better. "Okay. What are the odds?"

Before he could answer, Shadow saw the trees rustle behind him, and something flew out of the darkness.

"Get down!" she hissed at him as she simultaneously dived out of the way, rolled, and then fired a few arrows from her prone position, satisfied to hear a thump as their attacker fell out of bushes and to the ground, dead.

Shadow remained in a crouch, looking around warily as Niel crouched too, both utterly silent. Another rustle of branches sounded behind them, and a flurry of arrows embedded in the trunk of the tree only feet away. She immediately turned and shot half a dozen arrows back in quick succession.

"That's *your* fault," she hissed at him. "You distracted me!"

"I did not!" he hissed back. "You distracted me. You and your bloody sex life!"

"Shut up!"

An arrow hit a different trunk, this time from a different direction, and silently Shadow indicated she was going to go around. She cast her fey magic outward, feeling the trees' presence become stronger as she did so, responding to her earthy magic. Immediately her senses magnified, and she felt half a dozen men moving through the trees, converging on them. Once more, she cursed her stupidity for arguing with Niel about her sex life, shouldered her bow, and set about rectifying it, coming up on the closest man like a ghost and stabbing him through the throat before he even knew she was there.

She heard a strangled cry from the other direction, and knew Niel had found another. In a running crouch, she zigzagged through the undergrowth, picking off one, then another, until she found herself facing the remains of a stone wall and heard voices beyond it. She eased herself along it, finally able to see into the ruins of a room where a couple of Black Cronos members were talking, one man and one woman. She stepped out, shooting the man facing her first, but the woman was already diving to the ground as she threw a weird weapon at Shadow.

It was silver, shimmering in the light like it was molten metal, and it caught her bow, shattering it into tiny pieces. Shadow barely had time to register her shock that something had destroyed her fey-made weapon before the woman was on her, knife in hand. Shadow smacked her arm away and kicked her in the stomach, causing her to stumble backwards, and withdrawing both swords, whirled them around as she advanced.

Her opponent was slim and athletic, and her eyes had taken on a silvery sheen. She clenched her fist and seemed to draw a blade out of the air as she moved swiftly to block Shadow, and Shadow realised this would be no easy fight.

⸺◆◇◆⸺

For a few moments after the rumble of the blast, Nahum and the other man guarding the entrance waited, both keeping an eye on the stairs and each other. And then out of the corner of his eye, Nahum saw a flutter of movement.

Rather than dive for cover, he launched himself at the man opposite him, slamming up against a wall of muscle. But he wasn't aiming to knock him down; he was going to use him as a shield. He dodged around him, grabbing him around the throat and pulling him backwards.

He fought back hard, but it was already too late. Nahum felt him go limp as whatever had been thrown at him hit his opponent instead. Nahum dropped him and, accessing his throwing daggers, threw them at the woman who was sprinting towards him. His daggers were on target, but something odd was happening to the woman's skin. It shimmered, and suddenly it seemed as if her skin had become a shield. His daggers virtually bounced off her.

She was within feet of him when she launched herself, hitting him like a bullet, and with a shock, Nahum realised her arms felt like metal, and her face had a metallic sheen to it. Her hands fixed around Nahum's throat and closed tightly as she leaned into him, her breath hot on his face. He clamped his hands over hers to prise her off, but she was incredibly strong.

Screw this.

Nahum's wings unfurled and he lifted them off the ground, the woman's feet flailing and her grip loosening for a second until she wrapped her legs around his waist and tightened her grip once more. *That had never happened before.* He spun around, fighting to see as his vision blackened, and flew at one of the ruined towers. He slammed her back into a stone wall, powering through it, and then into the next. An explosion of rubble ballooned around them, and in free-fall now they plunged over the cliff and spun towards the surf that crashed into the rocks below.

———◆◇◆———

Niel was knocked off his feet by a blow between his shoulder blades, and he sprawled on his stomach as someone landed on his back, clasped his hair, and pulled back his head. In his peripheral vision, he saw the flash of a blade.

What the actual fuck...

Niel reared up and rolled over, pinning whoever it was beneath his considerable weight. An obviously male hand flopped on to the ground, clenching a nasty looking blade. He reached over, grabbed the thick wrist, and twisted hard before being thrown off.

The next several seconds were a blur of hard earth, muscle, blade, and the snarling face of some feral Black Cronos member who stank of dog. And then without warning, the man collapsed on Niel's chest, and blood gurgled from his mouth and onto Niel's face. Scrabbling to get clear of him, Niel threw him off and saw Shadow staring down at him.

"You okay?" she asked, holding her hand out.

"No!" he said, grasping it and hauling himself to his feet. "I am covered in this stinking cur's blood!" He wiped his face, smearing it everywhere.

"You look even worse now," she said, leading him to the entrance of the chamber. "Like some deranged zombie we like killing in those video games."

"You don't look much better yourself," he noted, seeing a slight limp to her walk and blood-soaked clothing. "Are you injured?"

"No. It's all from the woman I finally killed."

Then Niel realised her bow was missing, only her quiver of arrows strung across her back remained in place. "Where's your bow?"

"That bloody woman destroyed it!"

"Your *fey* bow?" He knew how strong her weapons were. She never let them forget it.

She grimaced. "Yes! I don't like these people or the way they fight. They pull weapons from nowhere, and grow weird armour." She paused as she saw the body on the floor. "Where's Nahum?"

Niel peered down the stairs. "Well, he's not down there." He scanned the trees again, wary of further attack, and asked, "How many did you kill?"

"Half a dozen. You?"

He looked at her resentfully. "Three."

She preened. "Never mind. I'm sure there's more. Do you think we should head to the chamber?"

"Let's wait, and if Nahum doesn't appear, maybe we'll go looking for him." He searched the sky. The moon was lower now, their surroundings darker, and he hoped he wouldn't end up stumbling across his brother's body. "Did you notice Mason wasn't with them?"

Shadow frowned. "No, I was too far back, watching the other direction. Do you think he's here somewhere?"

Niel didn't answer, instead staring through the grove towards the ruins. "They'll have driven here and have probably parked at the top of that lane we flew over. I bet Mason is insurance. I wonder if Nahum has gone looking for him." He lifted his axe, running his finger along the sharp blade. "You stay here, make sure no one else goes in, and I'll go check."

Twenty-Six

Harlan was in the middle of the group that stepped over the rubble of fallen stones and ventured into the next chamber. For a second, he stood just inside, letting his eyes adjust to the light, and heard murmurs as torches flashed around the space.

It was a large cavern that was a mix of natural cave and man-made structures. His flashlight illuminated crumbling columns rising into the air, and in the middle was a dark block of something.

Estelle conjured her witch lights, throwing them high above the group, obviously not as worried about revealing her true nature to strangers as the White Haven witches were. Her lights revealed more old-fashioned torches in brackets on the columns, and again she illuminated them with a quick burst of fire, and the cavern flared into life.

Harlan's first impression was that there had been a fight in here, or some sort of earthquake. Long stone tables were placed around the chamber, the surfaces crowded with bottles and jars, braziers, and other old-fashioned scientific equipment. But some of them had been smashed, tables split into pieces, surrounded by broken glass, or upturned. His blood ran cold as he saw metal gates set into the right-hand wall of the chamber at regular intervals, dark rooms beyond. They looked like either cells or storage rooms. He hoped for the latter. Overhead, what looked to be long strings of *something* were suspended over the entire place in a spider web design. He stumbled backwards as the resemblance struck him.

"Holy crap," he murmured to Jackson, who was next to him. "This is like that room in *Frankenstein*! The laboratory where he made the monster! But it looks like there's been a struggle here...a big one."

Jackson nodded absently as his gaze travelled the room. "I agree." He squinted up at the overhead lines that fed to a structure on the far side. "They're odd, considering the age of this place. I think they're for conducting energy." He focussed on Toto, who was directing his men to search the cave. His team fanned out, some heading to the tables, others searching around the far reaches. Toto then strode to the centre of the chamber, the other alchemists racing after him.

Harlan squinted at the blocky structure that squatted in the middle. "Is that a tomb?"

"Please don't say that."

Harlan glanced nervously around, noting that two Black Cronos guards were positioned on either side of the entrance, but with relief saw that Barak was close by. He caught his eye, and Barak nodded reassuringly. Ash was with the main group, but Gabe was conducting his own search of the room, while Estelle stood slightly apart from all of them, her sharp eyes appraising everything.

Jackson hurried to join the alchemists, but Harlan decided to see what was beyond the metal gates. He took his time, studying the columns as he went. Like most other things here, they were covered in painted symbols. Some of them were geometric in design; he'd seen similar ones before in books on alchemy.

He wandered amongst the stone tables, noting the dusty, grimy bottles that were lined up in rows, remnants of dried materials visible in some. At the side of one table, where it butted up against the wall, he saw wires travelling from a huge pottery jar on the floor up to the roof. The top was plugged with a cork, and Harlan caught the faint waft of something sharp. *Vinegar.* Examining the wires closer, he saw they were attached with clips to a rod that was sticking out of the pot, and it looked to be iron. A memory flooded back of an article he'd read on ancient batteries. It was believed that ancient civilisations had found a way to generate power, a type of crude electricity. *Was that what this was? A power source?*

He scanned the room, seeing the same huge pottery jars lined up at regular intervals all around the cavern and at the base of some of the columns, and looking up, he realised the columns weren't just for show—they supported the wires. *But what did they do?* It didn't seem as if they provided light; there were no rudimentary bulbs, for a start, and the torches already supplied that. And then as his eyes followed the web of wires, he realised not only did they lead to the structure at the far side, they all led to the alleged tomb in the centre.

Harlan's mouth suddenly went very dry. This was starting to seem more and more like some mad scientist's laboratory. Barak must have been watching his progress, because in seconds he was at his side, the big man looming over him.

"Are you all right?" he asked, his voice a rich rumble.

"No! Look at these wires overhead, and the pottery jars—and where they go. Right to the middle! I think the jars are a power source...ancient batteries!"

Barak was silent for a moment as he took it all in. "We had no such thing in my time. Explain how they work."

"I have the most basic knowledge only," Harlan said trying to retrieve what he'd read. "But eighty or so years ago, some guy discovered these pottery jars outside Baghdad—"

"Persia?" Barak asked, frowning.

"Well, Iran now, but yes. Anyway, they had copper and iron tubes in them, and they looked like a smaller version of this! They dated them to be over two thousand years old, and they discovered that they had been filled with vinegar or wine, which would start a reaction. Electricity! These are just much bigger versions...and there are lots of them."

"Interesting. Ash would know more, I'd put a bet on it. Have the others noticed yet?"

"I think they're too absorbed by the tomb—if that's what it is."

"It looks to be, but it's sealed for now, and there's a pretty big argument brewing down there as to how to open it." Barak glanced behind Harlan. "Have you looked beyond those grills yet? Because there are more wires leading through them."

"Are there?" Harlan whirled around and hurried towards them, Barak next to him. He peered into the first one and played his flashlight around the space.

"There's a bench along the far wall covered in rags, and," Barak paused, his eyes narrowing. "Bones. I can see them protruding through the rotted cloth. They're prison cells."

"Damn it. I'd hoped they were storage rooms." Harlan recalled Jackson telling him about human experimentation in the Second World War, and then he glanced at the members of Black Cronos placed strategically around the chamber, The Silencer of Souls next to Toto. "That's what these guys are, Barak. They're the results of experiments, but they clearly got stuff right."

Barak was already hurrying on to the next cell, and in each one they saw evidence of human habitation, with a hard bench along the back wall. "I wonder what they poisoned me with?" he murmured. "It triggered something in my blood."

A shout from the far side of the chamber caught their attention and they spun around, Barak already drawing his sword, Harlan cocking his gun. It was Stefan Hope-Robbins, and he was next to the structure the wires fed into. He called, "I've found a switch to the batteries. It may open the tomb."

Barak lowered his mouth to Harlan's ear. "I'm going to make sure our exit is clear. Stay sharp, Harlan."

Harlan nodded and hurried to the group. He found Ash at the back watching everyone, particularly The Silencer of Souls, who studied Gabe's actions with unnerving patience. For a moment Harlan just waited with him and watched the tomb. It was a step pyramid of four levels, surprisingly large up close, and seemed to be carved from a single block of white stone. Although Harlan thought it was unlikely to be made from one piece, he could make out no seams between blocks. Ornate symbols were carved onto the surface, and they seemed to crawl and writhe in the flickering firelight.

Estelle had positioned herself on the far side, alone, her face implacable as she watched the guards. Caldwell was arguing with Aubrey, Toto was arguing with JD, and Gabe had clambered onto the tomb and was examining the topmost level.

JD was gesticulating at an ornate symbol on the lowest tier. "I'm telling you," he said, shouting and red-faced, "that the jewel in the astrolabe must sit in the middle. It's part of the trigger, and must have been incorporated into the astrolabe's design."

"I admit that that has a certain logic, but it will destroy the astrolabe," Toto said, surprising Harlan that he should want to keep it intact.

"So? We're here now! We don't need the astrolabe any longer."

"Easy for you to say," Toto shot back. "It's not a part of *your* heritage!"

"You curdle-faced milksop!" JD spat. "Like a babbling clapper-claw! It is a wonder you have got as far as you have with your alchemical enhancements!"

Oh no. When JD started spouting Shakespearean insults, Harlan knew things were getting ugly. What was really worrying was why JD was helping at all. *Jackson had suggested JD was trying to stop this, but was he really?*

Toto's eyes hardened at JD's insult. "My team are the most enhanced humans you could ever wish to find."

"And yet Gabe and his team have decimated them!" JD yelled.

"Enough!" Stefan roared, and everyone fell silent and turned to him. At their reaction, Harlan started to wonder just who was in charge of Black Cronos. "Put the jewel in position now."

"Wait!" Jackson shouted, holding his hand up in a stop sign and leaping in front of the symbol on the tomb. "Is this really wise? We have no idea of what's in there, but we've all heard the rumours of a monster." He studied the alchemists' faces. "This looks like a tomb, and we all know it! All you need is the research. You don't actually have to open this." He appealed to each of them. "You're risking everyone's lives for this."

Toto sneered. "There is no research in here. My team has searched everywhere." His arm swept up to encompass the room. "It is a damp, cold cave. The tomb must preserve their research, too."

"But what if it's not here? Perhaps they stored the research elsewhere. These symbols might be some sort of code," Jackson pointed out. "Don't you think you should study them carefully first?"

He shot a desperate look at Harlan, and he felt compelled to support him. "I agree," Harlan said, moving to Jackson's side. "Potentially, you'll lose the chance if you open the tomb."

"I'm not an idiot," JD said scathingly. "I have already made a cursory examination of these symbols while you were skulking about, and they contain no hidden messages. Neither are they particularly magical. They are standard alchemical symbols—that's all."

Harlan gritted his teeth. "JD, I wasn't skulking about. I was investigating what was behind those metal grills. They are cage doors! Dead men are locked inside them! And in case you haven't noticed, some of this equipment has been destroyed—possibly in a fight. Please," he appealed, "can we think rationally about this?"

The alchemists, despite their differences, now shuffled together as if presenting a united front, and Caldwell stepped forward, throwing his shoulders back. "You must trust us on this. The symbols tell us nothing about the research, but that symbol there—" he thrust Jackson aside, "is the symbol for a new awakening, and it's clear the jewel must sit there. There's even a seam running around it! JD is right. It's a trigger, one we must activate." He turned to Gabe. "Thank you for your protection over the last few days, but we're here now. Your job is done."

Gabe gave a dry laugh. "I'm pretty sure it's not. What if the monster is in there?"

"It's a tomb. Therefore, whatever is in there, is dead."

"I'm glad you're so confident. Okay, go ahead. We'll pull back while you do your thing." He glanced at Harlan, Jackson, and finally Estelle, who was still poised for action on the far side of the tomb. "Let's give them some space."

Jackson looked as if he might protest once more, but in the end followed Harlan and Estelle to where Gabe and Ash had retreated to a safe distance.

"Right," Stefan said impatiently. "Can we get on with it?"

Aubrey had clearly decided to follow JD's earlier suggestion, as he had been fiddling with the astrolabe for several minutes. Now he finally prised the jewel out with a small blade and positioned it carefully in the centre of the ornate design. It clicked into place, and a whirring noise sounded deep within the tomb. Simultaneously, Stefan struggled to lift a long wooden lever next to him. It seemed stiff from lack of use, but he persisted stubbornly, finally flipping it up, and immediately there was another thump and thunk, and a strange fizzing noise filled the chamber.

Gabe drew everyone back even further. "This is going to be interesting. We need to be ready to go, to possibly fight our way out." He looked bleakly at the tomb. "I think there's a lot more in there than research papers. And potentially, whatever they find, Toto will want only for himself."

Estelle shook her head in disbelief, magic still balling in her hands. "I agree. And Caldwell is a fool if he thinks he's just going to walk out of here." She studied their surroundings. "If it looks as if they are going to kill us, or trap us, I'll tackle the guards next to Stefan."

"I'll take The Silencer of Souls and the guards on the other side of the tomb," Gabe said.

"Barak is planning to keep our exit clear and deal with the guards there," Harlan told them.

"Good. Then I'll take the remainder," Ash said. He leaned closer to Harlan and Jackson. "You two may need to stop Toto and Stefan if they try to prevent our escape. I don't think we need worry about the others—except maybe to rescue them."

"And what if something comes out of that tomb?" Harlan asked.

Gabe grimaced. "We can't let it escape, and that may take a team effort."

A flash of white light above them ended their conversation as electricity started to arc from what Harlan could only presume was some kind of ancient junction box, and then a white spark danced along the web of wires as the batteries fired up. Harlan wasn't entirely sure how it was working, but there was no doubt that it was. And something else was happening to the tomb. It radiated a pale light, weak at first, but as the wires continued to charge and electricity arced across their heads it grew brighter, until with a jarring, scraping noise, the top tier of the tomb split in half and slid open.

Harlan stepped back gripping his shotgun, as did the alchemists, and a breathless silence fell as everyone watched, transfixed. And then a roar sounded from within the tomb, something so primal and wounded that Harlan broke out in a sweat as he cocked his gun.

Twenty-Seven

N iel exited the grove and looked across the ruins to the vehicles parked in the distance. The grounds of the *château* were deserted and ominously silent, and there was no sign of Nahum, but he could see a couple of guards next to the vans.

Niel crossed the ruins cautiously, wondering how best to deal with the issue of Mason, and decided an upfront approach would be best. As he left the shadows, however, he sniffed dust and rubble, and frowned at the closest tower. *Was it his imagination, or was there more damage now than had been earlier?* He paused and listened, but heard nothing except the crash of surf below, so he set off again. With his axe secured to his belt, he held his hands up as he approached the van.

"Toto has sent me to check on Mason." He grinned. "An act of faith between us all."

Both guards looked at him suspiciously. They were tall; one heavily muscled, the other lean and mean-looking. Both had dead eyes.

The leaner one spoke. "I doubt that. Turn around and walk away. We only take orders from Toto directly."

"Oh, come on," Niel argued, half-joking. "They're all busy in the tomb. He hasn't got time to babysit you guys. Let me check on Mason."

The other man was staring beyond Niel, eyes narrowed. "Why are you alone?"

Niel shrugged. "Why wouldn't I be?"

"Our men are back there. They should have seen you approach." He rubbed his palms together and out of nowhere produced a long, slim blade like a rapier and pointed it at Niel. "Where are they?"

Niel ignored the question, instead saying, "That's a neat trick. How do you do that?"

He sneered. "We do it because we're superior to you in every way." He stared at Niel's face and chest and snarled. "Is that blood?"

Crap. He'd already forgotten about that and decided to ignore it. He feigned innocence, his arms outstretched. "I haven't seen anyone! I've just left my colleagues guarding the entrance with yours."

The man clearly didn't believe him, and he didn't waste words, because in a split second he lunged at him and Niel counterattacked, swinging his axe up to block him again and again as the man proved more agile than he looked. For the next few minutes, Niel was totally absorbed in fighting the guard. The other one just watched, his weapon at the ready, and Niel knew if he survived this, he'd be fighting him next.

Then something caught all their attention as a scream pierced the air, followed by a roar that sounded like Nahum. Niel saw a whirl of wings and feathers soaring above the cliff before it crashed through the closest tower, sending rubble flying as it headed towards them. Niel and his opponent dived to the ground, and as Niel cautiously lifted his head, he saw the other guard lying unconscious, blood pouring from his head, a huge stone block next to him.

Niel had barely time to see Nahum struggling with a woman who seemed stuck to him like a limpet, when he had to evade the jab of the rapier, and he leapt to his feet, swinging his axe with lightning-fast flexes. A blur of wings swept past him as Nahum plummeted to the ground, squashing the shrieking woman under him. He drove her onto the outstretched rapier of her fellow assassin, crushing him at the same time.

Niel jumped out of the way, and stood with his axe poised as Nahum extricated himself from the woman's grip, cursing as he did so.

"Herne's hairy bloody bollocks!" he exclaimed angrily. "She was stuck to me like bloody super glue. Legs like pincers around my hips, and her fingers were instruments of bloody torture." He gesticulated angrily at his neck and the ugly red marks circling it. "Look at it. It's a miracle I can even speak!"

"And yet you can, brother!" Niel said, amused. "The important question is, are your balls okay?"

Nahum looked down at his groin. "I bloody hope so. This may not have been my most sexually active few months, but it won't last forever."

Niel sniggered, and then quickly sobered as he looked at the dead woman, the rapier piercing her side. "You nearly impaled yourself."

"It would have been worth it to get rid of her. Have I killed the guy under her, too?"

Niel crouched and checked. "Yep. Smashed his head off a rock beneath him. That one though," he murmured, standing and pointing to the other man who had fallen first, "is still alive—just barely."

A rapping noise came from inside the van and a curt voice called, "Hello? Let me out!"

Niel pulled the door open, spotting a crumpled figure sitting inside, still partially bound, although someone had removed his gag. "You must be Mason."

The slim, grey-haired man looked up at him, alarm flashing across his face. "Yes, I am. You're not one of them."

"Nope. I'm one of the good guys," Niel said, quickly loosening the man's bonds. "Othniel at your service. And this," he gestured to Nahum, who stood next to him, "is Nahum, one of my brothers."

"Gabe's men?"

"The very same."

Mason nodded and staggered out, rubbing his limbs. "Are they dead?"

"Two are, but this one isn't," Niel said, nudging the fallen man with his foot. "He was hit by a rock."

"Well, he bloody should be," Mason said viciously, taking Niel aback. He wasn't a big man, but he exuded a lot of energy. *A man used to getting his way*, Niel realised, as he said, "Give me a knife."

"What?" Nahum asked, confused.

"A knife. I'll bloody well finish him off myself!"

Niel could barely believe his ears, and from the expression on Nahum's face, neither could he. "Are you kidding?"

"No! Knife, now!"

Nahum pulled one of his daggers free and handed it over, hilt first. Mason marched over to the man and with one swift movement, stabbed him in the throat. Arterial spray splattered out, covering Mason, but he didn't care. He wiped the blade on the guard's clothes, stood with a huge sigh, and turned to them with a grim smile.

"That's better. May I borrow this until we're out of here?"

"Sure," Nahum said, almost stuttering over the word. "Did he do something to upset you?"

"Animals. Abhorrent aberrations of nature." He shuddered. "The less that survive this, the better. Where is everyone?"

"The chamber," Niel told him. "But you should wait here. I'm going to check on them now."

"Not a chance. I'm coming, too. Lead the way!"

Niel had half a mind to tell him to stuff his attitude, but instead he rolled his eyes, glanced at Nahum with an exasperated expression, and walked away. They were only halfway across the ruins when a roar shook the ground, and they ran to the entrance.

<hr />

Shadow was waiting impatiently at the top of the steps. She was pretty sure there were no other Black Cronos members loitering in the bushes, and wondered how much longer she should wait for Niel and Nahum.

Suddenly, an epic, guttural roar rolled up the stairs, and without waiting to wonder what it could be, she raced down, swords drawn. She barely took in the huge carved doors and long chamber with the statue in the centre, focussing only on the shouts and another roar coming from beyond the broken wall at the end.

She vaulted over the stones and paused inside the threshold to let her eyes adjust to the flickering firelight and the onslaught of stimuli. A loud buzzing noise filled the chamber, echoing off the stone walls, and flashes of arcing white light fizzed at points across the roof, illuminating like a horror show the scenes underneath.

A massive, monstrous figure strode around the far side of the chamber, bellowing so loudly it made her wince. For a moment, she couldn't quite make out what it was. All she knew was that people were running everywhere. Some seemed to be attacking the figure, while others were running away—or being flung away like dolls. Shotgun blasts resounded, one after another, and some men seemed to be scrabbling around a tomb in the centre. A ball of fire soared through the air, smacking the hulking figure in the chest, but it didn't seem to impede it at all. Instead, it roared again and turned to charge. And that's when Shadow made out its features.

It was an enormous giant of a man with the legs and head of a bull. It reminded her of the satyrs from her world, except they were good-natured, cheerful creatures; this beast was enraged. And it was attacking everyone.

Shadow ran in to join her team who were spread in a loose circle around the rampaging creature, all of them darting to attack it, trying to distract it in one direction while striking from the other. But it wasn't working. Despite its huge size, it was agile, and insanely strong.

A few Black Cronos soldiers were already dead, but The Silencer of Souls was still alive, sticking close to a man with white-blond hair in the centre. Next to him were JD and Caldwell, all of them scrambling into and around the tomb, Aubrey's head just visible before he ducked into it again. And then Shadow realised something else. The surviving members of Black Cronos weren't engaging the creature—they were hanging back, watching her own team risk life and limb.

She ran to Harlan, who was closest and reloading his shotgun. "What's happening?" she asked, dragging him away.

"These stupid idiots released this thing from the tomb," he said, his eyes wild. "And now we have to stop it from getting out, all while trying not to die!"

"But we're the only ones fighting it, and so far, it's winning!"

A crunching noise made them both look up in alarm, and they saw Ash hit the cave wall, before slumping to the floor. He shook himself down and stood once more, this time his wings shooting out as he soared over the creature.

"Come and help us, then," Harlan said, about to run back to the others.

"Wait!" she grabbed his arm. "What woke him?"

Harlan frowned at her. "What do you mean? We opened the tomb!"

"The wires—the white lights! What are they?"

"Rudimentary electricity. Stefan released the tomb mechanism, potentially sparking the Minotaur to life, too—it's like bloody Frankenstein's monster!"

"Who's the blond man in the middle?"

"Toto, and the other guy next to him is Stefan Hope-Robbins. Both are sneaky shits—do not trust them!"

He shook her off and ran, but Shadow looked at the mass of interconnected wires running to the large box with levers and dials at the end, and then back at the figures in the centre.

There was a victorious shout from Aubrey as he emerged from the top of the tomb, shaking a fist full of papers. "I've found them!"

Toto pushed JD out of the way, scrambled up next to him and tried to grab them, setting off a huge scuffle in which Aubrey punched Toto, sending him sprawling off the tomb. The Silencer of Souls bounded up the tomb and threw herself on Aubrey, and both of them disappeared inside, papers scattering everywhere, and the remaining alchemists ran to collect them.

Nahum arrived at her side then. Mason was hanging back, wide-eyed with shock. "Shadow, we need to get out of here!"

"Not until we stop that thing—and Black Cronos!" She looked at the wires again. "I need Estelle. I have an idea. Where's Niel?"

"Fighting Black Cronos and trying to keep our exit clear. As soon as we arrived, they attacked. They've clearly decided it's time to eliminate us." Nahum's expression darkened. "Shit. The guards are moving in on JD and Caldwell, too. Okay, I'll get the alchemists out, you help stop that thing."

Shadow ran, zigzagging through the chaos to Estelle's side, narrowly avoiding being hit by a fireball. "Estelle, can you target the wires in some way? If electricity animated that thing, can we fry it using the same method?"

Estelle barely glanced at her, focussing only on the monster. "I can't move objects, Shadow! That's not my skill!"

"But could you channel the power somehow?" She pointed at the flashes of light. "I don't know much about electricity or how this is set up, but it seems that there's a lot of energy up there, just waiting to be used!"

Estelle paused, her eyes travelling from the large contraption against the wall to the wires that snaked overhead, and while she considered her options, Shadow watched Gabe and Barak engage the creature. Barak attacked with breathtaking speed as he barrelled in, his sword flashing, and Gabe went after the creature's blindside, managing to stab it several times. But nothing slowed it down.

The creature was covered in a multitude of deep cuts and stab wounds across its body and limbs. It bled profusely, and yet it wasn't tiring. She winced as it picked Barak up like he was a doll and hurled him away. Above them was solid rock, and even if Estelle could blast some of it free, they risked being buried alive in the collapsing cavern.

"They combined it with the power of Mithras, didn't they?" Shadow said, more to herself than Estelle. "That's why it has the head and limbs of a bull, but it was so much more than they expected."

Estelle launched another flurry of magic as it turned their way, and she looked exasperated. "Which explains why none of the spells I've used will work! They've somehow harnessed the power of the God! I've tried all sort of spells on it—to immobilise it, freeze it, burn it, clot its blood...many horribly destructive things I wouldn't ever dream of using on anyone else—and none of them work!" Shadow was shocked to hear that Estelle had morals, but Estelle was already speaking again, her eye on the wires. "It's possible to use that power, but I'd need to ground myself." She stared at the floor. "We're standing on earth and rock, but I risk electrocution."

That's all Shadow needed to hear. "Well, I'll leave you to work it out and go help my brothers." And then she ran to join the fight.

⬥◦⬥

Nahum waded in to break up the fighting alchemists before the soldiers did, pulling Caldwell away from Stefan, and JD from Toto. All of them were bloodied and bruising, with scraps of paper crumpled in their hands and shoved inside their clothing.

"You're all insane!" Nahum yelled. "Get out now, before we're all killed!" He pointed at the rampaging monster. "Are you all blind? Is that what you want?"

"Their research was flawed!" Toto said, his eyes icy. "I can build on it!"

Nahum hadn't got time for this. "You've made your own monsters—get out now!"

Toto faced him down. "There are more papers here. And I will get them before I leave!" He shook Nahum's hand off and clambered up the steps to the tomb, just as The Silencer of Souls emerged from the inner compartment. "Just in time, my dear. Help the guards finish these gentlemen off for me. They are not to leave this place," he said, ducking inside the tomb.

"Run, now!" Nahum shouted, pushing Caldwell and JD aside and punching Stefan out cold. *The less people who could interfere, the better.* "And drag him with you!"

He whipped around, flinging a dagger at an oncoming guard, and plunging his sword into the next.

Caldwell hadn't moved, despite the increasing threat. "But Aubrey—he was in the tomb!"

"Then he's already dead," Nahum told him. "*Go!*"

Nahum fought off another guard with deadly accuracy, and then faced the advancing woman. She was taking her time walking down the tomb, as if savouring her chance to kill him.

Suddenly, an enormous crackle of energy erupted overhead, and Nahum instinctively ducked as what appeared to be lightning flashed across the roof of the chamber, illuminating everything in a stark white light. It happened again and again, magnifying in its intensity as a huge electrical storm built up overhead. Forks of lightning flashed to the ground, narrowly missing him, but it caught The Silencer of Souls and threw her across the room, where she landed on all fours like a cat, her clothing smoking.

But she wasn't looking at Nahum anymore. She was staring at Estelle.

Estelle was standing apart from the others, and was surrounded by a nimbus of power like a gigantic Tesla ball, her bare feet dug into the earth as she radiated energy, pulling it from the wires that snaked around the cavern. Her arms were spread wide and she swept them at the monster, a massive bolt of lightning striking it in the chest and sending it flying into the cave wall. She followed it up with another and then another, pinning the creature in place with the onslaught until its body started to smoulder, and it bellowed with pain and fury.

Their team was already running for the exit—all except for Barak, who loitered by the tomb, watching Estelle. Nahum ran to his side.

"Barak, we have to leave!"

"Not without Estelle."

"But she's got this!"

"And she just might collapse because of the massive amount of power she's wielding." Barak regarded him steadily. "It's okay, Nahum. Just keep the entrance clear, and I'll see you outside." Nahum hesitated, clearly torn, and Barak's large hand clamped on his shoulder. "She didn't leave me, and I'm not leaving her. Go."

◆◇◆

Gabe arrived at the chamber's entrance after making sure everyone was ahead of him, and he paused on the threshold, keeping a wary eye on Barak and Estelle.

The chamber had turned into a death trap. The air smouldered, and the scraps of paper and the clothing of the fallen soldiers were already smoking, some bursting into flames. The whole place was ready to go up like a powder keg.

Jackson went to push past Gabe. "Gabe, I have to get back inside. Toto is still in there—in the tomb."

"You're as mad as they are," Gabe said, incredulous. "Look at this place!"

"Which is why I'm prepared to go. We need his knowledge about Black Cronos."

"You've got Stefan!"

"But I want Toto, too!"

Gabe stared at Jackson's stubborn expression. His lips were set in a tight line, his eyes narrowed. Then he glanced at Harlan at his shoulder, looking similarly determined. "*No.* You go and meet your extraction team. Ensure *everyone* is out of here. I'll get him."

"Gabe," Harlan grabbed his arm. "She's still in there—The Silencer of Souls. I saw her on the left. Be careful!"

Great jolts of lightning were sizzling through the air, and keeping his head low, Gabe sprinted across the chamber. It was hot now, and the air was so charged he could feel his hair lifting off his head like he'd stuck his hand in an electrical socket. He ignored it and the chaos beyond as he leapt on the tomb and looked inside.

It was a huge structure, with steps leading to the room at the bottom, and it seemed to Gabe that it was the place of the original experiments, as there was a wealth of objects down there. He presumed they had built the tomb around the monster. But there was no Toto here; only Aubrey's lifeless body was inside. *Shit.*

He looked around, studying the cavern from his elevated position, but he couldn't see him or the woman anywhere. All he could see were dead soldiers and smouldering fires. He'd already explored the cave earlier. There were no hidden doorways, no exits...unless they'd found something he hadn't.

Estelle was barely visible in the maelstrom of electrical energy she'd unleashed around her, but he could see the monster clearly. It was on the floor in flames, and if it weren't already dead, it would be soon. As much as he didn't want Toto or the woman to get away, this was no time to linger. He jumped down into the tomb, picked up Aubrey and threw him over his shoulder, and then headed to the ground level and Barak's side.

"Barak! How do we stop Estelle? It's time to go!"

Barak looked at him, panic-stricken. "I don't know. It's like she's locked inside that thing! I can't get close!"

Gabe looked at the contraption of wires and levers and the batteries running through the cavern and had an idea. "We need to destroy the panel," he said, yelling to be heard over the noise, and depositing Aubrey on the floor.

He grabbed a large stone from a broken column and hurled it at the rudimentary control panel. Barak followed suit, both throwing stone after stone until it shattered, sparked, and went dead, releasing Estelle from the maelstrom of energy that surrounded her. She collapsed on the ground, and Barak raced to her side, feeling her pulse, while Gabe picked up Aubrey again.

"She's alive," he said, scooping her up. "Let's get out of here, Gabe."

They were almost at the entrance when a secondary reaction started. A large humming, fizzing noise rose around them, and Gabe paused and looked back on the alchemists' chamber of horrors. One by one the rudimentary batteries exploded, flames climbing high and starting another wave of electric pulses, but Gabe didn't care. *With luck, the entire place would ignite.* He turned his back and raced outside.

Twenty-Eight

They all looked terrible, Harlan thought, as he surveyed his bedraggled team.
They were next to their car and the two vans belonging to Black Cronos. JD was sitting beside Mason, sipping bottled water and talking quietly. Neither had said much to Harlan, and he wasn't sure what that meant, but right now he was too tired to care. Barak was sitting with Estelle, who was now conscious but looked utterly drained. Nahum and Niel had just returned from patrolling the grounds, their stances still wary. Ash was talking to Caldwell, his hand on his shoulder, looking earnest but gentle. Gabe and Shadow were leaning against one of the vans, studying another larger white van parked a short distance away, this one belonging to Jackson's extraction team.

Harlan turned to watch, too. He hadn't really believed they would turn up. In the madness and chaos of this whole evening, he'd expected Jackson to be teasing him, like it was some great British wind-up on the sole American.

But he hadn't been lying. They were a unit of half a dozen men and women, with one wearing a bureaucratic suit. The others were dressed in military-style clothing, and they kept their distance from the rest of them—Jackson made sure of it. Stefan Hope-Robbins was groggy but conscious, and he had been cuffed and shoved, cursing and swearing, into the back of the van, his voice vanishing as the door banged shut on him.

Jackson returned to their group and resumed his interrogation of Gabe. "He must have been in there!"

"I'm telling you, he wasn't!" Gabe looked as annoyed as Jackson was. "I have no idea how Toto got out or where he went. I can only presume that woman helped him escape. And believe me, I am not happy she made it out, either."

"Damn it!" Jackson exclaimed, "Have we—"

"Yes," Niel interrupted. "We have searched the woods around the circle, and the ruins. They're gone. Whoever is left is dead, and you've got the bodies."

Aubrey's body and the dead Black Cronos members who had been killed in the ruins had been placed in body bags and loaded into the van, along with any equipment they could find.

Jackson sighed, and then brightened as he pulled himself together. "Sorry. You're right, we have. And we'll take their vehicles, too. With luck we'll find some more information in them. Toto would have been the prize, though. I think he's the real brains behind the enhanced humans."

Gabe grunted. "You should be able to get back in the chamber once the fires are out. I've checked the entrance. It's accessible."

Jackson grinned. "I know. We have a second team en route. This is actually better than we expected, in many ways."

"*What*?" Caldwell said, abruptly ending his conversation with Ash. He was smeared in dirt, his hair was a mess, and his clothing was torn, but his eyes blazed. "That is *our* chamber!"

Jackson folded his arms and regarded him steadily. "Your friend Aubrey is dead, and the whole place is a disaster zone. Are you really telling me that you want your Inner Temple to come here now?"

"Yes! If not to use it, at least to see it!" He looked down at the ground, shuffling his feet, and when he looked up again, his eyes were bright with unshed tears. "Aubrey was a brave soul, dedicated to learning our craft. We should honour him here. No one did more than he to find this place. You will treat his body well, won't you?"

"Of course," Jackson said gently. "We will get him home quickly and safely, and release him to you as soon as we can. And if you're sure you really want to, we'll ensure this place is safe before you return. Just be aware that we could be here for some weeks."

Caldwell patted his jacket that was looking very bulky. "And I will keep the papers I've found."

"Yes. But I want copies!"

"This is private!"

"This is the government you're dealing with now. Be grateful we're letting you keep anything."

Caldwell's lips tightened and he drew a deep breath in, but then he deflated like a popped balloon. "All right." He looked up at Gabe and Shadow. "Thanks for your help. We really couldn't have done this without you."

Gabe grunted. "One of you is dead. I don't really consider that a success."

"But we have some of the research at least, and we found the place," Caldwell insisted. "If only Aubrey and I had been here alone, that thing would have got out."

"You know," Gabe said thoughtfully, "we still haven't found your mole."

"There is no mole!" Caldwell said, annoyed.

Gabe refused to back down. "You're wrong, and now you're being wilfully blind. Someone—possibly Barnaby Armstrong—leaked that you had the astrolabe. *They* are responsible for Aubrey's death, because if Black Cronos didn't know about it, we wouldn't have been chased across England and France, and The Silencer of Souls wouldn't have sucked the life out of him."

Harlan almost felt sorry for Caldwell. He was desperate to defend his Senior Adepts, but there was no denying that Gabe was right. "I know you don't want to admit it, Caldwell, but there's no other explanation. When you get home, you need to be very careful who you trust."

"All right," he shouted. "Just leave it, please, for now. This is too much, on top of everything else."

"To be honest," Jackson said quietly, almost apologetically, "it will be something we look into. We will explore all potential connections to Black Cronos. But perhaps we should talk about that later," he added, as Caldwell glared at him.

An awkward silence fell for a second until Shadow said to Harlan, "You called it a Minotaur. What is that?"

He laughed. "It's a mythical bull-headed man trapped in a labyrinth. It's a murky tale, as all the Greek legends are. King Minos was sent a white bull to sacrifice to Poseidon, but it was so beautiful, he couldn't do it. To exact his revenge, Poseidon made the king's wife fall in love with it, and well...she had sex with it and gave birth to a bull-headed man."

Shadow looked horrified. "She did *what*?"

Gabe looked pale. "That's disgusting."

"It's a legend, of course!" Harlan said, trying to reassure them. "Not real. It's about the power of the ancient Greek Gods and the hazards of not paying them proper respect. King Minos put the Minotaur in the middle of a complicated maze, and then men were sacrificed to it."

"Is it a legend?" Ash asked, amused. "Because after what we've seen today, how can you doubt it? As you know, I am Greek, and have seen many strange things in my time. And we all know how vengeful Gods are."

Harlan did a quick calculation in his head. "The Minoan civilisation was during the Bronze age, right? Were you guys around then? Did you know him?"

"Maybe I'll keep that story for another time," Ash said, smiling. Harlan had a sudden vision of Ash in Bronze-age clothes, and thought he would suit that time very well.

Shadow, however, had heard enough. "Are we done here? I'm knackered and I stink, and after a shower, I want a drink on that stunning terrace."

"Agreed," Gabe said, stepping away and expanding his wings with a flourish. "Are you coming back, Jackson?"

"I think I will. I'll get the team to drop me off, but it won't be for a while yet." He turned to Harlan. "Can you drive everyone else?"

"Sounds good to me. Bourbon has never sounded better."

⬤

Shadow sipped her Cognac and leaned on the terrace railing, admiring the vineyards. The moon was sinking into the distant horizon, and it would be dawn soon.

She pulled a lightweight blanket around her shoulders to keep off the chill that had fallen in the early hours. It had been a long, crazy night, and she was glad that Gabe and her brothers had made it out of there alive. *Especially Gabe.* Even when he wasn't with her, he filled her thoughts. She would return to his bed later and sleep there...eventually. And she didn't care who knew it, either. When she imagined this turn of events, she thought she might feel prickly about it. Defensive, even. But actually, she didn't feel any of those things. In fact, she felt incredibly and unexpectedly comfortable about the whole thing.

She heard the Nephilim inside the house and smelled food. Despite the hour, Niel had decided to cook, proclaiming he was starving and that he would never sleep until he filled his stomach. At which point everyone else had requested food too, so now he was in there cooking bacon, eggs, and waffles with Harlan's help, who had also found bottles of whiskey and bourbon for the table.

Everyone was too wired after their exertions to even think about sleeping now. Caldwell had already settled at the end of the table with his newly found papers, half-destroyed and decaying, not surprisingly. JD and Mason joined him, and she was glad they were here. They knew him well, better than they did, and could comfort him as he mourned the loss of Aubrey. And of course, help him study his new acquisitions.

The back door swung open, and a slight figure slipped out wearing a long, elegant cardigan, and Shadow watched warily as Estelle joined her, cradling her own glass of whiskey. She leaned on the railing too, silent for a moment. They weren't friends, and she doubted they ever would be, but there was also no doubting she was a good witch.

Shadow forced herself to speak and be civil, wondering why on Earth Estelle had come to stand next to her. "That was some impressive magic you pulled off in there. Are you okay?"

"Of course," she said brusquely, immediately annoying Shadow. "It was hard, but I was equal to it."

"So, you pass out after every time you use magic?" Shadow couldn't resist saying.

"No!" Estelle glared at her. "That was a particularly big spell!"

"Herne's balls, Estelle! Calm down! Why are you so damn prickly? I'm not doubting you. I was impressed!"

Estelle's face froze, and she turned away abruptly. "I'm tired." There was a moment's silence, and then she grudgingly said, "You're a very good fighter. Shockingly fast."

Shadow couldn't help herself as she said, "I know. I'm fey." She stared at the vineyards again, feeling Estelle's animosity rolling off her in waves; she wished she'd just sod off and leave her in peace. "That bloody monster was virtually unstoppable. I've got bruises in places I didn't know I could. I think my hair is singed, too. How do you think *they* stopped it? The original alchemists, I mean. They sealed it in a tomb, neatly packaged and tucked away!"

"Good question," Estelle said, curiosity replacing her anger. "They obviously had a fight with it at some point. When we first arrived, we found broken tables and destroyed columns. They must have employed a fail-safe that we knew nothing about. Something alchemical. Perhaps with the aid of the research, Caldwell will find out."

"Perhaps. And," Shadow added, still brooding, "my beautiful bow was destroyed."

"But you can get another one, I'm sure."

"Not like that one," she said sadly, wondering where in fact she could get one made. Something she could talk to El about, perhaps.

They fell into an awkward silence, and Shadow wondered what Estelle wanted. She would never normally seek her out for conversation. And then it struck her. *Barak.* They all knew Barak liked Estelle—hence the bet. He'd often joked about how he liked her feisty nature, but he always made light of it. Frankly, Shadow was appalled. *But maybe there was something more there—for Estelle, too. Or was it just about the White Haven witches and her brother?*

Sick of standing in silence and refusing to move—she liked leaning against the railing and listening to the murmured conversations around her, and the clatter of the others inside—she said, "Caspian must not have been that pleased at you coming here so soon after he was attacked."

Estelle looked startled at that. "Caspian? I don't think he cares one way or the other. A break will do us both good. I'll probably stay on a few days, actually. You could all stay." She offered it casually, almost tentatively.

"Could we?" Shadow thought through the possibility. They had no new jobs to rush off to, and the witches were okay, although they may need their help soon with the missing witches who had betrayed them. "I guess we could, for a few days. I must admit I like this heat, and the *château*. It's very beautiful. I guess it depends if Caspian can manage without Barak and Niel for a few days longer. They do work for you."

"They work for Caspian, not me, and I know he's arranged cover for a few days. I'm sure he can cope," she said, a hard edge to her voice.

"Well, that's good to know," Shadow answered uneasily. "I'd have thought you'd be glad to see the back of us. Why don't we ask when the others come out?"

"Yes, let's." Estelle shuffled and stared into her glass. *Here it comes.* "Is it my imagination, or do you and Gabe have a *thing*?"

"Oh, yes. We have a thing. A big thing." She smiled. "I tried to pretend it didn't exist or would be bad for business, but what's the point in that? You only live once. And it was inevitable, despite the fact that he's a big, winged idiot," she said affectionately, not thinking he was an idiot at all. "And my brothers can only tease us so many times before they get bored and move on to something new. Although, I gather there was a bet that I'm not very happy about."

Estelle still wasn't looking at her. "They do tease, don't they? All of them. It's hard to know when they're serious."

"They do, but they're good men. Honest. Despite their wings they are essentially human, which means they come with all the crap that goes with that." She shrugged, mischievous. "Not fey, obviously, which is a flaw."

Estelle rolled her eyes. "Really?"

Shadow just laughed. "And they have nice muscles, too."

The door swung open again behind them, and Gabe's arms slid around Shadow's waist as he kissed her neck. "Ladies." He nodded to Estelle, and said to Shadow, "You smell good."

"That's because I've washed the smell of roasting monster off me."

He laughed, sending a shiver up her spine. "Food's ready. You both coming?"

"Yep." Shadow wiggled out of Gabe's embrace and looked at Estelle, who hadn't moved. "Come on, Estelle. If you don't get to the table quickly, it will all be gone. They eat like horses."

She trailed after them, and while Niel, Harlan, Nahum, and Barak delivered dishes to the table, everyone else settled into seats.

Shadow decided to broach the subject first as soon as everyone sat down—well, everyone except Jackson, who still must be at the chamber. "Estelle says we can all stay here for a few more days. What do you think?"

"I think it sounds fantastic!" Niel said enthusiastically. "Fine food, French wine, the heat! Yes, please."

"This heat reminds me of Greece, so that's a yes for me," Ash said, smiling.

"Fine with me," Gabe said easily, reaching for a dish of bacon and topping his plate up. He glanced at Nahum. "What do you think?"

"I think our brothers at home will be glad of the peace."

"I'd love to stay," Harlan said, looking at JD and Mason. "But it depends on what my bosses say!"

Mason looked as if he'd aged ten years. He'd lost his confident demeanour; obviously Robert's death had hit him hard, but he nodded. "I think you should, Harlan. I, however, will head back later today. I need to sort things out regarding Robert...talk to his family, address the staff. Take a few days, but make sure you're back for the funeral."

"Of course, I will be there. And then we'll talk." He stared at Mason for a long moment, and he just nodded.

What did that mean? Shadow wondered. *It sounded ominous.* "What about you, JD?" she asked.

He too looked haunted, but he still had that stubbornness around the eyes she'd come to recognise. "I'll stay a day—if Caldwell is happy that I help him with his new research—and then I'll head to the Paris branch."

Caldwell nodded. "Of course, JD. A day or so to gather my thoughts would be good. And despite what Jackson said, I would like to revisit the chamber before I go. Then I too must deal with Aubrey's death, and the implications for the order."

Barak smiled at Estelle and raised his glass. "That sounds like a plan, then. To the next few days."

Estelle returned his smile, and Shadow inwardly groaned as she raised her glass with the others. *What in Herne's horns had she just collaborated in?*

As if Gabe had read her thoughts, he nudged her and winked. "See? She's not so bad after all."

Thanks for reading White Haven Hunters: Books 1-3. Please make an author happy and leave a review.

Book 4 is called Hunter's Dawn, and it's out on May 26th 2022. You can pre-order it here: https://tjgreen.nz/books/hunters-dawn/

If you enjoyed this book and would like to read more of my stories, please subscribe to my newsletter at tjgreen.nz. You will get two free short stories, *Excalibur Rises* and *Jack's Encounter,* and will also receive free character sheets of all the main White Haven witches characters.

By staying on my mailing list you'll receive free excerpts of my new books, as well as short stories, news of giveaways, and a chance to join my launch team. I'll also be sharing information about other books in this genre you might enjoy.

Read on for a list of my other books.

Author's Notes

Thanks for reading White Haven Hunters Books 1 -3. I love Shadow, my stranded fey, and the seven Nephilim, and couldn't wait to write their stories. I'm also very fond of Harlan and the Orphic Guild. I know that together there'll be many opportunities for fun!

Shadow comes from the Otherworld of my series Rise of the King, about King Arthur. I thought that seeing as I had another fully realised Otherworld, it made sense to link her to that one. And I love crossovers and connected universes.

I'm intrigued by alchemy. It's such a huge, diverse, and ancient subject that it seemed to fit perfectly with the Nephilim. I'm not entirely sure where we'll end up going, but I'm looking forward to finding out. I am planning on a few short story prequels coming soon—for Shadow certainly, and hopefully Harlan and Gabe, too.

Thanks to my fabulous cover designer, Fiona Jayde Media, and to Missed Period Editing.

I owe a big thanks to Jason, my partner, who has been incredibly supportive throughout my career, and is a beta reader. Thanks also to Terri and my mother, my other two beta readers. You're all awesome.

Finally, thank you to my launch team, who give valuable feedback on typos and are happy to review on release. It's lovely to hear from them—you know who you are! You're amazing! I also love hearing from all of my readers, so I welcome you to get in touch.

If you'd like to read a bit more background on my stories, please head to my website, where I blog about the books I've read and the research I've done. I have another series set in Cornwall about witches, called White Haven Witches, so if you love myths and magic, you'll love that, too. It's an adult series, not YA.

If you'd like to read more of my writing, please join my mailing list. You can get a free short story called *Jack's Encounter*, describing how Jack met Fahey—a longer version of the prologue in the *Call of the King*—by subscribing to my newsletter. You'll also get a FREE copy, *of Excalibur Rises* a short story prequel. Additionally, you will receive free character sheets on all of my main characters in White Haven Witches—exclusive to my email list!

By staying on my mailing list, you'll receive free excerpts of my new books, as well as short stories and news of giveaways. I'll also be sharing information about other books in this genre you might enjoy. Finally, I welcome you to join my readers' group for even more great content, called TJ's Inner Circle, on Facebook. Please answer the questions to join!

https://www.facebook.com/groups/696140834516292

Give me my FREE short stories! https://tjgreen.nz/

About Author

I write books about magic, mystery, myths, and legends, and they're action-packed!

My primary series is adult urban fantasy, called White Haven Witches. There's lots of magic, action, and a little bit of romance.

My YA series, Rise of the King, is about a teen named Tom and his discovery that he is a descendant of King Arthur. It's a fun-filled, clean read with a new twist on the Arthurian tales.

I've got loads of ideas for future books in all of my series, including spin-offs, novellas, and short stories, so if you'd like to be kept up to date, subscribe to my newsletter. You'll get free short stories, character sheets, and other fun stuff. Interested? Subscribe here.

I was born in England, in the Black Country, but moved to New Zealand 14 years ago. England is great, but I'm over the traffic! I now live near Wellington with my partner, Jase, and my cats, Sacha and Leia. When I'm not busy writing I read lots, indulge in gardening and shopping, and I love yoga.

Confession time! I'm a Star Trek geek—old and new—and love urban fantasy and detective shows. My secret passion is Columbo! My favourite Star Trek film is The Wrath of Khan, the original! Other top films for me are Predator, the original, and Aliens.

In a previous life, I was a singer in a band, and used to do some acting with a theatre company. On occasion, a few friends and I like to make short films, which begs the question, where are the book trailers? I'm thinking on it...

For more on me, check out a couple of my blog posts at tjgreen.nz. I'm an old grunge queen, so you can read about my love of that here. For more random news, read this.

Why magic and mystery?

I've always loved the weird, the wonderful, and the inexplicable. My favourite stories are those of magic and mystery, set on the edges of the known, particularly tales of folklore, faerie, and legend—all the narratives that try to explain our reality.

The King Arthur stories are fascinating because they sit between reality and myth. They encompass real life concerns, but also cross boundaries with the world of faerie—or the Otherworld, as I call it. There are green knights, witches, wizards, and dragons, and that's what I find particularly fascinating. They're stories that have intrigued people for generations, and like many others, I'm adding my own interpretation.

I also love witches and magic, hence my additional series set in beautiful Cornwall. There are witches, missing grimoires, supernatural threats, and ghosts, and as the series progresses, even weirder stuff happens.

Have a poke around in my blog posts, and you'll find all sorts of articles about my series and my characters, and quite a few book reviews.

If you'd like to follow me on social media, you'll find me here:

Facebook, Twitter, Pinterest, Instagram, BookBub.

Also By

Rise of the King Series
A Young Adult series about a teen called Tom who's summoned to wake King Arthur.
It's a fun adventure about King Arthur in the Otherworld!

Call of the King #1
King Arthur is destined to return, and Tom is destined to wake him.
When sixteen year old Tom's grandfather mysteriously disappears, Tom stops at nothing
to find him, even when that means crossing to a mysterious and unknown world.
When he gets there, Tom discovers that everything he thought he knew about himself
and his life was wrong. Vivian, the Lady of the Lake, has been watching over him and
manipulating his life since his birth. And now she needs his help.

The Silver Tower #2
**Merlin disappeared over a thousand years ago. Now they risk everything to find
him.**
Vivian needs King Arthur's help. Nimue, a powerful witch and priestess who lives on
Avalon, has disappeared.
King Arthur, Tom, and his friends set off across the Other to find her, following Nimue's
trail to Nimue seems to have a quest of her own, one she's deliberately hiding. Arthur is
convinced it's about Merlin, and he's determined to find him.

The Cursed Sword #3
An ancient sword. A dark secret. A new enemy.
Tom loves his new life in the Otherworld. He lives with Arthur in New Camelot, and
Arthur is hosting a tournament. Eager to test his sword-fighting skills, Tom's competing.
But while the games are being played, his friends are attacked and everything he loves is
threatened. Tom has to find the intruder before anyone else gets hurt.

Tom's sword seems to be the focus of these attacks. Their investigations uncover its dark history and a terrible betrayal that a family has kept secret for generations.

White Haven Witches Series
Witches, secrets, myth and folklore, set on the Cornish coast!

Buried Magic #1
Love witchy fiction? Welcome to White Haven – where secrets are deadly.
Avery, a witch who lives on the Cornish coast, finds her past holds more secrets than she ever imagined in this spellbinding mystery.
For years witches have lived in quirky White Haven, all with an age-old connection to the town's magical roots, but Avery has been reluctant to join a coven, preferring to work alone.
However, when she inherits a rune covered box and an intriguing letter, Avery learns that their history is darker than she realised. And when the handsome Alex Bonneville tells her he's been having ominous premonitions, they know that trouble's coming.

Magic Unbound #2
Avery and the other witches are now being hunted, and they know someone is betraying them.
The question is, who?
One thing is certain.
They have to find their missing grimoires before their attackers do, and they have to strike back.
If you love urban fantasy, filled with magic and a twist of romance, you'll love Magic Unbound.

Magic Unleashed #3
Old magic, new enemies. The danger never stops in White Haven.
Avery and the White Haven witches have finally found their grimoires and defeated the Favershams, but their troubles are only just beginning.
Something escaped from the spirit world when they battled beneath All Souls Church, and now it wants to stay, unleashing violence across Cornwall.
On top of that, the power they released when they reclaimed their magic is attracting powerful creatures from the deep, creatures that need men to survive.

All Hallows' Magic #4
When Samhain arrives, worlds collide.
A Shifter family arrives in White Haven, one of them close to death. Avery offers them sanctuary, only to find their pursuers are close behind, intent on retribution. In an effort to help them, Avery and Alex are dragged into a fight they didn't want but must see through.
As if that weren't enough trouble, strange signs begin to appear at Old Haven Church. Avery realises that an unknown witch has wicked plans for Samhain, and is determined to breach the veils between worlds.

Avery and her friends scramble to discover who the mysterious newcomer is, all while being attacked one by one.

Undying Magic #5
Winter grips White Haven, bringing death in its wake.

It's close to the winter solstice when Newton reports that dead bodies have been found drained of their blood.

Then people start disappearing, and Genevieve calls a coven meeting. What they hear chills their blood.

This has happened before, and it's going to get worse. The witches have to face their toughest challenge yet – vampires.

Crossroads Magic #6
When Myths become real, danger stalks White Haven.

The Crossroads Circus has a reputation for bringing myths to life, but it also seems that where the circus goes, death follows. When the circus sets up on the castle grounds, Newton asks Avery and the witches to investigate.

This proves trickier than they expected when an unexpected encounter finds Avery bound to a power she can't control.

Strange magic is making the myths a little too real.

Crown of Magic #7
Passions run deep at Beltane - too deep.

With the Beltane Festival approaching, the preparations in White Haven are in full swing, but when emotions soar out of control, the witches suspect more than just high spirits. As part of the celebrations, a local theatre group is rehearsing Tristan and Isolde, but it seems Beltane magic is affecting the cast, and all sorts of old myths are brought to the surface.

The May Queen brings desire, fertility, and the promise of renewal, but love can also be dark and dangerous.

Vengeful Magic #8
When lost treasure is discovered, supernatural creatures unleash violence across Cornwall.

Midsummer is approaching and Avery, Alex, and the White Haven witches, are making plans to celebrate Litha, but everything stops when paranormal activities cause havoc. Smuggler's gold is found that dates back centuries, and a strange chain of events is set in motion; Newton needs magical help.

The witches find they are pitted against a deadly enemy, and they need the Cornwall Coven. But not all are happy to help – a few members have never accepted White Haven, and their enmity puts everyone in danger.

Chaos Magic #9
The rules have changed.

Reeling from the events that revealed other witches were behind the attack on Reuben and Caspian, the White Haven witches don't know who to trust.

The search for those who betrayed them tests their resources and their abilities, and as the fallout shatters alliances, they draw on their friends for support.

But it's not easy. The path they follow is dark and twisted and leads them in directions they can't predict.

Knowing who to trust is the only thing that may save them.

Made in the USA
Monee, IL
09 August 2022

11216389R00312